Books by E.E. Knight

ENTER THE WOLF: VAMPIRE EARTH VOLUME 1
(SFBC EXCLUSIVE 3-in-1 Omnibus)

Way of the Wolf

Choice of the Cat

Tale of the Thunderbolt

WAY OF THE BEAR

WAY OF THE BEAR

VAMPIRE EARTH VOLUME 2:

Valentine's Rising

Valentine's Exile

Valentine's Resolve

E. E. Knight

This is a work of fiction. All of the characters, organizations and events portrayed in this novel are either products of the author's imagination or are used fictitiously and are not to be construed as real. Any resemblance to actual events, locales, organizations, or persons, living or dead, is entirely coincidental.

First SFBC Printing: September 2013

Selected by Michael Phillips, SFBC Senior Editor

Published by arrangement with
The Penguin Group (USA), Inc./ The Berkley Publishing Group, Ace
375 Hudson Street
New York, NY 10014

Visit The SFBC online at *http://www.sfbc.com*

ISBN # 978-1-62490-772-2

Printed in the United States of America.

Contents

VALENTINE'S RISING

To those in uniform, past and present.
Thank you.

All along with singing river
A black mass of men was seen
And above their shining weapons
Hung their own beloved green
Death to every foe and traitor!
Whistle loud the marching tune
And Hurrah! me boys for freedom
'Tis the rising of the moon

The rising of the moon
The rising of the moon
And Hurrah! me boys for freedom
'Tis the rising of the moon

Well they fought for dear old Ireland
And full bitter was their fate
What a glorious pride and sorrow
Fills the name of ninety-eight
Yet thank God while hearts are beating fast
In manhood's burning noon
We will follow in their footsteps
By the rising of the moon

—"The Rising of the Moon" by John Keegan Casey

One

The Ouachita Forest, Arkansas, December of the forty-eighth year of the Kurian Order: The pines stand, colorless spindles under a winter overcast. The low mountains of the Ouachitas huddle dark all around, just touching the cloud sea. Water beads linger on bough, trunk, leaf and stone as though freshly dropped; the earth beneath the fallen leaves smells like decay. Birds overturn dead leaves and poke about the roots in silence, walking the earth as if too dispirited to fly. Brown ferns lie flat along the streambanks, under patches of frostbitten moss flaking off the rocks like old scabs. Even the wind is listless, seeping rather than blowing through the pines.

Naked outcroppings of stone, etched with lightning strikes of quartz crystal, project every which way from the ground like the work of titans who tried to pull out the mountain by its roots. The strata of the Ouachita slopes are jumbled, pushed up and twisted from a seismic pileup millennia ago. Thanks to the blind runs, box canyons and meandering crest lines of these elderly mountains, the landscape doesn't lend itself to habitation. These hills have been hide-outs of liberty-loving Indians, die-hard Confederates, and law-evading brigands—the notorious Younger gang used to hole up here with the James brothers. Between the stands of rock, the ferns' squashed-spider shapes lie in boot tracks and hoofprints forming a trail that suggests a similar hurried flight from authority.

The boot tracks have a source, noisily crunching over the hilltop's still-frozen ground. Six mud-stained figures walk with the oddly stiff motion of men on their last legs, strung out in front of and behind a lone horse pulling an A-frame drag supporting an unconscious man with blood-matted hair. Two dreadlocked men in blue-black uniforms share a blanket as they move, muttering to each other in the patois of the sunny island of Jamaica. Walking alongside the horse is the oldest of the group, a meaty-faced man of six-two, dark brown hair flecked with early gray and a boxer's shovel jaw. His clothing, indeed his whole body, has the look of having just emerged from a threshing machine. An improvised poncho is fixed about his waist with a wide brown belt. Dried blood stains the parts that dirt hasn't touched; bits of rag are knotted around wounds in his left leg and right arm. He moves the horse along with a switch, though the occasional lash does nothing more than send it lurching forward a quick pace and into the man leading it.

The lead shape, seemingly bigger than any two of the others put together, is of another species. So forbidding that one might think he was pried off a cathedral and placed among Arkansas pines as a prank, he moves along leaning toward his right side, one tentpole-length arm supporting his midriff. An even longer gun rides his shoulders, tied there by a bit of leather like an ox's yoke. He has bandages wrapped about the waist, a tight corset of brown-stained cloth that accentuates the width of the meaty, golden-furred shoulders above. The creature's eyes shift, widen, and even go a little wet as he spies a figure far away in the trees, jogging toward the file from ahead.

The young man the apish humanoid sees places his feet deliberately as he trots, for a trail in wet leaves on the hillside could be spotted by experienced eyes as easily as a line of signal flares. He favors his left leg, leading with the right up difficult patches of the hill. His shining black hair and bronze skin mark him as more than a spiritual relative of the Osage who once hunted these hills; he moves like them, flowing from spot to spot with the speed of a summer stream: sometimes fast, sometimes slow, sometimes deceptively still when he stops to examine the ground. He wears a simple black uniform, mud-splotched, set off by a strange bandolier of snake-skin with oversized loops, as if the sash had been designed to carry hand grenades, and carries a rugged submachine gun fed by a drum magazine.

His right cheek is scarred from the outer edge of his eye down. The wound, like a Prussian dueling scar, traces its pale way along the edge of his face, marring an otherwise handsome frame around brown eyes. The wary, intent gaze of a wild animal patiently reads the woods behind when he pauses to rest and lets the column come to a stop at its own pace. . . .

Have to turn again. The first zig left had been nine hours ago, to avoid a long string of soldiers walking at ten-foot intervals like beaters driving game. Then there'd been another left turn to avoid a watch-tower looking over a length of old highway. Now he'd spotted teams of men and dogs combing the banks of an ice-choked stream.

They were boxed in, no doubt about it. Every step the survivors of his Texas column took now brought them closer to the area around Bern Woods, where they'd been ambushed two exhaustingly long days ago. Since then no one in his party of survivors had slept or eaten hot food, and there wasn't much play left in their strings.

His head ached. Fatigue or dehydration. He took a drink from his canteen.

"What passes, my David?" Ahn-Kha said, sliding up to him using his legs and one long arm. The Golden One doesn't look at David Valentine; he keeps his eyes on the forest-cutting road below.

"We're cut off. A picket line. Maybe dropped off from trucks."

The Jamaicans, ex-*Thunderbolt* marines named Striper and Ewenge, dropped to their knees, unconscious atop each other within seconds of the column's halt. The man leading the horse spat a white bubble onto the forest floor. William Post, Valentine's lieutenant since their service together on the old Kurian gunboat *Thunderbolt*, dropped his bloody switch and joined David and Ahn-Kha. The drooping horse blew a mouthful of foam out from either side of its bit.

"How's Tayland?" Valentine asked.

Post glanced back at the wounded man on the dragging A-frame. "Unconscious. Strong pulse still. The horse'll be dead before him."

"We've got maybe twenty minutes, and then a picket line will be on top of us."

"I heard dogs behind," Ahn-Kha said. The Grog was the only one who didn't look dejected. He rubbed a bullet tip on his bandolier with the large thumb particular to the Golden Ones' hands.

"That's it, then," Post said. "We can't get back to Texas."

"Listen up," Valentine said loudly, and his complement of six—as recently as two days ago he'd been leading hundreds—was brought to life by prods from Post, except for Tayland. "We're boxed in. We've got three guns with ammunition still between us"—Valentine still carried his old PPD out of affectation; it was as impotent as one of the quartz-etched rocks jutting from the soil—"and I've not seen a hint of friendly forces."

Jefferson, the Texas drover at the horse's head, asked, "How many are coming after us?"

"More than enough."

He let that sink in for a moment, then went on. "I'm going to have to ask you to trust me. The Quislings love nothing better than taking prisoners."

"You want to surrender?" Post asked.

"Worse," Valentine said. "I want all of you to surrender. We fight it out here and we'll just be dead. Giving up, you have a chance."

"They'll feed us before they'll kill us," Striper said. "I'll hold my hands high, if it means hot tuck and sleep." His mate looked down, blinking at tears.

"I'll follow. I expect they'll take you back to Bern Woods; we've been heading that way for the last two hours, and we know that town is occupied. Perhaps something will turn up."

"I could play that I'm your prisoner," Ahn-Kha said. "They might keep an eye on me, but leave me free."

"No, I'll need you at the town."

"You want to see if there's any Quickwood left?" Ahn-Kha asked.

"I want the rest of our men. The wood will have to wait."

"How about a vote, Captain?" Post asked.

"Sure. Ewenge?"

All Valentine saw was the top of his hat as the man spoke. "Yes, sir. I give up."

"Striper?"

The Jamaican nodded. He took out a small eating knife and tossed it to the ground.

"Slave labor camp's not my style," Jefferson said.

"You're free to try to make it on your own."

"Okay then," Jefferson said. He knelt and relaced his boots.

"Tayland's still out," Post said.

Valentine handed Jefferson his canteen. "That leaves you, Will."

"Wonder if they'll send me back to New Orleans to hang as a renegade?"

"If that happens, I'll surrender and hang with you," Valentine said.

Post shrugged. "Sure. Don't do that though, sir. Just find my wife and tell her what happened on the *Thunderbolt*."

The only other refugee from the column couldn't speak. The horse just shifted a foreleg out and gulped air.

"That's it then," Valentine said. He walked around to the rear of the horse, and opened Tayland's eye. The pupil reacted to the light of the overcast, but the former Texas wagon-man showed no sign of regaining consciousness. Valentine nodded to Post, who untied the saplings from the horse's saddle. They lowered the litter to the ground, placing it gently on the winter leaves. Jefferson shook hands with everyone, accepted Post's pistol, received a few words of encouragement and some jerkey in wax paper from Striper, and ran southward.

"I couldn't run if the devil himself poked me," Ewenge said, watching him go. Jefferson waved as he disappeared from sight. The Jamaican marine mechanically removed the horse's saddle and wiped the sweat from its back.

"They'll be here soon. Walk around a lot and mess up the tracks," Valentine told Post. "If they ask about me, tell them I took off hours ago."

"What about me?" Ahn-Kha asked.

"You left now. Scared Grog running for tall timber."

"You'll leave tracks just like Jefferson, Captain," Striper said. "Maybe they follow you too."

Valentine nodded to Ahn-Kha, who was, as usual, ahead of his human ally's thoughts in throwing a blanket over his shoulders. Ahn-Kha bent over and Valentine climbed onto his back. He clung there like a baby monkey.

"One set of tracks," Post said. "Good luck, sir. Don't worry about us. Remember to find Gail. Gail Foster, her maiden name was. Tell her . . ."

"You were wrong," Valentine offered.

Post bit his lip. "Just 'I'm sorry.' "

Valentine thought of telling Post that he could tell her himself, but with hope vanished from the Ozarks like the winter sun, he couldn't bring himself to offer an empty lie to a friend.

Ahn-Kha ran, legs pounding like twin piledrivers in countersynch, clutching his long Grog rifle in one hand and Valentine's empty gun in the other. The trees went by in a blur.

They splashed up an icy stream, startling a pair of ducks into flight. If the freezing water hurt the Grog's long-toed feet, he gave no indication.

Valentine heard a distant shot from the direction of Post's group.

"Stop," he told Ahn-Kha.

Ahn-Kha took two more steps, and placed Valentine on a flat-topped rock midstream.

"You need a rest?" Ahn-Kha asked, blowing.

"I heard a shot."

"Maybe a signal?"

"Or something else."

Only the running water, wind and an occasional bird could be heard in the Arkansas pines and hardwoods. Ahn-Kha shivered. Valentine saw a fallen log upstream, felled by erosion so that it lay like a ramp up the riverbank.

"Let's cut back. Carefully."

* * *

It was Tayland. His eyes were shut, and he had the strangely peaceful look of the recently dead.

They'd just left him in the woods on his litter, wrapped in blankets that would soon be disturbed by birds or coyotes, a bullet hole dead center in his chest. The tracks said that a group of men and dogs had turned after Jefferson, but no one had bothered to follow the lone Grog.

As he said a few words of prayer over the deceased, Valentine remembered Tayland, wounded as they fled the ambush at Bern Woods, cutting the horse free from the traces of a teammate with a big bowie knife. He rooted around at the man's waist, and freed the knife and its scabbard.

The blade was sticky with its owner's blood.

"Shall we bury him?" Ahn-Kha asked.

"No. They might send a party back to get the body. You never know."

"The tracks lead back to town," Ahn-Kha observed. A wide trail showed that men walked to either side of the short-stepping prisoners. They'd probably put them in shackles.

Valentine nodded into the big, enquiring eyes and the pair turned to follow the trail.

If it weren't for the winter drizzle, the rider would have raised dust. Valentine watched him come into Bern Woods from the north, long coat flapping to the thunderous syncopation of his lathered mount's hooves. He clutched mane and reigns in his right hand, leaning far over his horse's neck so his left could wave a red-and-white-striped gusset above him, hallooing all the way.

Valentine waited and watched the guards in the south-gate tower smoke cigarettes. He felt strangely uneasy in his hiding place, near the foundation of a flattened house outside of town where he stowed his .45 automatic and clothes. He was concealed well enough, under a sheet-sized length of old carpet, planted with mud, leaves and twigs. He had used the carapace to crawl at a turtle's pace from the ruin.

It took only fifteen minutes of the forty or so before sunset for them to ride out again. The messenger trotted a new horse at the head of two clattering diesel pickups, beds loaded with support-weapons men, and tracking dogs riding in baskets tied to the cabin roofs. Behind the oil-burners a column of twos streamed out of Bern Woods, their horses tripping in the winter ruts of the broken road. Then a final figure appeared. Valentine drew an anxious breath. A Reaper. It strode out in a meter-eating quick-march, booted feet a blur under heavy cape and cowl.

The final figure explained his uneasiness while waiting. Something about a Reaper's presence gave him what an old tent-mate from the

Wolves had called the "Valentingle." At times it was so bad the hair on the back of his neck stood straight out, or it could manifest as a cold, dead spot in his mind. It was a capricious talent; he'd once walked over a Reaper lying hidden in a basement without a hint of it, but in another time and place he'd felt one on top of a hill a mile away. The Reapers, the praetorian guard doing the bloody work of Earth's Kurian Order that raised, and devoured, his species like cattle, had the ability too. They could sense humans through night and fog, rain or snow. Only through special training could men hide their presence; training that he had started when he was nineteen, seven long years ago. Since the ambush he'd—

Stop it. Since the ambush, regrets about his misjudgments while bringing his convoy home, his eagerness to turn the men and material over to the first Southern Command uniform he saw, had tormented him hourly, and he clenched his fists in frustration until bruises appeared in his palms. Valentine called himself back to the outskirts of Bern Woods and watched the column disappear up the old highway.

Ahn-Kha must have hit the bridge post. They had scouted the blockhouses to either end of the old concrete bridge—it turned out only one was occupied; three soldiers that hardly qualified for a corporal's guard—and Valentine told Ahn-Kha to pick off a man or two from the distance with his Grog gun an hour before sunset, before heading toward Tayland's body. The bridge was only a mile north of Bern Woods; they'd call for help from there.

His part was more of a challenge. After changing clothes in a lonely, recently abandoned farmhouse—he'd found a suitably smelly set of overalls, a knit coat and a shapeless woolen winter cap, and muddied his boots sufficiently so they wouldn't be an instant giveaway—he kept the snakeskin bandolier, wrapping it about his waist beneath the overalls. He wanted to be within the palisade around the old border-town before nightfall. Once in, he would have to evaluate which options were likely, which were possible, and which were madness.

He started a cautious creep toward the wall, down a ditch beside what had once been a short road heading west out of town, still beneath his moldering carapace. Even after he was out of sight of the guardtower he stayed in the ditch. He abandoned the carpet while still away from the wall, since a patrol would find it more suspicious up close than abandoned in the field.

Boarded-up windows and corrugated aluminum nailed over doors faced him from the backs of what had been the main street of the town. Many of the little roadside towns in the borderlands of the Ozark Free Territory were like this, walling the spaces between buildings with wire-topped timber blocking any ingress other than the gate; what had been a sleepy rural town was now a frontier fort.

It went dark with the suddenness of a clouded winter night. Valentine's night vision took over—another biological modification, courtesy of the Lifeweavers, the ancient enemies and blood relations of Earth's new masters. Colors muted but edge details stood out. The grain of the wall and blades of tired winter grasses formed their delicate patterns on his enhanced retinas. Valentine's nose picked up the town's evening aromas of wood smoke, coal smoke, tobacco, cooking and outdoor toilets. The last was especially noticeable, as his ditch served as an open-air septic tank at the end of a pipe running from under the wall. He slunk up on the sluice that served as the town's sewer from downwind. If a dog patrol came, there was a chance that the odor would mask his.

Valentine examined the sewer-pipe. The PVC plastic was not something he could wiggle through, but rainwater making its way into the ditch had opened a gap under that part of the wall. Child-sized hand- and footprints ringed the gap. He smelled and listened for a moment, then crawled for the break.

If he was lucky—which he hadn't been since leaving the piney woods of Texas, admittedly—the garrison of Bern Woods would be short enough on pairs of eyes that it would be all they could do to keep the gate, prison and tower manned.

Waiting had never gained him much, so he stuck his head under the gap. The sluice stood next to what looked to have been a chicken takeout, the remnants of its friendly red-and-yellow decor incongruous next to the Fort Apache palisade.

He drew Tayland's bowie knife and wiggled through. The fighting knife was the only weapon he carried. Being gunless kept him cautious and alert. It might also buy him a little time if he were captured. The only people allowed to carry guns in the Kurian Zone were those who worked for the regime; a quick harvesting in the grasp of the Reapers was the usual punishment for anyone else found with a firearm.

The town wasn't electrified at the moment. Valentine saw a few lanterns and marked the faint glow of candlelight from the upper stories of the buildings on the main street. He smelled diesel and heard a generator clattering some distance away to the south. Following his ears, he saw drums in a fenced-in enclosure next to a shed behind a stoutly built building.

Valentine got away from the wall as quickly as he could. The town seemed empty. He untied his long hair and mussed it with his fingers so it covered the scar on the side of his face, and pulled the hat down to his eyebrows. He took a slow walk toward the highway cutting the town in two, turning onto the main street at a gas station whose garage now sheltered broken-down horses instead of broken-down cars. He recognized the horse that had been dragging Tayland in an oil-change bay.

In the Kurian Zone you had to walk a fine line between looking like you were busy and drawing attention to yourself. He walked purposefully toward the one building lit with electricity.

A feed store still held feed, by the look of it, but the drug and sundry had been recently boarded up.

The brightly lit building turned out to be the town bank, complete with drive-thru teller, though it had become an antique store sometime before the cataclysm of 2022, judging from an old, rain-washed sign painted where once tellers had stood behind armored glass to service cars. Blue banners, with three gold stars set in a horizontal white stripe, hung from the flagpole next to the door of the bank/antique shop. A painted sign jutting from a pile of whitewashed rocks announced its latest incarnation: Station 46. Red-painted gallows stood just a few steps from the headquarters at what had been an intersection, dominating the central street like a grim plaza statue. There was no trapdoor, just a pair of poles and a crossbeam.

A tall sentry with a forehead that bore an imprint where it might have been kicked by a horse's hoof stood to one side of the door. Another man, proportionally older and rounder, sat in an ornate rocking chair with a shotgun across his lap. His sideburns were russet, but the sparse hair streaming out from under a pisscutter cap was gray. Both wore khaki uniforms with brown leather pads at the knees, shoulders and elbows, though the seated one had lieutenant's bars and a more elaborate uniform.

"Is this Station 46?" Valentine drawled, head tilted to match the poor leveling of the sign's face.

"Goddammit, seems like every day I hear that," the older man screeched. "The friggin' sign is out there, plain as paint, everything but a spotlight on it. But still I hear 'Is this Station 46?' from some shitheel six times a week and twice on Sundays. Never fails."

"So this is Station 46?" Valentine asked.

The aged lieutenant turned even redder. "Yes, dammit! This is Station 46."

"I'm to speak to the commanding officer."

"He ain't here, boy. I mean, that's me, seeing as he's out. Whatever the question is, the answer is 'no.' Now get going before I jail you for breaking curfew, you dunk."

Valentine was happy to swallow the abuse, as long as the lieutenant stayed angry.

"I was told by one of your officers to speak to the commanding officer, Station 46. That's what I'm here to do, sir."

The lieutenant leaned forward in his rocking chair. "What about?"

"My boy's watchin' two pen of hawgs bit north of here, 'round Blocky Swamp. There's a lot less hawgs in those pens thanks to some sergeant with a uniform like yours. He didn't pass any scrips or warrants, just took 'em. He told me if I had a problem with it to speak to the officer commanding, Station 46, Bern Woods. Walked all day, practically, as I do have a problem with someone just takin' my stock."

"What the crap, dunk? Haven't you heard yet? There's been some changes, boy. Southern Command's not riding 'round handing out scrip no more. That's all over and out."

Valentine widened his stance.

"I don't fight these wars, or know about it from nothing, and I keep my boys outta it too. I'm short salt and flour and sugar; thought I'd pick some up and catch up on the news after Christmas. But being short hawgs now too, I thought a trip to town was in order. I want to write on some papers and make a complaint."

"A complaint? A complaint?"

"That's correct, sir."

The old man wavered in perplexity, then looked at Valentine sidelong, under lowered lids, like a bull trying to make up its mind whether to charge or run.

"I'll take your statement," he said. "I don't expect you'll get the answer you're looking for, but I warned ya fair."

"Thanks. Would've saved us both some time if you'd done so in the first place," Valentine said.

The older man snorted and led him inside the command post. He held the door open for Valentine with a grin, and Valentine suddenly liked the aged lieutenant a little better, and hoped it wouldn't come to killing.

Little remnants of both the banking heritage and retail life of the building remained in the form of a vault and stock tables. Valentine looked inside the vault, where arms and boxes of ammunition stood in disarray from the hurried muster he had seen ride out of town. A few footlockers and gun cases with Southern Command notations on them huddled in a corner as though frightened of the new pegs and racks. Opposite the vault a row of rooms held prisoners, confined behind folding metal gates like those used to protect urban merchants' streetside windows from burglars. Valentine counted the men, his heart shrinking three sizes when he recognized their faces. Eleven remaining marines from the *Thunderbolt* sat in the bare, unlit cells—pictures of grubby despair. Post and the two Jamaicans occupied another cell. Two more, in Texan clothes, shared another; Jefferson passed him a hint of a shrug—he had dried blood from a cut lip in his beard. The other was a drover named Wilson. Guilt pulled at him with an iron hook. The marines took in Valentine with darting eyes but said nothing. The surviving teamster ignored him.

Valentine heard a hoot, and turned his head to see a pair of Grogs in loincloths. Simpler, shorter versions of the Golden One known as Grey Ones, they bore brooms and dustpans, cleaning rags and wood oil. They were the last of Ahn-Kha's team, the lucky pair who had made it all the way to Haiti and back. Not bright enough to understand Valentine's disguise, they chattered in excitement at his familiar face. Valentine took a step back.

"Hell, those things give me the creeps. You got them in town?" Valentine asked, feigning fright.

The Grogs gamboled up to him, hooting. Valentine put a long table between him and the excited pair.

"Must be the smell of pigs," the temporary commander mused. He pushed the Grogs off.

"Don't let 'em touch me," Valentine said. The fear in his voice was real enough. If the officer decided to point the shotgun and start asking questions, there wasn't much he could do.

"What's all d'excitement?" a musical voice asked, coming from the hallway behind the Grogs.

Valentine looked down at Narcisse. She was uninjured—assuming one didn't count the missing legs and left hand, old souvenirs of her escape attempts on Santo Domingo—and dressed in her customary colorful rags and bandannas. She "walked" by swinging her body on her handless arm, using the limb as a crutch. An accomplished cook was welcome in any army, and she'd been put to work, judging from the aluminum dish gripped in her good hand. Valentine's sensitive nose detected the aromas of hot peppers and thyme in the steaming mixture of pork and rice. Narcisse looked once at Valentine, and then turned to the officer, pivoting on her left arm like a ballet dancer on pointe.

The Grogs forgot Valentine at the smell of food.

"You ready to eat, Cap'n? Extra spicy, just like you asked."

The older man's nostrils widened. "Sure am." He picked up a yellowed piece of blank paper and a pencil, and handed them to Valentine. "Get lost, boy. Write down your complaint, then give it back to me."

"This isn't official; it doesn't have a seal," Valentine said.

"There's enough for your friend, Cap'n. He looks hungry."

He glowered down on Narcisse. "You're supposed to feed officers first, then the men, and the prisoners long way last. He can try for a meal at the church hall."

"Yes, Cap'n. Sorry, mister, I just do what I'm told. Thank you, Cap'n."

Valentine picked up the pencil. "Can I write this in here where there's light?"

"As long as you shut up and stay out of my way, you can do what you like."

Narcisse filled the officer's plate, and brought out a plastic water jug with a cup rattling on the nozzle. "You want me to take some to the boys in the tower, Cap'n?"

"No, they're on duty. We're short men with the Visor out with the riders."

"Yes, Cap'n. Apple cider?" For someone with only one hand, Narcisse acted the part of a servant with skill.

"There's some left? Sure. This is some fine spicy. I'm from Dallas, and I'll tell you that this is good cooking."

"Thank you, Cap'n."

The officer, who never corrected her when she called him "Cap'n," even ate with the shotgun in his lap. Valentine looked at the service pips on his sleeve, wondering why a man with so many years was just a lieutenant, and a junior one at that. Valentine wrote out his phony story in scraggly block capitals. The wall above him was festooned with wanted posters and poorly reproduced photos, perhaps a hundred in all. "Terrorism" and "Sabotage" looked to be the two most common crimes, though "Speculation" appeared on some. He recognized one face: Brostoff, a hard-drinking lieutenant he had served with six years ago when he ran with the Wolves of Zulu Company. There was a four-year bounty on him. Just beneath Brostoff was a half-familiar face; Valentine had to look a second time to be sure. A handsome young black man looked into the camera with calm, knowing eyes. Frat—listed in the handbill as F. Carlson—had a ten-year bounty on him for assassination and sabotage. Frat would be about twenty now, Valentine calculated. He'd last seen him when he brought Molly back to the Free Territory and reunited her with her family, when the youth was serving his term as an aspirant prior to becoming a Wolf.

Valentine watched Narcisse sneak a few spoonfuls out to the guard on duty, but when she stumped her way over to the men in the cells, the lieutenant growled at her. As she turned away from the prisoners' outstretched arms she gave Valentine a significant wink.

"*Dix minutes,*" Narcisse said, under her breath.

Narcisse had shown her talents before in Haiti and beyond, where her curious mixture of herbalism and *vaudou* rendered surprising results. She had once put a man named Boul to sleep with a mickey in his chicken. He had also seen fevered men recover and be walking around in perfect health a day after one of her infusions. Biochemistry or magic, she performed miracles with food and the contents of her spice bag.

Valentine counted the minutes and continued his scrawled essay on the loss of his fictitious stock, punctuated by plate scrapings and burps from behind. At last he heard the utensils laid down.

"Aww, I'm stuffed," the lieutenant belched. Valentine crossed out a misspelled word and wrote a new one above it with an eye on the lieutenant, occupied exploring one hairy ear with a pinky. The oldster looked thoughtful, then doubtful, and gave a little burp.

The lieutenant stood up so fast his chair fell over backward. He went to the door at a quick walk, picking up the shotgun on the way. "Watch things in here," he ordered the man outside, handing over the pump-action.

The tall younger guard entered, the shotgun looking like a child's toy in his grasp. "He okay?"

"Just finished his meal and left. Shithouse run, I suppose."

The guard sat down and put his feet on the table, shotgun in his lap. Valentine tried to keep his eyes on the paper, rather than the odd crescent-shaped dimple across the man's forehead.

"Oh hell, I got 'em too," the giant said, standing up. "C'mon, can't leave you in here alone," he added, grabbing some keys.

"I'm not—"

"Out, pig-man, or I'll throw you out," the private threatened, his eyes bright with anxiety.

Valentine relented, and the man escorted him out, and turned the key in the lock of the steel door. It looked like the only modification to the outside of the structure in dozens of years.

Valentine stepped aside on the porch. The guard hurried around the corner, undoing his suspenders with the shotgun under his arm.

He heard the lock turn.

"Daveed, I thought you'd never come," Narcisse said, smiling up at him. "Let me show you where they keep the spare keys."

The tall private returned, a little white-faced. His face drained even more when he unlocked the door and found a phalanx of rifles and shotguns pointed at him.

"You want to put the gun down?" Valentine asked from a corner, a tiny .22 automatic he'd found in a box marked "local confiscations" in his hand.

The private's eyelids fluttered and he toppled over in a dead faint.

"Beats shooting him," Wilson said, picking the dropped shotgun off the floor.

"About time we got a break. Andree, Botun, handcuff him and get him in a cell. Jefferson," Valentine said to the other Texas teamster, "keep your gun at his head."

"What did you put in the food?" Valentine asked Narcisse as his men tied the private lying against the bottom bars of a cell. Post was still in the vault, choosing weapons and ammunition for their flight.

"Cascara Buckthorn bark, child. Opens them up good."

They repeated the procedure when the lieutenant staggered back in.

"Fuck me," the old man groaned when he read the situation.

"No thank you," Valentine said, pulling the revolver out of the lieutenant's hip holster. "I'll leave that for the Hoods."

The man put hand to collarbone, as if to ward off the probing tongue snaking its way toward his heart already. "They'll have me."

"Hard luck."

"Like you care."

"Help me get past the gate and I'll let you get a running start for Dallas, Lieutenant. Or wherever. You might have a chance."

"Seems to me it's my choice of the frying pan or the fire," the old man said.

"A fight is the last thing I want," Valentine said.

"You're the leader of the column, right? Some kinda Indian scout for the commissary wagons? They said he had black hair and a scar."

"You going to trust this turncoat, sir?" Jefferson said. "I say we don't even give the Reapers the satisfaction. Leave the two of them hangin' with greeting cards for when they come back."

The old man stiffened. *Damn, almost had him.*

"Jefferson, make yourself useful in the kitchen, please. Narcisse is packing up, and we need food." He turned to the Quisling. "Look, Lieutenant . . . err . . ."

"M'Daw, mister good cop."

"I'm going to offer you a deal, M'Daw. Help us get away clean. You're a lieutenant; you must have some idea where patrols and so on are out. You get us out of this town without bloodshed, and I'll let you go in a day or two with food and water to walk to safety."

"*Shove, dunk,*" M'Daw said.

"Let me finish. The alternative is we kill every man of your troop in town. There can't be that many of them."

M'Daw said nothing.

"Hard way it is," Valentine said. He beckoned one of his Jamaicans. "Ewenge, keep an eye on this man. Post!"

"Sir?" his lieutenant called from the vault.

"We need to be ready to move in fifteen minutes," he said, removing his boots. He slipped a spare box of .22 shells in his overall pocket and picked up Tayland's bowie knife, then found a towel in the little kitchen atop a twenty-gallon water cask. "I'm going to make sure the streets are clear."

The streets were clear enough—a Kurian curfew had that effect. After test-firing the pistol a few times in the clattering generator shed—the tiny pop of the .22 could hardly be heard over the buzzing rattle of the generator—Valentine crept along the town wall, listening all the way. Only half the buildings in the little widening-in-the-road town seemed occupied.

He got his first rats at the tower. A Quisling, maybe seventeen and in a coat too big for his shoulders, stood watch in the bullet-scarred gate-tower as faint snores echoed from inside. The muzzle of a mounted machine gun pointed toward the sky, a canvas tube on it to keep the on-again, off-again rain from wetting it. Valentine waited until he moved to another corner, and heard a faint sigh and a heavy step as the kid crossed the sleeping sentry.

Valentine didn't take the ladder to the tower. Instead he jumped from an outhouse and ran along a beam that reinforced the wooden palisade, a six-meter drop to either side.

The boy turned as Valentine swung into the tower. Valentine shot him three times with the .22, wrapped up in an old towel to muffle the shots. He didn't watch the kid go down, tried not to listen to the bubbling of aspirated blood as he used the knife on the sleeping sentry.

He held the knife tucked under his armpit, shoved the gun back in the overalls, felt the warm blood on the floor of the tower with his chilled feet. Deep inside his lizard-brain, the shadowy part of himself, the part of himself that the rest of his soul hated, exulted.

Valentine lifted the beltless machine gun from its mount and went to the other side of the tower, overlooking the gate. The gate guard stood there looking up, perhaps trying to make sense of the strange clicks and clunks from the tower. Valentine threw the machine gun at him, readied the now-bloody knife again and followed the weapon over the side of the tower.

He missed the third rat with his jump. The man saw him leap and ran—Valentine noted that he limped—and as he gave a shout Valentine was on his back, knocking him down with a body blow even as the knife went into the guard's kidney. The man let out a hissing scream as Valentine straddled him, reaching for the .22. He pressed the gun to the back of the guard's neck and pulled the trigger. The .22 cracked like a small firework. Valentine pulled the body into an alley and took its coat off. Once he had the guard's coat and hat on he reloaded his gun, looking up the street. He saw a faint outline in an upstairs window above a former Ozark Shop 'n Swap.

Valentine trotted to the other side of town, keeping in the shadows. He saw another figure, also in a Quisling fatigue coat, moving down the street equally cautiously. Valentine waved him over, but turned his back so he could ostensibly keep watch in the direction he'd come from.

The man took a few cautious steps and stopped—maybe he'd spotted Valentine's lack of boots. Valentine threw himself into a doorway, putting comforting bricks in between himself and the Quisling, and drew his gun. He followed its muzzle out and saw the man dashing across the street to Station 46. Valentine fired one shot on pure instinct—missed—and lowered the gun. Post was waiting within Station 46, and there was plenty of cell space.

The residents of Bern Woods learned what was happening when they saw their neighbors in the street. Valentine posted Ewenge as a lookout, and as he returned from the tower he had thirty people vying for attention, for news, for some sign that the world they had known had been restored. They picked him out as the man in charge despite his mundane and musty clothes.

Valentine had no answers. The shadowy confusion reminded him of another night, in Oklahoma, when he'd had to leave the residents of the Rigyard after smoking out four Reapers. No matter which way he turned, another desperate face, another clutching hand—

"When are our boys coming back?"

"You can't leave us!"

"Reprisals. There'll be reprisals."

"They drained a man last week, right in front of everyone. Over a dozen eggs. A dozen eggs!"

He had no orders, no higher authority to consult. Instead of being a burden, it was liberating. The decision came easily. This time he could give them a running start.

He ordered Jefferson and Wilson to take what riding animals they could and arm the residents from the remaining weapons at Station 46, and then ride for the Texas pines as though the devil were at their heels—a metaphor not far from the truth. Trackers would follow the hoofprints, but the thick pine woods were only a few hours' hard ride, and every mile they went into East Texas would improve their chances of meeting guerillas—perhaps even the well-armed party he'd crossed Texas with.

Jefferson shook his head and showed Valentine a gap-toothed grin. "I left you once, sir. These Dallas brownshirts started a fight, took out three teeth. I want to be around for the finish. Wilson knows stock as well as I do, and any ten-year-old can figure out what direction south is."

The survivors of Valentine's ill-fated wagon train left as soon as they had gathered their necessities. He'd hoped to find some of the precious Quickwood he'd brought back from the Caribbean, but found just a trio of shot-up wagons. Valentine trotted out to the house where he'd hidden his clothes and .45 to retrieve them, but didn't take the time to change out of the overalls. The troops out hunting Ahn-Kha might give up and return at any moment.

He returned to the remains of his command. They were laden with all the food and water they could carry; even a flour barrel slung from a hammock tied to a pair of two-by-fours. The Grogs carried this last, happy to be moving in the company of men they knew. Narcisse rode on a marine's shoulders.

Valentine, pistol held behind the bib of his overalls, fell into pace behind M'Daw; left-right, left-right . . .

They shut the gate again behind them. "What'll it be, M'Daw?"

"I think the healthiest thing to do is tag along with you."

Valentine carefully lowered the hammer on his automatic, relieved. He had been nerving himself to shove the pistol into the old man's stomach, muffling the gunshot with paunchy flesh. "I'm glad you said that, M'Daw," he said, quite honestly.

Valentine's Cat-eye night vision caught motion at the base of the wall.

A pair of figures ran toward them. Valentine brought up his gun, but marked a woman's long brown hair.

"Sir, you clearing out?" the unknown man said as it began to rain. He had the dried-out look of a man with a lot of outdoor mileage.

"Mister . . . uhhh . . ." the woman put in.

"You can call me Ghost."

"My name's Rich Smalls," the man said. "This is my wife, Tondi. We got to find my boy."

"You'd better find him in a hurry. Mr. Wilson is leaving for Texas right now," Valentine said.

"We want to go," Tondi Smalls said. She was a short woman with straight, black hair below her shoulders, and pretty features marred by worry. Valentine guessed her to be six or seven months pregnant. "You're heading north, right? Our son's watching some horses in pasture. It's in that direction."

"We're going to be moving hard," Valentine said. "You sure you can keep up?"

"Would horses help?" Mr. Smalls said. "There's twenty or more horses in Patchy Pines. They'll be fresh and rested. Been on pasture for weeks."

"We'll need them. Show me, Mr. Smalls. You're a godsend."

"I could say the same about you, mister. It's been a hellacious year."

"I'd like to hear about it. Horses first. No tack, I suppose."

"Just rope, for leads."

"Bareback it is," Valentine said.

Smalls led the way down a bridle track, and fifteen minutes' walk brought them to the pasture.

The meadow circled a little cluster of pines and rocks, and was in turn surrounded by thicker trees, forming a badly cooked doughnut. The cold rain had faded into a drizzle, which would become snow as soon as the temperature dropped a degree or two more. Valentine, the crisis in town past, felt suddenly exhausted as he led his wet column northeast into the clearing. He heard stamping sounds of nervous horses under the trees as they splashed across a tiny creek swollen from the winter rain.

The meadow was too close to town. Valentine hurried his men toward a fire set under a rock overhang. Old cuts of carpet hanging from the rock made a shelter somewhere between a tent and a shack. Smalls ran ahead.

"Hank, you there? Wake up boy, your mother's here."

"Yes, Pa," a sleepy voice said from under the overhang. Valentine saw a bow and a quiver of arrows hung in the branches of a nearby tree. Joints of meat, cut from an animal that was probably a mule, also hung in the boy's camp.

A blanket-draped boy emerged, looking to be about thirteen years old and in the midst of a growth spurt. He wore brown corduroy pants, topped with a leather-trimmed blue shirt decorated with a gold star, similar to the one on the flag outside Station 46.

"Don't let the uniform bother you, sir," Smalls said, closing up the blanket on the boy's shoulders so it covered the star. "He spends a lot of time out in the woods on his own, and it's better if he's in the Honor Guard."

Valentine didn't have to ask what the Honor Guard was. Most Kurian Zones had it in one form or another; paramilitary training and indoctrination for the youth. A good record for a child usually meant safety for the parents. Valentine had seen a dozen forms of it in his travels under an assumed identity in the Kurian Zone, but he found it obscene here in what had been the Ozark Free Territory, as if his childhood church had been converted into a brothel.

"Hank, these are some Southern Command soldiers," Smalls said. "They're going to take us with them." Mrs. Smalls nodded.

"Uhh, with the horses?" the boy asked.

"Yes. Go and start rounding them up."

"Yessir."

"Just a second. Where'd these joints come from?" Smalls asked.

"Wounded mule. Wandered in two days ago with a wagon team; smelled out the other horses I suppose. I quick hid the wagon and the harnesses, and put 'em with our horses. Some searchers came through and didn't know the difference, so we're up five head for sly-trading."

"You say there was a wagon?" Valentine asked.

"Yessir. It was kinda shot up."

"Did the searchers find it?"

"Sorta. I put her the middle of the field like it'd been parked there when a team was unhitched. There wasn't much in it, just a big load of lumber, so they didn't look twice at it. They asked if I was gonna build a hut out here. I said it was for a smokehouse. I was more worried about them finding the Texas driving rig I'd tossed in the creek, or them noticing new horses missing brands."

"Where?" Valentine asked, so intensely that the boy shrank against his mother in fear.

"Sorry, Hank, is it? My name's David, and I was in charge of those wagons. Where is it?"

"Just the other side of these trees, sir. C'mon, I'll show you."

"Corporal Botun," Valentine ordered. "Keep everyone together here. C'mon, Jefferson, let's see what we can do with this rig."

Valentine followed the boy and Smalls, the tall Texas teamster at his side. At a word from Narcisse, the marine carrying her trailed along. They cut through a mixture of pine and hickory and came to the other side of the meadow ringing the boy's wooded campsite. The wagon stood there, its battered wooden sides dark and wet in the night's gloom. Valentine couldn't restrain himself. He ran and jumped up into the bed of the wagon like a mountain goat leaping to a higher rock.

A load of wooden four-by-four beams, coated with preservative resin, lay in the bed of the wagon. The raindrops beaded up and ran off like flowing tears. Tears that matched those on Valentine's face, concealed by the drizzle. He couldn't do anything about the dead men he'd failed. But now he could do something for those still living. Shaking, he turned to Narcisse.

"Quickwood," Narcisse said, looking into the wagon from atop the marine's shoulders.

"What kinda wood?" Smalls said.

Valentine sank to his knees in the bed of the wagon, running his hands along the beams. "Mister Smalls, I owe your boy a mountain of gratitude."

"Why's that? For finding your wagon?"

"A lot more. Hank might have just saved the Free Territory."

Two

Pony Hollow, Arkansas, Christmas Eve: One of the winter snowstorms that blows this far south dusts the Ouachitas with tiny pellets of snow. Less painful than hail and less treacherous than freezing rain, the snow taps audibly on the remaining leaves as it falls. The snowstorm provides the only motion in the still of the afternoon as curtains of it ripple across the landscape. Bird and beast seek shelter, leaving the heights of the rounded mountains to the wind and bending bough.

The ridges of the Ouachitas here run east-west, as if a surveyor had laid them out using a compass. But for the pines, the rocky heights of the mountains would look at home in the desert West; the mesalike cliffs rise above a carpet of trees, naked cliffs cutting an occasional grin or frown into the mountainside. Between the ridges creek-filled hollows are the abode of bobcat and turkey, songbird and feral hog. The latter, with their keen senses matched by cunning and surprising stealth, are challenging animals to hunt.

But one of the callous-backed swine has fallen victim to a simple speared deadfall of Grey One design, baited with a sack of corn. After thorough boiling, individual chops sputter in a pair of frying pans within a rambling, abandoned house. The fugitives enjoy a Christmas Eve feast—complete with snowfall. Horses are tethered tightly together in the garage, blocked in by the recovered wagon in what had been the home's gravel driveway.

A single guard watches over the animals from the wagon seat, a horse blanket over his head and shoulders. The hairy mass snags the snow pellets out of the wind as if it were designed to do just that. David Valentine, sitting under his sugar-dusted cape, whittles a spear point out of a piece of Quickwood with Tayland's oversized Texas bowie. His dark eyes look in on the celebrating men and Grogs.

"Pork chop?" William Post, former lieutenant of the Quisling Costal Marines, asked. He had found enough rags to complete an outfit of sorts, though the mixture left him looking like an unusually well-stuffed scarecrow. "It's practically still sizzling."

Valentine reached out with his knife and speared the chop. The meat was on the tough side, even after being boiled, but the greasy taste was satisfying.

"Merry Christmas, Val," Post said, his voice flavored with a hint of a Mississippi drawl. By common consent the formalities were dropped when they were alone together.

"Same to you, Will."

"My wife used to make peanut brickle and pecan pies at Christmas," Post said, his incipient beard catching the snow as well. There was a pause. Valentine knew that Post's wife had run away when he became a Quisling officer in New Orleans. "Narcisse is up to something with a pot of rice. I saw sugar out, too."

"Station 46 had a good larder. Sissy emptied it."

"Wonder what happened to that tall guard," Post said. "He didn't seem a bad sort."

"Not our problem."

"I know that. Can't help thinking about the poor bastard, though. I spent more time under them than you did. The choices are difficult. A lot of them don't cooperate with the regime as willingly as you think. Every other man's got a blind eye that he turns if he can get away with it."

"Yes. Those fellows weren't frontline material." Valentine stared off into the snowfall. "Where do you suppose their good soldiers are?"

"I think there's still fighting here and there."

"We've got one load of Quickwood left. We should try to find it."

Post nodded. "The men can't believe you went back for them, by the way."

"I owed them as much. Stupid of me to drop my guard, just because we were back in what I thought was the Free Territory. The ambush was my fault."

"Done with."

Valentine let it lie. He looked through the narrow windows of the house at the celebrating men. They weren't a fighting force anymore, and wouldn't be for a long time. They were survivors, happy to be warm, fed and resting.

"How's the radio holding up?"

His lieutenant had found a portable radio back at Station 46. "The Grogs love charging it up with the hand crank. I think they like to watch the lights come on. Lots of coded transmissions, or just operators BSing. I've gotten more information out of M'Daw."

"What does he say?"

"The Kurians only sorta run these lands; they're in the hands of a big Quisling Somebody named Consul Solon. Even M'Daw had heard of him. The rest I don't have facts about."

"He know anything about Mountain Home?" Valentine asked. The former capital of the Ozark Free Territory was tucked into the mountains for a reason.

"The president is gone. Don't know if he's dead or hiding. Smalls said the Kurians passed around a rumor that he joined up with them, but he doesn't believe it."

"Can't see Pawls as a turncoat," Valentine said.

"You ever meet him?"

"No. He signed my promotion. Used to be an engineer. He got famous before I even came to the Ozarks, the last time the Kurians let loose a virus. I remember he was lieutenant governor when I came here in '62. He became governor in '65 while I was in Wisconsin."

"Maybe he made a deal. Happened before," Post said. "Like the siege at Jacksonville when I was little."

"I doubt a man who lost his kids to the ravies virus would take to cooperating." Valentine tossed the gnawed pork chop bone to the ground. One of the horses sniffed at it and snorted.

"You coming in for dessert?"

"I'll sit outside a bit. I like the snow. We always had a couple feet by Christmas in the Boundary Waters. Kills the sound, makes everything quiet. I like the peace."

Post shuddered. "You can keep it." His old lieutenant returned to the house.

The Free Territory gone. It was too big an event to get his thoughts around just yet.

The idea of the resourceful, hardworking people having succumbed to the Kurians after all this time was tragic on such a scale that it numbed him. His father had fought to establish this land; Gabriella Cho had died to defend it, hardly knowing the names of thirty of its inhabitants. The risks he ran, his innumerable sins against God and conscience, all were in defense of these hills and mountains—or, more properly, the families living among them.

He kept coming back to the kids. He'd spent enough time on both sides of the unmarked border to know where he was just by a glance at the children. They played differently in the Free Territory, laughed and made faces at soldiers passing through—though they tended to be on the scrawny side. Their better-fed cousins in the plains or on the half-flooded streets of New Orleans or in the cow barns of Wisconsin startled easily and watched strangers, especially those with guns or enclosed vehicles, with anxious eyes.

Valentine preferred laughter and the occasional raspberry. The thought of Hank, turned into one of those painfully quiet adolescents . . .

All fled, all gone, so lift me on the pyre . . .

Defeat had always been a possibility, but the Ozark Free Territory had stood so long, it seemed that it should always stand. This is how the residents in the skyscrapers of Miami must have felt as they saw the '22 surge roll over the hotels of South Beach: *It's been there my whole life, how can it be gone?* There had been invasions in the past, some shallow, some deep. Territory had been lost, or sometimes gained, for years. He'd seen a grim battlefield after a big fight up in Hazlett, Missouri, and heard the tales of the survivors. But the Kurians were by nature a jealous and competitive lot, sometimes at war with each other more than the Free Territory. To coordinate the kind of attack that could roll up the Ozarks would require sacrifices the surrounding principalities weren't willing to make. During his years of Cathood in the Kurian Zone, Valentine had formed a theory that the Ozarks were a useful bogeyman for the brutal regimes. Death and deprivation could always be blamed on "terrorists" in the Ozarks, or the other enclaves scattered around what had been North America.

Had the Free Territory been on the verge of becoming a real threat? A threat that had to be eliminated?

Did the Kurians know about his Quickwood?

No. No; if they had, the Bern Woods ambush would have been carried out by swarms of Reapers, not Quisling red-hands.

Valentine reached into his tunic and put his hand around the little leather pouch hanging from a string about his neck. He felt the peanut-sized seeds of the Quickwood trees, given to him by the Onceler on Haiti, jumbled together with Mali Carrasca's mahjong pieces. Had his mission on the old *Thunderbolt* not been so long delayed—first in New Orleans before the voyage and then later among the islands of the Caribbean—he would have gotten back to the Free Territory with a weapon that might have made a difference. Quick-wood was lethal to the Reapers. The wood was a biological silver-bullet against the Frankensteinish death machines, aura-transmitting puppets of their Kurian lords.

Southern Command gone. Better than a hundred thousand men under arms—counting militias—defeated and apparently scattered or destroyed.

Regrets filled his stomach, writhed in there, like a cluster of wintering rattlesnakes clinging together in a ball. How much did the delay in Jamaica while the *Thunderbolt* was being repaired cost Southern Command? He could have pushed harder. He could have driven the chief away from his girlfriend; stood at the dry dock day and night, hurrying the work along. Instead he made love to Malia, rode horses across the green Jamaican fields, and played mahjong with her and her father. Malia . . .

Another if, another snake stirred and bit and he locked his teeth at the inner pain. Perhaps if he hadn't had his mind on the message from Mali about her pregnancy—*I'm going to be a father*, he reminded himself. He shoved the thought aside again as though it were a crime he hated to remember; he should have paid more attention to events after crossing back into what he thought was Free Territory, asked more questions, gotten to a radio. He might have avoided the ambush. . . .

His thoughts were turning in a frustrating circle again. He found he was on the verge of biting the back of his hand like an actor he'd once watched portraying a madman in a New Orleans stage melodrama. He was a fugitive, responsible for a single wagon rather than a train, running for his life with a handful of poorly armed refugees instead of the hundreds who had crossed Texas with him.

But he still had to see his assignment through. While he had never seen the plans, in his days as a Wolf he had been told that contingencies had been drawn up against the eventuality of a successful invasion. Southern Command had stores of weapons, food and medicines in the Boston Mountains, some the most rugged of the Ozarks. It didn't amount to anything other than a hope, but if some vestige of Southern Command existed, it was his duty to get the Quickwood into its hands.

There were obstacles beyond the Kurians. Getting north across the Arkansas River would be difficult. He had his shattered marines, a family with a pregnant woman, a Texas teamster and a Quisling he couldn't be sure of—and the precious wagonload of Quickwood. They were too many to move quietly and too few to be able to fight their way through even a picket line. He didn't know whether luck had gotten them this far into the Ouachitas or just Kurian nonchalance. The mountains were empty, almost strangely so; they had cut a few trails of large numbers of men, but only on old roads. If the Free Territory had fallen, he would expect the mountains to be thick with refugees: old Guard outfits, bands of Wolves, or just men determined to get their families out of the reach of the Kurians. Instead there was little but strings of empty homesteads in the hollows, fields and gardens already run to weed and scrub.

He looked down and discovered that he had finished his spear point. It was conical, and rough as a Neolithic arrowhead. They had no pointed steel caps for a tip of the kind Ahn-Kha had made on Haiti. Getting it through a Reaper's robes would be difficult.

The Jamaicans were singing in the other room. One of them had found a white plastic bucket of the sort Valentine was intimately familiar with from his days gathering fruit in the Labor Regiment, and employed it as an instrument with the aid of wooden-spoon drumsticks. With the backbeat established, the rest of the voices formed, seemingly without effort on their part, a four-part harmony. The rest, military, civilian and Grog, sat around listening to the calypso carols.

Narcisse, in the kitchen with Valentine, scooped some rice pudding onto his plate. She used a high kitchen stool and a chair to substitute for legs, moving form one perch to the other as she cooked.

"I used to have one of these with a turning seat in Boul's kitchen. Got to get me another someday. You'll like this, child. Just rice, sugar and raisins," she explained, when he raised an eyebrow and sniffed at it. "Okay, a touch of rum, too. It's Christmas."

"Rum?"

"I liberated the prisoners held in the officers' liquor cabinet back in town."

"You're a sly one. How did you make it inside that rigged-up jail? More magic?"

Narcisse spooned some more pudding into his cup. "Sissy's old, but she still has her game. Good thing I kept some coffee in my bag; those men back there didn't know a coffee bean from their earlobe. I ground it and brewed it, and before I knew it they had me in their kitchen. Just in case you didn't come back, I had them thinking that the Jamaicans were special farmers who knew how to grow coffee and cocoa and poppies for opiates. Was hoping to save their lives. Those soldiers believed me. Ignorance isn't strength."

"You know your George Orwell," Valentine said.

She shrugged. "Never met him. It was one of Boul's sayings." Boul was the man she cooked for before Valentine had brought her out of Haiti.

"Boul struck me as more the Machiavelli type."

"Daveed, you're troubled. You worried about the baby?"

Valentine was dumfounded. The letter Mali had left him with, with orders not to read it until he reached the Ozarks, had never left the pouch around his chest, where it rested among his precious seeds.

"Did Mali tell you?"

"Oh no, Daveed. I smell the child in her when we left Jamaica. She young and strong, Daveed; your girl'll be fine."

"It's a girl?" Valentine was ready to believe that someone who could smell a pregnancy could also determine the sex of an embryo.

"Daveed, you got to quit being a prisoner of the past. Forget about the future, too. Come back to the here and now; we need you."

Valentine glanced into the other room. Maybe it was the soft Caribbean tone of her voice, a bit like Father Max's. It reminded him he needed to confess. He lowered his voice. "Narcisse, there are people dying because I let them down. You know how that feels?"

Narcisse put down her spoon and joined Valentine at the table. Someone had spent some time varnishing the oak until the grain stood clear and dark—the Free Territory had been filled with craftsmen. The pattern reminded him of grinning demon faces.

"I've never been a soldier, child. Spent a lot of time runnin' from them, but never been one. The men, wherever they're from, even those ape-men . . . they believe in this fight too. They're not as different from you as you think. They don't follow you blind, they follow you because they know that if it comes to a fight, they want to look out for you as much as you want to look out for them."

"Think so? Narcisse, I ran outside of Bern Woods. I got up and ran."

"No. I saw Ahn-Kha dragging you away with my own eyes."

"I still left."

"Dying with them wouldn't have done your people any good. You saved yourself for the next fight. You saved the wood, at least some of it."

"That was an accident. A lucky accident. An officer belongs with his men. If he doesn't share their fate, he hasn't done his duty to them. It's the oldest compact between a leader and the led. Goes back to whatever we had for society before civilization."

Narcisse thought this over. "Was it wrong of them to surrender?"

"Of course not. It was hopeless from the start."

"But you fought, they fought."

"Couldn't help it. It was instinct."

"When you left, Daveed, that was instinct too, no?"

"Not the kind you should give in to."

"The past can't be changed, child. You keep worrying at it, you'll be doing the same thing as you did at the fight. Running away. Don't pick at a scab, or a new one grows in its place. Let the hurt heal. In time, it'll drop off by itself. Better for you, better for the hurt. If there's one thing I know about, child, it's getting over a hurt."

The Vaudouist didn't refer to her injuries often. She answered questions about them to anyone who asked, but Valentine had never heard her use them as a trump card in an argument before. Valentine let her unusual statement hang in the air for a moment.

"Narcisse, it sounds fine, but . . . a bit of me that isn't quite my brain and isn't quite my heart won't be convinced yet."

"That's your conscience talking. He's worth listening to. But he can be wrong . . . sometimes."

Valentine half dozed in front of the field pack with the headset on. Ahn-Kha snored next to him, curled up like a giant dog. Like most Quisling military equipment, the radio sitting on the table before him was ruggedly functional and almost aggressively ugly. Late at night the Quisling operators became more social, keeping each other company in the after-midnight hours of the quiet watches. Someone had just finished instructions on how to clear a gummed condensation tube on a still. His counterpart was complaining about the quality of the replacements they'd been getting: "Shit may float, but you can't build a riverboat outta it." Valentine twisted the dial back to a scratchier conversation about a pregnant washerwoman.

"So she goes to your CO. So what? She should be happy. She's safe for a couple years now. Over," the advice-giver said.

"She wants housing with the NCO wives. She's already got a three-year-old. She wants me to marry her so they can move in. Over," the advice-seeker explained.

"That's an old story. She's in it for the ration book, bro. Look, if a piece of ass pisses you off, threaten to have her tossed off-Station. That'll shut her up. Better yet, just do it. Sounds to me like she's—"

Valentine turned the dial again.

". . . fight in Pine Bluff. Put me down for twenty coin on Jebro. He'll take Meredith like a sapper popping an old woman. Over."

"Sure thing. You want any of the prefight action? Couple of convicts. It's a blood-match; the loser goes to the Slits. Over."

Valentine had heard the term "Slits" used by rivermen on the Mississippi. It referred to the Reapers' slit-pupiled eyes, or perhaps the narrow wounds their stabbing tongues left above the breastbone.

"No, haven't seen 'em. I'd be wasting my money. Over."

Valentine heard a horse snort and jump outside the cracked window, the way an equine startled out of sleep readies all four feet for flight. The sound brought him awake in a flash. A pair of alarmed whinnies cut the night air.

Ahn-Kha came awake, nostrils flared and batlike ears up and alert.

"Arms! Quietly now, arms!" Valentine said to the sleeping men, huddled against the walls in the warm room where they had enjoyed dinner. He snatched up his pistol and worked the slide.

Ahn-Kha followed. How so much mass moved with such speed and stealth—

"What is it, my David?" Ahn-Kha breathed, his rubbery lips barely forming the words.

"Something is spooking the horses. Watch the front of the house. Post," Valentine said to his lieutenant, who had appeared in his trousers and boots, pulling on a jacket. "Get the Smalls and M'Daw into the cellar, please. Stay down there with them."

Valentine waved to the wagon sentry, Jefferson, but the man's eyes searched elsewhere. Jefferson had his rifle up and ready. Two of the horses reared, and he stood to see over them.

Three Reapers hurtled out of the snow, black-edged mouths open, bounding on spring-steel legs. Three! He and all his people would be dead inside two minutes.

"Reapers!" Valentine bellowed, bringing up his pistol in a two-handed grip. As he centered the front sight on one he noticed it was naked, but so dirt-covered that it looked clothed. A torn cloth collar was all that remained of whatever it had been wearing. He fired three times; the .45 barked deafeningly in the enclosed space.

At the sound of the shots his men moved even faster. Two marines scrambled to the window and stuck their rifles out of the loophole-sized slats in the shutters.

A Reaper leapt toward Jefferson, whose gun snapped impotently, and Valentine reached for his machete as he braced himself for the sight of the Texan's bloody disassembly. Perhaps he could get it in the back as it killed Jefferson. But it didn't land on the sentry. The naked avatar came down on top of a horse; on the balls of its feet, like a circus rider. It reached for the animal's neck, got a good grip—Valentine almost heard the snap as the horse suddenly toppled. The Reaper's snake-hinged jaw opened wide as it straddled the fallen animal to feed.

The other two, robeless like the first and running naked in the snowstorm, also ignored Jefferson, chasing the horses instead. The Jamaicans' rifles fired in unison when one came around the cart and into the open, but the only effect Valentine saw was a bullet striking into a mount's rump. The horse dropped sideways with a Reaper on top of it.

Some instinct made the wounded animal roll its heavy body across the spider-thin form and came to its feet, kicking. As the Reaper reached for the tail a pair of hooves caught it across the back, sending it flying against the cart. It lurched off into the darkness, clutching its chest and making a wheezing sound.

The third disappeared into the snowstorm, chasing a terrified bay.

"Stay with the others," he said to Ahn-Kha, who stood ready with a Quickwood spear point. He threw open the door—and held up his hands when Jefferson whirled and pointed the rifle at him, muzzle seemingly aimed right between his eyes. The gun snapped again.

Valentine almost flew to the feeding Reaper. It heard him and raised its head from the horse, the syringelike tongue still connected to the twitching animal. It lashed out. Valentine slipped away from the raking claw. The momentum of the Reaper's strike turned its shoulder, and Valentine buried his knife in its neck, forcing it facedown in the snow as the tongue retracted, flinging hot liquid like a bloody sprinkler. He ground the bowie into the Reaper, hearing its feet scrabble for purchase on the snowy ground. It tried to shrug him off. Valentine brought up a knee, pressed on the blade . . .

The Reaper twitched as nerve tissue parted. In five seconds it was limp.

A blur—Jefferson's rifle butt came down on the back of the Reaper's head so that Valentine felt the wind pass his nose. Jefferson raised the gun up again.

"It's done," Valentine said.

Valentine pulled his knife from the Reaper's corpse, and Jefferson clubbed it again. "Jefferson, calm down. You might try loading your weapon. It's deadlier from the other end."

"Sorry, Captain. Sorry—"

Valentine ignored him and listened with hard ears all around the woods. Years ago, when he'd learned the Way of the Wolf, a Lifeweaver had enhanced his senses. When he concentrated on his senses—hardening them, in the slang of the Wolves—he could pick up sounds others would miss. He heard branches breaking in the snow somewhere, in the direction of the Reaper who had been kicked and then run. Valentine tried to make sense of the behavior. They had attacked randomly and hit the biggest targets they could see. Evidently they were masterless; their Kurian had probably been killed or had fled out of control range and they were acting on pure instinct. The severed-necked Reaper gave a twitch of an arm, and Jefferson jumped a good two feet in the air.

"Just a reflex," Valentine said.

"Should we burn it or something?"

"Get inside. Don't worry about the horses for now."

The Texan backed into the house. Valentine put a new magazine in his gun and took a few more steps around the yard, still listening and smelling. Nothing. Not even the cold feeling he usually got when Reapers were around, but his ears were still ringing from the gunshots inside, and the snow was killing odors.

He rapped on the door and backed into the house, still covering the Quickwood.

"Anything out back?" he called, eyes never leaving the trees.

"Nothing, sir," Botun said.

He heard a horse scream in the distance. The Reaper had caught up with the bay.

"Post," Valentine shouted.

"Sir?" he heard through the cellar floor.

"I'm going out after them. Two blasts on my whistle when I come back in. Don't let anyone shoot me." Valentine caught Jefferson's eye and winked. The Texan shook his head in return.

"Yessir," Post answered.

Valentine tore off a peeling strip of wallpaper and wiped the resin-like Reaper blood off the bowie. He considered bringing a Quickwood spear, but decided to hunt it with just pistol and blade: It would be vulnerable after a feed. He nodded to the Jamaicans and opened the front door. After a long listen, he dashed past a tree and into the brush of the forest.

A nervous horse from the other team nickered at him. He moved from tree to tree, following the tracks.

Valentine dried his hand on his pant leg and took a better grip on his bowie. He sniffed the ground with his Wolf's nose, picking up horse blood in the breeze now. He instinctively broke into his old loping run, broken like a horse's canter by his stiff leg, following the scent. He came upon the corpse of the bay, blood staining the snow around its neck. He turned and followed the footprints.

He didn't have far to travel. After a run that verged on a climb up a steep incline, he came to the Reaper's resting spot. Water flowing down the limestone had created a crevice cave under the rocky overhang. An old Cat named Everready used to say that Reapers got "dopey" after a feed, that with a belly full of blood they often slept like drunkards. This one had hardly gotten out of sight of the horse before succumbing to the need for sleep. He saw its pale foot, black toenails sharp against the ash-colored skin, sticking out of a pile of leaves.

Valentine heard whistling respiration. He put his hand on his pistol and decided to risk a single shot. He drew and sighted on the source of the breathing.

The shot tossed leaves into the air. The Reaper came to its feet like a rousted drunk, crashing its skull against the overhang. A black wound crossed its scraggly hairline. It went down to its hands and knees, shaking its head. Valentine sighted on a slit pupil in a bilious yellow iris.

"Anyone at the other end?" Valentine asked, looking into the eye. The thing looked back, animal pain and confusion in its eyes. It scuttled to the side, shrinking away from him. Valentine tracked the pupil with his gun. "What are you doing out here?"

Harrrruk! it spat.

It exploded out of the overhang.

Valentine fired, catching it in the chest. The bullet's impact rolled it back into the cave, but it came out again in its inhuman, crabwise crawl, trying to escape up the hill.

It moved fast. As fast as a wide-awake Reaper, despite its recent feeding.

Valentine shot again . . . again . . . again. Black flowers blossomed on the thing's skin at the wet slap of each slug's impact. It fled beneath a deadfall, slithering like a snake, trying to avoid the hurtful bullets. Valentine leapt over the trunk after it, bowie ready. He pinned it, driving the knee of his good leg into the small of its back, wishing he hadn't been so cocksure, that he'd brought Quickwood to finish it. He raised the blade high and brought it down on the back of its neck, the power of the blow driving it into the monster's spine. He tried to pull it back for another blow, but the black blood had already sealed the blade into the wound.

It continued to crawl, only half of its body now working.

Valentine stood up, and drove his booted heel onto the blade. If he couldn't pull it out, he could get it in farther. He stomped again, almost dancing on the back of the blade. The Reaper ceased its crawl, but the head still thrashed.

Urrack . . . shhhar, it hissed.

Valentine put a new magazine in his gun. It was beyond being a threat to anything but an earthworm or a beetle now, but he wouldn't let it suffer. He brought the muzzle to the ear-hole, angling it so the bullet wouldn't bounce off the bony baffle just behind the ear. He didn't want to risk the jaws without a couple of men with crowbars to pry the mouth open and a pliers to rip the stabbing tongue out.

He heard a sliding footfall behind, and turned, the foresight of the pistol leading the way.

It was the other Reaper, blood covering its face but cruel interest in its eyes. It squatted to spring. It had possessed instinct enough to approach from downwind.

Valentine emptied the magazine into it, knocking it over backward. Then he ran. Downhill. Fast.

It followed. Faster.

Valentine listened to it gain on him in three awful seconds, its footsteps beating a snare-drum tattoo. The footfalls stopped, and Valentine flung himself into the dirt in a bone-jarring shoulder roll.

It passed overhead, a dervish of raking claws and kicking legs. As he rolled back to his feet, he saw it fly face-first into a thick-boled hickory with a *thunk* Valentine felt through the ground.

Valentine had never felt less like laughing in his life. He continued his run downhill, blowing the whistle for his life, as the Reaper picked itself up.

He saw the house, and Post with the marines at the window. Jefferson, terror written on his face, pointed his rifle right at him.

Valentine dived face-first into the snow, sliding the last few feet down the hill.

Jefferson fired, not at him but over. More shots rang out, bright muzzle flashes reflecting off the dusting of Christmas snow like photoflashes.

The Reaper behind him went over backward. Valentine rolled over, pistol aimed in a shaking hand. Someone must have got in with a luck shot, for it lay thrashing, trying to rise. Failing.

"Hold your fire," Valentine panted. "Post, give me your spear."

"I'll do it, sir," Jefferson said, opening the bolt on his rifle and setting it down carefully. He reached behind the door and came out with a pick. "This is how we finish 'em in the Rangers."

"Careful now, Jefferson," Post said. "It might be playing possum."

Jefferson approached it, pick raised high. Valentine stood aside with his Quickwood stake. Jefferson needed this, after his fright earlier.

"Okay, dickless. Time to see what happens when you steal a Texan's horses."

"Damn, that fella right. That *bomba* doesn't have one," Botun said over the sights on his rifle.

Jefferson grunted, and swung the pick down. The Reaper brought up a limb to ward off the blow but the pick went home through its face and into the ground beneath. It stiffened into immobility.

Valentine turned to the marines at the windows. "Thank you, Post. Good shooting, men. Six shots, four hits. That's outstanding for a running Reaper." Valentine hoped the lighthearted tone didn't sound forced.

"On Jamaica bullets are rare, sir," a marine named Andree said.

He turned to look at the private. "In the Ozarks, men who can shoot like you are even rarer."

Three

Magazine Mountain, Arkansas, January of the forty-ninth year of the Kurian Order: A Southern Command Station Post once stood here, huts and wooden cabins placed to take advantage of folds in the ground and the canopy of trees for concealment and defensibilty.

Servicemen walking about on their duties added life and color to the camouflaged buildings. The Guards, the common soldiers in their neat charcoal gray uniforms and regimental kepis, would march past files of scarecrow-lean Wolves in fringed buckskins. The Wolves, rifles cradled in tanned fingers, assorted pistols and knives shoved in belts and boots, and no two hats alike, struck one as sloppy-looking when compared to the disciplined Guards. A Cat might be sleeping beneath an oak, head pillowed on rolled coat and Reaper-killing sword, exhausted after two months spying in the Kurian Zone, but still coming to full wakefulness at a gentle tap. Everyone from cur dog to colonel of the Guards would make room when teams of Bears entered the post. Southern Command's shock troops, wearing uniforms of patched-together Grog hide and bullet-ablative Reaper cloak, the latter's black teeth hanging from neck or ear, were people one instinctively avoided. Perhaps it was the forbidding war paint, or the scalps of Grogs and even Quislings dangling from belt and rifle sheath, or the thousand-yard stare, but whatever the source the Bears had an aura about them demanding a wide berth. Then there were the others in camp, the logistics commandos: scroungers who went into the Kurian Zone to steal or trade for what Southern Command couldn't make for itself, driving their wagons to the commissary yards and yelling at women to get their children out of their mule team's path. There were always civilians in camp, families of the soldiery or refugees waiting on transpor-

tation to other parts of the Freehold. There would be pack traders and mail-riders, gunsmiths, charcoal sellers with black hands, hunters trading in game for more bullets and farmers selling vegetables for government buckchits. It was chaos, but chaos that somehow kept the soldiery fed and equipped, the civilians prosperous (by the standards of the Free Territory) and, most importantly, the Ozarks free of the Reapers.

But that was before.

By that dark, wet winter of '71, the base of Magazine Mountain had only rats and raccoons standing sentry over burned huts or nosing through old field kitchens that smelled of rancid cooking oil. Bats huddled together for warmth in SCPO mailboxes, and the carts and pickup trucks rested wheelless on the ground, stripped like slaughtered cattle.

Heavy equipment rendered inoperable had a large red X painted on it. The same might be done with maps depicting the Ozark Free Territory.

"Goddammit, another fallen tree ahead," Post called from a rise in the road. He turned his horse and looked at Valentine for orders. One of Ahn-Kha's scouting Grogs squatted to rest.

"We might do better off the trail," Narcisse said to Valentine from her perch in the Quickwood wagon. Joints of horsemeat hung from a frame Jefferson had added to the wagon bed. It was too cool for flies. "These roads are almost as bad."

Smalls' son took the opportunity to put a taconite pellet in his wrist-rocket, a surgical tubing sling that he used to bring down squirrels. The boy ventured into the trees while Valentine thought. David looked at Ahn-Kha, who was sniffing the wintry air.

"Rain soon," Ahn-Kha said.

"The Magazine Mountain Station can't be far," Valentine said to Post. "Let's pull off the trail and camp."

There had been no more Reapers since leaving the house. The refugees Valentine led made agonizingly slow progress through the ridges of the Ouachitas, with occasional halts to hide at the sound of distant engines. They had seen no living human—though they had come across a Reaper-drained skeleton lodged in the crotch of a tree, giving Mrs. Smalls a warmer coat once it was pulled off the corpse and cleaned. A pack of stranger-shy dogs tailed them, exploring the surroundings of the campfire and digging up the camp's sanitary holes in search of choice snacks. Valentine had tried to tempt them closer with fresher food than something that had already passed through the human digestive system, but the dogs would have none of it. Every now and then he saw a wary, furry face appear on the road behind, proving that they were still being tailed. Valentine wanted the dogs with them. Dogs hated Reapers—or feared them—and usually whined or bayed an alarm if one was near.

Valentine waved Ahn-Kha and Post over.

"Sir?" Post asked.

Valentine looked up at the flat-topped loom of Magazine Mountain. "Post, we're near one of the big camps of Southern Command. I'm going to take Ahn-Kha and see what, if anything, is left. Pull off out of sight of the road, cover your tracks and camp. We'll go on foot; give the horses a rest."

"Chances are that fort's in Kurian hands."

"I know. That's why I'm bringing Ahn-Kha. Having a Grog along might confuse them long enough for me to talk my way loose, or get the jump on a patrol."

"How long you figure on being gone?"

"Less than a day. If twenty-four hours go by and you don't hear from us, act as you will. I'd say the Boston Mountains are your best chance, on the other side of the Arkansas River. If there's anything left of Southern Command, it should be there. Get the Quickwood to them. Don't forget the seeds."

Post fingered the pouch around his neck, identical to Valentine's, though it didn't contain any mahjong pieces. "I'll see it through, Val."

"Thank you. I'll probably be back in time for horsemeat and flatbread."

He took Ahn-Kha over to the supply wagon. They each threw a bag made out of old long-sleeved shirts over their shoulders. The shirt-sacks contained bread. Mr. Smalls rose from where he squatted next to his wife.

"Everything all right with you two?" Valentine asked them.

"Just a little tired, Mr. Ghost," Mrs. Smalls said, her belly prominent through the opening in the coat.

"We're stopping for a day or two. Fix yourselves up under the bed of the wagon. Looks like we might get some rain."

"Hank's been picking up sharp quartz crystals; there's lots of them in these hills," Mr. Smalls said. "If we attach 'em to the front of those wooden spear points, they might serve you a little better." He reached into his shoulder bag and pulled out a spear point.

Valentine looked at it. The boy had set a piece of quartz into the front, carving the wood into four prongs, like a gem-holder on a ring. Valentine tested the point on the quartz. It was sharp enough. "How'd he fix the quartz in so tight?"

"He soaked the wood after he carved it," Mrs. Smalls said proudly. "When it dried, it shrank down on the crystal."

"Good thinking," Valentine replied, handing it to Ahn-Kha for his opinion. The Golden Ones were accomplished craftsmen in their own right.

"This is fine work," Ahn-Kha agreed, fingering the point.

"Have him make some more, if he can," Valentine said.

Smalls nodded, and Valentine led Ahn-Kha off. They watched the Smalls boy search the tree limbs, but the squirrels were making themselves scarce. "Smart kid. In the Wolves we used to take boys on patrols, called them 'aspirants.' That spear point alone would have got him a place with my company."

"He thinks quickly. Remember what he did with the wagon."

"We could use another sharp set of eyes," Valentine said. "Want to bring him along?"

"He'd have a better chance at a squirrel with us," Ahn-Kha replied, his long ears twisting this way and that.

"Settled," Valentine said. He put two fingers in his mouth and whistled. "Hey, Hank, come over here."

The boy ran up to them. "Yes, Mr. Ghost?"

"We're going out on an all-night scout. You want to come?"

"Yes, sir!" Hank answered, his voice breaking with excitement.

"Go on, ask your parents. If it's okay with them, catch up to us."

"Thanks, Mr. Ghost," the boy said, and ran off toward the wagon.

Valentine and Ahn-Kha moved off into the woods. After a hundred yards, Valentine touched Ahn-Kha's shoulder.

"Time for his first lesson," Valentine said. "Keep going."

Valentine held his sheathed knife in his hand and waited next to the trail. Ahn-Kha disappeared into the brush, leaving a Grog-wide trail. Soon he heard the boy's footsteps as Hank ran to catch up with Ahn-Kha's furry back.

As Hank passed, Valentine stepped out from behind the tree. Quick as a Reaper, he got the slim youth in the fold of his left arm and put the sheathed knife to the boy's throat. Hank let out a squeal of fear.

"Just me, Hank," Valentine said, releasing him. "Don't pass so close to trees big enough to hide somebody."

"You didn't have to grab me!" Hank said.

"Your heart beating hard?" Valentine asked.

"Yeah. I don't like being grabbed."

"Then move a little more carefully when you're going through the woods. Long time ago, over on the other side of Arkansas, some friends and I weren't. They're both dead. The Hood stepped right out from behind the tree and grabbed Gil, as easily as you'd pick up a rabbit knocked out with your slingshot."

"Hood? That's another word for a Reaper, right? We were supposed to call them Visors."

"Do you know how it all works, Hank?"

"I know the Vis—the Reapers drink blood."

"A Reaper's like a puppet. There's another person pulling the strings. We call them Kurians because they're from another world, a planet called Kur. They use the Reapers to feed because it's less dangerous for them when they get the energy. The donor puts up a fight."

"That energy they get, it's something in us, right? Like our souls?" Hank said.

Valentine felt as if the boy had kicked him in the stomach. He thought back to the graves of his parents, brother and sister who fell in Minnesota when he was eleven. He had asked Father Max if their souls had been eaten. "Nobody knows. Yes, it's something humans have more of than other creatures. The man who raised me called it an 'aura.' There's more aura in an intelligent being than there is in a dog or something. That's why they feed on us."

"We walked past a Reaper once on an Honor Guard march. They had us out burning down houses. It didn't move. Just looked at us dead cold. Reminded me of a snake sitting on a rock."

"Dead cold, all right," Valentine agreed.

"So that's why everyone's scared all the time now. They're afraid the Reapers will get them."

"That's why people cooperate with them. The people who serve them get badges, or cards, or pieces of jewelry that mean the Reapers can't touch them."

Hank nodded. "Yeah, we heard some of that in Honor Guard. Our Top Guardian had some sorta certificate that signified his family was too important to reassign. I hated him, Dallas trash if ever there was."

"You grew up here in the Ozarks, right?"

"Yes, in the borders. My pa would go out into Texas and steal, or trade for horses. He sorta worked for Southern Command; at least they gave him stuff when he brought horses in."

"You remember what the Free Territory used to be like, right?"

"Yes, it all happened last spring, or last summer, really. I heard a lot of fighting. Then there were new people in charge. My pa was in Texas at the time; when he got back he said we had to do what they say for a while."

"You liked it better before they came, right?"

"Yes. Momma was happier. She hated it when Pa was in Texas though."

"I was gone for a couple of years myself. Now that I'm back I'm trying to find if there's any Free Territory left."

"Are we going to live there? Is there anywhere safe now?"

"I hope so, Hank. If there is, we'll find it."

They were refilling their water skins at a trickle when Ahn-Kha came back from his scout of the old camp.

"Everything's burnt out, my David. Picked clean. Lots of holes in the ground. If there were buried weapons, I'd say they've been dug up."

"No one there?"

"Tracks. I smelled urine."

"You speak really well, for a big stoop," Hank said.

Ahn-Kha stood straight, towering over the boy. "We call ourselves the Golden Ones. I grew up trading with men in Omaha. I translated for my people when I was David's age."

"What's old for a stoop?"

Ahn-Kha's ears folded flat against his head.

"About forty years older than you're going to get if you call him a 'stoop' again," Valentine said.

"You can call me Ahn-Kha, or Uncle, if that's too hard for you to pronounce."

"Uncle? My ma would smack me if I called a . . . Golder Ones my uncle."

Valentine decided to change the subject. "Hank," he asked, "what kind of scrounger are you?"

"Haven't had many chances. We'd just burn when we'd go out on the Honor Guard sweeps."

Valentine picked up a stick and put three parallel scores in the ground. He added a fourth, under them and perpendicular to the other three. "That's a mark for a cache. You know what a cache is?"

"Ummm . . ."

"It's a hiding spot. The mark would be on a tree or a rock. See if you can find one as we walk. Chances are it would be out at the edge of the camp. We're all going to go in and have a look around."

The crossed a series of gullies and came upon the camp, folded into the base of the mountain in the broken ground there.

The camp was in ruins, inhabited only by the memories in Valentine's mind. The Quonset huts were gone, the shacks and cabins burned to the ground. The smaller branches of many of the trees in camp were black-barked where the flames had caught them. Valentine saw again the old faces of his platoon, remembering the smiles of his men over mugs of beer in the canteen and Sergeant Gator's slow, easy laugh. He was a Ghost haunting a Southern Command graveyard, and in a few more years there wouldn't be anything left to mark a place where legends lived.

Ahn-Kha picked up a handful of dirt at one of the burned cabins and let it trickle through his hands, sniffing it. "Jellied gasoline," the Grog said. "Bad way to die."

Valentine kept an eye on Hank, who was examining tree bark.

"Is there a good death?"

"Among my people's warriors, we have a saying. 'A good death can come through battle, at a place that is remembered. A better death can come through heroism, sacrificing yourself in the saving of others. The best death comes late, after seeing grandchildren born, for then you've also had a life.' "

"There's a lot to admire in Golden One wisdom. Beats *dulce et decorum est, pro patria mori.*"

"What is that?"

"A phrase from Latin: 'It is a sweet and proper thing, to die for one's country.' That kind of death's neither sweet nor proper. Just ugly. Necessary sometimes, but not sweet and proper."

The allies stood in silence for a moment.

"It will be dark soon," Ahn-Kha offered as a change in subject.

"I don't want to sleep here. Let's make a camp farther up on the mountain. Somewhere we can hear."

"We could make it back to the wagon if we hurried."

Valentine found Hank's footsteps with hard ears. "I don't want to travel with the boy at night. I can hide my lifesign, and you don't show as human. Hank might get sensed if there are any more of those loose Hoods around."

"That was odd, to run across three masterless ones. Do you suppose that many Kurians died when they fought here last summer?"

"I hope so."

Valentine was getting tired of hoping. Ever since returning to the Ozarks, his hopes had been vanishing from his mental horizon like a series of desert mirages. Hopes that his Quickwood would make a difference in the war. Hopes that he might be able to return to the Caribbean, where Mali Carrasca was carrying his child—or daughter, according to Narcisse. Hopes that they'd find some vestige of Southern Command still in these hills. But if there was still hope to be found, it wasn't at Magazine Mountain.

Valentine ate his flavorless bread, and tried not to think of the plentiful fruits and vegetables of the Caribbean. Ahn-Kha was occupying

Hank with the story of the Golden Ones' battle against the General in Omaha.

"They would have rolled over us. But our Ghost found the railroad cars filled with the men who were operating the Reaper soldiers. He blew up some, burned the others where they were parked. The Reapers didn't go wild, like the ones with the horses; they just dropped in their tracks. Took the heart out of the rest of the General's men; they were used to having the Reapers at the front of the fight. In the confusion my brothers broke their chains and rose against them. But if it weren't for David, wounded twice—"

Valentine tossed a pebble at the Golden One. "Don't leave out the other details. Be sure to tell him how I almost had my head shot off," Valentine said, rubbing his aching leg. He pointed to the scar on his face. "An inch closer and the bullet would have taken the side of my face with it. Don't leave out the part where you found me in an interrogation cell, with my pants full of shit and a gun to my head. Ahn-Kha was the one who killed the General, Hank. I had a pair of handcuffs on at the time."

"Just wanted to know how you became friends," Hank said. "The sto—the Grogs I've seen don't mix with men."

"Grog is a word that covers a lot of territory, Hank. It's a term for the beings the Kurians brought to our world. Or maybe made, nobody knows, though the guys at the Miskatonic have some interesting theories. Technically you, a dog, and an oyster are all animals, but your similarities pretty much end there. Same with the Grogs. Some are as smart as Ahn-Kha, who's smarter than most men I know, but some aren't any brighter than a catfish. I think you're talking about the Grey Ones, like the Lucky Pair."

"Your ape things with thick ol' hides? They're called Grey Ones?"

"In my tongue, yes," Ahn-Kha said.

"The ones the Kurians use carry long guns. Fifty calibers," Valentine said.

" 'They'll take your head off at a thousand yards with 'em too, if you're fool enough to show yourself and not be movin'," a voice called from the darkness. "That's what Sergeant Samuels used to say, anyway."

Valentine came to his feet, hand on his pistol. He looked up to see a shaggy man in buckskins, coonskin cap on his head and a sheathed rifle cradled in his arms. Valentine noticed his hand was inside the sheath, though, gripping it so he could get at the trigger easily. Nearly half of the man's face was covered with a stiff leather patch, but the remaining eye was familiar.

"Finner?" Valentine asked. "Jess Finner?" Valentine suddenly felt like a sore-footed recruit again; he almost came to attention with chest thrown out.

Finner's eye took in the whole campsite, not resting on any one spot for more than a fraction of a second. "Yep. Was Sergeant Finner, Tango Company, up to a few months ago. Last time I saw you, Valentine, you were eating a watermelon the size of an anker of rum in Missouri. Heard you got a commission in Zulu Company under Captain LeHavre. He still alive, I hope?"

"I don't know. I'm no longer a Wolf. You look hungry, Jess. You want to come down and have a bite?"

"Maybe. If I do, know that you've got three rifles on each of you."

"Stand down, Sergeant," Valentine said. "I don't want an accidental shooting."

"Been watching your little procession for the better part of a day. Recognized you by the hair, at first. Limp's new. Saw you break off and thought it was time for a chat. I'm a bit curious about what you're doing out in the woods with a Grog, Valentine. What kind of rig are you wearing? That's not a Guard uniform."

"Its mostly a Coastal Marine uniform, dyed black. The bandolier is from a snake."

"Must have been some snake. Be more impressed if you had some friendly insignia, Valentine."

"Technically I'm a captain now, Sergeant, though you'll have to go on faith for that. I couldn't prove it any better to you than I could prove why I'm out here with a Grog. His name's Ahn-Kha, and he also outranks you. I've been out of the Free Territory for better than two years. Sort of a Logistics Commando operation."

"The boy?"

"Just a refugee. None of us are out here for fun. I'm trying to find any kind of Southern Command organization. If you can turn us over to one, I'd be obliged."

Finner took his hand out of the sheath. "No longer a Wolf, eh? Ain't no such thing, Valentine. Once you've looked into the eyes of Father Wolf, you're one until the day you die." He pushed the cap back on his head, revealing a greasy forehead. "Hell, whatever you are, it's good to see you again, Captain, sir," Finner said, holding up his hand palm outward in the Wolf salute. "I'm running with what's left of Southern Command here in the Ouachitas. If you want to meet the boys, just say so. They're only a couple hilltops away."

"I'll say so," Valentine said. "Ahn-Kha, take Hank and find the others. Tell them to camp quietly for another day, and wait for me. This should be the end of our trail."

* * *

"How did it happen, Jess?" Valentine said, as they walked in the loom of Magazine Mountain. The radio antennae Valentine remembered atop the rock-faced cliffs were gone.

Finner must have answered the question before to other fragments of Southern Command, searching for higher command like children looking for a missing parent. The words came out in a practiced, steady beat.

"Not sure. I was recruiting up in the Northwoods. Wisconsin this time, same's I do every year since you met me. It was August. Hottest one I can remember in a while, even up there. We had a little temporary camp south of La Crosse, where we picked up some food courtesy of the underground, and the boatmen said there'd been barges full of men brought across the Mississippi. Our lieutenant thought we'd better not try for the Free Territory until we knew which path was safe. He sent out scouts. Only one came back, and he said the riverbank south of St. Louis was crawling with Grogs. Captain Dorn finally showed up, and he left it up to us. We could scatter up north, or try to get through to the Ozarks. Most tried, a few recruits even. Well, they were right, the hills were crawling. We got picked up by some of those flying shit-eaters, and the harpies put the big ones on us. Legworms barreling through the brush like tanks with Grogs picking us off right and left as we ran. It was a massacre. No other word for it. I made it out, running south. Came across a week-old battlefield on the Crowley Ridge; our men were hanging in trees everywhere, getting picked at by crows. 'Round there I think I got some bad water, picked up a bug. Woke up in a hayloft; some farmers had found me wandering. Said I had a fever, babbled. I was about twenty pounds thinner. This family said the Kurians were running the show now, but they'd heard there was still fighting in the Ouachitas down by Hot Springs. Let's take a break."

Finner sat down and Valentine joined him, rubbing his tired left leg. Finner passed him a little stainless-steel flask. Valentine smelled the contents and shook his head, handing it back.

"I'd lost my blade and my gun while I was sick. When I felt well enough to move on they gave me a bagful of food and made me promise to say I got it in another village if I got caught. I ran into three deserters trying to make their way to the mountains in Kentucky, they said it was all over for the Ozarks. We'd been hit from everywhere—including up. They flew over at the beginning, dropping wild Reapers. Called 'em 'sappers.' I guess there were hundreds of 'em loose at one point."

"I've seen them. They're still running these hills."

Finner wiped his brow. "Southern Command had to send out teams of Wolves and Bears to deal with the sappers. Not enough reserves when the real attack came, though they tell me it wouldn't have made a difference."

"So when did you reach the Ouachitas?"

"Last summer. Gotta warn you, we're an ad hoc unit. Every man's there because he wants to be there; no parades or drill or courts-martial. Not enough supply to do anything but keep us alive. The fighting we do is purely to keep from getting captured. I wouldn't throw that 'captain' title around; the General wouldn't like it, unless he puts you on his staff."

"General who?" Valentine disliked it when someone was known only by the title "General." It reminded him of the leader of the Twisted Cross.

"Martinez. Twelfth Guards, formerly."

"Don't know him."

Valentine felt the darkness coming on. The air took on a wet chill.

"He wasn't a general before. He was colonel of the Twelfth."

"They had the tiger-striped kepis. Orange and black, usually stationed in the Arkansas Gap."

"Yup. Got the hell knocked out of them by troops coming in from Texas. That's who's running the Fort Scott area and the Ouachitas. Texans and Oklahomans. They must've stripped the Dallas Corridor bare; they say the invasion was over a hundred thousand men."

"How are they feeding them? Aren't guerillas hitting the supply lines? When I was in Zulu that was supposed to be our catastrophe assignment."

"Can't say. I spend my time scavenging, not on ops or recon. I've seen low-draft barges coming up the Arkansas. Cattle and rice."

"I came through northeast Texas. I thought the patrols looked slim."

"Yeah, the Ks in Texas think big. They're supposed to get a chunk of the Ouachitas. But there's some new bigshot organizing things out of the ruins in Little Rock. That's who's really running things hereabouts now. A man, if you can believe it. Ol' Satan and his gang of Kurians."

"Satan?"

"Solon. Consul Solon, his papers say."

Valentine's nose told him they were approaching the camp before they came across the lookouts. Latrine discipline wasn't a priority for this particular remnant of Southern Command.

"So this is what defeat smells like," Valentine said.

"It's not that bad. You get used to it. Hush, now, we're coming up on the pickets."

They were still in uniform, more or less. Mottled camouflage pants and gray winter-uniform tunics, many with hunting vests thrown over them; scarves and gloves made out of scrap cloth. Similarities ended at the extremities; there were a variety of hats, gloves and boots. Some of the men had resorted to cobbled-together shoes or sheepskin moccasins. A boy with a hunting bow whistled from atop a rock, and four men drew beads on them.

"It's Finner with a new 'un," one of the men said.

"Found a stray in the hills," Finner said. "Wolf, I know him personally, I'll vouch to the captain." Valentine wondered why he didn't mention Ahn-Kha or Hank.

"Then report to him," the one who recognized him said.

They passed the pickets, who dispersed again as soon as they moved up the hillside for the camp. Valentine's nose added other camp smells to the list headed by men shitting in the woods: smoke, tobacco, open-pit cooking and pigs. He heard a guitar playing somewhere; it drifted softly through the trees like a woman's laugh. To Valentine it seemed forever since last fall's wagon train, when he'd enjoyed the music of the Texans under the stars.

"Why didn't you mention the others?" Valentine asked.

"Didn't want your Grog friend hunted down. Standing orders, no alien prisoners."

"He's not a prisoner, he's an ally. He's worth those four pickets, and another six like them."

"All the more reason to keep him alive. Quislings we bury, but dead Grogs get stewed down to pig feed."

They topped a flat little rise, thickly wooded like most of the Ouachita Mountains, overshadowed by another hill whose summit was scarred with limestone on the face toward the camp hill. Valentine saw watch posts under camouflage netting among the trees of the taller hill. Tents were everywhere, interspersed with hammocks and stacked stones to hold supplies and equipment clear of the wet ground, along with little shacks and huts put together from everything from camper tops to bass boats. Evil-smelling trash filled the bottom of every ravine. There was no signage, no evidence of any kind of unit groupings. It reminded Valentine of some of the shantytowns he'd seen in the Caribbean, minus the cheerful coloring and kids playing. The men sat in little groups of four to ten, trying to get in a last game of cards by firelight. Valentine passed a still every sixty paces, or so it seemed, all bubbling away and emitting sharp resinous smells, tended by men filling squared-off glass bottles.

"Welcome home, Captain Valentine," Finner said.

This wasn't home. Not nearly. It looked more like an oversize, drunken snipe hunt. "Thanks."

"If you want some companionship, just look for one of the gal's tents with a paper lantern out front. They get food, washwater and protection as long as they're willing to share the bed once in a while. Sort of a fringe benefit of this outfit."

"Does this 'outfit' ever fight a battle?"

"We do a lot of raiding. General has us grab the new currency they're using here; we use it to buy some of the stuff we need from smugglers."

"Sounds more like banditry. Do you get overflown?"

"If the gargoyles come overhead, they only see a few fires. We don't try'n knock 'em out of the sky. We figure they just think there're refugees up here. We're far enough from Fort Scott so's they don't care, and the folks on the east side of the mountains have enough to do just controlling the flatlands."

"Many refugees?"

"No, unless they're Southern Command we send 'em elsewhere."

"Where's that?"

"Anywhere but here. That's part of what we were doing when I came across you and the boy and the Grog, keeping an eye out for runaways to warn 'em off. We got these higher hills around to cut the lifesign, but you never know when a Reaper'll be trailing along behind some broke-dicks to see where they're headed."

Voices rose to an excited roar from an opening in the trees, and Valentine's hand went to his pistol.

"Get him, Greggins!" someone shouted.

Finner shrugged. "Sounds like a fight. Interested?"

Valentine scowled and followed Finner downhill to a ring of men. Someone came running with a burning firework. In its blue-white glare he saw forty or fifty men in a circle, expanding and contracting around the action in the center like a sphincter. Valentine heard thudding fists, punctuated by roars from the crowd when an especially good blow was struck. He saw a few women among the men, some on top of the men's shoulders angling for a better view.

Instincts took over, even in the unknown camp. He elbowed his way through the press. "Make a hole!" he growled, then realized that Coastal Marine slang didn't mean much in the Ozarks. The crowd surged back around him and Valentine found himself with the back of one of the combatants sagging against him.

"No fair, that guy's holding him up," someone shouted.

A bloody-browed Guard corporal looked at Valentine over his scuffed knuckles. "Pull off, mister, otherwise he can't go down."

Valentine turned the soldier sagging against him, saw the bruised ruin of a face, then let go his grip. The man sagged to his knees, mumbling something in Spanish.

"Knees ain't down. Finish him, Greggins!"

The corporal stepped forward, corded muscles bulging from his rolled-up sleeves.

Valentine held up a hand. "It's over, Corporal. I'd say you won."

"What're you, his manager? Fight's not over until he's flat. He questioned my authority."

Valentine looked at the beaten man's uniform. "I see sergeant's stripes on him, *Corporal*. If I were you I'd be worried about a court-martial for striking your superior. Even if he were a private, a fistfight isn't the way we keep discipline."

Something in Valentine's voice made the man lower his fists.

"Now help him to his feet and get him to a medic. Better have him look at you as well. That eye doesn't look good."

The corporal took a step forward, then lashed out with a roundhouse. Valentine was ready for it, and slipped under the blow. He brought a driving knee up into the corporal's off-balance stance, and hammered him in the kidney with an elbow as the corporal doubled over. The corporal dropped, his mouth open in a silent scream.

Valentine looked at the circled men, not quite sure what they had seen in the blur of motion. "This how you do things now? Is there a sergeant in this circus?"

A man with a handlebar mustache stepped forward. "I'm a captain, Eighteenth Guards, East Texas Heavy Weapons. Who are you?"

"He's logistics, just come outta Texas, Randolph," Finner said.

"Don't see a uniform."

"I find my duties in the Kurian Zone easier to perform if I don't wear a Southern Command uniform, Captain." Valentine said, and a few of the men chuckled.

"I don't care for spies," Randolph said.

Valentine got the feeling Randolph wanted to see if he could be provoked into another exchange of blows. He reduced lifesign—the old mental technique that also did wonders for his temper.

"I know him, sir," Finner said. "Good man. Wolf officer."

"Disperse, damn you," Randolph said, rounding on the men. "Fight's over. Get some sleep." He turned back to Valentine. "Is that so? We'd better get you to the General, *Captain*, so he can decide what to do with you. We shoot spies trying to penetrate the camp, you know."

The men helped the brawlers to their feet. Randolph jerked his chin and put his hand on his pistol holster. Valentine walked off in the indicated direction, and the captain drew his gun. He didn't point it at Valentine, but the muzzle could be brought to bear easily enough.

Finner trailed along behind as they walked. Only Valentine had ears good enough to hear him click the safety off inside his rifle sheath.

"The General keeps late hours," Randolph said as they approached a vintage twentieth-century house. Lights burned inside and sentries stood on the porch. Where a swing had once stood, piled sandbags and a machine-gun post dominated the parked vehicles in the yard in front of the house. Valentine smelled a barbecue pit in the backyard.

"We've got a LC just in from Texas to see the General," Randolph said to the lieutenant who appeared at the other side of the screen door. "Or so he says."

"I brought him in," Finner added.

"Thank you, Sergeant, that'll be all," Randolph said.

"Let them in, boys," the lieutenant said. He had golden, braided hair and bare arms protruding through a Reaper-cloak vest hung with pistols and hand grenades. Four red diamonds stood out on the meat of his forearm. Valentine suspected he was a Bear. The lieutenant looked Valentine up and down. "I think I've seen your face. Can't place where though."

"Red River raid, sixty-five. You Bears hit the power plant and armory while two companies of Wolves raided some of the plantations. I was the junior in Zulu Company. Never got your name though."

"Nail's the handle. I was in Team Able. We had a hell of a skedaddle out of Louisiana on that one, as I remember, Captain . . . ."

"Ghost is what goes down on the paperwork for me," Valentine said.

Nail held out his hand. "Paperwork. That's rich." They shook. "Nice to see you alive, Ghost. Zulu got caught up in a fight on the Mississippi when all this started. I don't—"

"We can catch up later, Lieutenant," Randoph interjected. "I'm sure the General would like to hear this man's report. Colorful as the conversation is with all the Hunter code names." He turned to Valentine. "I take it you're a . . . hmmm . . . Cat?"

Valentine said nothing.

"Lots of us have family, beg your pardon, sir," Nail said. "It keeps them safe."

Randolph ignored the Bear and waved over an adjutant. Valentine's gaze followed the adjutant into the dining room of the house, where a long table piled with files and a sideboard covered with half-eaten trays of food and liquor bottles stood under dirty walls. Under a candelabra's light a man in red-striped trousers sat, a coat heavy with chicken guts draped over the chair next to him. He had a massive body and a small, balding head on a thin neck; the odd proportions made Valentine think of a turtle. General Martinez rose and threw on his uniform coat.

"Distractions, nothing but distractions," the General grumbled. He had the most perfectly trimmed Van Dyke Valentine had ever seen, as if he made up for the lack of hair on his head with extra attention to that on his face.

"Sorry to add to them, sir," Valentine said. "I'm looking for Southern Command."

"You're talking to a piece of what's left."

"My name is David Valentine, Cat codename Ghost, on independent assignment. I just came out of the KZ in Texas, sir. There wouldn't be a Lifeweaver associated with your command, would there?"

"They've gone to the tall timber, Cat. They're hunted even more than we are."

"I got jumped just across the Red coming out of Texas. I've got close to twenty mouths to feed and have no idea of what to do with them. Fifteen are trained soldiers, including some Grog scout-snipers. The others are refugees."

"Grogs? What unit has Grogs?"

"*Thunderbolt* Ad Hoc Rifles," Valentine said. It was near enough to the truth and saved explanations.

"Never heard of them. Still armed?"

General Martinez wasn't curious about what he was bringing in from Texas. Which was just as well. Valentine wasn't ready to trust him with his precious Quickwood. While they wouldn't use it to fuel the stills, it wouldn't be used to hunt Reapers, either. "Yes, sir."

"You said you came out of Texas?"

"Yes, sir."

"Well, Cat, we could have used a little more warning about what was building."

"I was further south. I only got to Texas—"

Martinez cut him off. "You'd be better off back there. Seems like every Gulag gun's here stamping out the embers."

Doesn't just look like a turtle, Valentine thought. *Snaps like one too.* Then he felt guilty for the thought. He'd been operating outside the military hierarchy for too long: his superior deserved his respect.

"Couldn't make it, sir. I've got some horses that need shoes, and my wagon could use a new team. I was hoping to draw from your commissary. Food and clothing and camp equipment would be helpful."

"None of which I can spare just now," General Martinez said. He paused in thought. "Let's have your team here. You can draw rations from the common pool for now. You'll have to lose the civilians. I've got a militia regiment I'm trying to turn into regulars; you and your veterans'd be a help with them."

"We'll keep heading north, sir. Can someone on your staff show me—"

"No, Valentine. I need every man who can shoulder a gun. We're bringing you in, that's an order. You'll be safer with us."

"I'm responsible for the civilians—I gave my word."

"Fine, we'll provide for them for a few days while we sort this out. I could attach them to a labor company, I suppose." He reached up and rubbed his beard with his knuckles, stroking first one side of it, then the other, making him less of a turtle and more of a cat sizing up a cornered mouse. "Randolph, take your light platoon and bring them in. I'm sorry I can't give you more time, Valentine, but other matters demand my attention. We'll talk again tomorrow. You know what to do, Captain Randolph?"

"Yes, sir," Randolph said, saluting and executing a neat about-face.

Faced with a direct order, Valentine could do little but obey. He saluted and left with Randolph. They descended the steps and joined Finner. "I feel like I've just been shanghaied," Valentine said.

Finner grinned, with the *schadenfreude* of a fox who has lost his tail seeing another fox lose his. "No, you've just been incorporated into the Bitter Enders. What's left they want to make sure stays till the bitter end. They've been shooting deserters."

"In other words, if the enemy doesn't kill you, we will," Randolph added. "Hate that it's come to that, but there you are. Six-bullet sentencing."

"How does that look stitched on a brigade flag?" Valentine asked.

Randolph let out a harrumphing noise that was half squawk and half bark. "Don't question us unless you've lived what we've been through. Valentine, the more I see of you the less I like you as an officer."

Randolph's light platoon was light on experience. Valentine doubted any of the soldiers were much over eighteen; beneath the dirt the majority looked like they should still be in school. They moved over the hills with youthful energy, however, and came upon Post's camp before noon the next day. Finner rejoined his Wolves, who appeared and disappeared in wary silence. Hank spotted the approaching column first, and when he saw Valentine he took off his straw hat and waved it.

"We've been ordered to rejoin Southern Command," Valentine said to Post as the two groups eyed each other. "These kids are here to make sure we do it." Ahn-Kha rose from a squat behind a wagon and some of the light platoon grabbed at their rifles.

"What are you doing with Grogs?" Randolph asked, hand on the butt of his pistol.

"As I explained to General Martinez, they're on our side and they're trained. They helped us in the KZ, and I expect them to be treated with the respect due any other soldier in Southern Command," Valentine said.

"And we speak," Ahn-Kha added. "Have those children take more care with their rifles."

"Seems suspicious, you coming out of the Zone with Grogs."

M'Daw rose from the campfire. "Mister—"

"Quiet, M'Daw," Valentine said. Then, to Randolph: "He escaped the ambush in his underwear, Captain, and the only clothes we could find that would fit him were Quisling. We don't have any dye, so I'd appreciate some, or a change in uniform for him. I don't want him shot by accident on standing orders."

M'Daw sat back down and huddled under a blanket in such a way that his stitched-on name didn't show.

"Let's load up, Post," Valentine said. "Ditch the lumber; we won't need to build shelters after all, and there's no point hauling it up that hill. Let's make Mrs. Smalls' journey as comfortable as possible."

"Yes, sir."

Valentine, Ahn-Kha, and the two Grogs unloaded the Quickwood while Post put the marines and the civilians in marching order. Valentine marked the spot, triangulating off of the peak of Magazine Mountain.

"Something wrong, my David?" Ahn-Kha asked as they threw another beam on the pile.

"I don't like the way this outfit we're joining is being run. I have no business challenging a lawful superior's methods, but . . . hell, I've seen groups of Chicago hookers that are better organized. I didn't come all this way to hand over the Quickwood to a bunch of outlaws."

"Do we have an option?"

"Southern Command is finished, if this is representative of what's left. I'm thinking we might be better off with your people in Omaha, or maybe mine in Minnesota. In six more months this crew is going to be robbing towns and trains to feed themselves, with the meanest knife fighter calling the shots. I want to see M'Daw and the Smalls safe, then we'll talk about taking off."

Ahn-Kha's ears sagged. "Better do it quickly. If they break the marines up into other units—"

"Randolph is coming," Valentine whispered. Ahn-Kha's ears pivoted to the sound of footsteps.

"Why's everyone got wooden spears along with their rifles?" Randolph asked.

Ahn-Kha growled an order, and led the Grogs back up to the wagon.

"For the feral pigs in these hills. Those are boar spears."

"One of your men said it was for killing Reapers. That black cripple said the same thing."

"Have to tell them something or they just run at the sight of one. They think it's got big medicine. But so far they've just been used on pigs."

"Hope you boiled the meat good. I've seen men die eating wild pig. You might want to have your men check their shit. Our doc has a great remedy for worms. Just tell him you need to be sluiced out."

"Thanks for the tip. Is there contact with any other pockets of resistance?"

"General Martinez gets his orders through special channels. When it's time to move we'll hear it from him. There's talk of a counteroffensive next fall, when the Kurians think the Ozarks are pacified."

"Seems to me they're pacified already. How many do you lose each week?"

"You won't get far questioning the General, Valentine. The men love him. He's daddy and Santa Claus and Moses all in one. Have patience, the Promised Land is there."

"The Promised Land is occupied. We don't have forty years. We shouldn't be acting like we have forty days. Inertia and illness are going to kill your General's army; the Quislings and the Kurians are just going to be buzzards feeding off the corpse."

"Look, Valentine, I'm liking you less and less by the minute. You ever talk to me like that again and I'll deck you. You weren't here when it was raining Reapers, or when we got blown out of Fort Scott by so many guns you'd think they had enough to land a shell every six feet. Martinez took five thousand beat-up men who were ready to surrender and pulled us back together. Southern Command put him in charge of the central Ouachitas after that. He's keeping us fed and armed without any help from a rear that plain vanished on us. Quit questioning him, or I'll turn you in as a traitor."

"In the Free Territory that trained me two officers speaking in private could criticize anyone without the word treason being thrown around. You swing on me anytime you like, as long as the men aren't watching. If you do it where they can see I'll have you up on charges for striking a fellow officer, Captain. Write up a report if you want. I'll be happy to repeat everything I've said word for word to the General."

They returned to the wagon, both simmering. Post had Narcisse and Mrs. Smalls in the wagon and everyone else lined up behind it. Randolph's platoon had been dispersed to form a screen. When all was ready, they hitched the team to the wagon and set off. Valentine elected to walk beside Ahn-Kha and the Grogs, picking the way southeast and ready to chop a path through the growth blocking the hill road if necessary. They forded a river and rested the team after the crossing.

"Why did you leave the Quickwood, Daveed?" Narcisse asked as they rested. Valentine was inspecting a wobbling wheel on the wagon, wondering if it would make it the rest of the trip.

Valentine glanced around, and found himself gritting his teeth at the gesture. He was used to looking over his shoulder in the Kurian Zone, but here, in the middle of titular comrades, the precaution grated.

"The boys we're joining up with, they're one rung on the ladder over the bandits on the borders between the Kurian Zones and the Freeholds. For all I know this General is getting set to go Quisling. He's keeping a lot of men who might be useful elsewhere liquored up and lazy. Their camp's in a state any junior lieutenant in a militia company wouldn't allow, but that doesn't stop them all from talking like they're the last hope of the Ozarks."

Mrs. Smalls rubbed her lumbar while her husband went to get her a drink from the river. "Some sergeant tried to disarm your funny-talkin' island men while you were with the Grogs. Mr. Post put a stop to it."

"I'm liking this Captain Randoph less and less," Valentine said.

"Whoo-hoo boys, horsemeat coming in!" a voice called from beside the road.

Valentine saw machine-gun nests set to cover the bend in the road running up against the taller hill of the camp. They'd been set up while there were still leaves on the trees and now looked naked against the hillside.

"We're here," Randolph said from the saddle of what had been Valentine's horse. The column had made good time; it was barely afternoon of the second day since setting out from the shadow of Magazine Mountain.

"This isn't much of a road, but it's obliging of the others not to patrol it," Post said.

Randolph's platoon led them up the hill, the Grogs and marines sweating to help the wagon up the incline.

"Damn, they got them ape-men with 'em," one of the idlers said, pointing with the stained stem of a pipe.

"Prisoners? I thought we were getting a new company," the other said. "It's not even a sergeant's platoon. *Thunderbolt Ad Hoc Rifles*—bah."

Word spread through camp and men gathered, hoping to see familiar faces. The Jamaicans, in their strange blue uniforms, excited some comment among the men with dashed hopes.

"Can I speak to a supply officer?" Valentine asked. "I have to feed and billet my men."

Valentine heard a buzz at the back of the assembled men. General Martinez strode through. There was something of Moses in him after all; the men parted like the Red Sea at his presence. Some removed their hats or wiped their eyeglasses clean as he passed, gorgeous in his braided uniform coat, Van Dyke aligned like a plumb line.

"Welcome back to the Free Territory, Captain Valentine," Martinez said. "Those rifles your men have; Dallas Armory, aren't they?"

"Yes, sir, we took them off the post at Bern Woods. Those were the ones who ambushed us coming back across the Red."

"Every man counts here. Every man is important," the General said, loudly enough for all to hear. "The Grogs are another story. They'll run back to their buddies as soon as they see 'em. Sergeant Rivers, shoot the Grogs."

A man with stripes sloppily inked on the arm of a long trenchcoat pulled up a shotgun.

"Sir, no!" Valentine said. "They're my men. Let me—"

"Shoot, Sergeant," Martinez ordered. The gun went off. A Grog fell backward, his chest planted with red buckshot holes, his legs kicking in the air.

Ahn-Kha ran from the back of the column, knocking aside Valentine's old marines as he burst through them.

"David!" Ahn-Kha shouted.

"*Druk*?" the other Grog said, looking from the kicking corpse to the sergeant with the shotgun. Its confused eyes turned to Valentine as the gun fired again.

Everything slowed down. The Grog wavered like a redwood with its trunk severed, then crashed to the ground. Valentine heard his own heart, louder in his ears than the gunshots, beating in time to Ahn-Kha's footfalls as the Golden One ran to his Grogs with arms outstretched. The smoking shotgun muzzle swiveled to Ahn-Kha as the red shell casing spun through the air. Valentine's hand went to his belt.

Valentine moved. Faster than he had in his encounter with the corporal the other night.

"Rivers," Valentine said, stepping behind the General with his .45

pressed to the back of Martinez's ear, "you shoot again and I'll kill him, then you."

"Valentine, have you gone—awwwk," Martinez started to say as Valentine grabbed a handful of goldenrod shoulder braid in his left hand and whipped it around the General's neck.

"Everyone calm down," Valentine said. "I don't want any more shooting. Post, don't draw that."

"Valentine!" Randolph shouted, pointing his pistol at Valentine's head in turn. "Let him go, right now."

"Men!" Valentine roared at the assembly. "General Martinez is under arrest for ordering the murder of soldiers of Southern Command. Randolph, you heard me tell him that the Grogs were part of Southern Command, under my authority. Twice. Uniform Code says no soldier of Southern Command can be executed without trial and unanimous verdict of three officers." Valentine decided not to add that the penalty for summary execution was a bullet in the back of the head.

"Southern Command is gone," General Martinez gasped. "There's no Uniform Code anymore."

"Then it's law of the jungle, Martinez. You're not a general, you're just some bastard who killed two of my friends. Last words?" Valentine thumbed back the hammer on the automatic.

"Shoot these bastards! Every one of them!" Martinez yelled.

"Guns down! Guns down! Keep order, there," a female voice shouted from the crowd.

Valentine looked across the heads of the crowd and saw men being pushed aside, before returning his eyes to the men around him. A stocky woman elbowed her way to the front. No, not stocky; short and powerful. She wore the cleanest uniform Valentine had seen yet in Martinez's camp, her muscular shoulders filling the Southern Command jacket in a way that would do credit to a Labor Regiment veteran fresh from six months of earth moving. Near white-blond hair disappeared up into a fatigue hat. The captain's bars on her collar were joined by an angled crossbar, forming a shortened Z.

The crossbar meant she was in the Hunters. Perhaps staff, but part of the organization that encompassed the Wolves, Cats, and Bears.

"You two," she called to Valentine's marines, "open the bolts on those rifles. Sergeant Rivers, lay down the shotgun." The men, even those who had never seen her before, obeyed. She looked over the situation, smelled the cordite in the air, and shook her head at the dead Grogs Ahn-Kha knelt beside. She turned to Valentine.

"Captain, you can put up the gun. I saw what happened from up the hill. General Martinez, it's my duty to place you under arrest for murder."

"I bet you're just loving this, aren't you, Styachowski," Martinez said. "I wouldn't fall asleep for the next week or so, if I were you. These men know their duty."

Styachowski's pallid features showed no sign of even hearing the threat, though her face had gone so white that Valentine wondered if she was about to faint at the sight of the bodies. Valentine released Martinez, carefully brought down the gun's hammer, and offered the pistol to Styachowski.

"Keep it, Captain Valentine. You're not under arrest. Neither are you, Rivers," she called over her shoulder. "But don't count on keeping those stripes, or the shotgun. You'll do your fighting for the next year with a shovel."

"Men!" Martinez roared. "Handcuff and gag this little bitch. Two-step promotion to any man—"

"The General's no longer in a position to give orders; he's relieved of command pending trial," Styachowski countershouted. Valentine couldn't help but be impressed by the volume she put into her roar. She coughed as she got her wind back. Perhaps she was ill; that might account for her pallor. "Corporal Juarez, I need you and your men to escort General Martinez to his quarters. Sergeant Calloway, have *Private* Rivers grab a shovel and start digging graves for the Grogs."

"But Grog bodies go—"

"Soldiers' bodies get buried on Watch Hill. That's where they'll go, right with our men."

Martinez glared at them from between two nervous soldiers. "Good luck finding three officers to convict, Styachowski. You and this other mutineer here both arrested me. You can't serve as judge and accusing officer. After I'm acquitted I'll try and hang you both for mutiny."

"Captain Randolph, find a place for Captain Valentine's people, please," Styachowski said. She nodded at Valentine, then turned and followed the corporal's guard up the hill.

"Post, have the men make litters for the Grogs. I'm sorry, Ahn-Kha," Valentine said.

Ahn-Kha looked up. Golden Ones cried; in that they were like humans. He held one of each of his Grog's hands in his own. "Nothing seems to change, my David. Always expendable."

"Ahn-Kha, I'll try and prove you wrong someday. First I want to see some justice done for the Lucky Pair."

The irony of the nickname tasted bitter, like hemlock in his mouth.

Valentine's only look at the trial came when he gave evidence, and he didn't like what he saw. The crisis in command required prompt action. The trial was held, without a preliminary inquiry, the next day in the old brick ranch-style home that served as a guardhouse. Perhaps it had once been a vacation home, or a quiet retirement spot at the end of a winding, mountainside road. The owner liked his architecture low and spacious: wide porches, wide doors, wide windows. Inside, a great brick wall bisected the house into a huge living area and smaller bedrooms, which now served as cells, thanks to the limestone blocks of the walls.

Tables and chairs were arranged, nearly filling the big living room, with the three judges pressed up against the longest wall and facing the prosecution, the defense and a witness chair between the two. The temporary commander of the camp, Colonel Abraham, had excused himself from the trial, as traditionally no officer who stood to replace an accused superior could serve as a judge. The next senior officer in the shattered chain of command was a colonel named Meadows, who presided over the trial. At other times he might have been a good officer, but all Valentine saw was a nervous man seated between Randolph and a lieutenant colonel who smelled, to Valentine's sensitive nose, of marijuana.

Meadows had only one finger to accompany the thumb on his right hand, which clutched a handkerchief used every fifteen seconds on his sweating brow. A throng of men outside, given no duties by officers sympathetic to Martinez, listened through open windows as best they could and added boos and cheers accordingly. Captain Moira Styachowski—Valentine learned her first name when she took his statement—acted as prosecuting officer. She performed admirably under the circumstances, which at one point included a rifle bullet coming through a window and whizzing past her ear. Court adjourned to the floor.

The rifle was eventually found, dropped in a stand of bramble, but not the shooter.

After the missed shot Valentine swore to himself that he'd get his charges out of the camp. This bit of Southern Command was turning into a madhouse of angry, well-armed drunkards. But how far could they get on foot with a pregnant woman, old M'Daw and a boy, with a grudge-holding General following?

Valentine told his story, and answered five questions from Styachowski, stressing that he had told General Martinez at the evening meeting the nature of his command and his use of the Grogs. He tried to keep his voice even as he told of the summary execution of the Grogs, simple but skilled creatures with whom he'd served for a year.

"Did it occur to you, Captain, that General Martinez and his men had been fighting those very creatures for years?" the officer acting as defense counsel asked, leaning down to put his face close to Valentine's, probably in an effort to intimidate. Both the defense counsel and the General had been drinking during the previous night as they talked over the coming trial, according to Styachowski, and his breath made Valentine turn his face toward the triumvirate of judges to avoid the fumes.

"He's been fighting Quislings, too. Does that mean he kills every man who comes into the camp?"

"Answer the question, Valentine," Randolph said.

"I've fought Grogs myself."

"That's still not an answer," Randolph said.

"I took it for granted that he's fought them."

The defense counsel nodded to Randolph. "Then why didn't you make it clear that they were Southern Command soldiers and not prisoners? Why didn't you give them uniforms?"

"I identified them repeatedly. I didn't have any uniforms to issue, and even if I had, they served as scouts in the Kurian Zone much of the time. That's what made them so useful. Putting them in our uniforms would have detracted from that. Even if they were naked, it shouldn't have made a difference because—"

Loud boos and catcalls came through the windows.

"You'll answer the questions asked, Valentine," Randolph said. "No more. You run on again and I'll have you arrested for contempt."

The men outside cheered that.

"I'm giving evidence; I'm not an official of the court," Valentine said. "You don't have that power."

"Don't go tentpole-lawyering with me," Randolph said, "or as soon as you get off the stand you'll be brought to a cell." The men outside cheered him.

Styachowski stood up, her lower lip swollen from her biting it. "Sir, can we close those windows and shutters? The circus outside—"

"Is of your own making. The camp is in disarray. This isn't a Star Chamber. The men have a right to know what's going on."

Valentine looked at Martinez's face. The General ran his knuckles down each side of his beard. Triumph shone in his bloodshot eyes.

So it was with trepidation that Valentine stepped away from the courtroom and went out onto the wide porch. An egg overshot his forehead and smacked the door's lintel, releasing a sulfurous reek.

"Next person throws anything deals with me," Nail said, stepping up and putting his thin frame in front of Valentine. The Bear was sunken-chested, but his tattooed arms were solid muscle and tendon. Perhaps it was just the aggressive stance, but his blond braides seemed to bristle. Men in Southern Command with regard for the integrity of their skeletal systems listened when a Bear made a threat; the catcalls quieted.

He escorted Valentine through the crowd using his elbows, an icebreaker smashing room for the larger ship behind. They made their way through the dirty camp. Nail found one of the squared-off green bottles, sniffed the mouthful that still remained inside and drained it.

"Goddamn that's vile, Captain." Nail sent the bottle spinning down the hillside, and after a faint, tinkling crash led Valentine uphill a short way on a trail. Valentine smelled more cannabis smoke from a cluster of men in a hollow.

"How long have you been in this zoo?"

"Long enough to know it's falling to pieces. If you ask me, a couple regiments of Quisling militia could sweep us off this hill. With slingshots."

"You can see it. Why can't the others?"

"The General got them out of a tight spot outside Fort Scott. These Guard brigades were the only ones to make it out of that pocket more or less intact, considering. Every time they thought they had us cornered, we got away. There's been some desertions, but no bad casualties since he took over. Food, light duties, wine, women and song. Everything a soldier could ask for, as long as they don't ask for a victory. Whatever else you want to say about the General, he knows how to slip out of a noose."

"I think he'll slip out of Styachowski's."

"You stepped into a private war, Valentine. Word around the campfire is Martinez tried to pull her pants off using his rank, if you follow." They crossed a narrow gully using a log bridge, with a rope strung as a handhold.

"When you say tried you mean—"

Nail winked. "Failed."

"He's been making her life hell ever since?"

"More like the other way around. She came out of Mountain Home GHQ, one of these invisible staff types that suddenly show up to fix screwups. Really sharp. Martinez made her his intelligence chief, but she quit. She landed in the quartermaster tents. If the men are well fed, I'd say it's because of her. The only ones to leave these hills are her scavenger patrols. Funny ideas, though."

"What do you mean?"

"She said she was a Bear."

Valentine raked his memory over. "I never met a woman Bear—but then I don't know many in your caste."

Finner shrugged. "No such thing. If she is one she's the only one I've ever met, too. I heard they tried it on a few women, but they died from whatever that goop is that the Lifeweavers pass out to the Bears at Invocation."

"We lost one when I became a Wolf."

"Yeah. Bears, too. But it's a hundred percent failure with women."

Valentine smelled a mass of humanity ahead, even upwind. "Now who are these?"

"You'll find out in about five seconds."

They passed down into a dimple in the hillside where Post had pitched their camp's tents. The tents were surrounded by a sea of uniforms. Guards, Bears, Wolves, even militia with inked insignia; all rose to their feet as Valentine and Nail crested the hill.

"It started at the Grog burial this morning," Post said, coming up to them. Ahn-Kha followed behind.

"I would have liked to have been there, but my testimony was required this morning," Valentine said.

"At first it was just the marines," Post said. "Then Finner and some Wolves came up, and others just kind of followed. Before the holes were finished it was in the hundreds. They had their guns; for a second it looked like a lynch mob. Then Ahn-Kha said something in his tongue—"

"The Third Lament, for the unjustly killed," Ahn-Kha added. "I practiced saying it so often in Omaha, I could recite it backward."

"When Ahn-Kha spoke everyone bowed their heads," Post continued. "When he finished, we all looked at each other. Like we'd all agreed."

"We're ready to come or go at your order, Captain," Nail said. "Every man here's had it with Martinez. We're ready for a change."

Valentine looked at the expectant faces, from old friends like Jess Finnner to strangers and back again. His stomach went tight and sour. The death of the Grogs and his actions had polarized the camp; if he stayed there would be open feuding.

He'd had enough of the torn bodies of friends and followers. A weary part of him had decided to vanish with what was left of the *Thunderbolt*'s complement. All he wanted to do was find a safe valley somewhere, then perhaps try for Denver in the summer. But he had to tell the gathering something.

"I'm glad you're here, all of you. I think . . . I know what happened to Ahn-Kha's Grogs was wrong. Right now in that cabin they're deciding if there's going to be a change, but even if there is, General Martinez will just be replaced by his Colonel Abraham."

"He's worthless!" a woman's voice opined from the crowd.

"Look what he's letting go on outside the guardhouse," another called.

"Enough. He's your superior officer, and mine too, for that matter. If this camp divides, it'll be destroyed. If you're unhappy about something, you're free . . . you're expected to bring it to the attention of your superior. I know you have the best intentions, but let's not give even the appearance of mutiny. The soldiery of Southern Command I see gathered here is better than that. The trial is being conducted according to the Uniform Code. Whatever happens is going to be legal, and it'll be our duty to accept the court's justice."

"They're breaking now," a boy called from the window, where he was listening to the voices in the guardhouse.

A restive mass of men, including Valentine, Ahn-Kha and those who had gathered at his camp, stood in the dark around the guardhouse, listening to the boy summarize the events inside. Colonel Abraham had placed a group of mounted soldiers around the court, putting them between the guardhouse and the men of any opinion. A massed fistfight had broken out when someone threw a rock at Ahn-Kha, and shouted, "You're next, stoop," but it ended when the horses waded into the fray.

Valentine waited, rolling and unrolling a piece of paper run off by the camp's primitive printing press. He had found it discarded in the camp.

SOLDIERS!

I write you from a cell, knowing the unjustness of the charges against me and sustained by your presence. I put my trust in the hands of God, for he is the final arbiter and whatever the outcome of my trial I can face him content that I have done right for you and for our Cause. I trust you to behave as the Loyal Hearts I know you are in this the darkest hour of our struggle. Carry yourselves as men of honor and obey until I am restored to command.

P. Martinez, General

Valentine reread the page-filling type. He admired the wording, equivocal enough to show Southern Command that he had asked the men of his command to keep order and obey those who had arrested and tried him, but he wondered if there wasn't an implicit threat in the final sentence. One interpretation of "Until I am restored to command" simply meant that he was confident of exoneration. A darker possibility could be that he was telling his loyalists that if he wasn't restored to command, he didn't expect them to obey those who had removed him.

Styachowski had been brilliant at the end, at least from what Valentine heard passed via the boy. The defense argued that it wasn't murder to shoot a Grog any more than it was to put down a mule, and that rules that protected a Southern Command soldier simply didn't apply to this case. After some back and forth the judges demanded that Styachowski give evidence that a Grog enjoyed the same rights as a Southern Command soldier.

After a pause—during which Nail predicted that they were sunk—Styachowski began a recitation of the court-martial of a sergeant in charge of a Grog labor detail recruited from the ranks of prisoners. One of the Grogs hadn't moved quickly enough to suit the sergeant; he shot the laggard as an example to the others. The wounded Grog died, leading to the sergeant being brought up on charges of murder by the Grog's keeper, a Mississippian named Steiner. Steiner pushed the case through both military and civilian officials, and testimony provided by Grog experts from the Miskatonic affirmed that the Grogs reasoned, felt emotions, formed attachments, created art, created tools and the tools to make more tools; indeed everything humans did. Because of the landmark nature of the case the sergeant, though found guilty, had his sentence reduced: even when he shot the Grog he did so in the leg, trying to wound rather than kill. The case was affirmed a year later when a barroom brawl between a Grog janitor and a riverboatman resulted in the death of the Grog and manslaughter charges against the sailor, who ended up serving a long sentence.

Martinez's consul ended its defense with an argument that Grogs were often summarily executed when taken prisoner, and the General was simply following a standard practice.

The three judges, having no chambers to retire to, went out to the old garage of the guardhouse to discuss the verdict. They could just be seen in the gloom within through a single window in the back door. Valentine's ears picked up Randolph's raised voice again and again. "Just Grogs . . . emergency . . . situation requires . . . indespensible."

Soldiers in the General's camp lit torches. The numbers had swelled in the darkness as others came off duty.

Finally, the front door opened.

The crowd quieted. Had Valentine been in a better mood, he would have smiled at the first display of discipline by the men since his arrival at the camp. He was finally able to hear voices from within the guardhouse, thanks to his Lifeweaver-sharpened ears.

"Bring him out of his cell," Meadows said. Valentine thought he heard Styachowski gasp, but he couldn't be sure.

There were footsteps, followed by the sound of chairs scraping.

"They're bringing him in!" the boy at the window shouted. The crowd froze; only the crackle of torches and the horses shifting weight from hoof to hoof came from the assembly.

"General Martinez," Meadows began, "this court recognizes your service to Southern Command. Every man here owes you a debt that cannot be repaid. However, the Uniform Code gives us little room for interpretation. As the code now stands, a guilty verdict in a willful murder case carries with it automatic penalties that cannot be suspended or commuted by this court in any way. Indeed, the only leeway given with a guilty verdict is life imprisonment instead of hanging, and as matters now stand there is no possibility of commutation from an executive authority since the governor cannot be reached.

"Though the charges are of willful murder, this court, in cooperation with the prosecution, has decided to find you guilty only of simple murder, which gives us the leeway to—"

"Guilty!" the boy shouted.

Martinez's supporters roared out in anger; Valentine heard no more. The mob threw two torches at the guardhouse. One sputtered out as it flew; the second landed on the timber roof, alight. Soldiers shot in the air, the muzzle flashes giving brief illumination to the mass of contorted, shouting faces. The most violent ran for the porch, gripping their guns like clubs to smash at the shutters and door. The guards ran inside, slamming the door behind them.

Nail barked an order and a triangle of men formed around Valentine, backs to him. They were Bears, big-shouldered giants who closed around him in a wall of muscle and attitude. Valentine, at six feet two inches, had to shift his head to see events around the guardhouse.

"Nail, can we get closer?" Valentine shouted.

"We can try."

"Ahn-Kha, let's get to the door," Valentine said.

Ahn-Kha's ears went back flat—the Golden One's equivalent of a man rolling up his sleeves—and he went down on all fours, using his two-ax-handle shoulders to clear a path like a bulldozer going through brush. The Bears followed, surrounding Valentine in a muscular cocoon. The horsemen were having no luck keeping the mob back; a few of the crowd had even been vaulted onto the roof. They extinguished the incipient fire, then continued stamping hard on the wooden eaves. Others kicked at the posts holding up the porch.

"They'll tear it down in a minute," Valentine said to Nail.

The door swung open. General Martinez appeared on the wide porch, holding his hands up for quiet. The men broke into cheers and whistles.

Martinez's small round eyes were sorrowful. He was sweating, even in the cool of the winter night. "Soldiers, soldiers! Quiet, men, quiet," he said, still moving his arms as if giving a benediction.

Even the men stomping on the roof stopped and waited for him to speak.

"I convinced them to let me speak to you. This madness has to stop. The camp is tearing itself apart because of these charges and this trial. As you have heard, the court-martial has found me guilty—"

Boos drowned him out until he held up his hands again. Valentine saw a self-indulgent smile cross his face, as if he found the whole proceedings to be a poorly executed practical joke.

"Yes, guilty, for doing my duty to the best of my ability. They are trying to destroy our army, the last, best hope for freedom for this land. Therefore I declare my emergency powers to be in effect, and these proceedings voided. This camp is in a state of martial law; the judges, Captain Styachowski, Captain Valentine, and any who helped them are under arrest for treason."

Valentine and Nail exchanged incredulous looks. The legalistic gibberish made no sense to them, as technically the soldiery of Southern Command had always been under martial law, from the moment they raised their right hands to be sworn in. A general in Southern Command had no emergency powers over his troops to invoke, any more than he had wings to fly. But the words sounded fine to the men, at least to the more stirred-up among them. Martinez stood aside while a dirty flood of them poured into the guard-house. Valentine heard fighting, a pained cry. A man flew backward out of the front window and lay on the porch, folded like a clasp knife, cradling his solar plexus and gasping for air. In a few seconds Styachowski was dragged out, held aloft by the mob with a soldier at each limb, followed by the judges, guns to their backs.

"General, sir, I've been on your side the whole trial," Randolph said, his mustache black against his fear-paled face.

"I'll make my mind up about you later, Randolph."

"None of the General's orders are legal," Styachowski shouted, held aloft by the mob. Blood ran from her nose as she turned to bite at a hand pulling her hair. "He's no longer in command. He can't—"

"Take her shirt off," someone shouted. Others cheered and whistled. Valentine heard cloth tearing.

"General Martinez," Valentine boomed, stepping up beside Ahn-Kha. "I started this. I arrested you. I held a gun to your head."

The mob quieted at this; the men wanted to hear the exchange between their idol and his usurper.

Valentine felt a hard hand on his shoulder. "What the hell are you—" Nail began.

"I'm the one responsible," Valentine continued, shrugging off the Bear. "Nobody had a choice once I arrested you; there had to be proceedings from that point on. This is still Southern Command. I'm the only one you should charge with treason."

"Randolph, here's a chance to redeem yourself," Martinez said. "Shoot that mutinous bastard right now. Here, in front of his pet Grog."

"Auuugh!" Styachowski shouted, still writhing atop her holders. "This is insane! Don't be an idiot, Randolph. Put me down, now!"

Valentine saw the desperation in her upside-down eyes.

"You'll be on the ground, all right," Martinez said.

Valentine stepped forward. "What's the matter, Martinez? Afraid to do a summary execution yourself? How come somebody else has to pull the trigger for you? You never been blooded?"

"Somebody shoot—" Martinez began. Randolph reached for his holster.

Ahn-Kha chambered a round in his long Grog rifle, and Martinez looked down the barrel of .50 caliber of death sighted on his chest.

Nail and his Bears came forward, again surrounding Valentine. "No," Nail said, slowly and clearly. A short submachine gun appeared like magic in his hands. "Anyone shoots, Martinez, and my team comes up on that porch. After you. We won't leave enough of you to fill a shoebox. Then we start killing everyone with a hand on Styachowski. Then everyone who tried to interfere with either of those jobs. How many of y'all do you think we'll get before we go down. Twenty? Forty?"

"Whose side are you on, *Lieutenant?*" Martinez said, making the rank sound like an epitheth. "Sounds like you boys are getting set to do the Kurians' work for them."

"That's so, General," the largest of the Bears said. He had the smooth, rounded accent of the rolling Kentucky hills, rather than the trans-Mississippi twang of Nail. He pulled a knife from his belt, tossed it in the air and in the second before he caught it again drew a tomahawk with his left hand. "But only if you start it. My finishers are out. Any blood spills, they won't go back in again without your guts strung on 'em."

"He's not a general, Rain," another Bear said. "Not anymore."

"Martinez is right," Valentine said. "Let's not do the Kurians' work for them. What'll it be, Martinez? A blood-bath?"

The Bears and Ahn-Kha must have made an impression. The crowd shrank away, perhaps not wanting to be the first to be tomahawked on Rain's way to the General.

"Name your terms, Valentine," Martinez said.

"First, nobody gets arrested for treason. Second, Styachowski and the judges walk out of camp with us. Somehow I think there'd be reprisals if any of us stayed. Third, you let anyone who wants to go with us leave. Peaceably."

"This is mutiny, Valentine."

"You have to have military organization to mutiny against. Your command is that of a warlord, maybe, but not armed service as Southern Command defines it."

"Then it's to the warlord to give his terms to those he's defeated. You and your men can leave. You may take personal possessions only. No Southern Command weapons, food, or equipment. You walk out of here as civilians, and I'll be sure to let my superiors know why that's the case. We won't be sorry to see you go; my men don't want to breathe the same air as traitors."

"He's awful free with that word," the Bear called Rain muttered.

"Try to get our guns. We'll walk out over—" Nail began.

"Wait, Lieutenant," Valentine said, putting a hand on his shoulder. "Nobody gets killed, that's good enough."

"Is this a surrender, my David?" Ahn-Kha asked in his ear.

"A tactical retreat, old horse," he said. Then louder: "You have it, Martinez. We walk out with just our possessions. Now let Captain Styachowski go. We'll be gone in twenty-four hours."

"This looks like a conference of war," Finner said the next day, as Ahn-Kha opened the tent flap. Styachowski, Post, Nail and, strangely enough, Colonel Meadows all sat around a folding camp table spread with maps.

"An informal one. Jess, they tell me you know the mountains east of here better than anyone. What are our chances of getting seven hundred people to the Arkansas River without using any Kurian-patrolled roads?"

"I don't see anyone smiling, so I guess this isn't a practical joke. Seven hundred?"

"That's what the numbers packing up look like," Colonel Meadows said. "Some are good soldiers, sick of hiding in the hills. Some are afraid that the General's gone loco." Meadows tapped his chest with the hand missing the fingers for emphasis.

"Styachowski says the hills are our only hope for moving that many without being noticed," Valentine added. "The Quislings stay out of the mountains because of those feral Reapers, except for big truck patrols. We'd hear those coming."

Finner looked at the maps. One, covered with a sheet of clear plastic, had a cryptic mark over where Valentine's refugees had been camping when the General added them to his command. "I was coming here to tell you that we've got two platoons of Wolves ready to go out with us. With them screening we might be able to do it. The lifesign will be horrendous. We'll draw trouble like a nightlight does bugs."

"And we'll be short, very short, on weapons," Post said. "It makes the route even more critical."

"How are you going to feed everyone, sir?" Finner asked.

"Working on it," Meadows said, with a glance at Styachowski. She looked tired.

"That's been most of the conversation. We'll take livestock. Like the myriads out of Egypt, we'll go with our flocks," Valentine said.

"What happens at the Arkansas? The river's watched and patrolled. I'd have trouble getting across with a platoon."

"Just get us there, Lieutenant," Valentine said.

"Sergeant, sir."

"You're going to be in charge of two platoons of Wolves. That's a lieutenant's command," Meadows said.

Finner looked nonplussed. "Any chance of turning down this promotion?"

"We get back to Southern Command, and I'll fill out the rank reduction paperwork myself," Valentine promised. "Let's give Finner some time alone with the maps."

"Don't need 'em, sir," the new lieutenant said.

"You'll at least need to know where we're starting. First waypoint is the old campsite where we dumped that load of lumber."

"Captain Styachowski, a word," Valentine said as they left the tent.

"Yes, Captain?"

"You still have friends on the old intelligence staff?"

"Staff? Friends? I had one nearsighted military analyst. She's coming with us; she doesn't like this moonshine brewery any more than I."

"I need everything you have on enemy organization on the Arkansas River."

"That's a lot of data. The river's their backbone running up the Ozarks."

"You've got to find us a way across."

"Short of stealing some flatboats or swimming the whole column, I don't see how we do it. Only bridges up are in Little Rock, and that's their new headquarters."

"Think about it for me."

Styachowski's eyes narrowed, but she spoke with a cheerful bounce to her voice. "I can't count on the waters parting, can I?"

"Sorry."

"Ah, well. When a Saint came marching into camp, I had hope—"

Valentine laughed. "What's the crossbar for?

"Hunter staff. I'm a Bear. Never made it on a combat team, though. Always some excuse."

"What did they invoke you for, then?"

"Didn't. I was sort of born into it. Only action I've seen was Hazlett, and that was in a mortar team."

"I was up that way. Didn't see the fighting, just the cleanup," Valentine said.

"Lucky. But it was a picnic compared to the last few months."

"One more thing. You had a rough time, at the trial and after. Are you okay?"

Her eyes narrowed. "What do you mean?"

"You don't look well. Have you been sleeping enough?"

She ran her hand through her hair and rubbed the back of her neck at the end of the gesture. "I always look like a slice of fresh death. Don't worry."

"I mean the fight at the trial. Hell of a thing to go through."

"I'm a bit numb still. I'm glad we have a lot to do . . . I'll just work till I drop tonight. Be better tomorrow."

"Don't short yourself sleep. Just makes everything worse." Valentine spoke from experience. "Sometimes a drink helps."

"I've had three drinks my whole life, Captain. Two of them were last night, after all that. Didn't help. Thanks for hearing me out about the Bear stuff. Lieutenant Nail just laughed. Our good General said I had too good a brain for fighting, and too tight an ass for uniform pants. I hope you'll give me a chance to prove myself."

"You proved yourself when you stepping in at the Grog shooting."

"I should have taken action before then. Been watching and waiting too long, should have followed my gut a long time ago. When he started letting the gargoyles overfly us without so much as a shot . . ."

She left the last to hang for a moment, and Valentine wondered at her absent stare into the distance. Then she swallowed and threw her muscular shoulders back. "Okay, time to round up some livestock and then sit down with a map. If you'll excuse me, I have a lot to do."

Colonel Meadows put himself between Valentine and Martinez as the column made ready to leave.

"You've nothing to fear from me, Meadows," Martinez said. He glanced up to Randolph, perched on a rock above. Randolph had decided to stay, and sat atop the rock, rifle in his lap, looking out at the assembled "mutineers."

"That whole farce was my fault," Meadows said. "You should have been tried from your cell in the guardhouse. You're a disgrace, but I'm the bigger disgrace for letting it happen."

Valentine looked out on the road, filled with files of people in their assortment of Southern Command uniforms, rain ponchos, coats and hats. Perhaps six hundred soldiers were interspersed with a handful of tagalong civilian specialists. Packhorses and mules, leashed pigs, chickens and geese in baskets, and a total of four wagons added to the noise and smell. Squads of Guard soldiers were relieving the men of Southern Command rifles, while others poked in the packhorse loads. A cold wind coursed through the hollow.

"None of the animals have a Southern Command brand," Valentine said, continuing the argument Meadows had interrupted. Ahn-Kha wandered up the file, cradling his long Grog rifle.

Out of Martinez's hearing, Valentine heard Ahn-Kha make an aside to Post.

"How'd you get a captured gun?" Ahn-Kha asked, touching Post's holstered .45. It was a duplicate of Valentine's; Post had given him one while they served together on the *Thunderbolt.*

"It's not Southern Command issue."

"Letter of the law," Ahn-Kha said. "A few dozen guns between all of us."

"For a column a half mile long."

Valentine turned his attention back to Martinez, still arguing with Meadows. "You think you can move this many through the hills? You're throwing away the lives of everyone here. I'll offer an amnesty. We can bring the command back together."

Meadows unhooked his pistol belt and handed it over to Martinez. "That 9mm is Southern Command issue. Wouldn't want to set a bad example." He looked at the men holding the horse teams. "Five minutes!" he shouted. "We get going in five minutes!"

"Don't be a fool, Colonel," Martinez said. "We need you. And these good men." His beady eyes glanced up and down the files of men. It seemed that those who still shaved and cleaned their uniforms were all lined up with Valentine.

"Martinez," Valentine said, "you don't have a command. You have a mob. They way things are going in this camp, you won't even have a mob much longer."

Martinez sneered. "Think so? I'll give you a prediction in return. We'll outlast you."

Four

The Eastern Ouachitas, Arkansas, February: In the decade before the Overthrow, the interstate between Little Rock and Hot Springs enjoyed a high-tech growth spurt. With key computer networks in prominent cities worldwide challenged by everything from terrorism to extended power outages, backup locations became the focus of a substantial slice of investment. In America's heartland, in the basements of non-descript office parks, fiberoptic lines connected servers waiting to cut into action should the need arise without the slightest interruption in data flow; "transparent redundancy," in the phrase of the times.

Southwest of the blasted ruins of Little Rock, off of one of the feeder highways to the old interstate, a chocolate-colored three-story with bands of black windows once housed claim and policy-holder records for one of the world's top ten insurance companies. In 2022 the building nestled in the Ouachita foothills looked a little like a giant slice of devil's food cake amidst its landscaping and parking lots. Now the lots are meadows, and saplings grow on its roof as birds fly in and out of paneless top-story windows; just another unraveled piece of the commercial fabric of a rich nation. The lowest floor shows some sign of recent renovation. Plywood has been nailed up over broken windows and horses graze behind the building in a paddock made from downed power-line towers. A few camouflage-painted pickups sit parked outside a barbed-wire festooned gas station between the highway and the office building. The battered office building looks peaceful behind a sign reading STATION *26.*

Except for the three bodies rotting in the noonday sun.

All male, all naked and all covered in a black mixture of rotting flesh and pitch, visited only by crows, they swing from a pylon that once held four lights above the parking lot next to the gas station. An uprooted stop sign stands in the parking-lot meadow between the bodies and the entrance road, redone in whitewash and black lettering—the two colors have run together in the hasty paint job—reading SABOTER'S REWARD.

"Bullfrog's been at it again," Finner said. "Sumbitch never could spell." He and Valentine crouched in the thick bush bordering the improvised horse pasture, examining the bodies from a stand of wintering lilac bushes, the western wind blowing the stench the other way. The rest of the column sheltered in the deeper woods a kilometer away, eating the midday meal out of their packs. The screening Wolves had been exploring the more open ground around the old office park and came across what looked like an inhabited office building. When they found the bodies they had summoned Valentine.

"Bullfrog?" Valentine asked.

"Sergeant Bill Frum. Top sergeant in the Guards, or so the men in his old unit say."

"A guerilla?"

"In a manner. He and his men joined up with Solon's crew in Little Rock and they gave him a commission. Only he's playing double agent or whatever you want to call it. He's got twenty or thirty diehards, twice that in part-time guerillas in the farms east of here, and about two hundred men scattered around who are supposed to be hunting guerillas. What they mostly do is look the other way."

Valentine reread the block letters on the sign. "So what about the bodies?"

"Camouflage."

"What's that mean?"

"His guerillas aren't really going up against the KZ forces. More like sneaking around and hitting the folks who cooperate. That burned-out farm we passed yesterday; I bet that was his work."

The scouts had reported bodies in the ruins, Valentine remembered.

"He's a good source of intelligence about the roads between the Rock and Hot Springs, for all that. Sometimes he sends a messenger, trades information or supplies he's been issued. In the last swap he told us they'd open the rail line south from the Rock again."

"He went to some effort to preserve the bodies. I wonder why?" Valentine asked.

"Shows any inspection groups that he's killing guerillas. I know he shoots deserters trying to get back home to Texas or Oklahoma. Picks off an occasional wildcatter come in from Illinois or Tenesseee to set up shop, and then burns down an empty house or two in fake 'reprisals.' Bullfrog likes a good bonfire. He burns anything used to trade with the enemy—from a cart to a farm, and buries locals who join up and are carrying arms."

"Buries?"

"Buries alive, in a coffin with an airhole of old pipe, so they have time to think about what they did. Then claims the guerillas did it. That's what Major Rojo used to say, anyway."

Valentine found himself feeling less contemptuous toward General Martinez and his moonshine-sotted camp. He'd rather have his men drunk and disorderly than burying people alive. Valentine squatted and crept away from the bodies through the new grass. Finner and his patrol rested among the newly mature trees that had sprung up in old landscaping.

"You said this is was pretty quiet area, Jess."

"Quiet's relative, Val," Finner said.

"Let's visit this setup," Valentine said.

"What, everyone?"

"No. Keep the column hidden in the hills. I want to visit this Bullfrog's lily pad and find out for sure which side he's hopped on."

Valentine crouched alongside a wrecked pickup covered in kudzu, and moved his hand as though he were throwing a dart three times. He could hear Styachowski's quick breaths behind. She'd vouched for the authenticity of Bullfrog's intelligence; as far as she knew his information had never led to the capture or destruction of Southern Command forces. Nail, looking back at him from twenty meters ahead, whipped his wiry arm in a wheeling motion forward and his Bears rose out of the ditch in front of the chocolate-colored office building—Valentine guessed it had once held a decorative pond—and entered, two remaining behind to cover. At another wave from Nail in the doorway, they ran in after him.

His old Wolf senses took over and he listened to the footsteps, the low calls, the crash of something heavy overturning.

"Blue Tick! Blue Tick! Blue Tick!" Nail called. The Bears had reached the door of the office building. Some boarded-over windows had STATION 26 stencilled on them.

"Running! They're running," Nail shouted.

Valentine rose and another thirty men rose with him. They trotted inside the swept-up but still water-damaged reception foyer; it stretched up through the building's three stories to paneless skylights, and dispersed to cover all sides of the building. Years' worth of plant life had established itself on the floors above so that roots and old extension cords and recent phone lines shared space on the wall. Valentine and Styachowski followed a pointing Bear named Ritter down a flight of stairs. Finner waited for them at the bottom. The landing was cluttered with suspiciously fresh blown leaves.

They stepped down an electric-lit corridor just in time to see Nail fling himself at a vaultlike door that was being closed.

"Open up, Sergeant Frum," Nail called. "Southern Command. Operations verification Squeak-Three."

"That's out of date," Styachowski said, coughing after the run.

Valentine examined the cinderblock walls. Heavy girders supported a concrete ceiling above. This Bullfrog had chosen his panic room, or hideout, or bomb shelter well.

"Southern Command hasn't set a new code for this year," Nail said. "It's the last effective password." Then, to the door: "C'mon, Sergeant, Squeak-Three. This is Lieutenant Harold Nail, Volmer's Bears."

Valentine pressed his ear to the cool metal and listened. If anyone stood on the other side of the door, he or she remained silent.

Finner pounded on the door. "Jess Finner here. For chrissakes, Bullfrog, gimme a break and open up. These Bears is just gonna blow you out otherwise. I'm not shitting you, ol' buddy."

Valentine heard an authoritative click from the door and breathed a sigh of relief. They had no explosives to make good Finner's threat.

The door opened and a brilliant beam of light filled the corridor. It hit Valentine's eyes like a knife, giving him an instant headache. Valentine could just make out light-frosted outlines of heads and gun barrels.

"Whoa there!" he said, holding out his hands. "Friends, okay? I'm codename Ghost, Cat of Southern Command."

"No Southern Command no more," argued a deep voice, smooth as buttermilk being poured.

"You call me 'sir,' Sergeant, and get that light off."

"Just making sure." The light went out and Valentine could see a dozen hard faces, guns ready, set against nondescript gray-green office décor.

"Just making sure, sir," Valentine corrected.

"I'm not blowing your head off, and I'm not calling you 'sir.' I might change my mind about one. Like I said, no Southern Command to say 'sir' to. They sold us out, just like they did my granddaddy in '22." A man proportioned a little like Ahn-Kha stepped forward, filling the doorway, and held up his hand, palm out. "Howdy, Jess. Had to make sure there wasn't a gun to your head. I'm Bill Frum. What can I do for you boys?"

* * *

It turned out Bullfrog was willing to do almost nothing.

Valentine sat among silent machines in the dusty basement room. A single candle made more shadows than light. He stared at the six dark boxes. Each about the size of an up-ended footlocker, the old computers—netservers, or so the tiny chrome letters next to the main power button said—stood like a squad of soldiers on parade. Bullfrog's men avoided this small, stuffy corner room, like Visigoths afraid to enter the heart of a Roman temple, fearing ancient, half-understood wrath. A little dusting and some power, and it would be hard to tell the past half century had even happened—

Except for some long-ago philosopher who'd written THE JOKE IS ON US on the wall, using a permanent marker to form the two-foot block letters.

He had to think.

His command was divided; the rest of the column was resting in the woods just under a mile away, while the team that penetrated the old office building stayed and mixed with Bullfrog's men, with orders not to reaveal anything about their numbers.

Bullfrog had taken the handful of guests on a tour of his domain, made cozy by gear plucked from the dead organs of Southern Command or issued by the Kurians. Crates of supplies covered with stenciled letters were stacked floor to ceiling along with guns, leather goods, bolts of cloth, camp gear, cooking pots, and medical and commissary supplies. The sergeant organized his command with a professional NCO's eye to detail and a mind for long-term operations. His men were clad in a variant of the old Louisiana Regular outfits Valentine had an intimate knowledge of from his days posing as a Kurian Coastal Marine in the Gulf.

Bullfrog wouldn't part with any of it, orders or no. He was overgenerous with what was lying around on the mess room tables and counters, offering the guests canned peanut paste smeared on heartroot, jerky, creamed corn, even root beer.

"No Southern Command no more," Bullfrog said each and every time the subject came up. "Just patriots and collaborators, mister, patriots and collaborators. We've gone underground. Literally. I got arsenals hidden all over the place for my Night Watch."

"You're guerillas."

"Yes," Bullfrog said, smiling so that his face seemed mostly made up of teeth. "Helluva war I got going here. I'm running both sides of it."

"And what do the Kurians get out of it?"

"A bunch of 'somedays,'" Bullfrog said. "I'm supposed to be recruiting. They're broke-dick on troops, not getting as much cooperation out of

Ozark folks as they expected, and the troops that took down Southern Command are heading home. They got soldiers running the lights and phones, driving trucks, running switches on the railroad. Most locals won't do anything unless you've got a soldier poking them along with a bayonet."

"What do you do with the ones who cooperate?"

"They get a warning. The Night Watch beats the hell out of 'em. After that—" He passed an index finger across his throat.

"We could really use some of those guns I saw in your armory."

"Can't. Strict inventory. Those are for the forces I'm supposed to be recruiting. They watch guns and gas like Jew accountants. There's never a pistol missing or a drop short. That's why they keep me as honcho hearabout. Figure if I'm honest about the small stuff, I'll be honest about the big stuff too."

Valentine felt hot and restless. He wanted to swing his arms and kick with his legs. Seeing the hoarded supplies appear and then vanish like a desert mirage frustrated him. If he could draw on Sergeant Bill "Bullfrog" Frum's stores in a substantial way his column might be able to make it the rest of the way to the Boston Mountains. They were already short of food; seven hundred people on the march couldn't live on the local rabbits and wild onions. Frum's obstinacy might mean the destruction of his column.

He needed release. An hour chopping wood might clear his buffers. What did that expression mean, anyway?

"Hell, sir, you look like a Bear warming up for a fight," a voice from the other side of the Arkansas broke in.

"What's that?" Valentine temporized, bringing himself back to the room with the dead servers.

Nail stood in the doorway, scratching the afternoon's growth on his face. The Bear officer put a half-eaten lasagna MRE on one of the old computers and crossed his arms as though he were wrapped in a straightjacket, pulled his heels together and rocked on them. Valentine realized that Nail was aping his pose. "You look like a stomped-down spring."

"About to go 'boing,' huh?" Valentine forced his body to relax. "I'll give you a warning before I snap."

"I've worked with Bears for six year, Captain. I'm used to it. It was more the staring-at-nothing look in your eye. You smell action in the wind?"

"No. I should get back to Post and Meadows."

"You know, sir, we've got enough men to empty this joint. Lots of stuff here we could use. Ol' Frum could say his headquarters got attacked unexpectedly."

"The sergeant's worked hard on his setup. I don't want to give the Kurians a reason to replace him."

"Still like to see Bullfrog taken down a notch. He's been the biggest buck of these woods too long; thinks he makes right and wrong. I don't like making war on civilians, ours or theirs."

Valentine felt a better warmth at those words. He saw a crack of light from Frum's locked-off door. "Neither do I. Follow me, would you?"

Valentine traced a line with his index finger under the THE JOKE IS ON US graffiti as he left. He nodded at one of Bullfrog's guerillas, dripping wet with a towel around his waist as he came back from the improvised bath—Bullfrog had turned an old janitorial closet into a one-man shower—and followed his ears to the canteen, where Bullfrog was shooting the breeze with Finner about the last few months.

"Troop trains heading back south and west lately," Valentine heard as he approached. "Borrowed troops heading home with boxcars of booty and prisoners. As long as the Night Watch keeps out of Little Rock and away from the lines, these hills stay quiet. If I touch the railroads I get a flying regiment sent—"

"Bullfrog, I'm taking over," Valentine said, cutting off the storytelling.

Bullfrog had one leg up on the table, the worn waffle pattern in the boot turned toward him, like a religious icon shifted to ward off evil.

"Taking over what?"

Valentine's heart tripped when he saw Bullfrog's hand fall to his holster.

Valentine stuck his thumbs in his belt. "Your unit. They'll be taking orders from me, until I depart."

"Doubt it. They answer to me."

"Never said otherwise. I outrank you. I'll give the orders to you, then you'll amplify, organize and carry out. Way it always worked in Southern Command."

Bullfrog sighed. "That again. I told you before, I don't—"

"You will, or I'll knock you into next week."

The sergeant stood up. Valentine's leveled stare hit Bullfrog just below the collarbone. "You think you can whip me?"

"If you won't take my word for it."

"If you're dead set on an ass-kicking, I'll oblige, Valentine."

"You've been around the Kurians too long. You're not the local demigod. Time to put you back in the chain of command, since you can't handle the responsibility." Bullfrog turned an intriguing shade of purple, took a breath—"I'm going to use these stores. And another thing.

I won't stand for any more reprisals against civilians," Valentine finished, delaying whatever was coming.

Bullfrog's rapid-fire laughter filled the mess room and echoed like a string of firecrackers going off: heh-ha-hehha-heh-ha. "I fight with my fists, not paper."

"That's your prerogative. I'm not filing a Jagger complaint."

Bullfrog wasted no time. He led Valentine outside. Word passed around among the men via the mysterious network that exists in any organization, always faster and more effective than any communications flowchart. As they walked out the thick steel door and up the stairs, everyone from Nail's Bears to Bullfrog's own headquarters staff followed.

Valentine took off his tunic as he exited the plant-cluttered office building. The cool air felt good as it licked across his hot ears. The sky had become overcast again; the late-winter rains looked to be building again. Meadows, guided by a pair of Wolves, was crossing the parking lot.

"Valentine," Meadows hallooed. "Since we're resting I wanted to—"

"Sorry, sir, busy," Valentine said.

Meadows' forehead wrinkled as Bullfrog removed his own jacket. "That you, Fa—no, Frum. Sergeant Frum?"

"Colonel Meadows," Bullfrog said, not bothering to salute.

"What's all this?" Meadows turned in a circle as he looked at the mixed contingent of men, some throwing suspenders over their shoulders or still pulling on boots as they emerged from the office building.

Valentine ignored him, but the remoter, calmer quarters of his brain filed away Bullfrog's familiarity with Meadows. "Men!" he said, not having to try too hard to sound fighting-mad. "An exchange of blows between officers of Southern Command is considered a court-martial offense by the Uniform Code, especially if there is a difference in rank. I picked this quarrel with Sergeant Frum; he's to be held blameless." Valentine spat into each palm and formed his hands into tight fists. "Sergeant Frum, do you hold me blameless under the Uniform Code?"

Bullfrog planted his feet. "You can count on it, Valentine."

"Tell the men, and Colonel Meadows, so he's a witness. I don't want to hang with those others."

Bullfrog somehow managed to shout using the side of his mouth, keeping his vision locked on Valentine. "He's blameless too, under the Uniform Code."

Valentine lowered his fists. "Sergeant, the Southern Command's

Uniform Code isn't a buffet. You can't pick and choose which rules apply. You either operate under it or you don't. You've just accepted its protection, and with its protection goes—"

"Bullshit!" Bullfrog shouted. "Tricks won't—"

He charged, arms up and reaching for Valentine's throat.

But Bullfrog was just big, and Valentine was a Cat. He sidestepped the rush, reached out and grabbed a handful of Quisling-issue collar, whipped his legs up and got them around Bullfrog's waist. They both went down, Bullfrog using his weight and strength to hammer Valentine into the ground.

Valentine got his forearm under Bullfrog's chin, an old wrestling move he'd learned—the hard way—from his old top sergeant in Zulu Company.

Bullfrog croaked in what Patel called his "hangman."

The sergeant gave one terrific shrug and spun, bringing Valentine sideways into the ground, but Valentine clung, battered and smashed by Bullfrog's weight, with the same tenacity as Rikki-Tikki-Tavi with his teeth locked in Nag the Cobra's neck. For the honor of his family Rikki wanted to be found dead with his teeth locked in the enemy, and for the honor of Zulu Company's champion wrestler Valentine clung to his choke hold despite the red-yellow-red flashes of pain from his ribs. Then Bullfrog went limp.

Valentine suspected a trick until he felt, and smelled, warm urine on his leg.

"He's done," Valentine said, getting to shaky legs and brushing himself off.

Bullfrog groaned.

"Somebody get the sergeant a towel," Valentine said, breathing into the pain.

"Enough of that, Captain," Meadows barked. He hooked Valentine with his good hand and his thumb and finger, pulling the Cat up. "You men, help the sergeant inside. Captain, you'd better have Narcisse look at those ribs. The rest of you, pay off your bets and get inside. Sun's going down."

Valentine's eyes rose to the tarred bodies hanging from the lamppost. Meadows nodded in understanding.

"Lieutenant Nail, take a detail and get those bodies down. Anyone else feels like fistfighting can work off their aggressions digging six feet down."

"You come back from a beating like no man I ever knew," Narcisse said the next morning, applying cool, water-soaked towels to Valentine's battered frame. Unfortunately, Bullfrog's substantial inventory didn't include an ice machine.

Valentine looked at his reflection in the washroom mirror. A great blue-and-purple mark on his chin was just beginning to show a hint of yellow through the skin. The right side of his rib cage looked like van Gogh's *Starry Night.*

"I've never broken a bone before," he said, feeling around at the soft spot.

Narcisse rapped him across the probing knuckles with her handless arm. "Leave it be, and it'll heal. Just a rib. Count yourself lucky; your lung stayed airy and you got lots of stuff holding that rib in place."

A heavy tread sounded in the basement corridor, and Ahn-Kha's bent-over frame appeared. There was now enough of a mixture of Valentine's column and the guerillas that Stya-chowski had judged it safe for Ahn-Kha to make an appearance. The Golden One bore a contraption that looked a little like a corset made of tube steel. He'd put it together using the frames of a stack of office chairs he found and leather scraps.

"I adjusted it, my David. Try it now."

Ahn-Kha could be as gentle as a cooing dove when he chose to be. The great arms, thick as well-fed pythons, wrapped themselves around Valentine and then worked the buckles on the brace. Valentine had always had good posture; constant insistence from first his parents, and then the more recently departed Father Max had given him an instinctive, erect carriage, but with the brace on he felt like a heroically posed statue, elbows slightly out. But he could breathe this time, unlike the preliminary fitting.

"Thanks, old horse."

He tottered out into the hallway, walking a bit like a drunk trying to conceal the extent of his load. He couldn't favor his bad leg, the way he usually strode. He made for Meadows, who stood at the far end of the hall, checking off supplies as they were distributed to Valentine's column. A somewhat subdued Sergeant—now Lieutenant, Valentine corrected himself—Frum stood just beside him, the bruise under his chin looking like a hangman's beard.

Colonel Meadows and Bullfrog were comfortable enough with each other that Valentine had suggested that Meadows stay at the hideout with whoever felt unfit for a try at the Boston Mountains. Bullfrog could find jobs for them as guerillas or in some of the settlements under his command. Meadows accepted, and with the help of a staff captain had begun to sort through the horde of Quisling supplies. Everyone seemed happier for it, like tired horses back in familiar stalls.

"All this stuff missing; it'll go against me at the next inspection," Bullfrog said.

"You'll be able to justify it."

"How's that?"

"You were doing your job. Recruiting and equipping warm bodies."

Bullfrog scratched his head, and Valentine turned to Meadows.

"Colonel, I think I'm fit enough to talk to the men. Could you get them together, please, sir?"

The men who couldn't fit underground had to be dispersed every night in case of a prowling Reaper, looking for lifesign where it wasn't supposed to be. Once the sun was well up they usually gathered for meals and news. There had been plenty of the first and not much of the latter lately, though everyone was looking better for a few days' rest. Styachowski popped up, dabbing a coffee mustache from her lips and showing her old snap-to-it briskness. She'd spent the past day combing through Quisling paperwork with the help of a corporal on Bullfrog's quasi-Quisling staff.

"I'll pass word around as soon as the morning patrol comes in," she said.

"Lieutenant Frum, you think you could send out your men as sentry? I'd hate to have a convoy come by for refueling and spot the whole bunch of us."

Bullfrog nodded. "Sure, Captain."

"Anything overnight?"

"Another train, pulling south; men returning to Texas and Louisiana, looked like," Frum said.

"The Ozarks seem good and pacified," Meadows said. "We're beat and they know it."

"Always interesting times, the pause between conquest and exploitation. I wonder if they're as organized as they think they are," Styachowski said. Valentine's selection of documentation from Bullfrog's files had given her quick mind enough to make a guess as to what the column's next move would be.

"Or if we're as beat as they think we are," Valentine added.

Valentine stood at one of the glassless windows above the entrance to the office building, on the second floor. Bullfrog hadn't gotten around to reclaiming this floor of the building yet. Birds flitted in one side of the building and out the other, zipping over low cubicles and around offices.

Creeper and broken glass crunched underfoot as he tottered to the window, glad that the men hadn't seen Ahn-Kha half carry him upstairs.

The men and women who had followed him out of General Martinez's camp sat around the door of the lot and in the notch leading toward the main entrance; unformed, unranked, a mass of faces and variegated uniforms—some still damp, Valentine noted, from a quick wash. Some elbowed others at Valentine's appearance, and faces turned up toward them. The chatter stilled.

The silence of their anticipation made Valentine oddly uncomfortable.

Valentine inflated his lungs, ignored the pain in his rib. "You all know about the Cats, am I right?"

"Yes, sir," a few answered back. Valentine thought about making them all holler a response back at him, but he wanted an honest conversation with the men, not an oration filled with theatrical tricks.

"They work behind the Kurian line," Valentine said. "Sometimes in their uniform. I've done it on more than one occasion."

He let that sink in for a moment before continuing. "We're making for what's left of Southern Command in the Boston Mountains. But if we keep going as we are, snaking back and forth, backtracking and sidestepping, we'll only show up sick, hungry, unarmed and tired—if we make it at all. If you men are willing, I know a way we can ride instead of walk, and join our comrades with rifles in our hands and ammunition in our cartridge cases."

They perked up at this. Even the jokers and snoozers in every informal assembly of personnel shut their mouths and fixed eyes on him.

"There'll be risks," Valentine continued. "But the risk of getting across the Arkansas River and through the lines with an unarmed column this big is about the same, by my calculations.

"So we have to balance the likely risks with the possible rewards. Anyone who isn't up for it, anyone who wants out of the game, can stay here with Colonel Meadows and Lieutenant Frum. Guerrilla service is just as honorable, just as important. But I have to make it to the Boston Mountains for reasons of my own. Anyone who wants to follow me, meet at the hollow where Lieutenant Post and and the Wolves are guarding the wagons."

"Then what?" Styachowski asked from among the audience. Just as they'd arranged when Valentine went over his prepared speech with her.

"Then we shave, strip and sew."

Five

The Ruins of Little Rock, Arkansas, February: The city never recovered from the nuclear blast inflicted on it in the death throes of the Old World. Though the fires went out and the radiation dispersed, the only life to return permanently was nonhuman. Pine Bluff, closer to the breadbasket of southeastern Arkansas, replaced it as a transportation hub; Mountain Home and Fort Scott surpassed it as government and military centers. At the height of the Ozark Free Territory's progress, it could boast of little more than a dock and a ferry in a cleared-out patch of rubble, though even that was based on the north side of the river; the south-bank heart of the city was avoided as if it were cursed earth.

The new rulers have a grander vision of a rail, road, and river traffic hub built on the decayed remnants of the old. The Rocks, as the locals call them, buzz with activity. The new human constructs have an anthill quality to them; low buildings made out of the blasted components of pre-2022 architecture. Some are already smoothed over by fresh concrete and white paint, and a more traveled eye might think of a little Greek town between hill and Aegean. The pilings and ruined bridges prevent barges from going farther up the river—only small boat traffic goes west to Fort Scott—so Little Rock is an amphibian marshaling yard. Warehouses and tents under the New Order's supply officers support the final mopping up and reorganization of the Ozarks. The river hums with traffic, and trucks and horse wagons fill transport pools as Consul Solon builds his capital.

One building stands apart from the others, avoided by all but a few humans who work on its exterior and still-unfinished upper floors. It is a Kurian Tower, home of one of the new masters of what had been the Ozark Free Territory. Other towers like it are going up in Pine

Bluff, Mountain Home, Hot Springs, and a dozen other, smaller towns. Only Consul Solon has seen them all.

Consul Solon. Little is known of him, save that he came from somewhere on the eastern seaboard. The name makes Quisling captains break a sweat. Children are hushed with warnings that Consul Solon will hear about misbehavior. An argument can be stopped with a threat to take the matter to him—a turn of events that might mean doom to both sides. Consul Solon is the man responsible for keeping human order in the various provinces of what was the Free Territory. He answers only to his Masters who have carved up the region: the dark princes of Fort Scott and Crowley's Ridge, the Springs, the Plateau, the Southern Marches, the Corridor . . . and other regions. Unlike much of the Kurian Zone, Solon is trusted to ensure the defense of all with a common force, rather than dozens of private armies in the hands of each overlord. Each Kurian has a Reaper representative at Solon's temporary headquarters at Fort Scott, the Consul's nerve center until the grander Consular Palace is built on the north bank of the Arkansas near Little Rock.

"Get out of the way of the trucks, like obedient little Quislings," Valentine ordered over his shoulder to Post, who signaled with an arm to pull the files off the paved road. Valentine leaned against the base of an old traffic signal pole on the outskirts of Little Rock and waved first to a motorcycle, then to the trucks as they passed on southward. Only ten feet of the pole remained; the rest of it lay in an overgrown ditch atop an engine block. But ample enough for leaning.

Valentine pulled off his helmet and rubbed his newly bald skull as he surveyed the column. The fuzzy-headed troops looked good enough in their Quisling uniforms, though they marched poorly. They were all shorn of their hair, and even the elaborate mustaches and beards—the pride and joy of many of the soldiers of Southern Command—had been left on the dead leaves in the woods near Bullfrog's station.

He had organized his footsore charges into three parts after leaving seventy-odd men and women tired of the trail or unwilling to face the risks of operating in the enemy's uniform. At the lead were Finner's Wolves, bereft of their beloved buckskins. They now wore the uniforms of the TMMP, an acronym for the Trans-Mississippi Mounted Patrol—the military police of Solon's newborn empire, entrusted with everything from guarding rail bridges to directing traffic. He, his officers, the Bears and the Jamaicans wore the simple, shapeless uniforms of recruits newly incorporated into the Quisling AOT—Army of the Trans-Mississippi.

At the center of the column, teams of four "recruits" each carried a Quickwood beam on their shoulders, faking exercises under the shouted direction of their NCOs. Mrs. Smalls rode in one of the wagons with the camp equipment; her husband and son led teams carrying the sick. The family had insisted on coming along, so that Mrs. Smalls could have her baby in the hospital reported to be in Little Rock. Valentine thought she stuck out like a cardinal in a coven.

Valentine watched the southbound trucks kick up gravel from the potholes with hungry eyes. In his days with the Wolves, a lightly armed convoy of six trucks falling into his lap would have been cause for celebration. He would have waited for signals from the observation scouts, then pitched into the convoy if his scouts flashed the all clear. The Quislings were sure of themselves if they were sending trucks with nothing more than a motorcycle and sidecar leading the way down the long road to Hot Springs. General Martinez must not have been too aggressive in the eastern Ouachitas over the winter, and Bullfrog only attacked the occasional Quisling target at night.

When the way cleared he got his column up and moving again. He stayed by his signal post, watching the men's faces as they walked toward Little Rock. A few looked excited, even eager to play the game, but others wore their fear like lead overcoats. They moved with the deliberative plod of men too tired and hungry to hope.

"Let's step out a little more, Calgary," Valentine called to a former Guard shuffling down the road with a hangdog expression. "We're having a hot meal tonight."

Calgary picked up the pace and smacked his lips, pleased for some reason to be recognized. Valentine felt better too. The weeks of starts and stops, double-backs, circling, hunger and cold in the hills, and soggy, fireless camps, keeping seven hundred men out of the way of Quisling patrols, were over. They were right where Valentine had placed his finger on the map at the conference the night they left Colonel Meadows and Bullfrog, and his column had all solemnly shaved their heads—starting with Ahn-Kha's destruction of Valentine's shoulder-length locks. At first it had been play, learning the AOT and TMPP ranks, working on their imaginary stories as mercenary recruits in Arkansas, or up from the swamps of Louisiana or the woods of East Texas, looking to seek their fortune in the new empire Solon was raising.

When they emerged from the hills and turned up the road for the old state capital, the men grew more and more anxious as the task became real, rather than just an imagined challenge in the future. At a rest halt, Valentine gathered the men and spoke to them as best as he could, relaying details of a plan he had kept from all save Ahn-Kha, though he suspected Styachowski had an inkling. When the time came to speak to them he had the men unharness the wagons and rest on a hillside, making a natural amphitheater.

"You all know I'm a Cat," he finished, booming the words out so all could hear. "As of today, you're all Cats too. We're going to pretend we're Quislings recruits. Lieutenant Frum has phoned in to headquarters here the happy news that he's finally met, indeed overfilled, his recruitment quota. We've got faked documents requisitioning us food, new clothing, shoes and weapons. You've all suffered because of shortages of those things. The Quislings in the Ruins have plenty, and we're going to trick them out of them, get across the river and rejoin Southern Command. Just keep your mouths shut. One loose tongue could do us all in."

So as they approached the Ruins, Valentine needed something to get their minds off their situation. Most of the men were worried they were walking right into a prison yard, the intermediate holding place leading to the inevitable Reaper embrace.

"How about a song, Jefferson. An old marching tune. 'Yellow Rose of Texas,' anyone?"

"Huh?" Jefferson said, looking down from his wagon.

"Narcisse, I've heard your singing. Give us a song," Valentine said.

"One everyone can sing?"

"If you can think of one."

Narcisse ran her tongue beneath her lips. "Lesseee . . .

"Mine eyes have seen the glory of the coming of the Lord:
He is trampling out the vintage where the grapes of wrath are stored;
He hath loosed the fateful lightening of His terrible, swift sword:
His truth is marching on."

The men took up the march with a will. They began stepping out in time; some, used to singing hymns or just musically inclined, added harmonies. Even the Jamaicans knew the words.

While the song lasted Finner fell in beside him.

"Captain, you sure about what you're doing?"

Valentine considered telling him to shut his mouth and obey orders, but the man who'd brought him south from Minnesota deserved better. "Commanding one of the worst marches in Ozark history. I'll let Consul Solon take care of transport from now on."

"But from the Ruins? Why not grab some boats and just cross at some quiet bend upriver? From a distance we'll look like a training march."

"Styachowski says the AOT is scraping men from every border station. Little Rock is a supply depot. New formations are brought there now, to be equipped before being sent elsewhere."

"If I had a suspicious mind I might be worried that you were marching everyone into a prison yard. That'd rate a brass ring and an estate in Iowa. If I had a suspicious mind, that is."

"Would it make you feel better to know that I'm keeping your Wolves outside the wire?"

"It'd make me feel better. Don't know about the rest of these lunks. How far outside?"

"About seven miles. I want you to camp around Mt. Summit. We won't be in Little Rock for more than three or four days, I expect. If this turns bad we'll make for you if we can. You've got a good view of the old Highway 10 from there. If I need to talk to you and I can't come myself, I'll send Ahn-Kha or Post. Just a nice ride in the country. We'll have one of these red bandannas tied on our heads."

"Red bandannas. Okay."

"One more thing." Valentine reached into his AOT officer's winter coat, a hanging mass of leather and canvas covered with bellows pockets. "Here's a report . . . well, several reports. Send a couple of good, and I mean real good, Wolves out to the Boston Mountains. They're to find whoever's in charge there and hand them over. A Lifeweaver would be ideal."

"I've got eight men who've run courier for Martinez up north. They know where to go."

"Keep those uniforms handy. You may need them again."

"Very well, sir."

"More responsibility than you wanted, I'm sure."

Finner rocked back and forth on his heels, keeping time to the music, fighting a smile. "I'm getting used to it. I think I'm better at this than I thought. Hope you didn't think I was accusing . . ." Finner let the sentence trail off.

"No. Stay suspicious, Finner. If I'd been more suspicious when we hit the Free Territory—oh, never mind. I want to pay this Consul Solon back with some of his own coin."

Finner and his Wolves left them while they were still in the hills. The road sloped down into the Ruins. It began to rain again. Valentine put an old green towel over his shaven head so the ends hung down like a bloodhound's ears and seated an old Kevlar helmet over it.

"This cover my scar?" he asked Post. "I'm worried I've made Solon's Most Wanted."

"Pretty much, " Post said, tilting his head to see the thin white line descending Valentine's right cheek. "It's shaded off, anyway. You can still see the bit by your eye. It's the haircut that makes the real difference."

"That wasn't a haircut, that was clear-cutting."

"Your teeth could use some coffee stains to complete the disguise. I've never known anyone who spends so much time brushing his teeth in the field."

"Every meal, the way my momma taught me." That memory caused a brief stab: the last time he'd seen them in Minnesota he was eleven and she'd—*stop it.* "If you'd ever seen a nice, runny oral infection you'd join me," he finished, a little lamely.

The column passed shells of buildings. Empty gas stations, strip malls with their glass fronts blasted out, foundations of homes that had burned and died grew closer and closer together as they came into the city limits. Gutted two-story structures gave way to piles of rubble, though the highway they walked on had been cleared. The debris lined either side of the road like snowdrifts.

The column sighted a guard post.

"Okay, Post, I'm going to talk to them. They'll probably take me to the CO of this scrapheap. If I'm not back in two hours, or if you hear shooting, just fade into the hills. Split up if you have to."

"Told me that, sir."

"I'm repeating it. Nobody, not even Ahn-Kha, goes in after me. We want them confused; fighting will unconfuse them faster than anything."

A sergeant with a corporal trailing behind like a heeled dog stepped from a little shelter at the spectacle of a quarter mile of humanity waking down the road toward his post. They wore tiger-striped cammies, with AOT yellow insignia at the shoulder. Valentine kicked his horse on and trotted forward. Ahn-Kha stepped in front of his horse and took the reigns.

"I heard you speaking to Post. If this turns, we're not to go in after you?"

"Not even you, old horse."

"If I can't go in after you, my David, I'm coming in with you."

"Post will need you if—"

"You'll need me more."

Ahn-Kha's ears went flat and the Grog took a stance a little wider than a riverside oak, four hundred pounds of roadblock.

"You'll be my bodyguard then," Valentine said, knowing when he was beaten, and not wanting to look like there was a crisis in his command.

They approached the guard station. Valentine hailed the sergeant from horseback.

"We're a day late, I know. Bad weather," Valentine said.

"A day late for what?" the sergeant said. He looked more at Ahn-Kha than at either Valentine or the unarmed column far behind. Valentine was suddenly glad Ahn-Kha had insisted on accompanying him.

Valentine glared, and turned his chin so the three pips on his collar showed.

"Colonel," the sergeant added, saluting.

"For outfit and transport, Sergeant. Recruits up from Station 26, District Commander Frum's HQ."

The corporal checked a nearly blank clipboard. "You're Colonel Le Sain."

"From Louisiana," Valentine said, opening a satchel. He passed down a wad of paperwork in an expandable waterproof envelope. "Route Orders are near the top. You'll see supply, transport, OI for each recruit and the roster's in the back, not that you need to concern yourself with the rest. Don't think you have to check off every name that passes; my officers are responsible for everyone getting on the barge. I take the heat if anyone deserts."

The sergeant took another look at the ID card dangling from Valentine's breast pocket. "Didn't they have transport for you on the road, uhhh, Colonel Le Sain?"

"Too cheap. Besides, it toughens 'em up."

"I'll let the general know you've arrived."

"When you do, mention that weather held us up. Hell, I'd better come along in case they have questions."

"Yes, sir. Corp, let the colonel and his stoop pass." The sergeant disappeared into his guardhouse.

Valentine dismounted and stepped over the chain hung between two concrete dragon's teeth blocking the road. "Up from Louisiana, sir? I used to serve in Texas, myself. Can't wait to get back." The corporal's face showed curiosity, not suspicion.

"I'm here permanently."

The guardhouse consisted of the remains of some concrete-and-steel professional building. Men in loose dungarees were rebuilding exterior walls from the rubble, fitting together more or less intact cinder blocks around electrical conduit already laid. Others worked on a superstructure to the building, building something that looked like a miniature aircraft control tower. The workers all had bright orange zipper pockets sewn on the breasts of their overalls.

"Forced labor?" Valentine asked the corporal.

"You know it, sir. At first it was lots of force and not much labor, but they've settled down."

"Good."

Valentine smelled the wet cement and waited while the sergeant passed responsibility up to lieutenant, and lieutenant to a radio. The lieutenant, a thirtyish man missing an earlobe, hung up the field phone and approached Valentine.

The Cat tried not to look relieved when he saluted. "Howdy, sir," he said, revealing a mouth full of black-rimmed teeth. "I apologize for taking so long. I'm sorry, but there's some confusion. They know about the men, but Brigadier Xray-Tango doesn't know you, sir." Valentine felt a cold sweat emerge on his back.

"I got my orders a month ago. Only thing to happen since then was a last-minute change; they had me set out from Fort Scott instead of Hot Springs. That got countermanded the next day; turned out they wanted me at Station 26 to command these recruits."

"Looks like when you got switched back, someone didn't follow up, sir."

"Order, Counter-Order, Disorder. Hot Springs had some confusion, too."

The lieutenant shrugged. He looked as if he was going to say something to Ahn-Kha, and thought better of it. "Brigadier Xray-Tango wants to see you and your orders before your men get billeted, sir. I suppose your Grog can go with you."

"Excuse me, son. 'Xray-Tango?' That an acronym you use up here?"

"No, it's a name. He's CO for this whole New Columbia area. He's new, too."

"I see. Wish they'd tell me these things."

"If you'll follow me, sir."

Valentine smiled. "I look forward to meeting the brigadier."

Little Rock's collection of warehouses and piers was Station 3, according to the sign over the entrance. Station 3 also had a motto: "Crossroads of the Future." Or so Valentine read as he stepped up the stairs and under a pre-2022 post and lintel in the neoclassical style. The rest of the headquarters building was a cobbled-together mix of wood floors, brick walls and beam roof. Communications passed from the radio room upstairs through old-fashioned air-pressure tubes. There was an audible *shoomp* as a new message arrived at the desk of an officer.

Another wrote outgoing messages in block letters on square-lined paper and sent them shooting back upstairs.

"The general will see you now, sir; your assistant can wait outside," a corporal said. He had the self-assured look of a ranker who was used to having officers at his beck and call. Ahn-Kha waited for a nod from Valentine, then went back outside.

The brigadier general had a corner office with narrow windows filled with the first unbroken glass Valentine had seen in the Ruins. What wall space wasn't taken up by windows had maps and bulletin boards on it. A liquor sideboard held trophies of figures in various martial arts poses instead of bottles. The desk smelled of recently applied varnish.

"Coffee?" Brigadier Xray-Tango asked. He had a neat uniform, with the same yellow star on the shoulder, and a hearty manner, under a haircut so close it resembled peach fuzz. Friendly but harassed eyes looked out from under bushy brows. There was something wrong with the face, though, and it took Valentine a moment to see it. Xray-Tango's left eye was open wider than the right; it wasn't that the right was squinting, it was more that the left lid stayed a little farther open. Valentine liked to look at a man's hands after his face, and as he poured the coffee Valentine looked at the work-roughened fingers. The nails were rimmed with a stain that matched that on the new desk, which was topped by a stenciled desk plate that read BGDR GENERAL S. XRAY-TANGO.

"Thank you, sir." Valentine sniffed the aroma from the thermos. "The real thing?"

"Privileges of rank."

"What's all the hardware for? Boxing?"

"Some. Ever heard of Tae Kwon Do?"

"That's like kickboxing, right?"

"A little. It's a martial art. I fought for my old brigade out west. Retired undefeated." He held out his left hand; on the finger next to a wedding ring Valentine saw a ruby red championship ring with "S X T" engraved beneath the "Single Combat Champion" title. "Can I see your orders, Colonel?"

Valentine sorted them and placed them in three piles on his desk. "Marching orders. Supply requisitions. Organization Inventory for the recruits. Y'all like your paperwork up here."

"That's a weak-looking OI," Xray-Tango said, glancing through the pages.

"Farm kids and men in from the borderland boonies. But they're good woodsmen. They know about moving through country and shooting."

"That territory organized?"

"Not as well as it should be. Most of them are the usual assortment of malcontents who chose carrying a gun over using a shovel in a labor camp."

General Xray-Tango's left eye twitched; a quick three-blink spasm, the third slower than the first two.

"You're moving kind of stiff, Colonel. Injury?"

"I came off a horse a couple weeks ago and broke a rib. I just got the cast off."

The eye twitched again and Xray-Tango took in Ahn-Kha's formidable frame.

"Why the bodyguard?" he asked Valentine.

"The Grog? SOP down there for anyone above captain, sir. Bodyguard. Master-at-arms. I don't know what you'd call it up here. He shakes up soldier and civilian alike."

"Kind of like your own personal Hood, eh? Not sure if I like that. A good leader shouldn't have to dole out summary justice. How often you use it?"

"I lost one on the way. I had to shoot a deserter. Just a homesick kid. I didn't know what kind of paperwork I had to fill out so I just made a report, countersigned by my second in command and the dead man's sergeant. We don't have dog tags but his work card's attached. That's how we did things in Natchez."

"That's the least of my worries, Le Sain."

"Why's that, sir?"

"To be honest, we've no record of you coming here. By Kur, I need you, that's for sure. All this rain with the spring thaw; I've got a command and a bunch of warehouses that might be underwater in a day or two. Consul Solon has zero, and I mean zero, tolerance for wheeling and dealing. So I'm going to have to do some checking. No offense to how they do things in Louisiana." The eye twitched again; *blink-blink-bliiink.*

"Don't follow your meaning, sir."

"I started out in the Okalahoma High Plains, Colonel. Not the most exciting place for duty. We had a captain out there, got bored with his duties and got himself a transfer to Lake Meredith. And when I say got himself a transfer, I mean he wrote one up, signed it and moved his troops a hundred miles just for a change of scenery. He figured he'd earned it after a lot of dusty years watching railways and cattle wallows. So happens he was a good officer and the Higher Ups let him get away with it. We've been after Frum at Post 26 for months to meet his recruitment quota for the year—and all of the sudden he's not just met it, he's over-filled it, with a Louisiana colonel to boot."

Valentine sipped his coffee, straining to keep his hand steady. The story was so close to his own that he listened for men moving in behind to put him under arrest, but all he heard from outside the office was typing.

"Now, could be you heard, down in your Louisiana boonies, that with the Ozarks getting pacified there'd be opportunity under the Consul's new system. Could be you decided that the way to a general's star would be to make yourself useful up here. Could be you knew there were fifty-seven brass rings given out over the last year, since we went in once and for all. Not just to generals either, but we got our share."

Xray-Tango opened his shirt, and there, hung from a golden chain, was a brass ring. *Blink-blink-bliiink.*

Valentine thought it odd. The brass ring–types he'd met usually displayed them on their right ring finger. The token indicated special favor in the Kurian Order. A wearer and his family would never be at risk of being sent to the Reapers.

"It happens that I like a man with ambition. I like an officer with initiative. I also like to hear the truth. I've got a way of knowing when someone's spoon-feeding me horse-shit and telling me it's applesauce. Leaves a bad taste in my mouth. So fess up. The orders for you to come up here didn't go through Fort Scott, or Hot Springs, did they?"

Valentine's bowels had turned to liquid as he sat in the chair, as if Narcisse had spiked the coffee with her emetic, and he decided to admit to as much as possible. "You're close to the truth, sir, but I don't want to say much more. I had some help along the way and I don't want people who've covered for me to get into trouble. Least of all anyone under me. My men, except for some of the new ones, trust me. I'm responsible for them, and if someone has to go to a Hood because of this, it should be me. It's my idea." Valentine felt strangely relieved with his confession—but would a partial truth set him partially free?

"No reason for it to go that far. I've just had over five hundred strong backs fall into my lap; I should be shaking your hand and buying you a bottle of Old Kentucky MM. You're in Little Rock—err, New Columbia, now, and I'm the lead longhorn in these parts. If your friends in Louisiana start asking about you, we'll play dumb. But I expect you to fit into the system here, or you'll wish you'd stayed in the swamp. Here's my command."

Xray-Tango stepped over to a map on the wall. It was a copy of an old Free Territory map, redrawn to take into account the realities of the new world. "This rockheap used to be the center of Arkansas. It will be again. We're at the crossroads of the river traffic and the road artery running the eastern side of the mountains, here. Makes an 'X,' as you can see. Within a year we'll have two new rail lines, one running down from Memphis over to Tulsa, the other down from St. Louis to Dallas. So there's a new 'X' going to be laid over the first. A line branching down from Kansas City to Fort Scott, and Fort Scott connecting Tulsa and points south and west is already running; Consul Solon had us working three shifts till that was done. But Fort Scott was promised to the Higher Ups in Oklahoma in return for their help with this. The new capital will be right here, at the intersection of all those Xs. This'll be the nerve center of the Trans-Mississippi Confederation."

"How many smaller states are there? I see a lot of borders."

"Twenty-six in all. Each one has its Higher Ups. Most just have one running the show. In this system Consul Solon's got rigged, we're supposed to call them 'governors.' But as you know, it's really Solon's land. Who's obeying who remains to be seen. He's keeping the peace between them, Kur knows how. He's even planning to set up some kind of court to work out disputes between them. You ever heard the like?"

"No. Natchez was—"

"I've heard it's a snake pit."

"I wouldn't say. But there were feuds all the time with the New Orleans Kur. They could use a court down there, too."

"Out on the High Plains I spent more time fighting with the boys out of Santa Fe than guerillas and saboteurs."

"I've been bushwhacked myself for scavenging in the wrong place at the wronger time," Valentine said.

"Can't say how you'll figure into this just yet, Le Sain. Right now I need disciplined labor more than anything, with the river rising. These hillbillies who used to be here weren't much on civil engineering; they didn't care if a bunch of ruins flooded. I've got two regiments of infantry and a fair amount of artillery, but it's on the other side of the river; there's still fighting in the Boston Mountains, and that's Solon's reserve. I don't dare use them. Over on this side I've got a few companies of reserves, my engineers, hospital and headquarters, and I'm hip-deep in quartermasters getting the river traffic where it's supposed to go. There are military police for the prisoners working on the river banks, and I'm trying my damnedest to get more."

"I'll put my men to work right away. I have a few with engineering experience. Sooner the job's done, the sooner we get activated."

"You *want* a combat command?"

"You bet."

Xray-Tango's droopy eye narrowed. "We'll see, Colonel. I'll have a lieutenant show you to a clear spot. You'll be in tents for a while, but I can get you running water and some gas stoves. If your men want better quarters, you'll be building them. You'll have more water than you can imagine, shortly. Now you get to spend the rest of your day filling out paperwork. This time it'll get stamped by me."

"Any chance of getting north of the river and seeing some action, sir?"

Xray-Tango smiled, triggering his eye again. "You are eager, aren't you?"

"Want one of those rings. You could give another brigade a break, sir. If they've been in the mountains all winter they'd appreciate time to refit."

Blink-blink-bliiink. "Let me run my command, Le Sain. You'll get your chance."

"Of course, sir."

"What kind of action have you seen?"

"Small-scale stuff, General. Skirmishes here and there. I've done a lot of ambushes and guerilla hunting. I've only heard cannon fired in training."

"Let's take it one step at a time. According to your OI, most of your command is green. Or is that falsified too?"

"They're a mixed bag, but I have some good NCOs. The men can shoot. You'd be surprised."

"I'll look forward to finding out what you can do, when the river's back under control. One more push when spring comes and things will be over with. It'll just be a matter of smoking out the remnants. I'm a busy man, otherwise I'd pour you another cup of coffee and warm it up with a touch of bourbon. I'd like to hear stories about life in the swamp. Do you have any questions?"

"Not a military one, sir. Your name, sir. It's—"

"Different, isn't it? My mother was a POW when she had me. I got put in an orphanage in Amarillo. There were a fair amount of us. The orphanage was run military-style, it even had a military name. 'Youth Recovery Center Four' was where I spent my salad days. They used the initials of our mothers. So I was always Xray-Tango. I never found out if I had been given a first name."

"The 'S'?"

The general's eyebrow trembled, but only for a second. "My wife used to call me 'Scotty.' She said I looked like one. The dog, I mean."

"Used to, sir? I apologize, sir. That's personal."

"It was quick. Heart attack. That's why I transferred to Solon's command. Couldn't take the flats out there anymore." *Blink-blink-bliiink.* "Too much empty."

An adjutant entered with a clipboard full of flimsies of radio communiqués. Valentine resisted the urge to glance at the top one as the soldier passed.

"That'll be all, Le Sain." General Xray-Tango lifted an order off his desk and dashed off a signature, then stamped it. "Corporal, give this to Lieutenant Greer.

"Oh, Le Sain. Good thing you were honest with me and I liked the shape of your shadow. I had two orders on how to deal with you sitting on my desk. The one going to Lieutenant Greer says he's to feed and uniform you and your command. The other said to shoot you and your officers. It's staying in my desk, just in case."

Lieutenant Greer was a sandy-haired monosyllabalist with the intent features of an owl. Though a young man, he was hard of hearing.

"Still lots of junk near the river at your camp, sir," Greer said. He spoke accentless English as though it were a foreign tongue. He walked beside Valentine, leading the column through the Ruins. Structural steel beams and plumbing fixtures poked out from the debris like leaning crucifixes in an old frontier cemetery. "Not all bad. Flat ground, good drainage. Old sewers, too."

They passed what must have once been multistory office buildings at the heart of the old downtown. One remaining spindle of girders had been left, and most of a tower clung around its central support. The spiral minaret reminded Valentine of the long, pointy shells of turret snails he'd seen on the beaches of the Caribbean. Laborers walked up the endless stairs winding around the structure, bearing bricks to the top.

"What's that suppose to be?" Valentine asked.

"The Residence," Greer said. "Eleven floors."

"Of"—Valentine paused and glanced around—"the governor?"

Greer averted his eyes and hunched his shoulders as they passed wide of the building. Valentine saw armored cars parked before it, covering the cleared streets outside the beginnings of a wall. A Kurian Tower, sticking there like a knife in the heart of the Free Territory. Valentine's throat went dry.

Greer murmered something so quietly Valentine thought he was talking to himself. "Two in the city. Brothers, or maybe cousins. Don't know names. Eight and five." Valentine guessed this last to be the number of Reapers each controlled, respectively. Reapers that needed feeding.

"Thirteen. Unlucky," Valentine commented.

"Don't worry now. Still plenty of prisoners. Much work to do. For now, they take only hurt and bad sick. This big state. I come from Indianapolis. Six years ago, bad drought, many farms die. Other Bloodmen from hills in south came, stole people. Then they fed on us in army."

"That's a hard piece of luck. This is a sweeter situation. That's why I came."

"Yes, sir. Duty with a future, here."

They continued north, almost to a little finger of a hill separating river from city, and reached their camp. It was a former city block now called "Dunkin Do," according to the old sign propped up among the rubble. The street had not even been cleared yet, and among the bulldozer tracks there were little piles of debris in hummocks, but it was still preferable to the mountains of shattered concrete elsewhere in the city. The block was circled by nine-foot posts, and rolls of barbed wire had been left out to rust in the rain.

"Was to be prison camp, sir," Greer said. "For after last push this year. But you can use."

Valentine wondered if this wasn't another warning from Xray-Tango that any nonsense would convert him and his men from allies to inmates in short order. He and Post trailed Greer around as he pointed out the water taps, already flowing, and the sewer outlets.

"Provisions tonight, sir, uniforms tomorrow, maybe stoves and fuel day after," Greer said. "Here's paperwork, sir. I fill some, you do rest, please, sir. Mostly just signatures. Officers can billet in garage, or stay in tents with men, up to you."

"Garage?" Post asked.

"You see soon. Underground parking. Like bunker, you know? Meet others. Good food, good times."

"We'll drop by," Valentine said. "Let us know when happy hour starts."

Greer's owlish eyes rolled skyward. "Happy hour, sir?"

"Never mind. I'll be here tonight, getting the men settled in."

They watched the men file into the camp, followed by the wobble-wheeled wagons. Jefferson cursed a blue streak, trying to get his team around a clump of reinforced concrete, its rods threatening horse leg and spoke alike.

"Questions, sir?"

"Who's in charge of supplying us?"

"Commissary Sergeant Major Tucker, in Quonset hut behind headquarters. Good man. Answer all questions. Usually answer is 'yes.' "

Tucker was more than just a good man. He appeared that evening like a horn of plenty, playing a sprited version of Beethoven's "Ode To Joy" on a silver concert flute. He showed up in the shotgun seat of a roofless, antiquated Hummer, interrupting the men as they were setting up their tents in military rows.

"General's orders," Tucker shouted, pointing with his flute at his cargo. "Fresh bread, fruit and veggies just up from the Gulf. Spring potatoes, winter cabbage, first peas and even apples. We've got beer in cask, but before I can issue that, we need to see what kind of workers you are."

The men forgot they were in the heart of an enemy camp enough to start cheering as he handed out the bounty. Cured side meat lay in baskets revealed as eager hands took the food.

"Whee-ooh, y'all need the showers rigged pronto, boys," Tucker said. "Ever heard of field hygiene?"

"We've been on the road for three days," Valentine said, stepping forward to help hand out the foodstuffs.

"You're up from Louisiana, they tell me."

"Sergeant Tucker, the smell's unfortunate, I know. They need some washtubs and soap more than anything."

"Coming tomorrow, sir."

"I'm only about half armed as well. I'd like to see that rectified."

"Guns are a problem, sir. You'll get a few for marksmanship, to familiarize yourselves with our models, but we don't have enough to arm all your men at the moment."

"That's unfortunate. Suppose there's an emergency and the camp has to turn out to defend itself?"

"We have contingency plans, sir. When y'all are properly integrated into the general's command, you'll be outfitted, but there's too much work to do here for now. You'll be in reserve a few months at least . . ."

"Months! I thought the fight was coming sooner than that."

"I can't say, sir. Those were the general's orders; he was specific about it."

Valentine recovered his mental equilibrium. "I haven't been fully briefed yet."

"Sorry you had to hear it from me, sir. But be glad for it; you'll have a better time back here. Those boys up north are dug in like ticks on a bear; burning them off isn't going to be a summer picnic. If you saw the hospital you wouldn't be so willful about it."

Months. Valentine spent two hours trying to fall asleep, staring at the silhouette of the Quickwood center pole in his tent. Using Quickwood to form their tents seemed as good a way as any to hide the material in plain sight.

Such a small thing, the Quickwood beam. But it was the source of all Valentine's hopes. He saw some of the men touching it as they passed, some with a reverence that brought to mind odd bits of mental flotsam about medieval pilgrims and alleged pieces of the True Cross, others caressing it as though it were a lover in passing. Even Post, who'd never shown any other signs of superstition, would give the tent-pole a double rap with his knuckles whenever he passed it in Valentine's tent.

The ruse might last six days, but more than a few weeks was out of the question. Sooner or later some fool would let something slip, a face would be recognized despite the shorn heads, an assumed identity would be dropped. There would be questions, and then, when he didn't have answers, more questions. From what he'd seen of the docks and warehouses, they were well guarded against any attack he could mount, armed as he was, even with his Bears. The Quick-wood had to make it to Southern Command, where it would be used to kill Reapers instead of hold up waterproofed canvas. But if he simply decamped and marched across the river, his chances of ever seeing the Boston Mountains were negligible.

Realizing sleep was impossible, he rose, dressed and found an ax. He wandered around the camp, nodding to the men on firewatch, until he found piled cords of firewood. David Valentine split fulls into quarters and quarters into kindling until he could drop into his bunk, body soaked with sweat even in the cold night air, muscles aflame, fretful thoughts finally beaten into numbness.

Six

The Arkansas River, February of the forty-eighth year of the Kurian Order: Part of the defense strategy of the Free Territory was simple inaccessibility. Southern Command tore up railroads leading into the Ozarks, broke roadbeds down, wrecked bridges, let forests grow over airstrips, and flooded bayous long since drained by the Corps of Engineers. As part of this strategy Southern Command rendered the Arkansas River unnavigable by destroying locks, sinking snags and pulling down levees, blocking invasion by water east from the Mississippi and west from the old river port on the Verdegris east of Tulsa. Four hundred feet of elevation from the Mississippi to Fort Smith were made impassible to anything other than shallow-draft traffic, thanks to the sand-clogged river and vigilant Guards at Arkansas Post and Fort Gibson. While both strongpoints changed hands several times over the course of the Free Territory's star-crossed history, they were always eventually won back.

Until now

In their months of occupation the Kurians have opened the river to some traffic between Little Rock and the Mississippi; small barges are again making the ascent to supply the armies still fighting in the mountains. But Nature takes her part in the conflict as well: a wet winter, early spring and heavy rains have raised waters to levels not matched since the floods of the nineteen twenties. The last controls, hydroelectric dams at the Jed Taylor and Dardanelle Lock & Dams, were destroyed as Southern Command fled to the mountains, leaving the river open to flooding. Only the fact that the levees were destroyed years ago, siphoning some of the water away in secondary floods, has saved the new masters of the Ruins so far.

But the river is rising.

* * *

The irony of the situation was not lost on David Valentine. He drove his men, enlisted and officers alike, in an exhausting war against the swelling Arkansas River. A wall of sandbags was the battle line. On the one side of the miles of sandbags, pumps and drainage ditches were the war materials of Consul Solon's military millstone, now grinding Southern Command into chicken feed. On the other side swelled a God-given natural disaster waiting to strike a blow for their Cause potentially more damaging than even batteries of heavy artillery with the town in their sights could hope to do.

Nonetheless he threw his men's bodies against the river. Even Ahn-Kha stood waist-deep in cold water, hardly stopping to eat, plunging his long arms again and again into the base of the levee, digging sluices for the pumps.

The endless labor inured his men to living hearth-to-hearth with the Quislings. When Tucker and his men handed out new AOT uniforms—a mottle of sea greens and browns, some with the look of reclaimed and redyed clothing about them—Post brought them in groups before Narcisse, who marked their foreheads in a *vaudou* version of the anointing of the ashes. She smeared them with a red paste and flicked them about the head and neck with a powdered white feather, chanting in her Haitian Creole. Even Styachowski submitted to it in good humor, after Narcisse explained to her and Valentine that it was just for show: The paste was winterberry with a touch of poison sumac to give it a tingle. Narcisse promised the men that the ritual would help them fool the enemy, guard their tongues and curse any who deliberately gave away their true allegiance so that any reward given by the Kurians would turn to ash and their hearts' blood to sand. Valentine watched M'Daw's face as he underwent the anointing; there would be a brass ring for him and land of his choosing if he were to go over to his old masters, and it would be so easy. So very easy. Just a word or two in the right ear at the wrong moment. The healthy respect for Narcisse's powers M'Daw had gained when she changed the old Quisling's bowels to the biological equivalent of a fire hose showed itself when he jumped at her touch as though she carried electrical current.

Valentine had considered assigning someone unobtrusive but reliable, like the Texan drover Jefferson, to keep an eye on M'Daw, but the old Quisling had been as willing as any on the march, and complained not at all. Valentine was inclined to trust him. Keeping track of worries in the current predicament was like following individual ants pouring from a kicked-open hill.

Mrs. Smalls was the only one excepted from the ceremony, though

Narcisse ministered to the pregnant woman as midwife and cook. She and her husband were confined to their tent. The baby had dropped, and they were expecting it to be born any day.

Valentine had Mrs. Smalls on his mind as he paced back and forth at the drainage ditch, watching the next two truck-loads of sand and bags make their way to the waiting shovel-wielding prisoners.

"Your shift was over a half hour ago, sir," Styachowski said. She passed him a hot cup of roasted chicory coffee, sweetened to a syrup with molasses. The mixture had been passed around as the closest thing to real coffee they could make in quantity.

Valentine gulped and looked through the steam at Styachowski. Even dripping wet she managed to look neat, though there were circles under her eyes, made worse by pallid skin and close-cropped hair. Styachowski had been tireless at the riverbank, still working when men twice her size dropped in exhaustion.

"I can go a couple more hours. Do two more dry in your bunk, Styachowski."

"I can—"

He swiveled his gaze to the prisoners. "Hey, you two there, don't pack 'em like sausages, or they'll burst under pressure."

"Sorry, sir," the prisoner with the shovel replied. He wore a faded Guard uniform with POW stenciled in orange across his back and down his pant leg.

"Sorry, Styachowski, you were saying?

"Nothing, sir."

"Then move along. I'll cover your duty."

"Neither of you ever quit," Styachowski said, looking down at Ahn-Kha. The Grog grasped a seventy-pound sand-bag in each hand and stuffed them at the bottom of the levee. "He's like a machine; I don't worry about him. You, on the other hand—"

"Can take care of myself. As you said, I spend my time shouting, not moving earth."

"Then why do you have mud up to your neck?"

"Clumsiness."

"I've seen you walk across a two-strand rope bridge without breaking stride. I doubt it."

"You'll spend eight hours in your bunk, Styachowski. That's an order."

She lifted her chin and opened her mouth—her cropped hair would have bristled were it not wet—but no sound came out for a second. "Yes, sir," she finally said. She waited to turn; Post and a corporal were trotting along the rim of the drainage ditch.

"Sir," Post said excitedly. "We've got a big bulge up next to where it's reinforced on that old park bench. "It looks like it'll give way any minute."

"Take Rodger's squad and shore it up," Valentine said, leaning around the wide shoulders of his lieutenant to take a look.

"It's in Captain Urfurt's section," Post added quietly, referring to the Quisling responsible for the length east of Valentine's. "He's dealing with a broken pump, hasn't noticed it and none of his prisoners are anxious to bring it to his attention. Know what I mean?"

"Shore it up, Will."

"But—"

"I'm not used to giving orders twice," Valentine said, his voice not a shout, but not conversational either. He'd never raised his voice to Post before, outside the din of battle. He rounded on Styachowski like a bar brawler who's felled one opponent and is looking to loosen some teeth in another. "Speaking of which, why aren't you in your bunk, Styachowski?"

"Sir," they both chirped, backing away to obey.

Valentine raised his mug. Some artist had painted a yellow star on it, and added "We Build New Columbia: Crossroads of the Future" in neat brushstrokes before glazing it. The incessant rain had already chilled the coffee. It tasted like dry leaves and old gum.

A whooping shout of joy came from his section of levee. Valentine saw two bedraggled men—the one with a hat belonged to his group, the other had the orange POW stenciling. Both men had skin the color of milk chocolate, long, handsome faces and similar silhouettes as they embraced.

Valentine had feared a moment like this. "Ahn-Kha," he said as he trotted over to the pair.

"Lord bless, Dake, I knew you made it out of the pocket. What gives, slick?" the one in the POW fatigues said.

Valentine thought his soldier's name might be Abica. Dake Abica sounded right in his head.

He heard Ahn-Kha's squelching footsteps behind. "You there, Abica," he shouted, as a sergeant hurried to interpose. "Come over here."

Abica put a hand on the arm of his relative—

"Alone!" Valentine shouted. "Ahn-Kha, keep an eye on that man."

"Be cool, Clip," Abica said. He approached Valentine.

The sergeant, a former supply clerk named Roybesson, joined him, instinctively placing herself facing both Valentine and Abica.

"Sorry, sir," Abica said. "That's my brother Cli—Clipton. Third Cavalry regiment, light artillery. He's smart and—"

"I don't need his Q file, Abica," Valentine said. "Roybesson, if those two speak again, you'll wish you'd been bit with Ravies Six. Got me?"

She blanched but answered quickly enough. "Yes, sir."

"Sir, we could—" Abica began.

"Private, we're going to talk to your brother in my tent. You, me and Ahn-Kha. If you don't do exactly as I say, Ahn-Kha'll kill your brother and you'll spend the rest of our time here in a tiger cage. Near the dike, so if it breaks we'll get a nice loud warning before you drown."

Abica's eyes flamed, and Valentine stared until Abica dropped his gaze to his feet.

"We go about this right, your brother will be in your tent with you tonight."

The private and his sergeant both unclenched their legs at that. Valentine forced a friendly smile. "We'll need some playacting out of you first, Abica."

The form read:

LIMITED PARDON

This document grants provisional immunity for any and all previous offenses against the Kurian Order. By signing it the pardon applicant renounces, completely and irrevocably, its former affiliations, begs forgiveness for its crimes, and asks for the privileges and benefits of fellowship in the human community.

I, ____,
seek a place within and protection of the Trans-Mississippi Extended District. I agree to obey the orders of my lawful superiors who will take my life forfeit if I violate this oath.

Sworn this (day)________ of (month)________, (year)________.

Signed:______________________________________

Witnessed:___________________________________

Recorded and sealed:_____________________________

A lined-off empty space in the lower right-hand corner waited for a cheap foil seal.

Valentine sat at his field desk, a slightly warped office table resting unsteadily on the plywood floor of his tent, hating himself for what he was about to do. This bit of playacting was the only alternative, and if it went wrong—

Cross that bridge when you come to it. The form, placed with a dozen others like it on a clipboard complete with tied-on ballpoint pen, rested next to an oversized shot glass.

The POW, his eyes shaded from the single bulb by his thick brow, stood before him. Abica stood behind, his sergeant just outside the tent. Ahn-Kha rested on his knuckles, a little stooped over in the confines of the wood frame and canvas. The drizzle outside grew heavier and lighter in fits, reminding Valentine of the sound of gentle surf on the Texas coast.

"Scotch?" Valentine asked, pouring some amber fluid from an unmarked bottle. He'd been told it was his whiskey ration, the designation just sounded better. "Cold work out there."

"You signed this?" Clipton Abica asked his brother. The skin was tight against his face, and Valentine saw his brow twitch.

"Had to. It was that or the boxcars, and I wasn't getting shipped to Dallas on a last ride. This is good duty, bro. Food's better—"

Valentine tapped the clipboard. "Son, the war's over here. We're reorganizing. It's better to be reorganizing than reorganized. I'm at full complement, but your brother asked very nicely. He's a smart man, and I always have room for another smart man."

Clipton Abica shook his head, looking at his brother rather than Valentine.

"Six years in and you'll get an allotment if you want. I'm about to make your brother a corporal, and I'm sure you'd rise too. Find a nice gal, or you can have your pick out of the pens waiting to go. It's hard but it's life. Any POWs we don't assimilate—" Valentine waved his hand out at the dripping water.

Abica broke in on the rain. "Do it, bro. Don't forget about Ma and Sinse and our cousins. They're caught up in this somewhere. Us being dead won't help them."

Clipton Abica picked up the brimming shot glass and smelled the whiskey appreciatively. "Better than strained brake fluid."

"You know it," Abica said.

The parolee tipped it into his mouth, put down the glass next to the clipboard, then with a lunge spat it at his brother and Valentine. He sent the clipboard skittering across the table at Valentine, who blocked it with his palm.

"Fuck both of you! Throw me—"

Ahn-Kha grabbed the man in a bear hug and dragged him out of the tent screaming and kicking. Valentine heard a few faint obscenities as Roybesson put him in handcuffs.

Abica looked out at the sight of his brother thrust into the mud, Ahn-Kha's sheep-sized thigh pressing into the small of his brother's back.

Ahn-Kha and Roybesson dragged him off.

"Why didn't we just tell him—"

"The truth?" Valentine asked. He refilled the glass and pushed it toward Abica. "We could have. But your brother's doing more for us back behind barbed wire."

"How's that?"

"They have spies among the prisoners. I'm sure of it. Your brother talking about what a rotten, traitorous, son of a bitch he's related to backs up all our stories."

Abica smelled the whiskey, looking more morose than his brother. Valentine thought he'd be sprayed a second time, but Abica drank it with a grimace. He shook his head. "I'm proud of Clip, sir. I'm proud of him. Dunno if I'd've done the same. I'm damn proud."

"How do you feel about yourself?"

"Like a shit."

"Welcome to the Cats, Abica."

"You don't owe me an explanation, sir," Post said later, in Valentine's tent. Valentine sighed, exhausted and wrung out. The faint smell of his whiskey shower made him feel like a barfly at last call. "But why didn't you just let the levee breach?"

The river was under control; the water level had stabilized. Reports from upriver said within a day it should fall. The rest of the struggle would be a holding action. Valentine wanted to be on his back in his bunk, but he couldn't be that discourteous to a subordinate, friend or no. He sat on the edge of his cot, rubbing the prickly growth on his skull. Ahn-Kha made a clattering noise outside as he fashioned an oil-drum cook-stove that could double as a water heater.

"We're being watched. No, it's not one of my feelings, it's logic. It may be Xray-Tango, or the bat-winged bastards in the tower. I don't know if they're suspicious, or just trying to figure out what kind of officer I am. But I had to go above and beyond. Xray-Tango said he liked initiative; he's getting it. Not that I'm going to cry another river if the levee falls; it's just not going to happen on my watch, or in my view."

Post looked out the tent flap. The drizzle had finally stopped. "Back on the old *Thunderbolt* I swore I'd never wear their uniform, or help them, again. But I'm killing myself to save racks of shells so they can be fired on my new side. It gets stuck in my craw, Val."

"Have the men said anything?"

"Not even jokes, at least in my hearing. They're scared of giving anything away. I would be too, surrounded by an army and minus a gun."

"They're working as hard as they would have if they'd been captured and put in a labor camp."

"They're better fed. I've been over to the prison camp."

Valentine shot a glance up at Post, who looked like someone had just stepped on his corns. "When were you there?"

"Day after we got here. I asked for a review of female prisoners."

Post was easier to read than a billboard at ten feet. "Your wife?"

"I always figured she headed here. It was the nearest Freehold to Mississippi."

"Will, you'll drive yourself crazy if you start searching every face for her. I've had a . . . person in my life. Was in my life. She's caught up in this somewhere, but if I start thinking about her, I won't be able to concentrate. I have responsibilities now."

Post looked at him sidelong. "Where was she last?"

"A village called Weening, just west of Crowley's . . ." Valentine stopped.

"Only human to hope," Post said.

"Being human is a luxury, at least these days. Feelings. Attachments. They stop you from doing what's . . . what's necessary. Someone called Amu told me I wouldn't be one anymore when I became a Wolf. I must have misunderstood what he was talking about."

"How long have we known each other, Val?"

"What, a year and a half? Since I came on board the *Thunderbolt*."

"You're the most human person I've known since my wife. Except when you do what's 'necessary.'" Post meant by this the wild night when the Reapers came up from the old Kurian submarine, and after sinking it Valentine had shot the submarines sailors struggling in the oily water. His emotions turned gray and cold whenever he remembered.

Valentine wondered if he could unburden himself. Confessing to not just the things he'd done, but worse, that he'd enjoyed, even reveled in—

"Colonel! Colonel!"

The shout even overcame Ahn-Kha's metalwork.

Valentine cast a regretful look at his bunk.

"Come in. What is it, Lieutenant Purcel?"

The company officer saluted, gasping. "Overheard on the radio, sir . . . Blue Mountain dam's gone."

"Oh, Christ," Post said.

"Guerillas blow it?" Valentine asked.

"Just went."

"Mr. Post, get everyone up. I don't care if they've just spent twelve hours shoring sandbags. Everyone to the levee. If Mrs. Smalls's had her baby, I want her holding sandbags open. If it's a boy, I want him shoveling. Mr. Purcell, if the general doesn't know it, pass the word along. I respectfully suggest that he empty the prison compound, and get those buckets of lard at the wire—wait, strike the last."

"Pass the word to the general—" Purcell began.

"Don't bother, Mister Purcell. Just run."

Valentine looked around the little tent, touching the leather sack at his chest. *It might as well all be swept away, but what about the Quickwood?*

"Ahn-Kha," he called, pulling on his tunic.

"Yes, my David?"

"Have the men bring the Quickwood to the levy. We'll use it to shore up. If it gives way, have everyone grab on."

Valentine and Ahn-Kha raced up and down the camp, gathering the men and deflating the tents by pulling out the Quick-wood center poles. He and the men ran to the levy, carrying the four-by-four beams in earnest rather than for exercise.

Styachowski was already putting the men to work. At other parts of the levee men were gathering, and Valentine walked the length, giving orders regardless of whose section it was. Farther back General Xray-Tango was organizing troops and prisoners alike, directing the flow of manpower to the dike.

The levee was already a sandbag sieve. Even Hank stood in the water, helping maneuver shoring timber against the sandbag wall. Farther down the levee a camouflage-painted bulldozer growled as it battled with the river, pushing walls of dirt against the drainage channel.

Valentine's men worked for hours, taking only handfuls of cold water from the river for refreshment. It was a blur of sandbagging and shoring for Valentine, all the while watching the debris-filled river as he slogged through the water on the other side of the levee. Darkness came, and still the river ran mad. Men began to drop to their knees in the water in exhaustion.

"We're losing it," Post said, watching Styachowski, up to her waist in water, direct shoring efforts. "I think it's going to go."

Valentine felt a personal animosity toward the river. It was like a living thing, determined to overcome him no matter how hard he drove himself and his men. "We're not beat yet."

Shouts and a scream. He spun to see a crowd jumping back from the levee, where part of a sandbag wall had collapsed.

"Get the bulldozer over here," Post yelled.

Valentine rushed to the site, Ahn-Kha joining him from the other side of the breach. A waterfall was coming through a notch in the levee; something had given way at the bottom and it had subsided.

"She's trapped, sir," one of the Jamaicans shouted. "It caught her on the legs as she fell."

"Who?" Valentine shouted.

"Styachowski," another said, forgetting to use her false name. "Captain Styachowski."

"It started to bulge and she jumped in with a shoring timber," Smalls said. "She was trying to place it—"

Valentine plunged into the swirling waters at the base of the fall, and began to feel around for her. He submerged. Under the water he felt a frantic hand grasp his. He pulled, but her body didn't yield. He felt around, and touched her face. Keeping a grip on her hand, he surfaced. Through cascading water, he looked up at the worried faces.

"Christ, get some of these bags away. I can feel her down there."

"That'll open the breach," a Quisling sergeant said.

"It's already opening."

Ahn-Kha plunged in next to him as Valentine shifted his back to protect Styachowski from the sandbags sliding off the pile. He felt her hand spasm in his.

The Golden One tore into the pile, hurling sandbags right and left. Others jumped in beside.

"No, Warren, more to your right, she's under here. Ahn-Kha, pull away just above my elbow. Watch your feet, you!"

The bulldozer approached, digging in and pushing a wall of dirt toward the rescuers.

"Hold that machine, dammit, I've got a man trapped!"

"Out of the way, sir, or when the breach caves you'll be trapped too," the Quisling sergeant shouted.

Valentine felt Styachowski's hand go limp in his. He screamed through the water falling all around him.

"What's going on?" Xray-Tango called, coming around the mound of dirt pushed by the bulldozer."

"She's trapped," Ahn-Kha said. "Officer Wagner," he added, remembering to use her false name.

"How long's she been under?" *Blink-blink-bliiink.*

"Five minutes, maybe," someone said.

"She's dead then," the Quisling sergeant said. "Bring that bulldozer forward."

"No! I've got her hand."

"Wait, Sergeant," Xray-Tango said. Valentine met his eyes, pleading with him. Xray-Tango shifted his gaze to the bulldozer, held up a hand. Then to Valentine: "Hurry, Le Sain."

Ahn-Kha plunged into the water and found the shoring timber Styachowski had been maneuvering. Valentine watched the Grog's back, matted fur shedding water, and saw muscles heave. The pile shifted. Knotted shoulders breached, and Ahn-Kha took a breath.

"Help me, you bastards," Ahn-Kha gasped. Valentine felt something give.

Valentine heaved at the lifeless hand, terribly limp in his. She began to move. He prayed she didn't have compound fractures in her trapped legs; she'd end up looking like Narcisse, even if she wasn't paralyzed.

Anxious arms helped him bring her up out of the water. Valentine laid her out on the mound of dirt pushed up by the bulldozer.

"Work the breach, back to work," Xray-Tango shouted. The men and a smattering of prisoners started relaying sand-bags. The bulldozer backed off and approached again from a new direction, digging into the ground.

Valentine saw none of it. There was just Styachowski, pale and limp beneath him, blue-faced and mottle-cheeked. He cleaned the froth from her mouth.

"Push on her legs and get the water out of her lungs," someone suggested.

Ahn-Kha knelt next to Styachowski, panting, water streaming from his body.

Valentine lifted his ear from Styachowski's chest. "That doesn't work," Valentine said, bending back her head. "Get a blanket, a dry one." He turned her head up, explored her mouth with a finger, and put his lips to hers. He forced air into her lungs.

"Get a medic, too," Xray-Tango shouted at the soldier going for a blanket.

"Ahn-Kha, push on her chest, here," Valentine said, indicating a spot. "Don't be gentle about it." He pressed his lips to her cold mouth again.

The Golden One worked her heart.

"Should we rub her hands and feet?" Xray-Tango asked.

"No," Valentine said between breaths. He was too busy to explain that it would draw blood away to the skin. She needed it in her brain, not her limbs.

Minutes in the wet dark passed, or perhaps just seconds. Hours? The only thing that mattered to Valentine were breaths, air into Styachowski's flooded lungs. Whatever time it took to run and get blankets had passed; the soldier returned with an armload.

Her eyes fluttered and opened. She coughed and heaved. Valentine rolled her on her side, and a mass of water and vomit came up. He held Styachowski through a series of wracking coughs, pulling blankets around her.

"Styachowski?" Valentine said as the coughing ebbed. Behind him the bulldozer was pushing the mountain of sandbags back into place. Valentine heard a beam snap and winced—he hoped that wasn't one of the Quickwood supports smashed.

Styachowski turned her face to see who was holding her. "God, Val—" she began. Valentine pressed his lips to hers, shutting her up. Xray-Tango turned away, perhaps embarrassed, and began to shout orders to the men helping the bulldozer. Valentine released her from the kiss.

"Dreams," Styachowski said.

"What's that?"

"Dreams," she said, and gathered herself. She burped, and glanced up at Valentine apologetically. "The wall fell on me, and I had dreams, or something. It was warm and pleasant, like I was being held by my mother as a baby. Then I woke up and you were there. Except my legs hurt."

A medic knelt at her feet. He ran his hands up her right leg, gently rolling it. He repeated with the left, and Styachowski cried out.

"There's a break. I don't think it's bad. Simple fracture; I don't feel any protrusions. We've got to get her on a stretcher."

"*Hssssssssssss*!" Styachowski sucked in air, closing her eyes. "It's throbbing. Am I bleeding?"

The medic splinted her. "It's the fibula, I think. Her knee's tore up, too. Abrasions."

"No, you're wet, you're not bleeding," Valentine said after looking at her legs. "Not badly. Bring the stretcher here."

The medic finished fixing the splint. Valentine took her shoulders and the medic her legs, and lifted her onto the stretcher.

"The infirmary at headquarters," the medic said to the men who took up the handles. "There's no hurry. Don't jog her."

"You can go too, Le Sain," Xray-Tango said, appearing at his shoulder. "Your captain there has things in hand."

"The breach?"

"God knows."

"Then I'll stay."

Like a close-fought battle, or a football match where the lead changes hands, the issue hung in doubt until the next morning, when once again the water stabilized. Then it fell, at a pace that could almost be measured with the naked eye.

"I wonder if something gave way farther down the river?" Post said, eating bread and cheese with dirty fingers as they sat together on a ready pile of sandbags.

"Some old Corps of Engineers dike," Valentine said. "Or Pine Bluff landing is underwater now." He was too tired to care about the whys; all that mattered were the whats. And the big what was that the water was going down.

The men were asleep in the mud all around, heads cushioned on sandbags or backpacks. The scattered groups of prisoners slept in huddles, like wallows full of pigs.

"You going to check on Styachowski, sir?"

"We should see about reorganizing the men. Work out some shifts. Wish we'd get some fresh bodies from the other side of the river."

Post stretched his arms and yawned. "They have problems of their own. The River Rats are flooded out."

"River Rats? I've heard that before, somewhere."

"The boatmen who work the barges and small craft. They've got a little town over there, from what they tell me. A couple of bars, music and girls included, a slop-house. Bona fide red-light district, sounds like. Some of the other soldiers go across for a good time, or to do a little black-market trading. They smuggle, too, of course."

"The soldiers or the River Rats?"

"Both, I suppose."

"I was wondering where Xray-Tango got his coffee," Valentine said. "Being in the Caribbean spoiled me. I've got a taste for the stuff, now."

"I'm ready to go back," Post said. "You're probably right. I'll never find her."

"Southern Command's not dead yet. There's Styachowski to think of, too."

"Go check on her, if you like. Ahn-Kha and I'll hold the dike."

Styachowski was asleep, her leg already in a cast, and after speaking to a nurse about her Valentine made himself comfortable. She was the only one occupying a bed in the infirmary; the real field hospital was on the other side of the river, in the old library. The nurses were keeping busy bandaging bashed fingers and wrapping sprains. A ruptured man groaned as the doctor probed his crotch.

Valentine made the mistake of putting his feet on her bed. The next thing he knew he was being kicked in the leg.

"Colonel," Styachowski said. "You're snoring."

He massaged the bridge of his nose until his eyes felt like focusing again. "Is it light out? How's the pain?"

"Better. They gave me a shot and I went out like a light. Codeine or morphine, I think. It's morning now. We're still in the dispensary, so I guess the levee held."

"The water was receding last night."

"New Columbia lives."

His stomach growled. "Aren't they going to feed you something? Wait, I'll go myself."

After retrieving bread, honey, and some kind of cooked cereal from the headquarters kitchen, he returned to Styachowski.

"You broke a leg once, sir?"

"No. It wasn't for lack of trying."

"You limp. I thought maybe—"

"An old wound. Line of duty."

Styachowski nodded. "You'll have to tell the story someday."

"When you're better."

"That'll be the day. I'm always down with something. If it's not a cold I've got a fever.

There was a long pause in the conversation while they ate. Valentine had never shared a meal in silence with a woman before. She probably needed to sleep again. "Can I get you anything before I go, Wagner?"

She shook her head, and Valentine relaxed a little, seeing her respond to her assumed name even under the influence of the painkiller. "No, thank you, sir. There is one thing though."

"What's that."

Styachowski glanced around the infirmary. "What's the policy here? Do they shoot the crippled horses, or send them . . . somewhere else?"

"Don't be silly. You're not getting out of my outfit that easy. I'm not going to let anything happen to anyone in my command. Especially to someone hurt doing her duty. The battalion's not going anywhere without you."

She sank back into her pillow. "Thanks, Colonel."

"I'll see if I can get you put back in your tent. You'd be more comfortable there, I think."

"Thank you, sir. But not just for that."

Valentine arched an eyebrow; she blushed and buried her face in her mush bowl.

"You wanted to see me, General?" Valentine asked

Xray-Tango thrust a curious, umbrellalike apparatus into the ground.

It was a five-foot pole with four arms projecting from the top. At the end of each arm hung a string with a washer tied to the end. The spear end, currently buried in the dirt of what had been an underpass, was tipped with metal.

Styachowski was back in the tent she shared with a female sergeant. The ground had dried up, and the river was down feet, not just inches. Mrs. Smalls was expected to deliver within hours. Men still worked the levee, but life was returning to what passed for normal in Consul Solon's Trans-Mississippi KZ.

Xray-Tango smiled. "I hope this isn't a bad time. I'll try not to keep you too long. Technically, I'm off duty. I keep what used to be called 'business hours.' "

"Curtiz said that, but he told me that I could find you here right now. I'm used to coming immediately when sent for. I'll be in first thing tomorrow, if you'd rather, General."

"No need. Unless you had plans for the evening."

"Maybe a trip to the screen center."

The south side of the river had two common rooms with projector screens, one for officers and the other for enlisted ranks. The soldiers lounged on everything from club chairs to old sofas watching the impossibly vivid colors on the pull-down screen. Valentine had put in an appearance at the officers' screen center and learned about the designer of a new riot bus, a biography of a woman who had produced an astonishing sixteen children, then an inspirational speech by a colonel who had won a brass ring in the rugged mountains in what had been West Virginia. He left to walk past Xray-Tango's headquarters and poked his head in the enlisted room, where a video of dancing showgirls on a Memphis stage had the packed soldiers drooling. An advertisement for a reenlistment bonus all-expense-paid trip to Memphis played immediately following. He hadn't gone back since and didn't intend to.

"Give the popcorn a miss. I think the butter is reclaimed machine oil."

"If you don't mind me asking," Valentine said, "what are you doing?"

"I started out as a section chief on the railroad. I still like to survey. You do anything to clear your head, Le Sain?"

"I swing an ax. To cut wood. I like turning big ones into little ones."

"I would have guessed music. Something artistic. There's a look in your eyes that makes me think you're the creative type. For Christ's sake, at ease, Le Sain. This is a chat, not an ass-chewing."

"Music's a good guess, sir. My mother used to sing. I had a little . . . recorder, that's what it was called. A recorder I'd play. Since you said this is just a chat, can I ask what that thing is, sir?"

"It's called a *groma*. It's an old Roman surveying tool. They used it to make straight lines. Works good for corners, too, but it's best for staking out roads." He leaned over, hands on thighs, to eyeball the lines strung with washers at the end, comparing them with the shaft. When he was satisfied that it was level, he sighted down the *groma* and waved a private holding a flag over a step to the right.

"No fancy optics," Xray-Tango went on. "The Romans built their roads straight, using that doohickey."

"They were great road builders, weren't they?"

"Yes. The old United States interstate system only built about half the miles that the old Roman network had. If you leave total lanes out of account, I imagine. They would have caught up, if they'd lasted as long as the Romans."

"Kur took care of that," Valentine said, keeping his voice carefully neutral.

Xray-Tango waited for another twitch to pass, then signaled to his private to place the little red-flagged stake. "You've had the usual indoctrination, I suppose."

"It varies from place to place."

"What's your wrist-cuff crib on it?"

Valentine had heard the Kurian catechism so often he was able to repeat it without thinking, half believing it. It had been drilled into him, twice weekly, at the community center meetings and Universal Church lectures in his time in the Zone. "Our planet was dying. War. Overpopulation. Pollution. Disease out of control. Mother Earth had a cancer called the human race. They came in and restored balance, brought order to the chaos. Kur did for us what we couldn't do for ourselves. Over half the population has proper food, shelter and health care now; everyone in care has access to the doctor. There are even dentists in a lot of places. New Orleans, for example. In Natchez we had to go to a plumber to get a tooth taken out."

"You know the words. You ever think about it?"

Valentine looked around to see if they were being overheard. "I think history gets written by the winners. The Old Regime had its problems, but they made some beautiful stuff. How many engines they built fifty or sixty years ago still run? Lots. If Kur makes anything that wonderful, they're keeping it to themselves. What's made now is clumsy by comparison, even when it works."

"The terrorists? The renegades?"

"They're right about them. Most of them are just misled. They don't know the Reapers are like white blood cells in an organism. If a piece of the body isn't working right, if it doesn't belong, if it's dead wood, it gets taken out to keep the rest of the system healthy."

"So you don't have problems with the system." He waved his assistant farther away to plant another stake.

Valentine's dancing heart missed a step. He'd found that among people who disliked the Kurians, they put a little extra stress on the phrase "the system" as a way of sounding out others who might share unorthodox opinions.

I've been running my mouth again. Is this a trap? Does he want to see how far I'll step into the noose? The problem was, he liked Xray-Tango for some reason, and when he liked someone, the dam on his garrulousness broke. This time, a breach could cost every man in his command his life. He needed to stuff a sandbag in his mouth, block it up like the river, before his tongue hung them all.

"I've done well under it," Valentine said, after a pause he hoped didn't betray him as thinking about his answer too much.

"Nothing's perfect under the sun. Come to think of it, even the sun up there isn't quite round. It's a bubbling sphere. Sends out some long arms of superheated gas now and then, if you look at it close. But the governors and their Reapers are in the here and now, not millions of miles away. When you're close to them, just like with the sun, sometimes you see the flaws. But we're a stronger civilization, thanks to them. Even if the system's ugly at times, doesn't work as fairly as it should."

"Are you saying something's wrong with the system, General?"

"I suppose I am, in a roundabout way. Thing is, if something doesn't work right, you either throw it away or you fix it. The poor bastards who used to live in this part of the country, they tried to get rid of it. It got rid of them, instead. I'm sure you've noticed as you get higher in the ranks it becomes more seductive. You know who Nietzsche was?"

"Ummm . . ." Valentine knew, but he wanted to let Xray-Tango talk.

"He talked about supermen, beyond old concepts of good or evil. You get to feel that way after a while. Beyond law, because there really isn't one, except don't cross the Kurians. Beyond morality, since there's no one to censure you—and as long as you do your job right the Higher Ups won't."

Valentine felt his admiration for Xray-Tango ebb. He'd heard too many upper ranks in New Orleans talk this way. *The supermen rise, and decide who shall rise behind them. The others have to die.* "Freedom," Valentine said.

"Yes, it's damn near perfect freedom. I've got a brass ring, so I know what I'm talking about. But you know what? While most use their freedom to put on airs, or lose themselves in drink, or vice—hell, I know a colonel who screws little boys and girls—some of us use it to improve things. You can improve the system. Not all at once, and maybe not outside where you hold whatever authority you've climbed to, but you can make a difference. Tell you the truth, Le Sain, it's pretty satisfying, helping those who don't have a choice about anything."

Valentine stood silently, until it became clear Xray-Tango expected him to say something. "I'm not going to argue with anything you've said, sir. But why are you telling me this, General?"

Xray-Tango turned. He accidentally bumped his *groma* and, before it fell, caught it up again in a blur of motion. Valentine hadn't seen anyone move like that, anyone who wasn't tuned up by the Lifeweavers, that is. Now he knew how Xray-Tango won all those trophies. He wondered if he was looking into the mismatched eyes of a Cat, deep undercover.

"I'm telling you this, Le Sain, because I've taken a shine to you. You're a good officer. I've decided I want you in my command. You'll have an enviable place in New Columbia—in the new Trans-Mississippi, one day. I want to put men in place who think like I do. Maybe together, we can build something worthwhile. Consul Solon's got the vision, he just needs men who can help him carry it out."

"Thank you, sir. But I've promised my command a chance to distinguish themselves, at least doing something other than hunting down the moonshiners."

"Are they that eager, or is their commander?"

"Action means promotion," Valentine said.

"You may get your chance soon. We're going to activate your brigade, refit them as light infantry. Once we've gotten through the final push up those mountains, we'll be in a position to promote you. Maybe even get you the ring you're sparking on."

"Thank you, sir."

"It's not quite as easy as that. You still need to speak to someone before you formally join AOT Combat Corps. Trust me, you'll come through with flying colors. You're intelligent, and you've already proven yourself where it counts. He might test you some more, but don't worry; I passed it and I'm sure you can, too."

Xray-Tango shouted to his assistant, "Sun's dying, son. Let's call it a day. We'll finish laying out the quad tomorrow." He picked up his Roman surveyor and shouldered it. "Hungry, Colonel?"

"I could eat."

"Good. Maybe our little meeting would go better over dinner."

Had Consul Solon slipped in early? The rumor, spread up and down the slop-pail lines, was that Solon was due in New Columbia, to check on plans for construction of his new capital city and especially his Consular Residence on the north bank of the Arkansas. He'd heard grumbling from the engineering officers, who were still clearing rubble with a single bulldozer while Solon's engineers had a crane, backhoe, cement mixer, and "the good dozers" up on his hilltop west of town. Supposedly, plans for the final push against the remnants of Southern Command were to be outlined, giving the generals in the field time to work out the details once the general strategy was handed down. Boats were already ferrying men from the hospital to clear bed space.

The worst cases went to the seashell-like tower still under construction. Some said that afterward their bones ended up in the cement mortar.

As they walked back to Xray-Tango's headquarters, Valentine marshaled his arguments to petition for a role in the offensive; he wanted all the operational knowledge he could get. The fact that Xray-Tango had offered to arm and activate his men could mean that the battalion was to take part.

The general led him past his sentries. His headquarters still buzzed with activity, though there were fewer present to be busy. Instead of taking Valentine to his corner office the general led him down a set of stairs, along a whitewashed warren of corridors, and around a corner to another sentry. This one had a different uniform than the other rough-and-ready soldiers in the general's command. He wore a dark, crisp uniform that was a cross between old Marine Corps dress blues and an SS ceremonial uniform. A bullpup assault rifle came to present as the general rapped on the door and opened it.

So Consul Solon's got his own version of the Praetorian Guard, Valentine thought as he passed in. He readied his mind for the interview with the new administrator of the Trans-Mississippi.

Then he stopped. This was an interrogation room. Complete with mirror at one end, a desk and a waiting chair.

Sitting behind the table in the bare little semicell was a Reaper.

Seven

New Columbia, March of the forty-eighth year of the Kurian Order: The Reapers.

For the residents of any Kurian Zone, fear of the Reapers is as natural an instinct as hunger, thirst, need for sleep or sexual desire. The Reapers come and go as they please, the eyes, ears, mouth and appetite of their vampire masters from Kur. Pale-skinned, yellow-eyed and black-fanged, one might think they had been designed to inspire dread; death incarnate, as painted with the fearful symmetry of Bosch. And one would be right. The Reapers are designed and grown by Kur to be their avatars among the human race, for the process of extracting the vital auras the Kurians use to extend their lifespan into immortality. When animating one of their Reapers, the Reaper is the Kurian and the Kurian a Reaper, the ultimate version of a puppet. The symbiotes consume humans—the Reaper feeding off of blood, and the Kurians restoring themselves through the energy created by all sentient beings. Even a plant gives off vital aura, though in such minuscule quantities that only one Kurian Valentine had ever heard of managed to exist off of it, and even that was at the cost of lassitude and an addict's pangs. Like their brother Lifeweavers, divided millennia ago by the great schism over immortality gained through consuming sentients, a Kurian can appear to humans in many forms, but even this is not sufficient to protect their precious lives—all the more valuable thanks to their belief that they've cheated entropy. So for the dangerous work of mingling with, and feeding off, humans, they employ a team of Reapers, going from consciousness to consciousness and place to place the way a pre-2022 human might flip cable channels.

The Reapers are instruments built to last. Cablelike muscles are fixed to a skeleton as light as ceramic and strong as high-tensile steel. They're strong enough to take apart a car without tools, and can run faster than a horse from the time the sun goes down to dawn. They wear heavy robes and cowls of bullet-absorbing material. Daylight is not deadly to either them or the Kurians, though it interferes with the link between puppet and master, and obscures lifesign, the ethereal emanations created by vital aura that the avatars use to home in on prey. So the Reapers restrict their dark purposes to the sunless hours.

Like the night David Valentine came in for his interview with a vampire.

"*have a seat, mr. knox le sain,*" the Reaper hissed. It had a dry, menacing voice, like old bones grinding against each other. Its skin had all the life and animation of a rubber mask; its heavy robes had a faint mustiness, but a sharper smell—like hospital disinfectant—came from the sleeve holes and cowl. Piss-colored eyes, as cold and unblinking as a lizard's, fixed on him. The Reaper's gaze escorted him into the room.

"Colonel Knox Le Sain, my lord," Valentine corrected, sitting in the armless chair across from evil. The presence of a Reaper made the everyday motion into a fall. It was poised, still, and every instinct in Valentine's gut told him that it would spring into action, a praying mantis going after an unwary fly. He wondered how many fearful tells could be read on his face, and tried to assume the complacency of one who is used to conversation with a Reaper.

"*that remains to be decided. do you know to whom you are speaking?*" The Reaper's face had all the expression of an Easter Island monolith.

"I haven't had the privilege of your lordship's acquaintance."

"I can handle introductions," Xray-Tango broke in. "Le Sain, you're in the presence of the governor of New Columbia, Lord Mu-Kur-Ri. You understand how this"—*blink-blink-bliiink*—"errr, works?"

"I know I'm speaking to his lordship's vehicle for interacting with us. At least that's how it was explained to me."

"*you're nervous, le sain.*" The Reaper used a quiet monotone, so Valentine wasn't sure if it was a question or a statement.

"Put yourself in my shoes. Wouldn't you be?"

"*we are beyond emotion. you need not be frightened. we simply wish to thank you for your service in our recent flooding. had the warehouses and their stores been lost, our preparations would have been delayed. it is time for this territory to be pacified, once and for all. it has already taken far too long. one concern remains.*"

Sometimes the Kurians liked to toy with their food. Valentine wondered if the ax was just slow to fall in this case, or if the creature was speaking the truth.

"What concern?" Valentine asked. He tried to lower his lifesign, worried that the Kurians could use it as a lie detector of some sort. He imagined jamming all his fear into a blue bag he could reduce to the size of a marble that he could carry about in his pocket.

"the origins of your ghost commission. our cousins in louisiana do not care to cooperate with us in tracing you. certain inconsistencies need to be explained."

Valentine tried not to react at the word "ghost," his code name. "Guilty. I'm not a colonel. I was a captain once, but I got busted back to the ranks. Got involved with the wrong man's daughter. I heard you needed men fast. Figured it would be a chance at a new start, fresh ground."

"Sort of a Foreign Legion, Le Sain?" Xray-Tango said. "Not a bad idea. They've got one of those on the Mexican border with California. From what I hear it's a success."

"the aztlan rangers do not concern us in the trans-mississippi, general. tell me, le sain, how are you at following orders? do you put your ambition ahead of your lord's trust?"

"My main ambition was to get out of the swamp. Then find a position where there was a chance of promotion. Done and done. You've already shown yourself hell-and-gone better than their lordships in Louisiana and Natchez. Food and uniforms are both an improvement up here. You said something about a reward?"

"we shall get to that. but where are my manners, colonel? general, have some food brought in."

Xray-Tango left. *"he is an efficient officer,"* Mu-Kur-Ri's caped mouthpiece said. *"he carries out orders intelligently. you would do wise to learn from him, in all things save one. he is a blade lacking an edge."*

"Meaning?"

"he is shy of the hard decisions that come with a man of his position and responsibilities. at times, to keep a machine running smoothly, worn-out parts must be replaced. do you think you could do better?"

Valentine shook his head. "No. I've shot a few men in the back, but I'm not much at stabbing them there. Running a command of this size isn't in the cards; I don't have the know-how." Valentine smiled. "At least, not now."

"then you have the spine to do what is necessary in our service?"

"Try me," Valentine said.

A soldier knocked and entered, bearing a tray of sandwiches and milk, carefully averting his eyes. Xray-Tango followed him in, carrying a coffeepot and a bottle filled with amber fluid.

"Sandwiches are all we keep handy here, Le Sain. I thought a toast might be in order, to welcome him to our command."

"we too wish to join your repast."

The soldier set down the tray, almost bowling Xray-Tango out of the way in his hurry to make it out the door. He mumbled an apology under his breath and a promise to look for dessert.

"Yes, my lord?" Xray-Tango said.

"le sain, a woman in your camp has just given birth. the squalling morsels are most delectable when new and slippery. go to your camp and retrieve it at once. general, go with him, and impress upon him our need."

Valentine rose from the seat on shaking legs.

"Come along, son," Xray-Tango said. "Let's not keep his lordship waiting."

They went through the headquarters, grim-faced and silent. Only when they were out in the darkness of the rubble-lined streets did they speak again.

Xray-Tango's eye twitched as quickly as an experienced operator could tap out Morse. "I didn't know that was coming, Le Sain. I figured they'd test you somehow. Had no idea that would be it."

"I've turned people in to them before, sir. But never an infant."

"Trust me, Le Sain. Don't think about it, just do it. Dealing with it beforehand just causes problems. Deal with it afterward."

"Voice of experience, sir?" Valentine asked, bitterness creeping into his voice despite himself.

"Just keep walking."

Valentine felt like sticking a knife into the general. He'd grown to respect the man; Xray-Tango was the first Quisling superior he'd ever met who inspired anything other than contempt and loathing. To see him so blasé about turning a newborn over to a Reaper . . . Perhaps he could stick him with words. "You might like to know he probed me about replacing you."

"I know. I asked his lordship to bring the subject up. How did you respond?"

"I said I wasn't up to it. At least right now."

"Le Sain, we're just sounding you out. There's ambition, and then there's ambition. If it drives you to be your best, that's great. If it drives you to try and undermine your superiors, well, I've still got that order in my desk."

"Sign it. I'm not handing that child over to him."

"Keep walking. I told you to shut up and trust me. Look, I didn't just have him ask you about that to see if you were the kind of person to supplant me, given the opportunity. I've got my ring now. I'm thinking about getting a piece of land and leaving all this someday. Not until we're established here, and not until I think I've got someone in place who thinks like me. Just trust me."

Valentine subsided into silence. He was sick of these conversations in the Kurian Zones, the questions and interviews with a purpose under a motive wrapped up in a trap. He missed the easier days of his service in Southern Command, surrounded by men he knew to be his friends, when every word out of his mouth didn't have to be parsed and weighed.

The Smalls had a little shell of a tent next to the hut Narcisse was turning into a larder. Mr. Smalls had been posing as a camp tinkerer, mending everything from boots to cots for the men. Valentine had thought they would escape notice, just part of the flotsam and jetsam every camp accumulated, civilians who begged a living doing odd jobs the ranks didn't wish to be troubled with. Candles burned within.

"Wait out here, please, sir," Valentine said. Xray-Tango's eye blinked, and he turned up his collar against the chill night air. Valentine turned to the tent. "It's Colonel Le Sain. May I come in?"

"We've got a healthy baby girl in here, sir," Narcisse called.

Valentine entered. "My respects, Mr. Smalls, Mrs. Smalls. Hank."

"This is the thirtieth baby I've brought into this world, Colonel. But this one's the most beautiful I've ever seen. Isn't she something?" Narcisse said. "She's just perfect."

Valentine looked at the little red thing, puffy and sqint-eyed. "Mrs. Smalls is the one deserving of the applause," he said. Mrs. Smalls, sweat-soaked and red, managed a smile.

Valentine forced the next words out. "I came myself because I was worried that if a nurse and some soldiers showed up, you'd be frightened. But every new baby needs its foot-prints taken, its name and place of birth recorded. It's the rules here. I thought I'd handle it myself, so I could expedite the paperwork and get your baby back to you as soon as possible."

Judas Iscariot, meet your spiritual scion, David Stuart Valentine, he thought to himself.

"That's nice of you, sir, but does it have to be tonight?" Mr. Smalls asked.

"Afraid so. It's to your advantage; as soon as the baby's recorded, you get the extra rations."

"Strikey!" Hank said. A growing teen's appetite was hard to reconcile with ration coupons.

Valentine knelt at the bedside. Though perhaps "bedside" wasn't the correct word, since little Mrs. Smalls lay on the floor, atop a mixture of old rugs and blankets, reinforced with pillows and cushions.

Valentine had to find a way to avoid Narcisse's eyes. "Did you see the birth, Hank?"

"No. My dad said I'd be in the way. Ahn-Kha helped me make a crutch for Styachowski."

"For who?" Valentine said. *Was the general listening to the conversation?*

"Captain Wagner," Hank corrected himself.

"That's more like it, Hank."

Mrs. Smalls bit her lip as Valentine pulled the baby from her breast. Narcisse had put the newborn in a cocoon.

"I should go along," Mr. Smalls said.

"Sorry, Mr. Smalls, it's past curfew for civilians. Don't forget, your status here is sort of informal. I don't want any more questions asked than the absolute minimum."

"Keep her out of the wind. Let me wrap her some more," Narcisse said, her voice quavering.

"I'll take good care of her," Valentine said. The bland lies were coming easier now. He took the blanket from Narcisse and together they put the infant under another layer. He got up and turned for the tent flap. The sooner he was away from Narcisse's eyes the better.

"Don't you need to know her name?" Mrs. Smalls said. Doubt crept up her face and seated itself between her eyes like a biting centipede.

Valentine felt like slapping himself. "Oh, yes, I do. I don't imagine you want to call her Jane Doe for the next sixteen years." The newborn began to make mewing noises.

"We've settled on Caroline," Mr. Smalls said.

"Okay, baby Caroline it is," Valentine said. "Back as soon as I can." He fled the tent.

General Xray-Tango had to double-time to keep up with him. "You're a helluva liar, Le Sain."

"I come from a long line of liars. We've gotten good at it over the last two thousand years."

The general either didn't understand the veiled New Testament reference or chose to ignore it. "Take it easy, Le Sain. It'll all be over soon. Then we'll get busy outfitting your command. Better days are ahead."

The baby was crying now: a tiny, coughing sound. She was so light! Valentine felt like he was carrying a loaf of bread in the blankets. Chances were he'd never get to hold his own daughter—if it was a daughter—and he wondered if she'd be as active as Caroline, who at the moment seemed to be fighting some internal discomfort. An impossibly tiny hand waved at him.

"For you and me. What about Caroline here?"

"Don't think about that now. Think about that tomorrow. You're following orders, remember that."

Following orders. The old out. But did he have a choice at this moment? He didn't so much as have his sidearm; wearing weapons was discouraged in camp for everyone not on police detail. It led to questions. He had a clasp knife in his pocket; he could kill the general and get his camp up. But how far would they get, unarmed, with a Reaper expecting him back? He sensed another one somewhere near the general's headquarters, aboveground and moving. For all he knew he was being watched at this moment. Maybe a dash west to Finner's Wolves—

No. It would be death for his command, and at the moment he was too rubber-legged with the thought of it to even run. He had to weigh his men's lives against that of the featherweight newborn. It came with the responsibility he'd first shouldered in Captain Le Havre's sitting room over a cool beer. If by some magic he were able to go back in time to that moment, he'd have turned him down and shouldered a rifle as a plain Wolf with Zulu Company. No decisions to make, just orders to follow. But wasn't that the same cop-out that had begun this line of thought? All he could manage was to plod next to Xray-Tango.

As his mind came full circle, he and Xray-Tango returned to the headquarters building.

"Steady now, Colonel. I've told you it'll be all right," Xray-Tango said, as they stood at the stairs leading down to the lower level. Valentine distracted himself by looking at the pattern of the cinder blocks in the walls. This was pre-2022 construction, certainly. There were conduits and plumbing fixtures going deeper into the earth. The Quislings, while clearing rubble above, were making use of the infrastructure below that survived the nuclear blast.

The Reaper had not moved since they left. It might have been a wax figure, sitting with palms flat on the table and head tilted slightly back, were it not for the eyes that opened at their entrance.

"give us the child, and let us fill our need," Mu-Kur-Ri's avatar said. The yellow eyes locked on Valentine. He felt a weightless, falling sensation, as though the slit-pupiled eyes were turning into canyons, the veins leading to them rivers, the yellow irises burning deserts. He was falling toward them, into them. The only thing he could put between his eyes and the Reaper's was the child. He held it out, breaking whatever hypnotic conduit drew him.

The Reaper took the baby. Gravity returned to the floor; Valentine's mind was his own again.

"There, you've got your answer, my lord—" Xray-Tango began, before choking on his words when the Reaper's hinged jaw went wide, like a snake preparing to eat an egg. It ripped away the swaddling clothes with a hand, opening the tiny girl's chest. The newborn had time for one brief cry, stifled instantly as the Reaper buried its face in the baby.

Valentine heard a soft suckling sound. He held himself up with the table.

Xray-Tango went white as a sheet. "Je—" he began, before staggering back against the wall. He slid down it as though he'd been shot.

The feeding didn't take long. Valentine counted vein pulses in the Reaper's pallid hand, held against the dead baby's bottom. After seven it lowered the child and closed its blood-smeared mouth. The yellow eyes were no longer dangerous, just drunken.

"most exquisite. when fresh there is a blend, a residual of the mother's full, mature body overlain with the delicate new energy. it sparkles, it sparkles. . . ." The Kurian lord favored Valentine with a grin.

Death discussed as one would a wine tasting left Valentine cold and nauseated. "If your lordship has no—" Valentine began.

"It wasn't supposed to be like that," Xray-Tango said, trying to stand on his feet but failing. He sat with his back to the wall, arm around a wastebasket.

"general, the idea of you setting conditions on my actions . . . it's just impossible. i hope you do not need a further lesson."

"But you agreed, this was just a test, the baby wasn't to be hurt."

"it didn't suffer," the thing said, approaching Xray-Tango. It dropped the drained newborn into the wastebasket with a empty, wet *thunk. "if, after all this time, you haven't learned that we take what we want, when we want it, perhaps—"*

The Reaper grabbed Xray-Tango by the scruff of the neck and lifted him like a kitten.

"No, I've got my ring, you can't!"

"i wasn't going to," it hissed. *"stop the games, general. this shell game you play with the pows, it stops from this moment. be grateful for them, otherwise we'd be more rigorous in looking for sustenance elsewhere."*

"It's for your lordship to say, of course. But in Texas and Oklahoma, you took so few. I thought that's all you required."

"we limited ourselves out of necessity. better times are here; we will enjoy the fat years as we made do during the lean ones. more prisoners, general. if you want to keep us happy, and keep your ring, you'll

gather more prisoners. the lives are up in the mountains. go up and bring us them to fill our need."

"I've made everything ready here. Logistics aren't holding us up anymore; it's the wet."

The Reaper turned to Valentine. *"le sain, we are told you hunger for combat command. distinguish yourself, bring the remainder out of the mountains, and you'll have a ring too."*

At last, a chance at honesty. "I'm ready to fight," Valentine said. Some of the warmth returned to his stomach. "Give us the guns. We'll show you what we can do."

"Consul Solon will deliver the Trans-Mississippi as promised, my lord. This isn't a riot, or a collective farm that's grabbed a truckload of rifles. Those are trained soldiers in those mountains, and damn tough ones, man-for-man. If you want those troops alive and functional at the end of this, we have to go about it properly."

"we are weary of reasons not to fight. general, it is our will that the colonel be transferred to a combat corps, as soon as his men can be readied. you will turn your fat clerks into riflemen, your construction engineers into artillerists. consul solon allows too much haft and not enough point on this spear he has forged; the terrorists should have been subdued long before now. there is disorder in texas. our cousins in illinois look across the great river with hungry eyes. new orleans hopes for us to hollow ourselves so they may fill the void should we collapse. the campaign must be brought to a conclusion, or even those with rings will be held accountable. now go and consider how you will do this."

Valentine wanted nothing more than to return to his cot and sleep. Sleep would bring oblivion. No more memories of the wriggling infant in his arms, or the blood being flicked from the tongue of the Reaper as it returned to its mouth.

Xray-Tango wouldn't let him out of the office. The general stood, holding himself up on his trophy sideboard, fish-mouthing as though he were about to vomit on his awards.

"I swear to you, Knox, on my mother's grave, I didn't know he was going to do that to the baby. We thought it up as just a test. See if you'd do it. If I'd known he really wanted it, I would have taken it myself. I can't let someone else do something like that. God, I've served them for twenty-three years. That's the worst thing I've ever seen."

Valentine looked out the window and saw Solon's banner on the pole in front of the entrance. In the distance, across the graded rubble, the bone white Kurian Tower shone in the glare of spotlights.

"Then you haven't seen much, sir."

"Well, maybe it was the worst thing I'd seen happen. We came across some bodies once—jeez, that's no conversation for a night like this. C'mon and have a drink. Steady our nerves."

"I've got to go see the parents. Want to come along and explain how it was all a mistake, sir?"

Valentine's icy tone stiffened the general. "You don't have to say anything to them. If they start anything, the MPs can—"

"No, I've got to do it myself."

"You're the opposite of my other officers, Le Sain. You avoid the pleasurable, and you take on the worst jobs yourself."

" 'If you want to prosper, do the difficult.' "

"Who said that?"

"My father."

He left Xray-Tango, passed through the wooden Indians in the headquarters manning late-night communications desks, and walked back to the battalion's camp. Dogs barked at each other in the distance as he crossed the scored scab on the old earth that was Little Rock.

He entered his "battalion" camp. He took no pride in the condition of the tents, the cleanliness and order, or even the painted river rocks along the pathway, markers his old marine contingent had made.

Candles still glowed within the tent. Valentine heard the regular breathing of Hank, and Mr. Smalls' soft snores.

"Ahem. Mrs. Smalls, may I come in?"

"How is she? That wasn't too long," the mother's voice answered. "Please come in."

Valentine let her absence from his arms speak as he entered.

"Mr. and Mrs. Smalls, I'm sorry. It's Caroline. There was a terrible accident. I was going down some stairs to the . . ."

The scream from Mrs. Smalls woke Hank and brought Mr. Smalls to his feet.

"It's a lie! It's a lie! Where is she?" Mrs. Smalls cried.

"God's sake, what happened? Tell us the truth," her husband said, while she still spoke.

Valentine had to turn his face partly away, as if he were facing a strong wind. "It's as I said. I slipped, it's my fault. You can't know how sorry—she never felt anything, her neck broke—"

Mrs. Smalls broke into wracking sobs. Hank looked from his grief-stricken parents to Valentine, and back again.

"Where's the body?" Mr. Smalls said. Valentine wished he'd get up and take a swing at him, anything was preferable to the bitterness in his voice.

"It's at the infirmary. Rules. Cholera because of the flooding . . . won't get it," Valentine muttered.

"Should've known. It didn't sound right," Tondi Smalls sobbed, clutching at her husband as though dangling from a precipice. Valentine met her gaze, begged her to stop with his eyes. There were no more lies willing to come out of his mouth.

"It was planned!" she went on. "What did you get for it? What did they give you? I hope it was worth it. I hope it was worth my baby! My baby!"

Valentine backed out of the tent, but her words pursued him.

"What was it? What was in it for you? What's my baby gone for? What for?" Her voice broke up against her grief and sank into hysterical sobs.

Twenty-four hours later. Dawn was far away. Empty hours until he had an excuse to do something stretched before him. He should be asleep. God knew he was tired . . . He'd spent the day on a borrowed horse, in a long fruitless ride along old state route 10, looking for Finner and the Wolves, and hadn't returned until dark. The lonely hours alone on horseback had given him too much time alone with his conscience. He'd eaten a few bites of food before retiring to his tent, but sleep was impossible. Eventually he just sat up and went to work with his pistol.

By the light of a single bulb—the Kurians were efficient at getting the camp electrified—Valentine sat cross-legged on his cot and looked into the open action of his .45. The classic gun was a fine weapon, in the right hands, and Valentine took care of it. He'd taken it apart, cleaned the action, lubricated the slide, then put it back together and wiped it down, rubbing the protective oil into the gun like a masseur.

He picked up a bullet and rolled it around between his fingers. The brass was pitted here and there, scratched. A reload. But the Texas outfitter who'd given him the box of ammunition knew his business with the lead. The nose was a perfect oval, like the narrower end of an egg. Valentine took a tiny file he kept with his gun-cleaning bag and made a tiny *X* across the tip of the bullet. The shell was a man-stopper, but the channels would help the lead flatten out, or even fragment, and churn through flesh like a buzz saw. When he was satisfied with the modification, it joined the others next to his leg.

The last was trickier. A private joke between him and his conscience. He went to work on it. It took him almost fifteen minutes to do it to his satisfaction, but in the end there was a little horseshoe. A symbol of luck. He regarded it for a moment, smelling the lead filings on the tips of his fingers. He took the horseshoe and added little lines on the ends of the arms of the horseshoe. Now it was an omega. The last letter of the Greek alphabet. The End. Also, oddly enough, an electrical icon indicating resistance. Perfect.

He picked up the empty pistol magazine, examined it, and set it firmly between his legs, open end up.

The eight completed bullets felt good in his hand.

Of course, a piece of him would live on, barring complications with Malia's pregnancy. Valentine couldn't decide if this made ending it easier or harder.

"The Valentine family," he said, feeding the one with the omega on it against the spring. First in would be last out.

"Dorian Helm, Gil, Selby, Poulos, Gator . . . Caroline Smalls," he finished, as reverently as if he'd been saying the rosary, kneeling in his room next to Father Max. He put the magazine in the gun and worked the slide, chambering Caroline. He extracted the magazine again, and took the last bullet. There was space for it now.

"Gabriella Cho," he said. "Thought I'd forgotten you, didn't you?" He blinked the moisture out of his eyes. The magazine slid back into the gun and he checked the safety. Handling the automatic with a shell chambered could be dangerous. He set the weapon down, admiring its simple lines. Then he placed it back in his holster. The holster was an ugly thing: canvas-covered something that felt like plastic within, TMCC stenciled on the exterior.

Valentine put out the light. Time passed, then Ahn-Kha was at the door.

"My David. The men are waking up. The review is in two hours. It would be best if we ate now."

"Coming."

Valentine put on the pistol belt. Ahn-Kha's ears went up in surprise when Valentine opened the tent flap.

"You still haven't shaved, my David? It's not like you."

"You're right, old horse. Let's hit the sink before breakfast."

Post was up already, shaving in a basin. Valentine took one just like it, filled it at the spigot and went to one of the shards of some greater mirror that the men looked into when cleaning their teeth or shaving. Valentine soaked his head for a moment to clear the cobwebs, and then shaved his face and skull.

"My David, is all well?"

"Right as rain, my friend."

"You've nothing to regret," Ahn-Kha said. "What happened was out of your control. Narcisse has spoken to the Smalls. They understood."

Post watched them for a moment before abandoning the officers' washroom. Valentine was glad of it; he was in no mood for his pity.

Ahn-Kha checked to see the room was empty before continuing. "You haven't been sleeping well. You're hardly eating."

"We have a review this morning. Let's look the part, old horse. Put a tent or something around you. I don't want to present one of my best men in just a loincloth."

"Tell me what holds your mind in such a grip."

"Hell, Ahn-Kha, things are looking up. The men are armed. Clean clothes, good food, they're getting healthier every day. All courtesy of Consul Solon. There's talk that in a few weeks we'll be transferred across the river. Once we're in the front lines . . ." He left the rest unvoiced.

"You have another agenda."

"Nothing for you to worry about."

He brought Styachowski her breakfast as the men turned out, sergeants checking the polish on their weapons and the state of their shoes. She'd been making herself useful in her tent with paperwork, since she could not move without aid of her crutch for weeks yet. Her cast was one blue-black smear of signatures and well wishes.

"Think you can hobble out for the review?" Valentine asked.

"I suppose."

"I want to introduce you as my second in command."

She frowned. "I've never been a line officer. The only command action I've ever seen was on the big bugout."

"Technically, you outrank Post and you're known better around here. You're familiar with the Ozarks. He isn't."

"Does he know you've decided this?"

"He's the one who suggested it. He wanted you in front of the troops, too."

"Well, the number-one uniform they gave me has never been worn. I didn't want to spoil the pant leg with the cast. Want to get busy with a scissors?"

Getting Styachowski dressed was something of a comic opera. Valentine tried to ignore the graceful shape of her small breasts under the white cotton T-shirt as he forced the leg of her pants up and over her cast. All at once the material slid over in a rush; he stopped himself from pitching head-first into her belly by grabbing her thigh.

"Sorry," he said.

"That's all right. Thanks, sir, I can finish the rest."

He turned his back as she hiked her buttocks off the cot to pull her pants up the rest of the way, and tuck her shirt in.

"The review is at nine-thirty. Looks like it's going to be nice spring weather. After it the men have a free day. See if the scroungers can set up a bar and some music. I have to go to a meeting."

"Xray-Tango going to have yet another bull session on finding a new crane and a road grader?"

"Solon's brought down some other Combat Command generals. There's going to be a discussion of the endgame for the Ozarks."

"You're invited?"

"Xray-Tango got me in. Our brigade figures in on the plans, somehow, so it's important enough for me to be there."

"Lucky you."

"Exactly what I was thinking."

The men were laid out before their tents along one of the cleared roads, six neat companies dressed according to height, in the wood-bark camouflage of AOT Combat Corps Light Infantry. Then there was Ahn-Kha's scout-sniper platoon in boonie hats, scoped rifles slung. The other men wore coal-scuttle Kevlar helmets and trousers bloused into new boots. Finally, the headquarters and support company, larger than any of the others, badges on their shoulders indicating each soldier's specialty. Nail's Bears were among them in a hulking cluster, assault engineer patches on their shoulders.

He had to hand it to the men running the AOT. What was requisitioned showed up, promptly and in the correct quantity. Very different from Southern Command, where if one put in a request for thirty assault rifles, in a month or two you might get a dozen rebuilt M-16s sharing space with a collection of deer rifles and Mini-14s with folding stocks.

Valentine had already been trained on the guns they'd be issued. The cases of rifles were now waiting to have the Cosmoline cleaned from them. The arms-smith who'd briefed him and his senior NCOs on the long blue-black guns introduced them as "Atlanta Gunworks Type Three Battle Rifles." The principal virtue of the "three-in-one" was its simplicity, but two features intrigued Valentine. With the addition of a bipod and a box magazine to replace the thirty-round magazine, they could do duty as a light machine gun. The interchangeable air-cooled barrel was a little nose-heavy, but the arms-smith showed him how veterans would balance it by adding a sandbag sleeve to the stock that also cushioned the shooter's shoulder against the weapon's kick. By swapping the regular barrel out for a match-grade version with flare suppressor, and adding a telescopic sight and adjustable stock, it made a formidable sniping rifle, throwing its 7.62mm bullet 1200 meters or more. He watched the arms-smith knock three 155mm shell casings off three posts at a thousand meters with three shots as a way of proving his point.

Valentine stood in front of the men, with Styachowski on her crutches to the right, Post to the left. A pair of motorcycles came around the corner from the direction of the headquarters, followed by an enormous black something, as wide as a Hummer but higher. Valentine had never seen a prewar sport-utility vehicle in such good condition before. Another truck followed, this one roofless, various subordinate officers arranged in the open seating. A diesel pickup rigged with benches in the bed brought up the rear.

The miniature column pulled up before Valentine's battalion. The cyclists lowered their kickstands. Valentine tried to look into the restored black behemoth, but the windows were darkened to the point that nothing could be seen from the side. The passenger door opened, and a man hopped out.

"Attend! Consul Solon is present."

A speaker on top of the SUV blared out an overamplified version of "Hail to the Chief" and Valentine stood at attention. The soldiers behind followed his example.

There was something childlike about the Consul, though he had the lined skin of a man in his fifties. He had the delicate features of someone who has survived extreme malnourishment, or even starvation, as a child. Overwide eyes, sparse brown hair, and rather thin lips looked out from a fleshless face bobbing on a scarecrow frame wrapped in a heavy coat and muffler despite the warmth of the spring morning. Valentine had not seen many movies in his life, but there had been a theater in Pine Bluff that showed old pre-2022 films on some kind of projector, and Consul Solon reminded him of a character in an old Bogart picture called *Casablanca.* There was a wariness to the eyes that reminded Valentine of the black-and-white image of Peter Lorre looking around the café.

Valentine took a single step forward, and Xray-Tango got out of the rear of the SUV. He trotted to join the little big man.

"Consul Solon, this is Colonel Knox Le Sain. You'll remember he and his troops were a godsend during the flood."

"Yes," Solon said with a nod to Valentine. None of the other officers were saluting the civilian coat, so Valentine didn't either. "The new battalion. You left the bayous for a healthier climate, as I hear it, Colonel. I like officers with initiative, Le Sain. I trust you'll restrict yours in the future to carrying out orders, rather than inventing your own." The Consul had a clipped manner of speaking, biting off the words. Solon's retinue carried out a small portable microphone, and strung a wire from the SUV to power it.

"Yes, sir," Valentine said.

He began introductions. Solon shook hands with Styachowski, thanking her for her injury sustained in saving the new capital of the Trans-Mississippi. He was polite with Post, but cut the interview short when Post hemmed and hawed out his respects. The lieutenants of each company stepped forward to meet him. Only one forgot himself so far as to salute Solon, but the Consul returned it in good humor.

As Valentine walked him back to the mike, Solon raised an eyebrow. "You have a big Grog there, Colonel."

"He's a good officer, Consul. Smart as a fox, and he tracks like a bloodhound. The men follow his orders."

"I'm not a fan of Grogs, Colonel. Putting them in any kind of position of responsibility, well, it's like Caligula putting his horse into the Senate."

"He's not like the gargoyles or the gray apes. He reads, writes and beats me at chess."

"Indulge yourself, then. But don't allow him to issue orders. The Grogs have no place in the Trans-Mississippi. There's already trouble with them further north."

He stepped to the microphone and faced the men. Post returned to his place in front of the infantry companies, and Styachowski her spot before the headquarters company, Valentine halfway between the two.

"Men of the Light Infantry Battalion, Third Division, Army of the Trans-Mississipi Combat Corps. Your comrades in arms welcome you. The civilized order you are part of thanks you. But before you can call yourself soldiers, with the pride and honor that title entails, you are required to take an oath to the Order I represent. Together we'll build a happier and more hopeful world. Please raise your right hands and repeat after me—"

Solon waited until he saw the hands in the air before continuing. Valentine spoke the empty words, listening to Ahn-Kha's booming voice behind him. "I do now solemnly swear allegiance to the Articles of the Consular Law of the Trans-Mississipi Confederation, to guard its integrity, to obey the orders of those officers placed above me, and to hold it above my life and those of its foes, foreign or domestic, or all I am and hold will be forfeit, until I am released from duty or am parted from service in death."

Solon spoke the words well. "Congratulations, soldiers, and welcome to the privileges of your new position. General?"

Another man stepped forward, part of Consul Solon's entourage. Solon handed him the microphone. He had streaming gray hair tied in a loose ponytail, and the same blue-black uniform as the guard Valentine had seen outside the Reaper's door, though his legs from polished boot-top to knee were wrapped in black puttees. The thinness of his legs and clear, hard eyes made Valentine think of some kind of predatory bird."

"Officers and men of the light infantry," the man said. "I'm General Hamm, of the Third Division. I'm your new commanding officer. We're the best division in the Trans-Mississippi, both now and once we're through mopping up that hillbilly rabble." Valentine wondered briefly how his hillbilly rabble felt about that choice of words. "You'll find I expect a great deal, but when this is all over, you'll get a great deal in return. In my old grounds in Texas, those who served me well in war found security in peace.

"Élan, right down to the company level, is important to me. Especially in my light infantry. You'll move fast and fight hard, grabbing ground and holding it until supports arrive. As a sign of your special bravery you'll carry a symbol, your bolo knife."

He looked over his shoulder. The diesel ground forward and stopped before Valentine. Hamm hopped up into the bed. "Help me, will you, Colonel? I like to hand these out personally."

There were long green crates within, like footlockers. Valentine lifted the hinged lid on one. Rows of sheathed machetes rested within. General Hamm picked one out and handed it to him. "Yours, Colonel. A handy little tool. Got the idea from those blades some of the 'Wolf' guerillas carry. You'll find I've improved the design."

"All the troops carry these, General?"

"No, just you lights. The heavy infantry get flak jackets and masked helmets. Consider yourselves saved a heart attack. That armor's Pennsylvania-built; it's hotter than hell down here."

Valentine unsheathed a blade. It was long and rectangular, a blade on one edge and saw teeth on the other. It widened slightly near the handle, which had a wire cutter built into the guard just above the blade. The metal was coated with a dark finish for night use.

Solon had retired to his SUV. Valentine, with the help of a corporal, handed up knife after knife to the general, who passed them out, each with a little word of commendation to the files of men brought forward to receive them. They returned to their company positions. The general took up a blade as well.

"You've got your blades. Your bolos. It was an old war cry, and soon you'll be shouting it again, when we go up into the mountains and get the poor bastards unlucky enough to be facing you. Let's try it out, shall we?

"Bolo!" he shouted, then lifted his hands to the men.

"Bolo," they shouted back.

"Not good enough!" Hamm said. "Booolo!"

"Bolo!" the men screamed back. "Booolooo!"

"Louder!" the general bellowed. He unsheathed the blade, brandishing it in the air. "BOLO!"

"BOLO!" it came back to him, a wall of noise. Valentine joined in, the scream so long repressed escaping. With it went some of his pain. He looked out at the thicket of waving, blackened steel. The general was right. He wouldn't care to be up against them either.

The next item on Solon's itinerary was a train ride. They took the ferry across to the north side of the river. Above them workmen and prisoners fixed I-beams to the pilings of the old bridge. Xray-Tango was rebuilding the railroad bridge first; the road bridge would come later. They stepped out of the ferry and took the short walk to the old rail yard.

The officers, a mélange of three generals, eleven colonels—including Valentine—and an assortment of accessory captains and lieutenants, ate a buffet served on the platform before boarding the flag-festooned train for its inaugural ride. The beginnings of the line to run, once again, west from the Little Rock area to Fort Scott had only been cleared a few miles northwest, but in those few miles it went to a station near Solon's prospective Residence, even now being constructed on a hill thick with trees, where once a golf course, lakes and the houses of the well-to-do stood. The nukes had flattened and burned house and bole alike, but a grander estate would rise from the ashes.

Valentine tried to keep his hand off his holster as he exchanged pleasantries with the braided Quislings. Solon was a gracious host, and introduced him to a few others as "Colonel Le Sain, a protégé of Xray-Tango." Xray-Tango introduced him to others as an officer nominated to command by Consul Solon himself. As the new officer in the coterie, Valentine received a sort of reserved attention. The generals nodded to him, the colonels seemed suspicious of him, and the lesser officers watched him. One lieutenant in particular pursued him, popping up at his elbow and clinging to him like a wart.

"Your Colonelcy would care for some more wine?" the unctuous lieutenant, a man named Dalton, asked.

"I'm fine, Lieutenant."

The man looked at the turned backs all around them, and lowered his voice. "A man in your position deserves a few comforts to forget the hardships of command. Ask anyone; I'm the sort that can make good things happen. I can make bad things disappear. *Pfssssht.*" He punctuated his conversation with sound effects. "You'd find me good company, and I'm looking for a good billet."

Valentine had already brushed off one captain angling for a staff position; he didn't want a Quisling with aspirations toward pimphood hanging around his camp. He asked Xray-Tango about it when they got a moment together on the train.

"Solon's at fault for it, really," Xray-Tango said. "He hands out promotions like a parade marshal throwing candy. They join his military advisor's staff until he can fob them off on someone. A lot of them are sons of important men in Dallas, or Tulsa, or Memphis. Anyone who helped him. Some of the officers had trouble fitting in back home, but they've done good service to the Higher Ups, so here they are. We've got generals who are illiterate, colonels who are pederasts; you get the picture."

"They should have gone down to New Orleans, then. They'd've fit right in." Valentine looked out the window as the train crawled west, blowing its whistle every minute on the crawling, festive trip. The official one. Another train with construction supplies had gone out on a test run a few days before.

"The bad ones have an unerring instinct for not getting themselves killed, have you ever noticed it? Colonel Forester took a bullet in the ear on the banks of the Black. General Cruz was sharing a foxhole with three men when a 120mm mortar round paid them a visit. Three privates got a helluva funeral, we had to bury them together because we couldn't tell who was who. Hamm's predecessor, General Patrick O'Connel, our best division commander last summer, had a birthday party and someone decided signal flares would really set off the cake. Six officers died when the house burned down."

"Idiots. But six? Fumes get them?"

"The fire spread fast. There were a lot of papers in there; they tried to fight it to save them. The general traveled with his own supply of gasoline. They locked it up good. Too good—no ventilation. *Whoof.*"

"The fire took a house full of people?"

"One or two made it. The general had an eye for the ladies. They traveled with him. He had this redhead. A real saddlebred—a little on the bony side, but pretty. She got passed on to Hamm like it was in the will."

"Privileges of rank," Valentine said, trying to sound as nonchalant. *Ali?* A fire would be just like her. But the rest didn't fit. Pillow recon, as Alessa Duvalier used to call it, wasn't her style.

The train swung and jerked as it crawled along the points. The track needed some work.

"What's Hamm like?"

"Third Division is a hell of an outfit, though they've really caught it since O'Connel died. They're scattered on the north side of the river now, refitting for the big push."

Valentine looked out the window. Ali would understand, if he could just talk to her. She'd been a Cat almost since puberty, had seen and done things that would turn a tough man's hair gray. He had been planning to put Gabriella Cho's bullet between General Hamm's eyes, right after removing Solon's head with Caroline Smalls', but now he was having second thoughts. After turning them over in his mind, he discarded his hopes. It was wishful thinking, to expect Alessa Duvalier to be wandering almost the same camp he was, even if she was a Cat.

The train finished its short run at a notch in the hills above what had been North Little Rock. Solon's party disembarked, more trucks—this time, hosed-down pickups—met them to take everyone up the steep grade to the estate grounds. Judging from the roadside placement of the posts marking where the fence would be, Solon had great plans for the grounds, if sheer acreage was any indication. A marble block the size of a crypt already bore the words STATION ONE–CONSULAR RESIDENCE in meter-high letters.

The hill flattened out as they rode to the top, and Valentine got his first view of the foundations of Solon's Residence. The vigorous young scrub forest that had been claiming the hillside lay in windrows up the gentle hill and at the top. A cluster of Quonset huts next to a pond housed the builders. The construction site, situated for a perfect view of the river valley to the west and the distant Ouachitas beyond, dominated a chunky, freshly cleared vista. As they drove closer Valentine got a better view of the future center of Trans-Mississippi power. There were basements, foundations and churned-up earth all around something that looked like it once was a college, or perhaps just a sturdy building that had survived the '22 devastation. A new roof had been put on it, surmounted by a cupola. The "college" formed the base of a great *U* of future buildings, some of which had the floors of the second story built along with the beginnings of walls. Georgian-style arched windows, minus the glass, were in place on the lower levels. It was reminiscent of the old Federal White House, expanded into a palace-sized villa.

The surroundings were just as impressive. The tallest hump of Big Rock Mountain, still forested, dominated the villa's "backyard."

Solon gathered his entourage at what would be the turnaround of his drive, in front of the new arched doors. Valentine angled his way through the press of officers to see Solon pointing out highlights. "There'll be a Grecian temple on top of the hill, one day. But that's the sort of finishing touch I'm saving until the masons are done with the important work down here. It'll be the finest view in the Trans-Mississippi, one day. Right now I call it the Lookout. I'll hike up there later, if anyone wants to join me."

He ushered the officers into the central hall. The interior had been gutted and turned into a grand entrance hall, branching off to the right and left to the rest of the villa. The entire back wall was missing, save for a balcony framework and supports for glass.

"This is going to open up on the inner patio. There'll be a pool and a greenhouse but, as you can see, it's just a big hole at the moment. At first I was going to get rid of this building. Old army construction, though the bricks were attractive. They'd turned the basement into some kind of hospital or dormitory. Come down, and see what I've done with it."

He led the party past a worker, who made haste to clear the way for the officers. "This is the Situation Room. There'll be a conference center and offices, and below, in the subbasement, a communications room and security bunker. The fixtures are in, but it's still missing some equipment." Solon led them into the conference center, separated by glass walls—complete with drapes for security—but as yet unfurnished.

"Now a brief meeting," Solon said, as his aides brought up a pair of easels.

Because of the lack of chairs, only the generals and colonels were allowed to sit for the meeting, and after it was over Valentine was grateful for the chance to walk again. After three hours of maps, orders, questions and arguments, he needed a break. Solon stopped for a meal, with a promise to answer question individually afterward. Access to the flush toilet was by rank, so Valentine grabbed a paper plate full of sandwiches and went up into the clean air and used the workers' outhouse.

He found an empty sawhorse and leaned against it, watching a bulldozer move earth. The sunshine made him feel even more enervated. He'd keyed himself up for nothing, as it turned out.

Two or three times during the meeting he'd rested his hand on his pistol. It would have been easy to draw it and kill five or six of the assembled senior officers. But as he came to the critical moment, the murder-suicide he'd been thinking about seemed more and more like an empty gesture as the emotionally frozen gears of his mind began turning again. A few deaths would not matter. The Kurians would have a hard time replacing someone as manifestly gifted as Solon, but the rest of the officers were easily switched cogs in the military machine. Or perhaps, when it came down to the sticking point, he lacked the courage to go open-eyed to his death.

Through the series of disasters—like falling dominoes he'd raced to stay ahead of—he'd been caught up in, he found himself in a unique situation. All the mistakes and misfortune had placed him in the enemy headquarters, handing him priceless information on the Quisling plans to finish off Southern Command. And his role in the operation couldn't have been better if he'd written the orders himself. His light infantry was assigned to probe the passes into the western Boston Mountains, looking for a lightly guarded route that he could seize so the rest of Hamm's division could put itself into the heart of what was left of the Free Territory's forces in their mountain redoubts. He could get what Quickwood he had where it was needed most, courtesy of the trucks of the TMCC.

The most tantalizing piece of information wasn't stated explicitly; Valentine had to put it together based on the questions from Quisling commanders from Tennessee, Okalahoma, Kansas and, especially, Texas. Solon was a strange cross between a venture capitalist and a military genius: he'd gotten command of large numbers of Quisling troops from all around the Ozarks, but the terms of the agreements were expiring. He'd made another set of deals, like a debtor trying to extend the due date of a loan for a few more months by promising interest greater than had been paid for the previous two years. He had until the end of summer to put paid to the loan, to conquer the Free Territory, before he lost eighty percent of his men. If he could clean up Southern Command's holdouts this spring and summer, he'd have enough to garrison his Trans-Mississippi with the help of the leaders of his Kurian substates, and send captives and prisoners off to the hungry neighboring Kurians, their bodies paying off his debts.

Valentine even found himself admiring his fellow officers. They asked intelligent questions, wrote notes in their order journals with smooth, elegant hands, and offered imaginative suggestions. There was efficiency, yes, but a certain amount of coldness, too, like greyhounds eager for the release of the rabbit, all eyes on the prize and not a thought for the men in uniform around them. A similar group of Southern Command officers would be more informal; there would be jokes and jibes and a good deal of smoke blowing.

"He's seeing everyone individually next," Xray-Tango said, breaking into his thoughts. The general gave a pine door-post an experimental rap. Valentine looked at the twitching eye and knew that Xray-Tango had received orders he hadn't liked.

"Did he give you what for about the bridge, General? Or getting the locks rebuilt?"

"No, nothing like that. That'd be sensible. He wants his house finished, so he can transfer his governement out of Fort Scott. The Twenty-three Representatives will be here soon."

"Twenty-three more Reapers? That won't be pleasant."

"These aren't so bad. I've seen them, all sitting around the conference table. They're more like zombies than anything; they just sit in their chairs until they need to see, hear and speak for the Higher Up at the other end. He feeds them pig blood, not people. Something about the distance, I dunno, they can't be animated right from so far away, and the ones closer have too much else to do."

"Then what's the matter, sir? You seem upset."

"I asked to retire after the big push. I'm feeling my age, Le Sain. Getting sick of making decisions for idiots who had the exact same decision put to them the day before. Then there's the . . . the stuff like the other night. It wears a man down."

"He turned you down?"

"He said he needed five more years to get the groundwork for New Columbia built. Promised me I could leave then. Bridges, highways, roads, factories, housing; he's even talking about an airport. The Kurians don't like anything bigger than bush planes in the air, but he's got this idea for a Trans-Mississippi air force burning in his brain. I'm just worried that after five more years, they'll want another five before I get my estate, and I've got my reasons for thinking that. You see, Le Sain, he promised me that when Southern Command was finished off, I'd be able to retire. I don't like a man who plays me like a fish. Can't stand people who are more convincing at making promises than keeping them."

"I'll go get my talking-to," Valentine said.

"You coming for the party later?"

"What party is that, sir?"

"You've been keeping to yourself lately. We're having a little celebration in the Blue Dome. You been in there yet?"

"No, there was the flood, sir. Since then I've been too busy fitting out."

"You owe it to yourself to live a little, Le Sain. Young man like you. Come along and have some fun."

"Odd you should say that, sir. I've told myself that just today. I thought there'd be some fun with this trip." He hooked a thumb in his gunbelt. "The day's not over yet."

There was only one miserable-looking captain still waiting when an aide shook Valentine awake. Valentine had pretended to snooze as he idled while Solon met with each officer; exhaustion turned his pretense into reality.

"The Consul will see you now," the aide said. He was ushered into Solon's underground office. The teal walls still smelled faintly of fresh paint. There was an oriental panel on the wall, three pictures, each in its own frame, separate works of art but forming a greater work together. The largest figure was of a warrior carrying a bow. Valentine looked in the corner of the office, where a recurved bow and a quiver of arrows had been placed.

"Colonel Le Sain," Solon said, looking up from his paperwork. "Our ambitious young newcomer. Please sit down."

"Thank you, sir," Valentine said, sitting in the club chair opposite Solon's desk. The Consul had shortened the legs on it, giving Solon a height advantage he didn't have when standing.

"I saw you admiring my bow."

"It's a handsome one, sir. Beautiful wood."

"My quiet center. I go away with the bow when I need to think. Or rather, not think, at least consciously. I'll take you out and show you, when we're less pressed by duty. Did you get caught up at the presentation?"

"Yes, sir. It was thorough, I'll give you that. There's only a little mopping up to do south of the Arkansas. North of it, it looks like you've got what's left of the opposition boxed in."

"They're more like a treed tiger. Properly prodded, they'll jump down. Unpleasant for whoever happens to be under them, but it'll be the end of the tiger."

"Could be dangerous for whoever goes up the tree to do the prodding, too."

"You understand your role, then. You wanted your shot at glory; I've granted your wish."

"They must be pretty hungry by now. Why not wait?" Valentine said.

Consul Solon's hangdog face tightened. "Evidently they'd prepared for years for this eventuality. Food and supplies deep in caves, mines ready in all the critical road junctures. And of course you're aware that our borrowed forces have to return home more or less intact."

"I caught that, sir."

"So headlong assault wasn't an option. It's our own fault. We didn't pursue promptly enough when they collapsed. It must have been some civil defense plan, to have so much put away for civilians, even. You know we've captured livestock up in the hills? I was tempted to take back some rings if my generals allowed them to get away with their chickens and sheep. Hopeless incompetence, but then what do you expect of forces that have been doing nothing but glorified police work and putting down uprisings for decades. They're gun-shy."

"Why not use Grogs?"

"The Grogs have their own concerns. The St. Louis ones only go to war for land; I'm not about to give up an inch of the Trans-Mississippi. Quite the contrary. Once we've got things under control here, we'll expand north. The whole Missouri Valley is crawling with them from St. Louis to Omaha; that'll change."

"The Higher Ups gave them that land in return for—"

"Don't be stupid, Colonel. That was a deal settled long ago. It wasn't with the Trans-Mississippi Confederation, either. I've spoken to the Twenty-three, and they're in agreement. You're seeing only the planting of a seed that will one day flower in the headwaters of the Mississippi, the Tenesseee, the Missouri, the Arkansas, yes, even the Ohio. That's why I came west, Le Sain. Elbow room. My days of sweating out strategies to control four more counties in Virginia or a town in Maryland are over."

"You're from the East, sir? I've always wanted to see it."

"No you don't. It's chaos."

"So you left? How did you manage that, if you don't mind me asking, sir?"

"You're a kindred spirit, Le Sain," Solon said, a twinkle coming to his basset-hound eyes. "If you don't like a place, your role in it, you get yourself out. I did the same, did you know that? My father was a senator in the old United States government. He didn't survive '22. I barely remember him. My mother struck up a relationship with a general who'd been useful to the Kurians. His lordship held a few towns around the Potomac in northern Virgina. I got my start as a courier; eventually I was running everything for miles around Harper's Ferry. The Kurians are such children in a way; if you're useful in getting them their candy, you can train them like Pavlov's dogs. I learned the art of politics. There must be generational memory in the land, for the whole area around what used to be the District of Columbia is home to the most backbiting, infighting group of Kurians you can imagine, all holding court in their little monuments around the Mall. A woman named Rudland, I believe she was from New York, organized them into a 'committee,' to cut down on the blood feuds. I'd help plead my lordship's cases before the committee, and if that didn't work, bribe a powerful member. Then a deal went wrong, and I had to—let's just say I left in a hurry.

"Not that it's been any easier out here. The soldiers I was originally going to use to flush out these backwoods killers suffered a setback when their Grogs revolted. Grogs are more trouble than they're worth; I've said it enough, you'd think someone would be listening by now. Those fools on the Missouri. It'll be a generation before that particular plan can be brought again to fruition. I'm not the first person to learn that if you want something done right, do it yourself, so I made deals to get the forces I needed. Though I haven't sought a reputation in the cannon's mouth, far from it. I earned my ring with words and ideas, not with bullets. They're more powerful in the long run."

"I'm still looking for mine."

"I'll tell you something an aging U.S. federal judge once told me. He had it on a plaque:

Vision without will fades like a dream.
Will without vision grows into a nightmare.

"The Kur are rich in will. I've never seen vision to go with it, so I'm supplying my own. As to will—well, you've seen what's being built in New Columbia. It'll be good. I'd like to think you'd stay out of desire to help me build here. But stay you will. Do you understand?" Solon curved his finger downward and tapped his desk to accentuate his words. "Stay. You. Will."

"Yes, sir."

"You've got an ambitious look about you, Colonel. I saw you at the meeting, looking around, wondering which of your fellow officers you could rise above. You're still a young man, and I'll indulge young men in that. At this rate you'll be one of my leading generals in a few years. Then you'll have it all: an estate, women, wealth. You're present at the founding of a country. Someday we'll mint coins. Maybe your face will be on one, if you distinguish yourself."

"I hope so. Did you have all this in mind when you came west?"

"New Columbia will be another Washington, another London, another Rome. Only better than Rome. Our temples will have real deities who give real rewards for an appropriate sacrifice. They will be Temples of Meaning instead of houses of superstition."

Valentine sickened at the thought of more white towers rising in the green Ozarks like that abomination across the hill, each one asking for its share of Carolines. His mother had been raped and killed again, and once again he trotted home just in time to see the horror. He couldn't keep the words in: "As long as we follow orders."

Solon looked at him with sad understanding—but then, with those basset-hound eyes, he had a face custom-built for the expression.

"Le Sain, if you've studied the history of China, you know it's been conquered many times. From the Mongols to the British. But in a generation or two, somehow it was China again. This land is the same way. We'll absorb the Kurians; when this fighting gets done with, we'll rebuild. They'll be powerful figures, certainly, like heads of corporations or governors. The real power was always in a set of oligarchs. They just happen to be Kurian now. But the rewards will go to the integrators, the ones who make it all work. Another constitutional government will rise, we'll have legislatures and courts, taxes and tollways."

"They'd let us have all that?"

"Why not?"

"Due process and all that might cut down on the flow of aura."

Solon leaned forward, steepled his fingers under his chin, and lowered his voice. "What makes you think I'd want that?"

"I'm not sure I follow you, sir."

"Every society has is share of drones: the uneducable, the lazy, the unproductive, the crippled, the sick. Then there are the criminals. Civilization has always paid some kind of price for their upkeep. With the Kurians in charge, they'll be fed into that furnace in the place of the talented. Only instead of the haphazard and arbitrary methods of today, it will be smoother, determined by courts and elected officials instead of this random slaughter. The robber barons will still take their toll, but it won't be at random anymore, they'll simply be a surgical instrument keeping the body politic healthy. Evolution did that for millennia, weeded out the unfit, but with our civilization the weeds were allowed to grow as well as the flowers. It's time to replant the garden of Eden. But first, we have to separate wheat from chaff. Every generation produces its share of each."

"I see."

"Do you? That unpleasantness with the baby the other night—yes, I heard about it. It upset you. If you want to be part of my bright future, you'll have to become used to that. Wheat and chaff, Le Sain. Wheat and chaff."

"You're a man of vision, sir. But sometimes the 'unfit' have hidden talents. Wasn't there a brilliant physicist named Hawking who only had use of his mouth? Van Gogh was crazy, Einstein's teachers thought he was retarded."

"You're well read for a bayou woodsman."

"I grew up in an old library, sir. Sort of a private collection. It started out with picture books and took off from there."

"You haven't been listening, Colonel. I've got the answers, so quit worrying about the questions. You see, we'll have courts, appeals.

We'll control the flow. The Kurians won't care how the plumbing works as long as the water keeps flowing. In the end, we'll have the real power."

Valentine left the Consul's office, hazy and flattened beneath a steamroller of a headache. He felt pressed flat by fatigue, as though the fading sun could pass through him as if he were a blood-smeared microscope slide. Consul Solon was persuasive. Valentine had to allow him that. He was also quite possibly a megalomaniac. It was a formidable psychological combination. No wonder Solon had come so far, so fast, in his quest for a federated empire of Kurian "states."

But like many ambitious conquerors, Solon had a problem. Would-be empire builders historically had two moments when even the smallest successful show of resistance might bring collapse. One was at the empire's birth, and the other was when it quit growing. Valentine doubted he'd live long enough to see the expansion stop.

That left turning Solon's Trans-Mississippi into a stillbirth.

Eight

New Columbia, March of the forty-eighth year of the Kurian Order: The Quislings and the Rats. Perhaps history has been overly unkind to Major Vidkun A. L. Quisling. He certainly loved his native Norway, but not so much that he let it get in the way of his ambition for political power through selling his good name and country to the Nazis. In that, at least, he is as dishonorable as his conscienceless namesakes. In the vocabulary of opprobrium against the Kurians, "Quisling" is considered perhaps the most obscene, for they thrive in the service of humanity's conquerers.

For those who spend time in the Kurian Zone, it is hard to be as bitter about the lower ranks. Armed service under the Kurians ensures life for the Quisling soldier and his family. It is hard to begrudge parents decent food to feed their children, a warm house and a few diversions. But some acquire a taste for the luxuries power brings and seek higher rank. They amass property, or gather art, or indulge their physical desires. Some become killers or sadists, exploring the freedom to taste that which is forbidden to others.

To the aid of the great ones with the power and money, there are always those willing to acquire their desires, legally or no. In New Columbia, those fulfilling, and profiting in, that service are the Rats. Not quite Quislings, but somewhere above the unfortunates living under the shadow of Kur, they live on the fringes of the law, their river boats giving them a freedom of movement and privacy that allows them to engage in lucrative smuggling. They have a strip on the north side of the Arkansas avoided by all save the river thugs, or those with the money to pay for a night in the dubious haunts of the riverfront. Most of them are clapped-together wooden establishments, already redolent of the unsavory activities taking place within. But there are a few substantial, finished buildings, complete with a touch of landscaping or a colorful coat of paint and expensive ironwork. Of all these, the most notorious—and expensive—is the Blue Dome.

As daylight faded Valentine hitched a ride into town with a pickup full of workmen, ignoring a pair of lieutenants who were waiting for more suitable transport. As the truck shuddered into second gear, one pulled a leather flask from within his shirt, passed it to a buddy, and with a practiced squirt shot a stream of the concoction within into his mouth before handing it back to the owner. He held it out to Valentine.

The Cat was tempted. After several sleepless nights, he'd spent the day keying himself up to kill a hatful of high-ranking Quislings, and then perhaps himself, only to find the moment, or his nerve, failing to live up to his destructive plan.

"What is it?"

"Joy-juice," the bearded laborer who'd produced the sack said. "Little wine, little homemade brandy, some fruit squeezings. Go on, Colonel, it's good stuff. Ain't blinded us yet."

Valentine shot some of the mixture into his throat, but didn't have the knack for stopping the stream yet. It splashed across his dress uniform shirt. He gulped it down. He'd had worse.

By the time the truck passed the markers at the bottom of the estate hill, they'd all had a round.

"How do you like working on the Residence?" Valentine asked.

"Good work," the man said, a few stray gray hairs on his head standing out against the black of his face and beard. "Ration book, and cash besides. No way I'm going back across the Missisisippi. There'll be good work for years. I can do electricity, plumbing, carpentry . . ."

Valentine felt for Xray-Tango across the river, trying to build New Columbia using captured Free Territory men, while the skilled workers, imported at God-knows-what expense, went to Solon's Residence.

"You don't live on the site?"

"Naw. Town's more fun. We all got a real house, even a couple of Tex-Mex women in residence for the chores and such. It's a sweet setup, Colonel. There's a diner in town, bars. They're talking about getting a movie-house going."

"I'm due at a party tonight. What's good to eat at the Blue Dome?"

The laborer smiled at Valentine with tobacco-stained teeth. "Shiiit, Colonel, what do you take me for? Only time I seen the inside of that place was getting the toilets running. Most of us do odd jobs at night, and old Dom, he pays well. But if I tried to walk in as a customer . . ."

"Exclusive?"

"Strictly for you officer-types and the rat-boat captains. What passes for society in these parts. But don't you worry; they'll treat you right, and the food'll stay down."

Valentine thought regretfully of the cigar box full of "Solon Scrip" back at his tent. He hadn't expected the day to end with dinner and drinks, so he'd left that morning with only a dollar or two tip money in his identification pouch.

The truck dropped him off next to a pyramid of rubble with a watch post atop it.

"Follow this street down to the river, Colonel," the workman said. "You'll see the Ragbag, a clothing-swap warehouse that'll still be open. Just to the right is the Blue Dome. No windows and only one entrance. It's got a neon sign with an arrow; you can't miss it."

"Thanks for the drink," Valentine said, after a second squirt from the leather flask. He offered two dollars in scrip. The laborer refused.

"It comes with the ride. Watch your money at the card table, and when you draw a flush, think of me."

The pickup bucked into gear and Valentine waved goodbye. He walked to the new riverfront of the north side of the Arkansas, at the edge of a little slope above the river proper, and thus safe from flooding. There were tent bars playing music, street vendors with food in carts, and everywhere men in deck shoes and woolen coats and sweaters, wearing knit caps or baseball-style ones with ship names sewn into the crown. A trio of muscular rivermen drinking behind a bar glanced at him, but shifted their eyes apologetically when they took in the uniform.

Valentine peered into the Ragbag's single window. The rest were still boarded up. Long tables and racks of recovered clothing were piled everywhere, and there was a cobbler in the corner tearing apart old shoes to recover the soles. He looked up the lively street and saw that a neon sign advertising the Blue Dome hummed from its position hanging out over the sidewalk. The joy-juice had assuaged his headache and left him sleepy.

The Blue Dome was a squatty block of masonry, better fitted together than most of the antheaps on the south side of the shallow Arkansas bisecting New Columbia, and painted to boot. There were no windows on the first story, and only shuttered, tiny slit ones on the second. Atop the building he could see the awning of something he guessed to be a penthouse; someone had gone to the trouble to hang basketed plants. From the alley between the Ragbag and the Blue Dome he heard the hum of ventilation fans and picked up the charred smell of meat on the grill. Valentine realized he was hungry.

Oddly enough, the Blue Dome's entrance was in the alley rather than on the main street. The aged stairs were pre-2022; he descended them to a new wooden door, which opened even before he knocked.

"Pri—oh, excuse me, sir, come right in," the burly doorman said, moving aside. Valentine stepped inside and halted, awestruck.

He felt as though he'd opened a worm-eaten wooden box only to find a Fabergé egg enclosed. Stuccoed walls opened up on an elegant room. Ensconced lighting behind delicate glass seashells drew his eyes upward to the glow of the Dome.

It stretched above a parquet wooden dance floor and stage to the right of the entrance. The concave surface was painted with some kind of luminescent blue material, which glowed in the reflected light of what Valentine guessed to be hundreds of small, low-wattage bulbs, giving the effect of a cloudless sky at twilight. Opposite him stood a massive wooden bar with polished silver fittings, a solid wall of liquor bottles behind it, and a bartender in a crisp white shirt and black tie standing ready. Between the bar and the stage, an elevated corner platform held a seated knot of musicians playing a quiet variety of jazz. The undomed part of the room stretched off to Valentine's left. Uniformed members of the TMCC sat around linen-topped tables. They stood on staggered burgundy-carpeted levels under the subdued blue light from what looked to be fifty miles of fiber-optic cable artfully wound into the ceiling and structural pillars. Around the edges of the room velvet-curtained alcoves were more brightly lit; Valentine could just make out green-topped gaming tables behind heavy burgundy curtains.

"Quite a basement," Valentine said to the doorman.

A man wearing the first true tuxedo Valentine had ever seen glided over to him. He had the coconut brown features of the subcontinent, and teeth as brilliantly white as his eyes. "Welcome, Colonel. I've been told of you and the service you did in the floods. Your first time here, yes?"

Valentine nodded.

"It was just a murky basement when I came here a year ago."

"You got in early."

"I'm an acquaintance of the good Consul's from back east. He's building a land of opportunity; when I heard his operations were a success, I was on the next train out of Baltimore. My name is Dom, and I'm pleased to meet you, Colonel. You are hungry, yes?"

"Yes," Valentine said. "You must have been building this place while they were still fighting."

"It is a principle of commerce as well as combat to get in first with the most. I'd like to think I've managed that. Your fellow officers wouldn't think of going anywhere else for an evening out, or a celebration."

"I can see why."

Dom bowed, then turned to a screened-off corner to Valentine's right. "Arsie, show Colonel Le Sain to General Hamm's table, would you? You're in luck, Colonel, you've got the best view of the floor from the whole restaurant. Enjoy your meal. If you wish to visit the gaming tables, they'll close for an hour at nine for the show, then they'll reopen."

A tall woman, all chestunut hair and silken skin in a cocktail dress that complemented the décor, appeared at Dom's side. Valentine saw a little tattoo of a faerie with heavy black eyeliner and lipstick winking out at him from her upper breast.

"Er, Dom, I haven't—"

"None of that, Colonel. Everything but your table stakes and bar charges tonight are courtesy of Consul Solon; your liquor is being picked up by General Hamm. Convenient, yes? That just leaves gambling money, and your name is good here; just show your identification to the cashier, last alcove on the left. It's as we're welcoming you to the Combat Corps tonight. I understand your battalion was formally recognized this morning. Congratulations, Colonel. 'Glory on your name, beauty on your arm, and a ring on your finger,' as they say. Speaking of beauty, Colonel Le Sain, I'd like you to meet Arsie, who'll be your escort this evening."

Valentine had sense enough, and joy-juice enough, to offer his arm. She was just an inch below Valentine's six-two. The soberer part of him wondered if Dom paired the officers according to rank or height. "Nice to meet you, Arsie."

"Congratulations, Colonel," she said, taking him across the dance floor to a long table set so it had a central view of the stage. A few other officers and men, some escorted by Blue Dome girls, sat and stood around the finger food on trays there.

"There's got to be a story behind your name, if you'll pardon the phrase."

"Ar Cee. Initials. RC."

"Which is short for?"

"I don't know. They said when I was a baby I was found in an old Royal Crown cola truck. You can say 'Arsie' if you like, Colonel."

"Call me Knox, please."

It was hard to tell just how false her smile was, but it did look a bit like the tattoo. "Thank you, Knox. Oh, you've got a stain on your shirt. Let me get some soda water," she said, hurrying off to the bar.

"Colonel Le Sain, welcome," General Hamm said, sitting at the end of the table with his boots up, stretching his stork-like legs. A purring, well-proportioned blonde was draped around his shoulders like a stole. "Old Extasy said you'd be coming. Welcome to the fun side of the Hard-Assed Third." He introduced Valentine to a uniformed blur of colonels and majors; some he'd met that morning, and others were new faces. There was a civilian in the mix, a sleepy-eyed man in an open-necked white shirt and black trousers. Hamm introduced him as Captain Mantilla. "Mantilla is a good man to know, Colonel. He's good at showing up where he's needed with what's needed. French wine, Italian clothing, Cuban tobacco, Mexican cabinetry, Belgian chocolate . . . he gets it all through connections down in New Orleans."

"I supply the liquor for the Blue Dome," Mantilla added, by way of proving his *bona fides*. He had fine whiskey lines about his hard eyes. "Unless you're well connected down in Nawlins, you'd have to go to Chicago or LA to get a decent single malt or cognac. We've got it right on the other side of that bar."

RC showed up with the soda water. She did what she could, using a table napkin Valentine wished he could use for bed linen, but the joy-juice resisted her efforts.

"Just stand close to me when we dance," Valentine suggested.

"Of course," she said.

"You're from around Natchez?" Hamm asked.

"I've done time in New Orleans, too." Valentine hoped any questions would fix on the latter; his year in the Quisling Coastal Marines would allow him to be conversant about its restaurants, bars and theaters.

"Don't much care for bayou types," Hamm said. "They don't stick in a fight. Not like Texans or Sooners. But I'm prepared to wait and see, seeing as you've got some Indian in you."

"Arsie's got a shot at getting some Indian in her tonight," a major guffawed.

RC waggled her eyebrows, and even Valentine had to laugh.

More food and drink arrived, and Valentine tore into pieces of steak served on thin iron spears, interspersed with vegetables on a bed of rice.

"The rice is native to your Trans-Mississippi," Dom said, visiting the table to see that the party was progressing and noticing Valentine's enthusiasm for the cuisine. "The vegetables come in from Missisisippi, since my usual sources in Texas are pricing themselves out of my reach at the moment. A tragedy, yes? The filet is from a friend's estate in Iowa. He feeds his cattle on a mash of corn and beer, swears by it."

"It is tender," Valentine said. He finished a mouthful and RC wiped grease from his mouth with a napkin.

"You'll need something to wash that down with, Colonel," a colonel named Reeves said. "You still haven't been initiated by the Division Cup."

"By Kur, you're right!" Hamm thundered. "The Division Cup! I brought it all the way here and forgot! Dom, brim it with hero's brandy, would you?"

"Of course, General, but the show—"

"Hold the show, damn you."

"Of course, yes, General."

The Blue Dome's owner returned with a silver two-handled loving cup. He presented it to the general, who took a sip, smacked his lips in approval, then passed it over to Valentine. Valentine looked at the cup, holding what looked to be a quart or so of liquor. The divisional insignia, a sneering, snorting donkey face with "Kickin' Ass!" emblazoned beneath, was etched into the side.

"It's not all brandy; there's sweetwater mixed in," Reeves assured him. "And a tab of Horny, to make sure you're up for the evening."

"You dosed it with Horny?" RC said. "I think I'm insulted, sir."

Not just his fellow divisional officers, but also others looked at him expectantly. There was nothing to do but attempt it, New Order aphrodisiacs or no. He lifted the cup to his lips and drank. And drank. And drank. He felt it running out the sides of his mouth and joining the stains on his uniform shirt and tunic. The men began to pound on the table, chanting, "Kick . . . ass . . . kick . . . ass . . . kick . . . ass."

It was empty. He crashed the cup back to the table hard enough to flip silverware over. The other officers applauded and cheered.

"Outstanding, Le Sain. Well done!"

The accolades whirled around his head as his stomach burbled its outrage. For a moment he was worried it would come back out faster than it went in, but through concentrated effort he kept it down.

RC kissed him on the earlobe. "Well done, Knox."

Valentine sat stupidly, staring at the band, which struck up a tattoo as a man in a red blazer appeared. His heart sounded louder than the big drum on the bandstand.

"Knox?" she said again, before Valentine realized she was talking to him. He tried to focus on her. "Knoooox!?"

"Yes?"

The man in the blazer must have told a joke; everyone was laughing. The band riffed.

"If you need to . . . hit the head, or whatever . . . it's—"

"No, I'm fine," Valentine said, fighting to make coherent conversation. "Warm in here, isn't it?"

"If you need to cool off I've got good air on . . ."

The band drowned her out with a flourish, and two pairs of female dancers each stepped out from either side of the stage. They wore what Valentine guessed were once called biking shorts and sports bras. They started a hip-hop dance number to pre-2022 techno that seemed designed to make Valentine's head throb. Valentine lapsed into silence and watched the girls through their routine, then some kind of magician came on stage and levitated a pair of them into a variety of pseudoerotic poses. RC gave the inside of his leg an exploratory squeeze.

"Ladies and gentlemen," Dom said, taking the microphone from the blazered master of ceremonies when the magician and the girls had gone off stage and the hooting faded. "We've come to the highlight of our show. Returning to our stage, after a too-long absence, is someone I'm sure you all remember well. She needs no introduction, so just let me say . . . Miss Tanny Bright!"

The jazz band exploded into noise again.

A woman marched out onto the stage, smiling and confident, basking in the cheers, applause and wolf whistles from everyone but David Valentine.

He'd even forgotten the witch's brew bubbling in his stomach in the shock of recognition.

Alessa Duvalier wore a stripper's version of the TMCC uniform. A peaked hat was perched on her glorious red hair, tipped so far over it must have been held on with hair pins. Thick layers of stage makeup covered her freckles. She wore a choker with some kind of medal on it, and a sleeveless fatigue shirt cut away to reveal her midriff, held closed by two buttons struggling against her upthrust bosom. A uniform skirt, which ended about where her thighs began, was cut up each side to the web belt. Her stocking-clad legs and patent-leather shoes made the most of her toned limbs. She carried two sheets of flimsies in her hand.

"Oh, how I miss him," she said, pretending to read the pieces of paper in her hands. "All I can think of is the last time we were together."

She looked across the faces in the audience, found General Hamm's eyes, and winked at him theatrically. The men guffawed, and Valentine heard twenty variants of "lucky bastard" muttered. She pretended to finish the letter. "And he's coming home! To me!"

The trumpeter in the band let loose with something that sounded like a bugle call. Duvalier planted her fishnetted legs wide, held the papers to her bosom, and broke into a dome-raising song, set to a marching beat.

"My sweetheart's slung his rifle
And marched away from me,
For duty sounds beyond my door
A call to destiny.
Waited true these lonely days
Until his letter came.
I saw the words: 'My darling,
We'll soon be one again!'"

It was a cheerful, upbeat song, and Duvalier marched across the dance floor, stepping high with her legs, swinging her arms in parody of a dress parade, touching and bouncing from man to man at the edge of the dance floor like a pool ball ricocheting across a billiard table. She ran her fingers up the arm of one, pressed her barely covered derriere against another, brushed a third's hair with her breasts.

Valentine felt the Blue Dome grow warmer, brandy and lust heating his blood.

The other dancers came out on the stage for the chorus, costumed in variants of Duvalier's getup. As they sang, she pretended to wipe the sweat from an officer's brow with the fake letter crumpled in her hand.

She lingered at Valentine's table, tousling the hair of each man as she continued the song. She sat on one's lap and sang into his face, then moved on to Valentine. She wrapped her arms around him and nipped him on the ear as she thrust her hands into his tunic, unbuttoned by RC in her efforts to clean his shirt. Valentine noticed, when her arms came back out, that she only had one sheet of paper in her hand. She kicked up a leg and planted a foot on the table, and all eyes went to her as Valentine buttoned his tunic over the note.

She finished the last chorus of the song at General Hamm's side, singing it to him. She hopped up on the table before him, feet planted wide to either side of his plate, joining the other dancers for the last chorus.

"Wait at the station
For the victory train.
We'll run from the siding,
Dance up lovers' lane,
Stroll along the river
Where first you became mine,
Lose all our worries
In my ring's golden shine!

The general helped her down and gave her a lip-smacking kiss. Valentine winced, feeling like a man who has just come across his sister in a brothel. Jealousy and disgust, infinitely fouler and more upsetting than the brandy and sweetwater, swirled and bubbled within him.

She looked around the table. "Good evening, Captain Mantilla . . . who's the new face?"

"Colonel Knox Le Sain."

"You don't like oldies, Colonel?"

"A bump and grind on top of my dinner puts me off my feed, funbunny," Valentine said.

"Colonel," Hamm growled. "I won't have you talking about Tanny like that."

"I'll give him funbunny," Duvalier said, reaching for a fork.

RC leaned forward. "The colonel just finished off the brandy in the Third Division Cup—and a tab of Horny. Cut him some slack, Ty."

Valentine's former mentor sat back down on Hamm's lap. She didn't flinch as Hamm rested his hand across her shoulder, fingertips touching her breast. Valentine looked away and back at the stage, nauseated.

"You're in for a messy night," Duvalier said, looking at RC.

"You never know," Valentine's escort answered.

"I am feeling a little—" Valentine began.

"I'll get you some air," RC said, as Valentine rose from his chair.

"No, I'm all right . . . or maybe not." Valentine hurried for the exit. The furniture and décor were an unearthly primary swirl around him. He staggered past the doorman and up the stairs. . . .

When the paroxysm passed he found he was resting against a Dumpster, sweating like a pig and feeling like a small rubber duck floating in a very big lake. He looked around, and reached into his tunic to retrieve the handwritten note. By the blue light of the neon sign, he read Ali's block-capital scrawl.

> Must See You AM Good
> Will be here one day more then to AFB
> Love the (lack of) Hair
>   Meeyao
>   T

Apart from her creative spelling of "meow" it was pure Ali; short, to the point and equivocal in case it ended up in someone else's hands.

Much of his education in operating in the Kurian Zone had been from her; though she was just under his age, she had twice his experience as a Hunter. While he wondered if she really was good, he was certain the "AM" referred to A.M. AFB probably meant the old air force base to the north as her destination. Hamm had his headquarters there for the refit; Valentine had been told his battalion was to move north and join him in another week or so. Xray-Tango had promised him more time on the range to practice with the new rifles.

For Valentine, it could not come soon enough. He wanted out of the Kurian Zone; Southern Command needed the Quickwood.

"Feeling better, Knox?" a female voice asked from somewhere across the Missouri line. He dropped the note into the Dumpster, startling a rat sniffing at the vomitus within.

He turned, half expecting to see Ali, but it was RC, holding a hurricane glass full of bubbling water.

"I brought you some more soda. It's good for more than just stains."

"You always this nice?"

"Inside there? Yes."

Valentine accepted the glass and took a mouthful. He spat it into the alley, then drank the rest.

"Better," he said, handing it back to her.

"Is the air helping?"

"Yes. Sorry I'm not converstational. I need sleep."

He couldn't take his eyes from the shadowy vertical line between her breasts. *Her chest was lovely, dark, and deep, but I have promises to keep, and miles to go . . .*

She put a hand on his forearm and drew it from the Dumpster. "My room's just around the corner. We could go up the back stairs."

"Nice of you, but I just need to sleep." If anything, she was more desirable in the muted light of the alley, every turning curve of skin a promise.

"Fine with me, Colonel. If I'm with you, I don't have to make nice in there."

Valentine looked at her, wondering if this was yet another Kurian Zone test or trap. *What the hell.*

"Lead on," he said, holding out his hand.

She took him down the alley and around the corner to the back of the Blue Dome. They went up a wooden stairway, the timbers of which were bolted onto the building like an afterthought. She walked him down a long common balcony.

"Yes, oh man, oh baby, oh my, yes, do it!" A female voice drifted through one of the windows.

"I prefer 'yes, do it, oh my, oh baby, yes,' myself," RC said, turning a knob on a windowless door.

"She gets good marks for volume," Valentine said.

"You wouldn't say that if you lived next to her."

It wasn't so much a room as it was a long closet. There was a double bed, with a single mounted above in such a way that it formed a half-canopy, a table, two closets . . .

"And a john, for the johns," she said, opening a narrow door. "There's even a shower. If we want a bath, there's a tub down the hall."

"You share the room?"

RC removed her shoes, frowning. "A dancer. Her name's Melanie. If the deadbolt's closed, she knows not to come in. There's a mattress in their dressing room, so she can sleep there tonight."

Valentine collapsed on the double bed, focusing on the ticking pattern on the mattress.

"Bedspins?" RC said, sitting down beside him.

"No. Just really, really, tired."

"Why's your gun off safety?" she asked, examining the gun he'd dropped beside him.

"Old habit, when I sleep in a strange place."

"Tricky with a .45. Don't worry, you're safe. The scuzzies might hit the boats, or the warehouses across the river. Never here."

"I see. You know your guns."

"Basic training starts at eleven for a girl in Dallas. The boys start at eight."

"Louisiana starts at fifteen."

"You don't talk like swamp trash."

"I grew up in New Orleans." Valentine thought he'd better get off the subject in a hurry. "Why'd you leave Big D?"

"You really want to talk, after a tab of Horny?"

"You're beautiful, RC, but I'm about to leave New Columbia. Still a little curious about you. You're authentically nice."

"Authentically nice. I'll take it."

"What's Dallas like?"

"I was on my back at twelve. You invest the capital you're given. I was pretty slender; the guys with a taste for . . . younger stuff . . . dug me until I was over eighteen. My face and hair didn't hurt. But once I passed twenty and had a kid, well, I wasn't worth much to my boss. Dom and Garrett, the doorman, were hunting up girls on the cheap.

Dom bought me out for next to nothing, and taught me to talk better and do my eyes right while he was building the joint."

"Where's your—"

"Son, they told me. New Universal Church youth center. Never even got a good look at him."

"Fresh start, huh?"

"Yes. Wasn't a real change, just on the outside. I'm still doing soldiers, still wondering if the penicillin they're giving me is the good stuff or not. I just wear a nicer dress is all. Appearances can be deceiving."

"Yes," Valentine said, drifting off to sleep.

"You ever wanted to change who you are?"

"Constantly."

RC might have been saying something else, just above a whisper, but he sank into an exhausted slumber.

Molly was moving beneath him in the darkness of the little basement room. He felt her bucking beneath him, clawing at his back, but the pain only made him thrust harder. Her eyes screwed up tight in orgasm, then opened as she screamed in passion.

Her slit pupils widened in their yellow irises as her tongue shot toward his breastbone . . .

Valentine woke, the sheets wet against his back, a rancid taste in his mouth as though someone had wiped his mouth with a discarded diaper.

"What's going on?" he whispered. There were thumps and a shout or two from below.

RC turned against him. "Eyuuhh? I don't hear anything."

Valentine felt a Reaper, somewhere below. Its presence pulsed with cold energy. He heard the crash of a table overturning.

"It's two in the morning," RC yawned. "They're just closing up downstairs. Sometimes they have to drag people out."

The Reaper moved into the street as RC spoke. He heard an engine start.

"They took someone out," Valentine agreed. He could picture the scene downstairs. The Reaper arriving, possibly with a human goon or two, and shaking someone awake. The horrible realization that they probably had less than an hour to live as they looked under the hood at the pale, emotionless face. Handcuffs, a waiting vehicle. "The Meet Wagons," they used to call them in New Orleans. Then the final struggle against its embrace: the last dance.

"God, your heart is pounding," RC said, pressing her palm to his chest. "That always happens when you wake up?" She was a shadowy presence beside him, nude, her long hair tied up for sleep. He felt her skin against his leg, softer than the sheets, save for the tickling tangle of hair between her legs.

"I startle easy," Valentine said. The Reaper was gone. He collapsed back on the bed.

Her hand moved lower. "Do you always get a gun when you're startled?"

Valentine's hand had moved to his gunbelt hung on the corner of the bed when he woke, but her attention was fixed on flesh, not steel.

"A gun?"

RC turned up the corner of her mouth as her hand explored him, tugged at his pubes, tested his shaft, cupped his testicles. "That's what I've always called them. Men take a lot of pride in them. Wave them around. They can be dangerous if mishandled." Something of a Texas twang came into her voice. "They shoot. Hell, you've got a real rifle, Knox." She began to stroke him, gently, before turning on the bed. Her nipple left a long, electric trail across his stomach. Her mouth met her hand, and he swelled in excitement. "Big game," she giggled, a string of saliva linking them.

He lay there, enjoying himself, until it occurred to him that Malia Carrasca's baby—his baby, their baby, was due soon. His orgasm, while apparently thrilling to RC, was just an empty series of physical sensations.

Valentine was on his third glass of water and was reaching for the pitcher again when he heard a knock.

RC rose and slipped a robe on her slight shoulders. "Melanie probably wants the room back. Don't worry, you don't have to leave until you feel like."

"I should be off anyway," Valentine said.

"Mel, gimme a break, woul—" she said to the door as she opened it. Duvalier stood there, her hair tucked in some kind of bag and a mask of creamy mud on her face. "Oh, Ty, hi . . . I've got company."

"I know, RC. Can I talk to him, in private? I need him to do something so I can surprise the Number One on his birthday."

"Umm, yeah . . . I guess."

"Just five minutes, sweetie."

RC looked at Valentine, hurriedly pulling up his trousers. "Knox, you remember Ty?"

"The singer from last night? Check her for forks," he said. "I'm sorry. I was a little drunk last night, Miss, uhhh, Bright. I didn't even know the general's birthday was coming."

"Thanks, sweetie," Ali said. She put a finger to her lips. "Shhhhh, okay? Secret mission."

"My lips are sealed," RC said, grabbing a basket of towels and soap and moving into the hall.

"Not hardly," Duvalier said, closing the door and shooting the lock.

"Tanny Bright?" Valentine said, after sweeping the balcony and the hall with hard ears. It was early morning, still; all he heard were RC's footfalls.

"I told him my real name is Ronny McDonalds, which he thought was even funnier. You missed my second number. Was she worth it?"

"I didn't know you could sing."

"Since this shit started I've sung in three different clubs. I'll let you in on a trade secret: The less she wears, the worse her voice can be. You look a bit green this morning."

Valentine poured himself more water, and offered his fellow Cat a glass, but she shook her head. "The 'hero's brandy' wasn't agreeing with me. I didn't even try to keep it down. My stomach generally knows best. Are we going to talk about anything important?"

She lowered her voice until it made no more noise than the breeze through the shutters. "God yes. I'm still active, under Mantilla. Are you in his contact group too?"

"I understand you're active under Hamm." He used sign language for this, the motions coming slowly thanks to brain-fog.

She switched over to hands as well. "Don't go there, Valentine. I thought you wanted to talk shop."

"You're right. Sorry, whatever you're doing is for the Cause. No, I'm not active. I was delayed getting back from Texas. I didn't return until just before Christmas. It's been nothing but disaster ever since."

Her hands again: "I just found out about you being here when I hit town. Southern Command got the report you sent with Finner. The overrun was already in full swing when I came up from New Orleans. I got the women and kids from your crew out. It's a story I don't have time for. They're safe down at Steiner Station."

"Steiner? Hal Steiner? Lots of rice paddies and a little fortified town?"

"That's the last place I was before this assignment. Steiner's place . . . it's grown. He's trying to feed and hide thousands of refugees in those swamps, plus a chunk of what's left of Southern Command.

Got it all phonied up to took like a little Kurian Province. It won't last forever."

"I know," Valentine audibilized this time, though he kept his voice down. "I've got the newest battalion in Hamm's division."

Her hands fluttered like fighting birds; she'd always been better than he at signing. "You say it like it's your fault. It's not. Being mistress to not one, but two, count 'em, two generals and an oily restaurateur wasn't in my plans when I got tasked with infiltration. Mantilla's one of us, too. Not a Cat, but he reports directly to the Lifeweavers. I haven't had the chance to tell him about you."

"You said you have orders from Southern Command?" he signed.

"From the Lifeweavers. They're in hiding, naturally. No sign of Ryu, but your old man Amu's been passing stuff back and forth to me through some Wolves and Mantilla."

"Anything for me?"

She rested her hands for a moment. "Yes, I've got orders. They want you to raise a ruckus behind the lines once the offensive gets under way. Theirs or ours, whichever comes first. Cut the north-south line through Little Rock so they can't shift their forces south quickly. Tie down as many of them as you can for as long as you can."

"If they can hold out a few more months, it'll be a different story. Consul Solon's about to send more of his army back to where they borrowed it. Texas, mostly."

"I've thought they seemed in a big hurry. This is just a guess, but I think something's in the works, Val. Southern Command's going to strike back somewhere unexpected, at least I hope so. If you can gum things up here—"

"I'll see what I can do. What's my line of retreat? Back west to the Ouachitas?"

"I've got nothing for you about that. They said just cause as much trouble as you can, for as long as you can."

With no orders where and when to run? Sorry, Valentine, right place, right time. You're a pawn in a good spot to tie down the King and Queen until they maneuver to take you.

"Who's my superior?" Valentine asked.

"I've no idea. I don't think Southern Command knows much more than that you're in here with some men. They're leaving it up to you."

"Well, there's more. I brought back something, something that kills Reapers. I put that in the report that went out with Finner."

"If you've got something that kills Reapers, start using it. Mantilla might be able to get some to the rest of Southern Command."

"It's just wood. It's some kind of catalyst, acts on the thickening agent in their blood. They seize up and die."

Duvalier pursed her lips in thought. "Wood isn't much help against artillery and armored cars. Speaking of Reapers, that's the second thing I've got to tell you. They arrested a captain on Hamm's staff. I've been stealing papers and I planted some on him to string this out a little more. I think Hamm's getting set to get rid of me. He used to bring his briefcase and what have you when we were together. No more. Kur knows there's a spy in his division. He's taking precautions."

"Good. I'm the new guy; they'll look at me."

"I doubt it. It's gone on since Hamm's predecessor, and they know it. I took him out, by the way. It was business and pleasure. He tried to pass me around like a party favor."

"That house fire. I heard the sad story. Sounded like your handiwork, Smoke."

She smiled and said in a whisper, "That's better than 'funbunny.' You know I wouldn't do the pillow recon if it wasn't for all this shit. The next incendiary device is going down Hamm's pants, then I'm blowing town."

"I'll try to light a fire of my own."

"Be careful."

"Sounds like the orders are to be destructive. That doesn't always go along with being careful."

"Well—"

"Ali, there's something you could do for me. Sort of a last request."

"Still Hornied up?" she said, incredulity written in block capitals on her forehead. "I thought that tall drink of water took care of you. Dream on."

He went back to sign language: "Get me whatever you can on Xray-Tango. He used to serve on the plains. He might even be semifriendly."

"That'll be tricky," she signed back. "I don't even know who's got the intelligence archives."

"Anything you can get me would help," he said.

"I'll see if I can get a message out. Maybe some Wolf can find you with the answer. How important is this?"

"It's important to me. He's got some strange qualities. Makes me think a parent of his might have been a Hunter. Sometimes things get passed down."

"I'll do what I can."

Valentine stood up. "That's always more than enough."

"Thanks, Ghost."

"Keep it safe, Smoke."

She gave him a quick hug and a peck on the cheek. "I've missed working with you, Val," she breathed in his ear. "You're one of the good ones."

Without further explanation, she left.

Valentine picked up his clothes, and looked around RC's shared room. There was a tiny stuffed bear sitting on a shelf in the closet above where the silk cocktail dress hung. He wondered about the little girl it had once belonged to.

He realized he was whistling as he descended the stairs, strangely buoyant. There was sunshine above New Columbia, though the clouds were building as they crept in from the west, but something more than the sun cheered him. RC had brought him an egg-and-toast breakfast after her bath, returning to the half-servant, half-girlfriend manners of the previous night. The taste of fresh eggs and butter wasn't it either. Perhaps it was just the knowledge that Ali was alive and well, and around to help. Despite the hangover he felt as though a door had been thrown open inside him; the world was giving him another day and another chance.

It crossed his mind that it could be the prospect of action. He'd been nervous and breathless since Duvalier's update; plans began to form in his head immediately, and with that momentum his mind shifted to a higher gear. He felt damnably close to precognitive, like a gambler pushing all his winnings onto the green double zero on the roulette table knowing the ball would fall to that slot on the next spin.

Raise a ruckus . . . raise a ruckus . . . Duvalier's words ran through his head like the trumpet's flourish in her rollicking song from last night. He realized where the tune he was whistling had come from.

He made his way through the alley, past the rat-infested Dumpster, and out into the spring sunshine. General Hamm, Reeves and a few of his other officers were enjoying a café breakfast outdoors.

"Coffee's hot, Le Sain, join us," Hamm called.

Valentine grabbed an empty chair. "Thank you. Just one cup, though. I've got to get across the river, General. The battalion is probably wondering what happened to me."

"They'll survive a few more hours. We had some funny business in the night, Le Sain. You've got some mud on your collar, by the way." Hamm stared at the stain for a moment, then continued. "One of my officers was taken away, and I don't like it. Williams. You remember him?"

"I met him last night," Valentine said, remembering the vigorous young officer, exchanging jibes with the rest of the table, frightened only by the bar tab he was running up. "But he wasn't on the trip out to the Consul's Residence."

"No. No, he wasn't. Apparently he went rooting through my papers while I was away."

"He had access to them?"

"He was my chief of staff's assistant," Hamm said, eyes leveled like firing squad muzzles at Reeves. Reeves looked a little pale in the morning sunshine.

Valentine tucked his collar under his tunic, hiding Ali's pasty smear.

"Who came—"

"The usual," Hamm cut him off. "By the time they woke me, he was gone, or I'd have asked some questions. I can't figure out why someone with access to my office would steal everyday correspondence. Something from the safe, yes, that'd be valuable to those crackers. But why steal letters about the state of the transport system in northern Arkansas . . . err, the Upper Trans-Mississippi? We're supposed to stop with the old state designations, by the way, Le Sain. Solon's orders."

"Because he wasn't a spy, someone wanted him to look like one?" Valentine said, feeling that it was a rhetorical question due out of Hamm's mouth within about five seconds.

Hamm leaned closer to him. "It's looking like there's a spy in my headquarters, Knox. We got royally raped last October, and I think it's because someone knew the hour and date we were pulling out of the line and sidling."

"Ask Solon for different orders for the offensive, or to move up the date, and keep them to yourself until the last minute, is my suggestion, sir. That or get a bigger safe."

"I'm wondering if I need a new chief of staff. I get the feeling you can organize and think for yourself. I need to replace Williams. You want the job? Staff work's a lot nicer than line duty."

"Sir, your offer is tempting, but I have to stay with my men—at least until all this is over. I want to see them blooded."

"Thought you were looking for promotion, responsibility. That'd come with a staff position. They make general more often than not."

"I am, sir, but responsibility is like water. It flows better from the top down."

Hamm murmured Valentine's words, trying them out on his tongue. "Hey, I like that. Mind if I use it in my next speech to the division?"

"I'd be honored, sir. But I need to get back across the river—oh, speaking of the river, where can I find Captain Mantilla? I'd like to put in an order."

"His tug's tied up at the wharf right now. It's battleship gray, with big blue letters on it. OGL. You need something, son?"

"Bourbon and tobacco. Not for me, for my officers."

"I like your style, Le Sain. I'm glad you're in my division."

The barge was even uglier than the old *Thunderbolt.* It looked like a couple of aluminum mobile homes piled on a raft, and needed a lot of rust-stripping before another coat of gray. Sure enough, gigantic letters stood out on the side just below the carbon-coated stack, OGL.

The anchor watch was asleep. A fleshy man, bald as Valentine and bronze-skinned by birth and sun, slept in the sun at the end of the gangway. An iodine-colored bottle rested between his legs.

"Excuse me, boatman?" Valentine said, venturing up the gangplank. He still felt as though there was an inch of air between his feet and the ground—and he couldn't stop looking at the bridge over the Arkansas River, and Solon's Residence hill beyond.

If anything, the snoring grew louder.

"Sir?"

Valentine came closer. The man was a dedicated napper, so much so that he sacrificed shaving and bathing in its pursuit.

Valentine flicked his fingernail against the bottle, eliciting a *ting.* "Closing time. Last call," Valentine tried, a little more loudly.

"Hrumph . . . umpfh . . . umpfh . . . double me up again, good buddy," the anchor watch said, coming awake in eye-blinking confusion.

"Did I guess the password?"

"Sorry there, sir. I was resting my eyes, didn't see you come up."

"They're still pretty red, friend. Eight more hours oughta do it. Can I find Captain Mantilla on board?"

"Engine room, I expect. He's usually there when we're not hauling." The anchor watch stood up and gave his belt a lift. "Follow the blue streak."

Sure enough, Valentine picked up a steady stream of grumbles and curses in English, Spanish, French and what he guessed to be Russian or Polish.

"C'mon, *panoche.* Loosen up, you bitch. *Kurva,* what's the matter with you this morning, you old *putain.*"

"Cap, this ol' boy's come aboard askin' for you," the boatman called down the hatch. "Wearin' a TMCC pisscutter and a turkey on his collar."

"*Merde.* Just a moment, Chief." Valentine heard tools being put down, and then someone coming up the ladder.

Mantilla's face appeared in the sun, smeared with grease like Comanche war paint. He furrowed his brows. "Morning, Colonel. Saw you last night but damned if I can remember your name."

"Le Sain, *mon frere.* I want to talk about getting a little extra cargo up here, the next time you come up the Arkansas."

"Thanks, Jim Bob, I'll take it from here." As the sailor moved back to his shady rest, Mantilla pulled out a cigarette and sat on the edge of the hatch. "What can I get you, Colonel?"

"I'm an old friend of Miss Bright's. You've done a few favors for her, and I need something similar. She sent me."

Mantilla took a sidelong look at him and blew out a lungful of carcinogens. "You stick your head in the noose first, Le Sain."

"When you talk to her faraway friends, you probably referr to her as Smoke. If you speak to the same people, call me Ghost."

"Pleased to meet you. How can I help?"

"I need something brought to Southern Command."

"Fair enough. I have to tell you plain, sir, that's getting trickier by the month. I can't guarantee anything. What is it, people, papers, photos?"

"Some wood. Just a few dozen four-by-four beams."

"You're shitting me."

"It's not really the wood, it's what's in the wood."

"Gold? Platinum?"

"If you don't know, you can't tell anyone. I just want to know if you can get them into the Boston Mountains."

"Boston Mountains? You're misinformed. That's just a screen. The Ozark high command's hiding out in the bayous in the southwest. Big Hal Steiner's got them hidden."

"Really?"

"Easier to feed them from the swamps and rivers. He's got rice up the wazoo, too. The part of your army that's holding out up north, it's mostways teams of your Bears and Wolves wearing Guard uniforms. The invaders got so busy blocking up the mountains they didn't catch the evacuation south. They think the whole southeastern corner of Arkansas is a Kurian backwater. All those Grogs Steiner has around the place has them confused."

"I've been there. You could hide an army there."

"They won't be hiding there much longer."

Valentine, already excited, hooked a thumb in his belt near his .45's holster. "When?"

"Soon. Within weeks."

"You a Cat, or what?"

Mantilla bristled. "Look, Colonel, let me have my secrets, too. We're on the same team, isn't that enough?"

"When you're on a team it's nice to know if you're talking to a quarterback or the towel guy."

"I'm more like the towel guy, Colonel. I'm due downriver yesterday. Can you get me your beams in double time?"

"How's tonight?"

"Tonight's excellent," Mantilla said, nodding approvingly and relaxing again.

"How you want to work it?"

"There's lots of shallows on the south bank, just downstream of the pilings from the first bridge. I'll ground her. I'll splash ashore and your men will rock me off using the wood as levers. That okay with you? Don't want to break open the Quickwood and have a bunch of gold fall out."

Valentine came to his feet. "Quickwood? How the hell do you know it's called Quickwood?"

"From you."

"How's that?"

"Call it intuition. Specific intuition."

"I thought only the Lifeweavers did tricks like that."

The enigmatic captain scratched an itch between his eyes. "Lifeweavers and us towel boys."

"Can you get me some bourbon and cigars? I told Hamm I was here to see you about that."

"Popular items. I keep them in stock. I'll drop them off tomorrow."

Valentine held out his hand. "Until tonight, then, Captain."

"Until tonight."

Valentine looked at the traffic waiting for the ferry and decided to hazard the footbridge for the railroad workers. The span was complete, track had been laid to both ends of the bridge and the wood-and-iron construct, Xray-Tango's first priority, would be ready to carry regular trains in another day or two once the sidings were coordinated. There had been a pontoon bridge, but it had been lost to the flood and never replaced. A few of the floats that weren't swept away were still pulled up on the riverbank.

He ascended the bank—one day there would be stairs, according to some wooden stakes pounded into the riverbank dirt. The trusswork was admirable; many of the top beams were recovered and straightened from the structural steel of Little Rock's former skyscrapers. Piled up ties waited for the crews to come and fix the rails to them. When finished, there would be a single track and a footpath wide enough for three men to walk abreast across the river, or a truck in an emergency. But the footpath would be finished last. For now, the workers had to either walk from tie to tie or walk across on the fixtures at the base of the trusses. Valentine chose the latter.

Valentine liked bridges. The engineering appealed to the mathematic, rational part of him, and their suspended airiness gratified his artistic side. He paused in the center and looked around New Columbia, from the northward bend in the river to the northwest, where Solon had his Residence on the steep-sided hill rising three hundred feet above the river, mirroring the wider Pulaski Heights opposite, then across the antheap where his soldiers had their camp, to the swampy flats of the former airport to the southeast.

Raise a ruckus.

He examined the south-side river wharf, where a barge offloaded trucks, a few artillery pieces and little tracked carries that reminded him of beetles. The cargo had probably come from one of the factories on the Ohio—he'd heard the Kurians had opened the river to barges all the way to the Mississippi. It made sense; cargo could be moved more easily on the water than by any other method. The guns were probably 105s, a cheap, simple gun his fellow TMCCers called "use 'em and lose 'ems." The Kurians, in their efforts to keep weaponry—and therefore humanity—at a pre–First World War level to prevent "the human predilection for self-slaughter" as the New Universal Church put it, frowned on most weapons greater than small arms or armored cars. Artillery was brought to a campaign, used and then destroyed when the fighting was over.

Logistics.

He'd heard a lecture in Pine Bluff from a Guard general, who'd modified Napoleon's dictum that "any lieutenant can plan a campaign, but it takes an unusual sort of soldier to carry one out." This general's version was that any lieutenant could fight their troops, but it took professionals to train and supply them so they'd be ready for a fight. Valentine was inclined to agree; in his days with the Wolves it seemed his days were filled with acquisition and distribution of food, water, bullets, bandages, boots, hats, antiseptic, salt . . . If they were lucky, there was only a shortage of one or two items on this long list of requirements for men in the field.

New Columbia was a tribute to the complexities of logistics. Solon was shifting his base from Hot Springs to his new capital, and Xray-Tango's brush hair was going gray in the general's efforts to keep up with the needs of the troops concentrated to the north and scattered to already-conquered stations west and south. Southern Command's factories were so much scorched earth. What had been the Free Territory was in chaos, and the scattered settlements were being concentrated into collective farms; they'd not be contributing to the TMCC breadbags until fall, if then. Every other day flat-bottomed barges were pulling up to the wharf and offloading, and soon the southern rail line back into Texas would be running more up from Hot Springs.

Wait at the station
For the victory train
We'll run from the siding . . .

Whistling again, in syncopation with his footfalls, Valentine crossed the bridge.

The delivery of much of his Quickwood had gone off without a hitch; Mantilla's tug showed up where and when arranged. He told Mantilla to ask Southern Command to strike as soon as possible, explaining what he had in mind. Time was critical, and they had to move while Consul Solon was still arranging his formations for the closeout moves in his bid to pacify the Ozarks.

"I can put the word in the Lifeweaver's ear, but whether Southern Command'll listen . . ." Mantilla said, shrugging. The night made his eyesockets black wells, unfathomable.

"One more thing, please."

"How can I refuse anything to the Cat who would dare challenge such a lion in his own den? What is it, *mon frere*?"

"I won't ask, but if you have contacts further downriver, especially near Pine Bluff, tell them to be ready to hit hard when I move. Civilian and militia uprising."

"Such an order can only be given by Southern Command's General Staff."

"Then Southern Command's General Staff can take it up with me."

"If you live. It is a forlorn hope, my friend."

"You know my orders; you passed them on to Smoke. 'Raise a ruckus.' The more widespread it is, the better."

"You are exceeding your orders, I think."

Valentine looked at the lights strung on the bridge like holiday decorations. "I think so too. It's still the right thing to do."

"We've got our orders to pack up and join the rest of the division," Valentine said to his assembled officers the next night.

The meeting was held in his NCO bar and recreation room, formerly a basement gym in one of Little Rock's office buildings. The crowd of sergeants, lieutenants, Bears and company officers kept Narcisse busy at the coffee urn. Everyone was eating dinner off of trays around a Ping-Pong table. The green surface was thick with three colors of chalk.

Nail and Ahn-Kha were lounging in wooden chairs outside the club, charged with preventing any interruptions for three hours. Post, the other officer with detailed knowledge of Valentine's plan, at least since last night when he'd gone over it with his select circle, was keeping an eye on things along with Hanson, the gunnery sergeant Valentine had also brought into the plan in its formative stages. Hanson had given the operation its name: Double Boxcars. The crap pit slang described Hanson's estimation of the scheme's chances of coming off as planned, rolling two sixes with two dice. Twice in a row.

"But even if it's a cluster fuck, we'll cause a hell of a lot of damage."

Styachowski had spent hours with Valentine writing on the Ping-Pong table that afternoon. She'd taken to wearing baggy cargo shorts because of her cast, and she'd loosened her shirt to give her more freedom of movement as she reached across the table to draw, fighting an occasional sniffle. Valentine coundn't help but admire her splendid body, though it seemed that her gymnast's legs and swimmer's shoulders had sucked all the vitality from the rest of her: she was still as pale and bloodless as ever, even on the hearty, well-balanced meals issued by Xray-Tango's commissary.

Her constant questions as she wrote out orders helped sort his own ideas. The men would have to get rid of their TMCC uniform tops; the rules of war, such as they were, allowed ruses in enemy uniform as long as the uniforms were changed before taking hostile action. The men would dispose of their tunics. Narcisse was already dyeing their undershirts black. To further distinguish friend from foe in the dark Ahn-Kha had suggested bandoliers of red demolition tape. There were rolls of it lying around, used to mark off areas known to contain mines, unexploded munitions or construction blasting.

Each quadrant of the table had a sketch of a critical zone in the plan: the wharf and supply warehouses, the train line running through New Columbia, the prison camp, and the Kurian Tower.

The last was the result of a cryptic comment from Mantilla as they'd loaded the beams onto the foredeck of his aged barge, after his faked grounding had been ended. "Good luck, Colonel. Be sure you hit the tower. Go down. Not up. The rat's in the cellar. Here's a little gift from the Redhead. You'll need it soon, I think." He'd given Valentine a bag with two bottles of bourbon. It had a false bottom. When Valentine found the hidden zipper he came up with his pair of Cat "fighting claws," and a little box with five flash-bangs inside. They were about the size of yo-yos, and each had a lacquered picture from a matchbook on it. Valentine recognized the matchbooks; they were bars and restaurants he and Duvalier had dined in while posing as husband and wife in New Orleans. A note from Duvalier rolled up in the box read:

G -The Good captain kept these for me, for you.
Luck - s

A second, rolling, blackboard stood against the wall, where Valentine had drawn the rail line running north from New Columbia, adding times for the trip up to Third Division's position.

If there were an unexpected visit from Xray-Tango, Styachowski's Ping-Pong table would be covered with plastic and a tablecloth, then heaped with food. Hopefully the visiting general wouldn't notice the detailed drawing of the Consular Residence along the way, and Valentine could look like he was giving a simple briefing about their shift north to join the TMCC's lines south of the Boston Mountains.

There were the usual questions. Dumb ones from officers who'd already had their role explained to them, and just wanted to hear it repeated again. Smart ones about what to do if there were a disaster at another component of the plan. Styachowski answered all questions, never once needing an assist from Valentine. She'd absorbed the details of Boxcars like a sponge taking in water, but had chafed at not having a more active roll in the operation.

"If the train's SNAFU, go to the barge," Styachowski said in answer to a question about failure in one part of the operation. "If the barge is underwater, go to the train. If they're both impossible, we'll get what we can across on the ferry."

Then there were the inevitable what-ifs. Valentine finally called a halt to it.

"Things are going to go wrong. Improvise. This plan boils down to getting to Objective Omega with everything you can haul. Supplies. Medicine. Prisoners. The tubes. But getting the men there comes first. I'd rather have you alive on the hill than dead trying to haul another mortar up there."

"But there's bound to be fighting," a sergeant said.

"At the docks and warehouses it'll be supply sergeants and clipboard-holders. Everything else, save the Kurian Tower, are sentries and police. Other than the guards at the prison camp, they're not used to carrying weapons every day. You'll outnumber and outgun them. The nearest real troops are watching the river and the roads from Pulaski Heights. If they move, their orders will probably be to go secure the Kurian Tower. They can't hurt us with anything but their mortars, and I don't think they'll fire into the town. If they do, they'll just help us do our job."

"As we said at the beginning," Post added, "we're like bank robbers. Scare everyone shitless, grab the money and haul ass before the cops arrive. And that's all." The men chortled at that. "How you scare 'em, how much you take and how soon the cops show up are variables we can't know until we're in the middle of the robbery. So you're going to have to do some thinking."

"What about the security guards?" Lieutenant Zhao asked, extending the metaphor.

Valentine tapped the corner of the map showing the Kurian Tower. "You don't have to worry about that. It's my job. Even if we don't get him, we should be able to stop him from coming after you with the Hoods."

Styachowski's face went blank. She would assume command of the operation if something happened to Valentine's group. "Okay, our train up to the front is in two days. Those of you on the train detail, watch them send out the train north tomorrow morning. See where the guards are. They'll be expecting spectators; it's the first train to cross the bridge. Be sure to cheer your lungs out as it goes over."

The meeting dispersed, but one soldier waited outside with the patience of a plowhorse. Jefferson, the Texas teamster, smoked a cigarette wrapped up in the distinctive gray-green paper of a discarded New Universal Church *Guidance* propaganda sheet.

"You had something for me, sir?"

"Two things, Jefferson. First, these." Valentine handed him a half dozen of the boxes of cigars he'd acquired from Mantilla in a waterproof canvas pocket. Jefferson smelled the tobacco as though it were a bouquet of roses.

"Thank you, sir." The teamster couldn't keep his eyes from narrowing in suspicion, though.

"You're right, Jefferson, it's a last favor. You've gone above and beyond the past couple of months. You were just supposed to get the wagons safely to a Southern Command outpost, and ever since the ambush outside of Bern Woods you've been running with us. Time for you to go home. If you'd like to try, that is."

As Jefferson smiled, Valentine could see the spaces where the

Quislings had knocked out teeth. "I sure would. But I want to be here for this fight."

"Sorry. I'm giving you my horse, a TMCC map and a courier warrant clearing you to Hot Springs. One favor, though. I've got some papers I'd like you to drop off with Colonel Meadows at Bullfrog's Station. Can you find it again?"

"Easy enough, if I've got the right ID." Valentine liked the cheery confidence in his voice.

"You can leave whenever you like, but the sooner, the better."

Jefferson took a long drag on the homemade cigarette, muscles at the corners of his mouth working.

"Out with it, Jefferson."

"You got some good men here, sir. I hate to leave them if a fight's in the cards. Feels too much like running."

"It's not Texas' fight."

"There's a lot who think that way. I'm not one of them."

Valentine offered his hand. "Jefferson, get to Meadows and you'll have done more for what's coming than a whole company of riflemen. And when you get back to Texas . . . there's no way I can make this official, but any pressure that could be brought to bear on Oklahoma or Dallas . . . it'll help us if they start screaming to have their troops returned."

"I'm a Ranger teamster, not a general."

"Jefferson, I'll write up a promotion for you to lieutenant in Southern Command. That'll make you an official emissary, if you think that'll help."

"It might at that." Jefferson tried a salute on for size. "Thank you, sir."

Valentine touched his eyebrow in return. "Take good care of that horse. He'll get you there."

With the paperwork done, Jefferson rode out after the midday meal. Afternoon gave way to a warm evening; spring was truly on the way. Valentine and Ahn-Kha sat on mats on the floor of his tent, playing mahjong with the pieces Carrasca had painted for him.

"It's a good plan, my David. Stop chewing on it and swallow."

"I feel like I'm making a mistake. I'm basing this on Solon's reaction. Suppose he just cordons us off and lets us sit?"

"Maybe we'll catch him in his hole."

"He's off to Pine Bluff, trying to hurry up the rail gangs and get his precious airfield built. Don't know why, since there aren't any airplanes to bring in. Then it's down to Hot Springs to see how the relocation of TMCC headquarters is coming."

"He doesn't want to put too many eggs in any one state, I notice," Ahn-Kha said, removing a green dragon pair.

"I shoulda seen that coming," Valentine said.

"Colonel! Colonel!" someone shouted from outside.

Valentine stood in a smooth motion, as if he'd been pulled up by wires. He went to the tent flap.

"Yes, Yvaro?"

"There's been . . . Sergeant M'Daw, he's stabbed, on the edge of camp. I think he's dying."

The night turned cold and unfriendly. *What in God's name?* With Boxcars so close he'd been having M'Daw watched. Valentine still wondered if he wouldn't return to his old allegiance when the time was right.

"Ahn-Kha, tell Lieutenant Nail about this, and have him bring a stretcher. Let's treat him here. Okay, Yvaro, what happened?"

"He'd turned in for the night. I thought so, anyway. Then I hear a shout from the latrine. It was him, and I ran over and saw him. Someone stuck him in the back with one of those wooden spears the Smalls made."

"Your breath smells like coffee," Valentine said. "You got a cup to help you through the watch, I suppose."

"How—yes, sir, sorry sir."

"Just take me to M'Daw. We'll worry about it later."

Valentine ran to the NCO latrine and showers. The men still lived in tents, but Valentine saw to it they had huts for shower and privy. The corporal panted, trying to keep up with Valentine.

M'Daw was unconscious. He lay behind the showers. He'd pulled out the spear and lost a lot of blood. Soldiers were gathered around, and one had a bloody dressing held tight against M'Daw's lower back. Across the mounds of rubble, the lights of the other installations of New Columbia were alive. Valentine did a quick search from the top of a ruined wall, but whoever had stabbed him could easily get away without being seen among the smashed buildings.

Hank Smalls ran up one of the hills toward the camp, crying. Blood ran from his nose and drops covered the front of his shirt.

"Hank!" Valentine called.

"Captain!" Hank sobbed, sinking to his knees.

"Raintree," Valentine called over his shoulder to one of the medics. "Help me here. It's the boy."

Valentine went to his knees and hugged Hank. The boy was a sniveling mess.

"Sir, my folks are running. Decided to run and tell the others about y'all. I din't know about it. Mister M'Daw tried to stop him and Pa stuck him."

Good God. We're dead.

"Where's he gone?"

"They want to turn you in. Did I do right?"

Valentine couldn't tell a boy that turning in his parents was the right thing to do, no matter the circumstances. Even as his mind regained its equilibrium, he grew angry with himself for not just telling the Smalls the whole truth. They knew he was lying. They'd just misinterpreted his lies.

"If you thought it was right, it was right. This is important, Hank; do you know where they were headed?"

Hank rubbed his eyes and climbed a mound of concrete to get a better view. He held a reinforcing rod and pointed.

Please don't let it be the Kurian Tower, Valentine prayed.

"That building."

Valentine followed Hank's finger. He was pointing at Xray-Tango's headquarters.

"Raintree, get Hank and M'Daw to the first aid tent. Do what you can for both of them."

Valentine had learned to run and think in his years with the Wolves. He ran to his tent, grabbed his gunbelt, and stuck his fighting claws in the cargo pockets in his pants. He took up the flash-bangs and his bolo knife, putting the first in his pocket and the second on his belt. *What else, what else?* He grabbed a few pieces of wax-paper-wrapped gum from the little box of luxuries beside his bed.

As he pulled his tunic back on, Ahn-Kha, Post, Styachowski, Nail and assorted faces gathered outside his tent, all in various states of undress.

"What's going on, sir?" Post, a flare gun in his hand, asked as he emerged.

"We've set a new record for things going wrong in an operation. It's started to fail thirty-six hours before the jump-off hour. Our masquerade is over."

"Miracle it lasted as long as it did," Nail said.

"No miracle," Narcisse said, appearing from the darkness. "Magic of the right hand."

Valentine took the gun and a satchel of flares from Post. "We're going to start Boxcars in thirty minutes; you all are going to be occupied. First thing is to get everyone up and ready. Don't go yet. I've got to run down a renegade. I'm taking Ahn-Kha. If you see a red flare from Xray-Tango's headquarters, we're aborting; head west into the mountains and do your best. A green flare from the Kurian Tower means commence Boxcars. Just hit whatever you can as soon as you can. Nail, your team has farthest to go, get your team to Alpha and I'll catch up. I've got to go confuse the issue. Post, get the pikes and stabbing spears, and the spare guns; I hope we'll need them. Make sure Ahn-Kha's platoon gets to the ferry. Styachowski, set up operational HQ at Alpha. You're in charge. Remember, red, run; green, go."

"Make it a go, sir, I've been running for near a year now," Hanson said.

"You're the best hope of the Ozark Free Territory. Act like it." Valentine gave them all a salute. "Ahn-Kha, let's go. Good luck, everyone."

The Golden One slung Valentine's old PPD—Ahn-Kha had made a few hundred Mauser reloads for it by hand—and trotted into the darkness.

"By now Smalls has had time to tell his story," Valentine said as they ran together, Ahn-Kha moving at his Grog canter using both hands and feet. "Xray-Tango's been woken up. Will they come for me or call an alert?"

"They'll ask Smalls more questions."

"Hope I can get there before Xray-Tango makes any decisions."

Ahn-Kha slipped the red flare into the gun as they approached the old bank. "My David, let's just fire this. We can get away clean into the hills. Much better off than when we walked up to the Ruins. We'll still cause them trouble in the mountains."

"Old horse," Valentine said, sticking a piece of chewing gum in his mouth. "I want them mad as hornets. I want Solon so peeved that he won't rest until I'm hanging from a gallows. I don't want to just be a distraction; I want to be an obsession. Put a green flare in. I'll be out in a couple of minutes."

Valentine left Ahn-Kha well hidden with a view of the headquarters building. With the gum softened he pulled it out of his mouth, shaped it and stuck a piece in each ear. He trotted out to the street, and came up to the guards in front of the building.

"Did some civvies just run in here? Man and a woman?" he asked the corporal.

"Yes, Colonel Le Sain, they—"

"Thank God. They don't come out the door, and if you see them climb out the windows, you shoot."

"Uhhh—"

"Surround the headquarters with your men. Right now, Corporal. I don't want them getting away with this."

Valentine ran up the stairs and into the light of the headquarters. One of Xray-Tango's staff had a field phone to his ear. He tapped the lieutenant on the shoulder.

"Yes, a security detail. Something's—" the man began, and then turned, recognizing him. "Just a moment," he said to the phone.

"There's been a murder in my camp. A sergeant is dead. I need to find General Xray-Tango."

"Downstairs, Colonel. Ummm . . . a man and a woman came in . . . it's rather confused, sir. You're to be taken for questioning."

"I've got some angry answers. Where are the Smalls?"

"Downstairs, with . . . Wait, sir, you can't go down there with your weapons."

Valentine took off his pistol belt and hung it on the chair in front of the lieutenant. "Easily done. Send the security detail downstairs, too, there's someone I want arrested."

He didn't wait for any more protests. He descended the stairs and listened for voices in the quiet of the basement offices. Even through gum-clogged ears he could hear questions and crying coming from a room down the hall, in a different direction from the one where he had his conversation with Mu-Kur-Ri's avatar. A military policeman stood outside the door.

"That was quick work," he said, looking behind Valentine expectantly.

Valentine advanced on him. "Sorry, Corporal, I beat the detail here. Where's that renegade, Smalls? I want you to put him under arrest for murder."

"He's being questioned now. Wait, sir, you can't—"

"You're under arrest," Valentine said. "Insubordination, for a start." The corporal shrank back as if Valentine had waved a hot poker at him.

The Smalls were already under what might be called intensive questioning. They sat in chairs, side by side, in a darkened room with a bright light shining on them from a desk set in the center of the room. Their questioners stood with backs to Valentine. He could see blood on Mrs. Smalls' hands and frock, the fear in Mr. Smalls' eyes at events spinning out of control.

An MP, three officers, Xray-Tango and the Smalls. Seven.

"Now it's not just Le Sain, it's the whole battalion? Seven hundred men?"

"Horseshit!" Valentine roared, unscrewing the bottom of his flash-bang. The trigger button popped out. *Armed.* "You left something behind, Smalls. Take a look, everyone."

"Le Sain, what—" Xray-Tango began, but Valentine shouldered his way through the questioners, pushing the general up against a wall, and slammed the flash-bang down on the table—triggering the button on the bottom. *Three seconds.*

The top was hand-painted with a vintage nude. Marilyn Monroe knelt against a red satin background, her arms behind her head, back arched, milky breasts lifted, a go-for-broke smile on her face.

He swung toward Xray-Tango, turning his back on Marilyn. He shut his eyes and shoved his hands in his pockets. "General, I'd like—" he said, and clapped his hands over Xray-Tango's ears.

Crack!

It wasn't a concussive explosion—more like someone loosing both barrels of a twelve-gauge—though even outdoors it left unprotected ears ringing. In the confines of the underground room the noise hit like a hammer blow. Even worse was the flash. Through his screwed-shut eyes Valentine still saw orange. Valentine popped Xray-Tango between the eyes with a strong jab. As the general's head *thunked* against the wall like a tossed coconut he followed through with a body blow to the solar plexus. Xray-Tango let loose with an asthmatic gasp and folded. Valentine slipped on his fighting claws.

He waded into the stunned Quislings. They were staggering around in ululating confusion, a six-player game of blind-man's bluff held under the influence of bad LSD. The confusion turned to screaming when Valentine opened the first throat with his claws. The questioning officer had caught himself in a corner. Valentine dug his claws into each side of the man's neck and pulled. The blood of opened arteries went everywhere. He raked another across the kidneys. The man went spinning in shrieking pain into Smalls, knocking both to the floor. Mrs. Smalls could still see; she turned her face from her husband to see Valentine advancing on her.

"You—not—no," she cried, more or less able to see what was coming.

He caught her with an elbow in the temple, and she sagged. He stabbed her husband in the Adam's apple, driving the extra-long straight middle claw into his voice-box. Maybe the Reaper would be in a forgiving mood, and delay killing him until he could tell the story in a few weeks.

But he doubted it.

It was awful, and it took too long.

Valentine looked around the abattoir. The knocked-over desk lamp illuminated walls splattered with blood, a floor painted in black and red depending on the fall of the light. The man with the slashed kidneys still twitched, in too much pain to rise again.

"General," Valentine said, lifting Xray-Tango to his feet. "General!"

"Spots. Alls I seeze spots," he said, drunkenly.

Valentine shook him in frustration.

"Scottie! Scottie!" he barked.

"Huh? Le Sain, what the hell—" The general's face fell into limp horror as he picked out a few details of the room with his damaged retinas.

"Everything the Smalls said is true. I'm a soldier with Southern Command. It's a rising, all over the TM," Valentine said, exaggerating the last a little. "I want you to join us. Fight the Reapers, instead of feeding them."

"God, the blood—"

"What'll it be, General? Fight or feed?"

"Ouch, you're hurting me, dammit."

Valentine felt a Reaper coming. Coming in anger, coming in fury, coming in haste.

"No time, General."

"Good God, they're all dead."

Coming fast.

"With me, General. You back me up, or I'll kill you. Give me that!"

Valentine gripped the pistol being taken from the general's holster. It turned into a wrestling match—which he had no time for. He raked his claws across the generals fore-arm, opening skin. The pistol came free. Valentine kicked it away, slipping off his claws.

He retrieved the gun, a standard KZ officer's revolver, rugged and reliable. He pulled back the hammer; the click sounded muted to his recovering ears.

"Out the door. I want you in front of me if anyone's shooting."

He heard banging somewhere below. In the direction of the Reaper. *Locked in an underground chamber? "In case of emergency, wake the vampire"?*

Xray-Tango poked his head into the hallway. Neither bullet nor Reaper claw removed it.

"It's clear. Don't get nervous, that thing triggers easy."

"Hurry, there's a Reaper coming."

"Jesus."

"The stairs. The gun stays pointed up as long as you keep quiet."

Valentine took a good two-handed grip on the gun. He heard a door give way and shoved the general with his shoulder. "It's coming. Upstairs! Upstairs!"

He pushed the general to the stairs and through the crash door at the bottom. As he slammed it behind them, he saw a shadow fly across the hallway and into the interrogation room. Mr. Smalls squealed—for the last time. Valentine shut the pathetically tiny bolt on the door.

"A bodyguard went nuts! Fuckin' tore everyone apart," Valentine shouted upstairs, pushing the general up in front of him. "That Hood's berserk."

An MP and another Quisling soldier stood at the top of the stairs, both pointing guns down at them.

"General?" Valentine asked, putting Xray-Tango between him and the rifles, just in case.

"Put up those guns, damn it. Run, run for it, boys. Or we're all dead!" Xray-Tango shouted, which was probably true enough.

Thank God!

Valentine got the general to the top of the stairs as the MP ran. Valentine heard another door downstairs torn off its hinges. He heard the scream of some other unfortunate pulled from a hiding spot. Probably the MP. That was enough for the TMCC grunt at the stairs. He put up his rifle and ran for the door, with a convincing "Get out of here!"

His example was one to be followed. The other officers and men made for the exits. One threw a chair out the window, and was about to follow it when a bullet whizzed by. One of the sentries outside, hearing shouts and confusion within, had shot in panic.

"What the—?" the private said.

"Try the door," Valentine suggested, grabbing his pistol belt and heading for the second story. "C'mon, General, let's call for help," he said, waving the pistol to point upstairs. Valentine smashed a red case on the wall and extracted the fire ax from within.

Either he was moving fast or the general was slow; it seemed an eternity until they came through the door to the radio room on the second floor. The rest of the floor was a cavern of future construction. Two operators stood next to the radios, both armed and pointing their weapons at Valentine and Xray-Tango. A trio of message tubes stood up from the floor like unfinished plumbing fixtures.

"Fuck! FUCK! Hold it right there, mister," the radioman with sergeant's stripes said, eyes bulging at the sight of the blood on Valentine.

"Holy shit," the other added, shaking like he had a jackhammer in his hand instead of a revolver.

"Watch those weapons there, soldiers," Xray-Tango said.

"I'm the only one who made it out," Valentine said. "If I were you two, I'd get gone. It's a bodyguard. It's going nuts."

"Jesus, that happened to my cousin in Armarillo," the shaking one said. "Like it got ravies. It killed thirty people before they stopped it."

"If you've got a way out of here that doesn't involve the stairs, I'd use it," Valentine said. "We'll call for help."

"It's my responsibility," Xray-Tango said, his eye twitching madly and the words barely getting out. "Run along, boys."

The men heard a crash below and decided they knew a sensible order when they heard it. They scrambled out the window and dropped to the ground below.

Valentine offered Xray-Tango the ax handle. "You want the honors?"

"Sorry, Le Sain, or whoever you are. I was true to you, best as I could be. You weren't straight with me."

"Could I have been?"

"That's a 'what-if.' I don't like to waste time with 'what-ifs.' I'm no renegade. I can't let you smash the radio. The only other unit strong enough to send for help is at the quartermaster office at MacArthur Park, down by the warehouses, and if you smash that one too, no one will get here in time. Assuming you cut the field-phone lines north on the bridge, and south on the poles, that is."

Valentine shared a smile with his former superior.

There was a scream from downstairs.

"Sorry, General," Valentine said. He swung the ax handle, connecting solidly with Xray-Tango's temple. He reversed the grip and, with three precise blows, left the radio in pieces.

Valentine hid behind rolls of weatherproofing, ax across his lap, lowering his lifesign. He pulled inward, concentrating on a point six inches in front of his nose, taking it *down, down, down . . .*

He became a prowling cat, a hiding mouse, a buzzing fly. A pair of ragged claws scuttling across the floors of silent seas. The Reaper came up and took in the ruins of the radio room. It hissed and picked up the general like a distracted parent lifting a child's dropped doll.

"general! general! wake! wake and tell what has passed."

Xray-Tango gave a moan as the creature shook him.

Valentine couldn't let the Reaper go to the window, see the men streaming out of his camp. He couldn't risk a single footstep behind him. It would mean a leap. He gathered himself, and readied the ax.

Even with its attention on Xray-Tango, it felt him coming. It was full night, when a Reaper's senses and reflexes become unholy. Valentine still buried the blade of the ax in its side, missing the great nerve trunks running up its spine. It dropped Xray-Tango.

"Melted butter," Xray-Tango murmured. At least that's what it sounded like to Valentine.

"*you!*" the Reaper spat.

Valentine fired Xray-Tango's gun into it, but he might as well have been throwing spitballs. It sprang.

He ducked, so fast that the air whistled as he cut through it. The Reaper sailed head-first into the framework of a wall, crashing through two-by-fours into the next room. Valentine ran, throwing himself out the window like a swimmer off the block. He jackknifed in midair, landing lightly, but his bad leg betrayed him and he sprawled into the dirt.

It flew out the window after him, ax-pinioned cape flapping like some hideous bat as it descended in a long parabola to the ground. It landed between him and the Ruins.

They faced each other. Valentine drew his .45.

"C'mon, you bastard," Valentine said, sighting on its yellow eyes.

It turned, looking over its shoulder. Valentine saw a hint of movement among the ruins and flung himself sideways.

A blast from the PPD illuminated Ahn-Kha's gargoyle features; the gun's rattle was music to his ears. The bullets caught the Reaper as it spun, knocking it to the ground. It tried to rise, but Ahn-Kha flattened it with another burst as the Grog took a step forward. Valentine rose, hand on the hilt of General Hamm's knife. Ahn-Kha stood, ten feet away from the crawling monstrosity, drum-magazined gun to his shoulder. He loosed another long burst, emptying the weapon. He lowered it, smoke pouring from the barrel filling the air with the peppery smell of cordite.

But the Reaper still lived. Valentine came up with the knife, pressed its head to the ground with his foot, and swung for all he was worth. The blade went in deep, severing its spine. The Reaper's limbs gave one jumping-frog spasm and went limp. Valentine pulled the blade out before the black tar clogging the wound could glue it in place like the ax head in its side.

Valentine kicked over the body as Ahn-Kha put a new drum on the gun. The Reaper's eyes were still alive with malice.

"Mu-Kur-Ri," Valentine said into the still-functioning eyes, for the Reaper's head still lived and could still pass on what it sensed to the Master Kurian at the other end. "The *Dau'weem* sent me to kill you. My name is David Valentine. I come for you now."

The Reaper tried to say something but Valentine swung again. The blade bit deep; the head separated. He picked it up by the wispy hair and sent it flying off into the darkness. He pitied the rat that might taste the flesh.

"Neither of us remembered to bring a spear," Valentine said. "We're a pair of idiots."

Valentine's eyes picked up a Quisling soldier or two, watching them from hiding spots. "The headquarters is clear," Valentine shouted at one. "The general's hurt. Call the medics. There might still be someone alive in the basement." He clapped his hands. "Hustle, hustle!"

The soldier scampered off.

"Let's go," he said to Ahn-Kha.

They trotted into the Ruins and circled around to the road paralleling the communications lines. Valentine surveyed the line of wires until he found the utility pole he wanted.

"Those are the field-phone lines south. Gimme that sling. I'll cut these; you'll need to do the ones at the railroad bridge. Flare gun, please."

"I can guess which one you want in it," Ahn-Kha said, slipping the flare inside and handing it to him. "I agree. It will be glorious, even if it fails."

Valentine attached the PPD strap to his waist after wrapping it around the pole. Using his claws, he shimmied up the pole easily enough. There was a crossbar for him to sit on at the top. There, four communications lines and one power line shared space on the pole. Careful to avoid the last, he took out General Hamm's light infantry machete and shoved the first phone line into the notch. He used the utility crossbeam as a leaver. *Twang*—it parted with a push. Valentine looked again at the knife, smiling wryly.

"Nice work, Hamm."

The other lines were easily severed. Ahn-Kha watched the road, ears twitching.

Valentine looked around at New Columbia from his pole-top perch. Here and there he picked out his companies, the red tape hung across their bodies muted in the dark but identifiable, moving silently toward their objectives. They'd been told to say their orders were to reinforce the guards at the vital spots: warehouses, dock, bridge, rail yard, prison camp. With all the confusion in the night, Valentine felt they would have a good chance of being believed. Searchlights were lit at the Kurian Tower, probing the darkness around the Tower as guards deployed to hardpoints and Mu-Kur-Ri braced for his coming. At the prison camp, a hand-cranked siren wailed as the guards turned out. He saw truck head-lights descending the winding road from Pulaski Heights. The Kurian had already sent for help.

Valentine cocked the flare gun. He looked down at Ahn-Kha. The Grog knew enough human gestures to give him a thumbs-up. He fired the pistol; the flare shot into the air with a sound like a cat spitting. The parachute opened and the signal drifted, a bright green star slowly descending, pushed by a wind from the southwest.

It sparked and sputtered across the sky on March 21, 2071, at 23:28—Captain Moira Styachowski made a note of the flare's time in her order journal. Valentine's Rising had begun.

Nine

New Columbia, March of the forty-eighth year of the Kurian Order: Risings. Widespread revolts in the Kurian Zone are rare, successful ones are exponentially rarer. While a number of the Freeholds of 2071 can trace their origins to uprisings against the New Order in the first decade of Kurian rule, since that turbulent period examples of large-scale rebellion hardly exist. The few exceptions succeeded only in cases of geographical isolation i.e. the Juneau Insurrection along the islands and coastline of southeastern Alaska and the more recent Jamaican revolt, or small populations on the fringes of the Freeholds who manage to hold out long enough for help to arrive: Quebec City, the Laramie Mountains, Las Cruces. Stacked against those few successes are the legendary slaughters at Charleston and the Carolina Coast, the Dallas Corridor, Cleveland, and Point Defiance between Mobile and Biloxi. Ten times that number as bloody, but not as famous because of the lack of surviving chronicles, could easily be named. Then there are hundreds, if not thousands, of small actions, where individual groups of desperate sufferers on a city block or two, at a collective farm, or within a factory managed to wrestle the weapons out of their keepers' hands and go down fighting. Sadly, we know virtually none of these stories beyond a faded scribble of names on a wall or a brief radio transmission like a cry for help in a ghetto night.

Whether it's two men with pistols or twenty thousand with a city, the Kurians are masters of suppressing risings. Even if one Kurian principality falls, the six surrounding immediately invade, with the twin goals of preventing the revolutionary virus from spreading and claiming new feeding grounds for members of their own hierarchy. Quisling soldiers know there are brass rings and ten-year exemptions to be won in putting down revolts; their vengeance is all the more brutal when they see their comrades strung up or lying in piles against execution walls. The Reapers return in an orgy of feeding. The aftermath is shown through slide shows at New Universal Church lectures and becomes the subject of homilies about the futility and madness of violence.

But while the flame of revolt burns, it burns brightly, fed by the liberated energy of the human spirit. Now it takes the form of a green flare falling slowly toward the center of Little Rock.

By the time Valentine got to the bottom of the pole the flare had returned to earth. Its green glow pulsed from behind a pile of debris-flattened automobiles stacked like rusty pancakes.

"This is it, old horse. I'll see you on the other side."

"My platoon has a good sergeant. Let me come with you."

"I'll be able to do this a lot better if I know you're waiting at the station. Otherwise I'll spend the next two hours worrying about what's happening on that hill. Get out of here."

"Until we meet again, my David . . . in this world or the next." They clasped each other's forearms in the Grog handshake.

"*Arou ng'nan*," Valentine said. Every language has a form of "good luck," though the Grog form was a little more prosaic, hoping that spirit-fathers would intercede on one's side.

They trotted off in opposite directions. Valentine stayed clear of the road, tracing the route out to the edge of the Kurian Tower that he had walked while forming his plans. The foundation of the tower and the construction grounds around it were floodlit, and searchlights from strongpoints atop the first story probed the night.

Nail and five of his six Bears were crouching in the cover of a filled-in cellar. Valentine looked at the faces above the guns pointed at him. The Bears' Quisling uniforms lay in a pile that smelled of kerosene. The Bears didn't need black T-shirts or red sashes. They were in their battle gear, the savage-looking Bear mélange of Reaper cloth, leather, combat vests, fur and Kevlar. Rain cradled a combat shotgun in chain-mail-backed leather gloves. Another Bear Valentine knew vaguely as Hack wore a massive girdle with Reaper teeth fitted into the leather. He held a machine pistol in one hand and one of Ahn-Kha's Quickwood spears in the other, its end decorated with eagle feathers like a Comanche war lance. Red, whose freckled face narrowed and ended in a jaw so sharp it looked like it could split logs, had Reaper scalps—at least Valentine hoped they were Reaper scalps—at his shoulder blades and elbows. More strings of black hair hung from the belt-fed machine gun so tied to his combat harness that it looked like part of him. Lost&Found had a shining cross over his heart and Brass, almost as wide as he was high, had painted his face so it resembled a skull. A red-eyed plastic snake head had been slipped over the mouth of his grenade launcher, and he'd wrapped the butt and grips with snakeskin and painted "The Fire Dragon" on the side of the support weapon.

"Where's Groschen?"

"He's got the Grog gun, forward. We like to have a good sniper ready when we go in."

"Signal him to pull back. I'm aborting this."

Nail exchanged looks with another Bear. "But the green flare—"

"We're still throwing the dice for Boxcars. We aren't going to hit the tower. I got an opportunity to throw a scare into Mu-Kur-Ri. He's protecting his precious aura with everything he's got. Going in there with some kind of surprise is one thing. Breaking down that door into the teeth of six or seven Reapers, and troops besides—I won't do it. In five more minutes there'll be troops from Pulaski Heights here. We'd have as much trouble getting out as going in."

"You're the boss," Nail said. He looked up and out of the basement and made a buzzing sound. "Damn, we're almost in spitting distance of that bas—Groschen's pulling back, he'll be here in two minutes."

"Very good, Lieutenant."

"Sir, you look like hell."

"I feel like it, Nail."

The men got to their feet, slinging their weapons. One gathered up the kerosene-soaked clothes.

"Why are you bringing those?" Valentine asked.

"A little ceremony," Nail said. "We'll save it for another day."

Groschen, now clean-shaven, returned to the basement, the long Grog gun over his shoulders. "The tower's off. Hope you aren't bleeding yet," Nail explained.

"No, suh."

"You may still get to do it tonight. They sounded the alarm over at the prison yard."

Valentine checked their line of retreat and led them out of the basement. When they were clear of the tower's sight-lines, Valentine gathered the Bears.

"Keep back about thirty feet. I like to be able to listen."

They cut through the Ruins, zigzagging around the graveyard of a civilization. They struck another field-phone line, strung on four-foot posts, and cut it. As they neared the road to the prison camp Valentine heard a mass of men moving away from the prison yard. Had they stormed it bloodlessly?

Lieutenant Zhao led his men up the road, away from the camp, in files at each side of the road. The men looked spooked. Valentine thought it best to call out from cover.

"Lieutenant Zhao. It's Valentine."

Zhao waved his right hand like he was wiping a table. The men crouched from the front of the lines and rolling backward, like rows of dominoes tumbling.

"Valentine who?" Zhao said. His hair was unkempt, his face was pitted from acne and he wore filthy glasses, but the only thing lacking in him as an officer was experience. Valentine had learned he was smart, hardworking and organized, which had led him to give him a company. But he'd evidently lost his head.

"Captain Valentine. Careful with the guns, men," Valentine said, stepping out from the rubble.

"Sir, did the Kurian go down?"

"I called it off. What happened at the camp?"

"The guard-tower had a machine gun for covering the yard," Zhao explained. "They slung it around and started shooting. Maybe they have night vision gear. We didn't go any farther. There's no cover for a hundred yards around the wire. I didn't want to risk those kind of casualties."

"Lieutenant, there's five hundred men in there, maybe more. Five hundred of our men, POWs. I want them back."

"I . . . I . . . I was using my judgment," Zhao said.

"I won't question it. Let's go have another look."

"We're going back?" a private said.

"If you were behind that wire, what would you want us to do?" Valentine said, looking at the objector. "Let's turn around, men. Who's in charge of your rear guard, Zhao?"

"Sergeant, umm . . . Franks is in charge of the tail of the column."

"I didn't say tail of the column. I said 'rearguard.' "

Zhao looked at his feet, miserable.

"Let's turn it around, Lieutenant. I'll scout ahead with the Bears."

"Thank you, sir."

Valentine and the Bears doubled the column.

"Christ, I hate all these little generators," Nail said. The lights of the prison yard glowed beyond the tumble of shattered buildings.

"Do you?"

"Of course."

"Be glad for them. I think Groschen is going to get his chance with that gun."

Time enough? Time enough? Valentine wondered.

Valentine had seen Kurian concentration camps by the dozens. This had to be one of the shabbiest he'd ever seen. The camp was wired into sections of thirds, one-third for women, the center third for guards and the most crowded part for the male prisoners. A single tower stood over the central common yard—judging from the road ruts, trucks came to pick up and drop off prisoners. The fence, just a series of stout poles to hold concertina wire was not even double layered, or electrified, or topped with razor wire. At each corner of the camp, outside the wire, was a sandbagged guard post. Prisoner and guard alike lived under prefabricated roofs; the walls were nothing more than pieces of tent and tarp, though the guards' tents in the center had openings that served as windows. Valentine's nose picked up the smell of corn flour baking in the only complete structure in the place—a Quonset hut set in the guards' section.

The guards' section was a frenzy of activity. The guards were piling up boxes and sandbags at either end of their Quonset; nervous men peered out from under their helmets, rifles ready. Zhao had thrown enough of a scare into them that they had abandoned the outer guard posts, but four men still remained in the tower. The machine gun that so frightened Zhao was positioned to cover the road.

"What do you think?" Valentine asked Nail, after having Zhao take his men and spread them out to the front of the camp. He watched another Bear, the quasi-giant Rain who'd bearded Martinez, heat the blade of his knife with an old liquid lighter, careful to keep well out of sight of the camp. Not that the men would have much night vision outside the brightly lit camp.

"Piss-poor layout, even for a temporary camp. Why do they still have all the lights on? It's like they want us to pick 'em off."

"Look at that," Rain said. "The poor bastards in there aren't waiting for us."

A trio of men were working at the concertina wire behind their tent in the tower's blind spot. Someone among the prisoners had been waiting for this moment; two men were working at widening the hole with pieces of wood as the first crawled through, cutting.

Valentine spoke: "Saves us the trouble. Nail, go back and tell Lieutenant Zhao to spread for skirmishing. Meet up with us there, at those concrete pilings that look like tree trunks. See them?"

"Sure, sir."

"Zhao should just demonstrate. It's not a real attack. I want them to shoot at the tower, once we start. If they kill them all the better. I just don't want that gun aimed at us. Oh, be sure to call out before you come up on them. They're nervous."

"Yes, sir," Nail said, disappearing into the darkness.

"Groschen, Rain, let's work our way around to the north side of the camp. Try and find something we can throw down on that wire."

By the time Nail caught up with them in a skeleton of reinforced concrete, the Bears had found an old metal fire door and pried it off its rusted hinges. It was a heavy, awkward burden, but Rain managed to get it up on his back.

"They're almost through the wire. What the hell are you doing?"

Nail looked up from the pile of TMCC uniforms he was lighting. "We're going Red, sir. It's a ritual. Haven't you ever seen Bears go into action before?"

"Not up close. The tower might see some of the light from that fire."

"Let 'em. Nothing makes the Quislings shit like Bearfire."

Valentine tried to keep his attention on the camp, but the little circle of Hunters going through their ritual distracted him. It was something out of another time and place, when men in animal skins nerved themselves for action through tribal custom.

They stared into the fire for a few minutes, sitting cross-legged and silently contemplating the blue-bottomed flames. First Nail began to sway; in a moment the others joined in, until they were moving in synch like seven metronomes, first right, then left, then right, all the while staring into the fire. When they were all moving in unison, exchanging grunts that meant nothing to Valentine, Nail rose onto his haunches and the others followed suit. Rain took out the knife he had sterilized, raised his Reaper-robe sleeve, and revealed a long line of little brown scars, hash marks running up to his triceps. He reached up with the blade and added another cut, parallel to all the others. He passed the blade to the next man, then sprinkled gunpowder out of a shell casing into the wound.

The knife traveled the circle, the men holding it out across to each other over the flames, until Valentine's own arm began to hurt in sympathy. The blade traveled from Rain, the one with the most scars, to Nail, and then to the others, each solemnly dusting the wound with the powder from their own shell casings. Valentine found himself wondering about hepatitis rates among the Bears.

When it was done Nail rose, a little drunkenly, and came up to Valentine.

"We're ready. They through the wire?" he said. Nail was enunciating a little thickly.

"Yes, men are starting to slip out. Someone's keeping them together at the edge of camp, though. Let's go meet them."

The Bears took up their assortment of weapons and the steel door. They ran, hunched over, up to the gathering point of the escapees.

"Someone's—" a tattered lookout said, before a Bear came from the shadows to clamp a hand over his mouth.

"Easy, men," Valentine said, holding out a hand as a couple of the prisoners took up rocks. "There's a Bear team here. Nice work on the wire. If you don't mind, we'd like to use it to get in. Who's in command, here?"

"I am. You've got a familiar voice, Bea—is that you, Valentine?" said Captain Beck, former commander of Foxtrot Company, and the officer who had Valentine drummed out of the Wolves.

"How's the arm, Captain?" was all Valentine could think to say. Beck had his right arm tucked into his shirt, Napoleon-style.

"Nerve damage. You back from Minnesota? What the hell's going on?"

"Long story, Captain. Gather the men here—"

"The women—"

"Please don't interrupt me, Captain. The team's going in for the women."

"Thank God for that. You wouldn't have a spare rifle or two, Lieutenant?"

Valentine didn't bother to correct him. "Nail?"

"We're light enough as is," Nail said. "Let us at those guards, we'll get you some guns, sir."

Beck nodded. "I like the sound of that. I'll take you into the men."

Valentine led the Bears through the wire, past an astonished line of men waiting their turn. "Keep it moving, men. There's going to be shooting, the more of you outside the wire the better."

"Gimme one o' them auto pistols an' I'll give—" one began.

"You'll get your chance soon enough, Corporal," Valentine said, looking at what was left of his uniform. "Move along, men."

They passed into a tent. The stench of the dark tent was palpable, a warm, cloying shroud enveloping them. The men didn't even have cots to lie on, there was just bedding on mats on the ground and some hammocks. "This and the barrack next to it are the only ones they can't see too well from the guards' hut." Beck said. "We were going to open some more holes in the wire from the outside so the others could get out."

The men gaped at the Bears.

"Do you have a signal system between the tents?"

"Yeah, we whistle," Beck said.

"Whistle them to keep their heads down, Captain, if you please."

"Johnson, do the 'watch out' tune. Alert for all barracks," Beck said. A rag-and-bone private let loose with three hacking coughs that could be heard a mile away and began a querulous whistling.

"Nail?" Valentine asked, looking through the tent flap. "What do you think?"

The guards were still piling sandbags around each end of the Quonset hut. Valentine could see a machine gun at the pile opposite the main gate, covering the back of the camp. *Too late, guys, we're already in.* The other Bears, at a signal from Nail, were opening window-sized gaps in the tenting.

"It's up to you, Lieutenant," Valentine said to Nail.

"They're worried about the prisoners storming the wire," Nail said. "We'll go in through the middle. Two grenades to each end of the hut. Hack, try and get yours behind the sandbags this time."

"Five seconds," Nail said, nodding to Valentine. The Bears pulled the pins on their grenades. He squatted, and motioned for Beck to get down. The men left in the tent fell to the floor. Two Bears threw, the others held the tent flaps open. Everyone covered their ears.

The cry of, "Grenade!" never came; the prison guards must have been some combination of inattentive and poorly trained. Just four explosions, less than a second apart.

"Blitz! Blitz! Blitz!" Nail shouted, tearing open the tent.

The Bears charged the wire. Rain went first. He threw himself at the wire like a breaching dolphin and crashed down on the concertina. He pivoted, holding the wire apart with gloved hand and boot as the other Bears stampeded over him. Valentine brought up the rear, pistol ready, but only smoke and pained cries came from behind the piled footlockers and sandbags. A severed arm had been flung into the wire—its fingers still moved. Groshen threw himself down in the space between the Quonset hut and the wire, his unwieldy Grog gun on a bipod and pointed at the tower. Hack covered the other end of the building. "Mother-fucker!" Lost&Found shouted. He made a tight fist and drove his leather-gloved hand through the aluminum in the side of the hut. Brass stuck the Dragon's snake-head muzzle through as soon as Lost&Found pulled his bleeding hand out and the grenade launcher hissed as he swiveled the muzzle: *fsssssh fsssssh fsssssh.*

Groschen saw a shot and took it, but Valentine ignored the .50 caliber report and its effect.

The grenades roared within the hut, blowing ventilators off the arced roof. Rain got to his feet and grabbed the aluminum in his chain-mail gloves. He planted a foot against the wall. Muscles on his back strained and he peeled open the aluminum side of the hut.

Valentine heard scattered gunfire; Zhao's company was shooting at the tower. He upbraided himself for not giving strict orders to only shoot the tower. The soldiers might start firing at his Bears in the confusion.

Rain extracted himself from the wire and pulled his knife and hooked ax. He plunged into the smoke boiling out of his improvised door. The other Bears followed drawing blades, hatchets and, in Brass' case, a folding shovel.

Nail followed his men in, machine pistol held tight against his shoulder.

Groschen shot again. "That'll teach you to peek," he muttered as he chambered another round.

Valentine heard screams from within the Quonset hut. A Quisling, blood running from his eyes and ears, stumbled blindly out the back door. He hit the sandbags and went over head-down-feet-up like a teeter-totter changing balance. Hack put a single shot into his armpit.

"We surrender. Surrender," a voice from the tower yelled faintly across the yard.

A pained scream bounced off the corrugated walls of the hut. He noticed Captain Beck at his side. "Helluva Bear team you have, Valentine."

Valentine had no time for him. "Throw your guns outta there," he shouted at the tower, his voice dry and hoarse in the smoke and cold night air.

The machine gun and some rifles flew out of the tower. One discharged as it hit the ground.

"Stop shooting, we surrender," the invisible Quisling shouted.

"Idiots," Groschen said. He picked up his Grog gun, holding it with the aid of a sling. "Let's go get them."

Valentine looked to Beck. "Wait here, Captain," he said. He shuffled crabwise to the sandbags covering the front of the hut. He followed his gun muzzle over the side. Two bodies and a third guard, whimpering out his confusion, lay there. The man must have been in shock, otherwise he'd be screaming, judging from the absence of his foot.

The man's pain still triggered instincts not wholly lost.

"Groschen, help this man."

"Sure thing, sir." Groshen drew a palm-sized automatic from his vest and shot the man through the ear. It was carried out with the same smooth, careless motion that he might use to toss away a gum wrapper.

"That's not what I meant," Valentine sputtered.

"Sorry, sir, but it's just a Kurpee."

Who are you to judge? Valentine had killed helpless men in anger, in desperation, in fear. He'd machine-gunned helpless sailors and murdered men in their sleep—and been giddy and sickened by the act. Maybe Groschen was better than Valentine after all; he didn't look like he'd enjoyed it.

"Coming out, Gross," Brass said from the doowary.

"Come ahead."

Brass came out, splattered with blood. "Even dozen. Rain's taking the heads now."

"You two, get the prisoners out of the tower. I'm going to see about getting the women out."

Groschen and Brass walked toward the tower, Groschen keeping his gun pointed up, holding it from the hip like a Haitian erotic fetish Valentine had seen in the Caribbean. He took one more look at the executed Quisling—he'd seen the man's face before, standing watch over prisoner labor. Whatever thoughts, ideas, dreams, or regrets had lived within that bloody head were forever lost.

Bullets flew. Shots from outside the camp made Brass and Groschen throw themselves to the ground. Valentine vaulted over the sandbag wall and landed on one of the splayed bodies.

"What the hell?" Nail said from the doorway.

"It's Zhao's company," Valentine said. "They're shooting at us."

"Fuck!" Lost&Found swore. For a man with "Born Again to Kill" written on his helmet, he had a distinctly un-Christian way of expressing himself. Brass and Groschen both hollered "Cease fire" as best as they could with their faces planted in the common yard's dirt.

"Doesn't that hurt?" Valentine asked, looking at Lost&Found's swollen hand.

"It will tomorrow. Don't worry, sir. She'll heal up."

Valentine caught motion out of the corner of his eye; a figure ran out to the gate of the camp.

"What's that idiot doing?" Nail said.

Valentine peeped over the edge of the sandbags. Beck stood in the open, waving a white rag with his remaining active arm. "Hold your fire!"

"My former captain," Valentine said. "Never short of guts."

There was another shot from the darkness. Beck didn't even flinch. He kept shouting and signaling.

"Boy's wiring is definitely not grounded," Nail observed.

Fifteen minutes later some order had been restored to the camp, now darkened by the destruction of the generator. Zhao's men were in a screen around it, their guns pointed in a less dangerous direction while Valentine organized his prisoners. Some blocks away a building burned; Valentine guessed it to by Xray-Tango's headquarters.

A quick headcount gave him five hundred twenty-seven men and sixty women. All were in this particular camp because they had been captured in Southern Command uniforms. Beck explained the half-assembled nature of their accommodations in a few terse sentences.

"The expected us to just be here a couple days. Then they found work for us, the flood started—a few days turned into weeks. Men were scheduled to ship to Texas, women to Memphis, by rail or water, whichever opened up first."

"Solon owes his neighbors for the loan of troops," Valentine said.

"Yes. We're the only currency the Kurians accept. During our captivity, their investment accrued interest."

This last was with a jerk of the chin toward the women. About one in four were visibly pregnant. Fertility drugs in the feed, perhaps.

"Don't let the expectants fool you," a woman who introduced herself as Lieutenant Colonel Kessey said, when Valentine waked over to the crowd of women wrapping up their belongings in bundles. "Most have combat experience." Kessey had an eyepatch and some burn tissue across her scalp, but put up a hard-nosed front as she organized her rescued women. "The guards used us like their common harem. They used to laugh and say we should thank them—pregnancy keeps you off work detail, saves you from the Last Dance."

"Can't say that I blame them," Valentine said.

She lowered her voice. "All the women get the lecture in basic. Rape Survival Strategy, given by women who've been there and made it back. I used to joke about it. 'In case of capture, break his balls.' Not so easy when there are six of them."

"How many can walk as far as the river?" Valentine asked.

"All of them, sir," Kessey said. "We have litters, just in—"

A scream from the Quonset hut cut her off. It was followed by another.

"Excuse me, would you?" Valentine said, hurrying off to investigate. Shouts blended in with the screams.

It was what he dreaded. The two guards captured in the tower had been strung up by their heels inside the hut. One had blood pouring down his body. Amid the bustle of Beck's prisoners grabbing weapons and anything else remotely useful, some of the vengeful prisoners had taken matters into their own hands. Two women, thin and hollow-eyed, stood in a circle of hooting men. Both had knives; one held the wounded guard's severed genitals before the other's eyes. Some of the male prisoners were tying together the legs of another man with a bloody wound in his leg, ready to string him to the ceiling fixture when the castrated man died.

"Stop that!" Valentine shouted. "Lieutenant Nail!"

Nail sat on an overturned desk, smoking a captured cigarette as he watched the show. "You want to interfere with those hellcats, you go right ahead," Nail said.

"Nail, you're relieved. Sergeant Rain!"

"You'll just have to relieve me too, sir," Rain said.

Valentine went over to the woman with the bloody knife. She'd already opened the trousers of the next man, who was babbling for mercy. Valentine took one look at his red, contorted face and held out his hand to the woman. "You there, hand it over."

She tried to give him her bloody trophy, with a smile. Valentine felt sickened, the way some go faint at the sight of another person's blood but can calmly hold a bandage over a pulsing wound of their own. Not many months ago he'd been the one mutilating corpses. He lifted his hand to push the slimy object down, out of sight of the others—

She flinched at the gesture, flinched with the fear in her eyes of someone who had been hit before, many times. Valentine felt a hard hand on his arm.

"Mister Bear," the other woman said. She had wide-set round eyes set beneath short white hair and a hard line of a jaw. "Yolanda has to wear a diaper all the time now. These men gang-raped her. They said her ass was too tight. So they took a knife and cut it so it'd open wider. That man bleeding to death, he had the blade, and this other piece of shit helped hold her down."

"Wasn't me, sir," the inverted man said. "We surrendered proper n'all."

Valentine looked into the haunted eyes of the woman who had stayed his arm, and then to Yolanda's face. He studied the profile; her darkly beautiful features reminded him of his mother's in another time and place.

"It's justice, sir," Nail said.

"No. It's not justice. It's vengeance." He looked down at the flushed face of the guard. "You decided to live like a savage, soldier. For that you get to die like one. Nail, I'm going to go out and talk to Lieutenant Zhao. I'll be back in fifteen minutes. I want this camp ready to move then."

As Valentine walked out, he heard Yolanda's friend address the strung-up man. "Fifteen minutes. Boy, you're getting off easy."

They left the camp with one of Zhao's platoons in front of, and one behind, the liberated prisoners. The third platoon walked to either side of the files. Some of Zhao's men had already managed to lose their red-tape sashes. Beyond the column, in the darkness that matched Valentine's mood, Nail and his Bears reconnoitered.

Valentine walked beside Zhao. The lieutenant had made a hash of things, and Valentine's anger could easily give way to what Zulu Company's Sergeant Patel used to call a "two-boot stomp" dressing-down. It might let Valentine blow off steam, but whether it would do the rattled Zhao any good depended on the resilience of the man. Dawn was still hours away, but already the Quislings were reorganizing. Here and there in the dark, isolated snipers were taking potshots at the column. So far all the shots were misses, but they were unsettling—especially to the unarmed prisoners.

"Sir, the company hasn't had enough time together," Zhao explained. "It's not like all these men have combat experience. Some were militia called up during the invasion. I've only got a handful in each platoon trained as infantry."

"Lieutenant, I know you feel like you've been asked for miracles. That you even got everyone to the camp, in the dark, along a route you weren't that familiar with is a credit to you. You got all this going at a moment's notice. Don't worry about the rest."

"That Captain Beck—"

"Beck's not in charge."

"What's going to happen at Omega, sir?"

"A lot of work."

"More fighting?"

"I expect. They'll be coming for us, though. We're going to play defense for a while."

"That's good, sir. I've had some experience with that."

"What was it like when you hit the camp? The first time, that is."

"I was scared. I saw their rifle barrels everywhere. I was scared more troops were going to come rolling down the road behind me while I was looking at the camp. When we started toward the wire and the machine gun opened up—I just lost it, sir."

Somewhere behind him Valentine saw the Abica brothers embracing. The younger playfully cuffed his older brother across the back of the head. *The green flare was the right decision. . . .*

"You acted according to your judgment. You were there and I wasn't. A machine gun can kill a lot of men in a few seconds. But remember what was in your head next time you see the enemy coming at you. I know it sounds like they're howling for your blood and nothing can stop them. Remember how you felt; sometimes the noise is just fear let loose. Now that you know their fear you can work it."

"How do you stop from being scared in the first place, sir?"

"Zhao, I asked my old captain in the Wolves that exact question. I'll tell you what he told me: Don't. It'll keep you sharp."

"Send a runner ahead to that post," Valentine said to Zhao, pointing into the darkness around the warehouses. "Make sure they're our men."

While Zhao organized that, Beck and Kessey rested their prisoners. Some of them had surreptitiously gorged themselves on food from the Quonset hut and were being quietly sick along the roadside.

"Once we're across the river, we'll be back in our own lines?" Beck asked.

"Captain, you're addressing a fellow captain, you know," Zhao put in, after his messenger moved off.

"Never mind that, Lieutenant. Captain Beck and I go back far enough that the niceties don't matter. In answer to your question, Captain, the only lines in the neighborhood are the ones we're about to draw. This is a deep penetration raid, you might say. My orders are to tie down as many troops as possible."

"Where do we fit in?" Colonel Kessey asked. "Don't worry about my rank, Mr. Valentine, as far as I'm concerned I'm under your orders. This is your op. I'll do as you say."

"Couldn't stand to see friends behind barbed wire, Colonel."

Beck shook his head. "Seems to me I once criticized you for rounding up strays, Va-Captain. Looks a little different to me now. Thanks for getting me out of the frying pan."

"We in the fire are glad to have you. What sort of mix do you have?"

"There's a few Wolves, incognito. They put on militia uniforms in case of capture. The rest are mostly guards. I have infantry, heavy weapons, signals, some engineers and mechanics. Backwash from the big bugout that didn't make it to the mountains."

"And you, sir?" Valentine asked Kessey.

"The usual mix. I've got a first-class gunsmith, you might find work for her. A couple of doctors and a nurse."

A runner interrupted their talk.

"We were hoping to link up with the prison party, sir," the private reported. "Captain Styachowski didn't know you'd be with them. She sent out a scouting party to observe the Kurian Tower, but they came back and said nothing had happened there. I'm to take you to her; she's down by the docks. She's made space for the prisoners on a barge."

"Good. Captain Beck, Lieutenant Colonel Kessey, if you could get them up again, please."

Valentine heard an explosion in the darkness. "What's that?"

"I think it's mortars from the Heights. They're dropping shells around the docks. It's blind fire, sir, they're not hitting anything but rubble."

"When the sun gets up that'll change. Zhao, get them moving. Best pace the prisoners can manage."

Styachowski was in the wheelhouse of the barge, using the radio there. The barge was to be used to get the men across in case of catastrophe at the railroad bridge. She held the microphone in one hand, a cane in the other, her face lit by instrument telltales. She visibly sagged in relief when Valentine appeared in the doorway.

"The train's almost empty now," Valentine heard Post crackle from the radio. "Still no action here. You want me to send it back? Over."

"Yes, send it back. Over and out.

"Thought something had happened to you, sir," Styachowski said.

"Some confusion at the prison yard." Valentine was relieved to see her alive and well.

A soldier ran up the side stairs and entered the cabin.

"Should the people from the work camp be put on board?"

Styachowski looked at Valentine. "You're in charge of the warehouses and docks," he said.

"Yes." The private backed out of the cabin and made a noisy exit down the stairs.

"What's the situation, Styachowski?"

Another mortar shell landed amongst the Ruins.

"The supply train to go north was just waiting there. I figured we could use what was on it as well as the opposition. Here's the juicy part. There were four 155mm guns loaded on flatcars and ready to go, along with a bunch of other goodies. Post had his men ride the rooftops, it was quite a sight."

"Have you heard from Ahn-Kha?"

"They took the bridge, no problem; just a couple of corporal's guards at either end. After securing it he went overland to Omega. Called us on

Solon's own transmitter. There was a little shooting. Someone was wounded up there, but he took the Residence intact."

"So where are the Quislings?"

"Sitting tight, waiting to be told what to do. I don't think it's sunk in to anyone what's happening yet, except maybe your Kurian in his tower. The prisoners we took here said they sent everyone with a gun there to guard him."

"How many prisoners?"

"A few dozen. Night watchmen type MPs making sure nobody pilfers, at least without giving them a cut. They're sitting under guard in the canteen here. We hauled Xray-Tango back, he was conscious for a few minutes and cursing you up and down. Seeing his headquarters on fire could have had something to do with that. I've collapsed into a little pocket here. I wasn't sure if I should burn the headquarters; I didn't want to give the mortar guys another reference mark."

Valentine wondered if he could have handled it half as well. "Nice work, Styachowski. I'm—we're lucky to have you with us. Really lucky."

She flushed to the corners of her eyes and wavered a bit in her at-ease pose. "It's been a nail-biter every second."

"What's this about sending the train back? That wasn't part of the plan."

"It was loaded. We couldn't fit everyone without dragging boxcars around. There's still plenty of stuff in the warehouse we can use."

"Do you have the manpower to load it before dawn?"

"We can try."

"Use the men we took out of the camp. Medical supplies, food, ammunition—especially for those guns. In that priority. Forget the rest. After the train pulls out send every pickup you have after it. They can bump their way over the bridge easily enough. We'll need transport to get it all from the station up the hill to the Residence. At first light set everything else on fire."

"Can do, sir. Excuse me, I'd better start giving orders."

"I'll give you my standard speech," Valentine said to the thirty-odd men under guard in a corner of one of the warehouses. The warehouses were shells of better-built structures that had survived the blast. Their drafty, burned-out interiors smelled of rat feces and cat urine, but they were space out of the rain. New walls of corrugated aluminum were wired onto the reinforced concrete. Styachowski's soldiers and the liberated POWs were filling hand carts and shuttling goods out the door in a frenzy.

"Anyone who joins us gets a new life in the Free Territory. You'll come with us as civilians. You'll work harder than you did under the Hoods, but you'll be able to do it with a clear conscience. This isn't an 'or else'; we're going to leave you somewhere safe. You might want to think about what'll happen when they start investigating all this. Angry Hoods aren't particular about allocating blame where it belongs. Heads are going to roll for this one. You might think about the chances of it being yours.

"This is Corporal Lopez," Valentine said, bringing forward the noncom after he gave his words a moment to sink in. "Any of you who want to take us up on the offer of a fresh start, just speak to him. Again, we're not threatening you with anything if you don't stand up. We leave that to the Kurians. Maybe you've got family back in the KZ, I don't know. Choice is yours, but make up your minds fast—we're in a hurry."

Valentine walked over to the sliding doors to the main aisle of the warehouse. One of the advantages of higher rank was the ability to stand around where and when you chose, just observing. He looked at the carts going out to the pickups and vans, rattling out their machine-gun-fire exhaust through straight pipes. Sacks of rice, cases of ham, tins of butter, dehydrated fruit, cotton balls and motor-oil . . . His real intent was to get a read on the faces, especially Xray-Tango, who had sat through his lecture in contemptuous silence. If anyone had his neck in a noose, it was he.

Xray-Tango remained seated, holding a washcloth to the side of his head.

Only three volunteers stood up to join Lopez. Valentine wondered if they knew something he didn't.

Two men, both POWs of Beck's, were wounded by long-range fire while the second train was being loaded. Valentine sent Nail and his Bears out to find the snipers, but they returned to report they'd shot and run.

There was only one company left, spaced out wide to cover the roads, rail platform, warehouses and dock. They knew they had to pull back and get across the river when Valentine's flare went up, or dawn, whichever came first. Valentine was watching the road leading to the Kurian Tower, where the remaining flames of Xray-Tango's headquarters gave him a good view of the road. The road wasn't concerning Valentine; what was approaching on it had him worried.

"Armored cars," Valentine said. "Snowplows, I think. Two of them. Pickups behind, double axles with light armor tacked on."

"Snowplows" was Southern Command shorthand for long, heavy armored cars with pointed prows for pushing through roadblocks. Armored cupolas with machine guns, or sometimes a 20mm gun nicknamed a "Bushwhacker" stood high and gave the gunner a towerlike view. They were built on the skeletons of garbage-truck-sized vehicles.

"They're in for a shock," Nail said.

"As long as our heavy-weapons guys know what they're doing."

"Two minutes," Valentine said. "I'll be right back."

Valentine gave his men, squatting next to their stovepipe-like recoilless rifles, a thumbs-up and ran back to the train platform.

"Styachowski! Roll, roll, have everything roll!"

She nodded and signaled to the man working the engine, a Quisling officer's machine gun bumping at her hip. A soldier helped her into the back boxcar. "The rest of you, fall back to the barge. The barge! Follow the women!"

Styachowski had used the female POWs after all. They stood along the road holding emergency candles. The lights weren't bright enough to be seen by the distant snipers, let alone the mortars on Pulaski Heights, especially with the warehouses beginning to burn. The men began to pull out, some carrying a last load between them, guided to safety by the candle-holding women.

Valentine pulled the flare gun from his shoulder bag and broke it open. He fired it. Before its parachute opened, he was already running back to the Bears. He glanced up and the white glare traced an angry scrawl on his retinas.

"Here they come!" Nail called, the growl of motors growing louder. Valentine could see the turreted tops of the armored cars above the rubble, coming toward them like the dorsal fin of an attacking shark. The Bears had arranged rubble to cover their heads and shoulders.

Valentine joined one of the teams with the light artillery. A box of forearm-sized shells was laid out, ready for loading, and a soldier knelt next to the tube, looking down a crosshairs bracket as he adjusted the barrel with levers.

"Let them have it as soon as you can," he told the gunner.

"Yes, Colonel," the man said. "Err . . . Cap—"

"Don't worry about it. Just put a shell into them."

The first armored car rounded the corner, the pointed prow on it filling the street.

"Clear!" the gunner yelled, but the other two in the crew were already well away from the back of the weapon.

It fired with a *whoosh*, more like a rocket than a shell. The backblast kicked up a shroud of dust, blinding Valentine for a moment. He heard an explosion somewhere down the road. The loaders opened the crossbars at the back and slid in a brassy new shell.

Valentine heard the Bears shooting. The front snowplow had been stopped, and smoke poured from the front. It was firing back; tracers arced from the turret, their brightness leaving strange echoes on his retinas. He saw vague shapes of troops exiting the armored car behind it before the recoilless rifle fired again.

"That's it. Wreck the tube," Valentine said.

"One more shell, sir," the gunner said, as the others loaded.

"Shoot and fall back." He raised his voice. "Nail, get out of it!"

More tracer streaks lit up the street. The gunner fired again, blindly. Valentine waited to see Nail and his Bears run for the burning warehouses, and pulled the gunner out by his collar. The loaders put another shell in the tube, and placed the spares beneath its massive tripod.

Tracer fire began to seek the recoilless weapon like a probing finger. "Better get going, sir," the gunner said, throwing a bag over his shoulder. He pulled out a shining new grenade.

Valentine looked up the street and made his dash. He gestured to the gunners, trying to encourage them to hurry. The gunner nodded to the other two and tossed the grenade in with the shells under the tube. The three of them ran.

From the platform Valentine looked at the rail bridge. He saw the tailgate of a pickup, bumping as the tires negotiated the ties. Men walked single file on the pedestrian walkway, crossing over to the north side. Others were setting charges.

"Nail," Valentine said, as the Bears came up behind him with the recoilless gunners. "It'll have to be the boat. They're getting set to blow the bridge."

Nail nodded, and they turned for the riverbank. A few members of the rearguard were hurrying for the dock. Mortar shells were dropping around the train station.

Nail clapped Valentine on the back. "We really—"

An explosion boiled all around them. Valentine felt a warm hand give him a gentle nudge. He realized he was on the ground. Nail lay facing him, his leg on top of Valentine's, like two lovers in bed.

"You okay?"

"Sure," Nail gasped. He started to pick himself up. Neither of his legs moved.

Valentine tried to help him up. "Rain, anyone . . . help!" His voice sounded like a far-off whisper.

"Legs . . ." Nail said, looking up at Valentine. He'd never seen fear in the Bear's eyes before.

Valentine picked him up in a fireman's carry and trotted down toward the pier. The barge waited, huge and comforting.

"Cast off, cast off," the sergeant handling the loading called. Zhao was running between little groups, clapping them on the shoulder and pointing toward the barge. Valentine saw his old marines from the *Thunderbolt* leave the piled sandbags around the dock—sandbags were easily found around the riverbank—and run up the gangplank to the barge. There was a hint of light in the sky; by it Valentine saw the main deck of the barge piled high with sandbags. The cargo carrier in front was filled with people, mostly prisoners from the camp, and Zhao's company.

"Bandages!" the sergeant called, looking at Nail and Valentine. "Take him to the foredeck, sir. The wounded are there."

Valentine boarded, and went forward. Just below the pilot house a man in splints and one of the women lay under blankets next to Beck's two wounded. Field medics helped Valentine lay Nail out.

"Sorry about this, Nail." The inadequate words made him want to bite his tongue.

"Don't feel a thing, sir. Hardly hurts."

"Shrapnel," the medic said. "His back's kind of tore up. I've stopped the bleeding—most of it."

Valentine heard the muttering boat engines gun, and the barge moved away from the dock, heading upriver.

"Can I get you anything, Nail?"

"I want to see."

"You want to see?"

"The bridge go."

Valentine looked at the medic, who shrugged. "Let me get this dressing finished. Then we'll see," he said. Valentine couldn't remember giving orders about having an aid station set up on the boat. One of Styachowski or Post's additions. He heard bullets plinking off the old scow. The side of the boat was an irresistible target for any Quisling with a rifle and a view.

They passed under the old pilings of the railroad span. Valentine heard the distinctive clatter of a Kalashnikov fired from the River Rats' town.

When the medic finished with Nail's dressing Valentine pulled a soldier and they carried his stretcher to the back of the tug. The screws were churning the muddy waters of the Arkansas. Behind them they could see the bridge framed against a pink sky. The warehouses were going up, a ground-level fireworks explosion.

"We fucked with them good," Nail said, his eyes bright and excited. "That sight's worth getting all tore up over." The sky was growing brighter by the second.

"C'mon, guys, don't wait and try and take a few with the bridge," Valentine said. "Just—"

Explosions ripped across the bridge, and wood and rails spun into the sky.

"What the hell?" Nail said.

The bridge still stood.

"Shit. Didn't they use enough C-big?" Nail said.

"It's not that," Valentine waited, hoping for the structural integrity to fail. The bridge still stood. "They used plenty. They just used it all at the bottom of the bridge, where it meets the pilings. Spread it out too much, too. They tore up the track good, that's all. On a truss bridge the load is all borne by the joints at the top. If they'd just blown out the tops of the span we passed under, it'd be in the river."

A mortar shell landed in the water astern of them.

"This boat trip's gonna get cut short," Nail predicted.

The barge edged toward Big Rock Mountain. Valentine felt it shudder. The soldiers went to the rail, concerned.

"We're aground!" someone shouted.

"Shit!" Nail said.

"Okay, just wade, swim, whatever," Valentine shouted. He ran forward, leaving Nail for the moment.

"Out of here. Over the side . . . just go!" he yelled. "Manfred, help the women. We need stretcher-bearers. Who wants to carry?"

Part evacuation, part shipwreck, they got the soldiers and some of the supplies overboard. Valentine stayed with the wounded until the stretchers were ashore. The water helped deaden the effect of the mortars; they did little more than create brief fountains of water as they exploded.

"There's still a lot of cargo on the barge," Zhao said, dripping from the armpits down.

"Forget it. We need to get up the hill."

It was easier said than done. The hillside rose two hundred feet at a 3:1 grade, where it wasn't a cliff. There was an old switchback road going up the side. Valentine sent up the stretcher-bearers in groups so they could replace each other. He stood among the trees at the base of the hill, watching the mortars drop shells into the barge. The Quislings seemed to be taking strange pleasure in wasting shells on the wreck, rather than dropping them on the hillside where they might do some damage.

He heard a heavy tread, and looked up to see a mountain of muscle.

"Good morning, Ahn-Kha," he said.

"I'm glad to see you, my David. It's been a long night."

"For both of us."

"Post and Styachowski arrive?"

"Styachowski is at the Residence now. Post is still unloading the second run."

"What's the TMCC doing about it?"

"At first light I heard some shooting, far to the north. My guess is two patrols ran into each other."

"So you don't think they've figured out where we are?"

"They'll know soon, my David."

"What do you think they'll do?"

"I leave outthinking them to you. I just try to outfight them."

"If you had to outfight me right now?" Valentine asked, looking across the river. He could just see the tip of the crane building the Kurian Tower, though he supposed the construction schedule had been set back.

"I'd try you soon, before you could organize. Today, tonight."

"Wouldn't hurt to pretend you're giving the orders across the river. Let's get up the hill."

It was full light by the time he approached Solon's Residence across the bulldozed hilltop. A bulldozer was at work, digging pits into the ground in front of the house beyond the turnaroud. Post stood in front of the entrance, giving orders. A truck pulled up and a team of men hurried to take the crates out and manhandle them inside. With the bed emptied, the pickup turned around and drove back down the road to the station.

Post looked up as Valentine approached.

"The hill is secure, sir. Ella, Daltry and Pollock have their companies north, east and southeast. We've got observers watching the river. Styachowski is holding the station until we get the rest up here, unless they come in force. This is a choice piece of ground. I can see why Solon picked it. Great view."

"Where are the wounded?"

Post pointed to one of the building shells. "Lower level of that one, sir. The doctors are getting set up in there. There was already a little dispensary for the construction workers, and they're expanding it. They could use some trained nurses. Dr. Brough's already bitching."

"I know of one. Get Narcisse in there as soon as you can."

"She's with the wounded at the station," Post said, shrugging his shoulders the way some men do at a heavy rain that can't be helped. "Nothing serious, but you know her. If someone's in pain—"

"I'm glad you had the sense not to stop her. Let's get the prisoners organized, Colonel Kessey—she's got an eyepatch, easy to spot—said she had some doctors."

"I saw her come over the hill," Post said. "She's talking to the men placing the guns now."

"Every company has Quickwood spears, right?"

"Having them is one thing. Getting them to use them is another."

"We've got today, at least. They won't hit us with Reapers until dark. Carry on, Will. Lieutenant Nail's been badly wounded by shrapnel. Hit in the back."

"Damn. You know, I don't think anyone's been killed yet? On our side, anyway. Who ever heard of that?"

"Maybe our luck's finally turned," Valentine said.

To the extent that there were still MDs, Major Brough deserved her title. She was a field surgeon with ten years experience in the Guards, and had seen everything metal could do to the human body.

"I'm not hopeful, sir," Dr. Brough said, when Valentine asked her about Nail. "Tore open his back. One kidney's gone, the other's probably damaged enough so it might as well be gone, too. His back's broken, and there's massive nerve damage. I'm surprised he was even coherent when they brought him in."

"He's a Bear. They're tough."

"I'm a surgeon. Lifeweaver mysticism isn't my field."

Valentine absorbed the news. Dialysis machines had gone the way of the dodo, as far as he knew. Nail was dead, it was just a question of how long.

"So he's still conscious?"

"I gave him a shot. I expected him to drop right off, but the morphine just relaxed him. He's in some kind of wide-awake shock, low blood pressure, fast heart rate, eyes a little dilated. Lots of perspiration."

"Mind if I have a word?"

"Go ahead. Sir, I have a request."

"Shoot, Doc. Anything for Nail."

"No, it's not that. I understand there's some kind of housing up here. If they've got a cookhouse, could you look for a refrigerator or a freezer? Without somewhere to store blood and plasma, wounded turn to corpses a lot easier. Your men have been stockpiling food and bullets. If it's going to be a fight, I'm going to need to do the same with blood. Some kind of donation schedule would help."

"Any coolers we find go to you."

"Thank you."

"If you need anything else, ask myself, Post or Styachowski. You'll get priority. But I hope you're very bored down here."

"Save the cheerful hero stuff for the troops. Years of amputations have made me a cynic."

Valentine walked over to Nail, who was resting on a folding cot. Nail's gear had been placed beneath the cot. Valentine picked up a tube he couldn't identify. It looked a little like a metallic zither. A waste-bucket with a blood-soaked dressing lay next to it, and the coppery odor brought back memories of the headquarters cellar. He didn't want to think about that for a while.

"They have you comfortable, Nail?"

"Yesss, sssir," Nail slurred. "Damn sorry I'm out of commission for a while."

Valentine lifted the canteen lying beside the bed.

"Water?"

"Yes, thank you, sir." He sipped. "I could use a meal. Been running around since the meeting."

"I'll see about it." Valentine wobbled the tube in his hand, like a baton.

"You like that, sir? You can have it. Brass came up with the idea."

"What's it do?"

"Gimme." Nail took it from him, aimed at the ceiling, and pushed a button. A dart flew out and buried itself there. Dr. Brough gave him a dirty look. Nail stifled a snicker like a schoolboy caught shooting spit-balls.

"There's a real serious spring inside. The winder's on the top, and you turn it clockwise to ready it. There's a safety at the front you need to flick off . . . To fire it you just push the button. I've got some Quickwood darts for it in my bag. I won't be needing it for a while. I hate being fucked-up and useless!" He pounded an unoffending blanket.

Nail wasn't speaking like someone with a shot of morphine inside him. Valentine had heard that Bears were hard to settle down after a fight.

"Lieutenant, I need your help. We might have some Reapers in our laps tonight. Do you think it would be better to space your Bears out with the companies to steady them, or should I keep them back here, and commit them when I know where the attack's coming from?"

Nail thought it over. “They’re used to working as a team, sir. Keep them back. Chances are the Reapers will just try to claw through your guys to get to the rear where they can do more serious damage. My team’ll clobber ’em.”

“Thanks, Nail.”

“Just give me a few days, sir. A week, then I’ll be back. Rain can run the team until then. If . . . if . . . I don’t, give him my bars. He’s earned ’em.”

“Nail, now that you’ve got some downtime, you want to write some letters? You have family, a girl?”

“I’m a Bear sir. My only family’s rooting through that supply dump out front looking for chow. If they find something to eat, have ’em remember me in here, laid out and hungry.”

Bear appetites were notoriously hard to sate. Valentine had seen them chew bark from the trees on the march through the Ouachitas after leaving Martinez. “I’ll see that you aren’t forgotten. It’s a promise.”

Valentine, exchanging a look with Brough, wondered how *it’s a promise* would look on Nail’s tombstone.

Ten

Big Rock Mountain, March of the forty-eighth year of the Kurian Order: Viewed from above, the outline of Big Rock Mountain looks like a cameo of a Regency buck, or perhaps Elvis Presley done during his last Vegas days. The Arkansas River flows west into the King's forehead, complete with lock of hair hanging down, where it's stopped by the cliff face of a quarry and turns south. After the small bulge of the nose the river passes a protruding jaw. The hill curves off east, gradually leaving the river, into an oversized collar tucked into the hair flowing down to North Little Rock. What was Interstate 40 runs up the base of the north side of the hill.

It's a picturesque prominence, named "La Grande Roche" by Bernard de La Harpe in 1722 as he traveled among the Quapaw Indians. The climb up the 580-foot hill is worth it, for the view west and east along the two gentle bends the Arkansas makes as it flows into Little Rock. Or so it must have seemed to the man who built a luxury hotel upon it for the swells of the Gilded Age. But hotels are a chancy business; the hilltop property became Fort Logan H. Roots, when men trained for the Great War in the swampy ground of Burns Park north of the hill.

Following a progression so logical that it verges on the sublime, the fort became a Veterans Administration Hospital for those shattered in the staccato series of twentieth-century wars. It became a warren of buildings, from elegant Grecian structures complete with solemn columns to the smallest maintenance shack and pump house, surrounded by parks full of oaks and a hilltop lake, memorials and greenways.

That was before the Blast. The twenty-megaton airburst, part of the nuclear fireworks that helped end the reign of man in the chaos of 2022, went off at ten thousand feet somewhere in the air between the Broadway Street and Main Street bridges over the Arkansas. It left nothing but foundations ten miles from the epicenter, barring reinforced concrete construction.

And a limb-shorn oak that had seen it all, like one of the shattered veterans of the former VA hospital.

The men were gathered beneath the grandfather oak. The tree, perhaps because it was partly sheltered by one of the great buildings, had survived the blast and the fires that came with it. It had the tortured look of a lightning-struck tree, scored on the southeast side and shorn of older branches from two o'clock to four, and from seven to ten, though knobby amputations showed where the once-leafy limbs had been.

Valentine looked at the expectant faces in the afternoon sun. They were haggard, unshaven, tired. Post and Styachowski had pushed them to the extreme of what could be expected of soldiers, and then beyond. The former POWs were mixed in with the men he'd brought away from Martinez—though they looked better, strangely enough, than when they first arrived.

Almost anything is perferable to being inside barbed wire.

Post has assembled a list of operational specialties from the prisoners. The hilltop redoubt was well supplied with ration processors—women and men who were experienced canners, food dehydrators, pickling and drying specialists. There were no herds to slaughter or bushels of fruit and vegetables to puree and seal. "If they come up the hill, we'll just can the AOT troops like sardines," Post said with a fatalistic shrug. Valentine had almost a whole motor pool from Pine Bluff; invaluable to Southern Command with their wrenches and hoists, but they would have to put rifles in their hands and cartridge cases around their waists.

In this he was blessed, as Southern Command had a tradition of rotating men between front line and support duties, allowing the freehold to rapidly convert support units to combat operations. All of them had heard bullets fly and shells land in dreadful earnest. He wished he had more time to get to know them. Post and Beck would have to rely on volunteers to put together an NCO grid.

The four big guns were spaced out like the bases on an oversized baseball diamond in the open ground in front of Solon's Residence, each in its own pit, dug by the bulldozer, and ringed with sandbags. The backhoe was still making trenches to the ammunition dump, buried deep beneath a layer of sandbags, dirt, railroad ties and rail beams. This last came from the dismantled rail line the now-destroyed train had run on to the station near the old interstate.

Apart from the occasional shell from Pulaski Heights, the only military action to take place in the last forty-eight hours was a skirmish already going into the Free Territory folklore as the Great Howling Grog Chicken Raid. Ahn-Kha had led two platoons into the outskirts of North Arkansas and snatched up every chicken, goose, goat, piglet, calf, sheep and domestic rabbit they could run down and stuff in a sack—at the cost of the commanding officer getting a buttock full of birdshot from a twenty-gauge—while a third platoon blasted away at the men guarding the partially blown bridge from a thousand yards. Ahn-Kha had been running from a henhouse with a pair of chickens in each hand when the birdkeeper peppered him with shot that had to be dug out by a medic named Hiekeda with sterilized tweezers. In tall-tale fashion, the circumstances of Ahn-Kha's wounding and subsequent extraction of the pellets were exaggerated until, in one version already being told over the radio, Ahn-Kha was sneaking past a window with a sow under each arm and six chickens in each hand when an eighty-year-old woman stuck a gun out the window and gave him both barrels as he bent to tie his shoe. The shot, in that particular version, had to be dug out by a Chinese tailor working with knitting needles used as chopsticks. But the raid was the Big Rock Mountain garrison's first offensive success of the campaign. As a bonus, a baker's dozen of forgotten milkers were rustled from their riverside pasture and driven up the two hairpins of the switchback road on the south side of the Big Rock Mountain.

"Men," Valentine said. "You've been following orders that haven't made much sense for three days straight. You've done your duty without questions, or answers that made any sense. I'm going to try to straighten you out now. Please pass on what I say to everyone who is on watch at the skyline."

The "skyline" was the men's name for the edge of the hillside, where a series of foxholes and felled trees traced the military crest: the point where the slope could be covered by gunfire. They didn't have a quarter of the trained men they needed to man the extended line; by using three companies he could place a soldier about every fifteen yards along the line, if he didn't cover the cliffs above the quarry with more than sentries.

"We were the first move in an effort to take back the Ozarks from Kur."

He couldn't get any farther; the men broke into cheers and the corkscrew yip of the Southern Command Guards. Valentine let the cheers stop. He said a silent prayer of gratitude for the high spirits of the men, tired as they were.

"We're about as far behind the lines as we can be. There are divisions of Quislings between us and the forces north and south, which will soon be driving for us."

Valentine knew he'd be roundly damned for what he was telling them; by the men if they found out he was lying, by his conscience if it was successfully kept from them. It was a guess at best. For all he knew, Southern Command was going to move toward Fort Scott or Pine Bluff. Since the men holding the Boston Mountains were a charade of an army, there wasn't a snowflake's chance in hell of being relieved from the north, and as for the south . . .

"We're in radio contact with Southern Command. They know about the blow we struck the night before last. We threw a wrench into the gears of the TMCC. You know it, I know it and the Quislings will know it when they start going hungry and running out of bullets to shoot at your comrades."

All that was true enough. With only Post in the basement radio room, he'd made a report to Southern Command, and after an hour's pause they contacted him only to say that he'd been promoted to major and was now part of "Operations Group Center" under the titular command of General Martinez. They told him that he was to tie down as many troops as possible and be prepared to operate without the direct support of Southern Command for an "indeterminate time frame." Valentine didn't think that clumsy phrase, or the mention of Martinez, would bring cheers.

"From this hill, with the guns and mortars taken in our raid, we command a vital rail, road and river crossing. Consul Solon had to give up his old headquarters at Fort Scott to the Kurians of Oklahoma. He was in the process of transferring it here. Now we've taken his new one, right down to his personal foam-cushioned toilet seat, which I placed under new management this morning." The men laughed.

"We're in a strong position with plenty to eat and shoot. I hope you like the view; you're going to be enjoying it for a long time. But the work has just begun. I'm going to put every man in this command under the temporary command of Captain Beck, the officer commanding the prisoners we brought out of Little Rock. I served, and chopped, and dug, under him. He's been in two corners as tight as this one, outside Hazlett and commanding me at Little Timber Hill, and I'm still breathing because he knows how to fortify. He's going to work you until you drop. Then he'll wake you up and work you some more, but you'll be alive at the end of this because of it."

Liar.

Beck pulled Valentine aside as Lieutenant Colonel Kessey took over the assembly.

"Major Valentine needed a trained artillery officer," she said, "and I, for my sins, happen to be one. I need more crews. The one I put together to set up the guns won't help me much to shoot the other three. Anyone who's got experience as a gun-bunny, cannon-cocker, or ammo-humper, please raise your hand. Not enough. Anyone who knows what those words mean, raise your hands . . . anyone who thinks they might know. Finally. Good news, you're all in the artillery now."

"What are the latest regs on friendly fire casualties?" Beck asked sotto voce.

"Be thankful they don't have to counterbattery the mortars on Pulsaki Heights just yet."

"We won't hear from them for a while. They shot their ready reserve and we've got the rest. That, or they're saving it for a charge up our hill."

"What do you need, Captain?" Valentine asked.

"Valentine, what happened after Little Timber . . . I'm sorry. This arm meant no more duty in the Wolves."

"It meant no more duty in the Wolves for me, too, Captain."

"That's my fault."

"Doesn't matter now. You're a helluva fortification engineer. The best officer I ever served with was Le Havre in Zulu Company, but if I had my choice of him or anyone else in Southern Command for this job, I'd want you."

Beck swallowed. "Thank you . . . sir."

"It won't be easy. We don't have anything like the men we should have to defend this position. You've got to make it look like we do. Sooner or later they're going to get around to trying us."

"The firepower we have is better than what we had in the Wolves. Supports, heavy weapons, mines. That counts for a lot."

"When the construction equipment is done with the artillery, it's all yours."

Beck nodded. Valentine saw his jaws tighten. Back in his days as senior in Foxtrot Company he'd known that meant Beck was thinking. Valentine reminded himself to give Beck Consul Solon's humidor of cigars. Beck enjoyed a good smoke while working.

"Rough out what you want and run it by Styachowski. She's sharp. I've told her and Mr. Post that you're in charge of getting us ready. They'll follow your orders. If there's anything I can do, let me know."

"You've done more than enough. How long are we going to have to be here?"

"How long were you going to hold that road to Hazlett?"

Beck thought it over. "It's like that, sir?"

"We've got to keep as many troops occupied as possible for as long as we can. We're right at the nexus of river and rail traffic in the Ozarks. We need to make sure they can't use it. At least not easily. We've got to protect the artillery covering the river and rail lines."

"Then I'll build a redoubt around these buildings and foundations. We have to figure on them getting on the plateau. More railroad rails and ties would be nice."

"There's the line running to the quarry. The Pulaski Heights boys might have something to say about us working right across the river from them."

"Maybe the 155s can say something back to them if they do."

Nail was a little pale, but he was eating and sleeping well.

"Better than I'd've expected," Dr. Kirschbaum said. Valentine didn't think she looked old enough to be a doctor, but wasn't about to ask her for a diploma. "Could be that kidney's in better shape than the triage report says. You should see this."

The doctor led him over to Nail. The Bear lay on a bed now; they'd taken mattresses from the construction huts and moved them into the hospital—along with the generator and a refrigerator that had been holding beer.

"Lieutenant, you've got another visitor," Kirschbaum said.

Nail managed a tired smile. "I'm about visited out, Doc. Unless he's got more of Narcisse's gumbo."

"You need a second nurse to handle your dishes and bedpans as is, soldier."

Nail drained his canteen and handed it to the doctor. "More."

"Do your trick first, Lieutenant."

"What trick is this, Nail?" Valentine asked.

"Check out my toes, sir."

They were wiggling.

"You don't have a battery under here, do you?" Kirschbaum said, pretending to check under Nail's bed.

"Ever treated a Bear before, Doc?" Nail asked.

"I've seen some DOAs. You boys take a lot of killing, judging from the holes. I'll leave you with the lieutenant, Major. Or are you going to ask him for a quickie, too?"

Nail winked.

Valentine swung around the chair next to Nail's bed. "I'm glad you're feeling better. What's in that gumbo?"

"Part of being a Bear."

"This isn't healing, Nail. This is more like regeneration."

"You know Lost&Found, sir? You know why he's called that? He's got me beat. He was dead, like body-getting-cold dead, and he came back. He was in the fraggin' body bag, sir. Zipped up and in a pile. He came to when the gravediggers picked him up. It's like a legend, this story. Sat up and asked his mom for griddle cakes. Three men there had simultaneous heart attacks. He kept the twist tie on the tag they stuck through his ear. We try to keep it quiet. In case we ever get captured, we don't want some Quisling cutting a notch in our arm just to see how quickly it heals."

Valentine found Narcisse in the basement of the hospital, pouring honey down the center of loaves of bread, risen and ready to go into the oven. She was organizing the kitchen with the help of one of the pregnant POWs and a former Quisling soldier, one of the three from the captured bunch at the warehouse, who looked about fifteen.

"Where's Hank?" Valentine asked. "I thought he was helping you out."

"He volunteered for the artillery. That woman Kessey came through earlier today, she adopted the boy."

"How's he doing?" Valentine had avoided Hank since the night they broke out of New Columbia.

"He told me he hated his parents. He hopes they're dead."

"No, he doesn't. Would it help if I talked to him?"

"Daveed, I don't know what you did when you went off that night. I don't want to know. I think it'd be best if Hank, he never know either. You tell him his parents, they run away."

"What makes you think they didn't?"

"Your eyes. They are your grief. They say, when you leave that place, you were dipped in blood."

"Enough with the juju stuff, Sissy. What have you been putting in Nail's soup?"

"Sausage, rice, celery, no chilis or nothing; the doctor, she say keep it mild—"

"That's not what I mean. He had nerve damage. It's healing. I'd heard Bears recovered from stabs and bullet wounds fast, but I've never known of a higher animal doing this."

" 'More t'ings in heaven and earth,' Daveed. If I knew how to make a gumbo that make cane-man walk again, I use him on myself and get new legs."

"Colo—Major, passing the word for Major Valentine," a soldier called in the hospital.

"Down here," Valentine yelled back.

A private from the command company made a noisy descent to the kitchen, a signals patch on his shoulder. "Major! Sergeant Jimenez needs you in the radio room. Priority broadcast from Southern Command. For all troops."

"Did you say broadcast?"

"Yes, sir, not direct communication. The Sarge said you needed to hear it."

"Thank you, Private. I'm coming."

Valentine stole a fresh heel of bread and dipped it in honey.

"You too bad, Daveed," Narcisse said. "This galley supposed to be for hospital."

"Impossible to resist your cooking, Sissy," Valentine said, moving for the stairs.

Word had passed among the men that something was up. There were a couple of dozen sandbag-fillers trying to look busy in front of the Federal-style command building. A new long-range radio mast had gone up atop its molding-edged roof since the previous day. The signals private held the door for Valentine.

"Does Jimenez have the klaxon rigged yet?"

"I helped him, sir. Klaxon, PA, he can even kill electricity."

"Quick work."

"To tell you the truth, sir, it was mostly rigged already. We just added the kill switch for the juice."

The radio room was a subbasement below the conference room where Solon had laid out his scheme for finishing off Southern Command. Solon had a sophisticated radio center. A powerful transmitter, capable of being used by three separate operators, was surrounded by the inky flimsy-spitters capable of producing text or images from the right kind of radio or telephone signal. Sergeant Jimenez had a pair of earphones on, listening intently.

"What's the news, Jimenez?"

"Oh, sorry, sir. Lots of chatter. Something big is going on down south. I'm scanning Southern Command and TMCC. Chatter north and south, but it sounds like there's action somewhere on the banks of the Ouachita."

"What about west? Anything from Martinez?"

"Not a word, sir. Like we don't exist."

"What did you call me here for, then?"

"There's going to be a broadcast from the governor. Thought you might like to hear what he had to say."

"I'm not the only one, Jimenez. Can you put this on the PA?"

"Uhh . . . wait, I can. Just give me a sec."

The radio tech rooted through a box of tangled cords in the corner, pulling up wires and examining the ends. He pulled out a snarl of electronics cable and unwound what he was looking for. Valentine put an ear to the headphones, but just picked up a word or two amongst the static. His eyes wandered over the Christmas-like assortment of red and green telltales, signal strength meters and digital dials. The apparatus was a Frankensteinish creation of three mismatched electronic boxes, placed vertically in a frame and patched together. The electromagnetic weapons that darkened so much of the world in 2022 took their toll on everything with a chip; the more sophisticated, the more likely to be rendered useless by an EMW pulse. Sets like this were an exception—restored military com sets with hardened chips. The Kurians frowned on any kind of technology that allowed mass communication; radios were hunted down and destroyed as though they were cancers. An illegal transmitter was a dangerous and practically impossible thing to have in the Kurian Zone. Only the most trusted of the Quisling commanders had them for personal use. Southern Command made transmitter/receivers by the hundreds, and receivers in even greater quantity, in little garage shops for smuggling into the Kurian Zone, and of course had encouraged the citizens of the Free Territory to own them as well, even if they were on the telephone network. Caches of radios had probably been hidden along with weapons when Solon's forces overran the Free Territory. If Governor Pawls was about to make a statement, chances were he had in mind speaking to those of his former citizens who still possessed theirs, and if they still had radios they probably had weapons. Valentine hoped for a call to rise. The Ozarks, especially near the borders, were full of self-reliant men and women who knew how to organize and fight in small groups. With his guns at the center of the Quisling transport network, the Kurians would have difficulty stamping out fires.

"We're live, sir. Just let me know when you want to pipe it through,"

Jimenez said. Valentine heard a voice through the padding on the earphones. He picked up another pair.

"When's the broadcast?"

"Soon, sir."

"I'm just getting static."

"I'll fix that," the technician said. He sat and worked the tuner. "Code messages again. Something's happening."

"Why aren't they doing it in the dead of night?"

"They usually do; reception is better. Maybe they want to get it rolling today, before the Kurians can react."

"Or tonight."

"Could be, sir. Oh, just a sec. Five minutes."

"Give me the microphone." When Jimenez handed it over, Valentine tested the talk switch. He heard an audible click outside. "Lend an ear, men. Lend an ear. We've got a broadcast coming in from the governor. I'm not sure what it's about, just that it's a general broadcast to what used to be the Ozark Free Territory. I figured you'd want to hear it. We'll pipe it over as soon as it comes on."

"They've got cassettes, so I can tape it," Jimenez whispered.

"For those on watch, we'll tape it and play it back tonight. That is all."

To pass the time Jimenez took Valentine through the shortwave spectrum. There were notes on a clipboard about where to find the bands for the Green Mountain men, the Northwest Command, even overseas stations like the Free Baltic League.

"Well have to set up a canteen where you can play the news," Valentine said. "Solon has enough office space down here; we can knock down some of these walls—"

"Just a sec, sir. He's coming on." Jimenez nodded to himself, then flicked a switch. Faintly, Valentine heard Governor Pawl's voice from the loudspeakers outside. Jimenez unplugged the earphones and the sound went over to the old set of speakers bracketed to the wall. Valentine had heard the old Kansan's rather scratchy voice on occasions past, explaining a new emergency measure or rescinding an old one, eulogizing some lost lieutenant or passing along news of a victory against the Kurians overseas.

"—and all our friends and allies who may be listening. Late last night, after speaking to Lieutenant General Griffith, my interim lieutenant governor, Hal Steiner, and what members of the Ozark Congress are with me at Comfort Point, I gave the order for the counterattack you've all been wating for in this, the darkest year of the Free Territory. A combination of weather, enemy movements and a fortuitous raid on the Quislings at the old Little Rock Ruins—"

"Hey, that's us," Jimenez said, smiling. Valentine nodded, listening.

"—I took as portents that it is time for the storms and shadows to disperse. Therefore I gave the order for 'Archangel' to begin."

"Archangel" must have meant something to the men outside; Valentine heard cheering.

"The first shot was fired before dawn this morning. As I speak, in the south we have seized Camden and are on the march for Arkadelphia; in the north we descend from the mountains and onto the plateau. So now I ask the men and women of the militia, when they hear the sound of our guns, to gather and smash our enemy, hip and thigh. Smash them! Smash them to pieces, then smash the pieces into dust. For the outrages inflicted on us, smash them! For the future of your sons and daughters, smash them! As you are true to your heritage of liberty, smash them! For the honored dead of our Cause, smash them! Now is our time. With courage in your heart, you will know what to do. With steel in your arm, you will have the means to do it. With belief in your spirit, you will not falter but shall see it through. We have lived through the night. Now let us make a dawn, together."

The broadcast switched over to a marching song of Southern Command, based on an old marching ditty. Valentine left the radio room and went out to see the men, the song ringing in his ears:

We are a band of peoples, granted through our creed
The Right to Life and Liberty: our Founding Fathers' deed.
But when those rights were taken, our duty then as one:
Cry "Never!" to the Kurian Kings, and take up arms again.
Never! Never! Our sacred trust . . . Never!
"Never!" to the Kurian Kings, we'll take up arms again . . .

Outside, Valentine heard the men join in the song. It spread across the hill, even to the pickets on the crestline. Though most of them couldn't carry a tune with the help of a wheelbarrow, they did slap their rifle butts, or shovel blades, in time to the "Never!" It was a rythmic, savage sound. He hoped the Quislings across the river were listening.

Valentine found Hank Smalls learning his duties as a "runner." The boy's job was to pass oral messages between the guns and the main magazine, headquarters, or the forward posts in the event of a hard-line breakdown with the field phones. He and a handful of other young teenagers were being escorted around the hilltop and taught the different stations still being put together by Beck and his construction crews.

"Can I borrow Hank a moment?" Valentine asked the corporal walking the teens around.

"Of course," the corporal answered. She had the nearsighted look of a studious schoolgirl entering her senior year, despite the "camp hair" cropped close to her scalp. Valentine stopped the children as they lined up, as though for inspection.

"Excuse me, Corporal." He drew Hank aside. "How are you getting on, Hank?" Valentine asked the boy. Hank wore a man's fatigue shirt, belted about the waist so it was more of a peasant smock. Mud plastered Hank's sandal-like TMCC training shoes, but the old tire treads were easy to run in and then clean afterwards.

"Busy. Lots to remember about fuses, sir."

"Are you getting enough to eat?"

Hank looked insulted. "Of course. Two hot and one cold a day."

Valentine had a hard time getting the next out: "Worried about your parents?"

"No." But the boy's eyes left his this time. Valentine went down to one knee so he was at the boy's level, but Hank's face had gone vacant. The boy was off in a mental basement, a basement Valentine suspected was similar to his own.

"Keep busy,"Valentine said, summing long experience into words. The boy looked like he needed more.

"Hank, I'm going to tell you something a Roman Catholic priest told me when I lost my parents. He said it was up to him to turn me into a man since my father wasn't around to do it. He'd never had kids, being a priest, so he had to use the wisdom of others. He used to read a lot of Latin. Roman history, you know?" For some reason Valentine thought of Xray-Tango and his *groma*.

"They had gladiators," Hank said.

"Right. A Roman statesman named Cicero used to say that 'no Roman in any circumstance could regard himself as vanquished.' You know what vanquished means?"

"Uhhh," Hank said.

"What Cicero meant was that even if you were beat, you should never admit that you were. Especially not to the people who'd beaten you."

"Like Southern Command keeping together even after all this," Hank said. The boy's eyes had a sparkle of interest, so Valentine went on.

"Cicero said a man had to have three virtues. *Virtus*, which meant courage in battle. Not minding pain and so on. You also have to have *gravitas*, which means being sober, aware of your responsibilities, and controlling your emotions. Even if someone has you madder than a stomped rattlesnake, you don't let them know they've got you by the nose, or they'll just give you another twist. Understand?"

"Virte—*virtus* and *gravitas*," Hank said. "I see. But you said there was another."

"This is the most important one for you now. *Simplicitas*. That means keeping your mind on your duties, doing what most needs to be done at the moment. In fact, I'd better let you get back to yours. I don't want to keep the corporal and the rest waiting."

"Yes, sir," Hank said, saluting. The vacant look was gone.

Valentine wanted to hug the boy, but settled for a salute. *Gravitas* required it.

All through the following day the sound of distant trucks and trains could be heard.

That night, though the men were exhausted from laboring on what was now known as the "Beck Line," they danced and cheered at the news that Arkadelphia was liberated, and the Quislings were falling back in disarray. Southern Command would soon be knocking on the hilly gates of Hot Springs, barely fifty miles from New Columbia.

They'd had their own successes. The mortar crews had prevented repair gangs from working on the rail lines during the day, and the occasional illumination shell followed by 4.2-inch mortar airbursts slowed the work to a crawl at night.

But strongpoints with machine guns were now all around the base of the hill, and the mortars on Pulaski Heights had begun to fire again, scattering their shells among the buildings of Solon's Residence. Two men laying wire for field phones were killed when a shell landed between them.

Big Rock Mountain added a life when one of the women gave birth. The eight-and-a-half-pound boy was named Perry after one of the dead signals men.

"That's pretty damn arrogant of them," Valentine said, taking his eye from the spotting scope the next day. It was late afternoon, and the shadows of the hills were already stretching across New Columbia. "Bringing a barge up the river in daylight."

"I'd say the river's too tricky to do it at night," Post said.

"Then we'll make it too tricky for them to do during the day."

They stood at an observation post above the switchback road running up the southeastern side of the hill, looking through a viewing slit with the protection of headlogs. There were snipers at the base of the hill good enough to get them, even with an uphill shot. There had been minor wounds among the work parties until three-man teams of counter-snipers had been sent down the hill to hunt out the marksmen. Valentine knew there was a gritty war of precision and patience being waged through scoped rifles two hundred feet below, but he had to keep his mind on the river, or rather denying its use to the enemy.

"They're trying to time it so they can unload at night," Post said. The barge was still far from the docks, behind the old brush-covered roadway of the interstate loop.

"I'd like to see if Kessey's guns can make a difference. Durning, you're forward observer for this side, I believe?"

The corporal in the post looked up. "Yes, sir."

"I want that barge sunk. Can you do it?"

"A crawling target like that? Yes, sir!"

Valentine listened to him talk into the field phone to Kessey, acting as fire direction controller, and the far-off squawk of the alarm at the gun pits. Kessey had decided that, because of the lack of experienced crews, she could only put two guns into effective action at once. The other two would be used once some of the raw hands gained experience. Within three minutes the first ranging shot was fired as the barge negotiated the wide channel around the swampy turd shape of Gates Island.

"Thirty meters short," the observer called, looking through the antennae-like ranging binoculars. Kessey tried again. Valentine heard her faint "splash" through his headset, letting him know another shell was on the way. Through his own spotting scope, Valentine saw the white bloom of the shell-fall well behind the barge. He took a closer look at the tug. Thankfully, it didn't belong to Mantilla. The observer passed the bad news about the miss.

"Sir, it's the damn Quisling ordinance. Their quality control sucks sewage."

"The target's worth it. Keep trying."

The Quislings on Pulaski Heights tried to inhibit the crews by raining shells down on the battery. Valentine heard the crack of shells bursting in the air.

The observer was happy with the next shell, and he called, "Howizer battery, fire for effect."

The shells traveling overhead whirred as they tore through the air. Valentine stepped aside so Post could watch.

"Keep your heads down, boys. Nothing to watch worth a bullet in the head," he called to a pair of men resting concealed behind rocks and earth along the crestline to his left.

"I think there were two hits to the cargo, sir."

"Secondary explosion?"

"No, sir."

"Probably just a cargo of rice then. Worth sinking anyway. Corporal, keep it coming."

The sun was already down beneath the trees behind them. Three more times the guns fired, with the forward observer relaying results.

"Another hit!" Post said.

"Sir, the barge is turning," the observer said.

"They cut loose from the cargo," Post said. "There's a fire on board. Black smoke; could be gasoline."

Even Valentine could see the smear of smoke, obscuring the white tug beyond. "Forget the cargo, sink that tub."

It was getting darker. Tiny flecks of fire on the sinking barge could be made out, spreading onto the surface of the water. There had been some gasoline on board.

The observer cursed as shells continued to go wide. Valentine could not make out anything other than the guttering fire.

"Illuminate!" the observer called.

A minute later a star shell burst over the river.

"Hell, yes," Post chirped.

Under the harsh white glare, Valentine squinted and saw the tug frozen on the swampland shallows of the northern side of Gates Island. The pilot had misjudged the turn in the darkness.

"Fuze delay, fuze delay . . ." the observer called into his mike.

Shells rained down on the barge. Its bulkheads could keep out small arms fire, but not shells. The star shell plunged into the river, but an explosion from the tug lit up the river. Another illumination shell showed the hull torn in two.

"We got her," the forward observer shouted. "Cease fire. Cease fire."

"Pass me that headset, Corporal."

Valentine put on the headset. "Nice work, Kessey."

"This isn't Colonel Kessey, sir," the voice at the other end said. "It's Sergeant Hanson, sir. She was wounded by the mortar fire. Permission to redirect and counterbattery."

The mortars on Pulaski Heights were scattered and in defilade; the number of shells required to silence even one or two was prohibitive. "Negative, Sergeant. Get your men to their shelters. I'm promoting you to lieutenant; you'll take over the battery. What's the situation with Colonel Kessey?"

"Blown out of her shoes, sir, but she landed intact. I'm hoping it's just concussion and shock. She's already on her way to the hospital, sir."

Valentine kept his voice neutral. "Thank you, Lieutenant. Over and out."

Later that night Valentine went through the solemn, and rather infuriating, ritual of composing his daily report to General Martinez. He labored over the wording at the end of the report.

> At approximately 18:20 we sighted a barge moving up the Arkansas River. Our howitzer battery took it under fire. After ten minutes sustained shelling the tug cast off from the sinking cargo. The battery shifted targets to the tug, which ran aground and was subsequently destroyed by howitzer fire.
>
> Counterbattery fire from the Pulaski Heights mortars caused two casualties. A loader was wounded in the foot and the battery Fire Direction Officer, Lt. Col. Kessey, suffered head trauma resulting in a concussion when a shell exploded near her. I hope to report that she will return to duty shortly, as she was still training and organizing her crews. The battery is now under the command of a first sergeant I promoted to lieutenant. Lt. Hanson completed the battery action.
>
> Enemy troops continue to concentrate in front of us. Eventually larger weapons will be moved to Pulaski Heights, making our current position untenable and offensive action impossible. The mortar tubes are dispersed and guarded from the river side, but I believe the New Columbia area to be open to attack from the hills in the west. I respectfully suggest that a movement by your command in our direction will allow us to control central Arkansas and pressure Hot Springs from the north as other commands push up to join us.
>
> My staff has a detailed plan worked out. Establishing closer contact would go far toward coordinating the actions of our commands to the benefit of Southern Command in general and the detriment of Consul Solon and the TMCC in particular.

Writing Martinez was an exercise in futility, but it had to be done, no matter what taste the task left in his mouth.

Valentine put a code card in the envelope and sent it to the radio room. He looked around the basement room that served as his office and sleeping area. If a man's life could be measured by his possessions, his life didn't amount to much. A little leather pouch of Quickwood seeds. A toothbrush that looked like an oversized pipe cleaner. Field gear and weapons. A report from Styachowski on her progress in organizing the POWs from the camp into battle-ready infantry. Pages of notes. A terrain sketch on the wall. He was a man of lists. Lists of officer rotations. Lists of Quisling brigades and regiments identified in the area—it had doubled in length in the past week. A list of needs for the hospital—God knew where he'd find an X-ray machine, why did they even ask? Xray-Tango. A man who wanted and needed to switch sides thanks to intelligence and conscience, but who couldn't bring himself to do it.

He collapsed into his bunk, palms behind his head. His scalp was getting past the prickly stage, and the returning black hairs on his head made him look rather like someone on a long walk home from prison; the visible skin of his scalp made even more odd-looking thanks to their presence. He let his hearing play around the headquarters building. Fresh construction made the most noise: hammers and electric saws turning Solon's future meeting rooms and art galleries into living space, with fainter splats from the ground floor above as windows were bricked up into firing slits. Typewriters clattered as clerks catalogued and allocated the stores from the warehouse raid. He could hear Post and Styachowski talking with the top sergeants and a smattering of lieutenants as they worked out the organization of the hilltop's men; many of the prisoners were getting their strength back after a few days of balanced rations and could now be blended into other units. From the communications center he heard field phones buzzing or jangling—they'd come away with two kinds, the ones that buzzed doubled as short-range radios, the jangling ones had been used by Solon's construction staff—now shakily melded together in a single network rather like Valentine's *ad hoc* command.

The Consul hadn't reacted to his seizure of the Residence as quickly, or as violently, as he'd expected. The Quislings under Xray-Tango had just concentrated on keeping him where he was rather than prying him off the hill. The forces they'd assembled could overrun him, at no small cost, but so far they hadn't moved beyond the engagement of dueling sniper rifles. Perhaps they couldn't afford a Pyhrric victory with Southern Command still on the move in the south.

Did they want to starve him out? He had just under sixteen hundred soldiers and captured Quislings—the latter were digging and hammering together log-and-soil fortifications under Beck's direction—that he could feed for months, if necessary, at full, balanced rations. After the canned meat and vegetables ran out he could still manage beans and rice for another ten or twelve weeks. They must have known the contents of the divisional supply train he'd made off with. Of course, the food would run out eventually, but not before Solon had to send most of his boys back to where he'd borrowed them, or Archangel had been decided one way or the other. A few shady Quislings had made contact with the forward posts, offering to trade guns and small valuables for food. Valentine's hilltop forces were, temporarily at least, better off than the besiegers. He could just wait for Southern Command to move up after taking Hot Springs, or the less likely relief from Martinez. If he were Solon, he'd destroy the the forces in his rear as quickly as possible, before turning his attention to the new threat from the south.

But you're not Solon. You don't know the cards he's holding; he knows exactly how many aces you've got. Except for the Quickwood. Valentine hoped a few dozen Reapers had already been turned to wooden mummies by the beams he'd passed to Mantilla.

A whistle sounded from outside. Barrage?

Valentine took up his tunic and ran through the officers' conference room, with Beck's proposed layout still on the blackboard. He entered the radio lounge, where off-duty men gathered to hear news and music piped in by Jimenez and the other operator.

"What's the whistle?" he asked Styachowski, who was sitting below one of the speakers, fiddling with Solon's old bow and quiver. She'd had an idea to use Quickwood chips for arrowheads. The cane she relied upon was conspicuous by its absence.

"Thought I heard someone yell 'star shell.' I haven't heard it followed up with anything. Maybe it's a psych job."

"Get to the field phones, please. I want you in the coms center in case it isn't."

Valentine hurried out to the front of the headquarters building. Sure enough, a star shell was falling to earth. A second burst far above the hill as the first descended. Valentine saw the men atop the building pointing and chatting. A few figures hurried to shelters, assuming real shellfire was on the way.

"Sir, you don't want to be standing there if a beehive bursts," a private behind the sandbag wall filling one of the arched windows called to him, referring to the flechette-filled antipersonnel rounds fired by larger guns.

The Cat stood, anxious and upset, listening to the night. There was a droning in the sky, faint but growing. Suddenly he knew why he was anxious. *The chills . . .*

"Reapers!" Valentine shouted to the men on the rooftop. "Reaper alarm!"

The sentry froze for a moment, as if Valentine were shouting up to him in a foreign tongue, then went to the cylinder of steel hanging from a hook on the loudspeaker pole atop the building. He inserted a metal rod and rang the gong for all it was worth. Valentine picked up the field phone just inside the headquarters entrance and pushed the button to buzz the com center.

"Operator," the center answered. Another star shell lit up the hill-top, creating crossing shadows with the still-burning earlier one.

"This is Major Valentine. Reaper alarm." He heard the woman gasp, then she repeated the message with her hand over the mouthpiece.

"Captain Styachowski acknowledges, thank you," came the flat response.

Ahn-Kha appeared in the doorway behind him, a golden-haired djinn summoned by the clanging alarm. He had a Grog gun in his arm and a Quickwood stabbing spear between his teeth. A second spear was tucked under his arm.

"This is going—" Valentine began, then shut up as he saw what was coming from the east. In the glare of the star shell, he saw a little two-engined turboprop, the kind used by pre-2022 airlines to hop a few passengers between small cities, roar into the light at a hundred feet. The rear door was open.

"What the fuck?" one of the soldiers on the roof said, watching. A figure plunged from the plane, trailing a cathedral train of material that whipped and flapped in the air as it fell. A parachute that failed to open? A second one followed it, and a third, all with the same flagellate fabric acting as a drogue for the plunging man-figures. Valentine saw another plane behind, a different make, this one coming for him like a missile aimed at his position, its daring pilot almost touching the treetops.

"Your shoulder, my David," Ahn-Kha said, as Valentine felt the barrel of the Grog gun fall against his shoulder. Valentine froze, a human bipod.

"*Nu*," Ahn-Kha said, and the gun jumped on Valentine's shoulder as the Grog fired.

The boom of the .50 echoed in the hallway. The plane reacted, tipping its wings to the side. At that height there was no room for error; the plane veered into the treetops. It roared through them to the music of snapping wood, then struck a thicker bole and pancaked. Exploding aviation fuel flamed yellow-orange in the night.

"Good shot," Valentine said, hardly believing his eyes.

"Good luck," Ahn-Kha returned. "I guessed to which side the driver sat."

The star shells lit up the first figure's landing in white light and black shadow. It hit the ground running, shrugging off the drapes of fabric attached to it. Only a Reaper could survive such a landing with bones intact . . . as did the next, and the next, striking earth to the sound of clanging alarm gongs.

Valentine watched, transfixed, and his "Valentingle" told him where the others were. To the west. Climbing the sheer face of the quarry, the one part of the hill almost un-climbable and therefore almost un-guarded. He took one of Ahn-Kha's spears.

God, two were headed for the hospital.

"Ahn-Kha, get the Bears!" he shouted, hurrying toward the hospital building. He ran past the old stable building that now housed the dairy herd. He paused in his race and threw open one of the barn doors. If these were the "unguided" sapper Reapers, they might be drawn to the heat and blood of a cow more than a lighter human.

A Reaper ran across the hillside, leaping from fallen tree to earthen mound like a child hopping puddles, making for the hospital.

"You! You!" Valentine shouted, waving his arms.

It turned, hissing, face full of malice, eyes cold and fixed as a stuffed snake's. It squatted, and Valentine braced himself for the leap.

Tracer cut across his vision like fireflies on Benzedrine. Men in a hidden machine-gun nest, covering the open ground between the buildings and the artillery pits, caught the Reaper across the side. It tumbled, closing its legs like a falling spider, and rose dragging a leg.

Valentine was there in two Cat leaps, but he must have looked too much like a jumping Reaper to the machine-gun crew. Bullets zipped around him. Valentine dropped to the ground.

The Reaper staggered toward him, one side of its body recalcitrant, like that of a stroke victim learning to use his worse-off half again. Valentine heard screams from the machine gunners: a Reaper was among them.

He rose, spear ready, and realized that once he used Ahn-Kha's point, he'd be unarmed. The nearest weapon was with the machine-gun crew, now dying under the claws of a sapper. Valentine ran for their gun pit, pursued by the half-leaping, half-staggering stride of the shot-up one.

The Reaper in the gun pit was feeding, back to him. Valentine jumped from ten feet away, landed atop its back and buried the Quickwood in its collarbone. The beast never knew what hit it; the Quickwood sank into the muscle at the base of its neck before the handle snapped off. Valentine's body blow knocked it flat. It stiffened, legs kicking and hands pulling up fistfuls of earth in black-nailed claws.

Valentine ignored the bloody ruin of the soldiers in the machine-gun nest, noting only that one was a promising soldier named Ralston, who'd qualified at the bottom in marksmanship with his rifle, but when given a tripod and the sliding sights on a Squad Support Gun, came to the head of the class with his accurate grouping. He tore the machine gun from Ralston's limp fingers and fired it in time to see the flash reflected in the eyes of the oncoming Reaper, lit up in the gun's strobe light of muzzle flash as it came toward him. The 7.62mm bullets tore through even the Reaper cloth, blasting back the staggering nightmare into a jigsaw cutout of tarry flesh and broken bone. What was left of the thing rolled around aimlessly, clawing at and opening its wounds in search of the burning pain within, a scorpion stinging itself to death.

He opened the gun, put a new ammunition box on the side, let loose the tripod catch, and ran for the hospital.

The next fifteen minutes were a blur, and would remain so for the rest of his life. Not that he wanted to remember any of it. The fight lived on in his mind as little snapshots of horror. The hospital, looking as though a scythe-wielding tornado had passed through it, leaving Dr. Kirschbaum and Lieutenant Colonel Kessey in mingled pieces. Nail standing, eyes bulging, holding down the Reaper as it stiffened with his spring knife in its eye, feeling its clawed hand digging bloodily into the muscle of his thigh, searching for the femoral artery as it died. The wave of Reapers, a dozen or more, coming across the hillside, throwing aside men like a line of hunters knocking over cornstalks for fun. One Reaper descending into the ready magazine for the 155s and a resultant explosion, lighting up the night and sending a railroad tie skyward like a moon shot. The Bears and Ahn-Kha meeting them, backed up by the *Thunderbolt*'s old marines, clustered in a protective ring around Valentine, pikes and guns working together to knock over the death-machines and then pin them until they stiffened. Styachowski, fear-whitened face like ice in the moonlight, carrying Solon's bow and sending an arrow into a leaping Reaper just before it landed on Post's back. When another Reaper broke the antique as she used it to ward off a blow that threatened to remove her head, she thrust up with another arrow held near the tip, putting the Quickwood into its yellow eye. Max the German shepherd, a pet of one of the construction engineers, licking the face of his dead owner, stopping only to snarl and stare at anyone who approached the body. The screams of panic from the maternity ward, where the pregnant women had drawn one of the sappers, a dozen men dying as they tried to pull it down as they protected the mothers to be with nothing but their knives and scissors. Hurlmer finally sticking a pike into it, his head torn off for the act. The fearful, confused eyes of the last Reaper to die, a wounded beast trying to escape by crawling amongst the cows, harried by bullet and pike until it died beneath a feed trough, corn-meal dust sticking to the blood coating its face.

All the while there was rattling fire from the crestline, as Quisling troops probed the hill.

At dawn there were fifty-three corpses lined up. Thanks to the backhoe and a lot of sweat from soldiers with shovels, each would have an individual grave. Woodworkers were hammering together the arrowhead tepee-cum-cross design of a Southern Command grave post and passing them on to painters. The men were gray and haggard after last night's bitter fighting and the probe up the hillside. Valentine pulled as many men out of the line as he could and gathered them by the graves. They had to follow a circuitous path to get there to avoid observation from the spotters on Pulaski Heights; any gathering of men in the open drew mortar fire.

Ceremonies weren't for the dead; they were for the living. There was a lay preacher to say the right words over the bodies. When they were rested in their graves, Valentine walked down the line of bodies in their shrouds, searching for words to add meaning to what had been random slaughter.

"We're in a siege, men. This hill is like a medieval castle, and the enemy is at our gates. That enemy, the TMCC, is in the first phase of taking a position by siege. It's called the 'Investment.' He's already put an effort into destroying us. Last night we killed eighteen Reapers, thanks to the Quickwood. Eighteen Reapers." Nothing else could explain the malevolent choice of targets: the magazine, the infirmary, the maternity ward. "That means there's more than one Kurian Lord in the area, perhaps four or five . . . even six. Not many Kurians can work more than two or three Reapers at once. Thanks to the rising that we began across the river, I suspect some governors have already been kicked out of their holes."

He picked up a handful of dirt, and tossed it on the row of corpses.

"Last night they tried to get our lives cheap. We kept the price up, thanks to the Quickwood, your courage and especially the sacrifice of those killed last night. Solon's investment isn't paying any returns yet.

"The fifty-three soldiers we're putting in the ground pinned down thousands of troops with their lives. Those mortars, and the guns that will probably soon support them, could be used outside Hot Springs, or against the Boston Mountains. The forces around the hill, from the snipers to the machine-gun crews, are looking up the hill at us instead of at Southern Command's Archangel operation. They're here because our guns are covering the rail and water nexus for Solon's territory. There's no fast and easy way around us; it means moving on broken-down roads, crossing bridgeless rivers. Nothing moves by water or rail, east-west or north-south, without our stopping it. They're not able to shift troops fast enough, and Southern Command's eating up what they can move piecemeal."

They liked the sound of that. Bared heads of all skin tones and hair colors, sharing a common layer of sweat and dirt, lifted, nodded, turned to each other reassuringly.

"Every town Southern Command takes is liberated partly by us . . . though at the moment we're doing nothing here but having the occasional mortar shell dropped in our laps.

"Unless we're lucky, the fifty-three here are going to have more company as the days and weeks go by. It could be that we'll all end up on this hill with them. If that's our fate, I hope we cost the TMCC as much as they did. If any of you want to say anything, now's the time."

"I've something to say," Yolanda, the woman who had mutilated the captured guards back at the prison camp, began. "It is not right for such men to go into the ground without a flag to be under. They are soldiers. Soldiers are their flag."

Free Territory flags weren't stocked in the warehouses we raided, the overtired part of him said.

"So I made them one. The men who came in to get us, I thought of them as I made this. Styachowski helped me with the wording, and Amy-Jo on the mortar team drew the animal."

She held it up. It was not a big flag. The base of it was red, rimmed with blue and gold roping . . . probably from a curtain somewhere in Solon's imperial Residence. In the center was a silhouette of a tusked Arkansas razorback in black, pawing the ground angrily and lowering its head to charge. Blue letters stood out against the red as if luminescent. DON'T FEED ON ME read the block-letter slogan.

The men laughed, not at the amateurish nature of the flag but at the pithy sentiment it expressed. They liked it. Valentine felt a little electricity run through the men as she turned it so everyone could see. It was a fighting flag: black and blue set against red, the colors of a brawl. A team could rally round the image of an animal—that was part of the Lifeweaver Hunter Caste appeal—and a savage boar was as good as any. Wily, tough, stubborn, a brute that would gore any animal that dared hunt it—and ugly as its mood when challenged—it suited the dirty funeral attendees.

Valentine went to Yolanda's side, and Styachowski came forward to admire the flag in the sun. Three parallel wounds, probably Reaper claw marks, stood out on her forehead.

"Let's have it up," Valentine said. "Ahn-Kha, where's the pike Hurlmer got that one with?" Ahn-Kha walked along the graves until he found the aluminum conduit pipe.

It took a few minutes to rig wire through the grommets and fix it to the pole. Valentine recognized Yolanda from the prison yard, but he only knew Amy-Jo as one of the heroes from the hospital fight. She'd snatched up the infant Perry and barricaded the babe and his mother in a bathroom, holding the door shut as the Reaper pried it off its hinges before it was swamped by pursuing men.

"Where do you want it, sir?" Yolanda asked.

"Here at the graves," Valentine said. "You said they deserved a flag above them. Can you think of a better place?"

"Make some more," Ahn-Kha said. "Or at least another, for the headquarters. This battalion needs an emblem."

"Hell, with the prisoners, we're a regiment," Styachowski said.

"Valentine's Razors," Post suggested.

The phrase passed up and down the ranks and more cheers broke out.

Valentine looked at his feet, embarrassed for the tears in his eyes.

Styachowski dug the pole into the ground and Amy-Jo and Yolanda found rocks to pile about its base. It wasn't a big flag, nor was it high off the ground, but every eye was on it as it flapped in the fresh spring breeze.

"What kind of shape is the battery in, Hanson?" Valentine asked, after the memorial service dispersed.

"Is 'piss-poor' an appropriate military description?" the new lieutenant asked.

"Can you quantify it a little more?"

Hanson scratched the growth on his chin. "Those Reapers that came up the cliff, half of them made straight for the guns. That suicide mission into the ready magazine—I lost men there. Ives, Lincoln and Lopez bought it in their gun pit. We found Streetiner in a tree. Smalls is missing, Josephs—"

"Smalls? Hank Smalls?"

"Yes. He was a designated as a messenger. When I heard the firing at the base of the hill, I sent him to tell the mortar pits to start preregistered fire missions. He never came back. There's still some woodland that we haven't searched yet. Maybe he ran and hid, and has been too scared to come out yet. Can't say as I blame him."

Valentine tore his mind away from Hank. He feared for the boy, but had to keep the rest of his command in mind. "How many guns can you have in action?"

"I'm jimmying the lists so I can keep three firing, sir. It won't be quick fire, and I'd like another twenty men to start training."

"We're thin as it is. But ask Lieutenant Post about it."

"Thanks, sir."

"Feel free to practice on the Kurian Tower. No shell fired at that is wasted, as far as I'm concerned."

"In all honesty, sir, I'm not sure I'm up to being battery officer. Could you give me a new commander? Like Styachowski? She knows the theory, and she's good at putting theory into practice."

It took guts for Hanson to tell Valentine that he didn't feel up to the job.

"I'll talk it over with her."

"Thanks, sir. We'll get 'em firing again."

"I'll talk to Beck about getting your ready magazine rebuilt."

"Yeah, it's probably landing in Berlin right about now."

Valentine finished his walk of the perimeter. The men were in better spirits than he would have expected; killing the Reapers and resisting the probe had made them confident.

What success they enjoyed should be shared with Beck's defenses. There were clearings along the easier paths up the hill for open fields of fire, and a series of foxholes and trenches, many lined with logs, for the men to do their shooting. They were still digging dugouts for the men to wait out shellfire, adding interconnecting trenches and access to the flatter hilltop so the men could bring food and water forward safely, and laying mines and wire along likely alleys of approach. Valentine saw one of Kessey's—now Hanson's—forward observers teaching the other soldiers the defensive fire mission zones. With the use of a simple code word, they could call in mortar fire on their attackers.

He returned to the headquarters building, and asked around for Styachowski. She was in her usual spot, beneath the speaker in the radio lounge, eating a bowlful of rice and milk. Her skin had that translucent look to it again; she'd been pushing herself too hard.

"What is that?" Valentine asked.

"Rice pudding. Narcisse made it."

"Don't you ever sleep? You were up all last night."

"Listening to the radio is like sleep. I can zone. What I really need is food."

"I'd still rather see you flat on your back."

"Major, under the Uniform Code, I believe you've just made a sexual suggestion."

Valentine snorted. "That's not what I meant and you know it."

"I was trying to make a joke. You look like you need one."

"Hank Smalls is missing. Since last night. Hanson sent him with a message . . . He never came back."

"A Reaper?"

"Could be. We never knew how many they sent in, just how many we killed. Poor kid."

"And naturally you're blaming yourself."

Valentine left that alone. "I did dig you up for a reason," he said. "I need your help. How would you like a change of duty?"

She brightened visibly. "The Bears? I know Lieutenant Nail's hurt again—"

"Sorry. Hanson isn't confident in his ability to run the battery. I want to put you in charge of it."

Styachowski pursed her lips. "I only know mortars."

"But you know the theory, right?"

"Of course."

"You've done everything I've asked you. You can do this, too. Those guns have to be kept good and lethal. They're the reason the Quislings are all corked up."

"Major Valentine, I've got a question for you, if you don't mind."

"Shoot."

"Last night, you sent me down into the communications bunker. That's the safest place on this hill. Even a Reaper would have trouble clawing through that door Solon had put in. Why did you want me there of all places?"

"I notice you didn't stay. You're my second in command. I couldn't risk us both being killed."

"I'll take over the battery if you take my place in the headquarters. I heard what you did last night, running around in the dark with Reapers everywhere. I've been scared all day thinking about it."

"Are you afraid of having to take command?"

"Not that. I—"

"Courier, Major Valentine," a staff soldier called. "A courier's come in. She's asking for you, and she said for you to hurry."

"She?"

"Yes, popped up on the west side. Pretty gal, red hair, says she's your mama but she's too young for that. I think she climbed the cliff, just like the Reapers."

"Where is she?"

"Eating in the main galley."

"Thanks." Valentine turned to Styachowski. "Sounds like we're getting intelligence. Want to come?"

"For news? Naturally."

They found Alessa Duvalier shoveling rehydrated scrambled eggs into her mouth. She had changed into an outfit Valentine knew as her "traveling clothes." She wore a long, deep-pocketed riding coat, wide-brimmed hat, hiking boots and a backpack blanket-roll combination.

"Hello, Ali. Tired of the showgirl routine?" He and Styachowski sat down opposite her. The cook brought a plate of fried potatoes and Duvalier loaded them with salt before digging in.

"They've got you boxed in tight here, Val. I had to wade across a swamp to even get to that damn cliff. This sort of reminds me of the day we met."

She still had her fast, deft hands, now working knife and fork instead of tying dressings. Both of them had added a few pounds since then. They shared a smile at the memory.

"Then it must be important."

"First, Hamm's back in town with his whole division. Another is moving for Pine Bluff. They won't be there for a couple days maybe; bad roads, guerillas, mines and no rail. Hamm's going to be going across the river in small boats to get south."

"You're not going along?" Valentine asked.

"He's always been unpleasant. Last night he was a bastard. Mean as a stuck pig. The Trans-Mississipi is crashing down around his ears, he's angry at everyone. Executed a junior officer himself."

"Anything from us?"

"Yes. Two days ago a Cat came in from Mantilla. He got your answer, and it's in this letter." She reached into her coat. "What good can come of it beats me. We had to run risks to get this to you. Hope it was worth it."

Valentine opened the envelope and looked at the page. A few bare paragraphs, handwritten, told him what he suspected.

"Where are you off to, Duvalier?"

"South. Every Cat's on the hunt for Solon. He was supposed to be assassinated at the outset of all this, but the Cat shadowing him missed. He disappeared and the Cat's dead."

"Damn. Hamm's division is moving on too?"

"He was supposed to dust you off this hill cheap. They were supposed to take you out while the Reapers were up here causing trouble, but there was some screw-up at headquarters. Only half his division got here in time. The Ks lost a lot of Reapers. I think they're gonna blame him."

"What happened that made you choose last night to leave?"

Duvalier's eyes shifted to her eggs. She added more salt. "He said something about wanting to climb this hill and piss on your body. Accused me of sneaking with you. I think I was going to be arrested. When he went to the CP, I took off; around morning I came up on some pickets along the old interstate north of you. They were talking about how you were still up there. Thought I might as well deliver the message before moving on."

"And check to see if I was still breathing?"

"I brought you along as a Cat. Call it a family interest. Hope the packet helps."

"Your soaking was worthwhile. What's your opinion on Xray-Tango?"

She shrugged. "Typical high-ranking goon. I did hear a rumor from Hamm. The Reapers took his wife away some years back. They thought she was a Cat."

"Remember our Invocation? The blood in our palms?"

Duvalier scrunched up her eyebrows. "Yes. Of course."

"Wonder if that's what passed on our abilities. Something in the bloodstream. Maybe she somehow passed on some abilities to him."

"I don't know Lifeweaver technomagic. Hope it's not something that would show up on some kind of blood test. Might make it easier for them to find us."

"Perish the thought," he said.

She finished her meal and drummed her fingers on the table, so fast each tap combined into a single dull noise. "Sorry I can't be more helpful. Don't try to figure Quislings, especially high-ranking ones. Might as well try to win over a scorpion."

Valentine took his eyes away from her hands. "Feel free to load up with whatever you need. I'd like to ask one more favor of you, though."

"What would that be?"

"The sound of your voice."

It felt a little like a producer doing radio theater that night. Valentine, Styachowski, Jimenez and Duvalier were crammed into the little room, each holding a page of notes. Jimenez twiddled the dials.

"We're on TMCC New Columbia band now," Jimenez said.

"Contact GHQ New Columbia, do you read? Over," Jimenez said. There was a pause of just a moment.

"GHQ here, reading five-five," the speaker crackled back.

"I have priority com from Colonel Le Sain on Big Rock Mountain to General Hamm. He requests that the general come to the mike, wishes to discuss terms of surrender, over."

"Nulton, cut the crap," the voice said.

"Check your RDF and signal strength," Jimenez said. "I'm just up the hill from you, over."

Valentine pressed the transmit trigger. "This is Colonel Le Sain, boy. Get the general to the radio rikki-tik, would you? Standing by."

"Ack—acknowledge," the voice responded.

Jimenez cut the static as they waited.

"You really think turning this into a soap opera will work?" Duvalier said.

"Life's been hard on him lately. I want to make it all my fault," Valentine said.

The minutes passed. "This is Stanislaw, GHQ New Columbia, with General Hamm online. Do you read, over?"

"Zippety do-dah," Duvalier said. "He went for it."

"Colonel Le Sain here. Put the general on the phone."

"I'm here, you turncoat," Hamm's voice cut in. "They said you wanted to do a deal."

"Yes. I'm in charge of guerrilla activity north of the river. I'm in a position to accept your surrender."

"Drop dead, dunk. Signing off."

"Any unarmed man who comes up the switchback road will be taken prisoner, no reprisals."

"Le Sain, if you called me here to joke around—let me tell you my terms."

"Hey, Hambone," Duvalier cut in. "Guess who this is?"

There was static at the other end.

"Yes, sir, I'm up here, too. You were right about one thing, Knox and I had a little fling. He's a man with a future, treats me good, and you know what they say about Indian guys—"

"Get stuffed."

Duvalier checked her notes. "I told him all about you, Hambone. To all those out in radio land, tune in at oh-one-hundred for a detailed description of just how pathetic General Hamm is in bed, complete with what he begged me to do to him. Sorry, General, Knox said this was just too good to keep from the world. We had quite a laugh."

There was no response. Styachowski took over the microphone, and Jimenez switched it to a different frequency.

"This is Ozark Central Command. Ozark Central Command to all stations. Latest intelligence has Third Division moving south of the river. Activate Zones Nuthatch and Finch, alert Jay and Crane. Authentication Z-4, repeat Z-4, P-9, repeat P-9. Signing off."

Jimenez killed the transmitter as she finished the farrago of nonsense.

"That'll give him something to chew on," Styachowski said, looking over at Duvalier.

"I hope he chokes on it," she said.

Valentine put Duvalier in his room, ordering her to get some sleep before her after-midnight broadcast. "Makes me feel like a whore, but if you think it'll help," she said, as Valentine transcribed a few bedroom details about General Hamm. Valentine wrote it so there were five minutes of gossip, then a teaser for the next night's performance, describing what Hamm liked to do to elicit an erection.

Then he had the observers fire a star shell above the river while the moon was down. There was no sign of boat activity; the Third Division showed a lot of activity in its posts.

He gathered Styachowski, Post and Beck for a late-night briefing.

"I want us to be extra alert this morning. Anyone else noticed an increase in activity?" Valentine asked.

"Yes, spotters saw a ferry shuttling back and forth upriver in the last four days," Styachowski said.

"I'd rather have that division busy with us than moving down to Hot Springs," Valentine said. "Earlier this evening we stuck a couple of banderillas in Hamm. Tonight Smoke is going to wave the red cape. He might charge at dawn."

"With the division?" Beck said.

"That's my guess. He'll try to overwhelm us. Captain Post, get every man you can into your line, but quietly. Captain Beck, I want you in the western command post. Send out pickets to listen—again, quietly."

"Yes, sir," Beck and Post said.

"Styachowski, have all your gun crews ready. Good people on the mortars; we'll be dropping shells close to our lines."

"I'll have everyone on station at 3 A.M."

"Major Valentine, report to the radio room, please," the PA blatted.

"Excuse me, please," Valentine said.

He made his way down the hall and to the stairs. There were crowds of men in the radio lounge, grinning and joking.

"Sir, we're going to be on the news," a private said.

"Really? Well, by God, we should be. You're causing Kur a lot of grief, for only fourteen hundred men. We're tying down something like ten thousand, you know."

"Go tell the Spartans," a better-read soldier commented quietly to a friend, but Valentine's ears picked it up anyway.

Valentine went down to the radio room, where Jimenez's relief was at the headset.

"I've got Baltic League on shortwave, sir. They're doing the news. In the news summary they mentioned us, and we're about to catch the repeat broadcast."

"Pipe it up, good and loud. Hell, put it on the loudspeakers."

". . . in the Caucasus continues," the vaguely English-accented voice announced. "Another Kurian Lord in the Rhone Valley went the way of his cousin last month when humanist guerillas seized his chateau, proving that the flames of resistance still burn in Western Europe. This is Radio Baltic League, broadcasting in the first language of freedom to humanity's patriots around the Baltic and around the globe, finishing the European part of the broadcast. Turning to America, an update on the news flash earlier. We have more details from Southern Command in the Ozark Mountains, lately the scene of heavy fighting. General Martinez reports that forces in his organization infiltrated, seized, and destroyed a major supply base on the Arkansas River, formerly the city of Little Rock. For those of you mapping at home, that's a major red-white-and-blue flag for our Cause. General Martinez's command has guns on a nearby hill commanding the entire town, and recently sank river traffic moving to resupply the forces engaged with Southern Command on the South Arkansas Front. He reports that the senior officer on the scene in command of the guns, Lieutenant Colonel Kessey, was wounded in the action, but has hopes for her speedy recovery. Congratulations to the daring and resourceful general, this morning's broadcast is in tribute to you and your men fighting on the Arkansas. Turning to other news from America, with spring coming to the Green Mountains and the Saint Lawrence Seaway—"

Valentine forced a smile across his face and went up into the radio lounge. The men gathered there looked like they'd been slapped.

"What the hell was that, sir?"

"Yeah, Major, that ain't right."

Valentine looked around. "What part isn't right? Did they get the location wrong?"

"No . . . no . . ."

"The lieutenant colonel is dead, but you can't expect them to know that detail. I've only just reported it."

"It's not that sir," Sergeant Hanson said. "They didn't mention you. Valentine's Razors. We're the ones that done it. Martinez, he's—"

"He's in charge of the central part of Arkansas. I send my reports to him, and he communicates them to Southern Command. They don't know everything that happened in his camp yet."

"But it's not right for him—" Hanson persisted.

"Sergeant, let's try to stay alive until this is over. They'll get the story right. It just takes some time. Get some food and rest, men. We might be busy tomorrow morning."

The next morning, they came in fire and thunder.

Duvalier's short broadcast gave the men a chuckle before they crept into Beck's fortifications. Soldiers always enjoyed a general getting his ego pricked.

The harassing fire started at three A.M., the mortars on Pulaski Heights peppering the whole hilltop with shells. Most of the men were in their trenches and posts, and those who weren't underground ran to safety in a hurry.

Valentine participated in the battle from the basement of one of the smaller buildings on the hilltop, between the gun pits and the western command post. All he saw of it was shellfire, all he heard of it was over scratchy field phone lines.

The men on Pulaski Heights came first. They'd obviously been given orders to pressure them with a river crossing, to look as if the attack were going to come by water. Styachowski dropped a few flechette shells among their boats, and the Quislings thought again about sacrificing their lives just to draw the attention of the artillery.

The listeners returned to their lines before light, with reports of men coughing, swearing and giving quiet orders. Beck ordered his handful of claymores—mines that swept the ground before a position with bursts of dartlike fragments like an enormous shotgun shell—placed above where they were concentrating.

When dawn came the artillery started. The divisional artillery was on the other side of Park Hill; Valentine wished he had a few trained men and a radio somewhere with a view. If Southern Command saw fit to send him a company or two of Wolves and a Bear team—

Their shooting was poor, compared to the mortars across the river. Shells landed all over the hill, damaging little but the turf.

The besiegers were at the bottom of the hill in the predawn gloom. Valentine listened in to the field-phone chatter. Kessey had her guns set up so the observers and officers on the line called the mortar pits directly without going through her, trusting the individual mortar crews to prioritize the use of their shells. Styachowski had been relentlessly training the men on the system ever since. The mortars went into action first, dropping their shells all around the base of the hill.

The assault came. Hamm struck from two directions, the north and the east, both driving to cut off the men at the tip of the finger of the hill extending eastward, to get control of the road going up the hill Valentine had used on his first trip to Solon's Residence. Styachowski used her guns to form a curtain of steel along the north face of the hill. Valentine paced and waited, watching the trees along the top of the eastern finger for signs of the Quisling troops. He forced himself not to call every time the firing quieted, and the company commanders had enough on their hands without him calling for status reports in the middle of action.

"Danger close! Danger close!" the voice of one of the forward observers crackled over the phone. He was calling in fire just in front of his own position—that the Quislings were partway up the hill this soon was troubling.

"Post, take over here. I'm going forward," Valentine said.

"There's no trench, Maj—" Post objected as he left.

Valentine had a soldier's eye for ground. His route to Beck's command post was determined by cover rather than directness. He scrambled through the fallen scrub oaks, along foundations of old buildings and then up a little wash to Beck's position on the north face of the hill.

Beck was at a viewing slit in his wood-and-earth bunker, looking west down the ridge pointing toward the train station. He had a band of dirt across his face the same size as the slit, giving him a raccoonlike expression.

"They're not having any luck from the east," Beck said. "Too much fire from the notched hill by the war memorial. They're coming up hard on the north side. Jesus, there it goes again . . . They're using flamethrowers. Sergeant, call in more mortar fire where that flame's coming from."

Valentine looked at the little gouts of flame as the sergeant spoke into his field phone, binoculars in his other hand. Beck passed his own glasses to Valentine. Valentine surveyed what he could of the north side of the hill; there were mottled TMCC uniforms all along it, all lying in the same direction like freshly cut hay.

Some gutsy company officer fired a signal flare, and the aligned figures stood and began to run up the hill. Beck tore the glasses from his face and flicked a switch on a fuse box. Explosions blossomed across the hill as the signal traveled the wire, little poofs of smoke shooting down the hill like colored sugar blown through a straw.

"The claymores," Valentine said. He saw the Abica brothers moving forward, great belts of ammunition about their necks like brass stoles.

"They're turning around."

"Lieutenant Zhao is back in the machine-gun post," a soldier reported. "He says they're heading back down the hill."

They tried again. According to Beck the second attack showed nothing like the patience and skill of the first. Hamm concentrated all his gunfire on the easternmost tip of the hill, until a permanent cloud of thrown-up smoke and dirt hung at the end of the hill, constantly renewed by further shellfire. But the men there held; the machine guns weren't silenced. As fast as they came up, they turned around and went down.

"We broke the second wave!" Beck's forward observer shouted. "They're running!"

"And the Third Division's bad luck continues," Valentine said. "Cease fire. Cease fire."

"Why?" Beck asked.

"Let 'em run. I want the others to get the idea. So next time they come, they have to start from scratch, not from halfway up."

"Hurrah for the Razors!" a soldier shouted as Valentine surveyed the devastated ridge. Stretcher-bearers braved sniper fire to bring in the wounded, and Valentine had come forward to see to those wounded. Pickups converted to ambulances were bumping across the shell-holed road to take them back to the hospital building.

God, and there's only one doctor.

"Valentine, time for me to be moving on," he heard, as he knelt beside a wounded man.

Valentine glanced up at Duvalier. "Interested in lugging a radio up Park Hill tonight?"

"No, sorry. Suicide isn't my style. I've got another assignment. They think Solon's outside Hot Springs. The Cats are concentrating. Someone'll get him."

"Is he so important?"

"Wherever he goes the Quislings do better, for some reason. He's like a lucky charm."

Valentine went back to cleaning the soldier's face. The man's elbow was torn up, and the skin on his forearm and hand already had a gray look to it. He'd never use his right hand again. "They won't try that again, will they, sir?" the private said, smiling.

"They're dumb, but they're not that dumb," Valentine said. "You taught them about touching hot stoves."

"It was them Bears, sir. They backed up our platoon. When the flamethrower burned out the machine-gun crew, they went down and got 'em, then held the machine-gun post, flames and all. We took the line back after that."

"Good teamwork, hero." He looked up at Duvalier. She stared at him, strangely intent. "Take off. It's getting dark. If you pass a TMCC mail pouch while you're sneaking through the lines, drop a note in for Xray-Tango; tell him I want to have a word."

Duvalier's lip trembled. "Val, if you guys get pushed off here . . . make for the south bank. There's good cover in the hills."

"We're here to stay, Ali. In the ground or above it."

She hugged him from behind; he felt her lips brush the back of his neck. Then she was gone.

There was a week-long respite from all save harassing fire. The Quislings were being careful with their shells, so only one or two an hour landed on the hill. Sometimes they would ratchet up the fire into a bombardment, so every time a shell landed Valentine tensed, waiting to see if others would follow. It was exhausting.

The only thing Valentine remembered about the period between the Third Division attack and the arrival of the Crocodile was Nail's recovery. Dr. Brough reported that one day the wounded Bear simply sat up and swung his legs off the bed, then walked downstairs for breakfast. He returned to command of the Bears and reorganized his tiny but ferocious group. With wounds from the Reaper fight healed, his teams were back at full strength.

Which was something that couldn't be said for the rest of the command. The bonfire they'd held to celebrate the victory was lit with the flames of Pyrrhus. The hospital overflowed with the bloody debris of his victory over his old general. Beck's line was a series of points; if the enemy came again as they had the first day of the attack, they would go through it like floodwaters through a screen door.

Then the first "railcar" struck.

The men called them that because it was what they sounded like as they roared overhead, looking like red comets of sparks. They may have sounded like railcars, but they struck like meteorites, causing the ground to writhe and shake in an explosive earthquake.

The shells landed all through the long night, every hour at the hour, precisely. The timing made the shelling even worse. Each man, Valentine included, dreaded the rise of the minute hand toward the top of the clock. One overshot the hill and splashed into the Arkansas River, while others killed men just from the concussion. Valentine saw one man with either a part of a lung or a stomach sticking out of his mouth. Others died without so much as a tooth being found.

The explosions drove man and animal mad. Max the German shepherd had to be put down after he attacked anyone who came near. The wounded in the hospital had to be tied into their bunks to keep from crawling under them, tearing out IV lines.

"It's the Crocodile, sir," a rummy-eyed old Guard said to Valentine in the blackboard-walled briefing room. Post stood next to him. "That's what we called it, anyway. They tell me from a distance it's all bumpy and green, and the tug tower sticks up like an eye."

"I've never heard of it."

"It's a Grog thing, out of St. Louis. She shelled us from twenty miles away on the Missouri, when we were dug in during the siege on the Bourbeuse in '61. She's naval artillery. She goes on the water and they move her around in an armored barge, like a battleship. I think they put the gun together on the banks, but nobody knows for sure."

"Solon's called in the Grogs? He must be desperate." Valentine wondered what kind of deal Solon had made to get the Grogs to aid him.

"You may get a chance to find out," Post said. "A messenger came forward at oh-nine-hundred, on the dot, under a flag of truce. He had a letter from Xray-Tango. I guess Hamm's been 'relieved' because it's signed General Xray-Tango, CINC New Columbia State, Trans-Mississippi. No demands, just a parley."

"Colonel Le Sain," Xray-Tango said, when Valentine emerged from the lines. Nail and Ahn-Kha stood alongside, Nail carrying the white flag. They met on an old residential road at the base of the hill. The growth had been blasted and burned by shellfire.

"General Xray-Tango," Valentine said. The general's spasm-afflicted eye sent out mental distress signals like Morse code.

"Both still alive, I see," Xray-Tango said.

"I should have shot Solon and you when I had the chance on that hill back in March. Would've been a nice change; the commanders kill each other and the privates live."

"What are you suggesting, a duel? We both take our pistols, walk ten paces and shoot? The winner gets the hill?"

"Save a lot of blood, General."

"You know it's ridiculous. Change of subject."

"You sent the message, General. What are we to discuss?"

"Your surrender. Prevent the 'further effusion of blood.' I believe that's the traditional wording."

"You're working for the experts in the effusion of blood, General."

"Forget it, Le Sain. I'll go back and blow you off that hill."

"General, suppose we step over under that tree and talk," Valentine said.

"That's better. A smart man knows when his bluff's called."

They walked along the old road at the base of the hill, leaving Nail, Ahn-Kha and Xray-Tango's aides looking across the road at each other. A red oak sprouted from a crack in the pavement, now big enough to offer them some shade in the late-morning sun. A dead apartment complex watched them with empty eyes.

"Just out of curiousity, General, what happened to Hamm?"

Xray-Tango's eye twitched. "He was"—*blink-blink-bliiink*—"relieved."

"Permanently, I take it."

The general said nothing.

"What are the terms, General?"

"Very generous, Le Sain. Very generous, indeed. These come from Solon and all the governors. Each has allowed their seal on the deal."

"I can just hear my last words as the Reaper picks me up: 'The seals are in order.' "

"It's got my name on it, too, if that means anything to you. It says you and your men can walk away. You can travel wherever you want, with your small arms. Join Southern Command's lines for all we care. Just get out of New Columbia."

"That simple, huh?"

"We kept it simple so you could understand it."

"I need to contact my higher ups."

"Oh, Colonel," Xray-Tango said. "I almost forgot. One more gesture of good faith for you. Bring him forward."

One of Xray-Tango's aides waved, and two soldiers stood up from the bushes, a slight figure between them. It was Hank. Valentine held his breath as they brought the boy forward, fearing some sort of sadistic display.

The boy had his right hand swathed in bandages. He was thin and haggard.

"What did you do to him?"

"That's a story, Colonel. He was being questioned, you see. By General Hamm himself."

Hank looked up at Valentine. He read pride, and something like defiance in the boy's eyes.

"I didn't tell them anything, sir," Hank said.

"No, he didn't," Xray-Tango continued. "Hamm took the boy to a charcoal grill. He threatened to cook the boy's hand there on the grate, smash it down like a hamburger with a spatula. Wanted to know who the spy at his headquarters was, like some kid would know. Your boy here stuck his own hand into the coals. Stared right at Hamm until he passed out. One of the men there puked from the smell."

"Hank—"

"Take him back with you. Your whole command, in the person of a prepubescent boy. What'll it be, Le Sain? Do they live or die? Does this brave kid live or die? Up to you."

Valentine pulled the boy over to his side of the road. "I'll see you later."

"You have until sunset. After then, anyone coming off the hill is dead. You've already had some deserters. This is your last chance."

"No, General, it's yours."

Xray-Tango stared with his owl eyes. "Pretty pathetic threat."

"You're fighting two wars, General, one with me and one with your conscience. The things you've seen, the people you've helped. You've been on the wrong side your whole life. You should have talked to your wife more."

"Huh?"

"She was a Cat. Same as me. The Lifeweavers train us to assassinate Kurians, Quisling generals, what have you. Maybe she was on an assignment, to kill you maybe, but she saw some hope in you, Scottie."

Xray-Tango's eye twitched. This time it didn't stop after three.

"That is . . . horseshit."

"Do you suppose they killed her quick, or slow?"

"Shut up. Shut up! I've made my offer. You have until sundown."

"They probably killed her. Maybe she was hung. In New Orleans I used to hear the guys in the wagons talk about a last ride for the women they—"

"Shut your fuckin' mouth!"

Valentine raised his voice in return. "What kind of sword is hanging over your head, General? How thick's the thread? You don't get us off this hill in hip-hop time and they'll haul you off, I bet. Brass ring or no. I saw one taken once. They jerked the ring right off, along with the owner's finger—"

Xray-Tango's eyes widened as he thought through the implications. "Balls," he howled. Xray-Tango's left fist exploded toward Valentine's jaw.

Valentine slipped under it, and just dodged a right cross that he only saw coming at the last split second. Xray-Tango moved fast for a big man. A jab by Valentine bounced off a beefy triceps. Xray-Tango paid it no more attention than a plowhorse did a fly.

Xray-Tango squared on him and the Cat's vision exploded into dueling rainbows; all the colors of the spectrum and a few Valentine didn't know existed danced to the ringing in his ears. He brought his forearms up to cover his face and saw a fuzzy apparition between his parallel radii.

Xray-Tango took the opportunity to work Valentine's stomach, the blows like the kicks of an entire team of mules. Valentine lashed out, but it only left him open for a combination that left him looking at the grass.

He fought for breath, took one and the mists cleared. He heard men shouting as he rolled to his feet.

Xray-Tango advanced, his fists turning tight circles in front of his massive shoulders. "Should have taken your dose and gone down, Valentine."

Valentine saw men from both sides gathering, emerging from their holes and trenches and piled-rubble redoubts to watch the fight. Even those who stayed behind with their weapons stood atop headlogs and sandbags to see the action.

Valentine tried a combination, but the big arms came up and he just missed losing part of his jaw to Xray-Tango's riposte.

"Who do you really wanna hit, General?" Valentine said.

Xray-Tango stepped in with lethal speed and tried the uppercut that had started the music still echoing in Valentine's ears, but the Cat stepped out of the way. The blows came like an artillery barrage, but every time the general's fist cut nothing but empty air. Valentine sidestepped, back-stepped, but there were no ropes to pin him, just an ever-shifting circle of soldiers.

"Shadowboxing, General. You're shadowboxing," Valentine gasped between breaths. "Quit fighting me and fight them!"

"They're fighting for the hill," someone in the crowd shouted as others came up. "A duel. General Extasy's winning against the Red Renegade!" An excited murmer went up from the crowd; every soldier's fantasy seemed to be coming true—the two big bugs fighting, instead of all the little worker ants.

Xray-Tango began to pant. "How are you going to win if you never hit back?"

Valentine bent under another combination, slipped under Xray-Tango's reach and came up behind the general, and tapped him on the shoulder.

"Did she ever ask you to desert, Scottie?"

"Narrr!" Xray-Tango bellowed, swinging laced fingers as though he held a sword to take Valentine's head off. Valentine ducked under it and the momentum of his blow carried Xray-Tango off balance. Valentine helped him to the ground with a cross.

The audience roared with excitement. "Southern Command is winning!"

"Extasy's a champ, you dunks," a seargeant from the other side shouted.

Xray-Tango rolled to his feet with the same grace that seemed so out of place in his big frame. Suddenly his feet were against Valentine's chest as he launched himself at Valentine with a two-heel kick, and Valentine felt something snap as both opponents fell backward to the ground.

The general rolled, got a hold of Valentine's leg and it was a ground fight. Against most other men Xray-Tango's weight would have ended the contest, but Valentine was a veteran of dozens of Zulu Company wrestling matches, often ending with Valentine facing the old top sergeant, Patel, before Patel won and went on to regimental competition. Valentine got ahold of an elbow and kept Xray-Tango's face in the dirt so he couldn't breathe. He forced the arm up, up—

Clack!

The arm suddenly gave way with horrid ease. Valentine sprang to his feet, let the general up.

"You're done," Valentine said.

"So are you," Xray-Tango answered. "We're going to roll up your men like—"

Valentine raised his voice toward the assembled Quisling soldiery. "The general lost. You're to retreat west, home to Texas or Oklahoma."

Dozens of faces suddenly brightened. An end.

"No!" Xray-Tango roared. "That wasn't what this was about."

"He's trying to back out of it," Valentine shouted over his shoulder to his soldiers. It was all lies; his men deserved more than lies, but if he could take the heart out of the Quislings, make them feel that their lives were being sacrificed after the general's loss of a duel—

"Back to your posts. Back to your posts. Open fire on this rabble," Xray-Tango shouted.

"Welshing Quisling!" a Razor shouted. Boos broke out on both sides.

"Back up the hill, men," Valentine said. "He lost and he's not squaring up!"

The two groups of men parted like magnets pressed positive to positive. Two floods of dirty soldiery retreated in opposite directions.

Valentine carried Hank up the hill himself.

Responsibility. Valentine had dreamed, on his long trip back across Texas, of being able to give up the burden, turn his command over to higher ranks. Let someone else make the decisions for a while, and lie awake nights because of the consequences. This was a decision he couldn't make.

He tried to consult higher authority. He had raised Southern Command on the radio, and got a colonel in Intelligence Operations who told him that "as the officer commanding locally, you're better able to evaluate the situation and reconcile your orders to keep as many as you can of the enemy tied down as long as possible, denying traffic across the enemy's road, river and rail network, rather than someone who had to be apprised of the situation over the radio."

"Thanks for nothing," he replied, fighting the urge to curse. He didn't want the techs in the radio room telling the others at breakfast that he'd lost it.

The anger at his superior officer was surpassed only by that with himself. He slammed the microphone down and retreated to his room. All over the camp, the story was spreading that Valentine and Xray-Tango had fought for New Columbia. Valentine had won, but the Quislings wouldn't leave. It made the men fighting mad, all the more determined to stay and win.

But Valentine lay in his bunk, feeling like a fraud.

The day's respite gave him a chance to gather the men in the open, in the afternoon sunshine. He gathered them at the grave site, where the fifty-three, now swollen to triple the original number, rested under their tiny hand-sewn flag. Valentine took in the faces. They reclined, his handful of Jamaican *Thunderbolt* marines, prisoners, Southern Command Guards, Bears, officers, NCOs and men, not a mass of uniforms, but a collage of faces. Faces he knew and trusted, under their dirt and bug bites. Only one or two had regrown the beards and mustaches they'd lost in the woods outside Bullfrog's phony station. Most had kept themselves as shorn as new recruits or in short, spiky hair—with showers a rarity, fleas, ticks and lice had multiplied.

He met the gaze of Tamsey, a corporal who'd shown him pictures of sixteen sisters. The boy had seen his mother die giving birth to his sixth sister, then his father remarried a woman with daughters of her own and jointly they produced more, and he knew every detail of each of their marriages. Next to him was a private named Gos, so nearsighted that he was almost blind, but an expert at feeding belts into a machine gun overlooking the switchback road on the southeast side of the hill. Gos could whistle any popular tune you could care to name, pitch-perfect. Amy-Jo Santoro, the heroine of the Reaper fight in the hospital, turned out to be an insomniac who sewed at night. She'd fix anyone's uniform, provided they gave it to her clean of dirt and critters; she had a horror of lice. There was Tish Isroelit, reputedly the Razors' best sniper, who'd stalked and then managed to bring down a Quisling colonel at dusk by the glow of his after-dinner cigar, shooting him through a closed window. She kept score by adding beads—Valentine had forgotten the exact ranking system, but it was color-coded—to braids in her chestnut hair. Sitting crossed-legged behind her was Denton Tope, a combat engineer whom everyone called "the Snake." Though a big man when he stood, he could press himself so flat to the ground one would swear his bones were made of rubber, useful for his trips out in the dark and wet to replace mines and booby traps at the base of the hill. He was always borrowing powerful binoculars at night to try to spot satellites among the stars. Dozens of other mini-stories, sagas that had briefly joined with his own and were likely to end on the churned-up hill, waited for him to speak.

"This is the deal," Valentine began. "There wasn't a duel for the hill, that was a private fight. Here's the truth: General Xray-Tango has given us until sundown to walk off this pile on our own. He'll escort us, with our rifles, anywhere we want. Hot Springs. Up north to Branson, maybe; see a show.

"Or we can stay here. Let them waste their time and bullets killing all of us, instead of Southern Command soldiers liberating towns and villages full of your relatives. Make sure there are a few less of them at the end of it all. At the end of us."

"So it's a life-or-death decision. How many of you know what the phrase 'Remember the Alamo' means?"

Hands went up all across the command. His command.

"I see a few who aren't familiar with it. It refers to a battle fought two hundred and fifty years ago, or thereabouts. Some Texicans under a colonel named Travis were holding out against a general named Santa Anna at a little abandoned mission station on the Rio Grande. They were outnumbered, surrounded, but they fought anyway, gave a man named Sam Houston time to organize his own counterattack. It became a battle cry for an entire war.

"How many of you remember Goliad?" No hands this time. "I'm not surprised. They were also a group of men in that same revolt against Santa Anna. They didn't fight like the men at the Alamo. They surrendered. Santa Anna executed every one of them.

"I'm not saying we'll be remembered, I'm not saying we'll be forgotten. What we do up here may have an effect on the future. Whether that future remembers us or not . . . it's not for me to say. I'll tell you another thing about the Alamo. Each of those men made a personal decision to be there. Some say they stepped across a line in the sand.

"I'm not doing anything that dramatic. Any of you who want to leave can get up and walk down that hill. I'm staying, and Ahn-Kha's staying. Each of the rest of you have a decision to make. You have until sundown to get out of town, according to Xray-Tango. He's going to kill the rest of us. Well, he's going to try.

"I'm going down to the radio lounge. The smart thing to do is run. It may not be the right thing to do, but it's the smart thing. The dummies can join me for a drink. We need to be back in the line at sundown. I expect the Crocodile will start firing again."

Valentine used his knife to cut open a carton marked "snakebite serum," from the medical quarters. Mantilla had given him the case that night he'd passed most of the Quick-wood on to Southern Command. He extracted a bottle of bourbon and broke the seal on the paper screwtop. He sniffed the amber contents. He flipped up two shot glasses on the bar.

"One drink for you, Colonel Travis, and one for me."

Travis didn't seem to want his, but Valentine left it there for him anyway. Ahn-Kha stood in the door.

"Good news," Ahn-Kha said. Nothing more. The Grog turned and went upstairs.

Valentine walked out the oversized doors, still on their hinges despite the shellfire. The soldiers stood in ranks, not neat, lines not dressed, and nothing but a proud expression was uniform, Post, Styachowski and Beck to the front.

"Thank you, men," he said, blinking back tears. "How many smart ones were there?"

"Nineteen," Styachowski reported. "Two were wounded. None of them women; they all wanted to stay."

Valentine saw a bright bandanna in the back.

"Couldn't get anyone to carry you out, Narcisse?"

"Didn't want to run again," she called. "Haven't had much luck with that; only have one arm left, sir."

Dr. Brough appeared with the case of bourbon. "Company commanders, to me. We've got some bottles to distribute."

"Okay, you dummies," Post said. "Back to business. Let's disperse, no point in getting killed all at once."

Valentine pulled the youngest member of his command aside as they dispersed.

"Hank, you sure you're fit to rejoin your outfit?" Valentine asked.

"Yes, sir."

Valentine disagreed. Hank looked sick.

"How's the hand?" Valentine said through gritted teeth. His nose picked up a faint, sweet smell from Hank's bandaged hand.

"Not so bad."

"Report to the doctor. If she says you're okay, you can get back to Captain Styachowski. She needs quick feet at the battery."

Hank turned away, dejected. Valentine whistled, and the boy turned.

"Hank, of all the men who stayed up here tonight, I'm proudest to have you with me."

The Crocodile opened up on them again as soon as the sun disappeared. The Grogs upped their rate of fire to three shells an hour, every hour. Their firing was wild at night, though the air-cutting shrieks and earth-churning impacts made sleep impossible. When dawn returned they began reducing Solon's Residence to rubble.

The men began to go as mad as Max the German shepherd.

One snuck out of his dugout at dawn and was spotted by an observer standing atop a heap of rubble, arms outstretched as though welcoming a lover's embrace as the sun came up in thunder.

Later they found a boot, Post reported, his incipient beard now going gray as well.

Sergeants had to put down furious brawls over nothing. The precise timing of the shells tightened everyone's nerves into violin strings as they waited for the next howl and explosion, leaving flung dirt floating like a cloud atop Big Rock Hill.

Valentine was coming up the stairs from the generator floor, where he'd been checking fuel feeds damaged by the shelling, and passed Styachowski in the stairwell when the 15:20 struck, burying its nose in the ground deep—and near—enough to cause a collapse at the floor above. Valentine threw himself at Styachowski, pushing them both into a notch under the stairs—unnecessarily as it turned out—and the lights flickered and died just as he smelled her hair and the feminine musk coming up from her collar.

They scooted up against an intact wall, Valentine covering his head as well as he could, and he felt a wave of dust hit him in the dark.

"You okay?" he asked, hearing rubble fall somewhere up the stairs. It sounded strangely far-off and muffled.

They sat there as the air settled. Valentine thought he heard a shout from above, but there wasn't a hint of light.

"I'll be dead soon, I think. It works on the mind. I'm smelling food, growing plants, coffee being warmed up. Listening to everyone."

"There's still hope," he said.

"You tell yourself that? Or just the rest of us?"

"They haven't whipped us. They aren't even close."

"That's not an answer."

He didn't supply one.

She pressed his shoulder with hers in the darkness. "You're an odd duck, sir. You look so . . ."

"So what?"

"Never mind."

"I'd like to know what you think. Might as well talk about something."

"How about that bacon we had yesterday? Talk about the bottom of the lot," she said.

"You've got me curious. I look so what?"

"Well, you look so soft, I was going to say. You've got really gentle eyes. They're scared, too. Sometimes. Like that night they dropped the sappers."

"I was scared. Till I saw you with that bow. You looked like you were at target practice."

She didn't say anything. He broke the silence. "Speaking of setting an example—I should go up those stairs and see—"

"No. Give it another minute. We're here, it's dark, and you smell . . . comforting."

"Is that a soft smell?"

"See, you are hurt."

"No. Interesting to see yourself through another's eyes. What another person thinks."

"I want it to be over. I'm down here in the dark pretending there's no fighting, no Crocodile. No memories of Martinez and his gang. You can't imagine how good it feels, to have all that gone."

Actually he could. Valentine had sought oblivion in lust in the past . . .

They sat in the dark, feeding off each other's warmth, conducted through her hard-muscled shoulder.

"Sir, why are you what you are?" Styachowski asked.

"You mean a Cat? And it's 'David' or 'Val' when I'm off my feet."

"Okay, Val. Why?"

"Why don't you go first?"

"I took up soldiering because I knew I could fight. When I was little, about six, I got into a scrap with a boy two years older than me. I beat him. When I say 'beat him' I really mean 'beat'—he ended up in the hospital. After that my mom told me about my dad. He'd been a Bear, in a column marching back from some fight in Oklahoma. Caught Mom's eye somehow, and they had a night before he moved on. She said she wasn't thinking—just doing patriotic duty she called it; I showed up nine months later. She said the hunting-men were like wild animals and I had to control myself and never lose my temper. The doc said that was superstition, but I dunno."

"Your mom may have been right. My father was a Bear, too."

"So you joined to be like him?"

"Something like that. I think it was my way of knowing him. He was dead by that time."

She sniffed. "Oh, I'm sorry."

"So the Bears didn't want you?"

"No. But I still want to be one. It's like this monster inside that wants to get out, wants to fight. I'm afraid that if the monster doesn't get to take it out on the enemy, it'll get out another way."

Valentine had never met someone with the same dilemma before. After a moment, he said: "You worried that you're a threat to others?"

"I meant myself."

Valentine brushed dirt off his kneecaps. "I wondered what my father's life was like fighting for the Cause, what made him give up and go live in the Northwoods. Now the only thing I wonder is how he lasted so long. There were other reasons. I believe in the Cause. I've got no time for the 'it's over, we've lost, let's just weather the storm, fighting makes everything worse' crowd. The Cause is no less just for being lost. Then again, being special appealed to me—meeting with the Lifeweavers, learning about other worlds."

He wanted to go on, to tell her that he worried that the Lifeweavers had also unlocked the cage of a demon somewhere inside him, to use her metaphor—even more, fed and prodded the demon so it was good and roused when it came time to fight their joined war. The demon, not under his bed but sharing his pillow, was a conscienceless killer who exulted in the death of his enemies at night and then reverted to a bookish, quiet young man when the fighting was over. He worried that the David Valentine who agonized his way through the emotional hangovers afterward, who sometimes stopped the killing, was vanishing. He could look at corpses now, even corpses he'd created—felling men like stands of timber—with no more emotion than when he saw cordwood stacked on a back porch. It made him feel hollow, or dead, or bestial. Or all three at once.

A voice from above: "Clear from here on . . ."

Valentine saw the flicker of a flashlight beam and got to his feet, reaching up into the dark to feel for the stairs above.

"Hellooo—" he shoulted as he helped Styachowski up.

"Stay put. On the way," a male voice called back from above.

Soldiers with flashlights, one carrying a bag with a big red cross on it, came down the stairs.

"Hey, it's Re—Major Valentine," one called to the other.

"That was fast digging," Styachowski said.

"There's not much of a blockage," the one with the medical kit said. "Just a wall collapse and some dirt to climb over. Ol' Solon built his foundations well."

Styachowski straightened her dust-covered uniform. "We're fine," she said, reverting to her usual brisk tone. "Let's get those lights in the generator room and see where the trouble is."

The last of her warmth left his skin as Valentine nodded. She turned, and he followed her and the soldiers into the generator room.

They had electricity within the hour, but Valentine wasn't sure how much longer he could transmit, so he composed a final report to Southern Command of two bare lines. He walked it down to the radio room himself.

Jimenez had the headset on. Jimenez took it off and threw it on the desk, upending a coffee cup. He didn't bother to wipe up the spill.

"They left Hot Springs yesterday. The official bulletin just went out."

"Then what's wrong? They're only fifty miles away. There's nothing between us and them."

"They're turning northwest. Heading for Fort Smith."

Valentine patted him on the shoulder. "There's a lot of Kurians in Fort Smith. Let's hope they get them."

"Right. Across mountains."

He placed his final transmission to Southern Command on the coffee-covered desk.

WE STAYED. WE DIED.

The shelling from the Crocodile went on for four more days. It was the closest thing to insanity Valentine had ever known. Nothing had any meaning except where the next shell would land. Styachowski's guns couldn't reach the Crocodile. One by one they were put out of action.

The radio room was buried by a direct hit, and Jimenez with it. The hospital had to go underground when a near miss blew down its southern wall. Beck died on the third day, torn to shreds as he turned the knocked-down remnants of Solon's Residence into a final series of trenches and fire lanes. Styachowski took over for him, pulling back what was left of her mortars and placing them in a tight ring of dug-out basements, along with a few shells they were harboring for the final assault.

They knew it was coming when the Crocodile's fire stopped. Thirty minutes went by, and the men gathered at their firing posts. An hour went by, and they began to transfer wounded.

The single remaining pack radio, kept operating by Post, crackled to life. For the past two days it had been rigged to the generator recovered from the kitchens. Post whistled and shouted for Valentine across the ruins. He hopped over a fallen Doric column, a piece of décor Solon fancied, and climbed down the wooden ladder to Post's dugout. A shell or two pursued him. Just because the Crocodile was silent didn't mean the mortars on Pulaski Heights quit firing.

"Urgent call for you, sir," Post said. "Scanner picked it up."

"Le Sain? Are you there, Le Sain?" the radio crackled, on Southern Command's frequency.

"Go ahead; not reading you very well."

"It's a field radio." Valentine heard distant gunfire over the speaker. "It's me, Colonel. The Shadowboxer."

"Go ahead, General. Another surrender demand?"

"It's Scottie to you, Knox. Or whatever. I'm the one that surrendered, using your metaphor. I took a few members of my staff on board the Crocodile. We wanted to see the gun in action, you see. For some reason the Grogs didn't think it was odd that I had a submachine gun with me. I shot the crew and pulled out a hand grenade. Grogs sure can run when they use all their limbs." He laughed, and it occurred to Valentine that he'd never heard Xray-Tango's laugh before. "Now I'm sitting between the magazine door and a shell. There's a dead Grog loader propping it open. This shell's a monster: it's got to be a fourteen-inch cannon. My driver and a couple of members of my staff are making their way around the other side of the gun through the woods. The Grogs are running for dear life. Regular Cat trick, isn't it? Infiltrate, assassinate. All that's left is the sabotage. I've got a grenade bundle in my lap right now."

"Scottie, I—" Valentine began. Post had an earpiece in his ear and a confused look on his face.

"Going to have to cut this short, Colonel." Valentine heard automatic fire. "My driver almost has an angle on me. Apologies to St. Louis, looks like they aren't getting their gun back. You know what the best part is, Le Sain?"

"What's that?"

"Since I started dreaming up this plan night before last, my face hasn't twitched once. God, what a relief, it's wonderful. Over and out."

Something lit up the sky to the east and Valentine felt the ground shudder. He counted twenty-two seconds. Then it came, a long, dull boom. Valentine went back up the ladder, and saw the top of a mushroom cloud climbing to the clouds, white flecked with gray at the edges. He watched it rise and spread.

Until the tears came.

The shells stopped, but not the attack. On the thirty-fifth day of the siege they came up the north face, like the wind behind a rain of mortar shells. They came up the east ridge; they came up the switchback. They came up everywhere but the quarry cliff.

The Beck Line collapsed.

Valentine's men tumbled backward toward the Residence. What was left of the gun crews dragged the one remaing gun back to Solon's prospective swimming pool and set it up there.

Even the headquarters staff turned out to stanch the attack. Valentine watched it all from a tangle of reinforced concrete, a conical mound of debris looking out over the hilltop beside what was left of Solon's Residence.

"Officer by the switchback road," Valentine said, looking through some field glasses. He and Ahn-Kha occupied one of the higher heaps of rubble. Ahn-Kha swiveled his Grog gun. His ears leveled and he fired, kicking up concrete dust.

"They'll zero that," Valentine said. "Let's move."

They slid off the mound and into the interbuilding trenches. Rats, the only animals that didn't mind shellfire, disappeared into hideyholes as they picked their way to the headquarters basement.

It still had a roof of sorts on it, three stories of collapsed structural skeleton. Among the cases of food and ammunition, Brough patched up wounds and extracted shrapnel with the help of her remaining medics. Bugs crawled in cut-off clothing, stiff with weeks' worth of sweat and dirt.

Brough didn't even look at the worst cases. After triage, performed by Narcisse, the worst cases were sent to the next basement over, which was only partially covered. There a few of the stronger-stomached women replaced bandages and murmured lies about recovery. That the men called the passageway to the next basement the "death hole" showed the general opinion of a sufferer's chances within.

Styachowski and Post bodily shoved the men into positions in the final series of trenches as the stream from the crestline turned into a trickle. They moved dully, like sleepwalkers, and collapsed on top of their rifles and slept as soon as they were told to stop moving. Soon, what was left of his command had to keep their heads down not just from mortar fire, but from machine-gun fire that swept the heaps of ruins.

Valentine looked around the last redoubt. In a year it would be a weed bed; in five these mounds would be covered by brush and saplings. He wondered if future generations would wander the little hummocks and try to pick out the final line, where the Razorbacks were exterminated in their little, interconnected holes like an infestation of vermin.

Hank was in the death hole. His burns had turned septic despite being dusted with sulfa powder, and Brough was out of antibiotics. The boy lay on the blankets someone else had died in, waiting his turn, keeping the tears out of his eyes.

"We sure stuck a wrench in their gears, didn't we?" Hank asked, when Valentine sat for a visit.

"With your help," Valentine said. "Wherever your parents are, they're proud of you."

"You can be honest with me, Major. They're dead; they have been since that night. You can tell me the truth, can't you? I'm tough enough to take it."

"You're tough enough."

Hank waited.

"They're dead, Hank. I went after them, and I killed them with the rest of the Quislings. They were telling about the Quickwood. About the ruse."

"My fault, sir," Hank said.

Valentine had to harden his ears to make out the tiny voice. "No."

"It is," Hank insisted. "I heard them talking after the baby—after you told us she was dead. 'We won't be sacrificed,' Pa said, and they started speaking with their heads together. I should have told you or Ahn-Kha or Mr. Post—but I didn't. Just Mister M'Daw and then it was too . . ." The boy faded back into sleep, like a child who has fought to stay awake until the end of an oft-repeated story but lost.

Valentine knew from fifteen years of regret what sort of abyss yawned before the boy. Agony rose and washed through him along with a gorge he fought to keep down, all the pent-up emotional muck of his losses breaking in his roaring ears and wet eyes. Maybe if he'd been tending to his ax and the kindling as was his duty that day, instead of corn collecting, he would have warned Mom of the trucks coming up the road to the house; she would have grabbed his sister and baby brother and gotten his father from the lakeshore—

Regret might haunt Hank, grind the child down, or drive him to God-knows-which bitter lengths to compensate for an imagined fault. Valentine couldn't allow that to happen to the boy—or man, rather. If anyone on the hill exhibited the manly virtues Valentine had listed when he sent Hank off to the guns, it was the septic boy in the cot.

Being able to forgive himself was a cause as lost as the Razors'.

There was still plenty of hot cocoa; it came in tins with little cups inside so all that was needed was a glass and hot water. He, Ahn-Kha, Post, Styachowski, Nail, Brough and Hanson met one final time. Their conference room was filled with wounded, so they gathered in the last artillery magazine. A few dozen mortar rounds stood, interspersed with sandbags, where once there had been hundreds stacked to the ceiling.

"You know what's always pissed me off about this operation?" Valentine asked.

"Your haircut?" Post asked. The officers had enough energy left to laugh.

"That railroad bridge. We never were able to bring it down."

"Isn't that in the 'too late to worry' file?" Nail asked.

"Not necessarily. If we get the men up and moving, we could punch through. Some of us would make it to the bridge. I doubt they've got reserves massed everywhere in case of a counterattack. Once we got off the hill it's only a mile."

"I'll go with you, my David," Ahn-Kha said. "I don't want to die like my father, in a burned-out hole."

"What happened to tying down as many troops as possible as long as possible?"

"Aren't you all sick of this?" Valentine said. "The dirt, the death? Sitting here and taking it?"

Styachowski and Nail exchanged looks. "If we do it, I imagine you'll need Lieutenant Nail."

"Of course I'd need him."

"Then I can't try my plan to save Hank," Dr. Brough said.

"What's that?"

"The boy, the one with the gangrenous arm. I've been curious about the resiliency of the Bears. I put some of Lieutenant Nail's blood in a dish with a bacterial culture. It killed it, like his blood was full of chlorine. I thought I'd try a transfusion; he and the boy have the same blood type. But it would take time for him to recover."

"You may not have that, Doctor. They'll attack again. I don't believe we're in any kind of shape to hold them off."

"Hank can't hold off the gangrene. It's system-wide."

Valentine finished his cocoa. "Nail, would you turn over your command to Styachowski? She's always wanted to be a Bear."

Nail tried walking on his wounded, mangled leg. He was still limping.

"I hate to miss out on a fight if my Bears are involved."

"I'll bring them back to you, if I can," Styachowski said.

The transfusion took place within the hour. It was done under fire; the Quislings launched a probing attack to see what sort of defenses the defenders still had. It left Nail drained, and after a tiny meal—by Bear standards—he drifted off to sleep.

As it turned out, they weren't able to try Valentine's plan that night anyway. The day's clouds dissolved and it was a clear night for the half moon. They'd be spotted on the river too easily. Valentine looked down at the bridge, and saw the white Kurian Tower beyond, shining under its spotlights like a slice of the moon fallen to earth.

The Quislings cleared the roads and brought armored cars up the hill. They prowled the edges of the ruins like hungry cats at rat holes, shooting at anything that moved. Styachowski and the Bears went out and buried what was left of the mortar shells where they had driven before. The next day they managed to blow the wheels off of one. It sat there, looking like a broken toy in a rubble-filled sandbox.

Then came the quiet dawn. The harassing fire slacked off, and the men were able to dash from hiding hole to hiding hole without anything more than a sniper bullet or two zinging past. Valentine was watching Hank sleep. He felt strangely relaxed. Perhaps it was because of the color in Hank's cheeks and his deep, easy breaths. The boy was on the mend. He worked out a final plan. His last throw of the dice, in the strange table run that had begun with Boxcars.

He talked it over with Ahn-Kha, Nail and Styachowski at the nightly meal. Post had been briefed early and would assume command of what was left of the Razors—mostly a noisome aggregation of wounded sheltering in dugouts and the basements of Solon's headquarters.

"It's worth a try," Nail said, looking at the weird, questionmark-shaped assault path Valentine had mapped out. He had a little of his energy back. "They won't be expecting it, after all this time, with them so close."

"It could take the heart out of them. Even more than the loss of

Xray-Tango," Ahn-Kha said. The Golden One's ears drooped unhappily. He'd been tasked with his supporting role.

"The only heart I'm after is in that tower," Valentine said.

Nail joined them despite his weak state. Valentine wanted to leave him and Styachowski both back at the camp, but they presented a strangely united front, and he couldn't argue with both.

Their chosen path to the river was down the cliff face above the quarry. Valentine had only rappelled once, long ago, in an exercise as a trainee. Valentine, Ahn-Kha and the Bears crept out of the trenches and moved west, where they fixed ropes to tree stumps.

"I would like to come on this, my David," Ahn-Kha said.

"Sorry. I need your muscles to haul us back up this rock," Valentine said. "Don't stay here and die. If you get overrun, try for the swampy ground to the north. Go back to your people."

Ahn-Kha looked over his shoulder at the shattered walls and missing roofs. "My only people are here, now. I will wait. Unless a bullet finds me, I will wait here, yes, even through another winter and another like that."

Valentine gripped arms with his old ally. "I'll be back sooner than that." He looped a line through a ring on a harness improvised from an AOT backpack, and dropped over the edge.

Naturally, he burned his hands.

The Bears loaded their gear onto an inflatable raft as Valentine applied antiseptic and dressings to his hands. The raft was a green thing that rose at each end like a sliced quarter of melon. A box containing four of them had been on the first train brought to Big Rock Hill. With a little luck and a little more dark, they might be able carry the Bears to the other side without being observed.

They waited by the riverbank as they half inflated the boat. It only needed to carry their gear, and the lower its profile the better. A warm breeze blew down the river for a change. Summer was coming on, and the frogs were welcoming it with creaky voices. Bats emerged from their riverside lairs in the quarry and hunted mosquitoes with meeping calls Valentine's hard ears could just pick out.

Valentine and the men were nervous. Even Rain, who had started a second set of slanted brownish scars on his left arm, shifted position and mumbled to himself constantly.

The Bears huddled together as they worked the little bellows that inflated the raft, keeping watch for patrols at the riverbank. The AOT had lost men on this side of the hill to snipers and had given up trying to occupy the narrow strip of ground between the cliff face and the river, but they could never be sure there weren't dogs loosed at night.

"What's going red like?" Valentine asked. He'd heard various stories, including one from ex-Bear Tank Bourne, but he was curious if different men felt it differently.

"You can't control it too well," Red said, patting the belt-fed gun on his lap. "All that has to happen is a gunshot and over I go. You get all hot and excited, like you've just won a race or something. Everything seems kind of distant and separated from you, but you have perspective and everything, so when you chuck a grenade it lands where you want it, not a mile away. Pain just makes you hotter and ready to fight more. It wears off after everything's all over, but once in a while Bears drop over afterward and don't wake up. Their hearts burst."

"You feel like you can run, or jump, or climb forever," Hack put in. "Sometimes you have to scream just to give it all somewhere to go. Here's something they don't talk about at the bar, though. Most Bears piss themselves over the course of it. Every single red nick I've got on my arm means I've come back with a pantload of shit."

Nail nodded. "I always go into action with an extra diaper under my pants. The guys in Force Apache wear kilts—actually, more like flaps—that's another solution."

"Glad I'm a Cat," Valentine said. "What about you, Styachowski, what do you want for a handle?"

Styachowski looked up from where she sat, knees hugged to her chest, one hand wrapped with a leather wrist guard for her archery. "I'd like to be named by my team."

"How about 'Guns'?" Nail asked. "From the cannon. Plus, she's got the arms for it."

Styachowski looked down, flexed her muscles. "Let's wait until after tonight."

The chill of the Arkansas River's current was enough to geld the seven men. The river flowed differently every few yards, it seemed; for a few minutes they had to kick hard to keep from being pushed downriver too far, then they'd hit a pool of slack water in the lee of some sandbar. They swam like pallbearers with a floating casket, four to each side. They made for a spot halfway between the Pulaski Heights and the bridge, near the place where Styachowski had been buried by the fallen sandbags the day the river ran mad.

When their feet struck muddy bottom again, they halted, and Valentine went up the bank for a scout. He saw that the rail bridge was lined with sandbags, thick with men and weapons points. Cable was strung about ten yards upstream, festooned with razor wire and looking as though there were more lines underwater, barring access to the bridge pilings. The boats would never make it through without a good deal of work with bolt cutters and acetylene torches.

But his Bears were on the enemy side of the river. In the distance, the concrete tower of the Kurians stood like a white tomb in the rubble-strewn grave of Little Rock.

Each pair of Bear eyes fixed on it like lampreys. Any chance at a Kurian was enough to heat their blood. He took the team up for a look.

He wished his blood could run hot like the Bears'; the spring night was no longer as warm as it had been when they were dry on the other side of the river. The water beaded on his oiled skin. The greasy coating served two purposes; it helped him resist the water and darkened his face and torso. His legs protruded out of camp shorts. He slipped some old black training shoes, preserved dry in the rubber boat, over his feet and put on a combat vest and his gunbelt, then picked up a cut-down Kalashnikov and an ammunition harness. He would have preferred the comforting bluntness of his PPD, but it was out of 9mm Mauser and the gunsmith didn't have the right molds for reloads. Finally he put his snakeskin bandolier of Quickwood stabbers over his arm and checked his bag for the presence of a battered old dinner bell that had, until a day ago, served as a Reaper alarm in one of the trenches.

He felt the mental echo of a Reaper in the direction of the bridge. It was in motion, crossing to the north bank. Wiggling up the bank and into cover, he checked the bank. In the darkness in the direction of Pulaski Heights he saw the twin red eyes of a pair of sentries smoking cigarettes. They weren't near enough for him to smell the tobacco, even though he was downwind. The sentries wouldn't hear or see his Bears, if they were careful.

Valentine inspected the remains of the buildings along the riverbank. He found an old outlet for the storm sewer system and waved the Bears over. The concrete mouth was wide enough to store the rubber raft. No words were necessary; the Bears took up their weapons silently. Styachowski had armed herself with a silenced .223 Mini-14 along with her bow. Valentine issued each Bear a Quickwood stabbing spear, almost the last of the precious supply. Ahn-Kha and the squad of Jamaicans, who proudly bore the informal label "Hoodhunters," had the few others.

They cut through the Ruins, skirting their old TMCC campsite. Their weeks at the camp—now occupied by a field hospital for those wounded in the siege—gave them a knowledge of the buildings that let them pick a route to cross the fallen city discreetly. They went to ground twice, once for a dog-led patrol that passed a block away, and a second time when Valentine felt a Reaper on his way to the hospital. Had the Kurians been reduced to feeding on their own badly wounded? Or did Mu-Kur-Ri fear to send his avatars far afield in search of auras?

They could see the Kurian Tower clearly now, no longer just a white blur in the distance. Valentine, then Nail, examined it through night binoculars from the vicinity of XrayTango's burned-out headquarters. The old bank had no flag before it as when Xray-Tango had made it his headquarters, though a few lights glimmered inside and a sentry paced back and forth behind it.

"Wonder how many are in there?" Nail asked. "Southern Command has to have driven a few out of their holes down south."

"I was hoping Solon had moved in," Valentine said. "I'd like to catch him in the temple of his gods." He swept the building with hard eyes, using the glasses and naked eyes alternately, naked eyes to spot motion, glasses to identify the source. "There'd be more guards if he had. Looks like the Quislings think the place is bad news."

"There's bars over the windows. And bunkers at the corners. How are you going to get through?"

"Don't worry about that. Just make sure you handle Xray-Tango's old building."

Nail smiled. "If there's anything they hate worse than Quisling soldiers, it's officers. They won't need a fire to look into to go Red."

"This is it then. When the shellfire starts, give me a few minutes. Then hit them. Look out for men on the roof."

"I didn't get the Bear bar on my collar by not knowing how to hit a building quiet. Take Rain at least, sir; he's worth a whole team of Bears."

"You're the hunter at the rabbit hole. I'm the ferret going in. I want to flush them, not fight."

"What if they hole up in a bunker and just work their Hoods?"

"Not your problem. Just get into that basement where I told you."

"Let me go with you, sir," Styachowski volunteered.

Valentine hesitated to say "no" and she filled the gap. "Lieutenant Nail and his Bears are a team; I haven't trained with them. . . ."

"Okay, two ferrets, Nail. See you below."

"One way or another, sir," Nail said, smiling as he gave a little salute.

Like a pair of rats, alternately hunting and being hunted as they went over—and under—the debris of old Little Rock, Valentine and Styachowski threaded their way toward the Kurian Tower. Construction hadn't stopped; they'd finished the second level and were starting on the third, even with the fighting across the river. It looked like an unevenly baked wedding cake with the layers stacked off center, or maybe a soft-serve ice-cream cone, Valentine couldn't decide which.

They found a rubble-filled basement loading dock just outside the glare of the tower's lights. The spiderwebs told them that the Quisling patrols didn't visit it, and they made themselves comfortable. They sat next to each other and looked up at the night sky through a gap above.

Valentine passed his time looking at the TMCC officer's handbook, a list of field regulations and procedures condensed to pamphlet size. He opened it to a page he had turned down and reread the passage he'd penned a tick next to. Even in their almost lightless refuge, the script stood out against the paper to his Cat-eyes as if it was on an illuminated screen. He finished and put the book back, trying to relax against the cold concrete. Rodents scurried somewhere farther inside the building.

The whistle-crash of the first shell ended the respite. The 155s came down with a terrifying noise—not as bad as the monster shells of the Crocodile, but unnerving all the same. He let five land to give the Quislings time to take cover, then nodded to Styachowski. They left their hideout.

They wriggled their way to a good view of the Kurian Tower, its white sides already smudged by the explosions. Valentine counted each shell burst; they arrived almost on the minute. After twenty had been fired, he grabbed Styachowski by the shoulder and they ran toward the tower, dodging their way through construction equipment and supplies. He heard one distant alarm whistle but ignored it. They made for the concrete bunker flanking the construction entrance to the tower. A scaffold with an electric elevator stood next to the entrance, on the other side of the bunker. Styachowski tore the colored tabs off a thick cylinder of a grenade, squatted listening to the fuse hiss—and threw it in the firing slit of the bunker.

"Hey!" someone inside shouted.

It would have been ideal if the next shell had landed at the same time as the grenade exploded, but they were seconds apart. The grenade went off first, followed by the louder, but farther off, explosion of the artillery shell.

Valentine had his own grenade to deal with. It was a green smoker. He pulled the pin and rolled it under a sluice on the steel curtain door of the construction entrance. It went off like two cats spitting at each other, and green smoke began to billow out from around the edges of the door. Valentine threw two more green smokers around the edges of the buildings. When the grenades were spewing he pulled the dinner bell from his bag and pulled out the sock he'd used to silence it. He rang it, loud and long.

"Gas! Gas! Gas!" he shouted. He rang the bell again.

"Gas! Gas! Gas!" Styachowski added, deepening her voice. She pulled out a pair of crowbars.

Valentine clanged the dinner bell for all he was worth, then tried the electric lift. No juice.

"We climb," he said.

Valentine went up first while Styachowski covered him, shrouded with green smoke. The gas warning had been taken up by men inside the building. Valentine heard a klaxon go off, three angry buzzes, followed by the triple "gas" call over the PA system within. He took the crowbars from Styachoski and pulled her up.

Valentine went up the scaffold to the platform on the first level. Styachowski joined him and they put their crowbars to work, pulling at a metal screen blocking a window. It was more of an iron grate than true bars, designed to explode an RPG aimed at the window. Nothing but cardboard stuck in a fitting for thick glass closed the window beyond, but the bars blocked them out.

Styachowski roared in frustration.

Valentine tucked his crowbar nearer hers. Together they pulled, shoulder to shoulder. Styachowski's muscles felt like machine-tool steel against his.

"Graaaaaa!" Styachowski heaved. She set her leg against the tower face. They pulled again—

The grate gave way, pulling the masonry at the top and bottom of the narrow window with it. Styachowski pulled an opening big enough for them to climb through.

Eyes wild and burning, Styachowski swung through, knocking the cardboard away. Wisps of green smoke could be seen within, and the gas alarm was still bleating its triple call every ten seconds. The tower's interior was still being worked on; the walls were nothing but cinder block coated with primer paint.

Valentine felt something crackling inside his mind, like a man running a sparkler firework across the field of an empty stadium. Or maybe two or three, waving and parting and separating like schooling fish. With them were the colder, darker impressions of Reapers.

"Downstairs! They're down, in the basement, heading north."

"How can you tell? I don't hear anything but that friggin' alarm," Styachowski asked from the other side of the room, covering the hall with her gun.

"I just do. Find the stairs."

The tower appealed to some kind of Kurian sensibility for architecture; the "stairs" were a tight ramp-spiral in a corner under the tallest part of the tower. Valentine could hear footsteps climbing the stairs above in between the klaxon bursts; the Quislings or construction workers or whoever were sensibly getting as high as they could above what they thought to be lethal fumes.

There was a change in the air as soon as they got underground. They came to a corridor; the lighting fixtures and flooring told Valentine it was pre-2022 construction. A man in a uniform with a gas mask over his face was leading another toward the stairs, the one behind had his hand on his leader. Neither could see much through the eyeholes in the dusty old masks, and they were going down the corridor like they were playing blind man's bluff. One had a radio bumping against his chest.

The Kurians were still below and moving away somewhere. Where was that rathole to Xray-Tango's old headquarters?

Valentine and the Bear hurried down the corridor, catching up to the men. Valentine heard the radio crackle.

"Townshend, Townshend, what's the situation? Is there gas in the tower?"

As Valentine passed him he lashed out with his fist, landing a solid jab in the radio-wearer's breadbasket. The man went to his knees, gasping. Valentine caught the other under the jaw with the butt of his machine pistol.

"Help—haaaaaaaaaaa—help," the radio man on his knees gasped into the mike. His battle for air sounded authentic enough. Valentine kicked out sideways, catching him in the back of the head. The Quisling's head made a sound like a spiked volleyball as it bounced off the wall, and he went face-first on top of the radio, unconscious or dead.

"Val, here," Styachowski said, checking a room at the end of the corridor.

It was a utility room. Snakes of cable conduit ran up from the floor and across the ceiling; boxes and circuit breakers lined the wall. Another stairway descended from a room beyond. The steel door had been torn off its hinges. Valentine recognized the nail marks of a Reaper. He picked up the mental signature of the fleeing Kurians again, this time clearer.

"You ready for this?" he asked Styachowski.

She nodded, giving him the thumbs-up.

He handed her two of his four Quickwood stakes. "Remember, they can make themselves look like a dog, anything. Just kill whatever you see. Unless it's another Bear, or me. No, strike that. If you see another me, kill him, too. I'll just hope you pick the right one."

"Yes, sir."

"Let's do it."

They went down to a boiler room, connected by another missing door—this one long since removed—to an arch-topped tunnel. Two Quislings, in gas-mask chemical weapon hoods, stood at the portal.

Styachowski's Mini-14 came up. She shot twice, the action on the gun louder than the bullet through the silenced weapon, and both men crumpled. As Valentine looked down the corridor she shot each Quisling again for insurance.

It wasn't much of a tunnel, only a little wider than the passageways on the old *Thunderbolt*. Old conduit pipes and newer wires ran along the walls and ceiling, lit here and there by bulbs encased in thick plastic housings like preserve jars. It smelled like damp underwear and bad plumbing.

Valentine went in first—trailing the psychic scent like a bloodhound—in the bent-over, lolloping run he'd picked up going through the underbrush in his days with the Wolves. He heard Styachowski behind; an occasional splashing footfall sounded as she hit a puddle in the damp tunnel.

He heard firing at the other end of the arrow-thin passageway.

The sparking mental impressions grew clearer. They were coming. With their Reapers.

Valentine pulled up. "They turned around."

"Shit! How many Reapers?"

"I don't know. Several." The corridor went dark. Styachowski pulled a flare out and lit it in a flash, then threw it down the corridor toward the coming Reapers. She reached for a fist-sized metal sphere on her vest.

She pulled the pin on the grenade. "Want to keep it?"

"No, throw it. When I tell you. If there's anything beyond Red . . . like Violet maybe, you might want to give it a try."

Styachowski pulled her bolo blade. It was a nice length for the tunnel. Valentine wished he had his old straight-edged sword. He felt oddly light and fearless. Just a mouth like dry-rotted wood and hands greasy with sweat and aching from rope burn. He shifted his grip on Ahn-Kha's stabbing spear.

The Reapers came in a wall of death, three of them, jaws agape like Cerberus.

"Now," Valentine said. Styachowski threw the grenade and readied her Quickwood stabber.

The Reapers ignored the bouncing explosive. It went off behind them, throwing them into the Cat and the Bear in a wave of heat and sound. Valentine's mind felt pain and confusion—his own, and that of the Kurians.

Styachowski went into the first Reaper like it was a badly stuffed scarecrow. Valentine could see the fight as clearly in the faint red glow of the flare as if it were daylight. She chopped off an arm, then buried her Quickwood into its neck. Another jumped on her back like lightning leaping sideways to hit a rod. It got its hands around her, claws reaching to rip open her rib cage, but Valentine plunged his stabbing spear into its shoulder, trying to hit the nerve trunks descending from the armored skull. The spear went through its robes and bit deep, eliciting an angry shriek, the loudest noise Valentine had ever heard a Reaper make.

Suddenly he was flying through the air. He crashed against the tunnel wall, held by the piece of steel that was the third Reaper's arm. Its eyes burned into his. Valentine slammed the side of his arm down in a chop against the Reaper's elbow, hoping to fold its arm like a jackknife, but he stayed pinned. The Reaper grabbed his other arm, forcing it to the wall so he hung in the crucifixion pose. Its narrow face drew nearer, jaws opening for the sweet spot at the base of his throat. The stabbing tongue stirred within its mouth like a serpent coiling for a strike.

Valentine brought up his knees, putting his feet on the demon's chest. It bore in, an irresistible force, folding him until his spine would snap—Valentine screamed in agonized frustration.

Styachowski's face appeared above the Reaper's. She was atop its back, her hands black with Reaper juice, her own blood pouring in a river from her nose. She brought her blade across its throat, grabbed it by the handle and tip, and pulled toward herself. The improvised guillotine cut through its windpipe and circulatory system, but the thing dropped Valentine and reached its queerly jointed arms around behind itself for Styachowski.

Valentine, his vision a red mist, brought both of his hands up, uncoiling with his body and helping the blade travel the last few inches. The Reaper's head went up and off in a gristly *pop-snap*.

The Reaper's body staggered off sideways, clawing at the air. The ambulatory corpse did a U-turn, crashed into the wall, and flopped over. There was shooting coming from the far end of the tunnel.

"Your hands!" Valentine barked, as Styachowski was about to wipe her sweating face. She froze.

"Oh, yeah," she said. Reaper blood was poisonous, whether swallowed or taken in through a mucous membrane. Even the best Hunters sometimes forgot in the midst of a fight. The tunnel was filling with smoke from the grenade, and the fight elsewhere.

Footsteps. Another Reaper charged out of the smoke, robes torn, one arm gone, its body riddled with bullet wounds. Valentine and Styachowski threw themselves against the passageway and it passed without noticing them.

"Fucker!" Valentine heard Lost&Found shout, spraying bullets up the corridor after it.

"Cease fire, Bear! You're shooting at us," Valentine shouted.

The bullets stopped.

"Sir! Sir! We got two of 'em. Two blue bat-winged bastards!"

Valentine could hardly see them through the smoke. He made his way toward the sound of the voices with Styachowski in tow.

"Reapers?" Valentine asked.

"We got two down. One got away from us."

"He got away from us, too. But I think he was running wild," Styachowski said, meaning its Kurian had been killed.

Valentine could better make out the haggard four now. They'd almost passed through the smoke. The Bears were missing Brass and Groschen.

"Where are the other two?" Valentine asked. He felt nervous somehow.

Nail jerked his chin up the tunnel the way the Bears had come. "A Reaper popped Brass's head off. Sorry, sir, couldn't be helped. Groschen is keeping an eye on the other end of the tunnel. The old headquarters had been converted to some kind of communications center. Lots of field phones and printing machines. We took it out."

Valentine didn't listen. There was a problem with the smoke. It didn't smell like anything. Smoke also didn't make noise as it crawled along the ceiling.

"One got away," Valentine hissed. "A Kurian. It's heading back down the tunnel."

Without further explanation he threw himself down the tunnel. In the distance he saw a faint figure, running for its immortal life. The Kurian could move. Not as fast as a Reaper. Nothing that wasn't engine-powered moved as fast as a Reaper.

It dashed through the door of the utility subbasement, Valentine almost on its heels. Its skin was the color of blue ice and it gave off a sickly sweet odor like marigolds. So intent on the chase was he that he bounced off the chest of the Reaper, which stepped out from behind the steaming boiler like a sliding steel door. The Kurian was safely behind it. The Kurian turned, looked at Valentine with red-black eyes, and then disappeared upstairs.

Valentine rolled backward and came to his feet.

The one-armed Reaper's eyes wandered. It extended its remaining clawed hand and pulled one of the boiler pipes free of its mount. Valentine heard the Reaper's skin sizzle against the hot metal, but the thing didn't even wince. It yanked the pipe out, so a firehose of steam flooded the passageway and the stairway behind it.

Then it advanced on Valentine.

"i know you," it hissed. *"our false friend from louisiana."*

"Valentine!" Nail shouted from behind him.

Valentine dropped to the ground. A hail of bullets filled the tunnel. The Reaper's face vanished in the tight pattern of a buckshot blast. It roared, and charged down the tunnel toward the sound of gunfire. With its eyes gone, it didn't see Valentine wriggling forward after Mu-Kur-Ri.

He heard fighting behind. Styachowski and Nail should be able to handle a one-armed, blind Reaper without him. He wanted Mu-Kur-Ri.

But the hissing steam blocked his way. There was nothing to do but . . . do it.

Valentine lifted his combat vest and got his head and arms tucked into as much of the material as he could, and held it closed over his face.

"This is for you, Hank," he muttered to himself. He took a deep breath; it wouldn't be pleasant to breathe in hot steam.

Later, when he'd forgotten the pain, he examined the burn marks in detail using a pair of mirrors. His lower back took the worst of it, from beneath his rib cage—where the combat vest ended—to the line of his camp shorts. That part must have been hit by steam shooting from the hose, and it turned into a girdle of scar tissue. The back of his legs got it badly enough that the hair only regrew irregularly, but there was less scarring there than above the line of his shorts. The thick cotton of the shorts and combat vest kept the rest of the damage to first- and second-degree burns. Painful enough, but they healed.

The pain drove him on instinct through the steam and up the stairs. He caught up to the Kurian and fell on it like a rabid dog. It squealed rabbitlike as he tore into the slippery mass with fists and teeth. Cartilage crunched under his knees, a pulpy mass of digestive organs slipped wetly through his fingers, then its rubbery skull finally gave out as he slammed it again and again and again into the concrete landing, still shrouded in green smoke. Then he collapsed atop the spongy corpse of Mu-Kur-Ri.

As he passed out he thought of Caroline Smalls.

The next thing he saw was Styachowski's face, gently rocking as it floated above him. A pleasant warmth gave way to pain, agonizing pain, pain like he'd never felt and would shoot himself to keep from feeling again. It was so bad he couldn't summon the energy to do more than whimper, his body paralyzed, living only in the endless moment of the burn's agony.

Think of something, anything, anything to drive the pain away!

"They think of a name for you?" Valentine croaked.

"Not yet," Styachowski said. She'd shoved expended cartridge cases into her nostrils to stop the flow of blood.

Nail patted her shoulder. "You did just fine, you're a Bear to be proud of. How about Ursa? Like the stars?"

"Wildcat?" Valentine said. "No. A woman who can be anything. A Wildcard."

"I like Wildcard," Styachowski said.

"No, if you like it, we can't use it. Unwritten law," Rain said.

Valentine turned painfully to Nail. "Make it an order, Lieutenant."

The Bear shrugged. "After all this," Nail said, "it seems we should call you whatever you like, Styachowski. Wildcard it is. The drawn card that turned out to be an ace just when we needed it."

"Wildcard, is he alive?" a voice that might have been Nail's said.

"He's alive."

It was torture to his skin to be lifted and carried. Sensibly, his consciousness fled.

He later heard about the scattering of troops from the Kurian Tower as Reapers ran amok, and the confusion that allowed Lieutenant Nail to carry him and lead the Bears back to the river, and how Lost&Found swam across with Valentine tied to an empty five-gallon jerrican to keep him afloat. As he heard the tale Valentine felt as though he'd lived it, but couldn't remember much except for vague impressions of floating. He rememberd shelling but no further large-scale attacks, just endless probes. He remembered Post's daily reports of units observed moving east through New Columbia, and the gun resting in the swimming pool running out of ammunition so that all the hilltop forces could do was watch. He remembered walking again, and giving up his bed to another wounded man and sleeping on a blanket on the concrete floor near where Narcisse worked the hospital kitchen and rubbed him with oily-smelling lotion.

Then came sounds of more trains in the distance and vehicular traffic around the base of the hill, and he managed to go outside. He'd meet the inevitable standing, even if he stood in bandages.

"Sir, you're needed on the west side." One of the pregnant women, in a man's service poncho which gave her belly growing room, reported from her station at the field phone.

Valentine made a stiff-legged journey. His bad leg ached all the time now, throbbing in sympathy with the healing burns. Ahn-Kha helped him up a set of stairs and they reached the observation point, what was left of Solon's grand balcony. Three soldiers knelt, sharing a set of binoculars, staring up the Arkansas River, a blue ribbon between the green Ozark hills.

"What in God's name is that?" Valentine asked.

The river was three deep in beetles. A flotilla of craft, none larger than thirty feet. Many towed everything from rowboats to braces of canoes.

"Reinforcements?"

"Depends on your point of view. Look—the mortars are shooting at them."

The tubes of Pulaski Heights were dropping shells into the mass of speeding boats, with little effect but wetting those inside.

Styachowski ran along the rubble-strewn base of Solon's Residence beneath them, tripped over a log and sprawled flat. She picked herself up, but didn't bother to wipe the mud from her chin.

"They're pulling back, sir," she called up, her voice squealing like a schoolgirl's in excitement. "Not the boats, the Quislings. They're coming off the hill."

"To oppose the landing?"

"They're just running," Styachowski said. "Running like hell for the bridge. A train just pulled out east, packed with men."

Valentine looked down the river, caught a familiar pattern. He snatched the binoculars out of the hand of the man next to him without apology, and focused on the boat trailing the leadmost pilot vessel. There was a flagstaff above the outboard motors. The State Flag of Texas flapped in the breeze.

The boats were a surprise to the Quislings as well. They abandoned the weapons on the Pulaski Heights and fled with the rest toward Pine Bluff. When Valentine was sure the hilltop was clear he brought up the wounded from their dreadful holes into the fresh air and sunshine. There were the dead to be sorted from the living, and sent on to the swollen, shell-tossed graveyard.

The Texans found him among the corpses, burying his dead.

"That's him. I met him in Texas," he heard a voice say. Valentine looked up and saw a Ranger he recognized, Colorado. The youth's shoulders had broadened, and what Valentine's nose told him was that motor oil stained the Ranger's uniform.

Colorado brought forward a bearded man. Valentine suspected that when the campaign started the colonel of the Texas Rangers was clean shaven.

"Nice to finally meet the famous Ghost," the colonel, whose name-tag read "Samoza," said.

The idea of a famous Cat struck Valentine as a bit absurd, and he fought down a laugh. If his nerves gave way now he'd fall on the man, laughing or crying or confessing, and none were appropriate to the moment.

"We've come all the way from Fort Scott for you," Samoza continued.

The words took their time in coming. Valentine's shocked brain had to inspect each one as it came out.

"Thank you. Southern Command couldn't even make it fifty miles," Valentine managed, looking out over the graves.

"Southern Command opened the door for us. Archangel was a joint operation from the start. The Kurians sent troops up from Texas to take you boys down. We figured if they didn't want it, we'd like it back. We got more besides."

It all hit Valentine like a warm wave. Intellect gave way to pent-up emotion like the dike that had swallowed Styachowski, and he found himself shaking, with tears in his eyes. He hoped his brain remembered it all and would be able to sort it out later. "What's that, sir?" he finally said.

"We linked up with Southern Command just outside Hope. Ironic, wouldn't you say? Then it was north into Oklahoma, and down the river to you."

"What made you come all this way?"

"A Ranger teamster named Jefferson made a lot of noise in East Texas. Claimed we had to go help the man who started it all. He fought alongside us all the way to Fort Scott and lost a leg there to shellfire. Haven't taken it yet but figured it could wait. You couldn't."

Valentine held out his hand to the colonel.

"You came all this way for a few companies of men?"

"We're from Texas, friend. We remember the Alamo."

Eleven

The Saint Francis River, August of the forty-eighth year of the Kurian Order: The land was healing with the people. In the weeks following the relief of the Razors at New Columbia, even Fort Scott changed hands yet again, to the combined forces of the Ozark Free Territory and the Texas Republic. Solon and his Kurian Council collapsed like a house of cards, fleeing in all directions. There were losses, irreplaceable losses, everywhere across the fought-over land. In the chaos in the Missouri Valley Grogs pushed south and the Kur in Kansas took a piece of the Ozarks around the lakes, and sent their Reapers into the Mark Twain Forest.

But the leaders of the newly wedded Texas and Ozark Free Territories would have something to say about that, in time. They controlled an area larger than any of the former states of the union.

David Valentine crossed the Free Territory with his pouch of Quickwood seeds. He planted one on a windswept hillside where a sergeant named Gator was buried. He placed another one outside a stoutly built barn near the Lousiana border—a crippled ex-Wolf named Gonzalez helped him relocate it, where a little patch of earth marked the location of the first man to die under Valentine's command. A few frontier farmers turned up for the ceremony. In time, the locals called it Selby's tree, and a Selby Meadows grew up around that barn. He placed a ring of Quick-wood trees at the ambush site outside Post 46, just northeast of the Red River, another on a devastated riverbank that looked like a piece of the moon, where the Crocodile had moored, and the rest shaded a cemetery on Big Rock Hill.

The rest save one. He took it to the empty little village of Weening on the Saint Francis. The inhabitants were scattered, the Carlsons had vanished and Tank Bourne was laid out, months dead, in his cellar. Valentine buried him in the shade of a willow tree by the river, and up near the riverside gate he placed his last seed in the rich Arkansas soil, soil that had once soaked up Gabreilla Cho's blood, and—though he did not know it—Molly Carlson's tears.

There was already a pamphlet printed about the fight at Big Rock Hill. It was rolled up in Valentine's bag next to his order book. He'd read a few pages—the author had relied on the collected radio reports from the hill for a day-by-day record of events, as interpreted for him by a decorated veteran of the Central Operational area named Captain Randolph—and given up after it described Lieutenant Colonel Kessey's brilliant rising in the prison yards of New Columbia, when a Quisling division was put to flight by men keen on avenging their outraged women. He'd heard they were renaming the battlefield Kessey Heights, which was fine with him. Her body lay on it.

Folded into the pamphlet, for protection rather than as a bookmark, was a radiogram from Jamaica.

TO: DAVID VALENTINE, SOUTHERN COMMAND
FROM: COMMODORE HOUSE, JAMAICA
CHILD AMALEE BORN 7LBS6 JUNE 19 BOTH HEALTHY MOTHER SENDS LOVE CONGRATULATIONS JENSEN

The Quickwood tree would have a nice life ouside Weening. He found a boy from the Peterson family—they'd been the first to see the empty homes of Weening for the opportunity they presented and move the extended family there. The boy was eleven and watched him through wary but intelligent eyes. He seemed old enough for the responsibility of watching over the tree. Valentine didn't want some clown clearing brush to cut down the Quickwood sapling.

Valentine tried to explain the importance of Quickwood to Mr. Peterson, but to the literal-minded man it came down to a tree that could grow a magic wooden stake that killed vampires. Valentine left it at that. There were things to do, so many things to do. Solon's dream of owning the Mississippi and its tributaries vanished with the consul, but far-sighted men from Texas to the Ozarks might be able to bring the evil man's idea to fruition—under new management, of course. Already there was talk of taking back New Orleans. Then the great gateway to the Caribbean would be open, a navy could be floated, and Southern Command would be able to put troops anywhere a keel could go.

And he could see his daughter.

Someday the Quickwood could be used properly. He'd returned to the Free Territory thinking the Haitian discovery would be a wedge he could drive into the heart of the Kurian Order, piercing it and breaking it up the way he did logs. But a wedge was only as good as the force driving it. All along, it had been cooperation between people, himself and Ahn-Kha, Styachowski and Post, Narcisse and Hank, Samoza and Jefferson, each doing their part in a whole that was even now being born.

How had the governor phrased it, after the formal military union of Texas and the Free Territory? "A new stake of freedom wedged between the Mississippi and the Gulag"? Something like that. Valentine liked to think of it as seed. A fast-growing seed, he hoped, and as deadly to the Kurian Order as the Quickwood he'd scattered over hundreds of square miles.

"Here you go, Gabby," Valentine said, covering the seed with moist earth fresh from the river. He knelt at the nongrave. "Keep it safe for me. Something happened this summer. A miracle. We took the worst they could throw at us—ended up the stronger for it. The Texans have the Dallas Triangle ringed in now, and we're sending captured artillery to finish the job. It's only a matter of time. I've got a daughter, if you can believe it. And here I've planted my last seed. It's a good day for me. It's a new beginning for us."

The future beckoned. The past, his regrets, his mistakes, all lay buried with the seed. No more looking back.

David Valentine glanced up at the hot noonday sun and wiped the sweat from his forehead, now beneath chin-length black hair, and wondered at the strange fate that saw him in the right place at the right time. Dreadful and deadly work still needed to be done, but it was work born of Hope.

VALENTINE'S EXILE

To the readers,
who carried me and my baby this far.

Only solitary men know the full joys of friendship.
Others have their family; but to a solitary and an exile
his friends are everything.

—*Willa Cather*
Shadows on the Rock

One

Dallas, March, the fiftieth year of the Kurian Order: Four square miles of concrete and structural steel smoke and pop and sputter as the city dies from the stranglehold of a siege.

Save for the sounds of streetfighting, hard to locate thanks to reflections from the skyscrapers, this city at war seems strangely empty. Scavenging black crows and wary, tail-tucking dogs catch the eye here and there, but human activity is nil. Vague stormlike rumbles mutter in the distance, and sudden eruptions of machine-gun fire from a few blocks away might be jackhammers breaking holes in a sidewalk in a more peaceful time. When men move they move in a rush, pouring from doorways and crossing streets in a quick wave before the whine of shellfire can catch them in the open.

Viewed from above, or on a headquarters map in one of the command bunkers, Big D is now a network of opposing circles.

The largest circle encompasses the great towers of the city center. Linked above the twentieth floor by spiderweb-like cables that allow the sure-tentacled Kurians interbuilding access without mixing with their human herds at street level, they show new holes and pits and hollows from the besiegers' guns and rockets. At street level mounds of debris and rubble stand in concentric rings, defended by batteries of guns manned by everyone from professional soldiers to minor functionaries in what until last year had been the affluent and sprawling North Texas Cooperative.

Surrounding that central axis are an assortment of smaller circles, ringing the central battlements like the chambers in a revolver's cylinder. The closest to the front lines are Texas regulars out of the Pinewoods and the Rio Grande belt; others to the north and east fly the tricolor of the Ozarks, and a few smaller ones filling gaps to the rear are clusters of militias made up of men and women freed from the heavy hand of the Cooperative.

Northwest of the city rests one of these smaller circles, surrounding an airstrip once called Love Field. The soldiers there are not placed to assault the city. The ad hoc unit occupying the airport grew out of the rising in Little Rock that opened Operation Archangel. They participate in the siege both as a sentimental gesture of gratitude to the Texans who plunged down the Arkansas River to rescue them and as being part of the gun-bristling ring that prevents an organized breakout. Their airfield joins the extreme left of the Ozark troops and the extreme right of the Texans.

Their regimental flag, a black-and-blue silhouette of an Arkansas razorback set under the joined Texas and Ozark flags, reads DON'T FEED ON ME. *Judged from a distance, the forces in this particular encampment, called Valentine's Razors by the veterans, aren't in shape to serve as anything but a supporting unit. Only a few mortars and machine-gun pits fill their lines, more for defense of the camp than for battering those within the city. Instead rolls of concertina wire on the open ground near the airstrip enclose cattle awaiting slaughter for the daily ration, and the airport's garages hum with the sounds of generators and power tools. On the march southwest from the Ozarks the Razors proved invaluable in getting captured Kurian vehicles operational again, and in turning cattle, wheat, pigs, and corn into grist for various regimental kitchens. Their aptitudes reflect the rear-area nature of many of the soldiers in the Razors, united by chance during the uprising in Little Rock.*

To a general of either side looking at a map and possessed of a modicum of intelligence, military and personal, the Razors are one of the least-threatening circles surrounding Big D.

But quality can rarely be judged from a distance.

The first clue is in the rifles that each on-duty soldier always has within reach: long, heavy-barreled killers with oversized banana magazines and integral bipods, some with telescopic sights, others with fixtures for high-capacity drum magazines. Souvenirs of the Razors' brief integration into Solon's Army of the Trans-Mississippi, they are the best battle rifles the famous Atlanta Gunworks produces. Thanks to the Type Threes, any soldier is capable of turning into a supporting fire unit in a moment, given a simple wrench and a belt of the proper ammunition.

Then there are the "prowlers." The mechanics of the Razors see to it that the best bits and pieces of Quisling wreckage make their way into the regimental motor pool, where they're assembled into armored cars and mortar transports. High-axled, fat-tired, covered with rocket-propelled grenade–stopping webbing, each swamp buggy-cum-armored car bears a pair of angry eyes, and sharp tusks and teeth, somewhere just above and forward of the front tires. A few have front electric winches formed into snouts, and the beds of many of the vehicles sport recoilless rifles, miniguns, and auto-grenade launchers. Other longer, heavier, double-axled trucks are built to carry troops, loading and unloading from doors in the backs or sides of the transports, and an assortment of trailer-pumps feed the gas tanks from captured gasoline supplies when on the move, or hold a reserve against supply interruptions when encamped.

The Razors shouldn't have worked. Soldiers thrown together under the most dire of circumstances couldn't be expected to stand up to a determined assault, let alone hold a precarious position alone in the heart of enemy country. The success of their famous stand on the banks of the Arkansas River might be considered a measure as much of their enemy's incompetence as their own mettle. But some credit must be given to the improvisational skills of the officers who organized the Little Rock Rising.

One of those men crosses the outskirts of the airstrip as the sun rises. His mottled dark green-and-gray uniform is thick with "Dallas Dust," an oatmeal-colored mixture of pulverized concrete, ash, and mundane winter dirt. Black hair tied in a pigtail hangs from his scalp, and a thin, white scar on the right side of his face only serves to show off an early spring tan, bronzing indicative of ample melanin in his genes. A shortened version of his Razor's battle rifle with folding stock and cut-down barrel bumps from its tight sling against leather battle webbing. The assault harness is festooned with everything from a wide-bladed utility parang to a gas mask hood, with flares for a signal gun at his hip and a "camel" water bladder over his shoulder. A veteran of the Razors would note the distinctly nonregulation moccasins on his feet, and infer that the Razors' operations officer, Major Valentine, was back from another of his "scouts."

David Valentine breathed in a last snootful of clean air and descended into the muskrat-den reek. He stepped down carefully, holding an uprooted young dandelion in his gun-free hand. The stairwell to the old terminal's sublevel was mostly gone. The entryway had been enlarged, replaced by churned-over earth paved with plywood strips dropping eight feet to the hole in the cinderblock side of the foundation where the basement door used to be.

The entrance to the Razorbacks' headquarters resembled an oversized anthole, if anything. It fooled the eyes that sometimes drifted high above the besiegers' positions.

He rested his gun in a cleaning becket and stood on a carpet remnant in the entryway to let his eyes adjust to the dim light within. Deaf old Pooter, one of the regiment's guinea pigs, rolled up onto his hind legs and whistled a welcome from his chicken-wire cage perched on a shelf next to the door. Valentine tossed him the dandelion.

"They didn't hit us after all," he told Pooter.

Pooter chuckled as a length of milky dandelion stem disappeared into his fast-working jaws.

If the Kurians dusted again, Pooter would expire in a noisy hacking fit, giving the men inside time to ring the alarm, lower the plastic curtains, and put on their gas masks and gloves.

Valentine was tired. He'd spent the last eight hours moving across the forward posts, keyed up for a battle that never came. Probably more than he would have been had there been action, the weird I'm-alive-and-I-can-do-anything exhilaration of surviving combat would have floated him back to the Razors' HQ.

On the other side of the door from Pooter was a sandbagged cubbyhole filled with salvaged armchairs resting among thousands of loosely bound pages from perhaps a hundred different pre-22 magazines and novels. A team of Nail's Bears, Razorback HQ's emergency reserve, lounged within, smoking captured tobacco and reading books or magazine fragments.

Except for one. The Bear Valentine knew as Lost & Found stood just outside the cubbyhole in the deepest shadow of the entrance, an assault rifle resting in his arms like a cradled child, a bucket filled with white powder at his feet.

Valentine took in the HQ air, perhaps ten degrees warmer than the morning chill of the Texas spring outside. The Bear tobacco, a faint fecal smell, brewing coffee, old sweat, drying laundry, gun oil, and a hint of cabbage stewing in salty broth rolled around in his nostrils.

"Morning, sir," Lost & Found said, looking out the door beyond Valentine. He prodded the bucket at his foot.

Valentine dutifully stripped off his combat harness and tossed it in the decontamination barrel. The rest of his clothes followed until he stood naked on the carpet remnant.

He took a handful of the boric acid from the bucket and gave himself a rubdown, concentrating on his shoulder-length black hair, armpits, and crotch. Rednits liked the warmth and tender apertures around hair follicles, and the battalion wasn't losing any more men to nit-fever.

Colonel Meadows had enough on his hands with twenty percent of the Razorbacks filling field hospital beds or recovery wards, eating leek-and-liver soup twice daily, getting their blood back up to strength.

Valentine went over to a bank of lockers featuring names written on duct tape plastered on new paint slathered over old rust, and extracted a uniform. Hank had put a fresh one in overnight, while Valentine was forward. Regular soldiers had to make do with the rumpled contents of the slop bins, but the Razorback officers each had a locker for their inside uniforms. When he was properly dressed in the mixed-gray-and-deep-green fatigues of the Razorbacks (Southern Command Mixed Infantry Division, for use of—some said the color scheme was reminiscent of a raccoon's backside) he put on leather-soled moccasins and followed the smell of coffee with his Wolf's nose.

He walked past the headset-wearing HQ radio/field-phone operator, whose gear was swathed in cheesecloth that smelled of kerosene, surrounded by six different NO SMOKING signs in English, Spanish, and French. The kerosene kept the electicks out. The little bastards ate electrical insulation and grew into three-inch sticklike bugs whose metallic chitin inevitably shorted out electrical equipment.

The boy with the headset, seventeen but scrawny enough to pass for fourteen, studied the flickering needles of the radio set as though divining runes. Valentine raised an eyebrow to the kid, got a head shake in return, and looked at the clipboard with the most recent comflimsies. There'd been some chatter out of Dallas the previous day that made GHQ-Dallas Corridor suspect a counterattack in the Razorbacks' area, but nothing had manifested last night.

Breakfast or a shower?

Valentine decided to give the boric acid a few more minutes to work and headed for the galley.

In the five weeks they'd occupied the airfield Narcisse and her staff had set up sinks, stoves, and even had a pizza oven going. Companies rotating to or from the forward positions always had a pizza party before creeping out to the strongpoints covering the approaches to Dallas. Narcisse wore no uniform, held no rank, and wandered between the battalion's kitchens and infirmary as the mood struck her, dispensing equal helpings of cheer and food, escorted in her wheelchair by a steadfast rottweilerish mutt who'd wandered into camp on the Razorbacks' trip south from the Ouachitas. The men and women whose job it was to aid and comfort the frontline soldiers obeyed the old, legless Haitian as though she were a visiting field marshall.

Valentine said good morning to the potato peelers, working under faded paint that once demarked a maintenance workshop, rinsed his hands, and poured himself a mug of water from the hot pot. He plopped in one of Narcisse's herbal tea bags from a woven basket on a high shelf, then covered his brew-up with a plastic lid masquerading as a saucer, and took the stairs down to the subbasement and the hooches.

He smelled the steeping tea on the way down the stairs. It tasted faintly of oranges—God only knew how Narcisse came up with orange peel—and seemed to go to whatever part of the body most needed a fix. If you were constipated it loosened you, if you were squirting it plugged you. It took away headache and woke you up in the morning and calmed the jitters that came during a long spell of shellfire.

Valentine had a room to himself down among the original plumbing fixtures and electrical junction boxes. In the distance a generator clattered, steadily supplying juice but sounding as though it was unhappy with the routine. Just along the hall Colonel Meadows occupied an old security office, but Valentine didn't see light creeping out from under the door so he turned and moved aside the bedsheet curtaining off his quarters.

His nose told him someone lay in his room even before his eyes picked out the L-shaped hummock in his wire-frame bed. A pale, boric acid–dusted leg ending in a calloused, hammertoed foot emerged from the wooly army blanket, and a knife-cut shock of short red hair could just be distinguished at the other end.

Alessa Duvalier was back from the heart of Dallas.

Valentine examined the foot. Some people showed the experience of a hard life through their eyes, others in their rough hands. A few, like Narcisse, were bodily crippled. While the rest of Duvalier was rather severely pretty, occasionally exquisite when mood or necessity struck, Duvalier's feet manifested everything bad the Cat had been through. Dark with filth between the toes, hard-heeled, toes twisted and dirt-crusted nails chipped, scabbed at the ankle, calloused and scarred from endless miles on worn-through socks—her feet told a gruesome tale.

A pair of utility sinks held her gear, reeking of the camphor smell of its spell in the decontamination barrel, her sword-concealing walking stick lying atop more mundane boots and socks.

"Val, that you?" she said sleepily from under the blanket, voice muffled by a fistful of wool over her mouth and nose to keep out the basement chill. She shifted and he caught a flash of upper thigh. She'd fallen into his bed wearing only a slop shirt. They'd never been lovers, but were as comfortable around each other as a married couple.

"Yeah."

"Room for two."

"Shower first. Then I want to hear—"

"One more hour. I got in at oh-four."

"I was out at the forward posts. Pickets didn't report you—"

She snorted. Valentine heard Hank's quick step on the stairs he'd just come down.

He looked at his self-winding watch, a gift from Meadows when the colonel assumed command of the Razorbacks. The engraved inscription on the back proclaimed forty-eight-year-old eternal love between a set of initials both ending in *C*. "One more hour, then. Breakfast?"

"Anything."

Valentine took a reviving spout-shower that kept Hank busy bearing hot water down from the kitchen. Valentine had been seeing to the boy's education at odd hours, trying to remember the lessons Father Max had issued at thirteen, and had put him in the battalion's books to make it easier to feed and clothe the boy. They shared more than just a working relationship. Both had ugly red-and-white burn scars; Valentine's on his back, Hank's on his semifunctional right hand.

"What's the definition of an isosceles triangle?" Valentine asked as he worked a soapy rag up and down his legs.

"All, no, two sides of equal length," Hank said.

"When all three are the same?"

"Equilateral," Hank said.

Hank also got the questions on degrees of the corners of an equilateral right. Tomorrow Valentine would get him using triangles for navigational purposes . . . it always helped to add practical applicability right away. In a week or so the boy would be able to determine latitude using the sun and a sextant, provided he could remember the definition of a plumb line.

"Haven't seen Ahn-Kha this morning, have you?"

"No, sir," Hank said, reverting to military expression with the ease of long practice.

Valentine hadn't smelled the Grog's presence at headquarters, but Ahn-Kha kept to himself in a partially blocked stairwell when he was at the headquarters. Ahn-Kha was evaluating and drilling some of the newer Razorbacks, mostly Texan volunteers who'd been funneled to them through Southern Command's haphazard field personnel depot north of the city. Southern Command tended to get recruits the all-Texan units didn't want, and Ahn-Kha knew how to turn lemons into lemonade. The first thing Valentine wanted recruits to learn was to respect Grogs, whether they were friends or enemies.

Way too many lives had been lost in the past thanks to mistakes.

Valentine asked Hank to go fill a tray, saw that the light was on in

Meadows' office, and poked his head in to see if his superior had anything new on the rumored attack.

"Forward posts all quiet, sir," Valentine reported.

"I'm not forward or quiet," William Post replied. His salt-and-pepper hair showed white traces of boric acid. "Narcisse made her chili last night." Valentine's old subordinate, an ex-Quisling Coastal Marine who'd helped him take the *Thunderbolt* across the Caribbean and back, and was one of the best officers he'd ever known, went back to sorting com-flimsies. Valentine's ears picked up a stifled burp.

"Anything happen here?" *Besides the usual morning gas.*

Meadows had the look of a man just up from a twenty-minute nap that was the only sleep he'd gotten that night. He closed his shirt, his missing-fingered hand working the buttons up the seam like a busy insect. "Not even the usual harassing fire. They're finally running out of shells. Big Wings overhead in the night."

Big Wings were the larger, gargoylelike flyers the Kurians kept in the taller towers of Dallas. Both smarter and rarer than the Harpies Valentine had encountered, they tended to stay above, out of rifle shot, in the dark. Some weeks ago Valentine had seen a dead one that had been brought down by chance, wearing a pair of binoculars and carrying an aerial photograph, grease-penciled icons squiggled all over the photo marking the besieging army's current positions.

"I had the A Company men turn in," Post reported. "The armored cars are still ready to roll, and C Company's alerted. Just in case."

"Thanks, Will," Valentine said. "Colonel, I still think they're preparing a surprise. I'd suggest we keep the line fully manned." Valentine regretted the words before his tongue stilled. Meadows was smart enough that he didn't need to be told the obvious.

"Our sources could be wrong. Again," Meadows said, glancing at the flimsy-basket next to his door. It was piled with messages that came in overnight but weren't important enough to require the CO to be awakened. The belief that an attack was due had been based on Valentine's intelligence, everything from deserter interrogations to vague murmurs from Dallas Operations that the heart of the city was abuzz with activity. There was no hint of reprimand or peevishness in his tone. Meadows knew war was guesswork, and frequently the guesses were wrong.

"Sir, Smoke came in while I was out," Valentine said. "I'll debrief her over breakfast."

Post gave Valentine a playful wink as Meadows read his messages. Duvalier's appropriation of Valentine's bed whenever she was with the Razors inspired a few jokes about Valentine's "operations." Valentine suspected that the best lines originated from Post's salty throat.

"How are the men up the boulevard doing?" Meadows asked.

"The boulevard" was a wide east-west street that marked the forward edge of the Razors' positions. Snipers and machine gunners warred over five lanes of former Texas state route from blasted storefronts.

"Unhappy about being on the line, sir," Post reported. Post had keen antennae when it came to sensing the regiment's mood. More importantly, he cared, and even better, he acted on their behalf. Post was a relentless terror to rear-area supply officers when it came to the well-being of his men. "They only got three days at the airfield." Comparatively fresh companies had been moved up in anticipation of the attack from the relative quiet of the old field.

"Let's rotate them out if nothing happens by tomorrow morning."

"Will do, sir," Post replied.

"I'll see to Smoke now, Colonel, if you don't have anything else," Valentine said.

"Thank her for me, Major. Grab a meal and then hit your bunk." Meadows tended to keep his orders brief and simple. Sometimes they were also pleasant. Meadows picked up the flimsies from his basket, glanced at them, and passed them to Valentine.

Valentine read them on the way back to the galley—or kitchen, he mentally corrected. Shipboard slang still worked itself into his thoughts, a leftover from his yearlong spell posing as a Coastal Marine in the enemy's uniform, and then living in the *Thunderbolt* after taking her from the Kurians.

01:30 *Potable water line reestablished to forward positions*
02:28 *OP3 OP11 Artillery fire flashes and sounds from other side of city*
03:55 *OP3 Barrage ceased*
04:10 *OP12 Reports train heard north toward city*

The OP notation was for field phone–equipped forward observation posts. Valentine had heard the barrage and seen the flashes on the opposite side of the city as well, glimpsed from between the tall buildings, making the structures stand out against the night like gravestones to a dead city.

The only suspicious message was of the train. The lines into Dallas had been cut, torn up, mined, plowed under, or otherwise blocked very early in the siege. Readying or moving a train made little sense—unless the Kurians were merely shuffling troops within the city.

Valentine loaded up a tray and employed Hank as coffee bearer, and returned to his room. Duvalier twitched at his entry, then relaxed. Her eyes opened.

"Food," she said.

"And coffee," Valentine replied, after checking to make sure she was decent. Hank being a teenager, he'd waited in the spot with the best viewing angle into the room and bed.

"What's the latest from D?" Valentine asked, setting the tray briefly on the bed before pulling his makeshift desk up so she'd have an eating surface.

"No sign of an assault. I saw some extra gun crews and battle police at their stations, but no troops have been brought up."

Hank hung up Duvalier's gear to dry. Valentine saw the boy clip off a yawn.

"The Quislings?"

"Most units been on half rations for over a month now. Internal security and battle police excepted, of course. And some of the higher officers; they're as fat as ever. I heard some men talking. No one dares report sick. Rumor has it the Kurians are running short on aura, and the sick list is the first place they look."

"Morale?"

"Horrible," she reported between bites. "They're losing and they know it. Deserters aren't being disposed of quietly anymore. Every night just before they shut down power they assemble representatives from all the Quisling brigades and have public executions. I put on a nurse's shawl and hat and watched one. NCOs kept offering me a bottle or cigarettes, but I couldn't take my eyes off the stage."

The incidental noises from Hank working behind him ceased.

"They make the deserters stand in these big plastic garbage cans, the ones with little arrows running around in a circle, handcuffed in front. Then a Reaper comes up from behind one and tears open their shirt. They keep the poor bastard facing the other ranks the whole time so they can see the expression on his face—they're all gagged of course; they don't want any last words. The Reaper clamps its jaws somewhere between the shoulder blades and starts squeezing their arms into the rib cage. You hear the bones breaking, see the shoulders pop out as they dislocate.

"Then they just tip up the garbage can and wheel the body away. Blood and piss leaking out the bottom, usually. Then a political officer steps up and reads the dead man's confession, and his CO verifies his mark or signature. Then they wheel out the next one. Sometimes six or seven a night. They want the men to go to bed with something to think about.

"I've seen some gawdawful stuff, but . . . that poor bastard. I had a dream about him."

"They never run out of Reapers, do they?" Hank put in.

"Seems not," Duvalier said.

Valentine decided to change the subject. "Okay, they're not massing for an attack. Maybe a breakout?"

"No, all the rolling motor stock is dispersed," she said, slurping coffee. "Unless it's hidden. I saw a few entrances to underground garages that were guarded with armored cars and lots of wire and kneecappers."

The last was a nasty little mine the Kurians were fond of. When triggered, it launched itself twenty inches in the air like a startled frog and exploded, sending flechettes out horizontally that literally cut a man off at the knees.

"I don't suppose you saw any draft articles of surrender crumpled up in the wastebaskets, did you?"

She made a noise that sent remnants of a last mouthful of masticated egg flying. "Na-ah."

"Now," Valentine said. "If you'll get out of my bed—"

"I need a real bath. Those basins are hardly big enough to sit in. How about your water boy—"

Hank perked up at the potential for *that* duty.

Valentine hated to ruin the boy's morning. "You can use the womens'. There's piping laid on and a tub."

Such gallantry as still existed between the sexes in the Razors mostly involved the men working madly to provide the women with a few homey comforts wherever the regiment moved. The badly outnumbered women had to do little in return—the occasional smile, a few soft words, or an earthy joke reminded their fellow soldiers of mothers, sweethearts, sisters, or wives.

"Killjoy," Duvalier said, winking at Hank.

The alarms brought Valentine out of his dreams and to his feet. For one awful moment he hung on a mental precipice between reality and his vaguely pleasant dream—something to do with a boat and bougainvillea—while his brain caught up to his body and oriented itself.

Alarms. Basement in Texas. Dallas siege. The Razors.

Alarms?

Two alarms, his brain noted as full consciousness returned. Whistle after whistle, blown from a dozen mouths like referees trying to stop a football brawl, indicated an attack—all men to grab whatever would shoot and get to their defense stations, plus the wail of an air-alert siren.

But no gongs. If the Kurians had dusted again, every man who could find a piece of hollow metal to bang, from tin can to wheel rim, should be setting up as loud a clamor as possible. No one wanted to be a weak link in another Fort Worth massacre that caused comrades to choke out.

Valentine forced himself to pull on socks and tie his boots, grabbed the bag containing his gas mask, scarves, and gloves anyway, and buckled his pistol belt. Hank had cleaned and hung up his cut-down battle rifle. Valentine checked it over as he hurried through men running every which way or looking to their disheveled operations officer for direction, and headed for the stairs to the control tower, the field's tactical command post. He took seemingly endless switchbacks of stairs two at a time to the "top deck"—the Razors' shorthand for the tallest point of Love Field.

He felt explosions, then heard them a second later. Worse than mortars, worse than artillery, and going off so closely together he wondered if the Kurians had been keeping rocket artillery in reserve for a crisis. The old stairs rattled and dropped dirt as though shaking in fear.

"Would you look at those bastards!" he heard someone shout from the control tower.

"Send to headquarters: 'Rancid,' " Valentine heard Meadows shout. "Rancid. Rancid. Rancid."

Valentine came off the last stairs and passed through the open security door. Meadows and two others of the regiment had box seats on chaos.

Whoever had installed the glass—if it was glass and not a high-tech polymer—had done the job well; still-intact windows offered the tower a 360-degree field of vision. In the distance the crenellated Dallas skyline—one bifurcated tower the men called "the Eye" stared straight at the field thanks to its strange, empty-centered top—broke the hazy morning horizon.

As he went to the glass, noting the quiet voice of the communications officer relaying the "Rancid" alert to Brigade, another explosion erupted in black-orange menace atop the parking garage—the biggest structure on the field.

Valentine followed a private's eyes up and looked out on a sky filled with whirling planes.

Not rickety, rebuilt crop dusters or lumbering old commercial aircraft; the assorted planes shared only smooth silhouettes and a mottled gray-and-tan camouflage pattern reminiscent of a dusty rattlesnake. There were sleek single seaters, like stunt planes Valentine had seen in books, whipping around the edges of the field, turned sideways so the pilots could get a good look at ground activity. Banana-shaped twin-engine jobs dove in at the vehicles parked between the two wings of the terminal concourses, one shooting rocket after rocket at the vehicles while the other two flanked it, drawing ground fire. A pair of bigger, uglier, wide-winged military attack planes with bulging turbofans on their rear fuselages came in, dropping a series of bombs that exploded into a huge snake of fire writhing between the Razors' positions and the southwestern strip.

"Who the hell are these guys?" Meadows said to no one.

The screaming machines, roaring to and fro over the field, weren't the only attackers on the wing. Flying Grogs in the hundreds, many the Harpy-type Valentine had first met over Weening during his spell in the labor regiments, swooped below the aircraft and even the control tower, dispensing what looked—and exploded—like sticks of dynamite at anything that moved. A few bigger wings—the true gargoyles of the kind Valentine had seen lain out—circled above, possibly waiting for a juicy enough target to be worth whatever they held in saddlebags hung around their thick necks.

The Razors fought back, mostly from their positions in the parking garages and the heavy weapons point around a winged statue depicting "Flight" near the entrance to the terminal buildings. Small groups of men or single soldiers fired from behind doorways, windows, or the sandbagged positions guarding the motor pool between the concourses.

Perhaps a gargoyle decided to hit the control tower. Valentine heard a heavy thud among the aerials on the roof, the scrabble of claws.

"Out!" Valentine shouted.

The trio looked up at the roof, apparently transfixed by the harmless scrabbling noises. Meadows' hand went to his sidearm, and the private fumbled with his battle rifle. In seconds they'd be dead, fragmenting brain tissue still wondering at the strange raccoonlike noise—

"Out!" Valentine said again, bodily pushing the private to the stairs with one hand, and pulling the communications officer from her chair with the other. She came out of her chair with her headset on; the headset cord stretched and unplugged as though it were as reluctant to leave its post as its operator. Meadows moved with dramatic suddenness as the realization of what might be happening on the roof arrived, and grabbed for the handle on the thick metal door to the stairway.

"I'll get it," Meadows said. Valentine, keeping touch with both the private and the communications officer, hurried down the stairs.

One flight. Two flights. Meadows' clattering footsteps on the stairs a half floor above . . .

The *boom* Valentine had been expecting for ten anxious seconds was neither head-shattering nor particularly loud, and while it shook peeling paint from the stairs and knocked out the lights, the three weren't so much as knocked off-stride.

Meadows joined them, panting. "The door must have held," he said.

Or physics worked in our favor, Valentine thought. An explosion tends to travel along the path of least resistance, usually upward.

"Maybe." Valentine said.

The impact of three more explosions came up through the floor, bombs striking Love Field somewhere.

"Orders?" Valentine asked.

"I'm going back up," Meadows said. "They might think they finished the job with one bomb. The radio antenna's had it for sure, but the field lines might still be functional."

"You two game?" Valentine asked the private—an intelligent soldier named Wilcox who was the military equivalent of a utility infielder; he could play a variety of positions well. Ruvayed, the lieutenant with the headphone jack still swinging at the end of its cord just below her belt, nodded.

Valentine clicked his gun off safety and brought it to his shoulder. "Me first, in case they crawled in."

Meadows brought up the rear going back up the stairs. Valentine reached the security door. Dust had been blown from beneath the door in an elegant spiked pattern, and he smelled smoke and the harsher odor of burning plastic. He turned the handle but the door wouldn't budge.

A kick opened it. The air inside had the harsh, faintly sulfurous tang of exploded dynamite.

As he swept the room over the open sights on his gun, Valentine saw naked sunlight streaming in from a hole in the roof big enough to put a sedan's engine block through. Older air-traffic consoles and the Razors' newer communications gear were blackened and cracked; the transformation was so thorough it seemed it should have taken more time than an instant.

The glass held, though it had cracks ranging from spiderwebbing to single fault lines. The quality of the stuff the old United States used to be able to make made Valentine shake his head in wonder yet again. Outside the planes still turned, swooped, and soared, engines louder now thanks to the hole in the roof.

But he kept his eyes and ears tuned to the new skylight, his cut-down Atlanta Gunworks battle rifle ready. Another tiny plane buzzed by, the noise of its engine rising fast and fading slowly over the other, fainter aircraft sounds. *Who the hell are these guys?*

Meadows pressed binoculars to his eye, scanning the ground in the direction of Dallas. "Not even mortar fire. It's not a breakout."

"Bad intelligence?" Ruvayed asked. "They thought *we* had planes?"

Another ribbon of fire blossomed against the parking garage facing the runway to the southwest. Valentine wondered about Ahn-Kha and Will Post. Both were probably at the hardpoints around the garages . . . why did they keep hitting that side of the airport? It faced the train tracks running out of the city, but the lines were torn up for miles.

Another of the tiny, fast scout planes buzzed low over the overgrown airstrip there. Save for his speed it looked as though he might be on a landing approach. The plane jumped skyward to avoid a stream of tracer.

"I wish we had some ack-ack guns here," Meadows said, binoculars trained up at some big multiengine transport circling the field. "All the high-angle stuff is close in to the city."

"Colonel," Valentine said. "Southwest. Look southwest, hitting hardest there."

"Field phones are shot," Ruvayed reported.

"Wilcox, hustle us up a portable radio," Meadows said. The private disappeared down the stairs.

The colonel searched the southern and western approaches to the airport. "Goddamn."

"I'd like to see what's happening in the garage," Valentine said.

"Go ahead. Pass the word that I'll be on the maintenance frequency, if I can get a radio up here. Send up a couple of messengers."

Valentine handed his gun and ammunition harness to Ruvayed. "Keep an eye cocked to that hole. And watch the balcony," he said. The control tower had an electronics service balcony just below the outsloping windows. Nothing but birds' nests and old satellite dishes decorated it, but it would be just like the gargoyles to land carrying a couple of sniper rifles.

"Yes, sir," Ruvayed said.

"Tell everyone to keep their heads down, Major," Meadows said. "Maybe this whole attack is a Kurian screwup. The mechanics moved a couple of stripped passenger craft the other day—from a distance it could have looked like we had planes ready to go."

"Yes, sir." Valentine nodded. He turned for the stairs. Meadows didn't care one way or the other about salutes.

"Goes doubly for you," Meadows called after him.

The violent airshow going on outside must have been running short on fireworks; only one more small explosion sounded during the endless turns down the stairs. The elevator to the control tower was missing and presumed scavenged—nothing but shaft ran up the center of the structure.

Valentine double-timed through the tunnel system and up to the first floor of the terminal. He trotted past empty counters under faded signs and motionless luggage carousels—the only part of the main terminal in use was a small area in front of the bronze Ranger statue (ONE RIOT, ONE RANGER read the plaque) where the consumables for the Razors were delivered every few days.

"Major!" A voice broke through the sound of his footsteps. A corporal with his flak jacket on inside out called from the other end of the terminal, "They're hurtin' on the west approach."

"Thanks. Tell the Bears to find Captain Post and be ready to counterattack if they hit us from the ground. Send messengers and a new field phone up to the top deck. Right away."

The corporal nodded and ran for the stairwell.

Valentine crossed over to the huge parking garages by scuttling under the concrete walkway to the upper deck of the lot. A wheelless ambulance in the center of the parking garage served as an improvised command post for the airport's close-in defense.

The air was full of smoke and a fainter, oilier smell Valentine recognized as burning gasoline.

Wounded men and burned corpses lay all around the ambulance. Captain Martin, a Texas liaison for the Razors, helped the medics perform the gruesome task of triage as he spoke to a pair of sergeants.

Valentine listened with hard ears as he approached. Enhanced hearing, a gift from the Lifeweavers dating back to his time as a Wolf, made each word sound as though it were spoken in his ear. "Everyone to the dugouts but the observers," Martin said. "Yes, treat it like a bombardment. We'll worry about an assault when we see one."

Martin recognized Valentine with a nod. "Weird kinda visit from Dallas. How did they pull this off?"

"I doubt they're from Dallas," Valentine said. "We would have seen them taking off."

More distant explosions—a series of smaller cracks that made up a larger noise like halfhearted thunder.

"I'm putting the men in the shelters," Martin explained.

"Good," Valentine said, not wanting to waste time explaining that he'd already overheard the orders given. "I'd like to take a look at the field south and west of here. Is there still an operational post where I can do that?"

Valentine saw Ahn-Kha approaching from a forward garage stairwell, a man draped on each powerful shoulder. Ahn-Kha's arms, longer than but not quite as thick as his legs, held the men in place in a strange imitation of the classic bodybuilder's pose.

Blood matted his friend's golden shoulder and back fur, Valentine noted as his old companion set the men down near the ambulance.

"He's worth three Texans," Martin observed. Martin was still new enough to the Razors to watch Ahn-Kha as though half fascinated and half worried that the Grog would suddenly sink his ivory fangs into the nearest human. "Ten ordinary men, in other words."

"The observation post?" Valentine reminded the captain, as Ahn-Kha checked the dressings on the men he had just set down. Enormous, double-thumbed hands gently turned one of the wounded on his side.

"Second floor of the garage, back of an old van. It's still wired to the phone network."

Valentine remembered. "I know it. Ahn-Kha!"

The Golden One nodded to one of the Razor medics as she wiped her hands on a bloodstained disinfectant towel and squatted beside the latest additions to the swamp of bleeding men. "Yes, my David?"

"Get your puddler and meet me at OP 6."

Ahn-Kha's "Grog gun" had become famous, a 20mm behemoth of his own design that resembled a telescope copulating with a sawed-off kid's swing set. The other name came from a skirmish the Razors fought outside Fort Worth, where Ahn-Kha reduced an armored car commander to a slippery puddle of goo outside his hatch at six hundred yards.

"Yes, my David." Over seven feet of muscle straightened. "I had to leave Corporal Lopez at the stairwell exterior door. He's dead, or soon will be," Ahn-Kha informed the captain.

"What the hell, Major?" Martin asked. "What's so goddamn important about blowing us off the planet?"

"We'll know sooner than we'd like, I expect," Valentine said.

Another bomb shook dust onto the wounded.

"Christ," Martin said, but Valentine was reminded of something else.

"Make sure the men have their dust gear in the shelters," Valentine said. He ran down a mental list of what else the Razors might need to stop a column, and the two reserve regimental recoilless rifles could be useful. "Get Luke and John operational up here too, with plenty of shells. But the dust gear first." Matthew and Mark were vehicle-mounted, and probably smoldering with most of the other transport between the terminals.

"You'd think we'd be drowning in it. Makes me think—"

"They're probably on their way already."

Valentine offered a salute. Martin's mouth tightened as he returned it—the Texans weren't big on military rigamarole, but there were ordinary soldiers present and the Razors knew a salute from their operations chief meant that the half-Indian major didn't expect you to speak again until you were ready to report on his orders—and hurried to the central stairway.

Valentine went up a floor to the last garage level before the exposed top and hurried to the rusty old van, parked just far enough from the open edge of the parking lot so the sun would never hit it. Though wheelless and up on blocks, missing even its headlamps and mirrors, the Razors kept it clean so that the carefully washed smoked-glass windows at the back and sides wouldn't stand out from the dirt and Texas dust of the nonlethal variety.

Valentine called out his name and entered the van through the open side door. Two Razors looked out on the Dallas skyline and the roads and train tracks running along the western edge of the airfield. Their ready dust-hoods hung off the backs of their helmets like bridal veils. Dropped playing cards lay on the van's interior carpet, the only remaining evidence of what had probably once been plush fixtures for road-weary vactioners.

"I've never seen so many planes in my life, that's for sure," one said to the other, a bit of the Arkansas hills in his voice. Valentine knew his face but the name wouldn't come. "Howdy, Major."

"Hey, Major Valentine," the other said, after relocating a piece of hard candy on a tongue depressor that the soldiers called a "postsicle." Captain Post had a candy maker somewhere in his family tree, and the men liked to suck on his confections to keep the Texas dirt from drying out their mouths. "We got hit after all, huh."

"I'm glad somebody noticed. Did it break up a good card game?"

"Depends. Lewis was winning," the Arkansan said.

"Sorry to hear that, Lewis," Valentine said. He vaguely knew that the tradition of canceling all wins and losses in an unfinished game had sprung up during the siege at Big Rock Mountain the previous year, and was thus hallowed into one of the battalion's unwritten rules.

"What do these aircutters got against the Razors, is what I want to know," Lewis said.

Valentine scanned the approaches to the airfield, then the sky. A larger plane, its wingspan wider than its body length, caught the sun high up.

Whoever's up there knows.

The second phase of the attack came within five minutes, as Valentine reported to Meadows through a field phone line patched into the portable radio now installed in the control tower.

"Holy Jesus!" Lewis barked.

The grass between the northwest-southeast parallel runways flanking the field bulged, then dimpled, then collapsed, sending a cloud of dirt to join the smoke still coating the field.

"Between the runways," Ahn-Kha shouted from his position at a supporting column. And unnecessarily, as Valentine locked eyes on the spot and brought up his binoculars.

A corkscrew prow the size of one of the old *Thunderbolt*'s lifeboats emerged into daylight. Striped blacks and browns on a pebbly, organic surface spun hypnotically as it rotated. Brown flesh behind—the snout pulsed, ripples like circular waves traveling backward to the hidden portion of the thing. It rolled like a show diver performing a forward twist and nosed back into the earth. Overgrown prairie plants flew as the giant worm tilled and plunged back into the soil.

"What the devil?" the Arkansan said, watching the creature dig, still spinning clockwise as it reburied itself.

Tiny planes whipped over the inverted *U* of exposed flesh.

"Tunnels, Colonel, they've tunneled to the airfield," Valentine said into the field phone. He consulted the map of the airfield and its surroundings, pinned to the carpeted wall of the observation van. "We need fire support to grid N-7, repeat N-7."

The tunneling worm's other end finally appeared, another shell-like counterpoint to the prow. Valentine marked an orifice at the very tip this time, though whether it was for eating or excreting he couldn't say.

The two identical warcraft, turbofans bulging above their broad wings, banked in from the west, aiming directly at the parking garages.

Valentine dropped the field glasses and the phone handpiece. Something about the crosslike silhouettes of the aircraft suggested approaching doom.

"This won't be good," Lewis said.

"Out! Out! Out!" Valentine shouted.

Ahn-Kha was already at the van door, perhaps ready to bodily pull the men from the observation post, but the three jumped from the van and ran for the central stairway.

They didn't quite make it.

Valentine heard faint whooshing noises from behind, over the Doppler-effect sound of the quickly growing engine noise. The men flung themselves down, recognizing the rockets for what they were.

The planes had aimed for the floor beneath theirs, as it turned out. Though loud, the only damage the explosions did was to their eardrums. A stray rocket struck their floor of the garage over at the other wing of the structure.

The van caught some of the blast from below. Their carpeted cubbyhole tipped on its side, blown off its blocks.

"Let's see if the phone's still working," Valentine said.

"What if they come around for another pass?" the Arkansan asked, teeth chattering.

"They've got to be out of fireworks by now," Lewis said.

"You alright, old horse?" Valentine asked Ahn-Kha, who was inspecting his puddler.

One business envelope-sized pointed ear drooped. "Yes. The sight may be out of alignment. I dropped it in my haste."

Back at the edge of the garage, in the shadow of a supporting column, Valentine gulped and met Ahn-Kha's eyes before cautiously peeping over the edge of the parking lot wall and surveying the field. A beating sound had replaced the higher-pitched airplane engines.

Helicopters!

Gradually Valentine made out shapes through the obscuring smoke of still-burning jellied gasoline and the more recent rocket blasts. A great, sand-colored behemoth with twin rotors forward, and a smaller stabilizing fan aft thundered out of the west. Smaller helicopters flanked her, like drones looking to mate with some great queen bee.

One of the little stunt planes flew in, dropping a cannister near the holes. It sputtered to life on impact and threw a streamer of red smoke into the sky.

Where's the damn artillery?

"Field phone's still good, Major," Lewis said, extracting the canvas-covered pack from the van.

"Spot for the artillery, if it's available," Valentine said, trying to give intelligible orders while racking his brain for what he knew about helicopter function. "Target that cherry bomb by the holes. And send Base Defense Southwest to Colonel Meadows."

"Base defense southwest, yes, sir," Lewis repeated.

Another plane roared by, seemingly inches from the garage, with a suddenness that momentarily stopped Valentine's heart.

"I do not like these airplanes," Ahn-Kha said.

Valentine watched the smaller helicopters shoot off more rockets, but these just sent up more thick clouds of smoke, putting a dark gray wall between the observation point and the holes.

"If we can't see them . . . set up the puddler. Lewis, any word on the artillery?"

"Sounds like they've been hit too, sir," Lewis said, taking his hand away from the ear not held to the phone.

The twin-rotored helicopter blew just enough smoke away with its massive blades so they could get a quick look at it as it landed by the hole.

"That's your target," Valentine said. "See the smaller rotor, spinning at the end of the tail? Aim for the center of that."

Smoke obscured the quick glance, but Valentine had seen something emerge from the hole dug by the worm, a turtlelike shape.

"Our mortars, anything, get it put down on that hole!" *They can shoot a hundred shells a day into the Dallas works, but they can't drop a few on Love Field.*

"Nothing to shoot at, my David," Ahn-Kha said, ears twitching this way and that, telegraphing his frustration. The Grog had his gun resting on his shoulder and its unique bipod. The gun muzzle was suspended by heavyweight fishing line from the bipod arching over it rather than resting atop the supports, allowing for tiny alterations and changes in direction, typical of creative Grog engineering, right down to the leather collar that kept the line from melting. The black-painted line acted as a fore sight when Ahn-Kha wasn't shooting through the telescopic sight.

Valentine felt impotent. "Tell Meadows it's a breakout," he said to Lewis. "I think the Kurians are trying to run for it with the helicopters."

"Why didn't they just land on a street in Dallas?" Lewis asked.

"We've got high-angle artillery there," Valentine said.

"Sir," the Arkansan shouted as the smoke clouds cleared. Some kind of bay doors had opened at the rear of the massive helicopter, which rested on thick-tired multiple wheels. The turtlelike thing, which looked to Valentine like a greenish propane storage tank crawling across the runway without benefit of wheels, tracks, or legs, had turned for the big chopper.

Ahn-Kha's gun coughed and Valentine's nose registered cordite. Ahn-Kha didn't bother to watch the shot. Instead he drew another highlighter-sized bullet from his bandolier and reloaded the gun.

But the smoke was back.

Valentine could just make out the helicopter through the thinning smoke. Explosions sounded from back toward the terminal, as another piece of the Razor military machine was blown up.

Ahn-Kha must have been able to see the rear rotor for a second—he fired again. Valentine marked the strange tanklike thing entering the rear of the helicopter . . . it was like watching a film of a hen laying an egg run backward.

"Where's the fuckin' support?" the Arkansan asked, voicing Valentine's thoughts exactly.

Valentine heard engines on the ground. He looked to the south, where a few of the Razors' strange conglomeration of transport and patrol vehicles—including two prowlers—were barreling past the statue of Flight at the edge of the airport buildings.

"Holy shit, the cavalry!" the Arkansan shouted.

Valentine recognized the salt-and-pepper hair of the man at the minigun in the lead prowler. Captain William Post. It was hard not to join the private in screaming his head off.

The aircraft spotted the vehicles too. A twin-engine airplane swooped in, firing cannon at the column. Valentine saw one big-tired transport turn and plow into the garage.

Ahn-Kha fired again, and the helicopter wobbled as it left the ground, rear doors still closing. The helicopter lurched sideways—perhaps Ahn-Kha had damaged the rear rotor after all.

The pilot managed to get the helicopter, which was skittering sideways across the field like a balky horse, righted.

Light caught Valentine's eyes from above and he looked up to see muzzle flash from a big four-engine aircraft above. Some kind of gun fired on the approaching vehicles.

But the Razors had guns of their own—and someone trained them on the staggering helicopter. Machine guns and small cannon opened up, sending pieces of fuselage flying. Black smoke blossomed from the craft's engine crown, instantly dispersed by the powerful rotors.

Ahn-Kha shot again.

The Razor vehicles had to pay for their impertinent charge. The military turbofan planes swooped in—Valentine grimly noted a desert camouflage pattern atop the craft—and fired from some kind of cannon that created a muzzle flash as big as the blunt nose of the aircraft, planting blossoms of fiery destruction among the Razor attackers.

Post's armored car turned over as it died. Valentine couldn't imagine what the wreck had done to his friend.

Like sacrificing a knight to take the enemy queen, even as the prowlers exploded the double-rotored helicopter tipped sideways, sending its six blades spinning into the smoke-filled sky as it crashed. The helicopter's crew jumped out with credible speed, and Ahn-Kha swiveled his cannon.

"No. I want prisoners," Valentine said.

One of the smaller helicopters swooped in and landed, even as tracer fire began to appear from the positions at the base of the garage, where gun slits had been clawed through the concrete weeks ago.

Ahn-Kha shifted his aim and began to send 20mm-cannon shells into the tail rotor of the rescue helicopter.

The concrete to the left of Ahn-Kha exploded into powdery dust. "Down!" *Was that my voice?* Valentine wondered as he threw himself sidways onto Ahn-Kha. Cannon shells tore through the gap between the floors of the garage, ripping apart the van. The Arkansan fell with a softball-sized hunk of flesh torn away from his neck and shoulder, and Valentine dully thought that he'd have to learn the man's name in order to put it in the report, and then the cannonade was over.

Lewis stared stupidly around, still kneeling next to the van, in the exact same position he'd been in a second ago, still holding the field phone to his ear.

Valentine heard the first *BOOM* of shellfire landing on the field. The artillery had come at last.

Valentine stood between the shell holes on the overgrown, cracked landing strip and surveyed the mess.

What was left of the attackers from the vehicles and the defenders of the garages had encircled the two holes and the downed helicopter. Valentine had seen Post borne away in a stretcher, but couldn't do anything but touch a bloodily peeled hand as the bearers rushed him to the medical unit.

The mysterious air raiders had rocketed their own helicopter before leaving, blowing what was left of the double-rotor airship into three substantial chunks—pilot cabin, part of the cargo area, and stabilizing tail.

The odd, green propane-tank capsule remained in the wreckage. Flames slid off it like oil from Teflon.

The Bears kept watch from the overturned earth of the Kurian wormhole. Valentine had poked his head in—the three-meter-diameter tunnel was ringed with strands of whitish goo about the thickness of his thumb, crisscrossed and spiderwebbed like the frosting dribbled atop a Bundt cake. Whether the digging worm creature (someone called it a "bore worm" but Valentine didn't know if the term came from *Hitchen's Guide to Introduced Species* or if the would-be zooologist had thought it up on the spot). The Bears also watched a pair of wounded prisoners, survivors of the transport helicopter who hadn't made it to the rescuing craft. A medic dressed a cut on one pilot's scalp just below the helmet line. The stranger submitted to the ministrations with something like dull contempt. The aircrew were lean, well-tanned men with oversized sunglasses and desert scarves. Both wore leather jackets with a panel stitched on the back, reading in English and Spanish:

NONNEGOTIABLE $10,000 GOLD REWARD
for the safe return of this pilot unharmed and
healthy to Pyp's Flying Circus **YUMA
ARIZONA/AZTLAN**. Negotiable traveling and
keep expenses also paid in trade goods.
**CONTACT PROVOST FT CHICO OR NEW
UNIVERSAL CHURCH—TEMPE
DIRECTORATE FOR INFORMATION
AND DIRECTIONS**

Each also had a patch reading PYP'S FLYING CIRCUS, featuring a winged rattlesnake, flying with mouth open as though to strike.

So the question of *who the hell are these guys* was answered. With another question.

But Valentine's mind was on that tank in the center of the wreckage.

Some of the men theorized it contained a nuclear bomb. Valentine suspected that the contents were a good deal more lethal to the human race long-term.

And everyone was looking at him.

Valentine paced at the edge of the wormhole.

"Nail, I want three Bears ready with demolition blocks. I don't know if it'll dent that thing, but it might rattle them."

Nail was a pigeon-chested Bear with long, sun-lightened blond hair, wearing captain's bars. Nail had been promoted after the fight on Big Rock Mountain, and was the leader of the toughest soldiers in the Razors . . . and probably Texas, in Valentine's opinion—and that meant the world, if you asked a Texan, but Valentine had learned not to argue with Texans in matters of regional pride.

"Ready? Send them forward now."

"No. I'm going to have a talk with them first."

"It's your aura, Val."

Ahn-Kha lifted his improvised cannon. "I'll go along, my David."

Valentine looked around, and pointed to a scrawny, fuzzy-cheeked Razor. "You come too, Appley."

"Yes, sir," young Appley said, uncomprehending but conditioned to respond to orders.

Valentine passed the boy his order book. "If we get some kind of dialogue going, I want you to look like you're taking notes."

"You want me to write down what they say?"

"If you want. Write your mom if you want; I just want you writing when anybody is talking. Can do?"

"Can do!" Appley said. Major Valentine only offered a "can do" to key jobs, and it was the first time the boy had heard the phrase applied to him.

"Great. Follow a little behind."

Ahn-Kha walked beside him. "Why such a youngster?" the Golden One asked, speaking from the side of his mouth—an eerie-looking effort, thanks to his snout and rubbery lips.

"Would you use that boy in an ambush?" Valentine asked.

"Of course not."

"I hope the Kurians think that too."

When he figured he was close enough, Valentine stopped and looked around at his feet. The Kurian vessel reminded him now of a pill rather than a propane tank. Or perhaps a malformed watermelon; the "top" half was a bit bigger than the bottom. Some kind of bright blue sludge clung to the bottom.

"Reminds me of heartroot come to maturity in a drought," Ahn-Kha said. Heartroot was a mushroomlike Grog staple.

Valentine picked up a piece of shattered glass and threw it at the tank. It bounced off. Valentine noted that the blue sludge shrunk away from the vibration. Perhaps a Kurian? They were bluish on the rare instances when they appeared undisguised. But why would it be hiding outside the tank?

"Anyone home?" he yelled.

The blue sludge quivered, shifted up the faintly lined side of the tank vessel. The lines reminded Valentine of the nautical charts and plots he'd seen on the old *Thunderbolt*.

"I've come to negotiate your relocation from Texas," Valentine yelled. He looked over his shoulder; the boy was scribbling. He was also cross-eyed when looking at something up close and Valentine stifled a snicker.

The blue goop bulged, then parted. Valentine startled, and no longer had to fight off laughter when he recognized a Reaper emerging from the protoplasm. The two-meter-tall death machines were living organisms linked to their master Kurian, used in the messy, and sometimes dangerous, process of aura extraction. The Reaper fed off the victim's blood using a syringelike tongue, while the Kurian animating it absorbed what old Father Max had called aural energies. Others called it soul-sucking.

Is that how they make 'em?

The Reaper climbed out of the blue sludge and lifted its hood, pulling it far forward over its face to block out the sun. Sunlight didn't kill them, unfortunately, but it interfered with their senses and the connection with the master Kurian.

Valentine silently wished for one of Ahn-Kha's Quickwood spear points or crossbow bolts. Two years ago Valentine had brought a special kind of olive tree–like growth called Quickwood back from the Caribbean. It was lethal to Reapers, but had been consumed in the insurrection in the Ozarks known as Operation Archangel the previous year.

"Look, they shat out a Reaper," Valentine said. The kid laughed, a little too loudly.

Ahn-Kha raised his long gun just a fraction.

Valentine revised his estimate of the interior of the tank. At one Reaper per Kurian, there could only be a dozen or so Reapers inside the tank. The flexible, octopus-crossed-with-bat Kurians could squeeze into nooks and crannies, of course, but the impressively built Reapers could only be packed so tight. And all breathed oxygen. At one Reaper per Kurian—there was a theory that without at least one Reaper to supply it with aura, a Kurian starved to death—that meant a dozen Kurians. Others claimed, with little to back it up but speculation, that the Kurians could "bottle" aura to last until a new Reaper could be acquired. Still others said a Kurian could absorb aura through its touch, a "death grip."

Experience told Valentine that if the third were true, the Little Rock Kurian who had died under his fists hadn't managed it in the last few painful seconds of its life.

"Far enough," Ahn-Kha said as the Reaper approached, raising his gun a little higher.

"*i shall speak for those within, foodling,*" the Reaper said, staying out of grabbing distance. Valentine had to concentrate to hear its low, breathy voice, always averting his gaze from the yellow, slit-pupiled eyes. Reapers had a deceptive stillness to them, like a praying mantis. Their grip was deadly, but their gaze could be just as lethal; the few times Valentine had looked closely into one's eyes he'd been half hypnotized.

Valentine took a step forward. "Use the word 'foodling' again and 'those within' will have to crap out a new negotiator."

The Reaper, apparently as egoless as a Buddhist statue, ignored the threat. "*your terms?*"

"First: You left behind a lot of men in Dallas. Tell them to surrender without another shot fired. No conditions, but officers and military police will be allowed to keep their sidearms, the combatants can keep individual weapons, noncombatants will be under protection of their own people. We're not taking them into custody. They can march wherever they want on whatever supplies they can bring out of Dallas. Second: What's left of Dallas, including artillery and transport, shall be turned over to us, intact. If both those conditions are met, we'll load your tin can on a transport and take you to any border region you like, along with any remaining of your kind that didn't manage to tunnel out of the city."

Valentine knew he had overstepped his authority—in fact this was more like running a track-and-field triple jump over his authority—but he wanted to make the deal before the Kurians had time to call for some other form of help. For all he knew flying saucers might already be on their way—

"*we no longer control dallas*," the Reaper said, even more quietly. "*certain handlers remain within, but the skulking soldiers of your breed inside are increasingly obstinate.*"

"Not my problem."

Valentine almost cracked a smile. In their millennia of scheming before taking over the planet in 2022, the Kurians hadn't accounted for human obstinacy. "*we shall consider*," the Reaper finished, though one of the Kurians within thought up the words.

"Don't consider too long. In fifteen minutes we're going to try high explosives. If that doesn't work we'll start piling tires around your capsule. Then we'll douse everything in gasoline and light it. You'd better have good air-filtration equipment in there; you burn oxygen, same as us, and a good tire bonfire can go for weeks."

The Reaper twitched in the direction of Valentine and Ahn-Kha shouldered his gun, but instead of the expected attack the Reaper lurched back toward the capsule and acted out a strange pantomime, or perhaps a game of charades where "jumping spider" was the answer. It lurched, it spun, it backbent—

Valentine heard his order book hit the ground behind him.

The Reaper fell over, then picked itself up. It returned to its previous position facing the three humans, holding itself stiffly and moving off balance, like a marionette with tangled strings.

"*we agree,*" it said, just before it toppled over again.

"I'd have given two more fingers to have seen that," Meadows said that night, rattling the ice in his glass. An orderly refilled it from an amber-colored bottle and disappeared back into the throng of officers and civilians at the celebration. The old Sheraton next to the interstate had seen better days—to Valentine it smelled of sweat, sour cooking oil, and roaches—but perhaps never such a universally happy crowd.

Valentine didn't feel like celebrating. William Post, possibly his best friend in the world apart from Ahn-Kha, had been maimed as he led the assault on the helicopters. The surgeons were fighting to save his life along with those of the other wounded.

Luckily that was the only fighting going on. The army of the North Texas Cooperative had marched out of its positions, and then the city, as the sun set.

"You bit off too much, Major Valentine," Brigadier General Quintero growled. Quintero had refused alcohol as well. He reminded Valentine a little of the negotiating Reaper; one side of his body sagged a little thanks to an old shell fragment that had severed muscle in his shoulder. "I can just tolerate those Dallas scoundrels relocating, but I don't like the idea of Texas truckers carrying that fish tank to Arizona."

Valentine liked Quintero, and if the general was speaking to him in this manner he could imagine what had been said to him since the afternoon, when Dallas broke out in white flags and the frontline troops cautiously advanced into the city.

"Could I make a suggestion, General?"

"Eiderdown quilts for the Quislings?" Meadows put in, trying to soften the scowl on Quintero's face.

Valentine ignored the jibe. "Route the Kurian 'fish tank' to Arizona via Dallas, with the drivers in a secure cabin-cage attached to a breakaway trailer. I'll ride shotgun if you need a volunteer. We won't be shy about telling passersby what's in back. Maybe a riot starts and you declare hostilities resumed and renegotiate the surrender more advantageously. Maybe the Kurians get pulped, and those Dallas troops get convinced that the only way they'll ever be safe again is to throw in with us."

Quintero turned it over in his mind, sucking on his cheeks as he thought it through. "You are a mean son of a bitch, Major. Excuse the expression."

"I'm glad you're on our side," Meadows added.

Two

Texarkana, April: The border town has turned into a staging area. Operations in the Texas-Ozark United Free Region move forward as the political leadership convenes in search of a way to govern the aggregation, already being called the TWO-FUR by the willfully dyslexic soldiery.

A new name for the region is in the works.

The city has become one of those chaotic staging areas familiar to those of long service. Units coming off frontline service bump elbows with freshly organized troops. Equipment and personnel swap by means official and unofficial, and creative middlemen set up shop to service needs ranging from new boots to old wine, aging guns to young women.

An old indoor tennis court serves as the local headquarters for the separate commands of the Texas and Ozark forces. There are warehouses and self-storage units nearby to hold gear scraped up by the Logistics Commandos or brought out of the Dallas–Fort Worth corridor. Most importantly of all, a hospital has been upgraded from a bare-bones Kurian health center to a four-hundred-bed unit that can provide care equal to any existing facility outside those patronized by the elite of the Kurian Zone.

Churches and temporary schools operate at the edge of "Texarkana Dumps," the current name for the collection of military facilities. Outside the perimeter of the Southern Command's patrols, a tar-paper and aluminum-siding shantytown has sprung up, accommodating refugees from the Kurian Zone as well as the illicit needs of bored soldiers waiting for orders.

Even the local wildlife seems to be in a state of leisurely flux. Crows and dogs and a few far-ranging seagulls trot or fly from refuse heap to sewage pit, with the local feral cats sunning themselves on wall top and windowsill after a night hunting the thriving rats and mice.

The soldiers fresh from the Dallas battlefield feel the same way. Fresh food, sunshine, and sleep are all that are required for blissful, if not purring, contentment.

The attenuated Razors' brief period of excited anticipation, carried since getting off the Dallas train and hearing about their billet, ended as soon as they saw the "hotel."

Even in its heyday no one would have called the roadside Accolade Inn worthy of a special trip. The subsequent years had not been kind to the blue-and-white block, four stories of stucco-sided accommodations thick with kudzu and bird droppings. Someone had put in screens and plywood doors, and each room's toilet worked, though the sink fixtures were still in the process of retrofit, having been stripped and not replaced. Neat cots, six to a room, sat against water-stained walls.

"Not bad," a goateed Razor said when Valentine heard him test the john's flush after washing his hands in the toilet tank. "Better than the sisters have at home."

Sadly, the attenuated regiment fit in the hotel with beds to spare. A third of their number were dead or in either a Fort Worth or Texarkana hospital.

The latter was Valentine's first stop after getting the men to the hotel. A First Response Charity tambourine-and-saxophone duo just outside the hospital door accepted a few crumpled pieces of Southern Command scrip with the usual "God Blesses you."

"Continually," Valentine agreed, though over the past year it had been a decidedly mixed blessing. The pair stood a little straighter in their orange-and-white uniforms and reached for pamphlets, but Valentine passed on and into the green-peppermint tiles of the hospital.

He made it a point to visit every man of his command; the routine and their requests were so grimly regular that he began entering with a tumbler of ice—he made a mental note to steal and fill a trashcan with ice before heading back to the Accolade—to spare himself the inevitable back-and-forth trip. But his mind wasn't at ease until he visited the last name on his list, Captain William Post.

Visiting hours were over by the time he made it to the breezy top floor, where Post shared a room with a blinded artillery officer.

"Well, just remember to be quiet," the head nurse said when Valentine showed his ID and signed in on the surgery-recovery floor. Dark crests like bruises hung beneath her eyes.

"Tell it to the FIRCs downstairs," Valentine said, as they started up again with the umpteenth rendition of "Onward Christian Soldiers," one of their supply of three hymns.

Post looked horrible. His cheeks had shrunken in, and the nurse had done a poor job shaving him. A little tent stood over the stump of his left leg and a tube ran from the region of his appendix to a red-filled bottle on the floor. A bottle on a hook attached to the bed dripped clear liquid into a tube in his arm, as though to balance output with input. Post's eyes were bright and alert, though.

His friend even managed a wink when Valentine rattled the plastic, metered hospital tumbler full of ice.

"How's it going?" Valentine asked in a small voice, as if to emphasize the words' inadequacy.

"They got the shrapnel out. Some small intestine came with it. So they say." Post took his time speaking. "No infection." He took a breath. "No infection. That was the real worry."

"God blesses you," the FIRCs chorused downstairs. Valentine agreed again, this time with more enthusiasm.

"You know what? They pulled maggots out of my eyes," Post's roommate said, as though it were the funniest thing to ever happen to anyone. "Got to hand it to flies—they go to work right away. I wasn't laying in the pit but three hours before the medics found me. Flies beat 'em."

"He'll be out tomorrow," Post said quietly, as though he had to apologize for the interruption.

"How much leg is left?" Valentine asked.

"Midthigh," Post said. "At first I thought it was a raw deal. Then I decided the shrapnel could have gone six inches higher and to the right. It's all perspective."

"We'll make a good pair, limping up and down the tent lines," Valentine said.

"You got to admire maggots," the man in the next bed said. "They know they only got one thing to do and they do it."

"I think I'll be spending the rest of the war in the first-class cabin," Post said, using old Coastal Marine slang for a retirement on a wound pension. "I've got to be careful about my diet now. So they say. There's a leaflet around here somewhere."

"Anything I can do for you?"

Later on Valentine spent hours that accumulated into days and weeks thinking back on his offer, and the strange turns his life took from the moment he said the phrase. He made the offer in earnest. If Post had asked him to go back to Louisiana and get a case of Hickory Pit barbecue sauce, he would have done his best to bring back the distinctive blend.

"Get my green duffel from under the bed," Post said.

There were only two items under the wheeled cot, a scuffed service pack and the oversized green duffel. Each had at least three kinds of tagging on it.

Valentine pulled up the bag, wondering.

"There's a leather case inside, little gold fittings."

It was easy to find; everything else in the duffel was clothing. The case felt as though it was full of sand. Valentine lifted it with an effort.

"Open it," Post said.

Valentine saw reams of paper inside. It was like a miniature file cabinet. Three manila folders filled it, marked (in order of thickness, most to least) "Queries/Replies," "Descriptions," and "Evidence." Valentine caught an inky whiff of photocopier chemicals.

Valentine had a good guess about the contents of the briefcase. Post had been looking for his ex-wife almost from the moment they stepped into the Ozarks. Valentine knew the details; Post had talked about her now and then when the mood hit, since the time Valentine met him while posing as a Quisling officer on the old *Thunderbolt.* William Post and Gail Foster had grown up in the Kurian Zone and married young. He joined the Quisling Coastal Marines, became an officer, fought and worked for the Kurians, in an effort to give them a better life. But the man she thought she'd married was no collaborator. As Post's career flourished their marriage dissolved. Gail Post became convinced he'd gone over to the enemy, and left. They'd always talked of trying to make it to the Ozark Free Territory, so Post assumed she'd come here.

Valentine opened the folio marked "Descriptions" with his forefinger. Mimeographed sheets headed MISSING-REWARD had a two-tone picture of a fair young woman with wide-set eyes, photographed full-face and profile. Perhaps her lips were a little too thin for her to be considered a great beauty, but then Kurian Zone identification photographs rarely flattered.

Post was a dedicated correspondent. Valentine guessed there had to be two hundred letters and responses paper-clipped together.

"There's three sheets on top of the Evidence folder. Take them out, will you Dave?" Post said. His head sank back on the pillow as though the effort of speaking had emptied him.

Valentine knew wounds and pain. He took out the pages—bad photocopies, stamped with multiple release signatures—and waited.

"I found her name. She was here."

"That's a damn miracle," Valentine said.

Post nodded. "I had help. Several new organizations were set up after you guys got the Ozarks back to reunite families. Then there was still the Lueber Alliance."

Valentine had learned about LA his first year in the Ozarks. Better than forty years old, it collected information on people lost in the Kurian Zone. Rumor had it the names numbered in the hundreds of thousands.

"Lueber found that first list for me," Post continued.

The page had a list of names, a shipping manifest with train car allocations—thirty to a car, relatively comfortable transport by Kurian standards.

Valentine didn't see a destination for the list. He flipped to the next page.

"That's just an old census. Showed she lived near Pine Bluff before Solon's takeover. Also Leuber."

Valentine had gone to a war college in Pine Bluff when the commander of Zulu Company offered him a position as lieutenant. He looked at the picture again, trying to associate it with a memory from the town. Nothing.

The third page was the strangest of all. It was a photocopy of a list, and the names were handwritten. Fifty names, numbered 401 to 450. TESTING STATION 9-P was the legend up at the top. Gail's name was in the middle, along with her age. His eyes found it quickly thanks to an X in the column marked "result." All the other names had blanks in the "result" column. Someone had handwritten "She's gone for good" at the top corner, though whether this was a note to Post or not none could say.

"What's this?"

"That's the oddball. Got it about a month ago. It came in an envelope with just my address on it."

Valentine looked at the attached envelope. Post must have received it just before they moved into the Love Field positions. Valentine could remember a change in Post, a resignation, but had attributed it to the strain of the siege.

He examined the document's envelope. Typewritten, obviously with a manual typewriter. Valentine deciphered the stamp—Pine Bluff again. But the post number wasn't the one for the war college. The Miskatonic? The researchers there studied the Kurian Order, probing unpleasant shadows and gruesome corners.

"No cover letter?"

"Nothing."

"How can I help?"

Post took a moment, either to gather thoughts or breathe. "You know people. The"—he lowered his voice, as though fearing comment from the blind man in the next bed—"Lifeweavers. Those researchers. Intelligence. I'd like to know what happened to her after she was taken. No matter how bad the news."

People herded onto trains seldom came to a happy end. Valentine had been in Solon's meetings, heard about "payments" in the form of captives going to the neighboring KZs. "You sure? Maybe you don't."

"She's still alive in my head," Post said.

"Exactly."

Post's lined eyes regained some of their old liveliness. "No, not that way. I always knew she was alive, even when I thought you were just another CM. Can't say how I know. A feeling. I still feel it. You know about feelings like that."

He did. Some inner warning system sometimes let him know when there was a Reaper around—the "Valentingle," his comrades in the Wolves used to call it. First as a joke. Then they learned to trust it.

"I can ask around." Post was right; he had a couple of tenuous contacts at the Miskatonic—the main scholarly center for research into the Kurian Order—and with Southern Command's intelligence. But that was pre-Solon. For all he knew they were dead or lost in the chaos civilians were already calling "the bad spell."

"Let me know the truth, whatever it is, Val."

"Can I have these?"

"Sure. I copied down everything in my journal."

Valentine rested his hand on Post's forearm. "Listen to the doctors and get better. The Razors need you back, even if you're stumping around on a piece of East Texas pine."

"I heard they were breaking up the Razors," Post said.

"From who?"

Post shrugged, and the effort left him red-faced. "Some doctor. Asked me what outfit I was with."

"Probably a rumor. Lots of stuff floating around military hospitals."

"Yeah, like turds in a bedpan," Post's neighbor said.

"A regular Lieutenant Suzy Sunshine, that guy," Post said. Lieutenant Suzy Sunshine was a Pollyannaish cartoon character in one of the army papers—*Freedom's Voice*—who turned any misfortune into a cheerful quip.

"I'll be back tomorrow," Valentine said.

"I'm not going anywhere."

Valentine left, upset enough to forget the ice.

* * *

The sun had vanished by the time Valentine returned to the Accolade. The Razors had set up some old car upholstery in the overgrown parking lot, and had gathered to drink and watch the sun go down.

"Bump, Major?" Ruvayed, the communications officer from the control tower, hollered as he passed. She looked off-kilter, like a dog back from the vet—part of her skull was shaved and a dressing blossomed in the bare spot like a white flower. She held out a tall glass.

"I need a major bump," another man added, flat on his back with a tepee of gnawed roasting ears, holding a lit cigar clear of the grass.

"Just have to check in," Valentine said as he passed, regretting the forgotten ice.

Meadows and Nail, the Bear leader, were going over personnel sheets, trying to work out store consumption and medical requirements for the men stabled at the Accolade.

"Wish staff hadn't snatched Styachowski back," Nail said, looking at the broken end of his pencil. "She went through paperwork like quicklime. Hey, Val."

"Maybe we need a piece of that blue blob they pried off the Kurian capsule," Valentine said. "I heard they're keeping it at Brigade. It eats paper."

The "dingleberry" was the only survivor of the Kurian capsule's trip through the defeated Dallas forces. The last Valentine had heard the Dallas Quislings were almost to Houston, being shepherded on blistered feet by mounted Rangers.

"Nail, can I have a moment with the colonel?" Valentine asked.

"Gladly. I'll grab a piece of twilight while I can." Nail drew a utility knife and went to work on his pencil point as he walked out the door.

"How's Will?" Meadows asked.

"Came through fine. I spoke to one doctor and two nurses. He's feeling a little low, but physically he's doing well."

"Send Narcisse over to have a chat with him. She's got a way of putting things in perspective."

"He said there's a rumor floating around that the Razors are through," Valentine said. His voice broke a little as he spoke. The Razors were a cross to bear, but also a matter of some personal pride.

Meadows sighed and sat down. "I wonder who blabbed. Smoke? I swear her ears detach and walk around on their own."

"No, she's not even in Texarkana. She heard about a Lifeweaver, supposed to be up in Hot Springs, and hopped a train to find him."

"I saw a Lifeweaver once. Or what a Wolf told me was one."

"So the rumor's true?" Valentine asked, wanting to change the subject. Wherever the Lifeweavers helping Southern Command had fled to when the Free Territory fell last year, they were taking their sweet time in getting back, and speculation didn't hurry them along.

"Sorry, Val. Look, the Razors only half existed as far as Southern Command was concerned anyway. They never liked experienced Wolves and a Bear team tied down to a regiment of Guard infantry anyway. That, and the men have specializations that are needed elsewhere."

The truth of his words made it hurt a little less. "When's it going to be announced?"

"Another day or three. We'll have a big good-bye blowout the day after the news; I've arranged for that."

Colonel Meadows understood the men and their needs better than Valentine. In his more introspective moments Valentine admitted to himself that he threw himself so much into the job at hand that he forgot about the stress it put on the tool.

"You can help, Val. In the morning there'll be decorations, then the barbecue starts. I've arranged for Black Lightning to play—according to the Texans they're the best Relief band in Southern Command. Stripper tent, tattoo artists, a back-pay distribution so you'll get the flea marketers in to provide some competition for the Southern Command PX-wagons."

"What do you need from me?" Valentine asked. If he couldn't do anything about the Razors dying, he could at least see to the burial.

"We need a bunch of transfer orders written. I've got a skills priority list; match it up with the men. Wish we had Will. For the party, I mean."

"Seems wrong to have it without him. I just told him the Razors were waiting for his return."

"Sorry about that. I didn't want to tell you until you had a night or two to rest up here."

"I'll sleep tonight. I intend to have a couple of sips of whatever Ruvayed is passing out."

"Consider yourself off duty for the next twenty-four."

Valentine had a thought. "Could you take care of one thing, sir? Pass something up? The general's signature would be helpful."

"What is it?"

"I'd like Post to be able to say farewell to the Razors too."

Roast pig is a mouthwatering smell, and it penetrated even the back of the ambulance. The vehicle halted.

"What's up your sleeve, Val?" Post asked. No fewer than four nurses and one muscular medical orderly sat shoulder to shoulder with Val, crowded around Post's bed on wheels.

"You'll see."

The doors opened, giving those inside a good view of the Accolade's renovated parking lot. The brush had been chopped away, tents constructed, and paper lanterns in a dozen colors strung between the tent poles and trees. Some nimble electronics tech had rigged a thirty-foot antenna and hung the Razor's porcine silhouette banner—Don't Feed On Me read the legend—to top it off.

Bunting hung from the Accolade's windows, along with another canopy of lanterns. Music from fiddles, guitars, and drums competed from different parts of the party. A mass of soldiers—probably a good third of them not even Razors, but men who knew how to sniff out a good party and gain admittance by performing some minor support function—wandered in and out of the various tents and trader stalls.

"Jesus, Val," Post said as Valentine and the orderly took him out of the ambulance. He looked twice as strong as he had on Valentine's visit the previous day—Post made a habit of coming back strong from injury.

"Hey, it's Captain Post!" a Razor shouted.

"Some secret debriefing," one of the nurses said.

"As far as the hospital's concerned none of you will be back for a day," Valentine said. "The only thing I ask is that someone attend Will at all times."

"SOP, Val. I can just holler if I need some water. John, set this thing so I'm sitting up, alright?"

The attendant and a nurse arranged his bed.

"If I'd known this soiree was going full blast," a nurse said, rearranging the cap on her brunette hair, "I would have brought my makeup."

Valentine pulled some bills out of his pocket and passed them to the head nurse. "For additional medical supplies. You can probably find what you need at the PX-wagons. If not, it looked like the strippers had plenty to spare."

"Ewwww," another nurse said.

"Oh, lighten up, Nicks," the head nurse said. "You're on first watch, then. I'll bring you a plate."

The men were already clustering around Post. "Great, great," Valentine heard Post saying. "Food's good. Only problem is, I was wounded in my right leg. They took the healthy one off."

"Just like 'em," one of the more gullible Razors said, before he saw what the others were laughing at.

The male attendant kept various proffered bottles and cups away from Post's mouth. "I want to hear some music," Post said. "Let's get Narcisse's wheelie-stool out and we'll dance."

"Razors!" the men shouted as they lifted the gurney and bore it toward the bandstand.

"That's a nice thing you're doing for your captain, Major," the nurse they called Nicks said. "He's lucky to have you."

"I'm the lucky one," Valentine said.

Black Lightning lived up to their reputation. Valentine wasn't sophisticated enough with music to say whether they were "country" or "rock and roll" or "fwap" to use early-twenty-first century categories. They were energetic—and loud. So much so that he kept to the back and observed. The crowd listened or danced as the mood struck them, all facing the stage, which was just as well because the men outnumbered the women by six to one or so.

The nurses kept close to Post, who had a steady stream of well-wishers, but seemed to make themselves agreeable to the boys.

Boys. Valentine startled at the appellation. At twenty-seven he could hardly be labeled old, but he sometimes felt it when he passed a file of new recruits. Southern Command had filled out the Razors with kids in need of a little experience—the regiment had never been meant to be a frontline unit in the Dallas siege—and they'd gotten it at terrible cost.

Or maybe it was just that the younger folks had the energy to enjoy the band. Most of the older men sat as they ate or smoked or drank, enjoying the night air and the companionship of familiar faces. A photographer took an occasional picture of those who'd been decorated that morning. Everyone had taken the news of the Razors' breakup well—

"What a surprise. Major Valentine alone with his thoughts," a female voice said in his ear.

Valentine jumped. Duvalier stood just behind him as though she'd been beamed there from the *Star Trek* books of his youth. She wore a pair of green, oversized sunglasses, some cheap kid's gewgaw from the trade wagons, and when the photographer pointed the camera at them, she had a sudden coughing fit as the flash fired.

"Didn't know you were back."

"After all this time, you still haven't figured it out, have you? I don't like my comings and goings to be noticed." Valentine noticed her slurring her words a little. He'd never known Duvalier to have more than a single glass of anything out of politeness—and even that was usually left unfinished.

"I thought you hated parties," Valentine said.

"I do, but I like to go anyway, and hate them with someone."

"You dressed up."

Duvalier wore tight shorts, a sleeveless shirt, and what looked to be thigh-high stockings in a decorative brocade. Her battered hiking boots just made the rest of her look better. "Wishing I hadn't. Some of your horntoads thought I was here professionally."

"Serves you right for getting cleaned up. Any bloodshed?"

"All the ears and noses in your command are accounted for, Major. Colonel Meadows asked me to find you."

"Speaking of finding people, I've yet to find anyone who saw you during our fight at the airfield."

She wrinkled her freckled nose. "I should hope not. Everyone but me was busy being a hero. As soon as the bombs started dropping I hid deep and dark next to a storm sewer leading off-field. You can't outsmart a rocket."

"If they gave out medals for survival you'd have a chestful. Speaking of which, is that the legendary red bra I see peeping out?" He reached for her cutoff shirt—

"Dream on, Valentine." She grabbed his hand and gave his wrist a painful twist, then pulled him toward the barbecue pit, her hand warm in his.

Colonel Meadows was carving pork, heaping it onto plates, and handing them out, at which point Narcisse would slather the meat with barbecue sauce and hand the plates out to the lined-up soldiers. Judging by their sticky lips, most were back for seconds.

"Daveed!" Narcisse said, spinning on her stool. "This recipe I learned on Jamaica—they call it 'jerked.' Have some!"

"In a second, Sissy," Meadows said. "We're getting a drink first. Spell me, Cossack."

A soldier prodding the coals stood up and took the carving knife out of Meadows' hand. Meadows tossed him the apron.

They filled pewter mugs from a barrel at the beer tent—it was poor stuff, as Southern Command had better things to do with its soil than grow hops—and found a quiet spot away from the band. Duvalier followed with a plate at a respectful distance. She had good hearing, if not quite Valentine's Wolf ears, and positioned herself downwind, back to the men but undoubtedly able to hear every word said.

Some fool fired off a blue signal flare to add to the festive atmosphere. It turned the beer black inside the mugs and added deep shadows to Meadows' eyesockets.

"Great party, sir," Valentine said, and meant it.

"We deserve it." Meadows was a *we* kind of officer. He held out his mug and Valentine touched his to it, the faint *klink* sounding a slightly sour note thanks to the pewter.

"An interesting letter in the courier pouch hit my desk the other day. This is as good a moment as any to tell you: They're offering you a Hunter Staff position."

Valentine felt his knees give out for a moment, and he covered with a swig of beer. "Staff?"

"Easy now, Val. It's a helluva honor."

Duvalier brushed past him on the way to the beer tent, and gave his hip a gentle nudge with hers.

"Not that you'll have a lot of time to show off your swagger stick. I hear they work you to death."

Valentine understood that well enough. Southern Commmand operated on a general staff system that selected and then trained a small group of officers in all the subsidiary branches of service: artillery, logistics, intelligence, and so on. The highly trained cadre then served as staff inspectors or temporary replacements or taught until promoted to higher command or, in the event of a crisis, they took command of reserve units.

The Hunters—the Wolves, Cats, and Bears of Southern Command that operated as special forces outside the borders of the Free Territory—had their own identical staff system that trained with the others and then performed similar functions with the smaller Hunter units. A couple of hitches in Wolf and Bear formations was enough for most; the veteran soldiers usually transferred to support units—or the Logistics Commandos if they still had a taste for operating in the Kurian Zone. But most still served Southern Command by belonging to ghost regiments that might be called up.

Captain Moira Styachowski, one of the most capable officers he'd ever met, had been on the Hunter Staff.

Valentine might end up in command of one of those formations. The role was wryly appropriate; he'd been nicknamed "the Ghost" when serving in the Zulus, his first Wolf company.

Meadows broke in on his thoughts. "Valentine, it's official enough so I thought I'd tell you. You're better than two years overdue for a leave. It'll take them a while to get your training schedule worked out. When we're done here you'll be cleared to take a three-months' leave. I'll miss you. It's been a pleasure."

And Valentine would miss the Razors. They seemed "his" in a way none of the other organizations he'd served with or commanded ever had. Seeing them broken up was like losing a child. "Thank you, sir."

He didn't feel like thanking anyone, but it had to be said.

He wandered back among the Razors, accepted a few congratulations with a smile, but all he wanted was quiet and a chance to think. Meadows had tried to add a sparkle to a bittersweet party, but all he'd done was ruin Valentine's enjoyment of the festivities.

Stow that, you dumb son of a grog. You're *ruining your enjoyment, not Meadows.*

Back in his days visiting the opulent old theater in Pine Bluff, they'd show movies now and then. He remembered sitting through part of one when arriving early for the evening's movie; the smell of popcorn and sweat on the seats all around him, unable to shut out even the blood from a tiny shaving cut on the man next to him with his inexperienced Wolf's nose.

The early show for the families was a kids' cartoon, full of bright primary colors even on the shabby little projector rigged to an electronic video-memory device. He recalled a bunch of kids' toys in a machine, and a mechanical claw that came down and selected one of the dozens of identical toys now and then. The toys responded to the mystical selection of the claw as though at a religious ceremony.

Life in the creaky, stop-and-start mechanism of Southern Command had never been so elegantly summed up for him. "The claw chooses!" Orders came down and snatched you away from one world and put you in another.

Duvalier proffered a fresh, cool mug filled with colder beer. "Guess that's it for Cat duty, far as you're concerned," she said. Her eyes weren't as bright and lively as usual; either her digestive troubles were back or she'd continued drinking. Valentine sniffed her breath and decided the latter.

The swirl of congratulatory faces wandered off after he took the mug, offered a small celebratory lift of the brew to the north, south, east, and west, and took a sip.

"Did you run down that Lifeweaver?" On second taste, the beer wasn't quite so sharp.

"No. There was a rumor one'd been killed by some kind of agent the Kurians planted last year. Guess Kurs' got their versions of Cats too."

Valentine had heard all sorts of rumors about specially trained humans in Kurian employ. That they could read minds, or turn water into wine, or redirect a thunderstorm's lightning. Everything from mud slides to misaddressed mail was blamed on Kurian agents.

Valentine shrugged.

"They'll get word to us. They always do, one way or another. Right?" Duvalier asked.

The last sounded a bit too much like a plea. Duvalier thought of the Lifeweavers as something akin to God's angels on Earth; the way the Kurians' estranged cousins presented themselves added to the effect. This cool and deadly woman had the eyes of a child left waiting on a street corner for a vanished parent.

"Mystery's their business," Valentine said.

She emptied her mug. "Want to blow this bash?"

The beer worked fast. Valentine already felt like listening to music and discussing the nurses' legs with Post. But he couldn't leave Duvalier tipsy and doubtful.

"Yes," he lied.

Her shoulders went a little further back, and more of the red bra appeared beneath her vest. "Lead on, McGruff," she said.

Valentine was pretty sure it was MacDuff—Father Max made his classes perform two Shakespeare plays a year—but couldn't prick her newly improved mood with something as trivial as, well, trivia.

The men were setting up some sort of chariot race involving wheelchairs, Narcisse, and a Razor with his leg in a cast from ankle to midthigh. By the looks of the clothesline traces and wobbly wheels on the chairs, the soldier's other leg would be in a cast by morning, but Valentine and Duvalier hollered out their hurrahs and stayed to watch. Narcisse's wheelchair overturned at the third turn—she didn't have enough weight to throw leftward to keep both wheels of the chair down in the turn—but she gamely hung on and was dragged through the freshly trimmed parking lot meadow to victory, garlanded by a dandelion leaf in her rag turban.

Duvalier pressed herself up against him as they jumped and cheered her on. As they wandered away from the race, she was on his arm.

"Seems like a staff appointment deserves a special celebration," she slurred as they left the crowd and passed under the Accolade's bunting.

"Careful, now," Valentine said as they made a right turn toward his quarters. "You're evil, teasing me like that."

She looked around and saw that the hall was empty. Then she kissed him, with the same fierce intensity that he remembered from the bloody murder in the Nebraska caboose.

"Let's. Now. *Right* now." She extracted a half-empty flask from within her vest and took a swig.

Valentine had desired her for years, and they'd come close to making love out of sheer boredom once or twice while serving together in the KZ. But the half joking, half flirting they'd done in the past had always been passed back and forth around a shield of professionalism, like two prisoners swapping notes around a cell wall.

"I wanna see what that little Husker cowgirl thought was so special," she said with a facial spasm that might have been a flirtatious eyebrow lift that suddenly decided to become a wink.

Dumb shit, why did you ever tell her that?

He pulled her into his room and shut the door behind them.

"Not drunk and not with us about to—" he began, fighting off her fingers as they sought his belt.

"Now who's the tease, huh?" she asked, falling back onto the bed as though he'd kicked her there. "You're a lot of talk and fancy words. Ahn-Kha's got bigger balls than you—"

That struck Valentine as a curious—and stipulatable—argument. They'd both seen Ahn-Kha any number of times, and the Golden One had a testicular sack the size of a ripe cantaloupe.

"Ali, I—"

"It's always *I* with you, Val. Ever notice that? I don't even want us to be a *we,* I just want one fuck, one goddamn, sweaty fuck with a guy I halfway care about. I spent eight months on my back for those grunting Quislings. Wasn't like blowing some eighteen-year-old sentry to get through a checkpoint 'cause I had a story about how I gotta get medicine to my sick aunt—I had to eat breakfast with those greasy shits and talk about how great they were and just once I'd like—"

And with that it was like all the air had left her lungs. She leaned over with her mouth open for a moment, a surprised look on her face—then she fled to the bathroom.

Valentine pulled his lengthening hair back from his eyes, listened to the mixture of sobs and retching sounds echoing off the tiles in the washroom, and let out a long breath. At the moment he couldn't be sure that he wouldn't rather face another air pirate raid than go into that room.

But he did so.

The mess was about what he expected. A horrible beery-liquor smell wove itself above and around the sharper odor of her bile, and she was crying into the crook of a vomit-smeared arm at the edge of the toilet.

He picked her up. After a quick struggle he set her in bed and took off her shoes and socks, and gave each rough foot one gentle squeeze.

"No, not now," she said.

"I wasn't."

"I got puke on my good bra."

"I'll rinse it out and hang it up."

"Thanks."

Her freckles looked like wildflowers in a field of golden wheat.

By the time he'd used a washcloth on her face and arm, rinsed out her clothes—and her socks for good measure—she was murmuring at some level of sleep. He put a thin blanket over her and cleaned up the toilet area, using a bowl as a wash bucket.

When that was done she was truly asleep, rolled into the blanket like a softly snoring sausage.

That night Valentine sat in his musty room with its vomit-disinfectant-and-tobacco smell and quieted his mind by laying out the three pieces of paper bearing Gail Foster's name. Black Lightning was still pounding away, the amplified music much reduced by the bulk of the intervening hotel.

He took a yellowed blank sheet of paper from his order book and drew a cross in the center, dividing the paper into four squares. He labeled the top left "Goal" and the top right "Known Known." The bottom left became "Known Unknown." Another scrape or two from his pencil and the bottom right box had the label "Unknown Unknown."

While it seemed like gibberish, the formula had been taught to him in his youth by the old Jesuit, Father Max, the teacher who'd raised him after the murder of his family. Father Max had told him (a couple of times—when Father Max was in his cups he sometimes forgot what he said) that the analytic tool came from a woman who used to work at the old United States Department of Defense intelligence agency.

It divided one's knowledge of a subject into facts you knew, facts you knew you didn't know, and the possibility of important pieces of knowledge out there that you weren't aware of until they rose up and bit you. But by diligent pursuit of the questions in the other two squares you slowly accomplished the goal, and sometimes found out about the third in time to act.

And when an Unknown Unknown showed up you had to be mentally prepared to erase even your Known Knowns.

Valentine had lived in the Kurian Zone, had even spoken to one directly, and all his experiences had left him with was the unsettling conviction that humanity's place in the universe wasn't much different than that of a *Canis familiaris*—the common dog. There were wild dogs and savage dogs and tamed dogs and trained dogs, and dogs knew all about other dogs, or could learn soon enough, but their guesses about the wider world (cars and phones and other phenomena) and a dog's place in it was limited by the dog's tendency to put everything in dog terms.

If he tried to put himself in the place of the practically immortal

Kurians, an endless series of doubts and fears popped up. The Kurians had laid waste to Earth once with a series of natural catastrophes and disease, so what was to stop them from unleashing an apocalyptic horseman or two if mankind became too troublesome? He'd seen on the Ranch in Texas that the Kurians were toying with different forms of life in an effort to find a more pliable source of vital aura than man, in the form of the ratbits. How much time did man have before the Kurians decided to clear off the ranchland that was Earth and raise a different kind of stock? Wouldn't a goatherd who got sick of bites from the billys switch to sheep?

Depressing speculation didn't help find Post's wife. He remembered his promise and picked up the pencil again. Under "Goal" he wrote: "Learn what happened to Gail Foster." He did some mental math as he transcribed Kurian dates (the years started in 2022, and after a brief attempt at calendar reform had reverted back to old-style months and days).

Known Knowns

Gail Foster lived in the Free Territory (Pine Bluff?).
— *was tested at station 9-P*
— *no other woman on the list had an X under "result."*
— *was shipped somewhere by the Kurians five days later.*

Known Unknowns

— *Shipped to where?*
— *Did test indicate a negative or a positive?*
— *Purpose of test?*

He checked the list of names on the Miskatonic paper again and wrote:

Why only females tested? (Fertility? Privacy? Expediency?)

The last was guesswork, for all he knew they tested all women, whether of childbearing age or not. There was the chance that they gave men the same test too, and for reasons of their own performed the tests separately—though the Kurians were not known for breaking up families and couples, it made groups of humans easier to handle.

Statistically, being one out of fifty in the Kurian Zone meant bad news for Gail Foster—formerly Gail Post. In his time undercover in the Kurian Zone Valentine had seen dozens—strike that, hundreds—of instances where the Kurians had culled humans into a large group and a small group.

The small groups never lasted long.

Were they checking for a disease or infirmity that meant she only had a short time to live? The Kurians used humans the way banks exchanged currency; perhaps a human only counted as a human if it could be expected to survive more than one year.

Valentine looked at himself in the shard of mirror on the wall. The single bare bulb in the wall cut shadows under his eyes and jawline. *You're a glass-is-half-empty kind of guy, Valentine.*

Maybe she scored supergenius on a test and was being shipped off to learn some kind of Kurian technology. Maybe she had a special skill that would keep her comfortably employed in the Kurian Order to a ripe old age.

Or maybe she showed up on some list as a refugee, and was shipped back to her original owners faster than you could say Dred Scott.

The other thing he'd learned from Father Max was that the first step in discovering a few Unknown Unknowns was to answer the Known Unknowns.

So much to do. He'd have Ahn-Kha take Hank to a boarding school. He didn't want the boy to become just another camp extra until he enlisted at fifteen. He'd have to arrange for transport for both of them, and for himself to Pine Bluff and the Miskatonic.

He had one promise to keep before starting this new page. Even if it was a page he didn't know that he was up to turning. Just as well Post had given him this. At least he had something to do with his leave other than fret.

Hank brought in breakfast. The boy looked as gray and bleary as a Minnesota October, and Valentine smelled more beer and vomit on him.

"How about a little yogurt, Hank?" Val said, holding up what passed for yogurt in Texarkana to the boy. He lifted a spoonful and let it drop with a plop.

"No, sir, I'm—already ate," the boy said, putting his burn-scarred hand under his nose. He fled, and Valentine chuckled into his bran mash.

"Are you up early or late?" Duvalier groaned. She rolled over and looked at the window. "Early."

"No, late. It's almost nine. I think everyone slept in."

She reached down into her covers. "Water?"

Valentine got up and gave her his plastic tumbler full.

"Val, we didn't . . ."

"Didn't what?"

"You know."

"You yodel during sex. I never would have guessed that."

"Dream on, Valentine." She rolled over on her stomach. "God, gotta pee."

She got up and dragged herself into the bathroom.

"This would have been a bad time of the month for us to do *that,*" she said from within.

"Do I need to get you anything from supply?"

"No, I mean—fertility and all that."

Valentine wondered for one awful second what his daughter looked like. She'd probably have dark eyes and hair; both he and Malita Carrasca were dark.

"I got basic hygiene first week of Labor Regiment," Valentine said. "Good soldiers don't shoot unless they've taken precautions not to hurt the innocent."

She laughed and then cut it off. "Ow. My head."

Someone pounded on the door hard enough that the hinges moved.

"Come in," Valentine called.

Ahn-Kha stood, blocking ninety-five percent of the light coming through the open door.

"Final review at noon, Major. Colonel's orders. Three generals will be in attendance."

"Thank you. Eat up—" Valentine said, indicating the tray. Narcisse always issued him three times the breakfast he could consume and there was a pile of sliced ham on the tray the height of a New Universal Church Archon's bible.

Ahn-Kha wedged himself between chair and desk.

"Generals, eh?" Duvalier said. "I'm going to make myself scarce. Striped trousers are for clowns."

Valentine looked at his row of battle dress and wondered which one could be pressed sufficiently for the occasion.

None of them, really. Whatever the Razors were all about, whatever was dying that afternoon, wasn't about creased trousers.

"I'm sorry, Valentine," Meadows said out of the side of his mouth as they approached the four generals on the bandstand that last night had barely contained Black Lightning. "He tagged along at the last minute."

Post and some of the other nonambulatory wounded sat behind them on the stand so they could see. The remaining Razors were drawn up in a great U of six attenuated companies in the open parking-lot space in front of the bandstand. Ahn-Kha stood with the senior NCOs, Hank with a group of Aspirants, and Narcisse watched from high on the shoulder of one of his soldier's husbands. In the center, a color guard of Bears took down the Razors' boar-silhouette flag. They did it badly, and the men coming together as they folded it looked like a mistimed football hike. The Bears did everything badly.

Except fight.

They presented the triangular folded flag to Meadows, who accepted it as he would a baby.

Valentine looked at the rows of men for what was probably the last time. They looked hard in their battle dress, hard in the relaxed way that only men who'd seen bloodshed could manage. But Valentine didn't see them as iron-thewed heroes. They were more like blown-glass sculptures, beautiful in their irregularity, their variety of colors, heights, and shapes. And just like the glass vessels, tiny shards of fast-flying shrapnel could convert them into a shattered ruin of gristle, blood, and half-digested food in an eyeblink. He'd seen it more than once, and once was enough for any sane man.

Their delicacy made them all the more precious.

Then he and Meadows turned and walked to the generals. Valentine knew each one by name, but only one from experience.

General Martinez.

The man who'd executed two of his Grogs, and would have killed Ahn-Kha right before Valentine's eyes, was the second-highest-ranking officer gathered at the ceremony, subordinate only to MacCallister, who'd supervised the drive on Dallas–Fort Worth. Valentine knew that he held some rear-area post as a reward for his resistance—such as it was—during Solon's brief reign over the Ozarks.

Old and very bad blood linked Valentine and Martinez. In the crowning irony, Valentine's whole rising in Little Rock and his defense of Big Rock Mountain had taken place under Martinez's command. But only technically; Martinez hadn't moved a man to his assistance when he was most needed.

There were salutes, and when the salutes were done, handshakes.

"Congratulations on your staff appointment, Major Valentine," MacCallister said from beneath a white mustache that mostly hid a missing incisor when he spoke.

"Richly deserved," Meadows put in.

They sidestepped.

Valentine gave Martinez a formal salute, returned equally formally.

"General," Valentine said.

"Major," General Martinez returned. He still looked like a turtle, even in his green-and-brown dress uniform. He didn't offer his hand.

Meadows led Valentine to a chair behind and to the right of the generals. He passed Valentine the Razors' flag.

"You deserve this more than anyone," Meadows said quietly. "They always were yours."

"Co—"

"Shut up, Major. That's an order."

MacCallister said a few words thanking the men for their bravery, devotion, and sacrifice. He read out the Razors' list of regimental achievements and citations, and explained that skilled men were desperately needed elsewhere, and it was his sad duty to order the dissolution of the battered regiment.

"A grateful Free Republic thanks you," General MacCallister said as he dismissed the men. Evidently progress had been made in the governance of the bits of four states that comprised the Freehold.

The soldiers had heard it all before. All of them knew about the Claw, and that the Claw couldn't be questioned. Even if they didn't call it that.

When it was done Valentine was expected at a late lunch with the generals. But there was something he had to do first. He went over to the line of wounded and spoke to each one. He ended at Post's elevated bed. Post looked better by exponents.

"Which nurse did you end up with?" Valentine asked.

"Which didn't he?" one of the men snickered.

"Sort of all of them and none of them, if you follow me, Dave," Post said.

Valentine handed him the folded flag. "I want you to hang onto this until you're better and we link up again."

"Hear you're going to be kind of busy on staff training. Maybe the higher-ups aren't nuts after all." As executive officer for the Razors, Post had spent endless hours in the Byzantine bowels of Southern Command procedures, trying to keep the Razors better supplied and better equipped than a half-forgotten rear-area reserve. "But why me? It's Meadows' flag."

"It's our flag," he said, and hoped Duvalier was lurking somewhere near—perhaps beneath the bandstand. "You're keeping it until I come back from leave. There's a few questions to be asked and a promise to keep."

Post's smile matched the Texas sun in brightness, and exceeded it in size.

"Thank you, sir."

Three

The Ark, Pine Bluff, Arkansas: Southern Command collapsed when Solon arrived, not in panic, but in a controlled implosion more reminiscent of a carefully demolished high-rise than a chaotic rout.

Stockpiles of foods, medicines, and especially weapons disappeared into predug and camouflaged caverns. Where caverns weren't available, basements sufficed. One of the most important of the Eastern Arkansas caches resided at SEARK—the Southeastern Arkansas College. Southern Command had several important facilities around Pine Bluff, including the main docks on the lower Arkansas, the old arsenal that produced munitions for the Freehold, the war college at the old University of Arkansas (an agricultural and technical university taught civilians on the same campus) and, in a nondescript building at the edge of campus, a group of scientists devoted to researching the Kurians, known by a few as "the Miskatonic." From machine tools to research archives, key resources were concealed on the overgrown campus of SEARK, or "the Ark." A whole greenhouse on the campus existed just to shelter plant growth that would be used to cover entrances to underground warehouses, and the more burned-out and disused a classroom building looked, the more likely it was that explosives could be found stored in the rusty darkness of the basement.

The Ark deception worked in Pine Bluff. Southern Command, in abandoning the arsenal, blew up piles of junk to make it look as though machinery was destroyed rather than hidden. The Miskatonic turned piles of old phone books into fine white ash in a bonfire outside the institute.

Pine Bluff, in the year after Solon's rule, is only a shadow of the lively riverfront town, with its markets and stores, blacksmiths and seamstresses. Some of the population still wears the dull yellows and oranges of Solon's Trans-Mississippi Confederation, others go about like hungry beggars as they look for lost friends and loved ones, searching for familiar faces from the shops and docks.

The Ark has a new lease on life thanks to its period as an archive. The Miskatonic has relocated from the burned U of A campus to McGeorge hall, three stories of red brick with freshly painted white pillars around the entrance and new-planted trees relocated from roof and doorstep. If the building's architecture reflected the facts and secrets locked within, it would be a dozen stories tall and carved out of black granite, with horns projecting from the roof and gimlet eyes peering from the gaps in the still-boarded windows. . . .

David Valentine stepped off the train even before it came to a full stop and landed neatly on his good leg. He checked in at the Guard Station and reacquainted himself with the modest sights of the hill-circled town, enjoying the sensation of being off the rickety train.

It had been a long trip up from Texarkana, thanks to the stop-and-start nature of nonmilitary travel. He spent a night in Hope, and learned that the famous unification of Texas and Arkansas forces had actually taken place in the nearby crossroads of Fouke. Southern Command, perhaps with an eye toward history, or realism about the soldier's eagerness to say they were present at the famous Texas-Arkansas-Fouke, had broadcast the news to the world from a minor general's temporary headquarters in Hope. Valentine spent ten dollars on an afternoon outing from Hope to the spot of the linkup (sandwich lunch included!) and saw the two state flags waving on a small hill next to a creek where beer and whiskey bottles from the celebration were still in evidence.

He wandered up and down Pine Bluff's main streets. Occupation seemed to have leeched all the cheery color from the town he remembered from his early days as a Wolf, studying at the academy. Vanished flower boxes, missing chalkwork advertisements on the brickwork, empty display windows where once mannequins had stood displaying everything from rugged smocks to ruffled wedding gowns, even the tired-looking berry bushes and picked-clean fruit trees filling every vacant lot related the occupation's story.

The lots made him think of Razors for some reason. Missing faces, dead or gone. He missed Hank most of all, even more than Narcisse or Ahn-Kha. Both could take care of themselves. But Hank had gone off to school with little enthusiasm. Valentine had tried to ease the parting by giving him his snakeskin bandolier, the same one he'd worn the night of the Rising in Little Rock.

"You deserve a medal, Hank, but this is the best I can do."

Hank ran his good hand across the oversized scales. "For real? For keeps?"

"For exceptional valor," Valentine said.

Hank hooked a finger in one of the loops. "Take a while to grow more Quickwood," Hank said.

"Fill it with diplomas."

At that Hank frowned—the boy saw himself as tried and tested as any of the Razors. In the end Valentine tasked Ahn-Kha with seeing the boy safely seated—and if necessary, handcuffed—at school.

He brought himself back to the present.

Valentine read the lettering next to a white cross painted on a walkway above the street, connecting two buildings at the heart of downtown:

HERE THEY HUNG JAMES ELLINGTON
FOR SPITTING UNDER THE BOOTS OF THE OCCUPIERS AS THEY MARCHED
THEY SAID HE WAS TO BE AN EXAMPLE
THEY WERE RIGHT

One of Valentine's happier memories was of his time spent in Pine Bluff as a student at the war college. Essays on the qualities of Integrity, Professional Competence, The Courage to Act, and Looking Forward; regulations on the care of dependants and children of his soldiers; sound management principles—Southern Command was nothing if not parsimonious—the multitude of identification badges . . .

Or the cheery efficiency of Cadet "Dots" Lambert, juggling student and instructor schedules with teenage energy. Valentine laid down circuitous paths so he could pass her desk and say hi between his early duties with Zulu Company, class, and meals. He'd never worked up the courage to so much as ask her to a barbecue—he'd been a scruffy young Wolf, a breed apart from the well-tailored guards and cadets who undoubtedly dazzled as they whirled the girl around the floor at military mixers that Valentine, with patched trousers, collarless shirts, and field boots always managed to miss.

He hoped Lambert hadn't been hung from the clock tower at the university. Or shipped off in a cattle car.

Which brought him back to his reason for the trip to Pine Bluff. The Miskatonic.

Valentine refreshed himself with a hotdog in heartroot at the diner, then wandered southward along the tracks to the old SEARK campus, now listed on the town map as the "HPL Agricultural and Technical

Resource Center." The entire SEARK campus was now surrounded by two rows of fencing topped with razor wire on either side of the streets surrounding the campus, enclosing as it did the war college, cadet school, and military courthouse.

Valentine showed his ID at the gate, surrendered his weapons, and signed in as a visitor.

"Have a fine one," the gun-check said, handing him a locker key on a pocket lanyard.

He heard distant gunfire from the other side of the railroad tracks as he entered, the spaced-out popping of a practice range. The cadets probably had a range day—it was a Friday and it would be just as well to stink them up on a day when they'd be a smelly nuisance to friends and family rather than their instructors—as most of the students looked to be in their late teens or early twenties. They looked so young. Elaborate razor-cut sideburns reminiscent of a bull's horns looked to be the new standard with the boys, and the girls were showing tight ringlet curls dangling from their little envelopelike caps.

Valentine, now closer to thirty than twenty, with three long trips into the Kurian Zone behind him that aged a man more than years or mileage, could shrug and disparage them as children. Except that the children had each been more or less handpicked and was studying morning, noon, and night in an effort to win their first brass tracks. Children didn't make PT at four A.M. and fall asleep on a pile of books at midnight.

There wouldn't be any old instructors to visit—frontline officers took a year or two off to teach, sometimes, but only the cadet school had permanent faculty and Valentine had ventured onto that campus only to take qualification tests. He took the sidewalk bordering the inner fence straight to the Miskatonic.

Their new building looked a good three times the size of the old one. Perhaps Southern Command had finally decided to take the scholars seriously. The Miskatonic researched how the Kurians and other dangerous fauna they'd "brought over" interacted and thought, instead of simply cataloging and quantifying threats.

Valentine had visited the "oddballs" inside now and then as a student at the war college, and had constant contact since in the form of debriefings every time he came back from the Kurian Zone. The debriefings were always by a variegated trio; a young student who served as stenographer, an intellectual-looking questioner, and then an older man or woman who silently listened, almost never asking a question him or herself, but sometimes calling the other two off into another room before the trio returned with a new line of questioning. He'd gotten to know a couple of the "oldsters"—by their faces, anyway—enough so that he hoped he could run down Post's mystery letter.

A pair of workmen bent over an addition to the entryway, adding a small brick blister next to the doorway. Valentine passed through a layer of glass doors. A second layer was in place, but the glass was missing.

The whole institution had a fresh-scrubbed smell to it. Valentine caught a whiff of wet paint from one of the halls.

Six feet of neatly uniformed muscle stood up from his desk. "Can I help you?"

Valentine wondered if the hand casually dangling at the edge of the desk had a sidearm in reach, or was hovering over the alarm button. Two more guards watched from a balcony on the second floor.

Procedures had changed since he was a student. The last time he'd just walked into the building and wandered around until he heard sounds of activity.

Valentine reached for his ID again, feeling a bit like he was still in the KZ. "David Valentine, for a follow-up to my 18 August debriefing."

The soldier made a pretense of checking a list.

"I don't have—"

"Sorry, Corp," Valentine said smoothly. "A few months ago I got a request for another interview. I'm just back from Dallas, and the creeps told me that whenever duties allowed, I was to report. Duties allow, so here I am."

"Could I see the request, sir?"

"It was in the regimental file cabinet, which fell victim to a 122 during the Dallas siege, and was buried with honors by every soldier with a drunk-and-disorderly charge pending. You want to phone the old man and unclog the pipes at your end, or should I hit the Saenger for the afternoon matinee and work on my complaint letter? Maybe I can get reimbursed for my hotel and expenses from your paycheck."

"Sorry, sir," the corporal said. "It's these pointy heads. They'd run this place like a fruit stand. You'd think security was the enemy. Could you wait a moment?"

"Why the new security?"

"Kurian agent. Six men shot each other running him down."

Valentine looked around for a chair in the foyer, but the only two in evidence held up an improvised coffee station for the workmen set up on one of the missing glass door panes. He settled for sitting on a windowsill.

"I'll wait. I think it was signed O'Connor. David O'Connor," Valentine said, dredging the name from his memory.

"Doubt it," the corporal said, a rugged military phone to his ear. "He bought it when they dropped Reapers on the campus."

"My mistake," Valentine said.

"His. He tried to capture one." The corporal connected with someone and turned ninety degrees away from Valentine to speak.

Whatever he heard made the corporal look at Valentine again.

"Yes, Doc." He replaced the receiver. "You want some coffee or anything, Major Valentine?"

"I'm good."

"One of the senior fellows will be right down, Major."

"And he'll hear how polite you've been as you've done your duty," Valentine said.

"Thanks. I mean it."

The two guards looking down from the balcony on the second floor lost interest, and Valentine heard footsteps over more distant construction noises.

A limp-haired woman wearing shapeless scrubs that looked as though they belonged in a hospital emerged from a door behind the security station and came around the desk, giving a friendly nod to the corporal as she passed. She extended her hand and Valentine shook it. She had an easy, confident manner that made Valentine think of the midwife from his youth in the Boundary Waters.

"Gia Dozhinshka," she said. Valentine wondered if he'd been greeted in an Eastern European tongue. "Zhin's the shorthand around here," she continued.

"David Valentine, or just Val. I don't think we've met."

"No, but I summarized your debriefs. Nebraska and the Caribbean, and I read your Wisconsin and Great Lakes material. Call me a fan. Let's go to an interview room. We can sit."

"New digs," Valentine said as they passed through a different set of doors under the balcony at the back of the foyer.

"We hid our low-level archives here when we got the order to bug out. Seemed easier to move Mohammed to the mountain afterward. No one's complaining. Central air, if you can believe it."

"I thought that was a legend outside the hospitals and Mountain Home."

"We've been blessed. That's what it seemed like at first, anyway."

A young woman pushed a cart down the hall. "Interview A, Tess," Zhin called.

They turned a corner and she opened a door to a room that had been subdivided by half-glass walls. Valentine saw two people speaking to a hairy-faced man with the look of a frontiersman, though even with hard ears he couldn't make out any words through the glass. She led him to a warren of enclosed cubicles. They circumvented most of them and went to a smaller office at the back, where she turned on a light.

"The chairs in this one are better. It's got its own sugar and such for coffee, too. Have to wait on Tess with your files. Anything to drink? Coffee? We have sage tea, courtesy of your Texas friends."

"Water would be good," Valentine said, spotting a cooler.

"Cups are up top. We don't have the kind that go in the little dispenser anymore."

Valentine got his drink and sat down at the bare table. Zhin settled herself opposite him.

"They decided you're worth guarding, it seems."

"We've come up in the world. Curse of being right."

"How's that?"

"A couple of our guys picked up on some strange dealmaking with the Texas-Kansas-Oklahoma Kurians. Solon hiring himself an army—but you know all about that. We figured we were going to get hit, and hard. Southern Command figured they were going to clean out the Grogs up and down the Missouri—Solon sent out a bunch of false intelligence indicating that. We ended up being right."

"But nobody listened," Valentine said.

"We were always outside the whole command structure. We'd give an opinion on this or that. What might work to pierce Reaper cloaks. Is there a way to disrupt the signal between a Kurian and his Reapers. What kind of ailments kill 'em. But since Solon's bid we've got to issue regular reports, assessments, and they're even starting to filter who we talk to and where we go so we don't lose 'assets.' "

"I met one of the filters at the security desk. Seems a reasonable precaution."

The young woman with the cart knocked and entered, pushing a collapsed binder with Valentine's name and some sort of catalog number printed on the outside. *Be interesting to take a look at the supplemental notes in that file,* Valentine thought. Pens, notepaper, and storage bags and jars littered the cart.

"Tess Sooyan, David Valentine," Zhin said, by way of introduction.

The young woman hid behind her hair and glasses. She sat down in the corner with a pad, leaving the table to Valentine and her superior.

"Used to be if someone saw a weird track or bone they'd bring it to us, and we'd hand out little rewards and so on, even if it was just another Grog skull. But the, oh, what do you want to call them, shifty types—border trash—they avoid us now. All the barbed wire and uniforms scare them away."

"Speaking of shifty . . . I've got a confession. I'm here under false pretenses. I didn't need a follow-up to my last debrief."

Zhin leaned back in her chair. "Oh?"

Tacitly invited to explain, Valentine extracted Post's note. "A friend of mine got this . . . I'm guessing it's from one of your people. He's looking for his wife."

"Probably one of the kids," Zhin said, showing the note to her assistant. "Still in school or fresh out of it, they start here running down public queries. They shouldn't be sending out copies of documents, though. Or passing on opinions."

"That might be Peter Arnham's writing," Tess said at a level just loud enough for Valentine to hear it. "He's on the Missing/Displaced network."

"Can you look into it?" Valentine asked. "My friend's a good man. Badly wounded outside Dallas. He's going to have to put his life back together after all this. It would help if he knew one way or the other."

Zhin put the message in her leather folio. "I'll get a group going on it."

"I'll owe—"

"No, we don't work that way. No favors, no bargains, and you needn't come back with a crate of brandy. If you want, we can put you up for a night or two on campus."

"I know the town. I'd rather not be behind wire. I'll look up the Copley, if it's still around. Maybe try for a bass in the reservoir lake."

She and Tess both made notes. "You might at that. No one was doing much fishing while Solon was running things."

Few pursuits can compare with fishing for a man looking for peace and quiet.

Two days later, enjoying his leave more than he'd enjoyed anything since parting with Malia, Valentine brought in a nice three-pound bass. As he tied up his aluminum shell he mentally inventoried the seasonings he'd picked up at the market after catching that catfish yesterday but had saved at the last minute in the hope of a better future catch: some green peppers, garlic, cloves, and a tiny bottle of what the spice merchant swore up and down was olive oil.

This particular lunker would be worth it.

He'd grill it over charcoal and hickory within the hour, and enjoy it with a syrupy local concoction everyone in town called a coke.

"Hey, Valentine," he heard a voice call. He looked up. "Reservoir Dan," the man who'd rented him the boat and tackle—and who accepted money only for bait " 'cause that's an actual expense" after seeing his Southern Command ID, stood at the pier, stubbing out one of the ration cigarettes Valentine had insisted that he accept. "Got a message for you—hey, you did good."

Valentine held the fish a little higher. "Got it near the stumps on the north side."

"You try that spinner?"

"That's what got him. What was the message?" Dan would go all afternoon about local fishing with the tiniest prompt.

"Some girl on a bike from the Ark. Said they ran your paper down and that you could come by anytime."

"I hope anytime includes after lunch," Valentine said. "Join me?"

"I'll bring the sweet potato pie," Dan said, smacking his lips.

Half a bass and a thick wedge of pie heavier, Valentine caught a lift on a military shuttle horse cart to the SEARK campus. Everything went faster this time, from surrendering his weapon at the gate to admittance to the Miskatonic.

This time Zhin brought him back to her office. The researcher had a deft hand at indoor gardening; assorted spider plants shot out tiny versions of themselves from the top of every file cabinet and bookcase, taking advantage of the window's southern exposure.

A young man she introduced as Peter Arnham, who seemed to prefer rumpled clothes two sizes too big for him, stood up nervously when Valentine entered.

"This isn't a trial, son," Valentine said. "I'm just doing legwork for a man who's missing his."

"I didn't know Hunter Staff Cats—Cats with the rank of major, anyway—did their own legwork," Arnham said.

"I'm not staff yet," Valentine said.

The Miskatonic researchers looked at each other and shrugged. He knew as little about their world as they did his.

"Everyone just sit," Zhin suggested. "This isn't a formal briefing, nothing like it."

They did so.

"Val, you're free to ask Peter here whatever you like. We don't know much about this; we're holding nothing back."

Valentine sensed an edge to her voice that hadn't been there before.

"You think I'm on an assignment?" Valentine asked.

"We know you work with cover stories and so on."

Valentine leaned forward. "No. It's really what I told you. I'm inquiring for a friend, a fellow officer, William Post. This isn't prep for an operation, not by a long shot."

"It's just that the mule list is a bit of a mystery to us too," Zhin said. "We thought maybe someone was finally looking into it."

"Mule list?"

"Just a shorthand we use," Zhin said. "Solon's departure left behind a real treasure trove of documentation—we've never gotten this complete a picture of human resource processing in the Kurian Zone before. We've had to add and train dozens of people just to sift through it all."

Arnham added: " 'Mule list' is a term we use because all these women appear to carry something the Kurians are interested in. We know it's not blood type or anything obvious, like Down's. About all we know is that only women are tested, and that if they come up positive for it they're immediately packed up and shipped off."

"How do you know it's a positive? List I saw just had an X under 'Result.' "

"Intellectual shorthand," Zhin said. "We just call it a positive. That's the kind of optimists we got here." Zhin and Arnham both chuckled.

"Why the 'she's gone for good' note?"

"I thought he deserved to know." Arnham stared levelly at Zhin. "I don't think that sort of thing should be kept a secret. Like I said, all the security shit is hurting us more—"

"Let's keep this on point, Peter," Zhin said.

Zhin turned in her chair to Valentine. "This Gail, your officer's wife, is most likely dead. Everything we know about the mule list says that they're put on priority trains with extra security and shipped out. Handling is similar to what happens when your Wolves or Bears are captured. We know Hunters are interrogated and killed at a special medical facility; that's been established. Doctors working for the Kurians do a lot of pathology on the bodies."

Valentine had heard rumors along those lines before.

"Have you looked into the family background of your mule list? Do they come from Hunter parents?"

"A few," Arnham said. "Not enough for a real correlation."

"What is the test?"

"Don't know. They take a small amount of blood. Like an iron check when you donate."

Valentine had given enough blood in Southern Command's medical units to know what that meant. A drop or two squeezed from a finger cut. "And then?"

"They drop it in a test tube. We know the negatives stay clear."

"How many show up as positives?"

"Less than one percent," Arnham answered.

"About one out of a hundred and fifty or so, looks like," Zhin said, checking another paper.

Valentine wondered if any of his known unknowns were filled in, or if this just represented a new unknown popping up. "But these women present a danger to the Kurians?"

Arnham's lips tightened. "I didn't say that. I said they were treated that way. Look, we're in the dark about as much as you. We're laying it all out there."

He rooted around in his folios and passed a binder to Valentine. Inside were six tabs. Each had a list from a testing station similar to the one he sent Post.

"Your girl's in the yellow-tabbed one," Arnham said.

Valentine nodded and flipped to the list. The sheets were the same as the others, a bare list of negatives. Female names, no particular ethnic background to them

Valentine's heart thudded before his brain knew why.

Melissa Carlson.

The rest of the room faded away for a second as the name held his attention. Melissa . . . Molly . . . the woman whose family had helped him in his trip across Wisconsin, who he'd gone to the Zoo in Chicago to save when she caught the eye of a sexually avaricious Quisling *nomenklatura* and murdered him. . . .

"You okay there, Val?" Zhin asked.

No result next to Molly's name. She hadn't been put on a train. Molly's sister Mary was just below her on the list; she'd been tested too, also no *X* in the result column.

But she had been tested. She'd been tested at the same location as Gail Foster. Why was she listed as Molly Carson? She'd married her Guard lieutenant . . . *What was his name . . . Stockton, no, Stockard. Graf Stockard.*

"Fine. You keep the big directories here, right? The Southern Command Military Census?"

"Yes, of course."

"Can I have a browse?"

"Sure. A name ring a bell?" Zhin guessed.

Not just a bell. A gong and clattering cymbals.

Four

Crowley's Ridge, Arkansas: Running southwest-northeast through the eastern part of the state, straight as though drawn on the map with a ruler, Crowley's Ridge varies from about two hundred to five hundred feet high, up to a dozen miles wide, and several hundred miles long. Once the next thing to terra incognita in Southern Command, with only a few precariously placed settlements hugging the Saint Francis, it is now considered the "civilized" eastern border for the defenders of the freehold.

The northeastern part of the state suffered literally earth-shattering devastation in the New Madrid quake and never recovered. Now the expanse between the Ridge and Memphis is a tangled floodplain for the newly feral Mississippi and its tributaries, like the Saint Francis, briefly bridged by a few pieces of road and a railroad line during Solon's tenure in the Ozarks.

Solon intended for Crowley's Ridge to be his eastern border and set up the outposts, along with a road and rail network to serve them. Southern Command's Guards were only too happy to assume their upkeep when Valentine's Rising and Archangel put Solon's incorporations into receivership. Now this series of Guard Outposts holds the line here, supplying smaller Hunter formations that explore the flat lands extending to the Mississippi and beyond.

Perhaps no area is more patrolled and contested than the corridor that runs along the old interstate that once linked Memphis and Little Rock. A few Kurians maintain their towers on the west side of the river within sight of Memphis, sending their Reapers into the wilderness to hunt refugees, smugglers, or out-and-out brigands, while Southern Command sends Cats and Wolves into the corridor to hunt the Reapers.

* * *

You're not doing this in order to see her, David Valentine told himself for the umpteenth time. She's smart, a good observer. Perhaps Molly even knew Gail.

No, her letters trickled off and you want to know why, a more honest part of Valentine said.

Shut up the both of you, someone whose name might be Superego interjected.

Valentine got the feeling he was being watched as he walked up the road running along the western side of Crowley's Ridge. Molly Carlson Stockard's name had turned up as residing at a military camp called Quapaw Post, and a quick message to the CO—Valentine justified it as a joint inquiry with the Miskatonic—revealed that she lived at the Post as a "Class A" dependant, which meant she didn't just live on post, but worked there as well.

A forty-mile train ride, ten-mile wagon hitch, and a two-mile hike brought him to this quiet corner of Southern Command, well north of the corridor.

He bore a full set of arms, as any serving officer in Southern Command did, even on leave. The Atlanta Gunworks assault rifle formerly shouldered by the Razors bumped against his back inside an oiled leather sheath to keep the wet and dirt off. The freehold had learned long ago that the more people trained to carry guns there were traipsing around the rear areas, the less likely they were to have to use them, whether threatened by the lawless or by the emissaries of the awful law that was the Kurian Zone.

He had to stop himself from jogging or falling into his old Wolf lope. He wanted to arrive more or less composed, not sweaty and bedraggled. He regretted that he didn't already have his staff crossbar, or he'd probably have been able to requisition a trap or even a motorcycle.

Quapaw Post didn't look like much; one thick concrete shell that probably enclosed a generator, armory, and fuel supply. A pair of identical, cavernous barns and a few wooden barracks, with a tower at the center for fresh water and sentries, rounded out the station. Miles of fencing stood along either side of the road and extended up into the oak-and-hickory-thick hills of the ridge and west into the alluvial flats, where the fields were subdivided into pasture and hay fields. Horses grazed and swished each other in the gauzy sun, and nearer to the road insects harvested the nectar of butterfly weed and wild bellflowers.

Evidently Quapaw Post supported Southern Command horseflesh. Horses on active duty needed a break as often—probably more often—as the men they carried.

Quapaw Post's CO, a captain by the name of Valdez, met him personally at the gate. Valdez varied his Guard uniform in that he wore camp shorts and leather sandals. Valentine got the impression this corner of Southern Command was not frequently inspected.

"A walking major?" Valentine heard the sentry ask his captain.

"Ex-Wolf. I checked him out; he's a good man on leave," Valdez said. "Oh, he can probably hear you by now, Crew."

"Long as it ain't a Bear, is all."

The Captain hallooed a greeting with Valentine a few strides away.

"Welcome to the Quapaw, Major," Valdez said. "You're welcome to my room, as I've got a cot in my office, or there's all kinds of space in the barns."

"If you don't mind flies and horseshi—" the sentry started.

"The barn is fine, Captain," Valentine said. The captain shook his hand and led him past some weedy sandbags to the official starting point of the base, a line of painted rocks. Valentine looked around. "Do you train the mounts here, or just feed them?"

"Both. That widow you asked about, Molly, she's one of our civilian trainers."

"Widow?"

"MIA technically, over six months, so that makes her a widow on the books."

"Does she know I'm coming?"

"I kept my mouth shut. But you know a small post."

"No sense wasting time. I'd like to see her."

"You're invited to a dinner with the other officers. Unless you'll be umm, otherwise occupied." Valdez made a point of nudging a path-bordering rock back into line, where it guarded some fragrant tomato vines.

"Tell your officers to dress down, this isn't an official visit. If they'd rather play cards over beer—"

Valdez brightened. "Your credit's good here, if you want to get in on a game. My kebabs are very popular if you like finger food."

"Sick horses have to go sometime. Glad to see border station duty's still the same." They turned up a little row of what looked like trailers with the wheels removed.

"You will want to get back to the electricity soon enough, I'm sure. Here we are."

Valentine recognized the bunkhouses. Known as "twenty by eights"—though a screened-in porch that could be opened on one end gave them dimensions closer to thirty feet in length—the easily constructed prefab bunkhouses were the backbone of Southern Command's dependant housing.

This one had the screened porch, and a thriving band of hostas living in the semishade under the floor, set a foot off the ground by concrete blocks.

Molly stood on the other side of the screen door. She seemed to shimmer a bit. Perhaps it was the water in his eyes.

A tiny, dark-haired figure clung to one of her legs. A tabby cat watched the drama from the tar-shingle roof.

"David?" she said.

"Hello, Molly." *Say something else!* "How are you?"

"I'll take your rig over to the barn," Valdez put in.

Valentine released his pack, grateful for something to do with his body.

When he'd had the barn office pointed out and said good-bye to the captain, Molly had the screen door open. She stood a few pounds heavier, her eyes were a little more tired perhaps, but her hair shone with its same golden glory. If anything, it was a little longer and fuller, drawn back from her cheekbones into a single braid. Some of the wariness that he'd come to know all too well on their trip back to the Free Territory still haunted her. She wore a civvied version of the old female Labor Regiment top, cheered up by a set of silver buttons, and a simple jean skirt with a built-in apron-pouch. She smelled like lavender.

The child had her creamy skin, or maybe it just looked light set against the boy's dark hair and eyes. If he and Molly had had a child the boy might have ended up looking like that.

"I'm sorry about Graf," Valentine said.

"Thank you. I'm adapting." Her eyes kept striking the scar on his face, then circling away, then coming back to it, alighting just for a flash before looking away.

Valentine was used to the reaction. In an hour or two, or tomorrow, it would just be another part of his face.

"You never told me—"

"This is Edward," Molly said, picking the boy up with an easy grace that suggested that she did it a hundred times a day.

"Edwid," the child agreed.

"Edward, say 'hi' to David."

The child didn't want to say hi and buried his face in his mother's neck.

"I smell like a long trip," Valentine said.

"Is that why you're limping?"

"I fell badly," Valentine sort of lied, leaving out the bullet entering his leg that precipitated the fall.

"He's two and he's got his own mind about people. Six months ago he giggled at strangers and grabbed their fingers."

Valentine did some mental math. If Molly had given birth about two years ago, the baby had been conceived at the end of his summer as a Quisling Coastal Marine in the *Thunderbolt.* Tripping over Post's square liquor bottles in the cabin they shared. The phony marriage to Duvalier. Had Molly's stomach quivered that August night the way it had when—

Stop that insanity. . . .

"I want to get cleaned up. Can I do that, and then we'll talk?"

"The only water in here is for the sink. We share flush toilets and showers at the end of the street. There's a hose that works at the stable, too; the vet room has a sluice in the center. Sometimes I'll just hook the hose in the ceiling there after work and shower."

"I'll do that. Back in an hour?"

"Do you want dinner with us?"

"Yes," Valentine said. Probably too eagerly. "If it's not trouble for you and Edward."

"You changed my whole definition of trouble," Molly said, but she smiled when she said it. "No, an extra plate is no trouble at all."

Dinner that night passed in uncomfortable small talk.

The bunkhouse had a tiny folding table that just fit the child's high chair and the two adults. A propane stove—natural gas was obtainable in the Ozarks, almost plentiful compared to some parts of the country—with two burners and an oven made up a tiny kitchen annex. A bead curtain partition separated a couple of twin beds that sat under a few pictures and a black-framed set of military ribbons and decorations.

Molly described, in broad strokes, her marriage to Graf Stockard, and life at home for her father and sister—her mother had finally succumbed to the illness that the doctors described only as "malignant cancer" (were there any nonmalignant varieties, Valentine wondered) while he had been crossing the Great Plains Gulag with Duvalier. She largely skipped over "the occupation," and somehow Valentine couldn't ask her about the testing as the horsemeat stew changed place with a strawberry cobbler on the table, if not in the smears on Edward's face. *Are you keeping your promise to Post or trying to get back into her bed?*

Of course conversing without really talking was an old habit of his and Molly's. They'd been that way ever since the zoo. She grew more animated when she described her duties as a civilian horse trainer.

When they said good night under a moth-shrouded lamp, both bled relief into the chill spring night.

Valentine spent the next day with Valdez, who wanted an opinion on some beadwork one of his men had found in a bush. On the way there he expounded on the virtues of sandals for soldiers, waxing eloquent on both their hygiene and durability benefits. They examined the site where the piece had been found, but neither Valentine nor any of the men could find tracks, and they returned to Valdez's office in the cool of the concrete redoubt.

"It's pretty dirty," Valentine said, evaluating what he supposed was a bracelet. "The leather's dried. Looks like Grog work, but I'm thinking a crow spotted it somewhere and decided to add it to his collection. Weren't the Grogs in this area during the occupation?"

"Fighting with the TMCC," the sergeant who brought it to Captain Valdez's attention added, referring to the Trans-Mississippi Combat Corps. Valentine had worn their uniform during his ruse in Little Rock.

"How'd it go with the Carlson girl?" Valdez asked after the sergeant had left, with an order to pass news of the find up to the brigade headquarters in Forrest City. He filled two glass tumblers with water and added a splash of something that smelled like it was trying to be gin.

"Why isn't she the 'Stockard girl'?"

"That *chulo* gave up on his family when he ran." Valdez opened an envelope resting in his in box, tossed it back like a fish too small to be kept, and sat down. He waved to a chair against the wall. Valentine pulled it up and thanked him for the drink by raising his glass halfway across the ring-stained desk.

"Ran?"

"Yes. I heard he and a few other cowards ran north into Grog land. He left a note saying that he'd send for her once he was established. I understand the Grogs sometimes employ men as mechanics and so on."

"She told you this?"

"No. As I said, it is a small post."

"Then what do you know about me?"

"From gossip? Nothing. But I've been around enough men to know when one is thinking about losing himself in a woman. You should do whatever you came here to do and leave again."

Valentine at once liked and disliked his temporary host. He liked the open way Valdez offered what could be construed as criticism, and disliked him because the criticism was so near the mark.

That afternoon he kept Molly company while she worked, cooling and calming the horses down after they'd been trotted on a long lead. Edward spent his days in the company of a B-dependant, an older woman who'd lost her husband and two sons to Southern Command's Cause.

They quit early when an afternoon drizzle started up.

Afterward, Molly hung the traces up in the tack room to dry.

"Is Mary still horse crazy?" Valentine asked, smelling the rich, oiled leather and remembering the preteen's currycomb obsession in Wisconsin.

"She discovered boys just before . . . everything."

"Where is she now?"

"They took her away."

"I thought she tested negative," Valentine said, and realized the implications of his words.

"Tested negative? What does that have to do with it?"

"I—"

"A gang of soldiers saw a fourteen-year-old girl they liked in a bread line and just took her." Valentine heard a fly futilely buzzing in a spider's web from the tack room's corner; in the stalls a horse nickered to an associate. Only human ears had the capacity to appreciate the grief in Molly's voice. "They killed her for the fun of it. According to our mouthpiece, they did get a trial and one of them was convicted for murder. Who knows what really happened."

"They do, for a start. I wouldn't mind talking it over with one of them."

"They're probably dead, Dave. Was it always like this in the Free Territory? When you talked about it with me in Wisconsin . . . seems like everyone's either dead or has dead family."

"You're not saying it was better back there?"

"No, not better. Easier. You always had the option of believing all the lies, too. Why are you here, David? It's not the sort of place soldiers spend their leave."

"Let's find somewhere to sit."

"I'll take you to my spot," she said, and extended her hand.

Valentine took it, wondering.

She took him out of the barn and to a portion of fence that projected from a side door. Extra hay bales sat here on wooden pallets, under a wooden awning to keep the rain off, a sort of ramshackle add-on to the aluminum structure that a pair of carpenters had probably put up in a day.

She scooted up onto one of the bales and sat looking at the springtime green of Crowley's Ridge, rising less than a mile away. "I like the view," she said. "Normally I eat with Edward and the other kids, but sometimes Carla takes the kids out for the day to the duck pond. Then I just eat my lunch here."

"Remember that day we sat on the hill and talked about your dad's setup for us?"

She tilted her head back with eyes closed. "Yes. God, I was young."

"You're still young."

"You're not," she said, startling Valentine a little. "Afraid of a little honesty? You're not that earnest young lieutenant anymore. You used to look at me. It gave me—kind of a tickle. Now you stare through me. Through that ridge, as a matter of fact."

"I'm here because your name came up in something we're looking into. A test that you—and your sister—took involving a blood draw."

"That's it?" she asked.

Valentine nodded.

"This has nothing to do with Graf?"

"Should I be asking you about him?"

"He's a good man. Was a good man. Guard duty was his world. When that went away he had nothing."

"He had you and a child."

"A prison camp's not much of a place for either. Don't you want to know about the boob test?"

Valentine wasn't so sure any more. "Why do you call it that?"

"That's what we called it in Wisconsin. They gave all the girls the same thing at about thirteen or fourteen. Just when you got your boobs so we called it the boob test."

"How do you know it's the same?" Valentine asked.

Molly twisted a piece of straw around her finger. "They did the same thing both times. Line up all the girls—well, it was all the women in Pine Bluff, I suppose, since they were just getting us organized. Usual health check with a tongue depressor and thermometer and listening to your heart and lungs."

"Okay."

"At the end they took a little wooden stick, smaller than a knitting needle, and scratched you with the end. Some gals got a big welt from it. To get released from the exam you had to show your arm. Most of us got a red mark, on some it raised a welt—it didn't on me or my sister—then, for those who didn't react, the nurse drew some blood and dropped it in a test tube."

"I don't suppose you asked—"

"Both times. They said it checked for infection."

"What happened when they put the blood in the test tube?"

"Nothing. It just dissolved."

"Do you remember if there was anyone who had it do anything else?"

Molly's face scrunched up. "Not in Wisconsin, but they only checked about eight of us. They plucked out some women from the group in Pine Bluff, I recall. A bunch of others kind of kicked up at that, and the women taken were yelling out messages to friends, but the soldiers said something like, 'They've got it made, they're going to Memphis priority style,' or something like that. Maybe it was just to calm everyone down."

"Memphis?" Valentine said.

"Yes, I'm sure about Memphis. Memphis in style."

"Wait here a moment, okay?"

"Sure."

Valentine trotted up to his pack and extracted Post's flyer. He returned to Molly and showed her the picture.

"Did you see her there?"

"That wasn't the woman I saw taken away. She was sorta black." She looked more closely at the picture. "She's pretty."

"She's my friend's wife. He wants to know what happened to her."

She yanked some more straw out of the bale and tossed it piece by piece into the breeze. "When they take you away it's never good. Never. That guard was just talking for the sake of talk."

"I don't suppose you saw the train leave or the uniforms of the men who took her."

"No. You know how they are with that stuff. Someone disappears through a door or behind a curtain and then they're just gone."

She stood up with a little hop. "Now. Your question's been answered. You can go."

"I wasn't the one who got married and quit writing," Valentine said. He saw her eyes go wet.

"Go join one of the nightly card games with Valdez and the corporals, David. Go and learn about a bad hand. We were a bad hand, that's all. You played it well back in Wisconsin, you did right by me and my family, but it was still a bad hand. Leave me—us—alone."

Valentine stood up too, and regretted it. He was a good six inches taller than Molly and the last thing he wanted to do was physically intimidate her. "What 'us'? You and me or you and your son? I've got a daughter, Molly. She's a thousand miles away and all I know is that she was born, but she's a piece of me. Just like you." He took a step back.

"A piece, you mean."

"Don't! Molly, just don't. It wasn't that way, not with us, not with Mo—Malita. Don't play with words and think that'll change what happened."

An arch collapsed inside her. "Crap," she said, and sniffled.

"You want me to go?"

"Yes. No—no. Do what you have to. You're built for it."

He spoke softly. "What's that supposed to mean?"

"One of the old hands in Weening used to say you Wolves and whatnot, the aliens came and took out your hearts and put in those of horses and pigs and lions or whatever to make you so you could stand up to them. You weren't human anymore, not on the inside."

"We drank some kind of medicine. That's it."

"You can eat with us tonight if you want. Or just leave—I'll understand. That trail you're on's cold enough." She turned and went quickly into the barn, and Valentine got the distinct feeling she didn't want to be followed.

She didn't want anything from him at all.

He borrowed a horse from Valdez—"We've got plenty that need exercise; take one!"—and rode the big quarter horse hard down to Forrest City. He posted a letter summarizing the relevant pieces of his conversation with Molly to the Miskatonic and saw to the feeding and care of his borrowed gelding. A few hundred dollars of back pay disappeared into the stalls and markets the next morning, and a hard afternoon's ride later he was back at Quapaw Post.

"What's all this?" Molly said at her screen door. Edward interposed himself in front of his mother.

Valentine set down canvas mailbags, and the child reached out with both hands. He was sophisticated enough to know what a big bag promised.

"Season's Greetings," Valentine said. "It's customary to give a little something in exchange for valuable information."

He reached in and extracted three bolts of fabric. "Denim, of course, and I hope you like that green. You're the kind of blond who can wear green."

A big bag of buttons came next. "Most of them match. I looked. I figured you could trade any you didn't like."

Shoes in various sizes for Edward came next, a heavy slab of bacon in waxed paper, great loops of sausage like ox yokes, some lemons and limes, candied dates, and a black-and-white ceramic cow that had probably once been a cookie jar.

He'd let Molly discover the cookies inside on her own, if Edward didn't first.

"Thought it looked like the cows in Wisconsin."

"Holsteins," Molly said, her hand at her throat.

Tea, powdered sugar, a bottle of brandy, even elastic-banded socks and underwear—luxuries all, smuggled from the Kurian Zone, no doubt, but it was considered bad taste to ask a trader questions beyond quality—all joined the growing pile on the tiny table.

"And some cans of jelly," Valentine finished.

"Jelly!" Edward said.

"You're too . . . too much, David. They were just words, and I was angry."

"I thought it was kind of refreshing. First time we'd been honest with each other since . . . well, your dad's basement."

Molly blushed, but just a little. "We were just about to have macaroni and ration cheese." The tiniest pause after "macaroni" told Valentine all he needed to know about what she thought of Southern Command's "cheese"—an oily yellow concoction that tasted faintly like axle grease. "I can fill another plate."

"Fine."

They ate on the steps of the porch rather than clear off the table. "It occurred to me on the ride back that I didn't know if you could sew," Valentine said. "I recall you were good with leather."

"Not like my mom. But I'm getting better."

One of Molly's civilian neighbors, a tight-faced, tan woman, walked by and took a second look at Valentine. Then she turned her face straight to home with everything but an audible *hmpff.*

After Edward went to bed they talked. Looking back on it Valentine realized that he talked and Molly listened. Beck and leaving the Wolves, Duvalier and training as a Cat, the Eagle D Brand in Nebraska's sand hills, the wild night of fire in the General's hangar, Jamaica, Haiti, ratbits, finding out that he'd be a father one rainy day in the Texas pinewoods. The deaths of M'Daw and and the Smalls, Hank. He raised his shirt and she touched the burns on his back.

He couldn't feel whether her fingertips probed or caressed. The surface nerves were mostly dead.

It felt so good to talk about it, maybe because Molly was a piece of his life dating back to before so much of it had happened.

"I can't sit anymore. There's a beautiful moon," Molly said. "You want to take a walk?"

Valentine wasn't sure he did. Or he wasn't sure of the part of himself that did, anyway. "What about Edward?"

"Mrs. Colbert can listen for him. She hears everything that goes on in the cabin anyway. It's all of eight feet away."

"Anything to help Southern Command's cheese along," Valentine said. "You'd think something that greasy—"

"What is it about soldiers and their bowels?" Molly asked. "You'd think with a woman and a moon and a warm night you'd just—"

Horse hooves clip-clopped through the gravel and turned up the little lane running between the rows of bunkhouses.

Four men on horseback leading a fifth saddled horse appeared. One of Valdez's men walked ahead, and pointed toward Molly's cabin.

Valentine could make out the uniforms even in the dim light. The two in back were Wolves; there was no mistaking the trademark soft buckskins and fringed rifle sheaths. The others wore the plain khaki and the round-brimmed "Smokey" hats of the Rounders, Southern Command's law enforcement branch.

Usually veteran Guards, the Rounders patrolled the roads and bridges of Southern Command keeping the population safe from "bummers"—people in the Ozarks without a stake of one kind or another, who were often conduits of everything from black-market antibiotics to military information—and outright criminals.

The Rounders often brought bad news to the harder-to-reach families as well. *Rounder on the doorstep* was a phrase that meant misfortune to most people living outside the towns.

"Rounders," Molly said, echoing his thoughts.

The horses stopped in front of her cabin and Edward appeared, seeking the comfort of her hem. She picked her son up.

Valentine went to the screen door of the tiny porch.

"You Major Valentine?" a man with jowls spilling over his frayed collar asked as he approached.

The Wolves stayed on their horses. One looked halfway familiar to Valentine—then it came to him; he'd been a Wolf at his Invocation, though the name escaped him. The Wolves' hands were conspicuously off their weapons.

"Could you step outside, sir?" The jowly man's laminated name tag said Goebbert.

"What's this about?"

"Just step outside, please, sir."

They ignored Molly and her wide-eyed child. As Valentine came out the Wolves got off their horses.

"You're a hard guy to find, Valentine," the other Rounder put in. He had cockeyed ears, like a hound listening to a raccoon on the roof. He handed a pair of handcuffs to Goebbert.

"Sir, please turn around and put your hands behind you."

Valentine's heart fired like a triphammer. *What the hell?* "What's this about?" Valentine repeated, sounding a lot less like a major this time.

"You're under arrest for murder," Goebbert said.

"Murder?" Valentine felt sweat everywhere.

Goebbert grabbed him firmly by the wrist. "Sorry, Major, orders."

They patted him down. Valentine winced as the hard hands traveled over the old scar tissue on the backs of his legs.

"David, what's going on?" Molly asked from her porch. She held Edward sideways, putting her body in between her son and the four strangers.

"It's got to be a mistake," Valentine said, looking again at the Wolf. Hammond, that was his name. The other young Wolves called him "Lightning" because he had a little tuft of blond hair in his brown.

"Might be," Goebbert said. "But we have to take you to court. Okay, Jim, he's in custody. Make a note of the time."

"Hammond, what is this?" Valentine asked.

Hammond might have smiled—his walrus mustache changed shape—though Valentine wondered why he would look pleased to be recognized by someone being arrested for murder. "We just got orders to make sure you come in. These boys were scared you'd get wind and take to the hills."

Molly had doubt in her eyes; she squinted against it as she might protect herself against dust.

"Molly, I'm not a fugitive. I wasn't hiding with you."

"Enough, Major," Goebbert said. "We've got to get you away. Help him mount, Hammond."

"Put him up backward. Fugitive mount," Uneven Ears said. "They say he's tricky."

The Wolves helped him mount. Sitting backward on the saddle made the night even more surreal. "My gear's in the barn—"

"It'll come along," the other Wolf put in.

"Where are you taking him?" Molly blurted, perhaps too emotionally, for Edward started to cry.

"Crowley Garrison Station, then on to Fort Allnutt, ma'am," Goebbert replied. Valentine craned his neck around and saw Goebbert shaking his head at his fellow Rounder.

David Valentine rode out of Quapaw Post backward. The soldiers came out of their cabins to see the "rogue parade," wondering faces glowing in the moonlight like jack-o'-lanterns.

They showed their paperwork at the gate, and carried out his gear on the Wolves' horses. Valentine, facing backward on his mount, carried only the memory of the fear in Edward Stockton's eyes. And the doubt in Molly's.

Five

The Nut, May: The Nut was an Arkansas State Medium Security Correctional Facility known as Pine Ridge before the Kurian Order, and would probably have remained another overgrown jumble of fence and concrete were it not for Mountain Home, the nearby town that fate selected to be the capital of the Ozark Free Territory (2028–2070).

There are any number of legends as to how Mountain Home ("Gateway to the Ozarks") became the seat of the Free Territory and the headquarters of Southern Command. The more colorful legends involve a poker game, a fistfight, a bad map, a general's mistress, or a souvenir shot glass, but the most likely story concerns Colonel "Highball" Holloway and her wayward signals column.

The colonel and her sixteen vehicles were one of hundreds of fragments fleeing the debacle south of Indianapolis that marked the end of the United States government as most Americans recognized it. While topping a hill northeast of Mountain Home two of her trucks collided, and Colonel Holloway established her signals company in the nearby town of Mountain Home. USAF General J. N. Probst, in charge of a substantial shipment of the first ravies vaccine, heard Holloway's test transmissions and rerouted his staff to make use of the army's facilities. Soon the fragments of everything from National Guard formations to a regiment of Green Berets were being inoculated and reorganized around Mountain Home. Civilians flocked to the protection of the military guns and vehicles, and a government had to be established to manage them. Some chafing in the first years as to whether Southern Command ran the Ozark Free Territory or the Ozark civilians ran Southern Command settled into the American tradition of military subordination to civilian authority—provided the civilians abided by the Constitution and held regular elections.

In those chaotic years the only law was martial—unless one counts the occasional lunchtime trial and afternoon hanging of looters and "profiteers" by horse- and bike-mounted posses. Military justice required an incarceration facility, and as the only other prison nearby was being used to house ravies sufferers in the hope of finding a cure, Pine Ridge became Fort Allnutt, named for its first commander.

Sometime after his death it became "the Nut."

The Nut is an asterisk-shaped building that might pass as a college dormitory were it not for the bars on the windows. Double lines of fencing separate it from the fields—the prisoners grow their own crops and raise their own livestock, and the better behaved they are the more time they get outside the wire—and subsidiary buildings have sprung up around it. Two technical workshops, a health clinic, the guard dorm, and the courthouse that doubles as an administrative center surround the six-story concrete asterisk. Finally there's "the Garage," an aluminum barn that houses a few wrecks used for spare parts. The Garage is where condemned men are hung, traditionally at midnight on their day of execution.

Valentine was proud of his memory, but in later years he never recalled his arrival at the Nut with any real clarity. Mostly he remembered a military lawyer reading the charges against him to a gray and grave presiding officer: torture and murder of prisoners under his supervision during the rising in Little Rock the wild night of what was occasionally being called Valentine's Rising.

Six men had died at the hands of the women he'd freed from the Kurian prison camp. They were guards who had used dozens of women under their supervision as sort of a personal harem. Valentine had never known their names and it was strange to hear them read out in court with all the formality that legal proceedings required—one wasn't known by any name other than "Claw."

Southern Command rarely tried its officers for the execution of armed Quislings—men caught fighting for the vampires were disposed of under a procedure informally called "bang-and-bury." Two generations of bitter feelings between the sides, and the Kurian habit of sending their own armed prisoners straight to the Reapers, had hardened both sides.

"The court finds cause for a trial." Valentine remembered that phrase. The judge declared that Valentine should be kept within Fort

Alnutt until the date of his trial, set for the end of the month: May twenty-third, to be precise.

This rapidity struck Valentine as strange; his knowledge of Southern Command jurisprudence was based on one bad hearing after the destruction of Foxtrot Company at Little Timber Hill and the occasional *Southern Command Bulletin* article, and it was rare to be tried within six months of one's arrest.

And with those words he went dumbly through the sanitary procedures at the jail entrance, climbed into shapeless baby-blue scrubs with large yellow *X*s sewn onto the back, each leg, and the chest pocket, and went to his cell.

His cell he remembered. As a major he got his own room in what his guard escort told him was the nicer wing of the Nut. There was a door with a small glass window rather than bars, and windows that would open to admit a breeze, though the sturdy metal frame was designed so that he couldn't crawl out.

The room had five one-foot-square green linoleum floor tiles across, and nine deep. The bolted-down bed bore a single plastic-wrapped mattress and a depressed-looking pillow in a cotton case that smelled like bleach, as did his combination sink and toilet. His ceiling had a brown-painted light fixture but no bulb: "They don't waste fluorescent tubes on cons, so the sun decides 'lights out,'" the guard said. "Hot chow in the cafeteria twice a day, and we bring out a soup and bread cart to the exercise yard for lunch. Questions?"

"How do I get a shave?" Valentine asked, rubbing his three-day beard.

The guard, whose name tag read Young, but looked as though his first name should be "Gus" or "Mick" or something else hearty and friendly, stuck his thumb in a belt loop. "There's two razors in the showers. You have to use them under supervision. Be sure to put it back in the blue cleanser—"

"I'm not a suicide."

"Didn't say you were. We keep an eye on sharp edges here. Lots of the guys just grow beards until trial."

Valentine looked at what appeared to be a hundred keys at the guard's waist. "Is there a library?"

"Mostly paperbacks held together with rubber bands, and porn. There's a bookcase or two for the highbrows. We've got a store with the *Provisional Journal* and *Serial Digest* for sale; you can earn money in the fields or with janitorial work. Kitchen's full up now."

"Thank you." The formal politeness came out despite the circumstances.

"No problem, Major Valentine. Good luck with the trial. There's a packet of rules and instructions under your pillow. We do an hourly pass through if you need anything."

"A lawyer would be nice."

"You'll have a meeting tomorrow or the next day."

His uniform "scrubs" were poorly finished on the inside. Loose threads tickled whenever he walked. By the time he finished biting off the stray threads with his teeth it was time for dinner.

Officers awaiting trial had a small cafeteria to themselves. Valentine ended up being at the end of the blue-and-yellow file escorted by Young and another guard to the central cafeteria.

Dinner, plopped onto a tray and eaten with a bent-tined fork and a spoon that looked as though it dated from the War of 1812, consisted of an unappetizing vegetable goulash with ground meat.

Two clusters of officers ate together at opposite sides of the cafeteria. A narrow man with long, thinning, butterscotch hair in the smaller of the two cliques looked up at Valentine and made a motion to the seat next to him, but Valentine just dropped into the seat nearest the end of the food service line—and immediately regretted it. He felt alone and friendless, as though already dead, forgotten and entombed in this prison. After dinner some of the men smoked, and Valentine went to the slitlike barred windows and enjoyed the breeze created by the kitchen extractor fans. The Ozarks were black in the distance, the sun masked by haze.

"Shooter or looter?" a reedy voice said.

Didn't even hear him come. Valentine felt thick and tired, brain too apathetic to even function—if he didn't know better he'd suspect one of the mild Kurian sedatives had been put in the food.

He looked at the man, short and close to bald, with an ivory mustache and growing beard, smoking a cigarette from a whittled holder. The eyes were crinkled and friendly.

"Pardon?"

"Shooter or looter, boy? You're the new squirrel in the nut. What they got you in for?"

Valentine tried to make sense of the metaphor and gave up. "Murder. Quislings."

"Then you're a shooter. That's those three over there." He turned his chin in the direction of the group with the long-haired man. "I'm Berlinelli. Malfeasance in the performance of my duties."

"Meaning?"

"Looter. I was doing what a lot of other guys were doing, on a larger scale. Siphoning gasoline and diesel out of captured trucks and selling it."

"I thought everyone in prison was innocent," Valentine said, a bit startled at the man's frankness.

"If you're a snitch it's no hair lifted. I'm pleading out."

"I haven't even talked to my lawyer yet. I need to write some letters. You wouldn't know where I could get paper, would you?"

"Who's running your floor?"

"The guard? Young, I think."

"He's a decent guy. Just ask him." He tapped his wooden cigarette holder on the windowsill and winked. "Got to get back to my tribe. It's Grogs and Harpies in here; we don't mix much."

"Thanks for crossing no-man's-land."

"Just a little recon. Mission accomplished."

Valentine asked Young about paper and a pen as they locked him back in his cell. The long-haired man was two doors down.

"Ummm," Valentine said. "Corporal Young?"

"Yes, Major?"

"Could I get some paper and a pencil? I need to write a few people and let them know where I am." And he should write Post and give him the findings of the aborted investigation, which amounted to a few more facts but zero in the way of answers.

"Sure. It's a standard SC envelope; just don't seal it. Censors. I'll slip them under the door gap tonight on my rounds."

"Right. Thank you."

Young unlocked Valentine's door. Valentine couldn't help but glance at the fixture of a secondary bar, a bolt that could be slid home and twisted, fixed to the metal door and the concrete with bolts that looked like they could hold in Ahn-Kha.

"Major Valentine," Young said. "I heard about you on my break today. The fight on that hill by the river in Little Rock. It's . . . ummm . . . a privilege."

Valentine felt his eyes go a little wet. "Thank you, Corporal. Thanks for that."

A sticklike insect with waving antennae was exploring his sink. Valentine relocated it to the great outdoors by cupping it between his palms.

He gave the insect its freedom. He used to be responsible for the lives of better than a thousand men. Now he commanded an arthropod. As for the general staff training . . .

"What the hell?" he said to himself. "What the hell?"

He met with his military counsel the next day right after breakfast—some sort of patty that seemed to be made of old toast and gristle, and a sweet corn mush. The officer, a taciturn captain from the JAG office named Luecke who looked as though she existed on cigarettes and coffee, laid out the charges and the evidence against him. Valentine wondered at the same military institution both prosecuting and defending him, and, incidentally, acting as judge. Most of the evidence was from two witnesses, a captured Quisling who'd been in the prison camp and a Southern Command nurse lieutenant named Koblenz who'd been horrified at the bloody vengeance wreaked by the outraged women.

Valentine remembered the latter, working tirelessly in the overwhelmed basement hospital atop Big Rock Mountain during the siege following the rising in Little Rock. He'd countersigned the surgeon's report recommending a promotion for her.

He'd sign it again, given the opportunity.

"They've got a good case. Good. Not insurmountable," Luecke said.

"And my options are?" Valentine asked.

"Plead guilty and—see what we can get. Plead 'no contest'—get a little less. Plead innocent and fight it out in front of a tribunal." She turned the cap on her pen with her fingers but kept her eyes locked on his as though trying to get a read.

"When you say 'not insurmountable' you mean?"

"Good. I like a fighter. For a start you're a Cat. We're hip-deep in precedent on Cats not getting prosecuted for collateral casualties. We can blame the women for getting out of hand—"

"I'm not hiding behind the women. Try again."

The pen cap stopped twirling for a moment. "If it were just the Quisling we could toss a lot of dust around. Lieutenant Koblenz will be tough; her statement is pretty damning." The cap resumed its Copernican course.

"She must have presented some case of charges for them to hunt me down so fast."

"She didn't file them. They talked to every woman who survived that camp and the battle. All the others couldn't remember a thing."

"Then who's behind this?" Valentine asked.

"Your former commander, General Martinez. I should say General Commanding, Interior, I suppose. He got promoted."

Valentine's head swam for a moment. When he could see the tired brown eyes of his counsel again he spoke. "He's got a grudge against me. I gave evidence at a trial—not sure if it can even be called that."

"Interesting. Tell me more."

Valentine tried to sum the story up as concisely as he could. He had come out of Texas with his vital column of Quickwood and was ambushed by "redhands"—Quisling soldiers who wore captured uniforms from Southern Command stockpiles. He had a pair of Grog scouts—they were smarter than dogs, horses, or dolphins and were far more capable fighters. The Grogs survived with a handful of others, and with a single wagonload of Quickwood made it to General Martinez, more by accident than design, at his refuge in the Ouachitas. Martinez had two of his Grogs shot at once, and it was only by putting a pistol to the general's head and arresting him for murder that Ahn-Kha survived.

The trial ended in a debacle and Martinez's camp was divided; many of the best soldiers decided to quit the place with Valentine. Ultimately they made it to Little Rock where the rising took place.

Captain Luecke remained poker-faced throughout the story, and only moved to set her pen down. "I don't know much about General Martinez, or what happened during the Kurian occupation," she said. "I spent it aspirating mosquitoes in a bayou. I'm going to ask for a delay in your trial date so I can prepare a defense, if you agree. Fair warning: It'll mean a lot more time for you in here."

She was a cold fish, but she was a very smart cold fish. As she packed up Valentine was already missing the smell of tobacco and coffee.

"Captain?" Valentine said.

"Yes, Major?"

"I'm not sure I want to fight this. I let prisoners get tortured and murdered right under my nose."

She sat back down. "I see. Guilty, then?"

"I . . ." The words wouldn't come. *Coward. You're quick to condemn others.*

"You don't have to decide this second. Can you do something for my satisfaction?"

"Yes."

"Give me the names of some of those women. And no, we're not going to point fingers and say 'they did it.' I just want to hear from all sides about what happened that night."

Valentine thought back to the too-familiar faces of the siege, especially those stilled in death. And not always faces: Petra Yao was only identified by the jewelry on the arm they found; Yolanda, who had to wear diapers thanks to the mutilation; Gwenn Cobb who walked around with her collar turned up and her shirt tightly buttoned afterward—rumor had it they'd written something on her chest with a knifepoint; the Weir sisters, who never talked about it except for their resulting pregnancies; Marta Ruiz, who hung her head and grew her hair out so it covered her eyes. . . .

Christ, those cocksuckers should have gotten worse.

Valentine felt the old, awful hurts and the heat of that night come back. The thing, the shadow, the demon that sometimes wore the body of "the Ghost" flooded into his bloodstream like vodka until his face went red and his knuckles white.

There were things a decent man did, whatever the regulations said, and let any man who hadn't been there be damned.

"Still want to plead guilty?" she asked.

Valentine tried lowering his lifesign. That mental ritual always helped, even when there weren't Reapers prowling. "Prepare your case."

The men in the exercise yard kicked up little rooster tails of fine Arkansas dust—Valentine hadn't seen its like even in Texas; soft as baby powder and able to work its way through the most tightly laced boot—as they walked or threw a pie-tin Frisbee back and forth.

He got to know his three fellow "shooters" there. They took their sourdough bread and soup out as far from the prison as possible and sat next to the six-inch-high warning wire that kept them ten feet from the double roll of fence.

Colonel Alan Thrush was the highest-ranking, not distinguished-looking or brimming with the dash one expects from a cavalry leader. He had short legs and the deft, gentle hands of a fruit seller. "Caught a company of Quislings doing scorched earth—with the families inside—on a little village called McMichael." McMichael had risen against the Kurians in response to the governor's famous "smash them" broadcast shortly after Valentine's move on Little Rock. "Left them for the crows in a ditch."

Unfortunately, his men left the customary set of spurs on the forehead of the Quisling officer in charge, and the commander of a column of infantry following made the mistake of pointing out his handiwork to a pink-cheeked reporter who neglected to mention the charred corpses in McMichael.

Colonel Thrush intended to fight out his court-martial. He said so, slurping a little beet soup from his pannikin.

Valentine was the only major.

Captain Eoin Farland was a clean-faced, attractive man whose wire-rimmed glasses somehow made him even better-looking. A reserve officer who'd been put in charge of a fast-moving infantry company in Archangel, he'd been far out on the right flank on the drive to Hot Springs. His men recaptured a town, stayed just long enough to arm the locals, and when he asked the local mayor what to do with six captured Quislings who had gunned down a farmer hiding his meager supply of chickens and rice, the mayor said, "Shoot them."

"So I did. I'd seen it done before in the drive, especially to Quisling officers."

"But he put it in his day report. Can you believe that?" Thrush laughed. "Shoot, bury, and shut up."

"Says the man who left bodies in a ditch," Farland said.

"Not better, that's for sure," the thin man with the long, honey-colored locks said. Valentine had learned that his last name was Roderick, that he held the rank of lieutenant though he looked on the weary side of forty, and nothing about the charges against him. Every time anyone asked, he shrugged and smiled.

"Are you asking for court-martial?" Valentine asked Farland.

"No. I'm pleading guilty. They've got my paper trail. Something's holding up the show, though, and my trial date keeps getting postponed."

"As does mine," Thrush said.

"What's gonna happen is gonna happen," Roderick said. "I'm asking for lobster and real clarified butter for my last meal. How about that? Better get it."

"Shut up," Thrush said.

"You start planning yours too, Colonel."

Valentine only got one piece of mail his first week in the Nut. It came in an unaddressed envelope, posted from Little Rock, and bore a single line of typescript:

HOW DO YOU LIKE IT?

"You've got a visitor, Major," Young said after the sun called lights out the next day. Valentine wondered if the guard ever got a day off. He'd seen him every day for a week.

Something felt wrong about moving across the prison floor in the dim light. Sounds traveled from far away in the prison: water running, a door slamming, Young's massive ring of keys sounding like sleigh bells in the empty hallway.

Valentine expected to be taken to some kind of booth with a glass panel and tiny mesh holes to speak through, but instead they brought him to a big, gloomy cafeteria on the second floor of the asterisk. Light splashed in from the security floods outside.

Young made a move to handcuff him to a table leg across from a brown-faced man in a civilian suit. Valentine was jealous of the man's clean smell, faintly evocative of sandalwood—in the Nut one got a new smock once a week and clean underwear twice.

Valentine wondered at the smooth sheen of his visitor's jacket. The civilian's gray suit probably cost more than everything Valentine owned—wherever they were storing it now.

"Don't bother, please," the man said, and Young put the handcuffs away. "It's an unofficial meeting. Won't you—"

Valentine sat down. He noticed his visitor nibbled his fingernails; their edges were irregular. Somehow it made him like the man a little better.

"Major Valentine, my name's Sime."

He said the name as though it should provoke instant recognition. Valentine couldn't remember ever having heard it.

Neither man made an offer to shake.

Sime tipped his head back and spoke, eventually. "I'm a special executive of our struggling new republic. Missouri by birth. Kansas City."

"How did you get out?" Valentine asked. Jesus, that used to be the first question he'd ask those fleeing the Kurian Zone in his days as a Wolf. Old habits died hard.

"My mom ran. I was fourteen."

"What's a 'special executive'?" Valentine asked.

"I'm attached to the cabinet."

"That superglue is tricky stuff."

"Quick but dusty, Major."

"You are going to come to the point of this?"

"Tobacco? Maybe a little bourbon?" Sime made no move to produce either, and Valentine wondered if some assistant would emerge from the shadows of the big, dark room.

"No, thanks."

"Trying to make things more pleasant for you."

"You could get me a bar of that soap you used before meeting me."

"How—oh, of course. Ex-Wolf. I'm very sorry about all this, you know."

Valentine said nothing.

Sime leaned forward, placing his forearms on the table with interlaced, quick-bitten fingers forming a wedge pointed at Valentine. "Are you a patriot, Major?"

"A patriot?"

"Do you believe in the Cause?"

Had the man never read his service file? "Of course."

"Body and soul?"

This catechism was becoming ridiculous. "Get to the point."

Sime's eyes shone in the window light. "How would you like to do more to advance the Cause than you've ever done before? Do something that would make the rest of your service—impressive though it is—look like nothing in comparison?"

"Let me guess. It involves the charges against me disappearing. All I have to do is go back into the Kurian Zone and—"

"Quite the contrary, Major. It involves you pleading guilty."

A moment of stunned silence passed. Valentine heard Young shift his feet.

Valentine almost felt the edge of the sword of Damocles hanging above. "That helps the Cause how?"

"Major Valentine. I'm personally involved in—in charge of, in a way, some very delicate negotiations. A consortium of high-level officials in the Kurian Zone—"

"Quislings?"

Sime wrinkled his nose and opened and shut his mouth, like a cat disgusted by a serving of cooked carrots.

"Quislings, if you will," Sime continued. "Quislings who run a substantial part of the gulag in Oklahoma and Kansas. They're offering to throw in with us."

"I see why you use good soap."

"Stop it, Major."

Valentine turned toward Young.

"Listen!" Sime said, lowering his voice but somehow putting more energy into his words. "We're talking about the freedom of a hundred thousand people. Maybe more. An almost unbroken corridor to the Denver Protective Zone. Wheat, corn, oil, livestock—"

"I see the strategic benefits."

Sime relaxed a little. Valentine felt nervous, his dinner of doubtful meatloaf revisiting the back of his throat. "Still don't see how my pleading guilty helps."

"These Quislings are afraid of reprisals. Maybe not to them, but to some of the forces they command. The Provisional Government organizing the new Free Republic wants to show them that we're not going to permit atrocities."

"Show? As in show trial?"

Sime turned his head a little, as though the words were a slap. He looked at Valentine out of one baleful eye.

"You have me. You also have this: plead guilty, and it comes with an offer. You'll get a harsh sentence, most likely life, but the government will reduce it and you'll serve somewhere pleasant, doing useful work. Five years from now, after we've won a significant victory somewhere, your sentence will quietly be commuted to celebrate. You could return to service or we could arrange a quiet little sinecure at a generous salary. When was your last breakfast in bed? I recommend it."

"I have the word of a 'special executive' on that? I've never heard that title before."

"Consider it as coming from your old governor's lips. He knows what you did in Little Rock. I'm speaking for him and for the other members of the Provisional Government."

Valentine took a deep breath.

"Do this, Major, and it'll be the best kind of victory. No bloodshed."

"That's the carrot; where's the stick?"

"You haven't given me an answer yet."

"Let's say I fight it out."

"Don't."

"Let's say I do anyway," Valentine said.

Sime looked doubtful for the first time. "The Garage." The air got ten degrees warmer in the dark of the cafeteria.

"Will you accept a counteroffer?"

"I'm a negotiator. Of course."

"Do you know Captain Moira Styachowski?"

"I know the name from your reports. She served with you on Big Rock."

"Get her in here. I hear that same offer from her, and I'll take it."

"Ah, it has to come from someone you trust. I feel a little hurt, Major. Usually my title—"

"I've had a gutful of titles in the Kurian Zone. You can keep them."

"I'll see what I can do. If she's on active service I might not be able to get her."

"She's the only—no. If you can't get her, get Colonel Chalmers. I've dealt with her before."

Sime extracted a leather-bound notepad and wrote the name down. "She's with?"

"A judge with the JAG."

"Very well. Thank you for your time, Major."

"I have nothing but time."

"Don't be so sure. Take my deal." Sime looked up and waved to Young.

The next day rain tamped down the dust on the exercise yard. The shooters and the looters stayed on opposite sides of the pie slice between the frowning brown wings D and E, trying to keep their pannikins full of lukewarm lentils out of the rain as they sat on long, baseball-dugout-style benches.

"Anyone got an offer from a civilian named Sime?" Valentine asked.

Farland and Thrush exchanged looks and shrugged. Roderick sucked soup out of his tin.

"We're getting pushed back again," Farland said. "God, it's like getting a shot when the doctor keeps picking up and putting down the big-bore needle."

Roderick stopped eating and stared. "I had rabies shots. Harpy bite."

"He said all this is more or less of a show. To convince some gulag Quislings that Southern Command won't just shoot them dead if they join us."

"News to me," Thrush said. He returned his pannikin to the slop bin and returned, twitching up his trousers with his deft little hands before he sat. It took Valentine a moment to remember when he'd last seen that gesture—Malia Carrasca's grandfather in Jamaica would go through that same motion when he sat. "You know, they might be firing smoke to get you to plead out."

"They've tried murderers before," Farland said. "My uncle served with Keck's raiders before they hung Dave Keck. But he killed women and children."

"And Lieutenant Luella Parsons," Roderick said. "When was that, fifty-nine?"

"She shot the mayor of Russelville," Farland put in. He wiped raindrops from his glasses and resettled them.

"Yeah, but she claimed he was working for them. Said she saw him talking to a Reaper."

"I heard they tried General Martinez himself for shooting a couple of Grogs," Roderick said.

"That makes sense," Thrush said. "If you ask me, it's a crime not to shoot 'em."

"Actually it was," Valentine said. "I was there. The two Grogs he shot were on our side."

"First I've heard of it. Were the charges dropped?" Farland asked.

Valentine shook his head.

"You made a powerful enemy, Major," Thrush said. "Martinez had a lot of friends in Mountain Home. He had the sort of command you'd send your son or daughter off to if you wanted to keep 'em out of the fight."

"Technically I was under him during Archangel. His charges are why I'm here, or that's what my counsel says."

"Bastard. Heard he didn't do much," Farland said.

"I wouldn't know. I was over in Little Rock."

Roderick grew animated. "Heard that was a hot one. You really threw some sand in their gears. What was her name, Colonel . . ."

"Kessey," Valentine put in. "She was killed early on in the fighting. Bad luck."

"What are you going to plead, Valentine?" Thrush said.

"Five minutes, gentlemen," a guard yelled, standing up from his seat next to the door.

Everyone was wet. Were they all bedraggled sacrificial sheep? "Haven't made up my mind yet."

Valentine grew used to the tasteless food, and the boring days of routine bleeding into one another and overlapping like a long hospital stay. He took a job in the prison library, but there was so little work to do they only had him in two days a week. He could see why men sometimes marked the days on the wall in prison; at times he couldn't remember if a week or a month had passed.

The weather warmed and grew hot. Even the guards grew listless in the heat. Young brought in two of the pamphlets produced about the fight in Little Rock and had Valentine sign them.

"Turns out I had a cousin in that camp your Bears took. One's for him and one's for his folks."

Part of his brain considered escape. He tried to memorize the schedule of the guard visits to his hallway, tried to make a guess at when the face would appear in the shatterproof window, but their visits were random.

Also, there was the Escape Law. Any person who broke free while awaiting trial automatically had a guily verdict rendered *in absentia*.

He slept more than he was used to, and wrote a long letter to the Miskatonic about the mule list. He labored for hours on the report, knowing all the while that it would be glanced at, a note would be added to another file (maybe!) and then it would be filed away, never to see the light of day again until some archivist went through and decided which documents could be kept and which could be destroyed.

He suggested that further investigation into the mule list was warranted. Anything important enough for the Kurians to put this kind of effort into—and apart from feeding and protecting themselves, the Kurians had few pursuits that Valentine was aware of—might prove vital.

Valentine signed it. His last testament to the Cause?

* * *

Letters arrived in a strung-together mass. Outrage and gratitude from Post, who was on the mend in a convalescent home and had installed Narcisse in the kitchen; wonder from Meadows; a few postcards from his former Razors who had heard about his imprisonment one way or another.

One offered to ". . . come git you Sir. Just send word."

Nothing from Ahn-Kha, which worried Valentine a little. The Golden One could read and write English as well as anyone in his former command, and better than many.

Valentine heard footsteps in the hallway pause, and then a knock at the door.

"Visitor, Major."

This time Corporal Young took him down to a regular visiting room, carrels with glass between allowed for conversation through small holes in the glass—or plastic, Valentine thought when he saw all the scratches. There were fittings for phones but it looked as though the electronics had been taken out.

He waited for a few minutes and then they brought in Moira Styachowski.

She wore good-fitting cammies with her Hunter Staff crossbar on her captain's bars. The only female Bear he'd ever met looked about as healthy as she ever did—just a little pale and exhausted.

"So they got you after all," Valentine said.

"I might say the same about you," Styachowski said in return, then her eyes shifted down. "I'm sorry, I shouldn't have said that. Dumb thing to joke—"

"Forget about it, Wildcard."

She smiled at the handle issued to her the night he'd been burned in the Kurian Tower of Little Rock. "You know who's behind this, right?"

"Yes, that Sime . . ."

"No, the charges. It's Martinez."

"My counselor told me. Seems like a sharp woman."

Styachowski looked down again.

"What?" Valentine asked.

"I was told, Val, in language that was . . . umm, remarkable for its vigor, to come here and tell you to work with Sime on this. The 'vigor' of the language employed made me ask a few questions of a friend at GHQ. So, for the record, take the deal."

Valentine lowered his voice. "Off the record?"

She leaned forward. "It's a setup for the benefit of some Oklahoma Quislings. According to my source at GHQ, Sime said, 'They need to see a few hangings to convince them.' Don't look like that. You've got your deal from Sime."

"Sime says. He's powerful enough to make it happen? Even with a Jagger judge?"

"The representatives"—she said the word with the inflection a bluenose might use to describe workers in a bordello as 'hostesses'—"are here and your trials are due to start. Luckily you were the last one arrested. The others will go first. They'll get their hangings."

"Is there anything you can do?" Valentine asked. So goddamn helpless in here. He felt an urge to lash out, punch the Plexiglas between himself and Styachowski. Perhaps even hit Styachowski, for nothing more than being the bearer of bad news. But the mad flash faded as quickly as it rose.

"I don't have much experience in this. A couple of classes on military law and that farce we had near Magazine Mountain sums up my experience."

"What about the newspapers? Your average townie thinks every Quisling should wind up in a ditch."

"Military trials aren't public. I'll see if I can talk to your counsel. If it makes you feel any better, Ahn-Kha is here. I set him up quietly in the woods nearby. I sent word to that Cat you're partial to but I haven't heard back."

"Who's your source at GHQ?"

Styachowski hesitated. "The lieutenant general's chief of staff, a major named Lambert. Says she remembers you from the war college, by the way."

Dots. Valentine had a feeling back then that she was destined to rise. She practically ran the war college as a cadet.

"Thank her," Valentine said.

"Val, if there's anything else I can do . . ."

"You've already exceeded expectations," Valentine said. "Again. Good-bye."

She visibly gulped. "You did right by those women." Styachowski got up and left, a little unsteadily.

Young escorted him back to his room/cell. "We turned away a visitor for you yesterday, Major. Guards say she was a bit of a meal. Red hair."

So Smoke had drifted into the vicinity after all.

"Turned away?"

"You're to get no visitors except by judge's order. Sorry."

"Is that usual?"

"Not for anyone in Southern Command. Sometimes we try Quislings, redhands, men caught as spies. They're kept I-C if it's thought they know something damaging if it gets out, but you guys are the first of ours."

"Should the lack of precedent worry me?"

"I only work here, Major. But, to tell the truth, it worries me."

Thrush got his trial the next day. He ate his dinner alone and the "shooters" didn't see him until breakfast (reconstituted eggs that tasted like bottom sand). He wasn't inclined to talk about the proceedings.

"My counsel keeps objecting and getting overruled," Thrush said. "Six witnesses for the prosecution. My defense starts today. There was wrangling over the witnesses, my counsel only got two in."

"Do you have any family or friends in the audience?" Valentine asked.

Thrush scowled, pushing his utensils around on his tray. "There's an audience alright. You never saw such a bunch of hatchet faces. Tight-ass Kansas types. I wouldn't be surprised if they are Quislings."

"I'm going to ask for noseplugs if they're there at my trial," Roderick said.

Valentine never saw Thrush again after that meal. Young, wary and somber, told him the verdict and sentence. Valentine wasn't surprised by the verdict but he was shocked at his reaction upon hearing the punishment. The Garage. Death by hanging. Thrush's sentence rang in his ears, rattled around in his head like a house-trapped bird frantic but unable to escape: Death by hanging.

Death by hanging. The Garage. Death by hanging.

Farland went next. The morning of his trial he was almost cheerful. "Hey, I've admitted it. I did wrong and I'll take what's coming, serve time and address cadet classes about humane treatment of prisoners if they want. The court's gotta see this as a case for mercy, right?"

His guilty plea just meant he had to spend less time in the courtroom before hearing his sentence. The trial was over and done with in thirty minutes.

This time, when Valentine asked, Young just shook his head. The guard had a hard time meeting Valentine's eyes.

In the yard that day Roderick didn't eat, he just rocked back and forth on his heels, whistling. Valentine felt he should know the tune but couldn't identify it.

" 'There's No Business Like Show Business,' Val," Roderick supplied.

"Roderick, what did you do that got you in here?"

Roderick shrugged. "Guess it doesn't matter now, since none of us will be telling tales. Rape and murder of a Quisling prisoner. She was sweet and creamy, and I figured they do it plenty to our people. She had the softest-looking brown hair, partly tied up in this red bandanna. Funny. If her hair didn't catch my eye, she would have just been another prisoner walking by. But I had the boys pull her out of line."

"They reported you?"

"No. I felt guilty about it afterwards. Talked it over with a chaplain. He turned me in. Guess I don't blame him. There's got to be a difference between us and them, or what's the point? I'm almost so I want their brand of hemp medicine." He made a hanging motion at his neck with his finger, both gruesome and funny at the same time.

Roderick's words stayed with him for hours. Roderick deserved his fate—if the men saw their officers behaving that way, they'd degenerate into a sexually charged mob the next time . . . *but wait*. How different were their crimes, really—save that Valentine amassed a higher body count? Eight men had died in horrible pain.

In the afternoon he met with Captain Luecke in a little, white-painted room with a big table. She looked a little haggard.

"I was handling Farland's case as well. I thought it was just going to be plea negotiations. I heard something about Sime making you an offer."

"What happened to Thrush?"

"He moved onto death row. They hung him at midnight last night. In front of the witnesses." She took a long drag at her cigarette, and the shaking in her fingers stilled for a moment as the nicotine hit her bloodstream. "Farland will go tomorrow night. Our guests can't afford to stay long. Do Sime's deal."

"Or end up like Thrush and Farland?"

"Maybe they're having you go last for a reason. After a few hangings, the bastards might be willing to see a little mercy."

" 'Blessed are the merciful, for they shall obtain mercy,' " Valentine quoted.

"This last week has been strictly Old Testament, Valentine. Like Leviticus."

"How did your checking on Martinez go?"

"It was quite revealing. I'm glad I wasn't at that trial. Were there really bullets flying in through the windows?"

"The prosecuting officer almost got raped."

Luecke sent a funnel of smoke at the ceiling lights. "There were times I thought a lynch mob coming for some overeager scalp-taker wouldn't be altogether a bad thing. But to see it in real life—"

"It worked out in the end. My defense?"

"You don't have one. Every witness I wanted to call met with the same response from the judge: *Major Valentine is on trial, not General Martinez. Denied.* Valentine, honestly, take Sime's deal. If anyone has the pull to get you off the hook, it's him."

"Pull? What kind of justice system is this?" Valentine asked.

Luecke lit another cigarette from the butt of her first as she took a last drag. "A kind I've never seen before. Take Sime's deal."

"If I don't?"

"I'll do my best. I have a feeling it won't be good enough."

"Can you get me a visitor? There's—"

"Sorry, no. Maybe after sentencing."

"That'll do me so much good," Valentine said.

"You're frustrated. I understand. Go back to your room and think it over. Sime's offer is our only hope."

"Our? You're not going to be standing in the Garage with a rope around your neck by the end of the week."

She crushed her cigarette. "You think I don't feel for the people I defend? It's a rotten world. A lot of the men who wind up here just got an extra spoonful of rottenness. Maybe they were born with it, or maybe it got fed to them in little mouthfuls over their lives. In either case, I do what I can for them."

Valentine put his head in his hands. *Keep it together, Ghost.* "I'm sorry. You've done more for me than I should expect, considering."

"If it makes you feel any better, Val, I did turn up one thing. I couldn't see much of it, but Southern Command did investigate Martinez. There's some kind of intelligence file that I saw cross-referenced in the docs. Whatever they were looking into came up negative, so the file got sealed. You wouldn't know anything about that, would you?"

"All I know is he shot two of my complement. And that he kept a few thousand men drunk and hiding in the hills when Southern Command needed them."

"We'll talk tomorrow morning. It looks like your trial is going to be on Thursday."

Two days.

"Thank you, Captain. You should eat—you don't look so good."

She pulled out a cigarette. "I'm paving my own trip to the Garage with these. See you in sixteen hours."

Valentine spent the next day in a kind of weary anxiety. They would try Roderick in the morning—he was not going to contest the proceedings, so it would go quickly—and then Valentine's trial would begin in the afternoon. He tried to write letters and found himself unable to find words, went through the motions of his job rebinding books at the prison library in a funk, unable to finish anything. He and Luecke met again, but found they had little to say to each other. She simply asked if he'd take Sime's deal. He shrugged and said that he hadn't made up his mind yet, and she said she had the statement for the tribunal ready if he did decide to plead guilty.

Valentine believed any speech she might make would be scrimshaw on a casket. What would happen to him would happen regardless. The only words that would count would be those that would place him in prison, or send him to the Garage.

The hours slipped away until sundown, and the prison slowly bled off the heat it had soaked in during the day. Valentine lay in his cot, arms and legs thrown wide to allow the perspiration to disperse.

There was a knock at the door and Valentine heard keys rattle.

"Room search," Young said.

Valentine knew the routine. They took him to a holding cell—this one had real bars—while two guards searched his room. The process usually took a half hour or so.

This time it took an hour. Were they worried he'd constructed some kind of weapon to use in court?

When they returned him to his cell Valentine noticed the usual cart outside, piled with his linens. Young looked at the other guard. "I'll take it from here, Steve-o."

"You sure?" the guard asked.

"I'm sure. Enjoy your dinner."

Steve-o, the other guard, extended his hand. "Good luck, Major Valentine."

"You mean good luck tomorrow, don't you?" Young said.

"Yeah. That's what I meant."

Valentine shook the hand.

"Just wanted to say I done it," Steve-o said. He wandered down the hall, whistling "There's No Business Like Show Business." Maybe he'd picked the tune up from Roderick.

"You've got a letter," Young said. He looked again at the envelope. "It says that it's not to be delivered to you until after your trial. But we had to check it anyway. No reason we couldn't check it before."

"Of course," Valentine said, wondering.

"Here you go. I get the feeling it's not from a friend."

Valentine saw the same plain envelope and paper. He opened the tri-folded message.

ENJOY THE HANGING. WISH I COULD BE THERE.

Young cleared his throat. "Kind of funny, this person being so sure of your verdict."

"Funny is right," Valentine agreed.

Young extracted a multitool pocketknife, unfolded a screwdriver, and cleaned a black mark from beneath his thumb. A red-painted key jangled from the ring on the knife; Valentine saw it glitter in the dim light coming in from his window. "I've never had a problem with my job before, Major. Most people wind up here, well, they deserve it. The ones that don't get spat back out, usually along with some who do. Better that way than the other. But in sixteen years I've never seen anything like this."

Young pointed to a laundry bag on his bed. "Fresh linens for your bed and a new smock," he said. "Girl in the laundry is new. I think she doesn't read so good. If they screwed up, I'll be back in an hour and fifteen minutes and I'll get you a new set of clothes." He placed the knife in his pocket. "Well, I got to get down to the yard. We got sick dogs tonight and until the vet is done looking at them, it's the two-legged animals that got to walk between the wire. I know the night before a trial is always slow. Hope you get some sleep, eventually."

As he turned, Valentine heard the pocketknife bounce off his boot and hit the floor. It slid under his cot.

"Damn cheap service trousers! Cotton my ass. More like knitted lint," Young said, and slammed the door behind himself—slammed it so hard it didn't close properly. Valentine didn't hear the dead bolt shoot home.

Valentine waited one amazed second, then put his slip-on shoe in between the door and the jamb so it wouldn't close accidentally. He checked his laundry bag. A complete guard uniform, right down to polished shoes and belt, hat, and hankerchief was inside. Valentine read the stitched-on name tag: YOUNG.

"Thank you, Corporal Young."

He got into the uniform. It was a bit roomy, but he didn't look ridiculous once he punched a new hole in the belt with the knife's awl. It was a handy little tool: two kinds of screwdriver, two blades, a saw/fish scaler, a can opener, a file, an awl, and a clipper—though the last didn't look up to the job of cutting the wire in the yard.

He put wadded-up papers—one of them was the mystery note—around his feet so they fit better in the size-twelve shoes.

It occurred to him that if he were to pass as Young at a cursory glance he'd need to be heavier. He wound a sheet around his midsection and put the belt back on at its worn notch.

Feeling hot with excitement he stepped into the hall, trying to walk with his head turned down and handkerchief wiping his nose. He'd never seen cameras in the hall of this part of the prison but he wanted to be safe.

He left the room behind with no regret. When was the last time he slept in the same spot so many days in a row? His cabin in the *Thunderbolt*, most likely.

He walked down the hall in the direction of the edge of the asterisk. Then he stopped in front of a door two down from his. Roderick's.

The man was guilty of an atrocious crime. But if the system was gamed—

Valentine looked through the window. The cot was empty—had Young arranged for two escapes? Then his eyes picked up a figure in the gloom behind the sink/toilet.

Roderick had cheated the hangman.

What looked like a twisted-up sheet was knotted around the sink tap. Roderick was in a sitting position, butt off the floor and held up by his sheet, face purple and tongue sticking out as stiffly as his legs.

He turned away from the window, and looked at the dim hallway light to get the image out of his retinas.

Every other time they'd brought him through the center of the asterisk, but there was a fire exit sign above a heavy door. While he knew some of the routes through the center of the building, there was too much chance of meeting another guard. Valentine tried the red key on the heavy lock, Roderick's purple tongue filling his vision every time he didn't concentrate, and the fire escape door opened. For an aged guard Young thought things through well enough. He listened with hard ears, and heard footsteps somewhere on the floor below.

Valentine slipped off the guard shoes, wincing at the sound of paper crinkling—the tiniest sounds were magnified when one was trying to keep silent—and padded down the stairs to the bottom level.

He searched the door frame leading outside.

The door to the exterior had an alarm on it. Valentine flipped up a plastic access cover and saw a keypad with a green-faced digital readout. Someone had written 1144 on the interior. Valentine passed a wetted thumb over the ink and it smeared easily—it was still fresh. He punched the numbers into the keypad and then hit a key at the bottom marked ENTER.

Nothing changed color.

Every nerve on edge, Valentine pushed open the crash door.

"Thank God for minimum security," he whispered. A real prison would have had at least two more layers of doors.

He put the shined shoes back on. While rugged enough for street wear, he wondered how long they'd last if he had to hike out. His good boots were in storage somewhere in the bowels of the prison complex.

The night air felt cool and clean, but the best thing about it was the amount. Free sky stretched overhead as far as even Cat eyes could see. Valentine drank in the Arkansas night like a shot of whiskey, and even the memory of Roderick's tongue faded . . . a little.

Keeping to the shadows, he walked around the edge of the building. Every now and then he stopped and pulled on a window as though checking to see if it was locked, all the while making for the pathway from the center of the asterisk to the gate in the double wire.

A few lights burned in the subsidiary buildings and the courthouse. Valentine stepped onto the path leading to the gate and strode toward the gate.

He heard high, feminine laughter from the gatehouse.

Valentine sneezed repeatedly into his handkerchief as he stepped into the flood of light around the twin vehicular gates. Valentine had seen the gatehouse in operation often enough; people were supposed to travel through the inside but guards desiring access to the area between the double row of fencing usually just had them open the gates.

Cap pulled low on his head, he looked into the window. Then stopped.

Alessa Duvalier sat on some kind of console, legs prettily crossed though she was in what Valentine thought of as her traveling clothes—a long jacket was folded carelessly next to her, her walking stick, which concealed a sword, next to it.

". . . so the blonde gives birth and asks the doctor, 'How can I be sure it's mine?' " They laughed.

"Shit, how did someone as ugly as Young end up with you?"

"Kindness," Duvalier said. "He's a very kind man."

"If you ever want to trade him in on a newer model . . ." the young guard said. He sputtered with laughter as he waved casually at Valentine—not taking his eyes off Duvalier—and Duvalier said, "Oh, let me!" She thumped something without waiting for permission and the twin gates hummed as they slid sideways on greasy tracks. Valentine nipped out of sight of the gate and walked quickly down the road.

Valentine heard a thump from behind, a door open, and then quick footsteps as Duvalier caught up.

She pulled him off the road and gave him a brief embrace, nuzzling him under the chin with her nose. "I can never leave you alone, can I?"

"My luck always turns whenever you're not around," Valentine admitted.

"If they arrested everyone who ever quietly shot a Quisling . . ." she said.

"Let's not mention arrests or prisons for a while, alright? As of this moment I'm a fugitive from justice subject to the Escape Law."

"It's not so bad. My whole life, I've been a fugitive from just about everything," she said.

"What's the plan?" Valentine asked.

"That's your end. But I've got a start under way. Oh, that Corporal Young's a good man. We need to burn those clothes."

"You've got replacements?"

"They're with Ahn-Kha."

She turned him into the woods and an owl objected, somewhere. Valentine heard the soft flap of bats above, hunting insects in the airspace between branches and ground.

They stopped to listen twice, then found a burned-out house. A transport truck with a camouflaged canvas-covered back sat in front of it. Valentine marveled at it. The ruins of the garage held a small charcoal fire and a very large, faun-colored Grog.

"My David," Ahn-Kha said. "We have escaped again."

"If we're still at liberty in twenty-four hours I'll call it an escape. Where'd you get the truck?"

"Styachowski requisitioned us a transport," Duvalier said.

Valentine stripped out of his uniform, and Duvalier flitted about gathering up the guard's clothing.

Ahn-Kha handed him a too-familiar dun-colored overall.

"Labor Regiment?" Valentine said.

"It goes with the truck," Duvalier said. "The big boy looks like he could do a hard day's work with a shovel."

"And you?"

She covered her fiery red hair with a fatigue cap. "I'm management. You two look like the all-day lunch-break type. Besides Val, you're the suckiest kind of driver."

"Where do we go?" Ahn-Kha asked. "My people will gladly shelter us at Omaha."

"We'd have to cross half of Southern Command. No, let's go east."

Duvalier climbed into her own overall and zipped it up over freckled shoulders. "East? Nothing there but river and then the Kurians. Until the Piedmont."

"I have an old friend in the Yazoo Delta. And I've got a mind to visit Memphis."

"Memphis? The music's to die for, but the Kurians see to it that you do the dyin'." She sprinkled something that smelled like kerosene out of a bottle onto the clothes and tossed them on the charcoal. They began to burn with admirable vigor.

"Ali, I've got my claws into a job. I'm wondering more and more about Post's wife, Gail."

"She's gotta be dead if she was shipped."

"No, she was some kind of priority cargo. I'll explain later. We need to go to the area around Arkansas Post on the river. Can you manage that?"

"Says the guy who just broke out of a high-security lockup thanks to me!" Duvalier chided.

"Medium security," Valentine said.

She tossed her bundle of traveling clothes and sword stick into the back of the truck. "How do I look?"

"You're better suited singing in the Dome than for the Labor Regiment," Valentine said.

"Gratitude! The man's got a vocablarney like a dictionary and he doesn't know the meaning of the word!"

"Please," Ahn-Kha said. "We had best be going."

The truck bumped eastward along the torn-up roads. A substantial piece of Consul Solon's army had been borrowed from the area around Cairo, Illinois, and points east, and they had employed a spikelike mechanism called a paveplow to destroy the roadbeds as they went home.

Patching was still being done, so most vehicles found it easier to drive on the gravel shoulder.

Duvalier drove, Ahn-Kha rode shotgun—with his formidable gun pointing out through the liftable front windscreen to rest on the hood—and Valentine bounced along in the back, feeling every divot the worn-out shock absorbers struck and hanging onto the paint-and-rust frame for safety.

About noon he felt the truck lurch to a stop.

"Just a road check," Duvalier said through the flap separating the driver from the cargo bed. "Rounders."

Valentine's stomach went cold. There was an old riot gun in the back, but he couldn't shoot his fellow citizens, even if it meant being rearrested.

"Afternoon, digger," Valentine heard a voice say from up front.

"Transport warrant and vehicle check. Jesus, that's some big Grog. He trained?"

"He's a citizen. Sick relief to Humbolt Crossing," Duvalier said, cool as ever. "There's the medical warrant. We've got an unidentified fever in the back, so you want to keep clear."

"Do we?" another voice said. "We'll have to risk it. Orders to check every vehicle. We had a breakout at the military prison in Mountain Home."

"Someone important, I take it," Duvalier said.

"David Valentine, part-Indian, black hair, scar on right side of face."

Duvalier again: "Never heard of him. He run over a general's dog?"

Valentine heard footsteps approaching the bed. There was nowhere for him to hide inside. He might be able to cut his way onto the roof. He reached for the knife, opened the saw blade . . .

"Killed some Quisling prisoners, they say."

"He use too many bullets?" Duvalier said.

"Whoa, Sarge, we got someone back here."

Light poured into the back of the truck, hurting Valentine's eyes and giving him an instant headache. The hole was only big enough to put his head through.

Valentine heard a harsh whisper from Duvalier.

"Well, well, well," one of the Rounders said.

"He doesn't look too sick," the one with sergeant's tabs agreed. "Wouldn't you say, slick."

That's it. Trapped. Back to trial.

"No."

"This look like our Quisling killer to you?"

The other squinted. "No, Sarge. Five-one and Chinese, three gold teeth; no way this is our man."

"I should get my eyes checked," the sergeant said, writing something down. "I need to erase, because I see a six-six black individual with a big tattoo of Jesus on his chest. Oh, crap, this stop form looks like shit now." He tore a piece of printed paper off his pad, wadded it in one massive hand, and tossed it over his shoulder.

"Anyway, it ain't our killer."

"No, that's not David Valentine," the sergeant said, winking.

"Too bad, in a way," the other said. "Old friend of mine, Ron Ayres, fought under him in Little Rock. I'd buy this Major Valentine a drink, if I could."

"So you've told me. About a hundred times," the sergeant said, closing the back flap.

Valentine listened to the boot steps return to the front of the vehicle.

"Okay, get your sick man outta here before we all catch it," the sergeant said. "I'd turn south for Clarendon about three miles along; there's an old, grounded bus shell with RURAL NETWORK PICKUP J painted on it alongside the road. No roadblocks that way to slow up your sick man, and I think this thing can make it through the wash at Yellow Creek."

"Thank you, Sergeant."

"Thank you for having such a pretty smile. Pleasant journey."

And thank you, old friend of Ron Ayres, Valentine thought.

Six

The Lower Mississippi, July: The river has reverted to feral since the cataclysm of 2022, a continent-crossing monster unleashed. The carefully sculpted and controlled banks of the twentieth and early twenty-first century are gone, or survive as tree-lined islands surrounded by some combination of marsh, lake, and river.

Even on the best and sunniest days, the Mississippi can only manage a rather lackluster blue between banks lined with opportunistic shellbark hickory, willow, and river birch. It is more frequently a dull navy, muddy brown at the edges, striped in the center by wind and broken by swirls or flats created by snags, shallows, and sandbars. Below the Missouri and Ohio joins, the flooded river is sometimes three miles wide, and moves at a steady four miles an hour toward the Gulf of Mexico, carrying with it rich loads of silt—some insignificant fraction of which will be dredged up and placed into the vast rice paddies around the partially flooded Crescent City. The rest accumulates here and there, gradually changing the course and shape of the Father of Waters.

The days of tugs churning up- or downriver with a quarter mile of linked barges are gone, along with many of the navigational aids. Barge traffic now looks more like a truck convoy, with various sizes of small craft and tugs pushing a few barges along the river in a long, thin column, led and flanked by small powerboats checking the navigability of the ever-changing river. The Memphis–New Orleans corridor is especially well guarded against quick strikes or artillery attacks by the roving forces of Southern Command, always on the lookout for a chance to seize a few bargeloads of grain, rice, or beans. If they are very lucky, sometimes they free a load of human currency from the Kurian trade system.

Of course the Kurians fight back, in a manner. Booby-trapped barges, or "Q-craft," loaded with mercenaries give the raiders an occasional unpleasant surprise.

There is one long stretch of river, flanked by a northward bend on one end and a southward hook downriver, that causes the barge captains to press close to the unfriendly western side. This is the "Tunica Sands," a stretch of river between Tunica and Memphis avoided by all the river rats as though it was cursed ground. Ten great, weed-choked casino barges on the eastern bank are now landlocked thanks to silt deposits all around their keels. Like a latter-day leper colony, the entire area is surrounded by fencing and watch posts.

Only the sick, under Reaper escort, go in. Only the Reapers come out again.

The big Cat hadn't changed much in the eight years since Valentine had last seen him. A little less hair perhaps, a little more waistline certainly, but he was still the big, half-aquatic athlete of the Yazoo swamps with a satchel full of apples. Everready had taught Valentine how to lower lifesign and move without being noticed over the course of one impossibly hot summer, and the fact that he'd survived to return proved the effectiveness of his tutor's methods.

The New Orleans Saints ball cap was gone, though. Now he wore a black, broad-brimmed hat that made him look like a missionary. Strung Reaper teeth rattled at his neck, and layers of bullet-stopping Reaper robe hung off his body in an oversized tunic that no sane man dared call a dress.

Finding him had been surprisingly easy. While casting about for a way to get across the Mississippi they came upon a "summer out" Wolf patrol in charge of monitoring river traffic. The Wolf patrol relied on Everready for information on the opposite bank in the Yazoo Delta between Vicksburg and Memphis, and the trio crossed the river in a birch-bark canoe with a guide who rested and camped with them at the rendezvous until the legendary Cat appeared to trade supplies for data.

Everready had no young Wolves to train this year, further evidence of the still-echoing disruption of Solon's occupation, and the continuing absence of the Lifeweavers. "Good to have you back, David," he said, upon greeting them. "Even an old swamp-hound gets lonely now and then."

So he was willing, after concluding his exchange with their Wolf guide, to take Valentine and company into Memphis.

"Only four ways into that town, barring being brought in in handcuffs and bite-guard," Everready said in their first camp on the trip north.

They looked like four spirits around their Yazoo swamp campfire, the humans under individual shrouds of mosquito netting, while Ahn-Kha followed the Grog manner by pasting his sensitive face and ears under a layer of mud.

"There's the river," Everready explained. "They check everybody at the river, and they're damn good at spotting fake documents, and most visitors are kept to the Riverfront anyway. Then there's the wall. There are gaps at the rock wall, of course, but the smugglers have gone to a lot of trouble to open them and watch 'em, and they won't let you through for free. Then there are the road gates, but it's the same problem, another document check. Most people who come to trade do it at Little City around Memphis, then the middlemen the Memphis authorities know and trust go through the gates with their goods."

"That's three ways in," Ahn-Kha said.

Everready shifted an apple stem to the other side of his mouth. "Yes, sir, Mister Grog, that's only three ways. The fourth is a bit tricky—it's up along the Tunica Run. Tunica's a dumping ground for those that got the ravies bug—Memphis buys 'em cheap off their fellow Kurians and dumps them in Tunica so there's always a feed on for their Reapers. Every now and then they release a batch on the west side of the river to give the Free Territory folks a little trouble, too."

Everready cracked his knuckles. "If you're careful, really careful, you can move north through the ravies colony. It's really just a big wall there, and one gate. They watch the gate and patrol the wall, but not too heavily. Ravies types aren't into engineering ways over or under the wall. Too busy chasing their own tails."

"So what's in Memphis that's worth all that security?" Duvalier asked. Valentine thought she looked like a silent-film starlet, with face glowing in the firelight behind the layer of netting.

"The banks," Everready said.

Her voice rose a notch. "Banks? There aren't banks any more."

"Yes, there are," Everready said. "Only kind of banks that matter to the Kurians. Big marshaling yards for the transhipment of humans."

"Tell her why," Valentine said.

"Logistics," Everready said. "Memphis is only a day's rail from every big city on the eastern seaboard, plus parts of the Midwest and Texas—the parts your boys haven't took yet, that is. It's why ol' FedEx was headquartered there, too. Some Kurian in Kansas buys tractors from Michigan; he sends authorization to the bank in Memphis to ship up three hundred folk or whatever the price was. They're on the next train to Detroit. Those yards are a sight to see. Let me ask you the same question. What's so important in Memphis that you're willing to risk going in?"

"We're looking for someone," Valentine said.

"Unless he got a job in one of the camps—"

"She," Duvalier corrected.

Everready shrugged. "Unless she got a job in one of the camps—wait, is she a looker?"

"She's attractive enough, but there's more to it," Valentine said.

"What do you mean, more?"

Valentine tried to explain the mule list to Everready as concisely as possible. The old Cat thought it worth another apple; he carved off slices for the other three and then gnawed at the remaining wedge himself.

The fruit tasted like candy to Valentine.

"There's this big ol' boy named Moyo who runs all the girls inside the wall. Always has his men checking inbound shipments for beauty. He's got a regular harem; half the large-scale pimps south of the Ohio buy from him. He employs bounty hunters to comb the hills east of here to bring in folks to swap out when one of his men spots a pretty girl. Kurians don't really care—what's the difference between one dollar coin and another? Moyo does a lot of high-priority transshipping. He'd be the first place I'd look for more on this mule list of yours, if it really is all women."

After that he and Valentine spent a few minutes looking at maps—Everready chuckled that he hardly used the maps anymore, he knew the ground between Memphis and Vicksburg so well—and planning the hike north.

"We should jog east a bit at the Coldwater. I got a store of captured gear you three can draw from." Everready flicked his fingers at Valentine's disintegrating guard shoes, and Valentine wondered if he was going to get the old lecture about how there's no reissue on feet.

"How's Trudy?" Valentine asked, jerking a netting-shrouded chin at Everready's ancient carbine. The well-oiled stock glowed in the firelight.

"Still saving my life."

"And the Reaper-teeth collection?"

"Seventy-one and counting."

"All from fair fights, right?"

Everready made a move to box his ears. "Valentine, how you think I got this old? Only time I even get into a scrap with a Reaper is when they's so disadvantaged it's hardly a fight a'tall."

* * *

Valentine woke to the smell of chickory coffee.

Everready and Duvalier were the only ones up. Ahn-Kha lay in a snoring heap, wrapped around his gun like a snake that had swallowed a bullock before retiring to a too-small tree.

He listened to the conversation as he shifted around, feeling for creepy-crawlies. He missed his old hammock.

"I didn't know Cats got as old as you. I thought we were all done by thirty."

"For a start, I stay in territory I know better than they do. I don't make a lot of trouble, I'd rather let my eyes and ears do the work."

"Don't the Lifeweavers ever have you—"

"I think they've forgotten about ol' Everready. But that's fine with me. I like to fight with my own set of priorities. I suppose that's how I ended up in this swamp."

"Seems lonely. Do you go into Memphis often?" she asked.

"No, they know my face there. Not that I wouldn't mind visiting the pros down at the Pyramid. Your pretty face makes me feel twenty years younger."

"Wish I could help—but . . ."

Valentine wondered what the silence portended.

"You're lucky. He's a good man. But be careful working with someone you got that kind of feeling for. The moment will come, maybe you'll have just a split second to move, and you'll move wrong 'cause of your feelings. You'll both wind up dead."

Valentine kept absolutely still.

Everready went on: "Don't look like that. Just one ol' hound's opinion. If I knew what I was talking about I'd have some hardware on my collar and be giving orders, right?"

"Let's see about breakfast."

"I'll check the crawfish traps. Better use the big pot. That Grog can eat."

Valentine waited to open his eyes until he felt the tip of Duvalier's boot. "You can wake up Ahn-Kha," she said. "When he stretches in the morning his gas drops the birds."

Everready's cache showed his usual craftiness. He kept medical supplies, preserved food, and weapons in several spots between the Yazoo and the Mississippi; the problem was keeping the gear away from scavengers. Humans could use tools and animals could smell food through almost any obstacle. In the Coldwater Creek cache he had solved the problem by burying his supplies behind a house and then placing a wheelless, stripped pickup body over it.

Ahn-Kha stood watch in a high pine while they excavated the cache.

"The engine block's still in this so she's a heavy SOB," Everready explained, retrieving a wire-cored rope from the house's chimney. The rope he fixed to the trailer hitch. Then he tied his Reaper-robe top around the base of a tree, looped the rope around it, and fixed it.

"Here you go, young lady," he said, handing the line to Duvalier.

She hardly had to lean as she applied a transverse pull to the center of the rope. The truck pivoted a few feet, exposing some of the dirt and a few hardy creepers beneath the pickup bed. Everready tightened it again and she slid the pickup body another meter toward the tree.

"Why the material around the tree?" Valentine asked.

Everready checked under the dashboard on the passenger side and then pulled out a folding shovel with a gloved hand. "So the bark doesn't strip. You'd be surprised how clever some scavengers are."

The heavy-duty garbage bags within had further items wrapped up inside them: a few guns thick with protective grease, boxes of ammunition, a large box of red pepper—ideal for throwing off tracking dogs—and a pair of shin-top-high camouflage-pattern boots.

"You and I have about the same size foot, I think," Everready said as Valentine grabbed up the snakeproof boots like a miner spotting a golden nugget. "There are some good socks rolled up in that coffee tin. An extra pair should make up the difference." Valentine smiled when he looked in the tin. It also contained a half-dozen old "lifetime" batteries with a logo of a lightning-bolt-like cat jumping through a red circle. Everready liked to leave the twelve-volt calling cards in the mouths of his kills.

He brought up a cardboard box full of a dozen familiar blue tins.

"Spam?" Valentine asked.

"Naw. This was part of a larger shipment going to the resistance farther east. I took a small expeditor's fee for getting the pony train there. There's plastic explosive inside the cans, you just got to pop the lid—there's even a layer of pork at the top." He passed up another bag. "Three kinds of detonators. One looks like a wind-up alarm clock, one's in this watch but you have to hook it to the batteries in this flashlight, and the others are straight fuses made to look like shoelaces, while the detonators are made to look like nine-volt batteries. Your armorers are clever."

Everready unrolled a chamois and handed a 9mm Beretta up to Duvalier. "This is a nice little gun, young lady."

"I'll take that Mossberg twelve-gauge," she said, pointing at a cluster of long guns. "Folding stock. Dreamy."

"Don't you think you'll stand out a bit in Memphis?"

"Not after I rope it up inside my coat."

"Your duster's going to look strange in this heat," Valentine said.

"Not if I'm mostly naked under it."

"Hope you're not looking for trouble in Memphis. Hard to get into. Harder to get out of. Valentine, since you're going to be posing as a reel looking to add a few new faces to his line, you'll want something with a little flash. I took this off a wandering guitar man in a swap meet card game."

He picked up a sizeable clear plastic food-storage container and broke the seal. A long, silver-barreled automatic pistol rested inside with a shoulder holster and spare magazines. The gun was nickel-plated and would reflect light from miles away—no wonder Everready stuck it in a hole. "You don't mind .22, do you?"

"For this kind of job I'd prefer it. It's quiet."

"Only took you four years and some to add that word to your vocabulary," Duvalier observed.

"And what else?" Everready said in his old talking-with-milk-chinned-young-Wolves tone.

"It's light so you can carry a lot, and it's a nice varmint round for when you get hungry."

"Exacto! Now let's get you a longarm. Where did I put that sumbitch?" He rooted through the guns and found a zipped-up case. "Here we are."

He extracted a gleaming bullpup battle rifle. "This here is real US Army Issue," he said, as another man might speak of a Rothschild vintage or a Cuban cigar. "Took this off some half-assed commandos outta Jackson eight years back. Called a Tacsys U-gun, 'u' for universal. There's four interchangeable barrels and actions so she can shoot 9mm, 5.56, 7.62 with a sniper barrel, or you can open her up and feed her shotgun shells. Used to have a silencer, but I rigged it to a rifle I lost. Sorry. Nice little four-power scope up top. Wish I could give you the grenade launcher for it."

Valentine checked the customizable sling. "This is great. But you keep Trudy?"

"A man doesn't give up on the girl he loves for a hotter model. Even if she's sporting polycarbon rifling.

"Good gear means flash in the KZ. Don't have the full manual but there's a card in the case that you should be able to figure out."

"Speaking of flashing, he could use a change of clothing," Duvalier said, already cleaning her Mossberg.

"Clothes will be a little harder, but I think I've got an old officer's trench coat in here. Very nice waterproofing and only one small, stain-free hole."

"You ready for this, Valentine?" Everready asked. "All your shots up to date?"

They rested atop a stripped Kenworth parked outside Tunica, within heavy-duty fencing and mounds of rubble blocking the roads south of the city, out of the line of sight of the nearest sentry tower, spaced miles apart on this, the less-critical south side of Tunica.

"So we just have to move slowly?" Valentine asked, loading the U-gun.

"Not so much slow as smooth," Everready said. "No sudden moves. I'm not saying a cough will set them off. Just that it could."

"Ahn-Kha, you'll be okay here for a few days?" Valentine asked.

"There is food and water. I will stay in the cab of this fine vehicle at night, and under those trees in the day. Are they less active at night?"

"Depends," Everready said. "If a few start prowling around, sometimes others join them. Then you get a mob mentality. They go off easier in groups."

Duvalier climbed up and hung off one of the rearview mirror posts and looked north into town. The mirrors themselves were gone. "I see one," Duvalier said. "By the traffic light that's touching the road."

Valentine saw it too. A distant figure staggered back and forth across the street, leaning forward as though trying to tie his shoes as he walked.

"Poor souls," Valentine said.

Everready slowly slid off the top of the truck. "Lots more, closer to the old casinos. That's where the missions organize themselves. That one's probably lost and hungry.

"Okay, kiddies, got your iodine?"

Valentine and Duvialier touched their breast pockets and nodded. Valentine had a big bottle, half full, courtesy of Everready's stockpile, and Duvalier had a stoppered hip flask holding the other half.

"You get bit, first thing you do is get clear and iodine it good. Even if you've had your shots the damn thing mutates sometimes, and who knows what strain is in there. Plus it'll save you an infection. Lots of these have hepatitis along with their other problems."

They started down the old road. "And don't shoot unless it's life or death. It'll just get 'em screaming, and between the shots and the screams you'll have a hurtin' of psychos on you before you know it."

Everready set an even pace, the old Cat rocking a little back and forth, like a ship rolling on the ocean. Valentine walked behind, U-gun across his chest in its hands-free sling. Behind him he heard the steady footsteps of Duvalier, pacing her feet to Everready's rhythm.

Valentine had only had one brief brush with ravies sufferers, on the Louisiana border. Southern Command generally shot those who succumbed to the disease once their minds went and they didn't understand what was happening anymore. He'd never seen the aftereffects before.

Seen? Smelled, more like.

Tunica had once been a pretty town, Valentine suspected, fragrant of the magnolias and dogwoods beloved by the residents. Now it smelled like a pig farm. Everready paused at the edge of what had been a park running through the center of town. The three of them stood opposite an old bronze statue of three weary-looking soldiers, the two on the ends supporting a wounded comrade in the center. Everready used the rifle of the one on the left to climb atop the bronze shoulders.

"The kudzu's been cut back from here," Duvalier said. The growth choked most of the rest of the park.

"Probably the Mission people," Everready said, covering his eyes as he looked around. Valentine heard cats spitting at each other somewhere in the park. "See those basins? Food and water. And there they are. Over by the pharmacy."

Valentine saw two heads bobbing among the growth. Both men, with stringy-looking beards. They moved like sleepwalkers, the second following the first.

"Careful now," Everready said. "If anyone hears an engine let me know; my ears aren't what they used to be. Memphis dumps off fresh cases in the center of town sometimes."

They crossed over to one of the main streets. Valentine saw that what he had thought were only two individuals were six; hollow-eyed, tight-cheeked, and knob-kneed. Some shorter women and even a child followed the first two.

Everready walked slowly and smoothly, like a man treading across a pool. Piles of feces lay scattered in the streets and alleys, drying in the summer sun. Valentine saw rats in the alleys, sniffing at the odious piles. Cats filled every shady windowsill and step, watching the rats. A pair of kittens watched them from beneath a wheeled Dumpster.

Valentine put his finger on the U-gun's trigger guard as the slow-moving train of people—or what had once been people—approached.

The two files passed each other, the ravies victims' faces spasming in a parody of vocalization, black-toothed mouths opening and shutting but no sound in their throats but dry wheezes. They looked sunburned and leathery. A few wore stained gray cotton smocks with URM stenciled on the chests and backs.

The little girl seemed a bit more animated than the rest; she pointed and waved.

Everready ignored her.

"URM?" Valentine asked when the group had passed.

"United Relief Missions. Old school Christians. Down at the riverfront. Memphis lets them operate sort of as independents because they keep these folks alive, or what passes for it."

"Looks like they feed themselves, too," Duvalier said, pointing at the corpse of a cat with her walking stick. The cat's midsection had been torn out.

"Wish it would rain," Everready said. "The town's a little better after a good rain."

They crossed a street, and Valentine saw a heap of bodies, mostly nude, on the steps of what looked like a neo-Georgian city hall. One kicked and another rolled over.

"Like hogs in a wallow. The cement gets cool at night," Everready said.

They passed through streets of homes, trees buzzing with cicadas, perhaps one house in three burned to the ground and the others crawling with cats and inhabited by crows. Valentine saw a larger flock gather and disperse around the crotch of a tree, and found the scavengers feeding on a corpse hanging in a backyard tree like a body draped over a saddle.

"That's Reaper work," Valentine said. "Last night, by the look of it."

"Uh-huh," Everready agreed. "When pickings are slim in Memphis they come down here to feed. Memphis buys ravies cases cheap from all across the country and dumps them here, sort of a walking aura reserve. I'm told they stay alive for years—till an infection gets them."

"I didn't know they still used it except to cause us trouble," Valentine said.

"I've heard of them dosing each other's populations when they feud. Or to put down revolts. See, nobody in the KZ gets inoculations except for Quislings."

"How much farther?" Duvalier asked. "This smell is getting to me. I'm getting sick. Seriously, Val . . ."

Everready pulled a little tin from his belt and set it on a stone-and-bar wall in front of one of the houses. He dabbed something from a green bottle on his finger. "Just camphor," he said, and wiped it under her nose. "Breathe through your mouth."

"Better," Duvalier said.

Another pair of rail-thin shamblers wandered near the corpse in the tree. Valentine could have counted their ribs. "I don't like how that one is looking around."

"Smells blood. Blood smell sets them off," Everready whispered, not taking his eyes from them as he mechanically repocketed his first-aid tin. "Best not to move, just stand here. Like those statues at the memorial."

Two crows held a tug-of-war over a piece of viscera.

"Oh God—" Duvalier said.

Valentine could never decide which sound hit his ears first after Duvalier's retch. The wet splash of vomit was certainly louder, heard with his right ear. The high-pitched wailing from the left startled him more, bringing back all the emotions of his first small-unit action as a junior Wolf lieutenant. Perhaps they arrived simultaneously.

Valentine clutched Duvalier's hand and pulled her to her feet. Her walking stick clattered to the ground and Everready grabbed it, unslinging Trudy and running with the carbine in one hand and the stick in the other.

"Follow me!" Everready called. "Don't shoot, you'll just draw more!"

Duvalier came off her feet again, wet-mouthed, unable to control her stomach. Valentine released his weapon and picked her up in a fireman's carry.

He followed Everready up a short slope to an intersection.

"Let me down, I'm okay," Duvalier said.

Valentine went to one knee. He looked back and saw a dozen or so figures running in a more or less arrow-shaped formation. At this distance their bare feet were so dirty that most looked as though they were wearing black shoes and socks.

Kudzu-covered, tree-filled service stations and fast-food restaurants lined the road leading toward the casinos, according to an ancient brown sign. Everready almost leaped across the highway toward a small doughnut shop. A shriek from the direction of the Mississippi let them know that trouble would soon be running in from a second direction.

"Why not the bank?" Valentine yelled. A little way up the road a stout-looking brick structure promised safety—for money or those fleeing psychotics—from behind a wall of scrub pine.

"Too big. Can't stop them from getting in."

Valentine heard footsteps just behind. So sick but able to run so fast . . .

He dropped behind Duvalier and turned, holding the U-gun by barrel and grip. A swift-running young screamer got the butt in his face as he reached for Valentine. He went down, rolling. Valentine shifted his grip and employed the gun in a credible backhand.

The screamer didn't get up again.

There was no glass in the door or the windows. Everready vaulted over the counter and entered the cooking line. The display cabinet held nothing but empty trays and an oversized wasp nest.

Valentine ran around a permanently parked car and entered the formerly white doughnut stop. Duvalier had tears in her eyes as she covered the front of the store with her pump-action.

"In here. Help me with this!" Everready called.

They fled into the cooking line, and Everready and Valentine moved a fryer to block the path to the narrow kitchen. The lighting seemed wrong—Valentine looked up and saw a hole in the roof. Weather or animal activity had enlarged it to the size of a picture window.

Everready emptied the damp mess resting within a plastic garbage can and wedged it above the fryer as Valentine heard screams from within the doughnut shop.

"Nice scouting," Valentine said, pointing to the hole in the roof.

"Hope they don't climb up there," Duvalier said, shifting her shotgun muzzle from the barricade to the roof hole.

Everready put his back to the fryer. Its rear was festooned with smeared warnings. "Planning nothing, never been in here to scavenge. I'd be shocked if there wasn't a hole in the roof of most of these places."

Pounding and screaming came through from the other side of the fryer, horribly loud, horribly near. Valentine fought the urge to run to the other end of the kitchen.

"Valentine, help me hold this—no, the plastic can, they're trying to crawl over! Girl, check the back, there might be a door!" Everready said.

Duvalier hurried to the other end of the kitchen and disappeared around a corner. Two shotgun blasts followed immediately.

"Oh shit," Everready swore.

Duvalier flew back into the kitchen, her coat billowing and bringing the smell of cordite as she turned and braced herself against a tall refrigerator. "There's a door. Or there isn't—that's the problem."

"How many?" Valentine asked.

"How many are there?" she shot back.

"Thousands," Everready said.

"Sounds about right," Duvalier said.

They came, more like a single organism comprised of screaming heads and waving arms than a series of individuals, filling the kitchen with noise. Valentine brought his U-gun to bear, feeling the pounding on the other side of the fryer against his back.

"The roof!" Valentine shouted, firing. "Go, Ali!"

"I can jump better than either of you. I'll cover you."

More appeared and Valentine didn't wait to argue. He stood on a prep table and tossed his weapon up through the hole, hoping he didn't overthrow and land it in the parking lot. He grabbed an electrical conduit pipe and pulled himself up, got his foot into a light fixture, and climbed. The roof was thick with growth, and disturbed butterflies hurried into the sky.

Everready passed up his gun to Valentine, and Valentine heard Duvalier's Mossberg.

"Forget the packs!" she shouted.

Everready made it to the roof with less difficulty than Valentine.

Duvalier crouched to spring up through the hole in a single leap and they were on her. She spun like a dynamo, slamming one against the fryer, even now moving from the pressure at the other side, screaming as another sank its teeth into her shoulder.

"Goddamn!" Everready swore as yet another grabbed her.

Though mad, though they felt no pain, her attackers weren't Reapers. She pushed one off, kicked another, punched a third, pale limbs and coat a whirling blur of motion. Everready shot a fourth with his carbine.

Valentine dropped back through the hole.

"No!" Everready shouted.

Valentine picked up her sword cane and used it as a club, swinging at the heads and arms coming around the fryer.

"Jump!" Valentine yelled as Everready shot another one down. Valentine struck a ravie on the floor as it clawed at her ankle; his kick broke its jaw.

Duvalier crouched and jumped, and went up through the hole like a missile.

Valentine drew the blade from Duvalier's sword stick. Using the wooden tube in his other hand, he battered his way back toward the office. He felt hands clutch at his canvas boots and broke the grip—if they were snakeproof they'd probably be ravies-resistant—then cracked one across the jaw.

"Val, where are you going?" Duvalier shouted.

"Lemme at that bite, girl!" he heard Everready say.

"Diversion!" he shouted.

Screaming his own head off, Valentine rushed into the office. The back wall had bloody splatters and buckshot holes. A staggered ravie, holding himself up on the desk, received Valentine's boot to his chest, throwing him back onto one coming through the door. Valentine pinned the fresher one like a bug on a piece of Styrofoam with the sword point and vaulted through the door, running.

"Olly olly oxen free!" Valentine shouted, banging a Dumpster with the wooden half of Duvaliers sword cane. "Come out, come out, wherever you are. London Bridge is falling down!" He hurried around into the next parking lot, banging on empty car hoods.

Ravies turned and began to run toward him, screaming. *Fine, better the oxygen flowing out of their pipes than into their bloodstreams.*

"Meet me by the casinos tonight!" Valentine shouted to the pair on the roof. He saw Everready applying a dressing and the iodine bottle to Duvalier's shoulder.

"Come out, come out, wherever you are!" Valentine called again. "Hey diddle diddle, the freak and the fiddle—"

The doughnut shop began to empty, and other ravies hurried up from the direction of the riverfront.

Just about. Just about!

"Ring around the rosy!"

The last few around the doughnut shop turned toward him.

"Warriors, come out to play-yay!" Valentine didn't know what childhood game the last one signified, but an old Wolf in Foxtrot Company used to employ the taunt on hidden Grogs, clinking a pair of whiskey bottles together.

He ran.

The ravies followed, screaming.

Ten minutes later and a mile away . . .

His bad leg ached, but he had to ignore it. Ignore everything but the staggered line of ravies running behind him. Valentine turned another corner, his third right through the suburban streets in a row. The pursuers were screaming less, growing weaker—which was just as well; he didn't know how long he could hold out.

Two more blocks, one more. He summoned the energy for one final sprint to the last turn, running with the sword cane like a baton in a relay race. His speed came at the cost of a deep, deep burn in his legs and lungs—

And there they were, a few stumbling ravies in a line, following the ones ahead of them, emitting an occasional strangled yelp. The very end of the long file of pursuers, formed into a wagon-train-like circle around six square blocks of Tunica suburbs.

Valentine marked the crash scene he'd seen the first time he ran down this street, impossibly compact cars piled into each other in a rear-end collision, looking like the skeletons of two mating turtles. He staggered behind the cars and sank to his knees, desperately trying to control his panting.

He peered between the cars, looking for his pursuers.

They followed his path onto the tree-limb-littered street, caught sight of their fellows, and ran to catch up to them.

Valentine was too tired to smile.

He crept through the underbrush of a lawn, counted twenty of the pack chasing their own tails. Already some were giving up, dropping to their knees and scratching at the accumulated leaves and pine needles in frustration.

Then he noticed the bite—or was it a cut? Must have happened in the doughnut shop; none of them had been close to him since—but something had made his elbow bleed. He applied his iodine and prayed. Under stress, some men's mouths spewed obscenity, others Sunday-morning verse. In this case, the latter felt more appropriate as the sting of the iodine took hold.

The cut had some angry red swelling around it by the time night fell and he walked, slowly and gently, down to the riverfront.

Two of the defunct casinos had electric light. Several had gigantic red crosses painted on their bargelike hulls, the universal symbol of help to whoever asks. Fire-gutted hotels lined the riverfront road. Valentine could picture the brilliant lighting above and around the multistory parking lots, the banners along the streets, the florid wealth of a gambling haven opening at the side of the Mississippi, beckoning like a Venus flytrap.

He kept out of the masses of somnambulists wandering under the lights, scooping handfuls of meal out of great troughs lining the streets.

Naturally, more food meant more piles of feces. And more rats eating the feces. And cats eating the rats.

He found an empty trough and passed a wet finger through it, sniffed the result. It smelled and felt like ground corn—hog-feed-grade corn, at that. Some rice and millet, too.

Valentine would rather eat the ants disposing of the leftovers.

"Val," he heard a hiss.

It came from the second floor of one of the hotels. He saw Duvalier's face in a window.

He floated into the shell of the fire-gutted building, a concrete skeleton.

She met him at the staircase with a hug, and they looked at each other's iodine-smeared wounds.

"Let's hope the vaccinations weren't just water," Valentine said. Rumor had it that ravies vaccine commanded a fantastic price in the Kurian Zone, and Southern Command had its share of the unscrupulous.

They crept upstairs. Cats (of the feline variety) scattered in either direction at their approach.

Duvalier and Everready had his pack and gun. Everready extended a piece of greasy waxed paper. "Cold chicken and a biscuit. From the Missions."

"What's next?" Valentine asked.

Everready threw a bone down the hall. A catfight started almost the second it landed. "I passed word to my contact in the Missions. He's going to get in touch with a trading man in Memphis, one of my sets of eyes in the city. Cotswald. Vic Cotswald. He'll take you in. Not the nicest man in the world, but reliable. He thinks I'm working for the Kurians down south, keeping tabs on things in Memphis. He knows me by the handle Octopus. Can you remember that? Octopus?"

"Great. What's my cover?" Valentine asked.

"I took care of that, Val," Duvalier said. "You're Stu Jacksonville, a new pimp on the Gulf Coast. We know the area from our time as husband and wife, so there'll only be a minimal amount of bullshitting."

"You sure you want to play a whore?" Valentine asked.

"Not whore. Bodyguard. Comrade in arms."

"Gay caballero?" Valentine asked.

"Lesbian, if you want to get technical."

Seven

Memphis: The dwindling number of old-time residents of this good-times city divide Memphis history into prequake and postquake. The destruction, the starvation, the Kurian arrival, the appearance of Grogs; all are linguistically bound together and organized by that single cataclysmic event.

When the New Madrid fault went, most of the city went with it. One of the few substantial buildings to survive the quake was the St. Jude Children's Hospital, whose grave granite now houses many of the city's Kurian rulers behind concentric circles of barracks and fencing.

The rubble left behind was pushing into piles. Eventually those piles were redistributed about the city, forming a fourteen-mile Great Wall of Junk in a blister based at the river that eventually had dirt piled on top of it to turn it into a true barrier. Now a precarious jeep trail circumnavigates the city atop the wall, except for three gaps to the north, east, and south.

The south gap is a subcarbuncle of its own, a fenced-in stretch of land between Memphis and Tunica full of livestock pens and grain silos, barge docks and coal piles, a supplemental reserve of food and fuel for the city in case events of war or nature cut it off from the rest of the Kurian Order.

Inside the wall, around the heart of the city, are the great bank camps, a temporary concentration of identical, wire-divided cantonments that stretch in some cases for miles. Once a tent city for those left homeless after the quake, the tents have given way to fifty-foot barracks, now wooden-sided, with windows and cooking stoves. Rail lines, sidings, and spurs stretch into the camp like the arteries, veins, and capillaries feeding the liver.

The residents go out of their way not to think about those in the camps.

Memphis still has some of its pre-2022 culture along Beale Street and in the "commons," the stretch of city bordering the waterfront. The commons are dominated by the ravaged and only partially glassed superstructure of the Pyramid. This mighty sports arena and convention center has canvas stretched over the missing panes, to admit air without the heat of the sun, giving it the appearance of an impossibly huge sailing ship squatting at the edge of the Mississippi, the trees of Mud Island separating its inlet from the main river.

The area around the Pyramid rivals Chicago's famous zoo as a center of dubious entertainments, though it is a good deal more exclusive, limiting its clientele to the River Rats, the men who work the barges and patrol craft of the great rivers of middle North America, and those brave enough to go slumming. The Pyramid itself sees a higher order of customer with appetites just as base. As a den where flesh is exchanged for goods or services, temporarily or permanently, the Pyramid has no rival on the continent.

While the city has any number of competing factions, captains of war and industry, mouthpieces both civil and Kurian, the commons and the Pyramid look to only one man for leadership. The great auctioneer Moyo has bought and sold more slaves in his forty years than many of the tyrants of old. Always to an advantage.

If anyone has gotten the better of him and lived to tell of it, even the old-timers of Memphis cannot say.

"You want to do what?" Vic Cotswald said.

Cotswald was a heavyset man, and puffed constantly, like an idling steam engine. He took up a substantial portion of the back cabin of his "limo"—a yellow-painted old Hummer.

"Learn about this fellow's setup," Valentine said. "Everyone's heard of Moyo. Why not do what he did, only somewhere else?"

They'd met at a roadside diner built out of a pair of old trailers fixed together and put up on concrete blocks. Duvalier looked a little wan and not at all herself. Valentine hoped it was just the pain of her wound and not the onset of ravies.

He'd know if she started trembling. That was usually the first sign. It might have been better to leave her with Everready in his casino-barge hideout, but she'd insisted on accompanying him into Memphis.

Valentine was dressed all in black. His costume was, in fact, a cut-down version of a priest's habit—it was the only well-made, matching clothing Everready could easily find at the Missions. Valentine had dyed the snake-boots to match on his own, and after cutting off the sleeves added a red neck cloth and a plastic carnation, scavenged from a discarded kitchen on one of the old gambling barges. He wore the gleaming pistol openly in its leather shoulder holster. The U-gun was zipped back up with the rest of their dunnage.

Cotswald wiped grease from his brow and sweat from his upper lip. "Of course everyone's heard of Moyo. Nobody moves deposits in or out of this town without him. The reason Moyo's still Moyo is that he doesn't let anyone get close to him who hasn't come up through his organization. He doesn't just hire Gulfies up to get a chance at the inventory."

Valentine had already learned two pieces of Memphis slang: deposits were the individuals in the bank camps waiting for transshipment to their probable doom; inventory was attractive women—and a few men and kids, he imagined—meant for the fleshpots, private and public.

"Octopus is a good guy. Pays well for the little scraps of information that pass my way. What are you offering?"

Valentine reached under his shirt and pulled up a simple lanyard that hung around his neck. A shiny ring turned at the end of the line. Everready had taken it off a dead general.

"A brass ring? Is it legit?"

"It's mine. You get me in to see Moyo, talk me up, and I'll give it to you. I'm sure you have contacts who can verify its authenticity. If it doesn't check out, you can blow the whistle on me."

"A coast ring's no good here."

"But it is good on the coast. Ever think of your retirement? There are worse places than a beach in Florida."

Cotswald broke into a fresh sweat. "A ring. You better not be doing a bait and switch."

"A *real* ring and a friend named Jacksonville. The higher-ups are putting me in charge of Port Recreation. Got to keep the plebes happy."

"When's the end of the rainbow, Jacksonville?"

"I'm rebuilding a hotel down there. Furnishings are on their way. I just want to see about some—inventory."

"I'm your man," Cotswald said. "Just be warned, stay on the up-and-up with Moyo. He's a razor, he is."

As they drove through the city Valentine got a feel for the people of Memphis. For the most part they were drab, tired-looking, clad in denim or corduroys. Hats seemed to be the main differentiator between the classes of the city. The workers wore baseball-style hats, turbans, or various styles of tied kerchiefs. Those who gave the orders wore brimmed hats—a broad-brimmed variety called a planter seemed to be the most popular.

Cotswald's Hummer wove through horse carts and mopeds on the way downtown—they took a turn riverward to avoid the jagged outline of the old children's hospital. It had sprouted tulip-shaped towers since the advent of the Kurian Order. A communications tower next to the hospital supported ball-like structures, like spider egg sacks, planted irregularly along the sides, a strange fusion of steel and what looked like concrete—but concrete globes of that size couldn't be supported by the tower.

Cotswald stared studiously out the opposite window, reading billboards for birth-enhancement medications. Something called Wondera promised "twins or triplets with every conception."

OUR GOAL: TRANQUILITY AND JUSTICE FOR ALL read another. WHY SETTLE FOR VITA*MINS*? GET VitaMAX—GUARANTEED SATISFACTION (HIS AND HERS).

Once in the summit of the city—the ground rose at the edge of the river before falling away sharply into the Mississippi—Valentine saw men and women dressed with a little more flash. Some of the women even wore heels. Many of the men sported suits that would cause heads to turn and mouths to gape in the Ozarks: broad-shouldered, pinstriped suit coats with matching trousers and patent-leather shoes in a variety of colors.

"It's a party town," Cotswald said as the sharp notes of an outdoor jazz trio came in through the open windows of the Hummer.

The car turned north onto a well-paved road and shot down an avenue of impressive new homes looking out over the breeze-etched river. The car slowed and turned onto a broader highway that went down the steep hill to the river. Valentine looked up at the riverfront homes. All had balconies, some had two or more.

In the distance to the north, seemingly sitting out on the river, he saw the blue-and-white checkerboard of the Memphis Pyramid.

"That's my house," Cotswald said as they slowed below a brownstone monstrosity, pregnant with a glass-roofed patio thick with potted plants. "Should say, the top floor is mine. I rent out the bottom floor to a colonel and his family. Helps to have friends in the City Guard."

"I admire the neighborhood," Valentine said. Duvalier tapped her fingers on her walking stick.

"But I'm hardly ever there. I usually sleep at the office. Hard to make good when you don't have your own bank, but I couldn't manage it. The faces get to me."

Valentine marked Cotswald as one of the Kurian Zone survivors who made himself as comfortable as possible without hindering the regime. *Born in a different time and place, would I shuffle loads of rice and beans in and out of my warehouses? Trade in a few luxuries on the side?*

Look the other way to avoid the faces?

Docks with tethered small craft filled the riverbank. Valentine saw the soldiers of the City Guard everywhere, the russet-colored cotton uniforms and canvas-covered sun-helmets going everywhere in pairs. Pairs searching boats, pairs driving in small vehicles Valentine had heard called "golf carts," pairs walking along the raised wooden promenades.

They got out of the way for the Hummer.

"South end of the riverfront is strictly family fun," Cotswald said as they passed into an amusement park. Valentine marked a merry-go-round in operation and a Ferris wheel giving a good view of the area. Many of the other rides were motionless. "You should see it on Jubilation Day, or Peace Week. People camped out all over the hillside. Great time. Except for the Year Forty-three shelling. The vicious bastards across the river dropped artillery shells all over the place the last night of Peace Week. Killed hundreds. Hasn't felt the same since."

"That was—" Duvalier began.

"Horrible," Valentine cut in. "Macon radio carried the story." He'd heard some Wolves talking about it after the Kurian propaganda broadcasts. Evidently they'd hired mercenaries to do it, then killed the three gun crews. A patrol from Bravo Company found the bodies and shell casings.

The Pyramid grew larger as they approached. Valentine had underestimated its size at first glance. It too had a superstructure capping it, a tall, thin tower with a mushroomlike top, a tiny umbrella perched atop the great canvas-colored structure.

Valentine had never seen anything that more perfectly summed up what Mali Carrasca called *Vampire Earth*: a ruin from the old world, a pyramid of power, with a Kurian at the very top, looking down on the foreshortened, antlike inhabitants of his domain.

"That's some setup Moyo's got."

"It's an old convention center," Cotswald said, wheezing a little more. "Kind of a city to itself. Every riverman on the big three has his own story about his visits there. The Chicago or Vegas or New York girls got nothing on Moyo's; he takes his pick from the deposits across half a continent."

"I'm going to make Jacksonville compete," Valentine said.

"Moyo was young once too," Cotswald said, eyeing the gap in Valentine's shirt that showed the chain to the brass ring.

"What do you do for him?" Valentine asked.

"Run a little booze and high-grade beef."

"He pay you with parties?"

"No, I don't go in for that—not that I'm disapproving of your line of work, Stu. He's got his own clothing lines. When his girls aren't working they're sewing. Some of the fashions you saw downtown, they come from his Graceland label. I sell 'em to shops as far away as Des Moines and Chattanooga."

Duvalier had fallen asleep in the back of the Hummer. Her eyes opened again when it came to a stop.

Cotswald had brought them to the north edge of the commercial docks. A fresh concrete pier and wharves built out of what looked like rubble sat in the shadow of what must have once been a great bridge across the Mississippi. A low, tree-filled peninsula hugged the Memphis side. A rail line ran up into the city from its main tracks, running perpendicular to the old east-west interstate. Valentine saw platform cars being loaded with bags and barrels from the river craft.

"That's the river shuttle," Cotswald said. "My warehouses are at the other end of it."

A narrow pedestrian bridge jumped a few hundred feet of rail line and jumbled rubble separating the Pyramid from the rest of Memphis. Houseboats like suckling baby pigs lined up along the river side of the Pyramid in the channel between the tree-filled island and the Pyramid's plaza.

"You get a lot of boat traffic in Jacksonville?" Cotswald asked.

"A few big ships and a lot of small, intracoastal traders. Looks like you've got your share too."

"That big white one up against Mud Island is Moyo's yacht. Hey, your girl alright?"

Duvalier had sagged against the side of the Hummer.

"You okay, Red?" Valentine asked.

"Just a little faint," she said.

Spiders of anxiety climbed up Valentine's back. "Let me take the packs."

"Thanks."

"Mind if I check your pulse?" Valentine asked. He lifted Duvalier's wrist and watched her hand. Still steady—no, *was that a tremble*?

She was bitten four days ago. She should be in the clear.

Valentine threw the satchel of "traveling supplies"—the pseudo-

Spam, chocolate bars, and a few detonators surrounded by fresh underwear and toiletries—over his shoulder, along with the bigger duffel carrying their guns. She used her stick to walk down to the bridge.

"I think I've got a little fever," Duvalier said. Cotswald puffed ahead, almost filling the sidewalk-sized bridge.

Cotswald explained something to the City Guard at the other end ". . . here on business . . . show the big gear a good time . . ." as Valentine gave Duvalier a water bottle.

"Val, I don't want to be walking around naked in that pen," Duvalier said. "If I got it—"

"You've got an infection from the bite, I bet. God knows what kind of bacteria they have in their mouths."

"Everready says it mutates sometimes. Maybe it mutated so it takes four or five days . . ."

Cotswald waved at them impatiently and they stepped off the walkway. The City Guards smiled and nodded.

"Welcome to Memphis. Roll yourself a good time, sir."

Valentine felt around in his pocket for some of the Memphis scrip—Everready sometimes used the lower-denomination bills for hygiene purposes, he'd accumulated so much of it over the years—and tipped the City Guard. He'd learned in Chicago to tip everyone who so much as wished you a good afternoon.

The bill disappeared with a speed that would do credit to a zoo doorman.

The Pyramid island had obviously once been parkland, but a maze of trailer homes had sprung up around it, separated by canvas tents selling food and beverages.

"Remember, Cots, I've got to get a peek at Moyo's operation if you want your ring," Valentine said.

"Stay away from the Common," Cotswald said, indicating the trailers and tents with a wave. "You hear stories about men disappearing. Don't know if it's shanghaied or"—he jerked his thick chin upward toward the Kurian Tower, a gesture almost imperceptible thanks to his thick flesh. "No society types go there, not if they want to avoid the drip."

Duvalier stiffened at the word "society." "Bastards," she said.

Cotswald furrowed his eyebrows. "Seems a funny attitude for a bodyguard to—"

"Her mother died from complications of syphilis," Valentine said evenly.

"Visitors with gold buy themselves housing," Cotswald went on, pointing to the other side of the island, where the houseboats were nosed into the protective dike around the city.

"Not too expensive, please," Valentine said. Everready's gold would only go so far.

"I'll arrange something for a budget. Let's go down to the rental agent."

They walked along the flood wall. Like most Kurian civic improvements, it was a patched-up conglomeration of sandbags and concrete. The river wall made the dikes of New Orleans look like monuments to engineering. Too bad the river was dropping to its summer low. . . .

"Seems quiet," Valentine said, thinking of the towering white propane tank on the river flank of the Pyramid. Most of the activity around the colossal structure involved men pushing crates on two-wheelers into the convention center. Valentine wondered at the lack of Grogs; in both Chicago and New Orleans their horselike strength and highly trainable intelligence were used for loading and unloading jobs everywhere. "Don't you have Grogs on your docks?"

"Moyo hates them. As to the quiet, everyone's sleeping out the heat," Cotswald said.

Duvalier's face ran with sweat, and her hair hugged her head.

"Let's make this quick," Valentine said.

They followed a path up the side of the flood wall and went down to the docks. Cotswald spoke to an enormous man sitting beneath a beach umbrella near the entryway to the boats.

"He needs to see the color of your coin," Cotswald said.

After a little bartering—Valentine had some difficulty with the man's accent—through Cotswald's offices they arranged for an old cabin cruiser at the rock-bottom price of four hundred dollars a week. In gold. One week in advance, and after the first day the second week had to be paid for or the rate would go to five hundred fifty dollars.

Valentine nodded at the terms. *We'll be gone before then. Unless Duvalier . . .*

Valentine sacrificed one of Everready's coins and got a pile of devalued Memphis scrip in return.

"Let me make sure those are Memphis bills," Cotswald said before Valentine could turn away. He thumbed through the wad. "Hold it, this fifty's in Atlanta dollars."

"Sorreh-suh," the rental agent slurred back.

Cotswald arranged the money and handed it to Valentine. "There's a couple of little markets inside the Pyramid. I wouldn't buy anything from the carts in the commons unless it's fruit or vegetables. They'll sell you dog and tell you it's veal. And don't buy the sausages unless you need stink-bait."

"Thank you."

"I have to attend to a few things in town. I'll be back tonight to show you around."

"Maybe not tonight. My security's not well. How about tomorrow night?"

"Even better. It'll be the weekend."

"Fuck it!" Duvalier barked.

Valentine took her arm. She flinched, but settled down when she saw who he was. "She doesn't like it when I fuss. C'mon, Red. Let's get you in the shade."

She still wasn't trembling. Valentine wished he had listened to old Doctor Jalenga from Second Regiment talk more about ravies. All he could remember is that when they started to spaz out the safest thing to do was shoot—

He'd agreed not to let her suffer—but now he wondered.

Cotswald followed them down the wharf, puffing: "Our arrangement. The—"

Valentine quickened his step, looking at the numbers painted on the cement alongside the moored houseboats. "You'll get it. Once you get me a tour of Moyo's setup."

"I need a chance . . . to check out that ring . . . before you blow town."

"As soon as I'm in the Pyramid."

Number 28.5. This was their boat.

It looked like a frog sitting between two giant white tortoises. The two-level houseboats on either side of the spade-shaped cruiser looked as though they were using the craft as a fender. It had once been a dual-outboard, judging from the fixtures.

Cotswald shrugged. "It's a cabin."

A man who was mostly beer gut and sunglasses sat under an awning atop the port-side craft. "Yello, stranger," he offered.

"Hello back."

"You'll want to wash your bedding out good," their neighbor said. "Last time that cabin was used, it was by the president of the Ohio-Nebraska. He kept his bird dogs in there. They scratched a lot."

"I'll be back tomorrow," Cotswald said, perhaps fearing becoming part of a decontamination press-gang. Valentine nodded.

"Stu Jacksonville, Leisure and Entertainment," Valentine said. "Thanks for the tip."

"Forbes Abernathy. I'm a poor benighted refugee from Dallas, adrift in the world and drowning my sorrows in alcohol and Midway pussy. Or that's what the wife said before she took off with a Cincinnati general. Does this boat look adrift to you?"

Valentine threw the satchel down in the stern of his housing and helped Duvalier in. "Not in the least."

"Now, your putt-putt; a strong storm comes and you'll be blown downriver."

"Thanks for the warning." He tried the key in the padlock holding the doors to the front half of the cabin cruiser closed. After a little jiggling, it opened.

He could smell the dogs. Or rather, their urine.

"Sorry, Ali," he said. He went into the cabin—it had two bed-couches set at angles that joined at the front, and moldy-smelling carpeting that looked like the perfect place to hatch fleas—and opened a tiny top hatch to air it out. There was a tiny washroom and sink. He tried the tap and got nothing.

"Thanks, Forbes," Duvalier said to him as she almost fell into the cabin and plunged, facedown, onto the bench.

Valentine knelt beside her and checked her pulse again. It was fast but strong. Still no trembling.

Another piece of Doctor Jalenga's lecture rose from the tar pit of Valentine's memory. A few people had proven immune to the various strains of ravies virus, or fought it off with nothing more than a bad fever. He crouched next to her—crouching was all that was possible in the tiny cabin—and touched her back. It was wet through, wet enough to leave his hand slick and damp.

She stirred. "Got any water?" Duvalier asked, rolling over. Her hazel eyes looked as though they were made of glass.

Valentine poured her another cup from his canteen. Perhaps a half cup remained. He needed to get them some supplies.

"Why are we back, David?" she asked.

"We're not back. We're in Memphis."

"That's what I mean. Back in the KZ."

"We're trying—"

"We're trying to die."

He put his hand on her forehead. It felt hot and pebbly. "We're doing no such thing."

"That's why we keep going back in," she insisted. "Every time we get out of the KZ, all we can think about is the next trip in. Now why is that? We feel guilty. We want to die like them."

"Rest. I'm going to see about food and something to drink." He unbuckled the shoulder holster.

He went up on deck, feeling alone and vulnerable. Such a tiny piece of information measured against the vastness of the structure above him—

After a moment's thought he locked the door to the cabin with the padlock again. The orblike superstructure atop the Pyramid seemed designed to stare straight down into the back of his boat.

Job at hand. Eat the elephant one bite at a time.

His neighbor had a comic book perched on his bulging stomach.

"Excuse me, Mr. Abernathy," Valentine called. "Is there a market around?"

"Inside the Pyramid. Plaza north. Jackson, was it?"

"Jacksonville."

"Where you two from?"

"The Gulf." Valentine jumped up onto the wharf. "Excuse me, my friend's feeling a little sick."

"You two ever been to Dallas?"

Valentine pretended not to hear the question and waved as he walked down the wharf as quickly as he could. The boat attendant saw him coming and suddenly found something to do inside a rusted catamaran.

Valentine ignored him and crossed a wide plaza to the Pyramid. From close-in the base seemed enormous, flanked by concrete outcroppings with pairs of City Guard doing little but being visible.

A towering stone pharaoh, leaning slightly to the left thanks to the earthquake, Valentine imagined, looked out on the main parking lot with its hodgepodge of trailers from the bottom of an entrance ramp.

He walked up the ramp and noticed dozens of chaise lounges on the southwest outer concourse. Women and men, mostly in bathing suits or camp shorts, lounged and chatted and drank while waiters in white shirts and shorts dispensed food and drink from a great cart. It struck Valentine as similar to the lunches in the yard of the Nut.

No double line of fencing topped with razor wire separated these people from their freedom. Habit? The security of position? One deeply tanned man snored into a white naval hat with braiding on its black brim, a thick ring of brass around his white-haired knuckle.

Valentine paid them no more attention than he would a group of lakeside turtles. He passed through a set of steel-and-glass doors and into the Pyramid.

Moyo kept his realm cleaner than the zoo, Valentine gave him that. The impossibly cool interior smelled of floor polish and washroom disinfectant. He was on some kind of outer concourse, advertisements for alcohol, tobacco, women, games of chance, and sporting events hung on banners tied everywhere. As he walked tout after tout, mostly teenage boys Hank's age, tried to hand him flyers. Valentine finally took one.

Black letters on orange card stock read:

Bloody "Cyborg" Action
Pulp Fontaine
(hook on right hand)
vs
The Draw
(solid aluminum left arm)
3 rounds or maiming
Friday July 22 9PM Center Ring
all wagers arranged by
Roger Smalltree Productions
"the pharaoh of fair odds since y37"
• **Payouts are Moyo Bonded and Insured** •
(Gallery of Stars Booth 6)

The teen squeaked: "Listen, sir, my brother's a locker warden. He says Draw's long-shotted to pay off big. Do a bet and you can pay a whole week on the Midway, say?"

"Say," Valentine said and moved on. A woman thrust out a mimeograph of a nude woman with snakes held in each outstretched arm. "Angelica the Eel-swallower!"

Four-color circus posters, bigger than life-size, screamed out their attractions as he followed an arrow to Plaza North.

Tammy's Tigereye Casino—Fortune Level
Rowdy Skybox • **Bring Your Attitude and Leave Your Teeth** •
M-certified Tricks and Treats at Zuzya's—
You've tried the rest, now get sqweeffed by the best!

Loudspeakers played upbeat jazz or orchestral renditions of old tunes Valentine couldn't quite categorize but which fell under the penumbra of rock-and-roll.

He found the food market using his nose. A lively trade from grill and fish vendors added to the aromas of cut melons, fresh berries, and tomatoes. At another stall fryers bubbled, turning everything from bread paste to sliced potatoes into hot, greasy delight, ready for salting.

His stomach growled.

He placed his hand on a pile of ice at the edge of an ice-filled bin holding two gigantic Mississippi catfish, resting on a semicircular counter, and felt the wonder of the wet cold.

"Mind! Mind!" yelled the woman behind the bins of freshwater food. "You buy? No? Shove off!"

Valentine settled on buying a five-gallon plastic jug full of water and some "wheat mix for cereals." Then he found a bottle labeled aspirin—it also smelled like it.

"You just bought that, son," the trucker-cap-wearing druggist said. He paid, glad that Memphis scrip was good in here.

Valentine sought out some food. The rotisserie chickens were reasonably priced and looked fresh—he had to buy a stick for them to put it on, and he topped his purchases off with a sugar-frosted funnel cake. He ate half of the last as he wandered, getting a feel for the layout of the Pyramid—or Midway, as the locals seemed to call it.

An area labeled the Arena seemed to be the center of activity; he heard a woman's voice warbling through a door as a pair of sandal-wearing rivermen exited. There were also two huge convention-center spaces, filled with wooden partitions turning the areas into a maze of tiny bars, tattoo parlors, and what he imagined were brothels or sex shows. Guards stood in front of the elevators, checking credentials and searching those waiting in line for a lift. Valentine guessed that Moyo's offices were somewhere upstairs.

Few visitors seemed to be around at this time of day; Valentine counted at least one employee for every tourist. Red-jacketed security supervisors ordered around men in black overalls with tight-fitting helmets; the footsoldiers bore slung assault rifles and shotguns, but twirled less-lethal-looking batons as they walked in pairs around the concourses, grazing from the food vendor stalls or being passed a lit cigarette by a marketer. Beefy old women pushed buckets and wheeled trash bins everywhere, their gray bandannas wet with sweat and PYRAMID POWER! buttons pinned to their sagging bosoms.

Valentine had done enough sightseeing and returned to the line of houseboats. His Dallas neighbor had disappeared. He hurried back to his small, rented boat, roasted chicken in one hand, water in the other. He set down the water jug and unlocked the cabin.

Duvalier came into the sunshine and reclined on the vinyl cushions—spiderwebbed with breaks exposing white stuffing threads—and drank almost her entire oversized canteen of water. Valentine mixed her up some of the cereal (IDEAL FOR CHILDREN AND SENIORS—ADVANCED NUTRITION! the label read) from the bag, and she ate a few bites with her field spoon.

"Gaw," she said, and tossed the rest to the Mississippi fishes. She leaned against the side of the boat and closed her eyes. He gave her two tablets of aspirin and she gulped them down, then gave him her cup to refill.

"Chicken?" Valentine asked

"You can have it. You get anywhere with this Moyo guy?"

"Haven't met him yet." He felt helpless against the heat coming up through her skin. "How are you feeling?"

"Weird dreams. Really weird dreams. Thought I was running in Kansas with a cop chasing me. He had giant bare feet with eyes in the toes. I know I'm awake now because you don't have flames coming out of your ears."

"I'm glad you're sensible. You were barking out profanity an hour ago."

"Give me a day or two. I'll be back up to strength—or I'll be . . . either way, you'll be on your way."

She slept, still sweating like a horse fresh from the track, in tiny doses all that night, waking Valentine now and then with brief cries. Not knowing what else to do, he stripped her and dabbed the sweat off her body. To add infestation to injury, both of them broke out in flea bites.

A firework or two went off outside, seemingly timed for the moments when she was sleeping. Forbes Abernathy made a noisy return to his boat about two A.M. with someone who communicated mostly in giggles.

Cotswald arrived the next day, dressed in a straw yellow linen suit. Valentine thought he had a ponderous elegance to him, but he still puffed and wheezed.

"Asthma," Cotswald explained. "Speaking of miseries, how's your bodyguard?"

"A little better," Valentine lied. Duvalier had visibly thinned as the fever wrung the water from her. Valentine, feeling almost as daring as the night he snuck into the general's Nebraska headquarters, had stolen a plastic bag full of ice from the fish vendor when her back was turned and used it to make a compress for her head. She now slept, perhaps a little more soundly thanks to ice and aspirin, in the flea-infested cabin.

He left her a note. Not knowing what the night might bring, he didn't lock her in the cabin. The only weapon he dared take was his little multiknife.

Cotswald puffed up past the stone pharaoh and into the cool of the Pyramid. The sun still seemed high, but the evening throngs were already milling around on the inside. The music played louder and livelier, and attraction barkers brayed. Rivermen in an assortment of outfits and assorted KZ thrill-seekers traveled in mutually exclusive clusters.

Women dressed so as to present décolletage, stomach, buttocks, and legs to advantage wandered through the crowd, selling shots of licorice-smelling alcohol called Mississippi Mud, or "party bead" necklaces of candy, aphrodisiacs, and Alka-Seltzers on a single convenient string, or hot pink Moyo-roses that could be presented to any working girl in tonight's theme costume—(Valentine overheard that it was a cheerleader outfit)—for a free tumble.

"Not that you really need one," a busty pimpette in a conglomeration of zippers and patent leather insisted to a young buck in a Mississippi Honor Guard uniform.

A faint cheer erupted from the arena as they walked the concourse toward the elevators.

"Fifteen-minute call for motorcycle jousting," a pleasant southern-belle drawl announced over the loudspeakers. "A reminder: The Jackson Rangers have gone all of July undefeated. Last year's finalists, Indianapolis Power, will challenge tonight. Ten minutes remain to get your bets in."

They shouldered past a group of off-duty soldiers extracting money from their socks and hats, and stepped into the line at the elevator.

"Destination?" a red-jacketed security man asked as he walked up to their place in the line. He had a bald head and the smooth-but-unenergetic manner of a headwaiter.

"Moyo's office," Cotswald said.

"You have an appointment, Mr. Cotswald?"

"Yes, we do. I made it through Anais."

The security man flipped through a three-ring binder. "Cotswald and Jacksonville. VIP visitor. Very good, sir." Two guards looked them up and down. "If I could just have you take off your coat, Mr. Cotswald," the security man said.

"Of course." Cotswald removed his coat and turned in a circle.

"Thank you. Excuse me, Mr. Jacksonville," the man said. "Step out of line and extend your arms, please."

Valentine submitted to a pat down from one of the guards. They extracted the folding knife. "I'm sorry, sir, no blades whatsoever," the supervisor said. He placed it in a gridwork of cubbyholes like a mail sorter and gave Valentine a numbered chit, and each of them got red plastic badges on lanyards.

"Please wear these around your necks at all times, especially when upstairs," the supervisor said. "Gordon will take you up."

They rode in silence. Gordon advised them to watch their step when the doors opened. Valentine made a move to tip him but Cotswald shook his head.

They exited the elevator, went down a short hallway lined with paintings of irises and turned, then passed into a wood-paneled foyer. A red-blazered security man holding another binder waited on a chair. A man with the most neatly trimmed hair and nails Valentine had ever seen smiled from his wooden desk at a nexus of hallways.

"Mr. Cotswald, how are you tonight?" Asian eyes that reminded Valentine of a picture of his grandmother crinkled in a friendly fashion.

"Keeping busy," Cotswald said.

"And this is?"

"Stu Jacksonville, Leisure and Entertaiment from the Gulf. This is Rooster. Stu's looking to upgrade his inventory."

"Excellent, just excellent," Rooster said. "You're wondering about the name. It's from my days looking for new talent in the rail yards. My hair used to stick up on top."

"Gotcha," Valentine said.

A voice shouted from behind leather-padded doors. "Christ on a popsicle stick, you're a fuckup. Rooster, I've got another ass that needs kicking in here!"

"Mister Moyo's having trouble with the lines up from Texas," Rooster explained. "Please excuse me. Won't you have a seat?"

"Oh, quit crying, you twat!" the same voice yelled. "Stuff the excuses!"

Rooster picked up a leather folio and passed through the double leather doors.

"I hate when he gets worked up," the security man said. "You want to go next?"

"You've got bad news too, I take it?" Cotswald asked, perhaps hoping for a piece of stray information he could sell to Everready.

"Desertions. Not of our people; the Memphis clowns. City Guard commander says we've got to start using our forces for exterior security as well as internal until they can get back up to strength. That means busting heads down in the commons, and no one much likes that."

"Maybe we should go first," Cotswald said. "Mr. Jacksonville is looking to spend a great deal of money."

"Then please, be my guest," the security man said.

One of the double doors opened again. A sullen-looking woman came out, holding the shoulder strap of her briefcase with both hands as though it were a lifeline in a hurricane.

Rooster had his arm gently touching her elbow. "Of course it's not your fault, Yayella. It's going to take a while for the reversals in Texas to be overcome." He guided her down the hall toward the elevators and Valentine followed the thread of the conversation by hardening his hearing. "We'll redirect traffic through New Orleans and coastal craft can get it to Houston. The deposits will arrive a little seasick, but they'll be safer."

Rooster glided back into the foyer. "We're next," Cotswald said, and the security guard nodded.

Moyo's office filled the entire east side of the Pyramid. Sloping glass looked out over Memphis' few remaining high-rise buildings and the gold-lit blocks of the former children's hospital in the distance.

Except for the striking slope to the glass, the office didn't look like a pimp's digs, full of exotic animal furs and silver barware, or a rail baron's throne room of oak and brass. Valentine was expecting some combination of the two. Instead Moyo's office seemed to be modeled on a small-town sheriff's: there was a battered wooden desk with a compact, easel-like computer on it, and a not-quite-matching credenza against a dividing wall next to the desk. A few tube-steel chairs were placed around the room, one opposite the desk and more against the walls. On the other side of the divider was a kitchenette where brewed coffee sat on a hot plate, a locked gun case, and dozens of aluminum file cabinets. The most esoteric features were fancy drop-lighting fixtures, throwing puddles of gold on the red carpeting and lending a warm tone to the room. The only personal touch was a curio cabinet filled with toy trains.

Two professionally dressed women played cards on a newsprint-covered table at the corner window. One had a diplomat bag with a laptop poking out of it, the other kept an old-fashioned steno pad at her elbow.

Opposite the women a corridor, complete with a steel-barred door better than anything Valentine had seen at the Nut, led to a darkened hallway that looked as though it went to the center of the Pyramid.

Moyo flicked off the computer screen as they entered.

Valentine thought Moyo had the junkyard-dog features of a man who bit down and kissed up, on the downslope of forty. A cigar that looked like it came with the desk protruded from the corner of his mouth.

"Mister Cotswald has a new associate, a buyer up from Florida," Rooster explained. "This is Stu Jacksonville."

"Jacksonville. Gene Moyo. Pleased." Moyo didn't look pleased, but placed the cigar carefully at the edge of the desk and came around the edge to shake hands. His hand felt like a wrench wrapped in desert leather. "Christ, Roo, at this rate I'm never getting down to the games. There's supposed to be a good match tonight."

"We won't be long," Cotswald said. "Just need a few permissions to look over your current inventory."

"Roo, call down to the box and tell them to hold dinner. Well, siddown, you two. Make it fast."

They pulled chairs as Rooster left.

Valentine wanted a look around the office, but didn't see how he could in his present circumstances. He surreptitiously felt around in his pocket.

"What's your line, Jacksonville? Pro or amateur?"

Valentine hazarded a guess. "My official title's Provisional Leisure and Entertainment Director. The port's growing."

Moyo put the cigar back in his mouth. "Learn something useful, son. No one with a title like that rises."

"It's a sinecure. I used to work coast security."

"Get the facial reconstruction doing that?"

"That would make a better story. It was an accident—I was careless with a rifle."

"What kind of numbers are you looking for?"

Valentine shifted in his seat to cover his hand's motion. "Thirty gals to start off. I'd like a seat at your auctions, too. I can see two, maybe three trips a year up here."

The cigar moved from the left side of Moyo's mouth to his right. "Payment?"

"Gold. I have enough for a substantial deposit."

"Let's see your color. Sorry, but you're a stranger to me."

Valentine placed a coin on the desk.

"Fort Knox mint. Very good."

"Mister Moyo, if you'd rather talk business at the game, I'm not averse to continuing negotiations down there."

"Anais!" Moyo barked over his shoulder.

The woman with the diplomat bag set down her cards. "Yes, Mister Moyo?"

"Get my weekly out. See if Rooster's got any last-minute additions, then you two can go home as soon as I'm done with my last appointment."

"Thank you, Mister Moyo," she said.

"Rooster!" Moyo yelled.

Rooster appeared quickly enough. "Take these gentlemen down to the owner's box. We have much inventory on hand?"

"New? Five or six girls at the most," Rooster said. "Sorry, Mister Jacksonville, a year ago we had half of Arkansas in here. At this rate there won't be another auction for some weeks."

"You can buy out of my joints, if you want, Jacksonville," Moyo said. "I've got a couple older gals who aren't half-bad managers, too. If the price is right you could hire one or two away from me."

"I appreciate your generosity," Valentine said, shifting his foot slightly.

Moyo put down his cigar again in the same wet groove. "Liquor in the box is on me, alright? Cots, you staying?"

"I need to see about my weekend shifts, and monthlies," Cotswald said. "Line In is piping the Sourbellies from Beal Street athenaeum tonight; thought I'd tune in."

"More ice for us, then," Moyo said, coming around the desk to shake hands again. "Rooster, take Stu down to the box and get him set up. Unless you want a quick look at the inventory?"

Valentine hated to think of the faces. "No, I'll check out your games. And your bar."

"Be down in an hour or so. I've got to go up and do my own reporting." Moyo inclined his head toward the barred corridor.

"You actually go up?" Valentine asked; no pretense was required for his incredulity.

"Just to an audience blister. You ever been in one?"

"No," Valentine said.

Moyo lost a little of his bristle. "My predecessor used to rub lemon zest inside his nostrils to keep out the smell. But it's the walls that get to me. That paste they use, it sucks water out of the outside air somehow. Everything on the inside's wet and dripping. When a big drop hits your shoulder . . . well, you jump. Feels like someone tapping you."

Valentine broke the silence that followed. "See you for a drink later, then."

"Sure. Whoa there, Stu, you missing something?"

"What's that?" Valentine asked.

"Looks like you dropped your roll." Moyo pointed. "It's right under the desk there."

There goes the excuse to come back up here . . . "Must have fallen out when I reached for my coin," Valentine said, flushing. "That would have been a pisser; that's my walking-around money." Valentine retrieved the bills he'd nudged under the desk moments ago.

"I'll forgo the ten percent finder's fee," Moyo said. "Rooster, give me the latest transport figures with destinations, then send in that ass Peckinsnow on your way out, would you?"

Valentine slipped the brass ring to Cotswald on the way out as Rooster collected his carryall from his desk. Valentine wondered how long it would take him to have it "checked out." While a brass ring meant little to a Kurian or one of their Reapers if it wasn't on the actual owner's finger, it was still a powerful totem when waved in front of the groundlings. Valentine just had to hope the circumstances of the ring's loss were not so well known as to have everyone connected to it, including Stu Jacksonville, immediately rounded up for the Reapers.

"If you're into music, maybe you can show me around Beale Street tomorrow," Valentine said.

Valentine watched Cotswald touch the ring in his pocket, fingering it like an exploring teenager. "Sure," he said absently.

"You'll find that little thank-you—what did Mister Moyo say,. 'finder's fee?'—useful if you ever get down my way," Valentine said.

"I'll have to do that before long," Cotswald said. Valentine felt sorry for the dreamy look in the man's eyes. Did confidence men ever feel guilty as they took their marks?

Valentine and Rooster exited on the "showcase" level. Cotswald continued down in the elevator.

Fresh paint covered the structural concrete here, and the lighting came from bulbs.

"Rooster, can I ask you a question?"

"Shoot, Stu. You don't mind if it's Stu, do you?"

"Not at all." Valentine liked using false names in the Kurian Zone. One more curtain between David Valentine and the vast darkness of the Kurian night. "Why the kindling up in Mister Moyo's office? My head porter has a nicer rig."

Rooster glanced up at the ceiling. "Affectation. He started out as a diesel mechanic. When they made him yard supervisor he got an office. It had that junk in it. To him, that first desk meant he made it. I don't mind—he gave me the previous director's outfit for my office. Solid mahogany and half a herd of leather."

"Do you intend to be the next director?"

"Almost there already. I run the day-to-day stuff, he gets the headaches. Personally, I like having him between me and them."

Valentine wanted to ask more about the day-to-day stuff, but they reached the box.

About a dozen people, not counting a food server and an impossibly beautiful young man tending bar, already lounged in the box. The wedge-shaped room was divided into a set of plush-looking seats arranged stadium-style and an entertainment area. A hot tub filled with ice prickled with the necks of beer bottles and sparkling wines. Harder liquors filled up a backlit case behind the bar.

A pair of televisions at each corner held scheduling information. "Closed-circuit TV," Rooster said. "Most of the skyboxes are wired. We've got a camera snafu so there won't be close-ups tonight. Getting replacement electronics takes practically forever."

Valentine looked over the attendees. One of the men had the look of an athlete, as big as one of the Razors' Bears, but his velvet skin had a far healthier sheen and only a neatly closed scar or two. Men and women in well-cut summer cottons were listening to the sportsman. Two obvious party girls eyed him hungrily from the bar.

Rooster introduced Valentine as a "hotel owner from Florida."

The box looked out over the three-ring circus at the center of the arena through tinted-glass windows. Valentine looked out on Moyo's entertainments.

The layout was familiar to anyone who had seen a circus. A hard wooden track, black with wheel marks, surrounded three platforms. The two on either end were more or less stages—one had a band on it at the moment, furiously working their guitars and drums—and the one in the center was an oversized boxing ring shaped like a hexagon.

Two decks for the audience, a lower and an upper, held a few thousand spectators. Valentine saw motion in the upper deck to his right, just beneath the ring of skyboxes.

"Admission is free," Rooster explained. "Some of the bookmakers own skyboxes. If you bet heavy with them you can sit up here."

Valentine caught motion in the upper deck, not sure of what he was seeing for a moment. Yes, that definitely was a woman's head of hair bobbing in an audience member's lap.

"I've heard of seat service, but that's taking it to a new level," Valentine said.

Rooster laughed. "Some of the cheaper gals work the BJ deck. They're supposed to be selling beer and peanuts and stuff too, but a lot just carry around a single packet or can. Lazy bitches."

"Outrageous," Valentine said. He looked up at the gridwork above. And froze.

The lighting gantries had Reapers in them.

Valentine counted three. One sat in a defunct scoreboard, occasionally peering from a hole like an owl. Another hung upside down from a lighting walkway, deep in shadow, neck gruesomely twisted so it could watch events below. A third perched in a high, dark corner.

"They always here?" Valentine asked. He didn't want to point, but Rooster was sharp enough to follow his eyes.

"Oh, yeah. That dark box, there and there; you have a couple more in each of those. Memphis' own version of closed-circuit TV. They never bother anyone." He lowered his voice. "Sometimes a contestant gets badly hurt. The injuries end up being fatal."

"Then why do they fight?" Valentine asked.

"Look at Rod Lightning's finger back there. Nice little brass ring and a riverside house. He trains cage fighters now. Sight of beetles bother you?"

"Not unless they're looking at me," Valentine answered, honestly enough.

Moyo arrived with a small entourage of river and rail men. Valentine took an inconspicuous seat and watched events below. Something called a "bumfight" began, involving a half-dozen shambling, shabby-looking men clocking each other with two-by-fours. It ended with two still upright and the blood in the hexagon being scrubbed by washer-women while a blond singer warbled from the stage near Moyo's box. He only had one brief conversation with Moyo.

"How do you like the Midway?" Moyo seemed positively bubbly; perhaps having another report over and done took a weight off—

"Better organized, and a lot less dangerous, than New Orleans," Valentine said. "There's nothing on the Gulf Coast like this."

"You checked out the inventory yet?"

"I've got a couple more days in town still."

"Rooster can set the whole thing up. I'm going to be on my boat this weekend."

"I think he's got a handle on what I need," Valentine said.

There was topless Roller Derby on the wooden ring—a crowd favorite, judging from the cheers. The metronome motion of swinging breasts as the woman power-skated had a certain fascination, Valentine had to admit. Then an exhibition of flame dancing. The first Grogs Valentine had seen on the Midway spun great platters full of flaming kerosene on their outstretched arms and heads. They arranged it so the liquid fire sprinkled off the spinning dishes and they danced beneath the orange rain. Valentine found it enthralling and said so to Rooster.

"God, I hate those things," Rooster said, on his third drink. "Stupid, smelly, ill-tempered. They're useless."

Attendants with fire extinguishers cleaned up after the dance as the Grogs cartwheeled offstage.

Then it was time for the main event. A cage descended on wires from the ceiling, ringing the hexagon with six wire barriers. He watched Pulp Fontaine turn the Draw's shoulder into a bloody ruin. *So much for long shots,* Valentine thought, as Fontaine accepted a victory crown from this month's Miss Midway.

"Ten thousand will get you her for the weekend, Stewie," Rooster chuckled. "Want me to set it up?"

"I don't roll that high," Valentine said.

The party in the box got louder and the stadium began to empty out. It was just after eleven. Rod Lightning left with the two bar girls. The announcer began to count down for kill-tally bets. Valentine wondered what that meant.

"Time to call it a night?" Valentine asked Rooster. "Thank you for your hospitality."

"Nope. One more special show," Rooster said. "Ever heard of a rat kill?"

"This have something to do with extermination?"

"In a manner."

Valentine watched twenty men of assorted sizes and colors being led into the center hexagon. Each had a black hood over his head. Some of the people on their way out hurried for the exits, but a good third of the audience stayed.

"What's this?" Valentine asked, a little worried.

"It's a rat kill," Moyo said from over his shoulder. "I'm going to watch this one. One of my yard chiefs is in there. Daniel Penn. He was screwing me on deposits, swapping out corpses for the healthy and smuggling them across the river."

Rooster made a note on a pad. "They're all criminals of one sort or another, or vagrants."

Some of the condemned men lost control of themselves as they stepped into the ring. Bladder, bowel, or legs gave way. Escorts in black uniforms shoved them into the cage and lined them up. Valentine saw a shot clock light up in the scoreboard—evidently one part of it still worked—set for sixty.

"And here comes the Midway Marvel," Moyo said.

"Jus-tiss. Jus-tiss! JUS-TISS!" the crowd began to chant.

Tall. Pale. Hair like a threadbare black mop. It was a Reaper, stripped to the waist, loose, billowing black pants ending just above its bare feet. It walked oddly, though, with its arms behind it. As it entered the cage he saw why—thick metal shackles held its wrists together.

"JUS-TISS JUS-TISS JUS-TISS!" the crowd roared, the attenuated numbers sounding just as loud as the thicker crowd had for the night's main event.

"The Marvel's got sixty seconds to off as many as he can. Record's fifteen for the year. All-time high is eighteen. Contest rules say that one always has to survive—even though we've never had a nineteen."

As they unshackled each man from his companions and removed his hood they read the crime, but no name. Number one was a murderer. Number two committed sabotage. Number three had been caught with a transmitter and a rifle. . . .

"Why no women?" Valentine asked.

"Haven't done women in a rat kill for years," Moyo said.

Fourteen, a currency forger, fainted when they took his hood off.

"Crowd didn't like it as well," Rooster said. "They booed when it killed a woman instead of a man. We have other ways of taking care of women. Would you—"

"No thanks."

A heavyset man in a black-and-white-striped shirt with a silver whistle entered the ring to more cheering. He wore a biking helmet and thick studded-leather gloves. The condemned men bunched up.

Valentine felt sick, suspecting what was coming. "Who operates the Marvel?" he asked.

"The one at the top of the Pyramid," Rooster said, lifting his glass a few inches for emphasis. "We only get to do one of these a month. You're lucky."

"You must have an unusually lawless town," Valentine said.

Moyo leaned in close. "I'll tell you a little secret. Only a couple are really criminals. The others are volunteers who took the place of a spouse or a relative in the fodder wagon. On a bad night only six or seven die, so they've got a better than fifty-fifty chance of making it back out."

That's the Kurian Zone. A lie wrapped in a trap cloaked in an illusion. "Jesus," Valentine said.

"Never showed up," Moyo said.

The referee held a black handkerchief high. Valentine was surprised to see that the Reaper's arms were still bound. Weren't they going to unleash it? Or would it simply break free at the right moment?

Sixty seconds, Valentine. You can get through this.

The referee let fall the handkerchief and backpedaled from between the Reaper and the trembling "rats."

As the fabric struck the floor the crowd cheered.

The Reaper sprang forward, a black-and-cream blur. It landed with both feet on the neck of the man who had fainted. Valentine almost felt the bones snap.

The referee blew his whistle.

"ONE!" the crowd shouted. Those still in the box counted along in a more subdued manner.

A convict grabbed another, slighter man by the arm and pushed him at the Reaper. Snake-hinged jaws extended and the stabbing tongue entered an eye socket.

Tweeeeet. "TWO!"

"Two," said the audience in the box.

The Marvel had a sense of humor. It head-butted the man who had thrown his companion into its jaws. Blood and grayish brain matter splattered across the damp canvas.

The whistle blew again. "THREE!"

"Three," Valentine said along with the others. The shot clock read forty-six seconds.

Another jump, and another man went down. The Reaper had some trouble straddling him before the tongue lanced out and buried itself in his heart. *Tweeeet.*

"Four," Valentine said with Moyo, Rooster, and the crowd.

"But it'll cost—"

Some of the men climbed the panels of the cage—not to get out, it closed at the top—but to make themselves inaccessible. The Reaper sprang up, jaws closing on a neck.

Whistle, cheers, and the shot clock read thirty-nine seconds. The Reaper threw the body off the way a terrier tosses a rat.

"SIX!" tried to hide behind the referee and got a leather-glove backhand for his troubles. "SEVEN!" was kicked off the fencing by another man higher up. "EIGHT!"

Valentine found himself yelling as loudly as anyone in the room.

Part of him wasn't faking. Another part of him was ready to vomit thanks to the previous part. . . .

Fifteen seconds left.

The Reaper hurled itself at the cage, and three men dropped off the fencing like windfall apples.

"NINE!" "TEN!" As the whistle and shot clock sounded, the Reaper lashed out with a clawed foot and opened a man up across the kidneys.

"Ten is the official count," the loudspeakers said. "Ten paid three to one. Check your stubs, ten paid three to one."

"About average," Rooster said. "Sorry you didn't get a better show, Stu."

The dripping Reaper folded itself onto the mat.

Eleven died anyway, screaming on the blood-soaked canvas.

Moyo said his good-byes. He looked exhausted as he drained the glass of whiskey he'd been nursing.

"How about a nightcap?" Valentine asked Rooster, who emptied his glass at the same time his boss did.

"Night's still young, and so are we, O scarred Stu." He refilled his glass.

"I've got a bottle of JB in my boat."

"Naw. Better liquor at my place," Rooster said. "You haven't really partied Memphis-style yet."

"Or we could hit some bars."

"I got something better than that."

"Better than the Midway?" Valentine asked.

"Better. I need to stop off at the security station first and check out some inventory. Meet at the big stone statue out front? Say in fifteen minutes?"

"How about I come with you?"

"No, you don't have the right ID for the security section. I'll be fast."

"See you there."

Valentine rode the elevator down—a more alert-looking guard worked the buttons after hours—and collected his pocketknife. He had to shrug off prostitutes—three women and a man, all with makeup headed south for the evening—on the way to the statue. The night had cooled, but only a little. The concrete seemed to be soaked with heat like the bloody canvas within.

Please, Ali, be coherent when I get back.

He caught sight of Rooster, leading a little procession of three individuals in oversized blue PYRAMID POWER T-shirts. All female, all teens, shackled in a manner similar to the twenty culls within.

"Got you a little souvenir, Stu." Rooster tossed him a black hood with the number ten on it. Valentine smelled the sweat on it.

"I had them tag it with the date. The one with the number the Marvel took is collectable."

Valentine wadded up the thin, slick polyester in his hand. "Who are these?" he asked, looking at the string of young women. Rooster held a leather lead attached to the first. A foot and a half of plastic line linked each set of ankles.

"I'm—" one began.

Rooster lifted a baton with a pair of metal probes at the end. "You wanna get zapped? No? Then shut it!"

"I just need to get a bag from my boat," Valentine said.

"Okeydokey," Rooster said.

"What's the plan for these three?" Valentine said as they walked.

"Inventory Inspecshun," Rooster slurred. "Fresh stuff, just off the train, that I picked out this week. Privileges of position and all that. They go back in the inventory hopper Monday morning." He glanced over his shoulder. "Provided I don't get a lot of lip," he warned. "Then it's back with the deposits."

"Three?"

"I don't mind sharing. I like to do one while the others watch."

Valentine looked at the trio. The youngest looked fourteen. He read silent pleas in their eyes.

"I think I'm going to bring my camera for this," Valentine said.

"Great idea!"

They walked slowly down the line of houseboats. Lights burned within some. Valentine heard moaning from the open window of another.

"Another Midway party!" Rooster said, as an orgasmic cry rolled out of the boat.

Valentine approached his boat. Their Dallas neighbor was apparently out for the evening.

"Red?" he called from the pier.

Duvalier popped out from the cabin like a jack in the box. One of the girls screamed. "The hell?" she said, gaping.

Duvalier had blood caked in her hair, under one eye, on her hand.

No time. Valentine brought his hand down, hard, on Rooster's wrist. He grabbed the butt of the club with the other hand, found the trigger, and released his grip on the wrist as he stuck the metal-tipped end against Rooster's breastbone.

A buzzing sound and the smell of ozone filled the riverbank air.

Rooster dropped, twitching, and he turned on Duvalier, expecting her to lunge, not knowing what he'd do to her. . . .

"Back off, Ali," he warned.

"Val, are you nuts? What's going on?" She sounded coherent, though her eyes blazed brightly.

"We're getting out of here."

"I was just going to suggest that."

"You want out of Memphis?" he asked the girls. Rooster moaned, and Valentine zapped him again.

"Yes," one said. The others nodded dumbly.

"Get in the boat."

He opened up the pocketknife and cut the bands between their legs, stuffed the hood in Rooster's mouth, and tied it down with the leather lead. He searched him, found a key to the girls' shackles, and transferred the restraints from the chicks to the cock.

"Who's the blood from?" Valentine asked Duvalier as they cut the lines from the little cabin cruiser to the wharf. Valentine made sure to leave a long lead at the front of the boat.

"Our Dallas neighbor," Duvalier said, pushing the girls into the cabin. "He insisted he knew me. I think he just wanted in my pants."

"Where is he?"

"Dead."

Valentine glared at her.

"Don't worry, I did him in his shower. Gave a blow job he never had time to forget. All the blood flowed into the boat drain."

"Except for what got on you."

"What's the plan now?"

"Thank God the river flows in the direction of Tunica."

Valentine hopped into the water and pushed the boat away from the wharf. The water was only four feet deep along the bank.

"Try and find something to use as a paddle," he suggested.

"Whaddya think you're doing, buddy?" someone called from another boat as they headed toward the river.

"Fishing!" Valentine yelled back. "Have a great weekend!"

The boat began to drift, and Valentine went around to the front and took up the line. He waded along the river, Mississippi mud, the real kind, treacherous beneath his feet. More than once his feet slipped on the bottom.

All Duvalier could find to use as paddles were dinner plates.

So he waded on, keeping close to the Memphis bank, until he passed Mud Island and got into the current. He fell into the boat as it slowly spun down the semi-intact bridge to the Arkansas side.

A few other pleasure craft were out, everything from ship-rigged sailcraft to linked lines of inner tubes, escaping the summer heat of the city but keeping well clear of the midchannel markers that evidently served as some kind of boundary. He parked the teenagers around the stern—their names were Dahra, Miyichi, and Sula, of Kansas, Illinois, and Tennessee respectively—and had them all hold plastic cups as though they were drinking. Valentine and Duvalier paddled with the dinner plates, weary work that required hanging off the side whenever the current threatened to carry them too close to a passing boat or the bank.

"The fever's down, I take it," he said to Duvalier as they caught their breath.

"Broke this afternoon," she said. "God, I'm tired."

Fewer and fewer craft were to be seen the farther south along the shore they drifted. They came to the second bridge. Only the piers nearest the shore were still connected with the road.

Valentine saw sentries on the empty bridge. It might seem odd to guard a bridge to nothing but a hundred-foot drop, but the vantage gave a superb view of the river south of Memphis.

"Ali, you get in the cabin with your shotgun. You three—pretend to be passed out," Valentine said.

After they passed under the bridge a spotlight hit them.

"You're coming up on the buoys," a megaphone-amplified voice called down. "Commercial and security craft only."

Valentine stood up, wavering. "My engine fell off," he yelled. "I need a tow!"

"Not our problem."

Sula raised her head and shielded her eyes from the spotlight. She jumped up on the front of the boat. "What unit y'all in?" she yelled, doing a thicker local accent than Valentine could manage convincingly.

"Bravo Company, Corsun's Memphis Guard," the voice called back, a little friendlier. "And you're about an eighth of a mile from being arrested."

"Well then, throw us a line," Valentine yelled.

"Bravo Company Memphis Guard," Sula yelled, raising her shirt. She hopped up and down in the spotlight. *"Whooooo!"*

"What's going on out there?" Duvalier asked softly from behind the cabin door.

"Distractions," Valentine said.

Approving yells broke out from above.

Then Sula sat down and hugged her knees, and they drifted until the spotlight went off.

"Nice improv," Valentine said. "Except it's likely to bring six patrol craft down on us."

Valentine knew vaguely that at the bend ahead a largish island divided the river. If they could reach it they'd be near the wall to the ravie colony.

A patrol craft even smaller than their boat plodded up the river on a single outboard.

"Are we in trouble?" Miyichi asked.

"Row toward the bank. Paddle!" Valentine urged. He leaned over and dug into the water with a dinner plate. Someone on the bridge with a good pair of night glasses would still be able to distinguish individual figures.

The boat turned sharply their way. A small spotlight or a heavy-duty flashlight lanced out through the river night.

"Keep down, you three," Valentine whispered. Then, a little louder, "Ali, small boat. If one sticks his head in the cabin, you blow it off!"

Valentine stood up and waved with both arms. "Hey there. Can you give us a tow?"

"Where's Miss Midway?" a voice called from the boat.

Sula stood up. "I was just funnin' with the soldiers. Didn't mean any harm."

Valentine tried his drunk voice again. "I'm sorry about her not keeping the flotation devices properly stowed, sir."

"Hey, Corp, let's turn 'em in as vagrants and take the bounty," a shadowy outline next to the flashlight said, too quietly for Sula to hear. Valentine felt a little better about what he was about to do.

"Let me do the thinking," the corporal said. "Get the man on board and handcuff him. If he's a Somebody we apologize and bring him home to mama. Otherwise we'll take a little snatch break with the girls before we collect the bounty."

Valentine opened his pocketknife to the longest blade and climbed up on the front of the boat, where Sula had done her exhibition, and knelt. He made a move to tuck in his shirt and stuck the open knife in his back pocket. "Toss me a line, there, sir. I really appreciate this."

The police boat came alongside. It had a small trolling motor and a big inboard. A waterproof-wrapped machine gun was lashed to a platform on the retractable top. Unlike Valentine's craft, the front was open, with more seating.

A lean man with corporal's stripes in a blue-and-white shirt tossed Valentine a rope. His partner wore a black baseball cap with a Memphis Guard patch sewn to the front.

Valentine leaned forward to catch it and went face-first into the river.

"Grab onto this, you idiot," he heard as soon as he surfaced. Sputtering, he grabbed onto the rope-loop boathook the corporal had extended.

"You're really racking up the fines, friend," the corporal said as he pulled Valentine into the boat.

You two or us. You two or us. You two or us, Valentine thought, working himself up for what had to come. He saw the other come forward with the handcuffs—

—and put his foot down—*hard*—on the corporal's instep. The knife flashed up and into the side of the man's throat. Valentine twisted his wrist as he pulled it out, opening the carotid artery.

The other dropped his cuffs and reached for his holster as his partner instinctively clapped a hand to the spurting blood. Valentine's fist seemed to take forever to cross the distance to the hat-wearer's face, striking him squarely between the eyes.

The gun quit coming up and spun off the stern.

Valentine threw himself after his fist and bodily knocked the man against the boat's side. The knife ripped into the Guard's crotch, digging for the femoral artery just to the side of the groin, then up and across the eyes.

A sirenlike wail and Valentine saw an explosion of light. He backed off, shaking his head, trying to think, to see. When his vision came back the man was on the deck, the blackjack he'd struck Valentine's temple with still in his hand. Duvalier was astride the railing, bloody sword cane in hand.

"Ali . . ."

"Not a bad killing," she said, nuzzling him. "But we have to go. Right now."

They transferred the people—including the bound Rooster—over to the police boat. Duvalier tossed over their dunnage bags as Valentine put on the river patrolman's baseball cap. They tied their now-empty boat to the transom on a ten-foot line. Valentine went to the control console and pushed the throttle forward. He didn't open it up all the way; too fast an exit might alarm the bridge watchers.

But they were still heading away from Memphis.

Valentine turned on the flashing police light. Perhaps the bridge sentries would think that the river patrol had spotted another craft and moved to intercept. They passed out of sight of the bridge behind the island, roaring down the river with a *V* of white water behind . . .

They rounded the island and rejoined the main channel of the river as it zigged back south again. "Ali, rig one of the cans with a timer," Valentine said. "We're into the ravies colony area now. We'll send this thing to the Arkansas shore and have it blow."

"Hope all this was worth it, Val," she said. "I don't think we're going to get another try at the Pyramid after this."

Valentine looked at the three girls in the bow of the police boat. "It was worth it."

Twenty-four hours later they stood in a dark lower deck of one of the old casino barges. A single lantern threw just enough light off the remaining bits of mirror and glass to reveal just how big, dark, and empty the former gambling hall was. Rows of broken-open, dusty slot machines stood like soldiers on parade.

It reeked of bat guano and mold.

Valentine, Ahn-Kha, Duvalier, and Everready surveyed their handiwork. Rooster was tied facedown on an old roulette wheel, his hands solidly bound to the well-anchored spinner. The rather haggard-looking deposit-and-inventory man couldn't see anything; his head was enclosed in a bag with the number ten written on it.

A small bowl of foul liquid—blood and musk glands from a sick old tomcat Valentine had shot with his .22 an hour ago—rested on the wooden bar for the players' drinks.

"Money, then?" Rooster said. "Moyo's loaded. He'll pay to get me back."

Dahra, Miyichi, and Sula sat on the stools next to the wheel so they could see Rooster's face. Valentine took the hood off.

"Okay, Jacksonville, I give up," Rooster said. The man was crying. "You win. What do you want? What did I ever do to you?"

"No, this is purely professional," Valentine said. "I need to know about a certain train."

"I deal with dozens of trains a week, man. How am I supposed . . ."

"No, this is right up your alley," Valentine said. "It's a really special train."

"Look, I have a dog. No one to look in on him. He's dying—"

"Listen to the question. A train. A special train, not deposits. All women on board. Routed through Memphis. Some sort of medical test selected them. Maybe joining with similar trains."

Slight hesitation. "I don't know anything about a train like that. Let me go and I'll find out for you—"

Valentine turned to the young women. "Looks like you're going to get to watch after all. Bring it in, Smokey."

Ahn-Kha stepped forward from the opposite end of the table, snuffling and snorting. Rooster tried to look behind himself, but couldn't get his chin around his shoulder.

"What's that?"

Valentine walked to the end of the table and used the saw edge on the pocketknife to split Rooster's pants at the buttock line.

"A big, bull Grog, Rooster."

Valentine winked at Ahn-Kha. The Golden One snuffled and snorted around.

"I don't like this," Rooster said. "I think we sent a train like that north somewhere."

Valentine dipped his hand in the smelly cat offal. "You'd better dig deep in your memory, before our bullyboy gets deep into you, Rooster." Valentine smeared the bloody slime up Rooster's crack.

"You can't mean—"

Ahn-Kha began to paw at Rooster, his giant, long-fingered hands taking a grip on his shoulder. He whined eagerly, like a starving dog begging for dinner.

"He thinks you're a female in estrus, Rooster."

"Holy shit, that's big," Dahra said, as the other two girls' mouths dropped open. "Pimp, my forearm's got nothing on this Grog—"

"Stop him!" Rooster shouted.

"Where?" Valentine said, leaning down and looking him in the eyes. "You're about a minute away from a lifetime with a colostomy bag, if you don't bleed to death. Where?"

Something brushed up between Rooster's spread cheeks. "Laurelton, Ohio. Laurelton!" Rooster shrieked.

"Pull him back," Valentine said, and Ahn-Kha grunted as he came off Rooster's back. Valentine threw down the hood. "Show me on this map!" Valentine said, opening an old, rolled-up state atlas.

He did.

Duvalier lifted the eggplant she'd been working between Rooster's buttocks, sniffed the smeared end, and made a face. The teens giggled.

"There, you've helped yourself out of a jam, Rooster," Valentine said. "Sorry about your dog, but we'll have to keep you here a few months. Once we've checked your destination out, we'll let you go free."

Rooster sagged in his bonds.

"What do they do with the women there?" Valentine asked.

Rooster, his nose planted on 11 Black, said: "I dunno. It's just very important that they arrive healthy. A doctor accompanies each train."

"How many trains?"

"One or two a year. Maybe a hundred total bodies."

Duvalier and Ahn-Kha exchanged shrugs.

Valentine picked up the bowl of cat guts and sent it spinning into the darkness. "Girls, watch Rooster for a moment. Don't take advantage of a pantsless man."

They went to a stairwell where a candle burned. "Everready, you think you can take care of those girls and keep an eye on that prisoner for the summer?"

Everready nodded. "Be a nice switch from fresh Wolves with the milk still on their chins."

"If we're not back by New Year's, I'll leave it to your discretion," Valentine said.

"Everready's home for wayward girls," the old Cat said. "I kind of like the sound of that. Maybe this old Cat should retire and take up a new line of work."

"In your dreams, Gramps," Duvalier said.

"Looks like I'm Ohio-bound. You two want to go back?"

"Never," Ahn-Kha said. "Will Post is counting on us."

"It does occur to you that you're looking for a needle in a haystack," Duvalier added. "Maybe a haystack that's been blown across half the country."

"You're going back, then?" Ahn-Kha asked.

"Maybe the ravies is finally kicking in," she said. "I'm game. But next time, Val, you're squatting under Ahn-Kha's junk and holding the vegetable, okay?"

Eight

The Tennessee Valley, August: Six former states lay claim to the Tennessee River, and benefit from the electricity it generates. Its tributaries are fed by the eighty inches or so of rain that drop on the Appalachian foothills, swelling the lakes behind the nine still-intact dams. Its total shoreline, utilized by man, bear, wildcat, ducks, geese, and wading birds, exceeds that of the entire Pacific and Gulf Coasts of the former United States.

The residents in the settlements around it pull pike, catfish, sauger, bass, and crappie from its waters, both to pan-fry and to plant alongside their seedcorn, a form of phosphate fertilization used by the Native Americans of the area three hundred years ago.

But there are still long stretches of river uninhabited and returned to the thickly forested banks of earlier times. The reason for the human flight: the skeeters.

Tennessee Valley mosquitoes are legendary for their numbers and virulence. With some stretches of the river overrunning flood control, swamps have formed, and the mosquitoes fly so thickly above the still water that they can resemble a buzzing fog. With them come malaria, bird flu, and some mutated strains of ravies—Alessa Duvalier could describe a bout with one strain in nauseating detail—so humans keep clear of certain stretches to safeguard their children and livestock.

There's still some river traffic in corn, soy, and grains (often concealing casks of white lightning and other illicit medications), and of course the quinine-gulping, citrus-candle-burning power plant workers and locksmen at the dams must be there. But the areas around the riverbanks and swamps belong to a few hardy individualists, fugitives, and those who hunt them—"mad dogs and warrant men" in the vernacular of the Tennessee Valley.

David Valentine encountered both in the summer of '72 at the Goat Shack in south-central Tennessee.

The heat reminded Valentine of Haiti, which is about as much as could be said of any hot day, then and for the rest of his life. Even in the shade he sweated, the humidity about him like a sticky cocoon, turning his armpits and crotch into a swamp as moist as either of the bottoms flanking the peninsula of land projecting like a claw into the lower Tennessee.

Everready's map had been accurate, right down to the "friendly" homes along the way where they could trade news and a few bullets for food, a hayloft hammock, and washsoap. But the Old Black Cat's knowledge of the area ended at the dipping loops of the Tennessee. From there they'd need another guide to get them to Ohio. And he only trusted one.

"Trains are no good. There are checkpoints at all the major rivers," Everready said as they talked routes on the top deck of a defunct casino. "You'll have to go overland. Only man who knows the ground I know of is Hoffman Price. This time of year you'll find him at the Goat Shack on the Tennessee. He can't bear to hunt in August."

The name, but not the man, sounded vaguely familiar to Valentine, but he couldn't place it.

"What's he hunt?"

"People. Real criminals, not Kurian fugitives and whatnot. Though I'm not sure that's from morals, it's more that they don't bring enough warrant money."

"What about guerillas?" Duvalier asked.

"He sticks his nose into no war—or feud, I should say. He calls the whole Cause a big feud. He's brought in a freeholder or two. Like Two-bullets O'Neil; he and his posse were going around hanging Quisling mayors and whatnot along with their families."

"What are we supposed to bribe him with?"

"Give him this," Everready said. He took off one of his Reaper-tooth necklaces, and searched the string. After a few minutes of fiddling he extracted two teeth and passed them to Valentine. One had the letter *h* carved into the root, the other the letter *p*.

"Tell him Everready's calling him on his debts."

Valentine watched the Goat Shack through his Memphis river patrol binoculars. Except for the horse tails swishing under a barn's awning and ATVs parked around the outbuildings, he'd suspect the place was deserted.

The Goat Shack certainly looked dilapidated—even abandoned. Glassless windows, the front door laid out across the wide porch, a few holes in the roof. The road-facing side had fresh cypress boards nailed on horizontally to cover a pickup-truck-sized hole. A dock, divided into an aluminum half by the shore and a wooden extension out onto the lake, ended in a boathouse. Pilings for other docks, perhaps swept away in some flood, dotted the whole riverside behind the house.

Goats rested in the shade of the porch. Valentine watched a tired-looking billy plunge his head into a water trough fed by a downspout and drink.

Valentine suspected it had once been a bar and restaurant for pleasure craft on the river.

A few feet behind, Duvalier lay flat on her back, her feet up on her pack. Ahn-Kha sat cross-legged with his back to the chestnut tree shading Valentine.

The smell of goats reminded Valentine of his first day as a Wolf.

"It just doesn't feel right," Valentine said. "It's like the place is waiting for us."

"We could try going north on our own," Ahn-Kha said. "I don't think this country is muchly inhabited."

"No, we need a guide," Valentine said. "Oh, screw it. Ahn-Kha, cover us from out here with your gun, would you?"

While he changed into the cleaner cut-down black clothes he'd worn in Memphis, Ahn-Kha unstrapped the leather belts around the blanket rolls containing his gun. Duvalier picked up her pack and slung her pump-action shotgun, then handed Valentine his U-gun.

They wandered off the small hummock the chestnut shaded and walked the broken-up road, more potholes than grade.

"What if this Hoffman Price isn't here?" Duvalier asked.

"We find someone else."

"Reaper teeth won't do us much good."

"I have some gold left."

"Just enough to be robbed of and left for dead."

Valentine put his arm on her shoulder. "As if you'd let that happen."

She shrugged him off.

The nanny goats lying on the porch watched them walk past a pair of motorcycles and up onto the porch. A mutt watched them from the shade beneath a truck up on blocks. Duvalier wrung out her neckerchief in the water trough and wiped the sweat from her deeply freckled face and neck.

Valentine heard the clatter of a generator.

"Ready when you are, Val."

"Hello the house," Valentine called. "May we come in?" The brilliant sunshine made every crack in the repaired section of wall a black stripe. There were bullet holes in the door frame and around the windows.

"You a warrant-man?" a crackly woman's voice called back.

"No," Valentine said.

"Then you're not welcome here. Be off."

"We're looking for a warrant-man, actually." Valentine heard movement inside, chairs being pushed back from tables, perhaps.

"Who?"

"Hoffman Price."

"Then come in, friend," the voice said.

It smelled like vomit in the big, welcoming room. It took Valentine's eyes a second to adjust. He instinctively stepped out of the door, and Duvalier followed him in.

A mountain of a woman, gray-haired and with a washed-out red halter top, sat on a stool at one end of a chipped bar with an electric fan blowing on the back of her neck, talking to a bearded man wearing what looked like a bathrobe. Valentine looked around what was evidently a bar. Sandbags were piled around the door and windows, and circled the entire bar at least to waist height. The floor was thick with grit, the ceiling with spiderwebs. The furnishings appeared to have been pulled out of boats and cars. Two men in leather and denim and linked chain sat at a far table, biker boots stretched out in opposite directions toward each other like the tails of a yin and yang symbol.

"Good afternoon, Black and Red," the woman with the crackly voice said, horrifying Valentine with her teeth. "I'm Greta. What can I get you?"

Duvalier was examining the wallpaper, to which was glued an assortment of wanted posters, from cheaply printed ten by twenties to full-color photos to what looked like fax paper.

"What does the house recommend?" Valentine asked.

"I like him," Greta said to the man in the bathrobe, then turned back to Valentine. "Polite goes a long way with me. I do a real mint julep."

"You're kidding," Valentine said.

"I shit you not, Black," she said.

He looked at Duvalier and she shrugged. "Two then."

"Being strangers, please put the guns on top of the sandbags there. Take a seat," Greta advised.

They disarmed themselves, but sat next to their weapons.

Greta got up from her stool, revealing a .45 automatic lying on the bar. She tucked it into a leather back-waistband holster and waddled off to a door at the back, next to the far end of the bar.

"You two got someone you're looking to bring in?" the man in the bathrobe asked.

Valentine shrugged. "You're not Price, are you?"

"He ain't allowed in here."

Valentine wondered at that. "Then I'd rather not discuss it."

"Just asking, Black," the man said. "I wouldn't jump your claim. I'm retired, like." He shifted in his seat and revealed a conspicuous lack of underwear.

"Peekaboo," Duvalier said, rolling her eyes at Valentine. He heard a grinding noise from the doorway.

Greta returned with two tall, thin glasses, the outsides slick with moisture. Valentine looked at the drinks as she set them down.

"Ice!" Duvalier exclaimed, putting both hands around the glass.

"Only ice machine for fifty miles," Greta said.

"We don't come here for the decor, Red," the man said.

"Close up shop, George," Greta said. "It wasn't a prizewinner in your best days, and nobody's going to pin a blue ribbon on it now."

Valentine sipped at the sweet drink. The alcohol dropped and hit like a sledgehammer driving rail spikes.

"My bourbon does have a bit of a bite," Greta said, and Valentine heard chuckles from the far table with the bikers. "How about some food?"

"We'd like to see Hoffman Price."

"He was up early fishing. He'll be asleep now."

"What kind of payment do you accept? I have some Memphis scrip—"

She put her hands on her hips. "Strictly barter, Black. I'll take three shells for that twelve-gauge, or five rounds for your pistol. That'll include lunch and those drinks."

Valentine counted out pistol ammunition.

Fifteen minutes later she brought them fried slabs of catfish and hush puppies, wrapped up in old wanted posters. They read the greasy bills as they ate. "Wanted on Suspicion" seemed to be the most frequent crime, followed by theft and fraud.

When they were finished she added another oily wrap to their table. "Now that you're done, you can take Hoffy his dinner. Saves me the bother."

"I thought he was sleeping," Valentine said.

"I saw his tracking Grog up and around. Means he's up. The boathouse is at the end of the dock, just follow the ferry line. You can leave your weapons. No one's going to touch them. Shack rule."

Valentine picked up the still-warm bag and found the back door. What had been an extensive cypress patio now looked like a piece of modern art made of bird droppings. An assortment of canoes and motorized rowboats lined the bank of the inlet protected by the finger of land.

"And outhouses hanging over the river. Nice," Duvalier observed, looking at the shacks at the end of the deck.

"Could be worse. Could be upstream," Valentine said.

They walked down the dock, boots clomping more loudly than usual on the planking. If anyone wanted to sneak up on Price, they'd have to do it in a canoe.

A raft ferry built out of an old twenty-five-foot pontoon craft was attached to lines stretching to a piling in the center of the river. Another set of lines linked it to the other side. Valentine saw a turned-over rowboat there. Some kind of sign stood over the rowboat, but it was too far away to read, even with the binoculars.

Two great wet hands rose out of the river near the boat shack. A Grog, the simple gray variety distantly related to Ahn-Kha, climbed out. It was a female. She rapped something against the dock and then stuck it in her mouth. As she chewed she watched them approach.

"Hello," Valentine said.

The Grog hurriedly whipped a second crayfish against the dock, then dropped it in her mouth. She chewed and looked at them as if to say "you're not getting it now, flatface."

She let them pass to the door, which sat crookedly on its hinges. Valentine knocked. "Mr. Price?"

God, something smells terrible. Is that the Grog?

"Yeah," a clear tenor voice answered.

"My name's David. Greta gave me your lunch. Can I have a word?"

"Door's not locked, son."

Valentine opened the door to the little shack, got a good view of river through the open door, saw a tied-up canoe—

—and was hit by a wave of odor that almost brought him to his knees. It was BO, but of an intensity he'd never experienced before.

He saw a man standing at a workbench, a disassembled Kalashnikov spread out on an oil-smeared towel. Smoke rose from a short pipe with a whittled bowl.

Duvalier stepped in behind. "Oh, Jesus," she gasped. She backed out and Valentine heard retching. Her stomach had never been the strongest—

The filthiest man Valentine had ever seen stepped away from the bench. Hairy shoulders, black with dirt, protruded from mud-stained overalls that seemed clean by comparison. Two bright eyes stared out of a crud-dark face.

Dumbstruck by the man's hygiene pathology, Valentine could only stand and attempt to forget he had a nose.

"I always enjoy the reaction," Hoffman Price said, putting down the pipe. Valentine tried to fixate on the faint odor of the tobacco, but failed. Price smiled. His teeth were a little yellow, but clean and fairly even. Valentine tried breathing through his mouth. "Greta used to call me 'breathtaking.' "

Valentine counted blood-gorged ticks dangling from the region about Price's armpits and ears and stopped after six. "Everready sent me. From the Yazoo."

"How is that old backshooter?"

"Same as always," Valentine said, not sure if he'd be able to make it across the river, let alone across two states, with this stench.

"Haven't seen him in . . . it's three year now. You looking for someone?"

The Grog hooted outside, and Valentine heard Duvalier say, "No, thanks. I like them cooked."

"Just a guide," Valentine said.

"Uh-huh. To where?"

"Just across the Ohio River. A place called Laurelton. I'll show you on a map."

"That's quite a trip, son."

"That's why I need a guide. Myself and two companions."

"That little gal out there up for mileage like that?"

"I've been to the Rockies and back with her," Valentine said, which wasn't quite true by about two hundred miles but sounded good.

"I'm on my summer holiday. Hope you've got a wheelbarrow full of incentive."

Valentine dug out the Reaper teeth. "Everready said he was calling in your debts." He held out his hand with the teeth in his palm.

"I'll be damned," Price said. He took them. Valentine resisted the urge to smell his hand to see if the odor had transferred.

"Pretty," Duvalier said, and the Grog hooted.

Price cocked an ear to the sounds outside. "Nice young gal you got. Some of the titty trash that gets brought into the Shack, they scream at her. But I have to say no, son. Too far, too long since I've been over the Ordnance ground."

"Ordnance?" Valentine asked.

"Big stretch of ground between the Ohio River and the Great Lakes," Price said. "They make the Kentucky Kurians look like amateurs. Decent bounties, but I like to spend autumn and winter down here."

"But those teeth," Valentine said.

"I'd do anything for old Everready. But you aren't him. That particular debt isn't transferrable."

"Money, then. I have some gold."

"Hard to spend when you're getting gnawed on by a legworm. I'll put on the ol' thinking cap, son, and try and come up with someone crazy enough for a round cross Kentucky. But no names come to mind."

The Grog came back in, leading Duvalier by the hand. She deftly opened a tackle box and showed her collections of costume jewelry, interestingly shaped pieces of driftwood, and some old United States coins. The two men stood in silence at the strange, interspecies feminine cooing.

"I see Bee's making herself agreeable," Price said. "Nice to see someone being kind to her."

"Dzhbee," Bee agreed, looking up at Price.

"He doesn't want to do it, Red," Valentine said, wondering if Grogs operated on a different olfactory level.

"What about the teeth?"

"That deal's with Everready; you got nothing to do with it," Price said.

Duvalier looked at him sidelong, as though afraid to stare. "That makes you a welsher," she said. "As well as a skunk."

"Ali!"

"You've got no paper on me," Price said. "And nothing I want. The door's just behind, unless you want to swim outta here."

She put her hands on her hips. "When's the last time you had a woman, Price?"

Valentine felt the boathouse spin.

"What's that talk for?" Price barked.

"I'm talking about a bonus. You can have me for the duration of the trip. Interested?"

She's gone nuts. What did that fever do to her?

A tar-fingered hand passed through the knots of greasy hair. Valentine saw some things he guessed were lice fall out. "Get out of here, both of you. I've had my fill."

She passed her right hand down her breast, to her crotch. "We'll be up in the shack if you change your mind. Till tomorrow morning. I'm a limited-time offer. C'mon, Black, let's get out of here."

They walked back up the noisy planks.

"What was that all about?" Valentine asked.

"Don't tell me you're jealous? Oh shit, I think some of that smell got in your hair."

"And you were talking about sex with him?"

"Val, I let that pig Hamm drip all over me in bed. This guy's just dirty on the outside. That Grog's sweet. There's no way he can be that bad or she wouldn't be that way. He'll come round. He just needs to think about it."

"Just when I think I know you."

"Ah, but you didn't hear my conditions. I would have insisted that he take a bath, first. I'm not interested in hosting a flea circus in my crotch all the way to Ohio. I only just got rid of the Memphis brood."

They negotiated a room with Greta ("It'll be cool enough to sleep about three in the morning.") and then went out to bring in Ahn-Kha.

Which turned out to be a mistake.

"We'll feed and water him, but he can't stay inside," Greta insisted. "Grogs are strictly outdoor animals."

Valentine, watching flies buzzing in one window and out another, thought the distinction between inside and outside largely moot. Especially with goat droppings under one table.

"Sorry, Ahn-Kha. They're big on rules here."

"Your poet Kundera said 'Only animals were not expelled from Paradise,' my David. I am not an animal, save in the same biological sense as that woman."

"And this isn't paradise, old horse," Valentine finished. "I'll sit outside with you."

Duvalier joined them on the porch with the goats, drinking ice water from a pitcher that had to be refilled every half hour.

Valentine watched the Goat Shack's dubious clientele trickle in as the sun set. He heard the ferry wheels creaking twice. Greta disappeared, replaced at the bar by a gap-toothed relative who shared her peppery hair color.

Duvalier produced a deck of cards scavenged from the casino where they'd interrogated Rooster with an eggplant. The idle evening on the porch passed pleasantly enough. Muscles sore from weary days on the road stiffened.

Perhaps a dozen patrons now passed time and swatted flies in the bar. Precious little commerce seemed to be going on; most of the groups of tables were swapping drinks for tobacco, or old newspapers for a pocketful of nuts. Many of the men smoked. Peanuts and jokes cracked back and forth across the tables.

Valentine watched a man in deerskin boots swap a pipe for an unfinished bottle. A sheathed knife dangled from a leather thong around his neck, and his belt held no fewer than three pistols. Considering the clientele and the quantity of weaponry, the Goat Shack was surprisingly peaceful. Or perhaps it was due to the clientele and the quantity of weaponry. . . .

Valentine felt guilty lazing on the porch. He should be doing *something.* Arguing about the nature of promises with Hoffman Price, wandering through the barroom asking for stories about Kentucky—instead he was looking for another heart so he could lay down a flush and take the pot of sixteen wooden matches.

Two men wandered up from the riverbank, one bearing a dead turkey on a string. They wore timber camouflage, a pattern that reminded Valentine of the tall, dark, vertical corpses of buildings that he'd seen in the center of Chicago. The one with the turkey turned inside with a word about seeing to a scalding pot. The other, a pair of wraparound sunglasses hiding his eyes, watched their game. Or perhaps them.

"What manner of Grog is that?" he asked.

"We call ourselves the Golden Ones," Ahn-Kha said.

The bird hunter took a step back, then collected himself. "The who?"

"Golden Ones."

"Golden Ones?"

Ahn-Kha's ears went flat against his head. "Yes."

"Didn't know there was them who spoke that good of English of your sort."

"Likewise," Ahn-Kha said.

"Definitely see you later," he said, staring frankly at Duvalier. She ignored him. The hunter followed his friend in. Ahn-Kha squeezed out a noisy fart, Golden One commentary on the stink left behind by unpleasant company. Valentine heard a couple of welcoming hallos from the inside.

"The mosquitoes are getting bad," Duvalier said, putting down two pair and taking the pile of matches.

"I'll see about dinner and DEET," Valentine said, rising.

Greta's generator ran two lighting fixtures, both wall-mounted, both near the bar. One was the lit face of a clock—someone had broken off the plastic arms, and whether the remaining stubs still told the time Valentine couldn't say—and the other a green neon squiggle of a bass leaping out of the water, a bright blue line projecting from its mouth. Perhaps a dozen customers sat in the gloom, save for the two huntsmen, who were looking at a wanted poster under the clock-light.

Valentine felt the stares of the company. Because they were outsiders?

"You wouldn't have a bottle of bug repellent, would you?" he asked the slighter version of Greta at the bar.

She shook her head. "No, sir. You and your girl could come inside. The tobacco keeps them out."

"If you don't like the skeeters, you could relocate off-river, tag," a shaggy woodsman suggested. "Take your pet and go."

"Earl," the bartender warned. "Goat stew and biscuits will be up soon, mister."

A third man joined the other two by the clock, getting a light. He joined in the inspection of the bill.

"I'll buy four servings," Valentine said.

"There's only three of you."

"The Grog's got a big appetite."

"We've only got goat. No spitted youngsters," the man called Earl said. Valentine didn't like the way he kept his hand near his open-topped holster.

"You won't even get goat if you keep that up," the bartender said. "Greta hospitalitied them herself."

Valentine walked away.

"Hey, tag!" Earl called as Valentine walked away. The bar went quiet. "Tag!"

Valentine went out the door, glad to have the pile of sandbags and a cedar wall between himself and Earl.

"I think we'll spend tonight on the porch," Valentine said.

"See you in country, tag," Earl bellowed.

"Hey, Earl!" someone inside called. "Come over here and roll one. Calm down."

"Everready should have hooked us up with guerillas," Duvalier said.

"They're up in the mountains east of Nashville, for the most part," Valentine said.

"It's a place to get across this river," Ahn-Kha said. "Perhaps there are no Kur this near. Even a Reaper would have trouble with the crowd inside."

The crowd inside chose that moment to spill out the door. The two turkey hunters and Earl came out of the bar, pistols drawn. Duvalier made a move for her shotgun.

"Hold it," a voice barked from the repaired section wall. "I've got two barrels of buckshot on you."

Valentine stood up, hands up and away from his weapons. "Now hold on. I don't want—"

"You got a warrant on you, tag," Earl said, a flashlight clipped to his pistol shining into Valentine's eyes. "You and this lady here."

"Mister and Missus David Rowan," the turkey hunter read, despite his sunglasses. "He's even got that scar. It's two-year-old paper out of New Orleans, but a warrant's a warrant."

Other bounty hunters came out of the bar, forming a rough semicircle around the porch. They didn't pull their weapons.

"Fifteen thousand dollars Orleans each, it says," sunglasses continued. "Five thousand per bonus for live delivery. Payable at any Coastal Marine station. There's one in Biloxi!"

Valentine did a quick count. There were sixteen men around, if he counted the one covering them from inside.

"That's real good money," one of the leather-clad bikers said.

"Forty thousand dollars is," Valentine agreed. "If you're in New Orleans. How many of you have been there?"

None of the men said anything.

"Okay, you've got us. Let's say you take us to Biloxi, and collect your two thousand five hundred each, barring any bribes you might have to pay."

"Shuddup and face down, tag," Earl said. "We ain't all collecting this."

"Says who? Let him talk, Earl," one in the semicircle said, his hand resting on his gun belt.

Valentine continued. "Let's say you get us down there without soldiers hoping for a promotion taking us away from you. Biloxi'll pay you alright, in New Orleans dollars. They print that stuff like toilet tissue. It can only be spent in New Orleans, unless you want to trade it into a hard currency exchange at a third of the value. Boat fare Biloxi to New Orleans was four hundred dollars when I was down there. A bad bottle of Orleans gin was sixty dollars. A room's over three hundred, if you don't mind cockroaches. How far's that two thousand five getting you now?"

"It's not getting shared sixteen ways," Earl said. "Now—"

A gunshot from just behind the doorway interrupted him.

Greta stood in the door, her shotgun pointed to the sky. Valentine's ears rang from the shot, and he wondered what it had done to Earl's hearing.

"Earl, you owe me one shell and these people an apology. Nobody serves papers at my Shack. Nobody."

"They ain't warrant-men," Earl said.

"He's right, Greta," one of the spectators said.

"I knew that when I gave them my hospitality."

Greta lowered the gun and placed it against the back of his ear. The turkey hunters got out of the way of the potential blast. "Earl, holster your piece and say your good-byes. You're off my peninsula permanently."

Earl put away his gun. "I'll pay up and go." He stared at Valentine. "But you three can't retire here." He raised his voice. "Any man wants to call himself a warrant-man, kill the Grog—he ain't subject to hospitality. Later we'll track down these two and share the reward. Meet me at the old county sign."

"You just do that, Earl. You just do that," a deep voice called from the darkness. Hoffman Price stepped forward, his Kalashnikov tucked under his arm so his hands were free to work his pipe. He got it lit and sent out a puff of smoke.

"And another Grog-lover sounds off," Earl said. "You throw down on me, you skunk, and Charlie'll blow you in half with his ten-gauge."

"Bee!" Price called.

Valentine heard wood shatter and turned to see a warrant-man crash headfirst through the repaired section of wall, ten-gauge bent around his neck like a dress tie. Bee swung out through the hole, treading on the unconscious Charlie, and extracted a pair of sawed-off shotguns from her boot holsters.

"Earl, you better shut up before I've got your whole rig for damages," Greta said.

"Didn't you hear, Earl?" Price said. "These folks hired me for a little trip to Chattanooga. They're under my protection." He raised his voice. "Any man comes to serve papers on them will interfere with my ability to earn my fee. Bee's my accountant when I'm in country. I refer all financial difficulties to her."

"Let's everyone calm down. We're leaving right now," Valentine said. "Pretend none of this happened."

Greta lowered her shotgun. "You ordered four meals, Black. You and Red and your big friend eat first, then you can leave. You might as well—Earl's picking up the tab."

* * *

The warrant-men, save for Earl, trickled back inside.

They ate at the riverside. "Lots of bad blood gets built up in this business," Price said. He posted himself downwind of Valentine and Duvalier, but it didn't help much.

After some head bobbing and a mutual dental exam, the two Grogs sat down next to each other. Ahn-Kha ate a few bites of his stew, then passed her the bowl.

"She speaks northern slope dialect," Ahn-Kha said. "I only know a few words."

Duvalier was already mopping up her remains with a biscuit. Valentine marveled at her appetite. "You really taking us on, or was that just show?" she asked Price.

"I'm taking you."

"Not through Chattanooga, I hope," Valentine said.

"That was just in case Earl gets the second big idea of his life and goes to the authorities, such as they are."

"What changed your mind?" Valentine asked.

"I got to thinking that I don't have too many more years in me to pay Everready back. If I have to step off, I'll do it clean. Plus Bee got a look at your big friend when he came down to the river to hit the shitter. She got excited. Bee gets lonely for her own, I think."

"I've had my mating," Ahn-Kha said. "She is dead. Besides, we are not dogs. Our strains do not mix."

"But you share some customs, looks like," Price said.

"I've been among her kind. Do not misunderstand me. She is well formed and agreeable." Ahn-Kha broke a biscuit in half and gave it to her. "I just could no more be a male to her than you could."

"I want to put a few miles on across the river before dark," Price said. He clicked his tongue against the roof of his mouth three times. "I have a mule. Bee and I will go load him up."

Valentine kept the food close to his nose as he ate his stew. "Is there a chance that you'll take a bath before we set out?"

"What, and spoil my camouflage?"

Duvalier looked up. "You're hoping to pass as a feral hog, perhaps?"

"No. Everready explained it to me years ago. I never could hide lifesign for shit. All the critters interfere with the Hoods. I don't read as human at any kind of distance." He walked up to the back doorstep and returned his plate.

"You want your other biscuit, Val?" Duvalier asked as Price disappeared into the stable.

"You got used to him faster than I did," Valentine said. "How did you keep your dinner down?"

"Greta in there gave me a bottle of clove oil. It's good for more than mosquito bites. A dab'll do you—provided you put it under your nostrils."

Nine

The Kentucky Bluegrass, September: The bluegrass itself is only blue in the mornings, and even then for the short season when the grass is flowering. The rest of the time it is a rich, deep green.

Poa pratensis *arrived in Kentucky by accident, used as padding for pottery on its way west to be traded to the Shawnee. Once thoroughbreds thrived on it. They have been replaced.*

Land of the dulcimer and bourbon (invented by an itinerant Baptist preacher), home to the most soothing of all American accents, Kentucky raises more than just champion livestock. Perhaps it's something in the water, for the state produces fiercely individualistic, capable folk under its chestnuts and between its limestone cuts. Abraham Lincoln and Jefferson Davis were born there, approximately the same distance apart as their future capitals of Washington, DC, and Richmond.

In its earliest days, the wooded hills of Kentucky were called a "dark and bloody ground." That appellation applies to Kentucky of the Kurian Order as well. The state is divided into three parts, somewhat resembling an O between two parentheses. The western parenthesis is the usual assortment of Kurian principalities bleeding the country from their towers along the Ohio, Tennessee, and Mississippi Rivers. The eastern parenthesis is the mountains of Virginia, home to a scattering of guerrilla bands at war with each other when they're not fighting the Kurians or those in the center of the state.

The center is the most unique of all. Clans of legworm ranchers, some comprised of Grogs, some of humans, and some mixed follow their flocks. They cannot herd them; the legworms are too obstreper-

ous and powerful to be herded, but they can be tamed and controlled under the right circumstances.

The same might be said of the riders.

"I've never seen growth like this before," Valentine said.

"You're looking at snake trails," Price said.

They stood in southern Kentucky, on a little knob of a hill looking out over a meadow. Price knew about moving cross-country. Bee usually took the lead, walking with her eerily careful grace. Then the three humans, taking turns with the compass and map to avoid getting trail-stale, followed by the mule. The mule was unusually cooperative for its breed, perhaps owing to a jaunty knit Rasta cap it wore, complete with fly-scaring dreadlocks. Valentine didn't dare look to see if the dreadlocks were simply sewn in or if they were attached to a scalp, and the mule wasn't telling. Ahn-Kha brought up the rear. At least once a day they zigged on a different course, heading north the way a sailing ship might tack against the wind.

What caught Valentine's eye about this particular meadow was the strange furrowing. Lines of thickly weeded earthen banks meandered across the field like a drunken farmer's tilling. The banks were perhaps a foot high at most, ran down little open spaces clear of smaller trees.

"That's sign left by legworm feeding."

Tchink tchink tchink—behind them Duvalier knelt over a spread out *Byrdstown Clarion*. The newspaper, a weekly melange of property and equipment for sale and lease, with a few stories about the achievements of local NUC youth teams, wasn't being used for the articles. Duvalier was pounding together two ancient red bricks pulled from a collapsing house, collecting the fine dust on the paper to be poured into an envelope and used as foot powder.

Bee snored next to her in the sun, her short-but-powerful legs propped up on a deadfall. The mule, a cooperative beast named Jimi, cropped grasses and tender young plants.

"I've known ground like this," Ahn-Kha said. "Older, though, more evenly grown up."

"You see, Val," Price explained, passing Valentine's binoculars back. His odor lingered on them, but Valentine pressed the sockets to his eyes anyway—after a critter inspection. "Legworms move in small herds; I've never seen over a dozen together. They pull up the sod with their mouths. They eat everything, leaf, stem, and root, and of course mice and voles and whatnot that get pulled up, then they crap it out the other end more or less constantly. The waste is pretty sweet fertilizer, and their digestive system isn't all that thorough, quantity over quality, so in the wormcast there's a lot of seeds, living roots, stuff that comes back. It grows extra lush and you get these little walls of vegetation."

"They don't mess with big trees," Valentine observed.

Price pointed at a thick oak. "They'll climb up and take some low branches. That's why some of these trees look a bit like umbrellas."

"Those trails will lead us to them, if we find fresher leavings," Ahn-Kha said.

"Sure," Price said. "Except with legworm tracks it's hard to tell which direction they're going. If you're lucky you'll come across a partially digested sapling. The way the branches get pressed down makes it like feathers in an arrow, only reversed."

Valentine wondered if it would be like Nebraska, with different "brands" sharing the same area. "How do they feel about trespassers?"

"Depends if they can make a profit off you," Price said.

They cut fresh worm sign two days later. After picking at the less-digested branches and shrubs, everyone agreed that the wide end of the cone was heading northeast.

"Five worms," Price said, counting the tracks. "Two big on the outside, three lesser in."

"Legworms mate in pairs?" Ahn-Kha asked.

"No, more like big orgies in the winter. Seriously," Price said, as Valentine raised an eybrow. "A legworm dogpile's a sight to see."

"What are we looking to get out of a bunch of worm-herders?" Duvalier asked.

Price whistled for Bee. "This is their land. I want permission to cross it. If we're lucky, they might bargain us up a mount."

"We don't have much to offer," Duvalier said.

"Your body is already spoken for," Price said.

"I've got some strong soap in my bag," she said. "Use it and I'll keep up my end."

"I thought humans made love face-to-face," Ahn-Kha said. Valentine wasn't sure he'd heard right until he looked at his friend. Even Price knew him well enough by now to know that one ear up, one ear out meant he was joking.

Catching up to the legworms wasn't as easy as having a clear trail made it sound. When moving without eating, a legworm goes at a pace faster than a horse's walk, similar to the Tennessee walking horse's famous six to twelve miles per hour run-walk. According to Price, they could pull up turf at a good three miles an hour, a typical walk for a human. A human on a sidewalk who isn't loaded down with pack and gun.

So they moved as fast as they could through the warm fall day, sweating and swearing at each new hill. Price and Valentine decided the course was arcing somewhat northerly, so they took a chance and tried to cut across the chord of the arc.

They never picked up the trail again. Other riders found them.

Bee pointed them out first. She dropped down on her haunches and let out a blue jay–like cry, pointing at a tree-topped hill. It took Valentine a moment to recognize what he saw. The legworm's pale yellow color was surprisingly effective camouflage in the shade of a stand of elms and oaks. Two figures sat astride it, probably human.

"Everyone wait here," Price said.

"Feels too much like a standoff," Valentine said. "Why not all go?"

"If you like, but as strangers we've got to approach unarmed." He unslung his Kalashnikov, held it up over his head, then placed it on the ground. He made a motion toward Bee and she sat next to his gun.

"Feel like showing off your famous charm school repertoire?" Valentine asked Duvalier. Behind them, Ahn-Kha kept a hand on Jimi the mule's halter.

"No. If there's a problem I like to disappear fast without anyone getting a good look at me."

"I shall stay back as well," Ahn-Kha said.

Valentine placed his U-gun on the grassy ground and set the pistol on top of it. He had to jog to catch up with Price.

"Let me do the talking, Val," Price warned as he lit his pipe. "They're tetchy around strangers."

"Any particular reason for it?"

Sweat ran lightly down the greasy dirt on his face. Price's filth was semiwaterproof, as impervious to rain as an oilskin. "Nobody likes them much. Most folks in the civilized world—beg your pardon, but that's how Tennesseeans see it, stuck between corn-likker-swilling guerillas west and east—avoid them like they carry a bad fungus.

"Even the churchies keep clear, except a few unreformed Jesus-pushers."

"Why do the Kurians let them be?"

"They get loads over the mountains, one way or another. Between the New York corridor and Chattanooga precious little moves by train; the lines are always getting attacked by guerillas, and you have to pay through the nose per pound. A legworm can haul as much cargo as a railcar. They and their brothers in Virginia are the main east-west smuggling artery for the whole Midwest. Not that they don't do legitimate runs too."

They hopped across two old wormtrails, little more than hummocks of summer-dried weeds, and entered the woods. Evergreens staked out their claims among the tough oaks and smooth-skinned hackberrys.

The two men astride the sixty-foot segmented worm wore black leathers fitted with an assortment of barbs like oversized fishhooks. A third had dismounted and stood near the front of their beast, a burlap sack of potato peelings and pig corn thrown under its nose. All three men wore their hair long, tied down in back and then flared out like a foxtail. All were on the grubby side, but didn't make an art form out of it like their guide.

Valentine had never seen a live legworm at rest. Its "legs" were hundreds of tiny, paired, black clawlike legs, running down the bottom of its fleshy hide like a millipede's. Oversized versions of the claws, growing larger even as the front of the worm grew thinner, pulled up the corn and the earth beneath, stuffing it into a bilateral mouth. Scimitar-like tusks, facing each other like crab claws, stuck out the front

"That's close enough, stranger," said the second man.

"Friendly call, high rider," Price said. "I'm Hoffman Price, friend to the Bulletproof, Worm Wildcats, and the Uttercross."

"We're Bulletproof."

"I know," Price said. "That's why I listed you first."

"Story!" the second man said. "And if it ain't, you know we don't like bums—"

"I know him, Zak," the one with the corncobs said, dropping his sack. He had a little gray in his red-brown hair, and a little more flesh around his middle. "He's no bum. He came and got that Swenson newbie. Maybe four years back. That Colt the Dispatcher carries, he got it from him."

"You wanna vouch for him, Cookie?" the one who'd been called Zak said.

"I'm just saying the Dispatcher knows him, is all."

"Where can I find the Dispatcher?" Price asked. "Is it still Dalian?"

Zak took a drink from a water bottle and passed it back. "Sure is. He's east. Soon as we've eaten we're moving on fast."

"Will you let us ride tail? Three human, two Grog. Mule in tow."

"You might be riding into trouble," Zak said. "One of our pods got jumped. The Dispatcher sent out a call."

"Our guns will secure the Bulletproof, as long as we enjoy the Bulletproof's hospitality," Price said. "You can count us on your side of the worm."

The man behind Zak pointed with a fingerless-gloved hand. "You know the words, but that don't mean much to me."

"He says he wants business with the Dispatcher, that's good enough for me," Zak said. "You can ride tail. Enjoy the music back there."

"Thank you, high rider," Price said. He touched Valentine and they turned.

"What did we just agree to?" Valentine asked.

"When you ride with the Bulletproof—any of the legworm tribes, really—you enjoy their hospitality. But you're expected to stand with them in any kind of a confrontation."

"You mean fight."

"Don't worry. When two tribes get into a feud they each line up on either side of an open field. There's a sporting match like lacrosse only with two contestants; all you have to do is cheer."

"What kind of feud?"

"Could be anything. Usually it's feeding ground. One group allegedly goes in another's area. It's hazy at best. About a third of Kentucky's divided up between the tribes. If they're caught, it's called an arrest but it boils down to being taken hostage. So they hold a contest. If the 'intruder' side wins, the hostages and their worms are released. If the 'intruded' side wins, a ransom and restitution are paid."

"Sounds rather civilized," Valentine said.

"Again, except for yelling, you won't have to do much."

Zac, Gibson—the man behind Zak—and Cookie gave them a quick legworm riding lesson, and issued them each a cargo hook and a climbing goad.

The cargo hook resembled a pirate's replacement hand, hanging from a chain whose links were wide enough for the attachment of lines. They used a pair to attach a long lead to the mule. The goad resembled a mountaineer's pickstaff, with a crowbarlike digger at one end and a long spike at the other. To mount the legworm, you plunged your goad into one of the many thick patches of dead skin—the worm's skin reminded Valentine of fiberglass insulation—and lifted yourself up to a height where a buddy could pull you the rest of the way up. Under no circumstances were you to use one of the longish whisker spikes projecting here and there from newer patches of skin in cracks between the dead material.

"They'll twist good if you grab a whisker," Cookie explained.

"Do they ever roll?" Valentine asked, though he knew the answer.

"Only if they're hurt," Zak said. "You abandon ship quick if that happens."

Bee went first. She plunged her goad hook up high, almost at the top of the worm thanks to her reach, then swung up on pure arm muscle. She accepted the rifles, then helped Price up, who then aided Valentine and Duvalier in their climbs. Ahn-Kha eschewed his goad; he stuck the implement between his teeth and jumped up, grabbing great handfuls of spongy skin, and clambered up with his toes.

"That's how the Grey Ones in the west mount," Ahn-Kha said. He attached his wood-framed pack, plunged the chained cargo hook into the creature's back, then casually gripped the chain with his long toes. Only the Grogs could sit astride the worm's broad back; the humans rode in a leaning sidesaddle fashion.

"Just like you're on a flying carpet," Cookie said. He looked at the strangers' faces. "None of you have heard of a flying carpet? Ignorants!"

"Everybody set?" Zak called back. His head was visible over the cargo netting holding down the trio's supplies.

"All-top and rigged," Price called.

"A lot of us don't say that anymore," Gibson said. "We just say 'yeah.' Try it, tender-thighs."

Zak reached back with a pole capped by something like an oversized legworm goad with a point on the end and stuck the hook down between the legs. That part of the legworm, right under Gibson, gave a little rise and they started ahead.

"You can stop bellyaching that people who aren't one of us aren't one of us anytime, Gib," Zak said, too quietly for anyone but Valentine to hear.

After the initial jerk of motion, the legworm ride made a believer out of Valentine. Whatever the legs were doing below, up top the creature simply glided as though riding on an air cushion. Little changes in the topography came up through the beast with all the discomfort of a cushioned rocking chair.

The mule was all too happy to follow behind without his pack.

Zak continued, "For all you know the gal's being brought to a tribe wedding, or the scarred guy's the Casablancan Minister of the Great Oval Office and Rosegarden traveling incognitpick. So be a good tribe or be silent."

Normally Valentine would be a little embarrassed at overhearing a dressing-down. Except he didn't like Gibson. But good manners won out and he diverted his hearing elsewhere: to the steady staccato crunch of the fast-falling legs. He'd forgotten how strange legworms sounded.

Marbles poured out of a bag in a steady stream onto a pile of crumpled paper, as Evan Pankow, a veteran Wolf, had described it in his first year of training.

The gentle motion of the legworm relaxed Valentine.

"You guys ever sleep up here?" Valentine asked.

"Only one at a time," Cookie called. "Other two have to keep each other alert."

The beast must have dipped its nose—if nose was the right word for the scowlike front end—and scooped a car-hood-sized divot from the earth with its tusks. Zak employed his legworm crook again and worked one of his three reins.

With the legworm in motion the "music" they'd been told to expect started. Like a massive balloon deflating, the beast dropped a cemetery-plot-sized mass of compost behind.

Valentine cautiously took a whiff. All he could smell was Price, and the other people and Grogs.

"Be thankful for small favors," he said to Duvalier as another colossal fart sounded like the horn of Jericho. The mule gave a start.

"It's always loud at startup," Price said. "Gas gets built up while it stands still. Give it a minute and you'll just hear a plop now and then as it makes a deposit."

Duvalier planted herself on the legworm's spongy back, holding her hook under her chin. "I don't mind at all if it means traveling off my feet."

Valentine wished he could see the reins better. The Grog's he'd encountered in Oklahoma used four, two set to either side. The men of the Bulletproof used three, one on each side and one up top. Valentine made a mental note to ask Zak about its utility.

He learned that and a great deal more at the dinner break. This time Zak fed the legworm on bags of peanut shells and ground-up acorn. Price's mule liked the smell of the nuts and joined in, chomping contentedly but rather messily compared to the legworm, who took earth, sod, and shell together in a single gulp.

"If we have to move fast, most of what we carry is food for the mount," Zak said. His face and forearms had dozens of tiny scars.

"How do you make it turn?"

Zak pointed to the rein. A metal loop projected from the beast.

"Yes, but what does that do?"

"Oh, you want the science teacher version? Well, a worm's such a big bastard, there's not much we can do that'll influence it. So we make it think that all its motions are its idea. All those whiskers are wired, so to speak, to an organ under the skin on either side that looks a little like an accordion. When it turns, to keep from rubbing against a tree or whatever, the accordion contracts and it turns. That rein is attached to the accordion, and when we pull it closed the beast turns."

"And keeping the nose up?"

"It's got a balancing organ kind of like your ear in the top of its front end. A little jerk makes it feel like it's out of balance, so it'll stick its head straight forward until the organ feels back in equilibrium. But if they're fed regularly they don't graze all the time. They don't need all that much if it's fair-quality feed. All the dirt they pull up in the wild is a lot of wasted effort."

"How does it breathe?"

"That's something. Here." Zak's leathers creaked as he squatted next to it. "Look underneath. That lighter flesh? We call that the 'membrane' but it's actually a good two feet thick. That thing gets oxygen into its bloodstream. Water don't make much of a difference, but they get sluggish as hell and try to find high ground—though sometimes swamp water will kill them."

"I've never seen one this close."

"Where you from?"

"Iowa. Got out young. My dad worked for, you know—"

Zak nodded. "Me too. Indiana. Practically grew up under a tower. The P worked electricity. Cool stuff, but not if you're reporting to one of those pale-assed jumpers twice a day."

"I left home at eleven," Valentine said. "Ugly scene."

"So what does the flea-ranch over there want with the Bulletproof?"

"I'm just trying to get from point A to point B."

"We'll be at camp a little after sundown. Don't fall off."

Gib drove the legworm a little faster through open country. After a few unheeded yawlps, the mule trotted behind to avoid being dragged. The rolling blue hills left off and they climbed onto the beginning of a plateau, where they gave man, grog, and mule a breather. Valentine saw wooded mountaintops in the distance.

"Keep your guns handy," Zak warned as night fell, looking over the landscape with a monocular. "There are guerillas in those mountains."

They struck a road and followed it to a waypoint town of a dozen empty homes, unless you counted barn owls and mice, a couple of hollow corner bars, and an overgrown gas station and market once dependent on the farm clientele.

Valentine marked fresh legworm furrows everywhere. Some ran right up to the road surface before bouncing off like a ricocheting bullet.

They passed up a rise, and a boy standing guard over the road and his bicycle waved them toward a commanding-looking barn. A pile of weedy rubble that might once have been a house stood close to the road, and a crisscross of torn earth emanated from it. Valentine guessed that from a low-flying plane the landscape would look like an irregular spiderweb. Legworms stood everywhere, pale blue billboards in the moonshine.

"Who's that with you, Zak?" a man afoot called.

"Visitors looking for the Dispatcher. I'm vouching, and I'll bring 'em in. Where is he?"

"Up in the barn."

Zak turned around, an easy operation on the wide back of the legworm. "We're here, folks. You'll have to leave your guns, of course."

"Um, how do we . . . ?" Duvalier asked.

"Get a newbie pole, Royd," Cookie called down.

"No, I'll help," Ahn-Kha said, sliding down the tapered tail. He lifted an arm to Duvalier. "Here."

Valentine jumped down, as did Bee and Price.

"Why not just jump?" Valentine asked Duvalier quietly. "I've seen you dive headfirst from two stories."

"Just a helpless lil' ol' thing without a big man around, Val," Duvalier said. "No harm in having them think that, anyway."

They got out of the lane and made a pile of their weapons and packs.

"Coffee's by the fire pit. Toilet holes are up in the old house," Zak said. "There's a lime barrel, so send down a chaser. Let me know when you're ready to see the Dispatcher."

"Bee—guard!" Price said to his assistant.

"Doesn't she have to use the toilet pits?" Duvalier asked.

"She's not shy," Price said. "And she always buries."

"I would just as soon not scoot my hindquarters on the grass," Ahn-Kha said.

Cookie stretched. "There's plenty of New Universal Church *Improved Testaments* up there. Help yourself."

Valentine wanted coffee more than anything. Duvalier took her walking stick and headed for the rubbled house.

They'd missed dinner, but a line of stretchers propped up on barrels still held bread and roast squash. Sweating teenage girls washed utensils in boiling water as a gray-haired old couple supervised from behind glowing pipes.

"Coffee?" Valentine asked.

"That pot, stranger," one of the girls said, tucking stray hair into a babushka. Valentine took a tin cup out of the hot wash water, choosing a mild scalding over the used cups tossed on the litters and plywood panels, and shook it dry.

It was real coffee. Not the Jamaican variety he'd grown regrettably used to while with Malia at Jayport, but real beans nonetheless. He liked the Bulletproofs even better.

The surge of caffeine brought its own requirements. He remembered to chase it down the hole leading to the unimaginable basement chamber with a ladle of lime.

McDonald R. Dalian, Dispatcher for the Bulletproof, was viewing babies he hadn't met yet when the Price-Valentine mission entered his barn.

The barn was a modern, cavernous structure that had survived its half century of inattention in remarkably good shape, thanks to its concrete foundation and aluminum construction. Small chemical lightsticks Valentine had heard called Threedayers in the Trans-Mississippi Combat Corps hung from the rafter network above.

Men, women, and children of the Bulletproof, most in their black leathers or denim, sat atop defunct, stripped farm machinery to watch Dispatcher Dalian hold court.

A half-dozen guitars, two banjos, and a dulcimer provided music from one corner. Another end of the bar had been turned into a food storage area; shelves had been cleared of odds and ends and replaced by sacks of corn and barrels of flour. A laundry also seemed to be in operation, with clothes and diapers drying on lines strung between stripped combines and the wall.

The Dispatcher had indeterminate features—a little Asian, and maybe a dash of Irish or African for curly hair, and a great high prow of a nose. Except for the curly hair, he reminded Valentine of his father, especially around the protruding ears and out-thrust jaw. He cooed over a sleeping baby as the proud mother and father looked on.

"She's grabbing my finger even while she's sleeping," the Dispatcher said. "Don't tell me she won't be a lead high rider some day."

The Dispatcher and the father of the child bumped their fists, knuckle to knuckle.

The flying buttress nose went up and turned. "Air strike! Only one living thing on the planet smells like that." He handed the baby back and turned. "Hoffman Z. Price has returned."

Price had his usual six-foot circle of solitude around him, even in the busy barn. "And grateful for the generosity of the Bulletproof, Dispatcher."

The Dispatcher opened a tin. "Tobacco?"

Price extracted his pipe and the Dispatcher took a pinch. "You picked your moment. We've got the better part of the tribe together."

"Is worm meat still profitable in Lexington?" Price asked.

"You're innocent of the ways of the trading pits as well as soap, brother. That den of moneychangers and Pharisees takes my meat and my belief in human goodness. I kid, I kid. But if it weren't for the Grogs in Saint Louis I'd be bankrupt. So I hope you're feeling generous. If I have another fugitive in my tribe I'll drive a harder bargain."

Valentine found himself liking the Dispatcher, even if he could be categorized as a Quisling and had a touch of tentpole-revivalist singsong to his words. There was no "step into my office," and as far as he could tell no retinue of subordinates and bodyguards one might expect of a feudal lord. The man carried out his business in the center of his people; any interested eye or curious ear could hear the latest.

A boy brought a spittoon made from an old motorcycle helmet.

Price pointed to Valentine. "I'm looking for a ride to the Ohio for five. We need food for same. Myself, Bee, David here, his friend Ali, and another Grog, an emissary from the Omaha area named Ahn-Kha."

Ahn-Kha didn't claim any titles, though in Valentine's opinion he deserved many. Valentine had to hand it to Price for adding a lot of sizzle to what was probably a very unappetizing steak.

"What does the job pay?"

"Two gold justices. Fort Knox mint."

"Hard currency. Lovely. But it won't pay for the kind of numbers you'd need to get up there safely. There are towers along the Ohio. That could be a dangerous trip, and the Bulletproof have no friends north of Lexington. I'll have to see if I can find you a lead rider willing to hazard a one-worm excursion."

"You seem to have most of them here. That man Zak seems capable."

"He is. I'll speak to him after tomorrow's challenge. He's a bit distracted at the moment. His sister was the lead rider for the legworm that started all this."

"Where should we camp?" Price asked.

"Bed down where you like, but keep clear of the campfires around that farm across the fields to the east. That's the Wildcat camp."

"May we use your laundry, sir?" Valentine asked. Everything he owned was long overdue for more than just a streamside rinse.

"Of course, umm, David," the Dispatcher said. "Our soap is yours. Did you hear me, Hoffman?"

As they walked back to collect the others Valentine had one more question for Price.

"I didn't know you could eat legworms. Even in the Ozarks we couldn't stomach it."

"You have to butcher them fast. The meat can be ground into pig feed. But there are other ways. Didn't you ever have a Ribstrip?"

Valentine remembered the preprocessed barbecued meat from his days masquerading as a Coastal Marine and in Solon's short-lived TMCC. Placed in a hard roll with onions and pickle relish, it was a popular sandwich.

"You don't mean—"

"Yeah. You put enough barbecue sauce on you can hide the taste. Ribstrips are ground and pressed legworm."

Human instinct is to join a crowd, and Valentine gave in to it the next morning. Everyone in the party save Duvalier came along to watch events.

At breakfast, mixing with the Bulletproofs, he'd learned a good deal about what to expect out of the contest. The challenge was fairly simple, a mixture of lacrosse and one-on-one basketball.

The two sides lined up at either end of an agreed field, roughly a thousand yards apart. At the Bulletproof's side, a line of short construction stakes with red blasting tape stood about ten yards out from the crowd, and the only one at the line was the Dispatcher.

Valentine decided there was probably an interesting story having to do with the rifle range of an experienced marksman behind it, but didn't press the issue. The two contestants each went to the center of the field, carrying only a legworm starting hook. The referee, usually either a medical man or a member of the clergy, would be in the center of the field with a basketball. He or she would toss it high enough in the air to dash out of the way before it came back into crook-swinging distance, and the contest would end when one contestant brought the basketball to his side.

"Why a basketball?" Valentine asked a Bulletproof rider who was also explaining the rules to his young son. Nothing was happening yet. The Dispatcher and some of his riders were meeting their opposite numbers in the Wildcats, presumably negotiating the recompense that would be paid.

"You know the answer, Firk. Tell him," the father suggested.

The boy shook his head and shrank against his father. Valentine turned away to save the boy embarrassment and looked out across the dew-spangled field, recently hayed. Opportunistic spiders had woven their webs on the stalks, creating tiny pieces of art like cut glass in the lingering summer sunshine. Some operational farms still existed in this part of Kentucky. Valentine wondered how they ran off grazing legworms.

"It's about the size of a worm egg," the father explained. "That, and basketballs are easy finds."

"No other rules?" Valentine asked.

"I see where you're going. You can't bring anything but the crook. You're stripped down to your skivvies to make sure. Not even shoes."

"Does one ever try to just brain the other and then walk back to the home side with the ball?"

"You get that sometimes, but both sides hate a plain old brawl. Slugging's no way to pump up your mojo, or your tribe's."

A stir of excitement broke out in the crowd when a wandering wild, or unreined, legworm dug a feeding tray toward the challenge field. A pair of legworms with riders hustled out at full speed for a legworm, about the rate of a trotting horse. By judicious use of the mount's bulk, the furrow was redirected.

By the time that ended the two parties had returned from the center of the challenge field. The Dispatcher looked downcast.

Valentine edged closer to the center of the line of people, but many others had the same idea.

He couldn't hear through the babble. "What's up?" people called.

Word passed quickly in ever-expanding circles. "The Wildcat challenger is a Grog! Some kind of import!"

"Ringer!"

"Damn them."

"Take a knee, everyone!" someone bellowed.

Everyone but the Dispatcher sat down. He looked around, nodded to a few, and spoke out to the squash field of foxtailed heads.

"Yes, you heard right. They've got a big Grog they're using in the challenge. Biggest one I've ever seen—even standing on all fours he's bigger than me."

Valentine judged the Dispatcher at about six-three. Ahn-Kha's size. Could there be another Golden One wandering the Cumberland Plateau?

"I saw a man challenge a Grog when I was eight," a well-muscled, shirtless man said, presumably the contestant, as everyone else had jackets or knits against the cool of the morning—warming fast as the sun rose.

"I remember that one," the Dispatcher said. "Fontrain died from his injuries. There's bad blood for this one. According to their Dispatcher, Tikka killed a man when she got taken into custody. Could be they're looking for payback.

"We're going to forfeit," he continued. "It's a hell of a ransom, but I'm not risking Tuck's head over a challenge."

"Might be a bluff," the shirtless man, presumably Tuck, said. "They're trying to get you to fold up by showing you a big, mean Grog. I'll go out there. It's my skull."

"And end up like Fontrain?" the Dispatcher said. "No."

"That means a feud," a craggy-faced woman sitting cross-legged next to Valentine said to everyone and no one. "Oh Lord, lord."

Valentine stood up. "Sir, I'll take a whack at this Grog."

Hundreds of heads turned in his direction. The Dispatcher straightened.

"You ever even held a legworm crook, son?"

"I've played grounders with Grogs," Valentine said, which wasn't quite true. He'd whacked a ball around with a cross between a hockey stick and a cricket bat a few times as Ahn-Kha taught him the fundamentals of the Grog game, and ended up bruised at all compass points.

Consternation broke out in the crowd; much of it sounded approving. "What do we have to lose?" "Leastways if he gets his head bashed in, it's no feud."

"Can we trust you, um, David?" the Dispatcher asked.

"I don't see how you can lose. You're ready to forfeit. Worst thing that could happen is that you pay the ransom anyway and get your riders back."

"Let David do it," the woman next to him called. "Let him take that Goliath."

The crowd liked the sound of that.

"Okay, boy, strip down and grab your crook."

"I've got one request, Dispatcher."

McDonald R. Dalian's eyes narrowed. "What's that?"

"Can I borrow a pair of underwear? Mine aren't fit for public display."

The crowd laughed.

Valentine stood behind a blanket held up by Ahn-Kha as he stripped.

Zak held out a white pair of shorts. "They look a little odd but they're the best thing for riding. They're military issue up in Indiana for their bike troops. Everything stays tucked up real tight."

"Thank you."

As he tried on the shorts Ahn-Kha spoke. "My David, let me try my luck at this."

"I'm from Minnesota, old horse. Born with a hockey stick in my hand."

"Then you will be careful out there."

"Since when am I anything but?"

"In what year were you born?" Ahn-Kha asked, ears askew.

"Be careful. If it is a Grey One, when they are on all fours and running they cannot turn their heads, or hear very well behind. He will not see you if you come at him from the side."

Neither would a freight train, Valentine thought. *Doesn't mean I can bodycheck it off its course.*

"Understood," Valentine said.

Price paced back and forth as Bee pulled up and chewed on dandelion roots. Valentine wondered where Duvalier had gone. But then a sporting event, even one as deadly serious as this, probably wasn't of interest to her.

The shorts were snug-fitting, running from his waist to mid thigh. The padded white pouch at the groin made him feel like one of the come-hither boys that strutted on the streets of New Orleans.

"Oh, that's cute," Price said.

"Better than the ones with three weeks of trail."

Ahn-Kha dropped the blanket and walked with Valentine, Price, and Bee to the center of the line of spectators. Valentine walked barefoot, testing the field's soil. Some murmured about the burns on his lower back and legs. The Dispatcher stood at the center of the line with the twelve-foot legworm crook, looking like a warrior out of some medieval tapestry.

"I can still order it called off," the Dispatcher said, the words just loud enough to travel to Valentine.

"I can't resist a challenge," Valentine said.

"Well, you look fit enough, 'cept for the limp. Hope you can run."

"I can run," Valentine said.

He tried the crook, an all-wood version of the one he'd seen Zak use. Its hooked end had a rounded point.

"Using metal isn't considered sporting," the Dispatcher said.

Damn, it's awkward. Like a vaulting pole.

"Any rule on length?" Valentine asked.

"Yes, it can't be over fifteen feet."

"How about, say, seven?"

"You must be joking. A Grog can already outreach you. You'll just be cutting yourself shorter."

"I'd rather swing a handy short crook than an awkward long one."

The crowd broke out in consternation when Ahn-Kha buried his old TMCC utility machete into the haft of the crook where Valentine indicated, and broke it over his knee.

Valentine tried the crook again. Now he could run with it.

Five hundred yards away, in the center of the field, the Grog waited. He looked huge even at this distance.

"Good luck, David," the Dispatcher said.

"Is anyone taking odds?" Valentine asked.

"You don't want to know," Price said.

"All you have to do is get the ball back to our line," the Dispatcher said. Valentine marked the stakes, stretching a hundred yards to either side, with the crowd spread out behind. "How you do it's up to you."

Valentine looked at Ahn-Kha. The Golden One's ears twitched in anxiety, but one of the great limpid eyes winked.

Valentine raised his arm to the crowd and turned to walk into the center of the field, stretching his arms and legs as he went. The legworm ride yesterday had tasked his muscles in a new way, a trace of stiffness which gave him a good deal more cause to doubt. He wondered how the Bulletproof would feel about a valiant try . . .

The "referee" wore taped-up glasses and a modest crucifix. He carried a basketball under his arm, and leaned over to speak to the Grog as Valentine approached the halfway point. Valentine noticed a pistol in a holster, with a lanyard running up to the referee's neck.

The Grog rivaled Ahn-Kha in size, almost as tall and a good deal wider of shoulder and longer of arm. Pectoral muscles like Viking roundshields twitched as he shifted his half ton of weight from side to side. The Grog's legworm crook lay before his massive hands as though to establish a line Valentine would never cross.

"You're Tuck?" the referee asked.

"Change of programming," Valentine said. "I'm David."

"David, your Wildcat opponent is Vista. Vista, your Bulletproof opponent is David. Don't touch me or you forfeit. Interference by anyone else also results in a forfeit for the interfering side. This mark"—he indicated a pair of flat river stones—"is the center of the field, agreed to by your respective Dispatchers."

The Grog yawned, displaying a mellon-sized gullet guarded by four-inch yellow incisors, capped with steel points, top and bottom. The great, double-thumbed hand picked up the long crook.

The referee held out the basketball. "The object of the contest is to get this ball to your own line. The game begins when the ball hits the ground, and ends when the winner brings it home to his own goal line. I'll fire my pistol in the air to indicate a victory."

Valentine noted the hook on Vista's crop had been chewed to a sharpened point, and hoped that his intestines wouldn't end up draped over the loop at some point.

"Any questions?" the referee finished, stepping to the two stones in the center.

Neither said anything. Vista glared at Valentine. Valentine stared back. The referee held out the ball between them, and when he lowered it for the bounce-toss the Grog was looking away.

"May the best . . . ummm . . . contestant win."

The referee tossed the basketball straight up into the air and back-pedaled out from between man and Grog, quickly enough that Valentine felt air move.

Valentine heard a faint sound like a distant waterfall and realized it was cheering, cut with a few whistles. He felt not at all encouraged, and took a few steps back out of clobbering range as Vista raised his crook—*No sense getting my head knocked off the second the ball hits.*

The damn thing took forever to fall. Was it filled with helium?

The ball struck. Valentine's brain registered that it took a Wildcat bounce, helped along by a quick swing of Vista's crook that Valentine didn't have the length to intercept.

But Vista went for him instead of the ball. The Grog leaped forward, using one of his long arms as a decathlete might use a pole, and upon landing swung his crook for—

The air occupied by Valentine. If Vista didn't want the ball, Valentine would take it. Valentine sprinted after the ball, now rolling at a very shallow angle toward the Bulletproof on its second bounce.

The instinct to just go toe-to-toe with Vista and decide the contest in a brawl surged for a moment. But he'd lose. Valentine looked back to see Vista galloping toward the ball, crook clenched at the midpoint in those wide jaws. Grogs running on all fours looked awkward, but they were damn fast—

Valentine cut an intercepting course.

Vista, you messed up—the Grog's crook had the hook end on Valentine's side. Taking great lungfuls of air, Valentine poured it on. He reached forward with his own hook, Vista's head invisible behind the mountainous shoulders—

—and latched his hook to Vista's. Valentine planted his feet to bring the racing Grog down the way a cowboy would turn a cow's head.

The field smacked Valentine in the face as he landed, yanked off his feet by five times his weight in charging Grog. The crook slipped away like a snake.

By the time he looked up again Vista had retrieved Valentine's crook, and used it to give the ball a whack, sending it farther toward the Wildcat line. Vista left off the contest. Instead of following the ball to a likely victory he advanced on Valentine, long crook in his left hand, held hook out, and Valentine's shorter one looking like a baton in the right. Apparently the Wildcat Dispatcher wanted to teach the Bulletproof a lesson.

You wily gray bastard. You suckered me!

Animal triumph shone in Vista's eyes. Valentine tasted blood from a cut lip. The referee ran across the periphery of Valentine's vision, moving for a better angle on events.

Valentine stood up, swiping the dirt from his knees as he watched Vista advance, and ran his tongue along the inside of his teeth.

Vista raised his twin weapons and bellowed, stamping his feet and banging the crooks together.

Valentine raised his middle finger in return.

The Grog knew what that meant. It charged, wild-eyed.

Valentine ran away.

He felt the long crook tug at his hair and ran harder. Vista couldn't sprint with weapons in his hands, so the Grog paused. Valentine used the precious second to achieve some distance, then settled into his old, pounding Wolf run, pretended his aching left leg didn't exist.

Vista gained on him, slowly, but only by sprinting full tilt. And the Grog couldn't breathe as well with two crooks crammed into its bear-trap-like mouth. Valentine slowed a little, listening to the footfalls behind, but didn't dare look back; a trip and a sprawl would be fatal.

Vista slowed. The Grog's eyes no longer blazed, but were clouded by new doubt, and it came to a halt perhaps a hundred yards from the Bulletproof line.

A shout from somewhere in the line: *"Hrut ko-ahhh mreh!"*

Valentine glanced back and saw Ahn-Kha, making a sawing motion with one of his mighty arms.

Vista screamed back, words or pure rage, Valentine couldn't tell. Vista dashed off at an angle southward, running an oblique course for the Wildcat line.

Got you now!

Valentine's crook spun past his nose and he sidestepped—and caught it as it bounced in the air. This time he heard the cheers clearly. With fresh energy he tore toward the Wildcat side and the distant ball, hidden by a gentle fold in the earth.

Sorry, Vista. You'll keep your temper next time.

But the Grog had unguessed-at reserves. It pounded up behind Valentine, sounding like a galloping horse. Valentine risked a glance over his shoulder and saw Vista running in a two-leg, one-arm canter, the long crook raised to catch him—

Vista swung and Valentine blocked. Valentine shielded his back against another blow and hurried on, then got a painful rap on the knuckles that opened his hand, and he lost his crook for the second time.

He could run better without it anyway.

Now for a real burn.

Valentine ran, extending his sprint. Were he still a fresh Wolf of twenty-two with an uninjured leg he would have left Vista gaping behind. As it was he increased the distance, but only just.

The ball would be an awkward thing to carry. Under his arm he wouldn't be able to run with a proper stride; held in each hand he'd be running upright, not a natural human motion. He could kick it, but what if he mistimed an approach and missed? If only he had a satchel . . .

Valentine spotted the ball and changed his angle. Vista slowed behind him, perhaps conserving his wind to intercept Valentine on his sprint back. Even more distance yawned between them.

The referee caught up on both of them.

Valentine reached the ball and the Wildcats booed. He ignored the catcalls.

Vista pulled up, perhaps forty yards away, and blew air like an idling train engine. He left ample room to cut an intercepting course.

Valentine dropped his shorts. Someone on the Wildcat side had enough of a sense of humor to whistle, a twittering wolf whistle.

He picked up the ball and stuffed it into the elastic waistband, then closed most of the waist in his fist. The ball was too big to go out the leg holes.

Vista cocked his head, oddly doglike with ears outstretched.

Holding the ball in the improvised sack, Valentine ran straight at him.

The Grog, perhaps fearing another trick, widened his stance and rocked back and forth, crook held loosely in his right hand.

At three strides away Valentine feinted right, away from the crook—then leaped.

He tucked the ball into his belly as he flew through the air, not wanting it batted away as he went over Vista's head in a great Cat leap.

It swung its crook where Valentine should have been.

Valentine landed lightly on his good leg, had a bad split second when Vista's thrown crook struck him in the ankle, and ran, feeling rapidly growing pain from the blow.

Valentine managed to open the distance between them, and Vista let out a strangled, winded cry.

The Bulletproof danced and shouted behind their markers, some urging him on by circling their arms in wheels toward the red tape.

Valentine crossed the line—a gunshot sounded, and old instincts made him flinch—and fell into a mass of Bulletproofs. He felt a sharp slap on his bare buttock, and looked to see the craggy-faced woman giving him a gap-toothed grin.

Valentine turned to look at his opponent. Vista collapsed to his wide knees, pounding at the turf with great fists. He took the basketball out of his underwear, gave up trying to reach the Dispatcher, and tossed the ball in the air.

Limping, Valentine went out to Vista. The Grog jumped up, snarling.

Valentine offered his hand.

The Grog snatched him up by the arm and lowered his head with mouth gaping to bite it off at the wrist. Another shot sounded and the Grog pulled back, a bleeding hole in its cheek.

Valentine spun out of reach.

The referee trotted up, pistol held pointed at the Grog. "Back to our side! Back!"

The Grog emptied a nostril at the referee and turned away.

The referee lowered his gun, looked at Valentine from beneath a sweat-dripping brow. "You, sir, are one dumb son of a bitch. Congratulations."

"Thank you," Valentine said, rubbing his wrist.

Ahn-Kha loomed up. "My David!"

"I'm fine. A little bruised."

The Dispatcher and Zak joined them, the former with the basketball, the latter holding Valentine's clothes.

"What did you yell?" Valentine asked, remembering the scream from the sidelines. "He forgot all about me."

"I accused his mother of the lowest-caste choice of mates," Ahn-Kha said. "Such an insult can only result in a duel. He started to answer me when you ran."

"Maybe you'd better stay in camp when David goes to collect his share."

"Share?" Valentine asked.

"You won. A portion of the recovered herd is yours."

"And I owe you a great debt," Zak said. "Dispatcher, may I go along and collect my sister?"

"Go in my place. But keep away from the Grog. One blood contest a season is enough."

The Wildcats fell back from their side of the field as they crossed, Valentine holding the basketball up as though it were a torch per Zak's instruction.

A huge legworm, longer than the one Valentine had ridden into the Bulletproof camp, led six unreined worms onto the contest field. Valentine watched them pull up soil, weeds, and hay stubble like plows.

Three riders sat astride the broad back, in the "flying carpet" sidesaddle-seat Valentine was beginning to recognize.

"That's Tikka, she's the reiner," Zak said.

Tikka had sun-washed, caramel-colored hair, plumed into a lusher version of the foxtail her brother wore, and the tan, windburned face of a woman who seldom knew a roof. The man behind her was shirtless, with bandages wrapped around his midsection. The third rider, a beefy, gray-haired woman, evidently kept the tradition of the third rider being older.

"Watch the whiskers on the unreined legworms," Zak advised Valentine. "Tikka! Look at the trouble you caused," he called.

She dismissed him with a wave. "Talk to the herd."

Zak turned to Valentine. "The Dispatcher won't allow us to ride together. Too many brawls."

"I thought it was cousins who liked to fight in these parts."

Zak winked. "Fight . . . or kiss. Fact is, I don't feel guilty about either. I'm adopted."

Valentine spent the day mildly worried. Duvalier had tucked a note in his pack

> Checking out the other camp
> Back tonight
> —Meeyao

and had not returned.

Valentine found himself a minor celebrity in the camp. As he limped around on his sore ankle, Bulletproof children came up and bumped him with their fists and elbows. He explored the camp with Price, trying to stave off the coming stiffness by keeping his muscles warm. He looked at some of the carts and sledges the legworms towed. Many held loads of fodder, or sides of meat, but one, under guard near the Dispatcher's tent, had a generator and racks of military radio gear.

"There'll be a party tonight," Price said. "Weather's nice and the herders will disperse."

"The little contest this morning," Valentine said. "Does anyone ever not pay up when they lose?"

"That's why they bring together as much of the tribe as they can. Sort of like wearing your gun at a poker game."

Valentine and Ahn-Kha did laundry at the washtubs. The other Bulletproofs doing washing insisted on giving them soap flakes and the outside lines for drying their clothes. A woman carrying six months of baby under her tie-front smock hinted that Valentine would be getting some new clothes that night. "They're going round for donations," she said.

By nightfall a raucous throng of legworm herders surrounded the barn like a besieging army. Their rein-pierced mounts stood along the road ditch in lines, eating a mixture of grains and hay dumped into the ditch.

Valentine didn't feel much like joining. His legs had been filled with asphalt, his ankle had swelled, and his shoulder blade felt like a chiropractor had moved it four inches up. He stayed out in the warm night and ate beans from a tin plate, scooping them onto a thick strip of bacon, and watched Ahn-Kha make a new pack for Bee out of a legless kitchen chair the Golden One had traded for somewhere.

"Everyone wants to see you," Zak said, coming out of the darkness. "Dispatcher himself asked for you."

"I'm tired, reiner."

"Just for a moment. You're Bulletproof now. You've got to have a sip."

"A sip?"

"It's where we get our name. What did you think it meant, Kevlar? We've got some char-barrel-aged Kentucky bourbon."

Valentine scraped off his plate into the legworm-feed bucket. EVERY BITE ADDS AN INCH was written on the side. "You should have opened with that, Zak. I'd have been up there already."

Inside the barn, a wood-staved cask big enough to bathe in stood upon two sawhorses near the band, each of whom had a sizeable tumbler tucked under their chair as they scraped and strummed and plucked away. Tikka, in a fringed version of her brother's leathers, gave him a welcoming hug that allowed Valentine a whiff of leather-trapped feminine musk, then took Zak's hand and pulled him away. The Dispatcher poured drinks into everything from soup bowls to elegant crystal snifters, with the help of Cookie at the tap.

Valentine entered to applause and whoops. He kept forgetting he was supposed to hate these people. Perhaps they'd bred the legworms that destroyed Foxtrot Company at Little Timber Hill. But they'd carved out a life, apparently free of the Reapers. He had to give them credit for that.

"Our man of the night," the Dispatcher said, his nose even more prominent thanks to its reddish tinge. "How do the victory garlands feel?"

"They're turning purple," Valentine said, accepting a proffered thick-bottomed glass from Cookie. A quarter cup of amber liquor rolled around the bottom.

"Some Bulletproof will take the edge off."

"Just a splash, please, sir. I—don't hold my liquor well."

"It's that cheap radiator busthead you flatties brew in the Midwest, is why," Cookie said. "Bulletproof's got aroma and character."

"It blows your damn head off," Tikka said. "That's why we called it 'bulletproof' in the first place."

"Enjoy," the Dispatcher said, raising his own glass and bringing it halfway to Valentine.

"Bad luck not to finish your first taste," someone called from the audience.

Valentine touched his glass to the Dispatcher's, and several in the crowd applauded.

The liquor bit, no question, but it brought an instantaneous warmth along for the ride. Cheering filled the barn.

"He's Bulletproof now," the Dispatcher called to the crowd, noticing Valentine's wince. "Bring out his leathers!"

A parade of Bulletproof wives and daughters came forward, each holding a piece of leather or armor—a jacket with shoulder pads sewn in, pants, boots, gloves, a gun belt, something that looked like spurs . . .

Valentine stood a little dumbly as they piled the gear on his shoulders and around his feet. It was a dull gunmetal color, and made him think of a knight-errant.

"Zak," the Dispatcher called. "Where'd he get to? *Zak!*"

"Right here," Zak called, coming in from the gaping doorway to the barn, Tikka in tow, both looking a little disheveled.

"Zak, show David here how to wear his leathers."

Valentine, Zak, and Tikka picked up pieces of his new outfit and went outside. He'd seen breastplates like the one they strapped on before. They were an old army composite, hot as hell, made you feel like a turtle, but they could stop shrapnel. "You got ol' Snelling's rig," Zak observed. "He was a good reiner, if a bit flash for the Bulletproof. Dropped stone dead of a heart attack one hot summer day while climbing his mount. You never know."

"No, you don't," Valentine agreed, glad this Snelling hadn't been felled by a sniper working for the Cause.

"Zak says you're a flattie?" Tikka asked. She had a siren's voice, and her melodious accent begged a man to sit down and stay a while.

"Iowa," Valentine said. "But I left when I was young. I spent a lot of time in the Gulf."

"That where you picked up those scars?"

"Pretty much. What's this on the sleeve?" A series of hooks, reminding Valentine a little of sharpened alligator teeth, ran down the outside seam of the forearm of the jacket.

"Serrates," Tikka said. "They're for digging in when you mount, or hanging on to the side."

Zak showed him how to fix the spurs, which were a little more like the climbing spikes utility linemen wore to reach their wires. They could be flipped up and locked flush to the inner side of the boot. Locked down, they projected out and down from his ankle.

"Some guys put them on their boot points. I think that looks queer," Zak said.

Valentine explored the padding in the jacket shoulders and elbows. Military Kevlar plates were buttoned into the back and double-breasted front. The pants had stiff plastic caps on the knees and shins.

"You can take the bulletproofing out, but we generally wear it. Can be a lifesaver."

Valentine felt a bit like a porcupine. His old Cat claws would fit right in on this outfit. He could wear them openly and they'd just look like another set of spikes.

"How do you two kiss without harpooning each other?" Valentine asked.

A smile split Tikka's tan face and her eyes caught the firelight. "That's just part of the fun."

"Don't make fun of the leathers," Zak said. "A lot of effort goes into each one."

"Fine stitching," Valentine said. He wondered about the hides, though; they were thicker and pebblier than cowhide.

"I don't mean that. That's legworm egg-casing, stretched and dried. Getting it is trickier than threading a full-grown legworm for reins. You have to go into a breeding pile and get the egg right after it hatches, because it rots fast if you don't get it scraped out and dried. You have to help the little bugger inside out of it, or he'll eat almost the whole thing, and if you hurt a legworm grub doing that the adults stomp everything in sight."

"It's kind of a rite of passage for our youths," Tikka said. "They have to go into the winter dogpiles and check on the eggs. When they come out with a hide, they're considered full-grown members of the tribe."

"Thank you for skipping that step with me," Valentine said. "I'll wear it with pride."

"But be careful, Dave. There are lots in town that look down on riders. You'll get called a hillbilly and a Grogfucker and worse. Some think riding herd on a legworm's the same as cleaning up after a gaunt."

"He looks too fine for that kind of talk, Zak," Tikka said.

"How do you do the foxtails in your hair?" Valentine asked.

"Easy," Tikka said. "There's a cut-down pinecone attached to the tie. Some braid their hair around it. I can show you. Now that you've got a few worms, you should look the part."

"Zak, I want to talk to you about that. I'm passing through. Hoffman Price brought us up here in the hope that we'd get a guide to the Ohio River, up around Ironton or Portsmouth. I'll swap you my share of the recovered beasts for a ride."

Zak shook his head. "I've got a bigger string a little to the west. I'm leaving early tomorrow to get back to them."

"Then I'll drive you," Tikka said. "That way I'll get my string back."

"He's already got a girl, Tikka," Zak said. "You'll have to excuse my sister, Dave, she's man-crazy."

"Any girl who doesn't want a husband by twenty and babies after is man-crazy, in my brother's opinion," Tikka said. "Zak, you know you're the only one for me."

" 'Only one' when I'm around, that is. And that's just 'cause I keep saying no to a train."

She tried to stomp him with her heavy riding boot but Zak danced out of the way. "You're a fresh piece of wormtrail, Zachary Stark."

"What in the hell are you wearing, David Black?" Alessa Duvalier asked from the darkness. She wore her long coat, black side turned out, and carried her walking stick.

"And that's the girl, Tikka," Zak said, grabbing for her long hair. She dodged out of the way and got behind Valentine.

"Apparently I'm Bulletproof now," Valentine said, striking a Napoleonic pose. "What do you think?" Tikka played with his hair.

"I'm tempted to get your pistol and test you. Starving, is there any food left?"

Valentine smelled blood on her. "Sure. I'll show you. Excuse us."

"Let's hurry. Starved."

Valentine led her up to the food tables, and she cut open a loaf and filled it with barbecue. They went back to their camp in the empty field.

Ahn-Kha and Bee were wrapped up in a fireside game that involved piling buttons on a rounded rock.

"Price is walking his mule," Ahn-Kha said. "Did they offer us transport, my David?"

"Oh, he's got a ride. Count on him," Duvalier said.

"What have you been up to?" Valentine asked.

"I didn't miss your performance this morning. I just watched it from the Wildcat side. I was checking out these camps. There's some bad blood between these, um, tribes."

"You've made it worse?" Valentine asked.

"Of course. We might want to shift a little more to the west. When it got dark I offed a couple of the Wildcats and left a note warning them not to use Grogs in any future contests. They were already stirred up because someone got shot when they captured those Bulletproofs. When they see what I did to the bodies it ought to put them over the edge. A lot of their riders were upset that they let it go with just a contest. This should put them right over the edge."

Ahn-Kha sent a cascade of buttons down the side of the rock and bowed to Bee. He got up and went over to the wrapping for his oversized gun.

Valentine rose and looked across to the ridge with the Wildcat campfires. Had some of them gone out? He should have counted. Captain Le Havre would have taken a piece out of his ass for that kind of sloppiness. He picked up his U-gun.

"Wait here," Valentine said. "If shooting starts, let's meet at the creek we crossed just before we turned in here."

"Val, what are you doing?" Duvalier said.

"I'm going to warn them."

"Why? The Bulletproof will probably win; there're more of them. It'll get a good war started between these assholes."

"There are kids all over the place."

"Nits make lice, Val," Duvalier said.

"Is that who you really are?" Valentine asked.

"Whose side are you on, Ghost?" she called after him. "I know the answer: your ego's."

Valentine hurried up to the barn, the new leather pants creaking as he trotted. His ankle hurt, but seconds might count.

"Yes, you look fine in your leathers, Bulletproof," a woman called from the door of the barn. The party was still in full cry, and Zak and Tikka were stomping the concrete with bootheel and toe in syncopation, another quarrel forgotten. Valentine ignored his greeter and went straight for the Dispatcher.

The crowd parted, alarmed at the U-gun. Valentine carefully carried it pointed down, his hand well away from the trigger area. Zak stepped in at his rifle arm. "Dave, there's no need—"

"Watch that weapon, David," the Dispatcher said. "What's going on? Pants too tight and you're looking for the tailor?"

A few laughed.

"Dispatcher," Valentine said. "Our Grogs were down looking at the contest field. They went off to some bushes to—you know—"

"And?" the Dispatcher asked.

"They saw the Wildcats. Some of them on their worms, armed, others gathering."

"Coming this way?" the Dispatcher asked.

"The Grogs just ran back. Armed riders is all I know."

The Dispatcher upended his glass of bourbon onto the concrete. "Carpenter, get to the herd riders, have them try to lead the wild worms west. Mother Shaw, take the children out to the cover-field. Everyone else who can shoulder a gun, get to the rein-worms. Lead riders Mandvi, French, Cherniawsky and McGee, with me. David, you and your people with Zak; Zak, get them clear."

"You might see some fancy riding after all," Tikka said.

The crowd dissolved, and the musicians cased their instruments, if not sober at least sobered.

Zak brought Valentine to his legworm at the road trough. Other riders were climbing on board, bawling orders to the teenage boys watching the mounts—

—when a rocket cut across the sky, leaving a sparking trail. It exploded overhead with a *BOOM* that rattled Valentine's bones.

The legworm reared but Zak settled it.

Zak extended a hand, but Valentine found that with the hooks and spikes in his costume, climbing the side of the legworm was possible without assistance, as long as another shell didn't fire.

"What the hell was that?" Valentine asked, the boom still echoing in his ears.

"A big firework, sorta. Scares the worms. They're trying to make the mounts bolt."

Valentine saw one worm humping as it headed down the road, a rider raising dust as he was dragged. The others had their mounts under control, more or less, and turned them toward the barn.

Another rocket exploded, but it only served to hurry the legworms in the direction they were already going. Zak reached their campsite.

"Get on!" Valentine called. "We've got to ride out of here. Where's Price?"

"I don't know," Ahn-Kha said. "Still off with his mule." Valentine helped the others up.

Bee looked alarmed, and refused to mount. She let out a shriek into the night. Ahn-Kha barked something at her and reached out, but she slapped his hand away and ran off toward the road.

"I'll drop you off with the kids in the cover-field," Zak said. "You'll be safe there."

"Take us to the fight," Valentine said.

"The Dispatcher—"

"The Dispatcher's going to need every gun," Valentine said. "We've got three. Right?" He looked over his shoulder at Duvalier and Ahn-Kha.

Anh-Kha nodded. He had his cannon and Price's Kalashnikov. Duvalier patted her shotgun. "I'm happy to plant a few bobcats."

"Wildcats," Zak said.

"Then let's get online."

Valentine looked down at his U-gun. The only ammunition he had for it was Everready's 5.56mm. He wished he had a real sniper load. He looked at Duvalier's shotgun. The Mossberg would be useless in anything but a close-quarters fight. "Ali, take Price's rifle."

"Be sparing," Ahn-Kha said. "There is only one magazine."

"Where's the rest?"

"In boxes." Ahn-Kha rummaged around in the battle satchel that contained spare bullets and gear for his gun, and handed him the box.

Cookie and Gibson joined them and the legworm slid quickly down the hill to where the other riders were gathering. Cookie had his ear to a headset, coming from a handcrank-charged portable radio.

Another rocket exploded over the massive barn. Yellow-white sparks ran down the tin roof.

"They're good with the fuses over there. Probably been cutting them all day. So you're a brother rider now," Gibson added to Valentine.

"Seems like," Valentine said. Zak lined up his legworm behind another. Just behind them, in the center of the column of legworms, the Dispatcher waved a flashlight. The column turned and the legworms went single-file up toward the barn.

"If we go to battle line you, the girl, and the Grog can cling to the cargo netting," Zak said. "Keep your heads down."

Valentine learned what battle line was as soon as they crested the hill and turned their line north. Another sky-cracking explosion over the barn sent a legworm humping over from the other side of the hill, its riders hanging on for their lives. The line of battle-ready legworms twitched, but stayed in station front to back.

"They're coming. Flank facing offside," Cookie called, listening to his headset.

Zak and his team slid off the top of their worm, as did riders all along the battle line, digging their hooks, goads, and spikes into the thick patches of dead flesh. Women and teenage boys with rifles, hooks looped around their chests and attached to their ankles, joined the fighting line, adding their guns.

The column moved in the direction the fleeing legworm had just abandoned. Valentine readied himself for what would be on the reverse slope of the hill when they topped it.

Cookie slapped his thigh, headset to his ear. "Zak, we got 'em. They're in the field, not halfway across, in open order."

Cheers and foxhunting hallos broke out all across the Dispatcher's line of legworms as the news spread.

Zak's mount crested the hill and came down the other side, turning slightly as it followed the worm directly ahead.

Twenty or more legworms crept—or so it looked in the distance—in three columns across the contest field toward the Bulletproof camp.

Valentine took comfort in the thick length of legworm between him and the Wildcats. It was like shooting from a moveable wall. He thought of stories he'd read of fighting warships, their lines of cannons presented to each other. In naval terminology, the Bulletproofs were "crossing the T" against the oncoming Wildcats.

The Dispatcher's legworm followed theirs, and the one behind his let loose with a whooshing sound.

"The pipe organ's firing!" Gibson yelled. "Yeeeah!"

Streams of sparks cut down the hillside and exploded in the earth among the columns. The Wildcat legworms began to turn and get into line to present their own bank of rifles to the Bulletproofs, but the mounts kept trying to get away from the explosions.

Machine guns from the front Wildcat legworms probed their line, red tracers reaching for the riders. Another Wildcat firework burst above and Valentine felt the legworm jump, but it had overshot.

The Bulletproof column accelerated. Zak employed his sharpened hook to urge the legworm along and close the gap that opened between his mount and the one ahead. Zak still had his rifle slung; his job was to keep his beast in line, not fight.

Now the two masses of legworms, the Bulletproof's tightly in line and moving quickly, the Wildcats' in an arrowhead-shaped mob, converged.

Ahn-Kha sighted and fired. "Damn," he said, loading another shell. He shot again. "Got him."

A legworm in the Wildcats turned and others writhed to follow or to avoid its new course. Ahn-Kha picked off another driver.

"That's some kind of shooting," Cookie said. Ahn-Kha ignored him, fired again, swore.

The front end of the Bulletproof column began to fire. It had run ahead of the Wildcats; the marksmen got an angle on the exposed riders clinging to the right sides of their mounts.

The Wildcat column dissolved into chaos. Each legworm turned and hurried back toward their camp as fast as the hundreds and hundreds of legs could carry their riders.

Cheers broke out all across the Bulletproof line.

"That's how you win a scrap!" Gibson said. "Tight riding. Damn if Mandvi can't point a column."

"It's because we were ready for them," Zak said, nodding to Valentine.

"Cease fire," Cookie shouted, radio headset still to his ear—though no one but Ahn-Kha was shooting. The Wildcats retreated in disorder.

Valentine hadn't used a single bullet.

More rounds of Bulletproof were being issued as riders danced jigs. Other legworms, still with armed riders, circled the barn at a distance, though the scouts had claimed that the Wildcats were decamping and heading for higher ground to the east.

"Zak, I take it you're willing to give our friends a ride north, now," the Dispatcher said. "And if you aren't, I'll make it an order."

"Of course I'm willing. I'm willing to dig a hole to hell if that's where they want me to drive my worm."

"Your sister can go watch your string," the Dispatcher said.

"Wormcast." Tikka kicked a stone.

Duvalier hung on Valentine's arm, but it was play; she felt stiff as a mannequin. "Better luck next time."

"What's your destination over the Ohio?"

"We're trying to find an old relative," Valentine said. "She's come up in the world, and we're going to see if she'll set us up."

"Take Three-Finger Charlie, Zak," the Dispatcher said. "He's got connections with the smugglers. Tell him to trade egg hides if he has to, I want these folks set up so they can pass through the Ohio Ordnance in style."

Hoffman Price led his mule into the circle of revelers. "I was scavenging for mule shoes. He found a mess of wild carrots, and they were fat and sweet so I pulled up a bushel."

"You missed—" Zak began.

"I know. I saw it from a couple miles away. You Bulletproofs throw one hell of a party. Fireworks and everything."

Price looked at the bourbon-sloppy smiles all around. "What? Don't y'all like carrots?"

Ten

The Ohio River Valley, September: North of the bluegrass in the upper reaches of the Ohio River lies a stream-crossed country of woods and limestone hills. Rust-belt ruins, dotted with an occasional manufacturing plant, line the river. North of the river is the Great Lakes Ordnance, a network of Kurian principalities in a federation of unequal ministates huddled around the middle Great Lakes. South of the Ohio are coal mines and mill towns, under wary Kurians who have staked out claims bordering on the lands of the legworm ranchers.

No one much likes, or trusts, anyone else. But this is the industrial heartland of the eastern half of North America, such as it is, producing engines, garments, footwear, tires, even a bush-hopping aircraft or two, along with the more mundane implements of a nineteenth-century technology. Their deals are made in New York, their "deposits" are exchanged in Memphis, and their human workers are secured by mercenary bands of Grogs hired from and directed by the great generals of Washington, DC. As long as they produce, even slowly and inefficiently, the material the rest of the Kurian Order needs, and keep the Baltimore and Ohio lifelines open, their position is secure.

It was here that David Valentine lost his forlorn hope of a trail.

Valentine, Price, Bee, Ahn-Kha, and Duvalier stood at the Laurelton Station a week later in a blustery rain.

Zak and the other Bulletproofs departed after depositing them in the care of a man named McNulty, a River Rat trader and "labor agent" friendly to the tribe on the south bank of the Ohio.

They'd ridden into a shantytown right in the shadow of a grain-silo Kurian Tower—only the most desperate would resort to such real estate in broad daylight—with Price's mule happily munching hay in a flatbed cart being towed by the powerful legworm. After introductions at the River Rat's anchored barge-house and one last round of Bulletproof bourbon in farewell, Zak turned over six full legworm egg hides, cured and bound in twine. Valentine only parted with them after McNulty gave them Ohio ID cards, ration books, and an up-to-date map of the area. The map was annotated with riverbank areas that were hiring and cheap lodgings—all with the password "BMN."

McNulty probably took a cut of any business he referred.

With a week's familiarity, Valentine could see why the legworm-egg leather was so valuable. It breathed well, and though it became heavy in the rain the wet didn't permeate to the inside.

They followed the riverside train tracks to the turn-in for Laurelton. Price told them what he could about the north side of the river. He had returned fugitives to the Ohio authorities once or twice, but had never been much beyond the river. Bee stuck close to him here under the somber sky—autumn had arrived.

The residents kept to their towns. Patrolmen on bicycles, most armed with nothing more than a sap, rode the towns and highways. The officers looked at Price's Kalashnikov as they passed—the rest of their longarms were wrapped in blankets on the mule—but made no move to question them. Valentine saw only one vehicle, a garbage truck full of coal.

The ground reminded Valentine of some of the hills near the Iron Range in Minnesota, low and jumbled and full of timber. But where the forests in the Northwoods had stood since before the Sioux hunted, the forests in Ohio had sprung up since 2022, breaking up and overrunning the little plots carved out by man.

So when they cautiously turned the bends nearing Laurelton, only to find more windowless houses and piles of weed-bearing brick, he couldn't help feeling deflated.

There was a station, if a single siding counted as a station. The track continued north, but the height of the weeds, trees, and bracken suggested that a train hadn't passed that way in years. Valentine even checked the rust on the rails to be sure. In his days as a Wolf he'd seen supply caves hidden by saplings and bushes specifically pulled up and replanted to discourage investigation.

Deep oxidation. He could scrape it off with a thumbnail.

"Fool's hope," Valentine said. "Rooster either lied or didn't have correct information from the Kurians. Maybe they divert the trains to keep the final destination secret."

Price unloaded his mule to give the animal a breather. "The debt is settled. I feel for you, David. Long way to come to find nothing. It's happened to me."

Post would know he'd tried his best. How many vanished a year in the Kurian Zone? A hundred thousand? A half million? But how do you laugh in a legless man's face and tell him the last rope he's clinging to isn't tied to anything but a wish?

The narrow road bordering the track was in pretty poor condition. It certainly wasn't frequently traveled.

Why here?

Price filled the mule's nosebag and Bee rooted inside one of the abandoned houses for firewood. Duvalier stretched herself out next to a ditch and took off her boots.

The hills around Laurelton were close. A hundred men, properly posted, could make sure that whatever transpired here couldn't be seen by anything but aircraft or satellites.

Ahn-Kha poked around the road, examining potholes. "Strange sort of road, my David," Ahn-Kha said.

Valentine joined him. Like the tracks, it ended in weeds to the north. The south part—

—had been patched.

Valentine trotted a few hundred yards south.

There was a filled gap in the road at a washout, recent enough for the asphalt to still be black-blueish, rather than gray-green. The Kurians weren't much on infrastructure maintenance even in their best-run principalities; they didn't like anything that traveled faster than a Reaper could run. . . .

Valentine examined the weeds and bracken bordering the station. Sure enough, there were three gaps, definite paths leading from the tracks to the road. Quick-growing grasses had sprung up, but no brambles or saplings, though they were thick on the west side of the tracks.

"A farewell feast," Price said, revealing a sausage wrapped in wax paper and a loaf of bread. "Unless you want to come back with us."

Valentine handed him Everready's Reaper teeth. "More than earned. If I had another set I'd give them to you, with my initials written on them."

"If you see the old squatter again, let him know I appreciate being able to repay the debt. What are you going to do next?"

Valentine rubbed his chin. He needed a shave. "You said you'd brought in men to the Ordnance?"

Price consulted a scuffed leather notebook and extracted a card from a pocket. "Yup. I'm 31458 here in Ohio." He passed it to Valentine.

The card had the number, and some kind of seal featuring a man in a toga holding one hand over his heart and the other outstretched, over a pyramid with an eye at the top. "Meaning what?"

Price shrugged. "Dunno. They always recorded my number when I brought a man in, though."

"How hard is it to get one of those?"

"I didn't even know I had to have one. They gave it to me when I brought my first man in. I was going to stop at one of the cop stations and look at what kind of warrants are out. Long as I'm up this way, maybe someone's hiding out in Kentucky I can bring in. Make the trip profitable in more than a spiritual sense."

"Mind if I tag along?"

"Not at all."

"Let's walk along the road on the way back to the river."

After lunch they walked single file down the side of the road. Valentine stayed in the center of the road, crisscrossing it, checking blown debris, the patchwork repairs, anything for some kind of sign. He found a few old ruts that he suspected were made by heavy trucks, but they were so weathered that he could only guess at the type of vehicle.

"So we did all this for nothing?" Duvalier asked when they took a rest halt. "We're just going back?"

There was a welcome tenderness to her voice; she'd been cold since Valentine had turned the mutual slaughter she'd tried to start into a victory for the Bulletproof.

"Wherever they take the women, it has to be pretty close. I want to start searching. Seems to me it's got to be within a few miles. Otherwise they'd bring the train somewhere else, or right to where they want them. We'll just start searching, using a grid with the station as a base point."

"Why are we still with Stinky, then?"

"To set us up as bounty hunters. It's not far from what we're really doing, and it would explain us poking around in the woods."

"I don't like it here. These hills and trees, all wet and black. It's like they're closing off the sky. I haven't liked this job; just one misery after another."

Valentine looked up from yet another worthless mark that wasn't a track. "I'm glad you're here. I'd have been hung months ago if it wasn't for you and Ahn-Kha, most likely."

"The Lifeweavers were watching over us all back there. But they don't know about us being here. How can they know we need their help?"

Duvalier's worshipful naivete when it came to humanity's allies took strange forms sometimes. "Not sure how they could help us now," Valentine said.

"Something would turn up. A piece of luck. Like the general's train showing up in Nebraska."

"After we crisscrossed three states looking for him. Would have been better if the Lifeweavers had arranged our luck to hit when we passed a dozen miles from his headquarters without knowing it."

She planted her walking stick. "You think everything's chance."

"No. If it were, I wouldn't still be alive."

After Price flagged down a patrolman on the riverside highway, they stopped in the little Ohio-side town of Caspian. An Ordnance Station, part police house, part customs post, and part post office had the latest warrant flyers posted in a three-ring binder. Valentine and Price went inside while the rest visited a market to buy food.

"Look what the river washed up," an Ohioan with a package said to his friend as they passed in on their way to the postal clerk.

Price helped Valentine select a handbill. Valentine wanted a female, thirtyish. "Not much to choose from. Guess Ohio women are law-abiding. Except for Gina Stottard, here."

"Stealing power and unauthorized wiring," Valentine read. "A desperado electrician."

"She's all there is."

"What do I do next?"

"Follow me."

Price took three handbills of his own—the top man had killed a woman while trying to perform an illegal abortion—and went over to a blue-uniformed officer behind a thick window. She blinked at them from behind thick corrective glasses.

"Copies of these, please," Price said, sliding the handbills under the glass along with his warrant card. "And—"

"Gimme a moment," she said, and went to a cabinet. She got a key and disappeared into another room. Ten minutes later—perhaps she'd worked in a coffee break—she returned with the copies. They were poor-quality photocopies, but still readable. "Six dollars," she said.

"My associate needs a bounty card."

"That makes it sixteen dollars. You could have said so. Have to make another trip to get one."

"I tr—I'm sorry."

Fifteen minutes later she returned with the form. It had a numbered card on it similar to Price's. Valentine filled it out using his Ohio ration-card name—Tarquin Ayoob, not a name Valentine would have chosen on his own; it came off his tongue like a horse getting wire-tripped—and passed it back under the partition. She counted the money, stamped both the document and the bounty card, then took out a scissors and cut the card free.

"What's the number for?" Valentine asked.

"If you got a prisoner in tow you can get free food and lodging at any NUC door, they just need the number. Counts as good works for the Ordnance Lottery. Bring in a man or even a useful report and your number goes in that week. You can buy tickets, too. This week's pot is half a million. Care to enter?"

"Doubt we'll be in the Ordnance long enough to collect," Price said. "I thank you, officer."

They left the station and reunited with Duvalier and the Grogs at the riverbank, sharing a final meal. Apples were growing plentiful, making Valentine think of Everready. Price pulled up the mule's feet and inspected them one by one as Bee held the animal.

"This is really good-bye," Valentine said.

"Watch your curfew around here, son," Price said. "Folks button up really tight. If you're solid-silver lucky, the police pick you up and throw you in the clink for breaking.

"I'm going to be poking around in Lexington for a bit. Ohio fugitives head there, more often than not. There's jobs at the processing plants, and the West Kentucky Legion isn't too choosy about who it takes on. I'll check in at the depots."

"Can I come back with you that far?" Duvalier asked.

Valentine almost dropped his apple. "You want to give up?"

"This led nowhere, David. I don't want to stumble around ground I don't know. I feel like we stick out here. Everyone talks different, wears different clothes."

"Give me three more days," Valentine said.

"How far away will you be in three days?" Duvalier asked Price.

"I could dawdle along the river here for a bit. I never got my vacation in at the Shack. I owe myself some fishing."

"Three days' worth?" Valentine asked.

"Three days."

"Lots of people here on bicycles," Valentine said. "Price, where do you suppose we can rent some?"

Price treated himself to a motel room. He found one with a distinctly nondiscriminating owner when it came to personal hygiene, Grogs, mules littering the weed-covered parking lot, and where the occupants poured their night soil.

It turned out you couldn't rent bicycles, and no money would buy a bike capable of supporting Ahn-Kha. By parting with yet another gold coin to a bike and moped dealer under a canopy of festive plastic bunting, he and Duvalier each got bicycles with tires, functioning brakes, storage baskets, even clip-on flashlight headlamps that charged by pedaling.

After some exploring with Ahn-Kha they found a house deep in the woods, not quite a cabin and not quite a shack. While it rested at a tilt thanks to the absence of a foundation, there was a functioning well and Ahn-Kha got water flowing into the house again with a little tinkering and a lot of root cutting.

The weather turned fair again and Valentine and Duvalier bicycled together, almost unarmed—he brought the .22 pistol, she her sword-carrying stick—starting at the nearest crossroads to the end-of-the-line station and working their way outward, following roads heavy enough to support trucks.

Valentine kept turning them to the north and east, into hillier and more isolated country. He couldn't say what drove him into this particular notch of Ohio. Perhaps it was a line of three legworms patrolling a ridge, glimpsed as they crept through the trees at a distance. Or it was the one true military convoy that passed them coming out of it; three tractor trailers, with Grog troops in supporting vehicles and venerable five-ton cargo trucks.

They were only questioned once, by a pair of policemen also on bicycles. Valentine showed his card and the warrant for the renegade electrician, explaining that he'd learned she had a cousin who lived out in these woods.

"Don't think so, Ayoob," one of the patrol said. "Even during deer season most around here know to avoid the point country. You're better off searching the other side of the river."

So on their third day they risked a predawn ride along the river road to get into the hills early. Other than the good condition of the roads in the region, he couldn't point to anything but a feeling.

"Another feeling. Is it because you can't go back?" Duvalier asked. "Is that why you won't let this go? You need something to do, even a ghost chase?"

Valentine chewed a wild bergamot leaf and tossed its purple-pink flower to Duvalier. "You've been good company. After today you can go find the Lifeweavers. But be sure to tell them about this."

She nuzzled his cheek. The half quarrel had faded.

"Wish we could find out where that's going," Valentine said as they breakfasted on bread and cheese. A green-painted military truck turned off from the river road and approached their position. Black smoke belched from its stack as the truck shifted up.

"Can do," she said, putting the flower between her teeth and picking up her bicycle. "Watch my coat."

"Ali—"

She pedaled madly in the same direction as the truck, and brought her bike alongside. She reached out and grabbed a tie for the cargo bed's canvas cover.

Valentine watched her disappear.

He had little to do over the next three hours but refill their water bottles and worry. When she came coasting down the hill again she had a huge smile.

"I've got a date for tonight," she said, pulling up her bike and accepting a water bottle. "Nice guy from New Philadelphia. Lance Corporal Scott Thatcher. He plays the guitar."

"Thought you were leaving tonight."

"Don't you want to know what I found?"

The jibe Valentine was working on died half-formed. "You found something?"

"It's big, it's well-guarded, and Thatcher didn't offer to take me to lunch inside, even with a lot of hints. You wanna see?"

Valentine picked up his bike as Duvalier shoved her coat into the basket on the back of her bike.

"What is it?" Valentine asked as they pushed up the hill.

"I'm not sure. It looks kind of like a hospital. There were ambulances out front, military and civilian. Big grounds, double-fenced."

They topped a hill; another loomed on the other side of a narrow gully. The road took a hairpin turn at a small stream. "I don't suppose your Corporal Thatcher illuminated you?"

"He said he was just a delivery boy."

A truck blatted through the trees. They pulled their bikes off the road and watched it negotiate the gulley. It was an open-backed truck, filled with an assortment of uniformed men, some in bandages, some just weary-looking.

"Okay, it is a hospital," Valentine said as they remounted their bikes. "Why all the security, then?"

They finally saw it from the top of the next hill.

"This is probably as far as we should go," Duvalier said. "There's a watch post at the end of the trees."

Valentine couldn't see much through the trees, just a few salmon-colored building tops, at least a dozen stories tall. The ground leveled out past the hill, flat ground and a straight road to a guarded gate beyond a half mile or so of open ground. Valentine looked through his mini-binoculars. Yes, there was a little watch station, about the size of a lifeguard's house at a beach, near the break in the trees.

"Three layers of fencing, with a road between," Duvalier said. "Outer layer is electrified. Innermost layer is just a polite six feet of glorified chicken wire. He dropped me off at the gate. The gatehouse looks normal enough, but ten yards out to either side there's tenting over something. I'm guessing heavy weapons."

Valentine did some mental math. This place was perhaps twenty minutes from the train tracks, in trucks driving forty miles an hour.

"Oh, Thatcher gave it a name."

"He did?"

"He called it 'Zan-ado.' "

"Xanadu?" Valentine asked.

"Yeah. Mean anything to you?"

"I've heard the word. I don't know what it means. A fairyland or some such. You hanging around for your date?"

"I'm meeting him in Ironton."

"Ahn-Kha and I will check this out. Tonight."

They said good-bye to Price while Duvalier biked off to keep her appointment. Valentine decided he could trust Price with a message to Southern Command. Someone needed to know about Xanadu.

If Price was willing to act as courier.

Valentine insisted on a farewell drink. Their supply of Bulletproof had been much reduced in trading, but they still had a few stoppered bottles.

They drank it inside the filthy motel room, windows and doors wide open to admit a little air.

"Price, you ever run into any guerillas?"

"I avoid them if I can. I've had my guns commandeered off me. They've threatened to shoot Bee, too."

"If you could get a message through to the Resistance, you'd really help the Cause."

"*The Cause*. Not that shit again."

"It's the only—"

"No! You don't tell me about the Cause, boy." Price took a drink. "I know your Cause. I know Everready's Cause."

"How did you come to know Everready? What happened with those teeth?"

Price took another long swallow. "Don't suppose you ever heard of a place called Coon County?"

"No."

"Won't find it on your old maps. Nice little spot, up in the mountains near Chattanooga, north of Mount Eagle. Called it Coon County because of Tom Coon, roughest son of a bitch you ever met. I bet he killed near as many Reapers as Everready. Ol' Everready was our liaison officer with Southern Command. Got radio gear and explosives through him.

"We had a bad scrape and lost twenty-six men, captive. Colonel Coon, he had some Quisling prisoners of his own. We kept them around pulling plows or cutting wood, that kind of stuff. He went in, alone, to negotiate. We figured they hung him, since he vanished for a month. But wouldn't you know, he came back with twenty-four. Said two had been killed before he could get there, and he exchanged the survivors for twenty-four of our prisoners.

"A few weeks later this big operation got under way, Rattlesnake I think it was called. Lots of guerillas involved. I missed it because I had Lyme disease. Tick bite. Put me on antibiotics and finally got a transfusion from old Everready.

"Then Colonel Coon came back. He looked tired, but he took the time."

He stared out the window, looking at his mule grazing in the field across the road. Valentine wondered what visions he really saw.

"Coon sat by each bed in the hospital, told a few jokes. He asked me how my wife was doing, if the baby had come. He had that kind of memory.

"Then the Reaper showed up.

"It wasn't any kind of a fight, any more than pigs in a slaughter pen put up a fight. Doc Swenson tried to get to a gun; he went down first. A nurse ran. I remember Coon wounded her in the leg. Kneecapped her.

"The Reaper took a friend of mine, Grouse, we called him. The woman next to me blew air into her IV and died rather than have the Reaper take her. I just froze up. I couldn't move a muscle. Not even my eyes, hardly. It killed the nurse right at the bottom of my bed.

"It fed and Coon started staggering around. He was speaking so fast—you ever hear someone speaking in tongues, David? Like that, words coming out as fast as voltage. The Reaper started dancing, doing this sorta waltz with the nurse's body as it jumped from bed to bed. Some of her blood and piss got on me as it swung her around, hit me right in the eye.

"That's when Everready came in. He gave it a face full of buckshot and stuck a surgical knife in its ear. Then he drowned Coon in the slop bucket where they emptied the bedpans. He picked me up like I was a six-year-old girl and ran.

"Well, there were Reapers everywhere. Coon had led them right in. They got everyone in Coon County, even—even my wife."

Price passed the bottle back to Valentine.

"Everready told me about how he'd heard from the Lifeweaver what a seductive thing it was, to feed on another man's spirit like that. He said humans could do it same as the others with the right training—kind of like what the Lifeweavers do to men like Everready. I thought they got to Colonel Coon when he went to bargain about those twenty-six men, but Everready said it was probably even before that. I felt dirty, living when Na—everyone else died."

"What's Coon County like now?" Valentine asked.

"Just another Kurian Zone, David. I gave up the war then. How are we supposed to win when they can grant a man immortality for joining in? The Kurian Zone ain't so bad. The Reapers feed behind closed doors, it's like it's not even happening. A person gone now and then, like they walked off into the country and never came back."

Price looked at him sidelong.

"Even the end's not so bad, they tell me. The Reapers, they look into your eyes and you see pretty meadows full of flowers and sunlight, or everyone you know who's dead welcoming you, urgin' you on, like. You don't even feel the tongue going in. That doesn't sound so bad. A good Christian doesn't fear death."

"He doesn't hasten it, either," Valentine said.

"Young and idealistic. You want to talk 'hastening' death—you've been in battles. Who's got the better deal, the man in the Kurian Zone has plenty of food on the table, leisure time to spend, a family if he wants—children, even grandchildren if he keeps his nose clean—compare that to you boys in the Ozarks. Get drafted, what, sixteen is it now? Break your back in labor units until a rifle becomes available, and then you're dead by twenty. How many virgins you buried, David? What kind of life did they have?

"Only people I'm setting myself against are those that want to make other people's tiny slice of life a misery. Murderers, rapists, child touchers, swindlers. That's my cause."

"You're forgetting the biggest murderers of all."

"You say. I say all they're doing is making it sensible and orderly. You get an orderly birth, an orderly life, an orderly death. I've come across dozens of folks running from the Kurians. Or at least they started out that way. Two, three days later they're hungry and cold and they ask me to lead them to food and shelter, thank me for putting them back in the Order, even if it's an NUC waystation with a Reaper in the belfry. They want the Order."

"Keep telling yourself that, Price, if it makes you feel better. Wish I'd known the man Everready saved."

"You missed him," Price said. "I don't. Let's talk again in ten years and see if you're still so sure of your Cause."

Valentine rode his bicycle and Ahn-Kha loped along, his gear tied to Valentine's handlebar and on the back of his bike. A distant whistle sounded curfew as the sun disappeared, and Valentine walked the bike off the road.

They slept for three hours, long enough to give their bodies a break, then moved through the hills more cautiously. Valentine kept his lifesign down, and hoped that his old ability to feel the cold presence of a prowling Reaper hadn't been dulled by disuse. Sure enough, there was one in the gully with the hairpin turn on the road, keeping watch.

They put earth and trees between themselves and the Reaper, threw a wide loop around—

And Valentine sensed another one, a dark star on his mental horizon.

It reminded him of the installation he'd come across with Gonzo in Wisconsin, before their disastrous encounter with a sniper.

He and Ahn-Kha backed off, put another half mile of woods and wildlife between themselves and the sentry Reaper.

"I might be able to get through them alone, old horse," Valentine said. "You don't make human lifesign, but you make enough for them to get curious."

"I could go first. When it comes to investigate, you—"

Ahn-Kha was no fool. The Golden One knew exactly what he was saying, that he was willing to draw a prowling Reaper and trust Valentine to dispose of it before it killed him.

"No. A Reaper goes missing and they'll know someone's poking around. Go back to the house, keep to thick cover, and wait for me. Or Duvalier."

"What will you do?"

"I'm going to get past the Reaper sentries. Then keep down until the day watch comes, if any. If I'm lucky, I'll be inside the sentry line and outside the wire, and I can get a real look at the place by daylight. At dusk I'll creep out again."

"If you're not lucky?"

"You and Ali get back to Southern Command. Hopefully they'll try again with a better-prepared team."

"I remember having this conversation before. We only just found you. Would it not be better to look around from inside the wire, my David?"

"Of course. How do we do that?"

"It is a hospital. One of us just has to be sick enough."

Valentine nodded. "I know a couple of old tricks. One or two can even fool a doctor. Let's get back to Ali first. If this blows up in our faces, I have a feeling we'll never get outside that wire again."

Valentine, Ahn-Kha, and Duvalier stood at the crossroads. The river road stretched off east and west, the road leading to the well-guarded hospital branching off.

She didn't discuss her "date" the previous night—save to deny that she got anything of use out of the soldier. "He's going on a long patrol. He offered to see me again in four days."

"Are you going to wait for him?" Valentine asked.

"Depends if you and the jolly gold giant here go through with this insanity."

"It will work," Valentine said.

"Price left us a bass boat," Duvalier said. "And I've still got our Spam. How much action do you want?"

"Just a little fire or two on the other side of the river. Tonight. Nothing too hard."

"And your illness?"

"A little ipecac and other herbs with unfortunate pharmacological side effects."

"Will that be convincing enough?" Ahn-Kha asked, scanning the road and woods. "I think I see your dinner, Alessa. My David, may I see your pistol?"

Valentine handed over the gun. Ahn-Kha checked it over, then pointed it at his neck.

"Ahn—"

The gun went off with a sharp crack. Valentine and Duvalier stood dumbfounded. Blood and flesh flew from the Golden One's neck. He lowered the gun to his elbow and shot himself through the arm. Then again, at the hip point.

Valentine tried to wrestle the gun from Ahn-Kha's grip, burning his hand on the barrel, but the Grog was too strong. It fired again.

"Urmpf," Ahn-Kha grunted, releasing the gun.

"What the hell, man?" Duvalier asked.

"No need for insults," Ahn-Kha said. "I just decided—"

"You wounded yourself to get into the hospital?" Duvalier asked.

"Why not just shoot yourself once?" Valentine asked, putting the gun back on safety and digging for his first-aid kit.

"One bullet wound with powder grains around it might be self-inflicted. How many desperate cowards avoid combat by shooting themselves four times? But I fear the last penetrated my intestines."

"I'm sorry," Valentine said. "I thought you'd gone mad."

"I knew what I was doing. Pass me that disinfectant."

"You should get going," Valentine told Duvalier. "If you pass some of our local constables, have them send an ambulance."

Duvalier gathered up her stick and pack, and wheeled her bicycle over to Ahn-Kha. She kissed him on the ear. "You taste like a muskrat. Don't let him leave you."

Valentine glared at her.

"I'll hang around at Price's motel," Duvalier said. "They made him pay for a month because of the Grog. If you make it back out you can find me there. Unless, of course, I get the feeling I'm being watched. Then I'm gone."

Valentine applied dressings, then sat Ahn-Kha on the saddle of the bike. The tires immediately flattened, but it served as a convincing conveyance for a wounded Grog, with one long arm draped around Valentine's shoulder. Birds called to each other in the trees; they both could lie down and die and the birds would still sing on.

"How you doing, old horse?"

"The wounds burn."

"They'll get you patched up. Hope that supply truck passes soon."

"I can walk all the way there if I must."

No supply truck came, but a white ambulance snapped deadfall twigs as it roared through the riverside hills. It didn't employ a siren, but there was no traffic to hurry out of the way.

Valentine sat Ahn-Kha on the weed-grown shoulder and stood in the roadway, waving his arms. The ambulance, tilted due to a bad suspension, came on, unheeding, lights flashing—

Then swerved and braked, stalling the motor.

The driver spoke through the wire grid that served as his window. "You almost got yourself killed, quirt." His associate used the stop to light a cigarette.

"We're trying to get to the hospital. My friend's wounded."

The clean-shaven pair in blue hats exchanged a look. "A Grog? Try the—"

"I'm hurting too. Can we—"

"On a call, sir. We'll radio back and have you picked up." He nodded at his associate, who touched a box on the dashboard.

"Thank you. Thank you very much."

"Don't move. Another ambulance will be along." The driver got the engine going and moved off.

"Curbside service," Valentine said, taking out his pocketknife.

"My David, what are you going to do?"

"We're both going in wounded."

Valentine raked the knife twice across the outer side of his left hand. He'd been anticipating the pain, which made it all the worse.

"Defensive wounds," Valentine said.

"I hope we have no need for a real dressing. This is our last one," Ahn-Kha said.

"Just give me some surgical tape and a scissors. I'll close them with butterfly dressings. Those two in the ambulance might have noticed that I didn't have a big dressing on my hand."

"I will cut the tape. You're bleeding."

Valentine spattered a little of his own blood on his face to add to the effect.

Ahn-Kha deftly cut notches into each side of the surgical tape and handed the pieces to Valentine one at a time. A butterfly bandage used a minimal amount of tape directly over the wound, gripping the two sides of skin with its "wings." Valentine splashed on stinging disinfectant, then used three bandages on one cut, two on the other.

It took twenty minutes for the second ambulance to arrive—a gateless pickup truck painted white. The driver was a single, older man with a ring of flesh adding a paunch to his chin.

"You two're the walking wounded, I'll bet."

"That's us."

"Hop in the back. There's a water jug there, don't be afraid to use it. Bring your bike if you want."

A yellow plastic cooler with a cup tied to a string was stuck in one corner of the pickup with a bungee cord. Valentine put the bike in, then he and Ahn-Kha climbed into the bed. The truck sagged.

"Hoo—he's a big boy, your Grog. Now hold on, I'm going to drive gentle but I don't want to lose you when I turn."

The driver executed a neat three-point turn.

Valentine spoke to him through the open back window of the pickup. "I'm Tar Ayoob. What's your name, sir?"

"Beirlein, Grog-boy. I never seen his type before. He some special breed?"

"They got them up in Canada," Valentine said. "They're good in the snow. Big feet."

"Oh, Sasquatches is what he is, huh? What do you know."

"I'm told this is the best hospital south of Columbus," Valentine said. "Hope they're right. My friend's got a bullet in him."

"We'll patch him up. Don't worry."

The pickup negotiated the hairpin turn, climbed out of the gulley in second gear, then came out of the trees and Valentine finally saw Xanadu.

It filled all the flat ground in a punchbowl ring of wooded hills. Most of the structures were salmon-colored brick or concrete, save for some wooden outbuildings.

Duvalier was right; a triple line of fencing, one polite, two lethal, surrounded the campuslike huddle of structures. Guards at the gate made notations on a clipboard and handed Valentine and Ahn-Kha stickers with red crosses on them. In the farther corners of the expanse of grass between buildings and fence Valentine saw dairy cows. There looked to be a baseball diamond and a track closer to the gate.

The four biggest salmon-colored buildings looked like apartments Valentine had seen in Chicago, except those had been built with balconies, and large windows. Each one was as long as a city block, rectangular, and laid out so they formed a square. Valentine counted twelve stories.

A long, low, three-story building of darker brick extended from the four, and was joined to a concrete jumble, tiered like a wedding cake, that had ambulances and trucks parked in front of it.

The ambulance didn't stop in front of the hospital. It continued to drive around back, past what looked like three-story apartments.

"Hey, what about the emergency room?"

"Your Grog goes out to the stables. Don't worry, our vet's treated Grogs before."

The pickup drove to a pair of barns, giant old-fashioned wooden ones with an aluminum feed silo between. The truck pulled up to a ranch house with a satellite dish turned into a decorative planter. Valentine saw another, distant barn. Fields with a group of Holsteins and a group of Jerseys were spread out to the wire. A guard tower, hard to distinguish against the treetops, could just be seen.

Xanadu's footprint covered several square miles, perhaps the size of downtown Dallas. If it was a concentration camp of some kind, it was a pleasant-looking one.

A blond woman in a white medical coat, a stethoscope around her neck, came out on the porch of the ranch house and walked to the back of the truck. A man in overalls followed her out, holding what looked like a set of shackles. "This is Doc Boothe, Tar."

Doc Boothe had one of those faces that hung from a broad forehead, progressing down from wide eyes to a modest nose to a tiny, dimpled chin. "How cooperative is he?"

"Extremely," Ahn-Kha said. The vet let out a squeak of surprise. "Unless you try to put manacles on me."

"A patient who can talk. You're a DVMs dream. What's your name?"

"Ahn-Kha."

"I'm Tar," Valentine said. "We're out of Kentucky, Bulletproof tribe."

"And another Kentucky quirt shows up looking for Ordnance medical attention," the man with the shackles observed. "They need to patrol the river better."

The vet ignored both her helper and Valentine, except to say, "Leave your guns in the truck for now. We've got a safe inside. Ahnke, come into the operating room."

She led them in past kennels filled with barking German shepherds and pointers. She unlocked and opened a gray metal door. The tiles inside smelled of disinfectant. Dr. Boothe checked to see that they were following, then turned on a light in a big, white-tiled room. A heavy stainless-steel berth, like an autopsy table, dominated the center of the room.

"It's not right to treat him in a vet office," Valentine said.

"I've got experience tranquilizing large animals. And I'm comfortable around them. I know you're worried, but he's in better hands here than in the main building. They slap bandages on and send everyone to the sanitarium in Columbus. Okay, Ahnke, on the table. Do you want to lie down? Make it easier for me to reach. You ever had a reaction to pain medication?"

"I've only had laudanum," Ahn-Kha said.

"This is better, it takes the edge off." She opened a cabinet and took out a box of pills, shook three out, and poured him a cup of water. "Pepsa!" she called. "Gunshot tray."

Ahn-Kha swallowed the pills.

A plump woman in blue cotton brought in a tray full of instruments. Valentine recognized a probe and some small forceps. The doctor removed Ahn-Kha's dressings.

"Pepsa, take a look at the legworm rider," Boothe said. "He's got some cuts on his hand. Unless you object to being treated by a vet assistant."

"I'd rather stay with my tribemate."

Pepsa gestured into a corner, and Valentine took a seat. She took up Valentine's hand and looked at the self-inflicted wounds, then got a bottle and some cotton balls.

"Does that hurt?" Boothe asked Ahn-Kha as she cleaned the wound on his neck.

"I'm not worried about that one."

"We'll get to your stomach in a moment. Neck wounds always worry me."

"He has a lot of neck," Valentine said.

"Must have been some brawl. You've got some graining."

"We walked into the wrong room," Valentine said.

"It happened in Kentucky?"

"Yes. A few hours ago."

"Uh-huh. I can still smell the gunpowder on you, Bulletproof. You two didn't get drunk and get into a fight or anything?"

Pepsa professionally dressed Valentine's wound without saying a word. By the time she was done the doctor had a light down close to Ahn-Kha's stomach, injecting him just above the wound.

"You've got a lot of muscle in the midsection, my friend," Dr. Boothe said. She probed a little farther and Ahn-Kha sucked wind. "Uh-huh. I think we can forget about peritonitis. I don't want to dig around without an X-ray."

Xanadu had no shortage of medical equipment.

"Is Pepsa a nickname?" Valentine asked as the nurse gave him his hand back. She nodded.

"Pepsa's mute, Tar. You done there, girl? Get him the forms. Put down whatever bullshit you want, Bulletproof, then we'll talk."

Valentine liked the doctor. Her careful handling of Ahn-Kha impressed him. That, and the fact that apparently she gave a mute a valuable job in a land where disabilities usually meant a trip to the Reapers.

Pepsa led Valentine to a lunchroom. A quarter pot of coffee—real coffee according to Valentine's nose—steamed on a counter in a brewer. Above the poster a placard read "FALL BLOOD DRIVE! *They bleed for you—now you can bleed for them!* Liter donors are entered in a drawing for an all-expense-paid trip to Niagara Falls." Valentine filled out the forms, leaving most of the blocks empty—like the eleven-digit Ordnance Security ID, which occupied a bigger area on the form than name.

The vet dropped in and sat down, rubbing her eyes. "Calving last night, now your Grog. He'll be fine, but I will have to operate."

"Will it be a hard operation?"

"Toughest part will be opening up those layers of muscle. But no.

Kentucky, since you're not Ordnance you'll have to pay for these services, cheap though they are. What do you have on you?"

"Not much."

She stared at him. "I know there are a lot of rumors about this place. That it's some kind of Babylon for high Ordnance officials. Or that strings of happy pills get passed out like Mardi Gras beads. I've heard the stories. I'm not saying you two jokers tried to get in here by doing something as stupid as putting some small-caliber bullets into each other. But Xanadu's no place you want to be.

"What it is, in fact, is a hospital for treating cases with dangerous infectious conditions. Anti-Kurian terrorists got it in their heads to try a few designer diseases lethal to the Guardians, and there's been some weird and very dangerous mutations as a result. That's why we've got all this ground and livestock, the less that passes in and out of those gates, the better. Just in case. Do you know how diseases work, microorganisms?"

"Yes, little creatures that can fit in a drop of water. They make you sick."

"Uh-huh. So every breath you take behind these walls is a risk, and the closer you get to the main buildings, the more danger. So you should thank your lucky stars you were treated out here."

Valentine nodded. *Interesting. Is it all a cover? Or is there a project I don't know about?*

"After I operate we're going to keep your friend here for three days of observation. Don't worry, you'll have a bed, but you'll work for it. Consider it paying off your debt for your partner's medical treatment. Once you're out of here, go back to Kentucky and tell your buddies. This isn't a drugstore, it's not a brothel, and it's not a place to come get cured of the clap with the Ordnance picking up the tab. It's a scary lab full of death you can't even see coming. You understand, or should we start writing it on the sides of the legworms you sell us?"

"I understand," Valentine said. "Thank you."

Eleven

Xanadu, October: Summer lingered that year between the Great Lakes and the Appalachians. In eastern Russia and Mongolia the bitter winter of '72 came hard and fast, leading to starvation in the Permafrost Freehold. In the Aztlan Southwest El Niño blew hot, making a certain group of aerial daredevils licking their wounds in the desert outside Phoenix ration water. Florida, Georgia, and the Carolinas drowned under torrential tropical storms hurtling out of the mid-Atlantic one after another, ushering in what came to be known as the mud fall.

Ohio could not have been more idyllic, with cloudless days reaching into the midseventies and cool nights in the high fifties, perfect weather for sleeping under a light blanket. There was plenty of time for apple picking and blueberry gathering, and the turkeys had grown extra large in that year of plenty.

David Valentine always remembered that first fall of his exile as a grim, disturbing business under a kindly sky. Perhaps if he'd been lazier, or argumentative, or a thief, he and Ahn-Kha would have been thrown out of Xanadu with the Golden One's sutures still weeping. But after his first day in the fields he found the biowarfare scare story implausible, and became determined to find out what lay behind the neatly tuckpointed facade of those reddish bricks.

The job offer didn't come as much of a surprise. It happened over dinner in the "field house"—a small apartment building that reminded Valentine of Price's motel, essentially a line of tiny rooms, two sharing one bath, that housed the lowest of the low of Xanadu's laborers: the "hands."

Up one step from the hands were the service workers, who mixed with the hands at their shared recreation center just behind the hospital. The fixtures made Valentine think it had originally been built to be a large-vehicle garage, but now it held Ping-Pong tables, a video screen and library (full of dull-as-distilled-water New Universal Church productions), and a jukebox ("Authentic Vintage MCDs").

The service workers performed cafeteria and janitorial duties inside the main buildings. Valentine learned his first night there that they expected the hands to do the same for them. He learned how to cook "factory food,"—washtub-sized trays of pastas, vegetables, and sweet puddings. Every other night there was meat from the Xanadu livestock. Beef predominated, which Valentine found remarkable. Even during his hitch as a Coastal Marine he'd only been fed chicken; beef was saved for feasts before and after a cruise.

A step above the service workers was the security. There weren't many of them, considering the evident importance of the facility. Enough to man the two gates (there was a smaller one to the east) and the towers, and to keep guard at all the main building doors. Valentine could have stormed the place with a single company of Wolves, had he been able to get the company that deep into the Kurian Zone.

And made it past the cordon of Reapers.

The security forces lived and worked from the long building almost connecting the hospital with the salmon-colored apartment blocks.

That was all Valentine could learn about the self-contained community in his off hours. During the day he worked on the plumbing for a fourth barn, stripped to the waist and digging the ditch for the piping. He recognized make-work when he saw it; a backhoe could have completed the digging in a day.

"You ever think of joining the Ordnance, Tar?" Michiver, the chief hand, asked him over his plate of stew at one of the long cafeteria tables in the rec center. Michiver had a nose that looked like an overgrown wart and ate slowly and stiffly and with a bit of a wince, like an old dog.

"I like the soap and the flush toilets," Valentine said, truthfully enough.

"When I saw you pull up with your big Grog in that leather outfit, I thought you were just another Kentucky quirt. But you put in a real day's work and stay sober at night."

"That's not hard when the nearest liquor store's ten miles away."

Michiver's eyes puckered as he leaned close. "Ordnance duty is nice, if you put in the hours. Three hot meals a day, good doctors and dentists, Lake Ontario cruises for your vacation."

"I'm not much on the Church, though."

Michiver rested his head on rough hands. "It's just one day a week.

I've gotten good at sleeping with my eyes open. Heard one lecture about the importance of recycling, heard them all."

"So are you offering me a job, boss?"

"For you and your Grog, assuming he's willing to work. When that new barn goes in I'll need a supervisor, you could be it."

"I was thinking of joining up with the Kentucky Legion."

"And get your head blown off? Chasing guerillas up and down the hills is alright for some, but you've got character and intelligence. I see it plain. We could use you here."

"Doc Boothe warned me off about diseases."

"Hands work outdoors; you're not cleaning up after the patients inside. I've been here fourteen years and I've never seen anything but colds and flu and a bit of pneumonia in the winter. Don't concern yourself with what's going on up at the Grands."

"You sure seem eager to have me. That means there's a catch."

"I'm no spring chicken, Tar," Michiver said, rolling a lock of gray hair between thumb and forefinger. He had an I GAVE MY LITER button on his shirt. "If there's a catch, it hasn't caught me."

"Do I have to sign a contract or anything?"

"Ohio's booming. Hard to find reliable men these days; everyone wants city work under the lights. You Kentuck aren't so hot for jump joints and dazzle halls. Don't worry about contracts, you can quit whenever you like. Forget about your tribesmen. No one in Kentucky's in a position to say boo to the Ordnance. Stay the weekend at least. Saturday's a half day and we're having a dance in town at the NUC hall. The Church is bringing down some husband-hunters from Cleveland and the beer's all the way from Milwaukee, if you're partial to that poison." Michiver made his points poking the table, each poke nearer to Valentine as though trying to herd him into saying yes. "Great way to end your week here, either way—what you say?"

"I say fine."

Ahn-Kha watched him get dressed for the dance—leathers on the bottom, freshly washed blue chambray workshirt up top—and offered only one piece of advice: "Don't drink. Doctor Boothe says Michiver doesn't touch a drop of alcohol."

Valentine wished he had something other than work boots to put on his feet. "I'm more interested in getting friendly with the security staff. There's one odd thing about this place; except for the people in charge of the various departments, and that vet's nurse, seems like no one here's worked here longer than a year or two. Except friend Michiver."

Ahn-Kha gave that a moment's thought. "Perhaps you either get promoted or rotated out."

"I get the feeling Michiver's offer is a wiggling pink worm inside the mouth of a very big snapping turtle."

"It gives us time to look down the turtle's throat, my David."

Valentine waited in front of the staff apartments, a little apart from the crowd of off-duty hands and service workers waiting for the buses into town. A last bottle of sealed Bulletproof was tucked inside a plain paper bag he cradled. He watched those waiting to go to the dance. A few passed around a silver flask, more smoked. The women wore golden metallic eyeshadow and heavy black liner, apparently the current style in Ohio.

A dozen of the security staff all waited together in a line against the wall, like the schoolkids too cool to be out on the playground.

Doctor Boothe rode by in her little four-wheeler—an electric golf cart tricked out for backcountry. She used it to get from animal to animal on Xanadu's horizon-spanning acreage. She stared at Valentine for a moment, then picked up her bags of instruments and turned indoors.

Three buses took them into the riverside town. Valentine managed to take a seat next to one of the security men, but he either stared out the window or spoke to the two of his class in the seats just ahead during the half-hour trip. The church hall turned out to be a quasicathedral with attached school; the dance was set up beneath raised basketball backboards in what had been the gymnasium. A raised stage was built into one end of the gym.

Red and blue streamers formed a canopy overhead and decorated the refreshment tables—provided by the Ohio Young Vanguard, Actualization Team #415, according to a sign and a jar accepting donations. A teenage girl, eyes bright enough to be the result of Benzedrine, thanked him for his five-dollar donation and offered him a four-color pamphlet.

THE ORDNANCE AND NUC THANKS ITS HEALTH SECURITY WORKERS OF XANADU read the banner over the raised platform at one end of the gymnasium. Dusty red curtains half closed off a stage, hiding the lighting gear for the musicians. At the other end folding tables and chairs had a few balloons attached.

A nostalgic hip-hop dj-backed band ("lame" pronounced one of the security staff) laid down a techno beat as they entered, and the chief bandsman started exhorting the crowd to enjoy themselves as soon as the workers trickled in. The music echoed oddly in the high-ceilinged, quarter-lit gym, making Valentine feel as though he'd just stepped inside a huge kettledrum.

Valentine knew a handful of names and a few more faces, and once he'd nodded to those he knew he sat down on the basketball stands and read the tri-fold pamphlet the Young Vanguard girl had given him.

7 Civic Virtues we grow inside, as our bodies grow outside:

1. *Humility—we understand that mankind has been pulled back from the brink of self-destruction by wisdom greater than ours, giving us hope.*
2. *Hope for the Future—we know we can build a better world if we just listen to the quiet voice in our hearts.*
3. *Hearts that know Compassion—to act for the better of all, we pledge our minds, and the mind's servant, the hand.*
4. *Hands Busy in Labor—we pledge to work and sacrifice so that the following generation may live happier lives.*
5. *Heroism—we stand for what we know to be right and pledge our lives to the future; our word is our bond.*
6. *Honesty—we must be honest with others, for only then can we be honest with ourselves.*
7. *Healthy Bodies and Minds—we pledge to refrain from partaking of any substance that might cloud mind or pollute body.*

Pictures of particularly outstanding Vanguards and their Ordnance sponsors filled the back. Valentine more than half believed it all. The Churchmen knew how to keep their flocks all moving in the same direction—straight to the slaughterhouse.

The male-female ratio equalized a little when a pair of local Churchmen arrived with a contingent of single women. Their clothes and stockings marked them as city girls, looking like peacocks dumped in a headwater barnyard, and smelling of desperation. Or perhaps that was just the name of the perfume. The Churchmen divided the group in two parts and led their subflocks around, making introductions.

"Take a heck of a lot more than applejack to get me to take a run at one of those boxies," one of the security men said to his mate.

"Try a blindfold," another agreed from behind a thick mustache.

Valentine sidled up to the trio. "I've got an untapped bottle of Kentucky bourbon, if you like."

Thick Mustache sneered. "Take a hike, cowpuncher."

"My—" Valentine began.

"Get lost, quirt," the one eyeing up the women said. "You're not making yourself look good, you're making us look bad."

Valentine felt the room go twenty degrees warmer. "We could talk more outside, if you like."

"I'll share your liquor, new man," a female voice said in his ear.

Valentine startled. Six feet of creamy skin stood barefoot next to him, her heels dangling loose from one hand and a clutch purse in the other. She was at least a decade older, but high-cheeked and attractive in a shoulder-padded dress. Or simply more skilled with makeup and clothing than the rest of the women in the gym. Valentine wondered if she'd come in by a different route—she'd neither arrived on the buses nor been escorted in by the Churchmen.

"Looking hot, Doc P," the security man who'd called Valentine a "quirt" a moment ago said.

The woman cocked her head, an eyebrow up. Even Valentine, thirty degrees out of the line of fire of the stare, felt a chill.

"C'mon, you 'bot," Thick Mustache said, pulling his companion away.

"What's your name?"

"Tar. Tar Ayoob."

"Tar? Like in 'nicotine and . . .' "

"Short for Tarquin," Valentine said.

She transferred her shoes to her purse-holding hand. "Fran Paoli. I work up at Xanadu too."

"I'm liking it better and better there," Valentine said, shaking her offered hand. She laughed, but lightly.

Valentine showed her the bottle.

"That's real Kentucky Bourbon, I believe," she said.

"Care for a snort?" Valentine asked.

"With water," she said. "About 5ccs."

"How much is that?"

"A shot glass."

When Valentine returned from the refreshment table with two ice-filled plastic cups of water, she stood next to a paper-covered table festooned with balloons reading "Happy Birthday."

Valentine set his glasses down and held out the chair for her. "Why did you take your heels off?" he asked.

"I can be sneaky that way. Besides, it makes me feel sexy."

It also makes you two inches shorter than I am, Valentine thought. "I didn't know we'd have any doctors in attendance."

"I'll be it. Oriana and I came down to the waterfront to do some shopping."

"And you just couldn't resist the music and the decor?" Valentine passed her drink to her. She sipped.

Fran rolled the liquor around in her mouth, and swallowed. "No. I wanted to meet you."

"You're very direct."

She looked up as the liquor hit. "Whoo, that takes me back. I did a term with a field hospital down your way."

"Wanted to meet me?" Valentine insisted.

"When you get a few more years' . . . oh . . . perspective on life, let's say, you run short on patience for gamesmanship."

Valentine watched more uniforms flow in. Couples began dancing, doing curious, quick back-and-forth movements, one part of the body always touching. Hand gave way to arm that gave way to shoulder that gave way to buttock that turned into hand again. He felt like a scruffy backwoodsman at a cotillion.

Good God. Ali's here.

She wore a plain woolen skirt and a yellow blouse that flirted with femininity, but went with her flame-colored hair. Lipstick and eye makeup were making one of their rare appearances on her face. A soldier who looked like a wrestler's torso on a jockey's legs was introducing her to one of the Churchmen. Valentine wondered if he was looking at an infatuated boy or a dead man.

"Do you want to dance?" Valentine asked.

"You don't look like the slinky-slide type."

"Is that what that dance is called?"

"It was when they were doing it in New York ten years ago. God knows what it's called out here." Her thin-lipped mouth took on a grimace that might be called cruel.

Valentine tried a tiny amount of bourbon, just enough to wet his lips and make it appear that he drank. "So how did you know you wanted to meet me?"

"Moonshots."

"Is that something else from New York?"

"No," she laughed, a little more heartily this time. "Have you been in the Grands yet?"

"The four big buildings? No."

"I have a corner in Grand East. Top floor." She said it as though she expected Valentine to be impressed. "Apartment and office. I've got a nice telescope. Myself and some of the nurses have been known to take a coffee break and check out the hands. We call a particularly attractive male a 'moonshot.' It's hard to get a unanimous vote from that crew, but you got five out of five. The hair did it for Oriana—she's the tough grader."

"There's not a bet having to do with me, is there?"

"Admit it. You're flattered."

"I am, a little." He picked up his drink. "Don't go anywhere." He took a big mouthful of his drink, headed for a corridor marked "bathrooms," and turned down a cinder-block corridor. He found the men's. An assortment of student- and adult-sized urinals stood ready. He went to the nearest one and spat out his bourbon, thinking of an old Wolf named Bill Maranda who would have cried out at the waste.

Alessa Duvalier tripped him as he exited. He stumbled.

"You're a rotten excuse for the caste," she said, keeping her voice low and watching the hallway. "Have you found her?"

"No. Just as tight on the inside."

"So how do you like pillow recon?" she asked. "Is she tight? Or is the bourbon loosening her up?"

"Haven't had a chance to find out, yet."

"According to my date she's big-time. You be careful. I've moved to the NUC women's hostel, by the way. My would-be boyfriend was horrified by my accommodations. Bed checks."

"I've got a chance at an upgrade too, methinks."

She pressed a piece of paper into his hand. "Phones work around here, but you get listened to," Duvalier said. "If you need to run, leave a message at the hostel that your migraines are back. I'll get to the motel as soon as I can and wait. Do they allow inbound calls up there?"

"I think there's a phone in our rec center. I'll call with the number."

"Good luck." She made a kissing motion in the air, not wanting to leave telltale lipstick. She dived into the women's washroom, and Valentine went to the bar for more ice.

He chatted with Fran Paoli for thirty minutes or so, learned that she'd been born in Pennsylvania and educated in New York. She found the Ordnance "dull enough to make me look forward to *Noonside Passions*," evidently a television show, and wouldn't discuss her work, except to say that it required specialized expertise but was as routine as the NUC social. But it promised her a brass ring and a Manhattan penthouse when she completed her sixteenth year at Xanadu.

She couldn't—or wouldn't—even say what her area of medical expertise was.

Paoli waved and another woman approached, with the purse-clutching, tight-elbowed attitude of a missionary in an opium den.

"Oriana Kreml, this is Tar, our moonshot babe. Tar-baby! I like that."

"The market was a joke. 'Fresh stock in from Manhattan' my eye. Are you done presenting in here?"

"Oriana's a great doctor but a greater prig," Fran Paoli laughed. "Would you like a ride back, Tar-baby?"

"Thank you," Valentine said.

"Then let's quit the Church. Crepe paper gives me a rash."

They took Valentine outside to the parking lot. A well-tended black SUV huffed and puffed as its motor turned over. It was a big Lincoln, powered by something called Geo-drive.

"Would you like to drive my beast, Tar?" Fran Paoli asked.

"Would you forgive me if I wrecked it?" Valentine said. "I'm not much with wheels." Valentine liked cars, the convenience and engineering appealed to him, but he didn't have a great deal of experience with them.

He climbed into the rear seat. The upholstery had either been replaced or lovingly refurbished. A deep well in the back held a few crates of groceries. Valentine smelled garlic and lemons in the bags. The women in front put on headsets.

Fran Paoli turned on the lights and the parking lot sprang into black-shadowed relief. Music started up, enveloping Valentine in soft jazz. She turned the car around and drove down a side street until she reached the river highway. Two police pickup-wagons motored west. Valentine wondered how many unfortunates they carried to the Reapers. Two each? Three? Nine? Valentine stared out the window as the red taillights receded into demon eyes staring at him from the darkened road. They blinked away.

"You and your hobbies," Oriana said quietly.

Fran Paoli turned up the music, but Valentine could still hear if he concentrated. "So I like to go to bed with more than a good book."

"Someday it's going to bite you."

"Mmmmm, kinky. But don't fret. I can handle this hillwilly."

"He's after status and that's it. Don't fool yourself."

Valentine looked for Reapers in the woods as the truck approached Xanadu, but couldn't see or sense them. The security guard hardly used his flashlight when the SUV reached the gate. Fran Paoli waggled her fingers at him and he waved twice at the gate, and the fencing parted in opposite directions.

She drove up a concrete, shrub-lined roadway and pulled into a gap under the south tower. "Two-one-six, entering," she said into her mouthpiece, working a button on the dashboard, and a door on tracks rolled up into the ceiling. The SUV made it inside the garage—just—and parked in the almost-empty lot. A few motorbikes, a pickup, some golf carts, and a low, sleek sports car were scattered haphazardly among the concrete supporting pillars like cows sleeping in a wood. A trailer with an electric gasoline pump attached was set up on blocks near the door.

"You'll like the Grand Towers. You mind helping with the groceries?"

Valentine took two crates, Oriana one.

They walked past a colorful mural, silhouettes of children throwing a ball to each other while a dog jumped, and Fran Paoli passed her security ID card over a dark glass panel. An elevator opened. It smelled like pine-scented cleanser inside. Soft music played from hidden speakers.

"Home," Fran Paoli said, and the elevator doors closed.

"You don't have to hit a button?" Valentine asked.

"I could. It's voiceprint technology. A couple of the techs on the security staff like to tinker with old gizmos."

"I wish they could get an MRI working," Oriana said.

Valentine looked in his boxes on the ride up. Foil-wrapped crackers, a tin of something called "pâté," a bottle of olive oil with a label in writing Valentine thought looked like Cyrillic, artichokes, fragrant peaches, sardines, a great brick of chocolate with foil lettering . . .

The elevator let them out on a parquet-floored hallway. If there was a floor higher than twelve the elevator buttons didn't indicate it. Lighting sconces added soft smears of light to the maroon walls.

Fran Paoli held Oriana's groceries while she let herself in. "Good night. Call if you want your rounds covered."

"Thanks, O."

Oriana thanked Valentine as she took her box of foodstuffs—slightly more mundane instant mixes and frozen packages with frost-covered labels. Her door had a laminated plate in a slide next to it: ORIANA KREML, MD.

"I'm at the end of the hall, Tar-baby," Fran Paoli said.

She led him down, putting an extra swivel in her walk. Valentine clicked his tongue against the roof of his mouth in time to her stride. She twirled her keys on their wrist loop.

The door at the end read EXECUTIVE MEDICAL DIRECTOR. She opened it and Valentine passed through a small reception office—a computer screen cast a soft glow against a leather office chair—and a larger meeting room with an elegantly shaped glass conference table. Floor-to-ceiling windows reflected only the darkness outside and their faces. Lights came on as she moved through the space to a frosted-glass partition. Valentine marked a telescope at the glass corner she passed.

A casual living space and then a kitchen. Valentine set the boxes down on a small round table, and extracted the fresh fruits and vegetables.

"Stay for a drink?" Fran Paoli asked.

Fran Paoli snored softly beside him in postcoital slumber.

Her makeup was on the sheet, him, and the oh-so-soft pillowcases, and she gave off a faint scent of sweet feminine perspiration and rose-scented baby powder. She made love like some women prepared themselves for bed, following a long-practiced countdown that evidently gave her a good deal of pleasure.

Valentine thought of "Arsie," the professional he'd met at that Quisling party in Little Rock. Was this how it was for her? Did she feel like her body was an apparatus as her customers took what they wanted?

Valentine engaged in the lovemaking with—perhaps clinical detachment was the right word. It had been fun; Fran Paoli's hunger for him, the way she discovered his scars and touched them, licked them, gently as though drawing some mixture of the pain they represented and taking pleasure from them, both motherly and sexual, healing and arousing; while he'd become instantly erect at the first touch of her full, falling breasts and flesh-padded hips. She touched his erection, squeezed it as though testing its tensile strength, clawed and gasped and bucked out her satisfaction with its quality, and then brought him back again after he spent himself into the black-market condom—a thin-walled novelty that made Southern Command's prophylactics feel like rain ponchos.

"You can get a shortwave radio easier than these," she said, and she passed him the second plastic oval.

But he'd learned little, other than Fran Paoli's expertise with a bathtub razor, from the "pillow recon." She still wouldn't talk about what she did.

She woke him briefly when she got up, though she tried not to. Valentine dozed, feeling the sun change the quality of the light in the apartment, heard a vague whirring sound, remembered that he'd seen some kind of pulley-topped treadmill. Then she woke him for sex; sweaty, clean-faced, with her hair tied in a ponytail and her muscles hot from exercise. In the morning light the dark circles under her eyes showed, along with the sags at the backs of her arms, and the topography of the deposits on her thighs, but he came erect and she rode him like a final exercise machine.

"Tar, you are a treat for sore thighs," she said, and collapsed backward, still straddling him. He felt her hair on his ankle. He couldn't see her face, and had the strange feeling he was speaking to her vulva.

She pulled herself up. "I need a shower. There's another bathroom right next to the outer office if you need to use it. You can help yourself to anything you like in the kitchen. No homesies for your Aunt Betty, though. Poppy-seed crackers and Danish Havarti are too hard to come by."

"I should check in at the barn," Valentine said. "The livestock don't take days off."

"If I'm still in the shower when you're dressed, feel free to just leave. When I got up I phoned down to the security desk and let them know you were my guest last night. Just take the yellow card on the counter for the elevator."

He investigated the kitchen, and found bananas and orange juice. The "orange" juices Southern Command issued had a grainy taste, but this had real pulp in it. Valentine ate two bananas and explored the apartment. There was an office off the conference room, but it was locked. He could jimmy or pick it easily enough with something from the kitchen, but after she walked naked from the bathroom to go to her bedroom dresser for clean underwear he decided against it.

Fran Paoli didn't keep much that revealed anything about herself as a person in her apartment. He saw a photo in the bedroom of her as a teenager, atop a horse, in a khaki uniform with a peaked cap tipped saucily on her head. A gray-haired man in a tweed sport coat, with a forced smile, hung in a frame on the wall. A sad-eyed china spaniel sat on top of what might be a candy dish on the kitchen counter. It was chipped and scratched, but the dish contained nothing but a couple of bands for her hair.

He looked out the windows. The conference center looked out on the grounds, barns, and wire in the distance. The living room was set so you could look at the other three "Grand" buildings. All had the tall windows at the top, and he saw a few desks and living room furniture in the others. The rows of windows below were darkened and many were shaded. They told him nothing except that if there were one room per window, that made a lot of rooms, over three hundred per building. Twelve hundred rooms.

Between the four "Grand" buildings was some kind of common space, nicely laid out with lots of bistro tables around the edges near trees and planters, and a long pool at the center under greenhouselike glass. People were swimming what looked like laps, but in a leisurely fashion. He couldn't tell much about them thanks to condensation. Others were sitting at the bistro tables, enjoying what remained of the soft fall air, but from so high up he could tell little by the tops of their heads. All were wearing either blue or pink scrubs.

Pink and blue. Pink and blue.

He set his glass of orange juice down on an end table. Valentine strode into the conference center and looked at the telescope. He tried lifting it. He could stagger, just, with it. He looked at the smaller "finder" scope—it could be detached from the larger. He twisted a screw, freed it, and went back to the living room. He looked from pink to pink down in the plaza.

The patients were all women. He'd expected that. They were thin, some sickly looking, most with tired, limp hair. He'd expected that too, as he'd seen it often enough in the Kurian Zone.

Almost all were pregnant. Some bulging, some with just a swelling. He hadn't expected that.

The shower turned off. Valentine picked up his orange juice and drained it as he returned the spotting scope to its rest, lined up with the telescope. He hoped he hadn't screwed up the alignment too badly. He pointed the large scope at the barn, adjusted the counterweight, and made it clear that he'd been screwing with the optics.

When Fran Paoli came out of the bathroom, her hair in a towel, he was washing his glass in the sink.

"Just leaving," he said.

She gave him a kiss on the neck.

"I don't suppose you'd like to come to my place, next time," he said.

"You're cocky." She unwrapped the towel and began to work her scalp with the dry side.

"No next time?" he asked.

"Of course there will be, Tar-baby. You're so tight. I don't feel like I've begun to unwrap you yet."

"I'm in room—"

"While there's a certain thrill in those old, stained mattresses down there, I'm a bit worried about fleas. How about we meet halfway? I might work in a picnic tomorrow—I've got a spare afternoon. You can tell me where you got those hot-assed pants. I would love to have a skirt of that leather. Is it kid?"

"More like bug."

"Is Michiver still running things out in the fields?"

Valentine tried to read her brown eyes, but failed. "Yes."

"I'll get you the afternoon off tomorrow, if I can make it."

"Great."

"And tell that old knob we need a golf course, not more cows. I'm really sick of the one-hole wonder on the north forty."

"I'm the bottom man in the totem pole in the barns, Fran-tick."

She laughed. "*Frantic*. Tar-baby, I love it. You'd better go, or you'll really see frantic. I'm due on my rounds."

Valentine slapped her thin-robed bottom as he headed for the door. She stopped him with a whistle and passed him a yellow piece of plastic. "Here. Elevator won't work without this. Just slide it into the slot above the buttons. There's a diagram."

"Thanks."

He winked as he closed the door behind him and walked down the hallway. The lighting had been altered; it was brighter and cheerier this morning. He went to the elevator, feeling like a male black widow spider who's crossed the female's web and inexplicably lived.

He swiped the card in the reader according to directions. As an experiment, he hit the button for the sixth floor, but the elevator took him to the ground floor.

Valentine exited at a high-ceilinged lobby. Cheerful, primary-colored murals of square-jawed agricultural workers, steel-rimmed medical men, and aquiline mothers told him that those who passed through this lobby were

CREATING A BETTER TOMORROW

and that

PROGRESS COMES WITH EACH GENERATION

A rounded, raised platform held a few of the security staff. Two women in blue scrubs, one holding a plastic water bottle, the other a Styrofoam coffee cup, chatted near a bank of wide-doored elevators that evidently didn't go all the way to the top floor. Valentine walked toward the doors leading to the patio and pool area.

"Hey, hand!" one of the security men called.

He couldn't pretend not to have heard. He turned. "I'm sorry?"

"Your yellow building card. Turn it in."

Valentine fished it out of his pocket, reached up to place it on the desk. "Here you go."

He went back toward the doors, pretending not to see the other exits.

"Am I getting smarter or are they getting dumber?" the security desk said to his friend. "Hand!"

But Valentine was already passing out the doors.

He headed across the slate bricks. The intertower area smelled like flowers and cedar chips, which were spread liberally around the landscaping. Two women in pink, both copiously pregnant, nibbled at ceramic bowls, eating some kind of breakfast mix with beat-up spoons. Valentine's nose detected yogurt. Both were rather pallid and looked as though they needed the morning sun.

Another group of four, no visible swelling inside the loose pink outfits, kept company by one in blue, worked on each other's hair and a pitcher of tomato juice. Valentine passed through the greenhouse doors and down a short ramp to the swimming pool deck. Chlorine burned his nostrils. Two dozen heads bobbed in the wide lap lanes. Others were lined up at one end of the pool, talking, waiting their turn.

No two swimming suits were alike; there were hot pink bikinis and big black one-pieces. Maybe the pool was the one place the women got to express themselves with clothing.

"Come on, ladies," a man in shorts with a coach's whistle exhorted from a short diving board. "Keep swimming. Gets the blood flowing. Gets the bowels moving. I want to see healthy pink cheeks—yo, can I help you?"

The last came when he spied Valentine.

But the words barely registered.

Gail Foster, formerly Gail Post, waited at one side of the pool with the next group.

Her hair and cheeks were thinner, but the big green eyes and delicate, upturned nose were unmistakable. With her hair wet and flat, idly kicking the water as she talked to the woman next to her, she appeared childlike, so unlike the ID photo from Post's flyer where she stared into the camera as though challenging the lens to capture her. She didn't even look up as the man with the whistle hopped off the board to approach Valentine.

"Just taking a shortcut," Valentine said, tearing himself away from Gail's face.

"Don't disturb the expectants. Turn right around and—"

"Right. I'm going." Valentine retreated back up the ramp.

He walked around the greenhouse to the east side of the patio, looking for a hose, a rake, anything. But there were no groundskeepers or tools in sight. He removed his work boot and went to work on the leather tongue with his pocketknife, tearing it. If questioned, he could say that he was trying to get rid of an irritating flange.

He managed to idle away a half hour. A new group of women marched out of the south tower in single file, white robes held tight even in the warm morning air. Valentine looked at the knobby knees and thin legs, and wondered what kind of diet the women were on. They looked like gulag chars who hadn't been on full rations of beans for weeks. Once they passed in another group walked two-by-two back into the tower, led by one of the medical staff in blue scrubs.

Valentine went to work relacing his boots so the laces presented fresh material to the eyelets.

Like clockwork, another group came out, this time from the west tower, and Gail Foster's exited. It was hard to tell under the robes, but all seemed to have about the same level of swelling in the midsection. Same routine, led like chicks behind a blue mother hen.

Damn. West tower.

Valentine put his boots back on and hurried back to the road leading to the pastures.

A faint beep sounded from behind. The vet, Dr. Boothe, sped up on her little four-wheeler cart. "Want a lift?"

My weekend to be offered rides by women.

Valentine hopped into the seat next to her. The trail tires kicked up gravel as she set the electric motor in motion again. "What did I tell you about falling for the bullshit here?"

"I like being indoors every night. I've seen too many bodies in the woods."

She looked at him and away again, quickly. "Impolite to bring up such matters."

"It's all the same bullshit, Doc. Depends on how much you want to shovel off."

"Give me a break. You're part of it now. You were, even in Kentucky."

"There's being a part and taking part. Your assistant, for example. How'd she get past the genetics defect laws?"

"Pepsa? She wasn't born that way. She's from a tough neighborhood in Pittsburgh. She complained once too often, and that's what happens to complainers there. They ripped out her tongue. She still complains—just does it on that little pad of hers."

"So what's with all the pregnant women?"

She took a breath. "They're highly susceptible. You know how the Ordnance is about birthrate."

"I don't, actually."

"They're here so the babies can be saved."

"Don't want anyone going before it's decided. Nice and orderly." Price had that right, anyway.

"Don't talk to Michiver that way, Ayoob. I wish you weren't talking to me."

She pulled up to the veterinary station. The guard dogs in their kennels barked a welcome.

"I imagine you're supposed to turn me in," Valentine said.

"If it comes to protecting my position, don't think I won't. You and the Grog are nothing to me. Nothing."

"Except someone you can be honest around."

"You want honest? I don't like people. That's why I'm a vet. Now get out, I've got some cows to inseminate."

Valentine got out and went over to greet the dogs. He nodded to Pepsa, busy cleaning out the kennels. Dr. Boothe stared at him for a moment, then drove away.

Michiver seemed to know more than he was willing to say as he greeted Valentine at the farm office. "Heard you had a good time after—err, at, the dance, buck." Out back a feed truck clattered as the winter's stores were transferred to the silo. A group of hands ate sack lunches on the porch.

"A lively night," Valentine agreed. "Where do you want me today?"

"You can have the afternoon off. Be back for evening milking. Let the machines do the titty-pulling for a change."

"I give him a month," one of the other hands said to his lunch mates.

"He's colored," a big piledriver of a man named Ski said as Valentine left. He didn't bother to lower his voice; Valentine hardly had to harden his ears at all to pick up the commentary. "And a Grogfucker to boot. She'll keep him around to show off to the other doctors at the holiday parties. He'll get his dismissal papers right before New Year's."

Valentine seethed. He took a walk to let the anger bleed off. Watching cows had a magical soothing quality to it, something about the tail swishing and contemplative chewing always put him in a better mood.

The cows of Xanadu were rather scrawny specimens. Compared to the fat milkers in Wisconsin or the small mountains of beef he'd seen in Nebraska they looked fleshless and apathetic—despite the good grass and plentiful water.

Of course, with characters like Ski taking care of them, anything was possible. He probably left nails or bits of wire lying around. Cows aren't overly bright in their grazing, and they're never right again once a wire is lodged in one of their stomachs.

Valentine found Ahn-Kha scooping grain. The Golden One was

alone, and the cascade of grain going onto the conveyor as it went up to the silo gave a lot of covering noise. He hopped up onto the side of the truck.

"I met a doctor last night and got inside the towers. I saw Gail."

To his credit, Ahn-Kha didn't miss a stroke with the shovel. "I knew this would be the end of the trail. I am surprised she is still alive."

"Give me that. You shouldn't be pushing."

Ahn-Kha passed him the shovel. It felt good to move the mix of corn and feed grain. "This is some kind of baby factory. I've heard stories of women otherwise unemployable just being warehoused while they gestate. Once they recover they go through it all over again."

"Then why all the security?"

"Remember the Ranch? The Kurians might be tinkering with the fetuses. I've wondered why they don't make their own versions of Bears."

"Too hard to control, perhaps. My David, where were you born?"

"The lakes in the Northwoods. You know that."

"But do you? You've told me before it was a strange childhood. Never seriously ill. Never a broken bone. Healing from cuts overnight."

Valentine shoveled harder. "Bear blood, passed down. Like Styachowski. If someone was breeding a more pliable human, it didn't take."

Fran Paoli continued to see him on her strange schedule as the weather turned sharply colder.

Valentine loved autumn up north, the bannerlike colors of the trees, the wet, earthy smell of leaves falling and rotting. He found excuses to work near the wire where he could see the trees, smell the woods.

They saw each other strictly on her terms. Her duties sometimes left her with as much as a whole day free, and she would tear up the roads in her big Lincoln to get them to a show in Cleveland and then back down again. Once she brought him to the south Grand and they made love in an empty conference room on the top floor where a few spare mattresses were stored, for medical staff working long shifts to take breaks.

Valentine never asked her about putting him to work in the towers. He never asked her for so much as a ham sandwich. She bought him two sets of clothes, a fine-material suit with a double-breasted jacket—he feigned ignorance with the necktie knot, since the only one he really knew how to make was the tight Southern Command military style—and some casual, slate-colored pants with a taupe turtleneck made of an incredibly soft and lightweight material she called cashmere.

"You need more than cash to get that these days," she said, observing the results when he put it on and stood in front of the framed floor-length mirror in the corner of her bedroom. "You need connections."

"My whole life I've never had a connection."

"Which is why you're milking cows. I'm not even that great of a doctor, but I'm running a whole department here thanks to connections I've made. Why haven't you asked me for a better job? Every guy I've dated wants me to set him up in an office."

Preguilt flooded Valentine before he even said the words. "You're not like any woman I've ever known, Fran. I didn't want you to think I was . . . what did Oriana call it . . . 'after your status.' "

"You're so young."

Valentine let that rest.

"A brass ring won't just fall into your lap, you know. You're smart. Haven't you figured out that you need to be angling for job security?"

"If I don't like it in the Ordnance I'll just go back into Kentucky, or sign on as an officer in a Grog unit."

"That's a waste. Any stump-tooth can fill out requisition forms for Grog infantry. You need to get yourself into a field Kur needs here. Something not just anyone can do. That's why I chose obstetrics. Kur looks ten thousand years into the future, and about the only certainty is that you need babies to get there."

"The kind of education I have doesn't lend itself to medical school," Valentine said. The bitterness came of its own accord, surprising him.

"There's nursing. You could put in a year here, then go off to Cleveland or Pittsburg for classroom work."

"You could arrange that?" Valentine said.

"I'll speak to the director. Be right back." She turned her back to him, then turned around again and sat on the bed.

"She said you might fit an opening," Fran Paoli said, patting the spot next to her. "Let's do a follow-up interview to be sure."

Valentine managed to wheedle a job for Ahn-Kha out of it as well. Ahn-Kha went to work in the laundry of the main hospital building—the amount of clothing and linen generated by the hospital and the four Grands was formidable. Ahn-Kha discovered two other well-trained Grogs, the simpler Grey Ones, working in the bowels of the hospital, also filling and emptying the washers.

They left the grotty little hand housing and moved into the cleaner, but smaller, apartments for the service workers.

"Less than two weeks in Xanadu and already you're improved," the housing warden said. He carried an assortment of tools at his belt and a long-hosed can of bug spray in a hip holster. "I want your Grog to shower outside, though, or you're outta here. He can use the hose. First sign of fleas and you're outta here."

The room had a phone, and even more amazingly, it functioned. Valentine couldn't remember the last time he'd stayed in a room with a working phone.

They put Valentine to work in the South Grand to begin. His "nursing" duties involved bringing food and emptying the occasional urine bottle, and endless tubes of breast milk.

He learned a little more of the "baby factory" routine. The women had their children at an appointed date and time, always by caesarian. Up until that time they were two to a room, with high cubicle walls in between giving the illusion of individual apartments. After giving birth, they were "rotated" to a new building and given a new room. If they hadn't had a window before, they got one the next time.

Each room had a single television.

A modicum of deal-making took place having to do with television choice and the window side of the room The television had four channels; channel three exhibited a parade of tawdry dramas including the staple *Noonside Passions.* Would Ted turn Holly in to gain the brass ring he'd so long wanted, though he did not yet know she was carrying his child, and would her sister Nichelle ever get out of the handsome-yet-despicable black marketeer Brick's webs? Channel six showed a mixture of quiz shows, courtroom contests where curt, black-robed Reapers impassively heard evidence and assigned monetary damages, divorces, or inheritances, then self-help or skill-improvement sessions in the evening; channel nine broadcast children's programming in the day and then music, either with the musicians or with relaxing imagery at night; channel eleven was the only station that broadcast twenty-four hours a day, providing nothing but propagandistic Ordnance newscasts and bombastic documentaries about mankind's past follies.

Valentine worked four floors in his new blue scrubs, madly during mealtimes, slowly at other hours. Two days of twelve-hour shifts, then a day off, then two more days of twelve-hour shifts, then a day off and a half day—though the half day usually consisted of either training or NUC lectures or some kind of team-building make-work project. His charges were all in their second trimester. Though the women looked wan and drawn thanks to their pregnancies, they were cheerful and talkative, or spent long hours on sewing projects for Ordance soldiers (rumor had it the semen that fertilized them came from decorated combat veterans). He wondered if Malita Carrasca had been this upbeat during her pregnancy. He wondered at the weight loss; the mothers to be he'd met over the years had mostly put on weight.

"It's the quick succession of pregnancies," another nurse, an older woman with years of experience, told him as she lit up in the emergency exit stairway, the unofficial smoking lounge. Valentine had taken to carrying cigarettes, and even smoking one now and again—it was the easiest excuse to get away from his duties for a few minutes. "They have six and then they retire to the Ontario lakeshore and run a sewing circle or a craft workshop. Nice little payoff. But hell on the body while you're cranking them out."

"Diet, Tar," the hefty nurse who counted off meals as they went on Valentine's cart said. She was his immediate supervisor for mealtime duties. "These doctors are all protein-happy. Throwing pregnant women into ketosis. Protein, fats, fiber, and more protein is all they get. And enough iron for a suit of armor. Liver, onions, supplements."

"It gets results," Valentine said. "They're happy enough."

"That's the medication talking. Every woman here's buzzier than a beehive."

Valentine got a chance to test his supervisor's opinion the next day. Every time Valentine got a chance, he looked out one of the windows facing the patio area and the greenhouse below, trying to get a feel for the rhythm of Gail Foster's schedule. Other than a trip to the pool every other day, she never seemed to join the other groups of pink mothers to be.

He wondered if there was a reason for that.

Then one day, as he served lunch, he saw her again, sitting at a table with a book open before her. She had one of the thick, white robes around her body and a towel around her neck.

Valentine finished passing out his meals to the women who ordered food delivered to their rooms—most ate on the second floor, in the cafeteria—and then hurried to the elevator and went outside, ostensibly for a smoke.

Gail Foster sat wrapped up in her book and white terrycloth. He tried to read the title, but it was in a cursive script hard to see at a distance. He walked up at an angle, getting out of the mild fall breeze so he could strike a match.

The smell of the match lighting reminded him of that long-ago escape from Chicago's Zoo.

It looked like the elaborate cursive script of her book read *A Dinner of Onions,* but Valentine couldn't be sure. Gail studied the pages before turning, as though she had to learn the first chapter for a test.

"Good book?" he asked.

She didn't respond. Valentine watched her eyes. When she got to the bottom of the right-facing page, instead of turning it she went back up to the top of the left-side page again. Was she memorizing the novel?

"Not many patients here like to read," Valentine tried again. He took another step forward, blocking her light. "What's it about?"

She turned, looked up at him. "I'm sorry?"

"Your book. What's it about?"

"Some people. I don't know."

"You feeling alright?" Valentine asked. She seemed distant.

"Very well. Doctor says I'm doing very well. But I need some sun, you see?"

Valentine took that to mean he should get out of her light. "Your accent, where are you from?"

"Down south."

Nothing to be gained by waiting, though he felt as though he were having a conversation with a child. "Do you ever want to go back?"

The words slid off her like the water in the pool. "Back where?"

"Down south?"

"No. I have to stay here so the baby can come. It's part of being a healthy mom. There are four parts to being a healthy mom, did you know? Diet, Exercise, Care, and Attitude. I had to work on my attitude most of all, but it's much better now."

"Obviously," Valentine said, giving up. "Do you ever wish you could be with your child after it's born?"

Her eyes grew even larger. "Oh, no. Our children go to special schools. They learn, from their very first weeks, how to lead mankind out of darkness. The Long March to the Future. It would be selfish of me to want to keep my baby from that. That would be a very bad attitude to have."

"Absolutely," Valentine said, finishing his cigarette. Post had once told him that he and Gail had their falling out over an abortion. She did not want to bring a child into the world just to be disposed of at some future date by the Kurian Order.

Was there anything left of that woman?

On off days Valentine and Ahn-Kha went out to "the grotto"—a low pond ringed by trees on the southwestern perimeter of Xanadu—and plotted out how an escape might be engineered. They would eat and talk, then throw a fooball back and forth when they needed to think. At the next break they would talk again. The escape had to buy them enough time to get across the river before an alert was sent out and a pursuit organized.

They developed a plan, but it was like a string of Morse code, a group of dots and dashes with gaps in between. The biggest problem was the security system. Thanks to some postcoital perusals of Fran Paoli's file cabinets—he turned the television on after shutting her door to allow her to sleep in peace—he had learned that Gail was in room 4115 of Grand West, and that she was scheduled for her caesarian in early December. Valentine's ID would get him into his building and onto his assigned floors, plus the common areas for staff, but he couldn't even get access to a floor above or a floor below his levels, let alone a different building. Ahn-Kha could bring laundry into the basements of any of the four Grands, but couldn't access the elevators.

His conversations with Alessa Duvalier grew increasingly anxious. She wanted to know how his head felt.

"Go back home if you like," Valentine said. "Or are things getting heavy with Lance Corporal Scott Thatcher?"

"Soon to be Sergeant Thatcher. He's talking about getting married, said it makes a big difference in how the officers look at you when promotion time rolls around."

"That's wonderful," Valentine said.

"I'm counting the days until he pops the question. I hope your schedule lets you come to an engagement party."

Cooperation from Gail would make all the difference in the world. During daylight hours the women were free to visit their outdoor patio, or even a strip of park bordering the north tower. But how to get cooperation from a woman who had to think long and hard over whether she'd finished a page in her novel or not, and what action to take about it once she did?

"We need someone who can drive. Drive really well," Ahn-Kha said as the days began to run out in October. There was frost on the ground most mornings now.

"That might be doable," Valentine said. "You think we could trust the doc?"

"Your lover? No—"

"I meant Doctor Boothe. I've seen her with pickups and that little ATV. She says she hates people. Maybe she means she hates the system."

"She is risk-averse," Ahn-Kha said. "She does her job, wraps herself in it like a cloak, my David."

"There's one bit of skin showing. That assistant of hers, Pepsa, she's protecting her, hiding her. I wonder if she'd get her out with us."

"And why are we leaving?" Ahn-Kha said.

"I'll come up with a reason."

Evenings at the rec center were typically a bore, and that night was no different. The cavernlike garage had a few games of cards going, an almost-unwatched video, a pickup basketball game, and a "reading circle" where a group of nurses took turns reading a novel—a tattered old gothic about some siblings locked in an attic by a cruel grandmother—and performing the different voices. The only things new were several taped-up orange flyers for the Halloween Dance at the NUC hall, and a table where some of the workers were sewing together odds and ends and adding colored feathers or glitter to masks and hairpieces. The result was more Mardi Gras than Halloween. Valentine wasn't planning on attending. Since he had been to the previous dance, and his lover didn't feel the need to go trolling again, he offered to work that evening.

He opened a "coke" and took a swig of the syrupy concoction with its saliva-like texture. Xanadu cokes had never seen a cola nut but they did give one a brief rush of caffeine-charged glycemic energy.

The pickup basketball game had a lot of noisy energy. Valentine watched Ski, the hand who liked to call him "Grogfucker," sink a three-point shot over the heads of the other hands. An easy man to dislike. Valentine counted heads, nerved himself.

"You've only got five players. Need a sixth?" he asked.

They ignored him.

Valentine set down his bottle and moved around under the basket.

"Clear out, Nursey," Ski said. "Boys only." The jumble of arms and legs shifted back to the basket to the beat of the bouncing ball. Ski tipped it in and Valentine reached out and snatched the ball. He gave it an experimental bounce.

"How about a little one-on-one?" Valentine asked, looking at Ski. The others lined up next to Ski.

"How about you fuck off," Ski said. "Before I bruise up those pretty little eyes."

Let's get it over with, big boy.

Valentine bounced the basketball off Ski's forehead, feeling oddly like he was facing Vista again. He caught the ball on the rebound.

"Naaaah"—Ski let loose with a scream, charging at Valentine with fists flailing. He was big, but a sloppy fighter. It would have been so easy for Valentine to slip under his guard, take his elbow, and use the big hand's momentum to tip him over the point of Valentine's hip. Instead Valentine put up a guard as Ski rained blows on him. He put his head down and rammed it into Ski's stomach. Ski gripped him by the waist and they locked.

A couple of the others saw Ski winning and joined in. Valentine felt himself pulled upright, took the better part of a punch on the temple, a grazing blow to his chin, then another in the gut. Air—and a little coke—wheezed out as his diaphragm contracted. He tasted blood from a cut lip—

Then they were pulled apart, Ski by two of his fellow hands, Valentine by a burly blue arm. Valentine realized it was one of the security staff, talking into his radio even as he put him on the ground with a knee across his back.

Xanadu's security arrived faster than he would have given them credit for—perhaps they were better than they appeared—and didn't let the fight go with a simple "shake hands." Valentine, Ski, and a third hand all made a trip to the long security complex between the hospital and the Grands, where they were put into whitewashed cells to cool down. Valentine gathered from the exchanges at the admissions desk that Ski had caused trouble before, and Valentine had been scooped up in the administrative overkill. Almost as an afterthought they fingerprinted him.

Valentine sat in his cell with a rough brown paper towel, wiping the ink off his hands, wondering—

He'd been printed before in the Kurian Zone. A set of fingerprints existed in the Great Lakes Shipping Security Service, inserted there as part of the long-ago operation that brought him to the Gulf Coast with a good work record that could survive a detailed background check. He imagined the Ordnance had some kind of connection with the GLSSS, and he just might be able to explain away a connection if the old "David Rowan" identity pinged.

But if the connection was made to the renegade officer of the late *Thunderbolt* . . .

Valentine felt a Reaper's presence in the building. Somewhere above.

A warty, one-eyed officer had the three brawlers brought up a level so they stood before his desk. The Reaper lurked somewhere nearby, not in the room. Valentine felt cold sweat on his belly and back, and his eyes searched the desk and file cabinets for something, anything, that could be used as a weapon.

"Brawling, eh?" the officer said from his paper-littered desk. His desk plate read LIEUTENANT STRAND.

"Hot blood, Strand," Ski said. "Nobody was aiming at murder."

"Little too much hot blood. You didn't join in the blood drive this fall."

"I get woozy when they—" Ski said as his companion winced.

"Corporal!" Strand said. "Take them over to the hospital. Liter each, all at once. They won't feel like fighting for a while."

"I get spells—" Ski's accomplice said. Valentine felt only knee-buckling relief. Anything was better than the hovering Reaper.

They were marched over to the hospital under a single-security-officer escort. The security man had a limp worse than Valentine's. Perhaps a sinecure at Xanadu security was a form of payoff for commendable Ordnance service.

"A nice, big bore. Right in the leg," the security man told the nurse.

Noonside Passions was on in the blood center. Valentine concentrated on it as they jabbed the needle into his inner thigh. Ted's evidence against Holly had mysteriously disappeared, and the episode ended with Nichelle's revelation that she'd stolen it—not to protect her sister, but to force her to steal gasoline for Brick's smuggling ring . . . even as Brick started seducing a virginal New Universal Church acolyte named Ardenia behind Nichelle's back.

"That bastard," the rapt nurse said as she extracted the needle. Valentine didn't know if she was referring to Brick or the guard, who was holding a hand-mirror up to Ski to show him how pale he was getting. "One liter, Ayoob. You're done. You'd better lie for a while until I can get you a biscuit. Coffee?"

"Tea. Lots of sugar."

"All we have is substitute. How about a coke? That's real syrup."

"Great," Valentine said as he passed out.

Footsteps in the hall. A blue-uniformed, mustachioed security man turned a key in Valentine's cell. "Ayoob. You're being released to higher authority."

Valentine found he could stand up. Just. Walking seemed out of the question at the moment.

"C'mon, Ayoob, I don't have all night."

Had the fingerprints been processed?

The guard led Valentine out from the catacombs, up some stairs, each step taking him closer to the Reaper, past a ready room, a briefing area, and out to the entryway.

Away from the Reaper!

Valentine caught a whiff of familiar perfume.

"Tar-baby," Fran Paoli said, from across the vastness of the duty desk. "Your face! You need to see a doctor."

The damage wasn't as bad as it looked.

She took him back up to her apartment, dressed the small cut on his cheek, and gave him a pair of cream-colored pills that left him relaxed, a little numb, and with a much-improved opinion of Kurian Zone psychotropics.

"There's a little halloween party tomorrow night at the top floor of Grand North. You won't need a mask."

"I might be working."

"I'll get you off," she said, snapping the elastic waistband on her scrubs. He liked Fran Paoli better in her plain blue scrubs than in any of her more exotic outfits that were designed to impress.

"Undoubtedly. But I don't know that I should miss any shifts. I think I have to keep my nose clean here for a while. If they even let me keep my job. Otherwise it's back to Kentucky."

"Let me worry about your reputation. And your job. Besides, it's going to be a fun party. North has this beautiful function space, and even Oriana's going to get dressed up."

Valentine found it easier to talk with his eyes closed. He felt as though he were drifting down a river on a raft, and opening his eyes might mean he'd have to change course. "I don't have a costume."

"Yes, you do. That biker getup of yours. I've been working on something to match all those spikes."

"Easily done."

"You nap. I have to get back to the wards—I'm missing an operation." She left.

Valentine didn't nap. He wondered—agonized—about the efficiency of the fingerprinting procedures. Would it go in an envelope, off to some central catalog for a bored clerk to get around to? Or would it be scanned into a Xanadu computer, which would spit out a list of his crimes against the Kurian Order as fast as bits of data could be shuffled and displayed? How long before that long, low building, resting at the center of Xanadu, a crocodile keeping watch on his swamp, woke up and came for him? The Kurian Order, like a great slumbering dragon, could be tiptoed around, even over, by a clever thief. Make too much noise, though, rouse it through an attack, and it would swallow you whole without straining in the slightest.

The sensible thing would be to blow this operation, tonight; take Ahn-Kha, find Ali, and be across the river in Price's bass boat before the next shift change.

Could he face Post, tell him his wife was a drugged-up uterus for the Kurian Order? Better to lie and tell him she was dead.

He wouldn't even be able to bring the news himself. He was an exile, condemned by the fugitive law. Ahn-Kha or Duvalier would have to find him in whatever rest camp was helping him adapt to an artificial leg and a shortened intestine.

Getting her out, hopefully in time to beat the fingerprint check, would mean he'd have to bring more people in on the effort. Could he trust the doctor?

Madness. He was right back where he started.

Would William Post do the same for you? How much can one friend expect of another?

No, that's a cheat. The question here is what is a promise, hastily issued from beside a hospital bed, a tiny promise from David Valentine, worth?

Doctor Boothe yawned as she came to her surgery door. "Ayoob. What happened?"

He tried to show the good half of his face through the strip of chained door. "A fistfight with Ski and a few hands. Can I come in?"

"It's eleven at night."

"It's important enough."

She shut the door and Valentine heard the chain slide. He looked around. The cool night air was empty.

She brought him into the tiled surgery and turned on a light. "What's so important, now?"

"I'm leaving the Ordnance. Going back to Kentucky."

"Good for you."

"I was wondering if your assistant might like to come. Anyone with veterinary training would be welcome there."

"Pepsa? A rabbit-run? Why should she do that?"

"She's mute. I'm surprised she hasn't been culled out of the herd before this."

"How dare—"

"Just cutting through the bullshit, Boothe. Or are you the type who only likes to see half the truth? I know people. We could get her somewhere safe from the Reapers, a lot safer than your dog kennels and dairy stalls."

"We?"

"Me. Ahn-Kha. You. Someone on the outside. I don't want to say more."

"You just offered your heart up, you know that. You'd be gone tonight if I told security. I'd get a seat at the head table at the next Ordnance Gratitude Banquet."

Valentine didn't want to kill this woman. But if she moved to the phone— "If you're such a friend of security, why haven't our guns ever left your office? Or have they?"

She couldn't help but look over her shoulder at the corridor to her storage room.

Boothe seemed to be fighting with something lodged in her throat.

"You could come along," Valentine continued. "Disappear into the tribelands, or relocate into Free Territory."

She frowned. "Free Territory's a myth. Some clearing full of guerillas does not a nation make."

"I've been there."

"As if it's that easy."

"I didn't say anything about it being easy."

She lifted her chin. "Let me talk to Pepsa."

Valentine followed her with his ears and listened from the surgery doorway as she went into a back room and spoke to Pepsa. The quiet conversation was one-sided; Valentine couldn't see what Pepsa communicated back on her kiddie magic tablet. This would be an all-or-nothing gamble. Every person added to a conspiracy doubled the risk.

Dr. Boothe, with Pepsa trailing behind in a robe, joined him in the surgery. Pepsa looked at him with new interest in her gentle eyes.

"You have people who can help us get all the way to Free Territory?"

Valentine thought it best to dodge the question. "There are plenty of animals to take care of there. Herds of horses."

Pepsa wrote something on her board.

"But you do have people outside Xanadu to help us get away?"

"Absolutely."

Boothe and Pepsa exchanged a look. Pepsa wrote again.

"What do you need us to do?" Boothe asked.

"We need some food that can be preserved. Pack some cold-weather clothing and camp-mats, and have it all ready by tomorrow afternoon. Make some excuse for not being available until November first or second. And one more thing. I need a quick look in your pharmacy."

Valentine walked all the way back to the rec center to use the phone there. He could have used the phone in Boothe's office, but just in case she or Pepsa turned on him, he could warn Duvalier.

The phone rang fourteen times before a gravelly voice at the hostel answered it. "Yeah?"

Valentine asked to speak to Duvalier's Ordnance ID pseudonym.

"No calls after nine."

"It's urgent. Could I leave a message?"

"She'll get it in the morning, Corporal."

The attendant must have thought Valentine was Duvalier's would-be boyfriend, Corporal Thatcher.

"Tell her my migraine is back. I'll come by tomorrow night, then we can get to the party."

"Migraine?"

Valentine spelled it.

"She'll get the message at a decent hour. Reread your phone protocols, Corporal—dating doesn't give you special privileges to disturb me."

"Tell her some new friends will be along. We'll have transport."

"I'm not a stenographer, son. Call her tomorrow."

Valentine thanked him and replaced the receiver. Next he'd have to wake Ahn-Kha. He looked at the craft table with the Halloween costumes.

Xanadu had its share of children, and while it was still light out they paraded around in their costumes from building to building, collecting treats from the security staff at the doors.

The kids sang as they collected their candy.

A Reaper, a creeper
Goes looking for a sleeper
Wakes him up, drinks him down
And packs him in the freez-zer.

Valentine, dressed in his Bulletproof "leathers" and carrying a large brown market bag full of costuming, was a little shocked to hear the realities of life in the Kurian Zone expressed in nursery-rhyme fashion. He watched one young child, dressed in the red-and-white stripes of a frightening, bloody-handed Uncle Sam, pull his cowgirl sister along as they sang. He'd been at sea during his other Halloween in the Kurian Zone, so he couldn't say if it was a widespread practice. Or maybe on this one night mention of the real duties of the Reapers was allowed.

Valentine passed in to Grand East and nodded to the security staff. They were used to him by now.

"Nice costume, Tar. You really rode those things?"

"Sure did," Valentine said, trying to put a little Kentucky music into his voice.

Valentine went to the smaller of the elevators, the one that went to the top and garage floors, and rode up.

He couldn't help but pat the syringes stuck in the breast of his legworm-rider jacket. His .22 target pistol was tucked into the small of his back, held in place by three strips of surgical tape. Hopefully he wouldn't need it.

Fran Paoli just yelled "come in" at his knock. He hurried in, wondering just how—

And he had his answer when he saw her.

She stood in the doorway of her bedroom, a gothic queen spider in thigh-high boots thick with buckles. Black eyeliner, spider earrings, a temporary tattoo of a skull on one fleshy, corset-enclosed breast.

"Sticks and stones may break my bones, but leather and chains excite me," she quoted.

"What on earth do you use boots like that for?" Valentine asked.

"Turning men on. Is it working?"

"I'll say. Come here, you naughty girl."

She giggled, and came up and kissed him. She tested the hooks on his forearms, and looked down at the spurs.

"You're dangerous tonight," Fran Paoli observed.

"You've no idea."

He sat on the arm of her sofa and threw her across his knee, raising the torn, black-dyed taffeta miniskirt. A black thong divided her buttocks. He gave her backside an experimental slap.

"Ohhhh!" she cooed.

"I may just have to tie you up so other men don't get a chance to see this," he said, snapping the thong. He hit her again, harder.

"Nothing I could do about it," she said.

He hit her harder. She gave tiny giggle-gasps at each swat.

"My, what a strong arm you have," she said, lifting her now-splotched buttocks a little. Valentine extracted the syringe from his jacket, pulled the plastic cap off with his teeth, and held it in his mouth while he spanked her again, even harder. He felt both ridiculous and a little aroused.

"Uhhh—" she gasped. He transferred the syringe to his hand and injected her, threw it across the room behind her, and struck her again.

Six more swats and she was limp and moaning. The large-animal tranquilizers had their effect.

She slurred and tried to caress him as he transferred her to the bedroom. He kissed her several times, gagged her with her bathrobe belt, and tied her up in the closet using pairs of pantyhose and leather belts.

She offered no resistance save a dopey-eyed wink.

"Now you just wait there for a little while," he said, and kissed her on the forehead. He shut the closet door.

Valentine took her keys from the dresser, and her blue ID card. He pocketed them and rode the elevator to the basement.

He'd worked out every move in his mind, gone over it so many times a sense of unreality persisted. Was he still lying in bed, planning this? Was it his real hand reaching for the big Lincoln's door, his bag he placed on the passenger seat, his foot on the accelerator as he backed toward the fuel pump?

The pump clattered loudly enough that he wondered that the whole building didn't come to investigate. He topped off the tank, and filled the two spare twenty-liter plastic containers she kept in the back. He climbed into the driver's seat, and put on the seat belt and com headset. He started the SUV and turned it toward the garage door.

"Two-one-six, leaving," he said into her mouthpiece, pressing the com button on the dash.

"Dr. Paoli?"

"Tar Ayoob, running an errand," he said.

"Two-one-six, leaving," the voice acknowledged. "Enjoy the party." The garage door rose.

Valentine pulled the SUV around to the west tower, parked it in plain sight under a roadside light, and trotted over to the basement door with his bag. He knocked, and Ahn-Kha, in his laundry overcoat, answered.

"Here," Ahn-Kha said, and passed Valentine some blue scrubs.

The boots looked a little funny under them, but he'd pass. Once Ahn-Kha checked the basement hallway, thick with conduits and junction boxes, Valentine went to the larger, gurney-sized elevators and pressed the up button.

Ahn-Kha brought a wheelchair out from around a corner. They were easily found all over the building, but it never hurt to be prepared.

He pushed Fran's blue card in the slot and went up to the fourth floor.

Halloween decorations, traditional orange-and-black paper, festooned the hallway over the honor-in-childbearing propaganda. Vague noises of something that sounded like a Chevy with a bad starter came from the central common room. Valentine walked behind the wheelchair to Room 4105.

The outer cubicle was empty. A woman lay in the next bed, sleeping—but it wasn't Gail.

He knew Gail Post's schedule by heart. She'd already been fed, and it was getting to the point where the women were usually expected to be in their beds, asleep.

He crossed the building to the common room. Twenty-odd women watched spacecraft blow up a model of long-ago Los Angeles. Vacant, tired eyes reflected the sparking special effects.

Gail Foster sat right in the center.

A nurse popped up at the door. "Can I help?"

"Gail Foster. Follow-up X-ray."

She glanced at Valentine's ID badge, but didn't examine it closely. "Follow-up to what?"

"Not sure. Dr. Kreml's orders. They should have called. She wants it taken tonight."

"That one," the nurse said, pointing.

Valentine tapped her on the shoulder. "Gail, I need you for a moment," he said.

"Sure," she said absently. Valentine helped her to the chair by the door. A few of the other patients exchanged looks, but most watched the movie.

The nurse who had questioned Valentine was at the center console, speaking into the phone.

No choice.

He wheeled Gail to the station. The nurse turned to watch him.

"Is there a problem?" Valentine asked.

"Just checking with central."

"Should I wait?"

"If you don't mind." She turned and checked a clipboard again.

Valentine hated to do it, but he took out the horse tranquilizer. With one quick step, he got behind her and jammed it into her neck. He pulled her down, one hand on her mouth, and waited until her legs quit kicking.

"You certainly got her cooperation," Gail said.

"Let's not have any attitude tonight, okay, Gail?" Valentine asked as he pulled the nurse into a file room. He found a length of surgical tubing and tied the door shut.

Gail offered a *wheeeee* as he raced her down the hall to the elevator. On the ride down he stripped off his scrubs.

"I've never been here before," Gail observed as they entered the basement corridor. Ahn-Kha helped her get dressed. "Oh, pretty," she remarked, as Valentine slipped a feathered mask on her.

They walked her out to the Lincoln, Ahn-Kha half carrying her across the road. The Golden One climbed in the back cargo area where his disassembled puddler waited, along with Valentine's weapons.

"Keep her quiet back there, and out of sight," Valentine said.

He drove the Lincoln around the building perimeter to the veterinary office. "Glad you remembered the heavy coat," Valentine said as Dr. Boothe slipped into the passenger seat.

"You give good instruction. Is this Paoli's rig?"

"I like to make an exit," Valentine said.

Pepsa's eyes widened as she saw Ahn-Kha in back.

Valentine passed out masks to Dr. Boothe and Pepsa. "Just on our way to a party, okay? Once we're past the gate, you'll be driving."

As they rolled around the hospital the headlights illuminated a figure at the roadside in harsh black and white, gleam and shadow. A pale face, exaggerated and immobile as a theatrical mask, held them like a spotlight.

A Reaper.

Boothe sucked breath in through her teeth. Valentine's heart gave a triple thump. The Reaper could upend the Lincoln as easily as it might lift a wheelbarrow. Then what chance would they have, still within Xanadu's walls. If it moved he'd have to—

But it didn't.

After they passed it crossed the road behind them. How could it not know they had an expectant mother inside the SUV? Of all forms of lifesign, a pregnant woman's was the strongest, and Valentine had one experience involving a Kurian and an infant's lifesign that he'd rather die than repeat. Perhaps the Kurian animating it was sick, or sated, or . . .

Someone was letting them go.

The gate warden hardly looked at them as they followed a bus full of Halloween partygoers out of Xanadu. Ahn-Kha lay flat in the back cargo space, holding down Gail Foster. "Have a good time, Dr. Paoli," the sergeant said. Valentine nodded and Boothe waved in return.

Pepsa tapped her hands against the leather seats as Valentine pulled away from the gate. "We've done it!" Boothe said.

"We've done it, alright," Valentine demurred. "Now what are they going to do about it?"

Twelve

Escapes: Nearly every part of the Kurian Zone is traced with "pipelines," or channels for escapees to reach safety. Other networks supply guerillas and underground information distributors, and a few do double, or even triple duties as criminal organizations involved in smuggling and black-market trading. In the better-run networks, each person at a pipeline junction only knows her links in the next stage of the operation, making it harder for a pipeline to be rolled up. Generally, the less that is known about a pipeline the safer it is to travel.

This has a drawback, however. Without careful preparation work, operatives who venture into unfamiliar territory will have no idea who to trust and who not to, as the man next door in the New Universal Church hostel might be the local pipeline operator or a Kurian informer.

A grim vocabulary exists among those who shuttle material, human or logistical, through the pipelines. Shutdowns and spills are bad, involving loss of a route, and a penetration is the worst of all, indicating that the Kurians successfully uncovered a line and cleaned it up after their "mole" crept its way through. A "rabbit" is an escapee that makes a try for freedom without any guidance whatsoever. Rabbits are useful in that "rabbit runs" divert resources that might otherwise be used to uncover a real pipeline.

Like a cottontail's dash for cover, most rabbit runs are fast, panicked, and quickly finished.

Valentine switched places with Boothe as soon as they passed out of the light of the gates. It was a cloudy evening and the woods were black as a mine shaft. Only with wide-open Cat eyes could he distinguish a tree trunk or two. He relaxed a little once they passed where he had sensed the Reaper pickets on his reconnaissance and made it out of the hairpin-turn gully—if Valentine had chosen a spot to ambush the big-framed Lincoln, it would have been there.

The Reapers, if they were out there, hadn't caused the "Valentingle"—but with his blood loss, and nervous exhaustion after the strain of the past few days, his wiring might have loosened.

Boothe drove skillfully, just fast enough to choose the best way to negotiate the patched road without bouncing her passengers around too much. The rugged suspension on the truck helped. In the rear cargo area, Gail counted the bumps, but lost track at sixty-seven.

As they took the river road into town Valentine saw what looked like bonfires in the hills, on both sides of the river.

"What's all this?"

"Hell night," Boothe said.

"Meaning?"

"Kind of a tradition. Old, emptied houses get burned to the ground on Halloween night. Farther out it's grain silos and barns."

On this one night the town sounded lively. People crisscrossed the streets burning everything from road flares to candles in grimacing, fanged pumpkins. Valentine wondered at the pumpkins—Reapers had pale skin, not orange in the slightest, and a yellow squash might better reflect both skin tone and their long, narrow skulls.

They pulled up on the street leading to the NUC hostel. It, too, was burning. Firefighters and police fought the blaze with hoses.

"I thought you said only abandoned buildings?" Valentine asked.

Boothe stopped the four-wheeler well away from the conflagration and its attending crowd.

"Could be some drunk got carried away. I should see if anyone—"

"No," Valentine said. "Stay here."

He got out of the vehicle. A man in football padding sat on the curb, drinking from a bottle within a paper bag.

Valentine heard a high-pitched whistle from the other side of the street. Duvalier and a man in the shale-colored uniform of the Ordnance, old US M-model rifle over his shoulder and a duffel in his hand, ran across the street and to the Lincoln.

"You weren't kidding about transport," Duvalier said. "Tar, meet Corporal Scott Thatcher."

Valentine remembered him from the dance. Thatcher had a bony face, but everything was pleasantly enough arranged.

"You sure about this?" he asked. He meant the question for Duvalier but Thatcher spoke up.

"I want out, sir. Passage all the way if it can be arranged." He lowered his voice. "Free territory."

Valentine didn't like it. The boy could win a nice position in the Kurian Zone by turning them in. He was certainly armed heavily enough to take control of the escape, with a pistol at his hip, an assault rifle over his arm . . .

Is that what you really think? Or is it Alessa finding someone?

Valentine's first escape from the Kurian Zone, leading a few families of refugees with a platoon of Zulu Company's Wolves, had been betrayed to the Reapers. He wouldn't let it happen again.

On the other hand, an Ordnance uniform, stripes, and knowledge of the region—assuming Thatcher could be trusted—would come in handy.

"He's okay, Val," Duvalier said. For her to use his real name like that must mean something. "He knows the ground. I trust him. So can you."

"We'll see."

"Says the man who manages to come out the gates with three, count 'em, ladies and gentlemen, three women. New personal best?"

Valentine ignored the jibe. "You'll have to put your duffel up top," he said to Thatcher. "The rifle can go in back. Give me that pistol."

Thatcher passed him the weapons. Valentine handed the assault rifle back to Ahn-Kha in the cargo bay.

"Take shotgun," Valentine said. "And remember, another shotgun's in the seat right behind you."

Valentine wondered how they'd all fit. Duvalier crouched in between the driver and passenger seats, next to Thatcher, with Valentine and Pepsa in the seats behind.

"Fire your doing?" he asked Duvalier as they pulled away from the fire and the growing crowd.

"Yes. But it's just a diversion. In another half hour the police headquarters is going to lose their fodder-wagons and fuel depot."

Pepsa took a startled breath. "I had a feeling you were more than just a boy heading home, Tar," Boothe said.

"You thought of everything," Thatcher said. "But it's not the police we have to worry about, it's the Ordnance."

"A girl has to keep busy," Duvalier said.

In the back, Ahn-Kha assembled his puddler.

"West on the river road," Valentine told Boothe.

"Where you planning to cross?" Thatcher asked, excitement bringing his words fast and hard.

"Route ten bridge," Valentine said. "Just a mile ahead here. Saw it when we were biking. It gets a lot of traffic."

"Yeah, 'cause it's open to civilians," Thatcher said. "You'll at least get a flashlight sweep. Go up five more miles and cross at Ironton Road. That's an Ordnance checkpoint. There's a Kentucky Roadside popular with all of us up a ways there. Better all around."

"Well?" Boothe asked.

"Ironton Road it is," Valentine said.

Duvalier gripped Thatcher's hand and nodded, but Valentine felt like it was a mistake. He handed her a party hat.

The old, rusty trestle bridge had been blown up at some point. New girders and railroad ties had been cobbled together to close the gap.

"Don't worry, we've taken trucks over it," Thatcher said as Boothe slowed. Valentine checked the magazine of Thatcher's 9mm, then chambered a round.

They made it over the gap with no more than the sound of tires rumbling across the ties.

A lighted guardhouse at the other end had a couple of uniformed men in it. The Lincoln's headlights revealed two chains, running from either side of the bridge to a post in the center, more of a polite warning than a serious obstacle. Yellow reflective tape fluttered from the center of each length, looking like a dancing worm in the headlights' glare.

"I'm supposed to be asleep now," Gail announced, an angry tone in her voice.

"Oh great, we have a med-head," Duvalier said.

"Keep her quiet in back, there," Valentine said to Ahn-Kha. He heard a squeak.

Boothe rolled down her window as they approached the checkpoint. She swerved into the left-hand lane to pull up to it.

"Hey there, Cup," Thatcher called. He passed over an ID card. Valentine didn't know if it was Ordnance slang or a nickname, but the man's shirt read "Dorthistle." "Five and a lost Grog going to Beaudreaux's. Back by sunup."

The sentry looked at the card, then placed his flashlight beam on Thatcher.

Boothe began to glance around and Valentine stiffened. If he was on the ball, the sentry would notice the fight-or-flight tell. She was looking for a direction to run. Valentine yawned and returned his hand to the butt of the pistol next to his thigh.

Valentine heard the phone ring in the guardhouse.

"Line's up again," the man inside said. "That was quick."

Shit shit shit.

"You going to unhook or what, *Private,*" Thatcher said. "It's Halloween and we need to raise some hell."

A soldier inside picked up the phone.

The private went around to the center post and placed his hand on the chain.

"Border closed, alert!" the soldier with the phone shouted from inside the guardhouse.

"Ram it," Valentine shouted. Boothe sat frozen, her hands locked on the steering wheel.

The guard by the chain stepped back, fumbling for his rifle as the butt hit the post.

"Christ, go!" Duvalier said.

Valentine opened his door and aimed his pistol through the gap at the white-faced guard, lit like a stage actor by the Lincoln's beams. A whistle blew from somewhere in the darkness.

Pop pop pop—the flash from the pistol was a little brighter than the headlights; the guard spun away, upended over the chain.

The noise unfroze the gears in Boothe's nervous system. She floored the accelerator.

The Lincoln hit the chain, bounced over something that might have been the post going down, or might have been the guard, and Valentine heard a metallic scream that was probably the front bumper tearing.

The Lincoln gained speed.

"Turn the lights off," Ahn-Kha boomed as he looked out the back windows. "Don't give them a mark to aim—"

Bullets ripped into the back of the Lincoln. Ahn-Kha threw himself against the back of the seats, wrapping Gail Foster in one great arm and Pepsa in the other.

"Agloo," Pepsa yelped. Gail screamed.

Valentine felt the Lincoln head up a slight rise, then turn, putting precious distance, brush, and trees between them and the checkpoint.

"Everyone okay?" Valentine asked.

"Some glass cuts," Ahn-Kha said. "Post's mate is hit in the foot. Let me get her shoe off."

Gail yelped again. "I want to go home," she wailed.

"I believe a toe is missing," Ahn-Kha said.

Pepsa nodded at Valentine.

"Pepsa, take my bag. See what you can do," Boothe said.

Ahn-Kha shifted to give her room to get in the back. Valentine heard his friend wheeze.

"Glass cuts?" Valentine said.

"I fear it may be more than that, my David," Ahn-Kha said.

"Who's David?" Boothe asked.

"Just drive, please."

"I could go faster if I turned on the lights."

"No," Valentine and Thatcher said in unison.

"Go left here," Thatcher said. "Good road."

Valentine, smelling blood, his stomach hurting as though he'd been mule-kicked, saw a distant patch of flame; a house burning over by the river. Somewhere there were people dancing in firelight. Somewhere Reapers were asking questions. Boothe made the turn, heading south.

The bumper ground as it scraped the road surface.

Ahn-Kha let out a gentle cough. "My David. I saw headlights hit the clouds far back. I believe we are being followed."

How far would the Ordnance chase them into Kentucky?

"Stop the car. I'll drive," Valentine said. "Doc, check out Ahn-Kha. Do what you can for him."

Valentine slipped into the driver's seat, and got the sport-utility vehicle moving as soon as he heard the back door close. Boothe switched places with Pepsa in the cargo area. Ahn-Kha kicked out a bullet-starred window.

You can do this. Nothing to be afraid of. You've driven before. Badly, but you've driven.

He could see farther than Boothe, and pushed the engine up past forty miles an hour. They ate miles. Every now and then the Lincoln hit a pothole with a resounding thump.

A flash blinded him. "You need help," Boothe said.

"Watch the light back there," Valentine said. Boothe had been using a flashlight to look at Ahn-Kha. Sudden increases in light gave him an instant headache.

Valentine spotted a legworm trail, the distinctive rise and thick vegetation cutting across a field.

"I'm going to go off-road," he told Thatcher.

Thatcher pushed a button on the center console, engaging the four-wheel drive. "Slow down. They'll see tire marks otherwise."

Valentine applied the brake, felt the Lincoln change gears. Automatic transmission made a huge difference in driving effort.

He turned onto the legworm trail. Any tree big enough to stop the Lincoln was avoided by the creature. The ground looked easier to the east, so he followed another legworm trail leading that way. He listened to the car cutting through weeds and grasses.

"I've done all I can," Boothe said. "The external bleeding's stopped, for now."

Valentine found another road, got on it, and took it for a mile until it intersected with one in even worse condition, but at least he was heading south.

"We're still being followed," Duvalier said. "Looks like a motorcycle."

Valentine didn't need the confirmation. He felt them behind, a presence, the way you felt a thunderstorm long before its first rumble.

"Stop the car, my David," Ahn-Kha said. The Golden One hoisted his puddler, then waited until they could hear the faint blatt of the motorcycle engine.

"Cover your ears," Ahn-Kha said.

The gun boomed. Gail screamed. Valentine watched the motorcycle light shift, wink out.

"That'll learn 'em," Duvalier said.

Valentine put the car in gear again. He watched the colon blink on the dashboard clock. Had all this happened in only twenty minutes?

He pushed the Lincoln, daring himself to wreck it, locked on to a distance a hundred yards in front of the car as if watching for downed tree limbs was the be-all, and end-all of his life. Which it might be, if he struck a big enough object in the dark.

"They're still behind," Ahn-Kha observed ten minutes, or six hundred or so clock flashes, later. "Gaining, it would appear. Perhaps they have Hummers."

"Shouldn't have shot that poor Cup," Thatcher said. "They wouldn't be after us like this otherwise. I bet there's a locator in this rig."

"You people are crazy," Gail said. "They say I'm the one who causes problems. They must have never met you." Her voice sounded raw and tired.

Valentine crossed legworm trail after legworm trail, recent mounds with just the beginnings of growth on them.

Ahn-Kha coughed again. "My David, I have a suggestion."

"I don't want to hear it," Valentine shot back.

"They are going to catch up with this truck sooner or later. Would it not be better if we weren't all in it when they did?"

"Ahn—"

"Let him talk," Duvalier said.

"I cannot walk far. Let me lead them on a wild Grog hunt. When they catch up, I will grunt and pretend that I am simple. They will think a trick has been played, that a poor dumb Grog has been put at the wheel to lead them away."

"Lots of Grogs know how to drive. They're good at it," Thatcher said.

Valentine looked at Duvalier, but she wasn't listening, or was only half listening. Her lips were moving in steady rhythm.

"Four minutes behind," she said. "I marked that hilltop."

She began to fiddle with her explosive-packed Spam cans, a detonator, and a fuse. She threw one out on one side of the road, and then the other went into the opposite ditch.

"You'll have to get royal-flush lucky to take one of them out," Thatcher said.

"I'm not trying for that. I just want to fool them into thinking they've been ambushed."

Valentine drove past a burning barn, collapsed down to the foundation and mostly sending up smoke by now. The Lincoln plunged into a thicket and he had to slow down. He found another legworm track and cut off the road again, splashing through a stream. The wheels briefly spun as they came up the other side, then they were out into broken country again. Following the legworm trail, he found yet another farm service road running along a rounded, wooded hill. They were in real back country now. It would be dangerous to go off-road—not that the roads in this part of Kentucky were much better.

"They're still behind," Duvalier said.

Valentine wanted to wrench the steering wheel free of its mount, throw it out the window, turn around, and smash the Lincoln into their pursuers—

"Enough, my David," Ahn-Kha said. "Let me take the wheel."

"Val, it's the only way," Duvalier said.

"Alright. But I'm coming with you."

"No," Ahn-Kha said. "You've kept faith with me. You must still see Gail back. I may be able to fool them. With you, there will be too many questions."

Valentine stopped the Lincoln in the middle of the road. "We have to hurry. Everyone out. Thatcher, don't forget your gun and duffel."

Ahn-Kha climbed out the back and came around to the driver's door, helping himself stand up by putting his long right arm on the side of the Lincoln, puddler cradled in his left. He was a mess, his back peppered with bandages and streaked in blood, a thick dressing on the back of his firepluglike thigh. Duvalier stopped before him, then stood on tiptoe to kiss one whiskered cheek. She looped her oversized canteen around the Golden One's neck. "I want this back, you hairy fuck. You hear me?"

Ahn-Kha murmured a few words into her ear.

"Oh, dream on," she laughed, wiping away tears.

Valentine could only stand, tired and fighting his headache, fiddling with his gun. Would it be better for their pursuit to come upon all their bodies, stretched out next to the flaming Lincoln? Perhaps with every dead hand posed with middle finger extended?

"We'll meet another dawn, my David," Ahn-Kha said as he reclined the driver's seat all the way so he could squeeze up front. He tossed the puddler onto the passenger seat.

"If we live to see another dawn," Valentine said.

"If not, we'll meet in a far better place," Ahn-Kha said. One ear rose a trifle.

"Good luck, old horse," Valentine said. He placed his forehead against Ahn-Kha's, hugged him, felt the rough skin and the strangely silky hair on his upper back.

Ahn-Kha squeezed the back of his neck and the Lincoln drove away.

"Off the road! Fast," Valentine said. Issuing orders in his old command voice, then picking a route up the hill, kept him from staring after the receding Lincoln. The best friend Valentine ever had, or would ever have, left only a little blood on the road. "Thatcher, lead them up that hillside."

Duvalier pulled the whining, pregnant Gail Foster into the bush, opening a gap in the bramble with her walking stick. Dr. Boothe and Pepsa followed her, Pepsa searching anxiously down the road for their pursuers. Valentine spotted one of Duvalier's Spam cans, unopened and unwired, left in the center of the road, and picked it up with a curse.

Valentine closed the gap in the brush behind them by forcing a few tree limbs down, and limped after his party, giving his tears their time.

Halfway up the hill they froze and counted the pursuit. A column rolled up the slight incline: another motorcycle, two Hummers, a pickup with dogs in it, and two five-ton trucks. A platoon of Wolves or a team of Bears could knock hell out of them, but he and Duvalier would waste themselves against it.

Without Ahn-Kha's reliable strength alongside him, he felt like a piece of his spine had been plucked out.

"He did it," Duvalier said as they saw the pursuit convoy crest another rise in the distance.

They crested the hill, and thanks to its commanding view Valentine went through Thatcher's inventory. He'd brought some good topographical maps of Kentucky, and between the two of them they made a good guess as to where they were. Several lights could be seen between the hill and the northern horizon, but they were so distant he couldn't tell if they were electric or burning homes.

"What do you suppose that is?" Duvalier asked, pointing southwest.

"I don't see anything," Boothe said, but she couldn't without Cat eyes.

A garbage pile, perhaps? It looked like a plate of spaghetti the size of a football field.

"That's a legworm dogpile," Valentine said. "Look at all the tracks."

"What, that hump down there?" Thatcher said, squinting to try to make out what they were talking about. "I saw three of them all tangled up once after a snowstorm."

"Let's get off this ridge," Valentine said. "Take a closer look. Maybe some of their tribe is around."

Valentine pointed out a tree at the bottom of the hill, and had Thatcher find a path toward it. Gail's breathing was labored and Duvalier gave her the walking stick. Valentine hung back to check the rest spot, and waved Duvalier over.

"You dropped this in the road," Valentine said, giving Duvalier back her can of explosive-filled meat.

She looked at it, puzzled, and whipped her bag off her back. The wing locks were still clicked shut. "Then it jumped out on its own."

"Someone left it?"

"Everyone was in a hurry to get out of the truck. Maybe it got kicked out in the confusion."

Valentine only remembered the sound of feet hitting the ground. "Let's not leave anything to luck, good or bad," he said.

They caught up to the others at the bottom of the hill, and walked out into the horseshoe-shaped flat with the legworm dogpile roughly in the center. What might have been utility poles at one time could be seen against the horizon, a few miles away. The peak of a funnel-topped silo and a barn roof showed.

Legworm trails crisscrossed the ground everywhere, but none looked or smelled fresh. Maybe their minders were on the other side of the valley.

Gail collapsed, crying. "Legs won't hold me up anymore."

Boothe listened to her heart and breathing with her stethoscope. "She's healthy, just out of condition."

"We can rest for a little," Valentine said.

Then need came, terrible need. Valentine felt them on the towering hill behind, moving like an angry swarm of bees.

Reapers.

They'd home in on the lifesign—he had a pregnant woman, and

bitter experience told him that Kurians hungered for newborns like opiate addicts sought refined heroin; he might as well be running with a lit Roman candle—and that would be the end of them.

"We're in trouble," Valentine said.

"What—" Duvalier began.

"No time," he snapped. He handed her his rifle. "You and Thatcher head for those telephone poles. Doc, you and Pepsa go into those woods and find low ground. Lie flat, flat as you can." He tossed her Thatcher's 9mm.

"Reapers?" Duvalier asked.

"Coming down the hill." Boothe went as white as the cloud-hidden moon. "Hurry." He grabbed Gail's wrist. "I'll lead them off. Maybe I can lose them."

You won't. Too long until sunup.

"How?"

"Interference." *Price's critter camouflage, writ in sixty-foot letters.*

Valentine took Gail's wrist and pulled her to her feet.

"Hate this," she said. "I want to go to my room. Please? This endangers the baby."

He could feel them coming, but caution had slowed them, stalking lions reevaluating as the herd they'd been stalking scattered.

Gail's legs gave out. Valentine picked her up in a fireman's carry, hoping it was safe to carry an expectant woman this way.

"Those chain things sound like wind chimes. I like wind chimes," Gail said. "Are we going back to the Grands soon?"

"Very possible," Valentine said as he ran.

From a hundred feet away the legworm pile looked like a gigantic lemon pie with a lattice-top crust—baked by a cook who was stoned to the gills. The legworms had pushed banks of earth up into walls, forming the pie "tin," and had woven themselves at the top.

Valentine reached the bank and climbed up it, sending dirt spilling. He went down on one knee, set Gail on churned-up ground, and caught his breath.

They were coming again. After him. Fast.

"I don't want to run anymore," Gail said.

"Good. We need to crawl."

He pulled her beneath a smaller legworm's twisted body, back set to the elements, shaggy skin flapping in the wind like an old, torn poster. They descended into the dark tangle, and perceived a faint aqua glow from within.

Valentine felt like he was back in the ruins of Little Rock, negotiating one of the great concrete-and-steel wrecks of a building downtown. Legworms lay on top of each other everywhere, a sleeping pile of yellow-fleshed Pickup Sticks.

The air grew noticeably warmer as he pulled Gail deeper into the nest.

The legworms were not packed as tightly at the bottom. Valentine felt air move. He followed it, and the glow.

"Don't like this," Gail whispered.

"Don't blame you."

And came upon the eggs. The legworm bodies arched above and around, making a warm arena for their deposits.

About the size of a basketball, the eggs had translucent skin. The glow came from the growing legworm's underside; the soft "membrane" had blue filament-like etchings of light, transformed into aqua by the greenish liquid within the eggs.

"Smells like old laundry in here," Gail said.

"Shhh."

Valentine saw deep pock marks in the skins of the larger legworms at the center. The eggs must have dropped off. Black lumps, like unprocessed coal, lay scattered between the living eggs. Evidently only a few eggs made it to whatever stage of the metamorphosis they now enjoyed.

Stepping carefully, Valentine crossed the egg repository, hoping the baby legworms were giving off enough lifesign to confuse the Reapers' senses.

He heard-felt-sensed motion behind.

A string of Reapers entered the egg chamber, clad in their dark, almost bulletproof robes, the first staring about as if to make sense of the small glows and vast shadows.

Valentine shoved Gail toward an A-shaped arch in a legworm's midsection. She turned around to protest, and her big eyes grew even wider, until they seemed to fill her face.

Gail shrieked. She instinctively reached for him, putting his body in between herself and the others.

As one, six Reaper heads turned in their direction. Valentine drew his .22 target pistol.

The lead Reaper dismissed the threat with a wave, a grotesque wigwag of its double-jointed elbow. It had a burn-scarred face, making its visage that of a badly formed wax mask.

Valentine pointed the gun at Gail's head. She squeaked.

The Reapers spread out, but came no closer.

"keep calm, brother," the leader said in the breathy voice that al-

ways brought Valentine back to the terrors of the night Gabriella Cho died. *"no one need die tonight. be warned: hurt her and we will peel off your skin and leave you raw and screaming."*

He switched the sights of the pistol to the Reaper's yellow gimlet eye.

Valentine tried to still his hand.

"you believe you can stop me with that?"

"Not me," Valentine said.

And shot.

He aimed at an egg, shot, switched targets, and shot again, as quickly as he could pull the hair trigger. The gun felt like a cap pistol in his hand.

But the bullets had an effect.

They struck the eggs and tore through them, sending fluid flying, splattering the Reapers. The egg chamber suddenly smelled like old milk. He stifled a gag.

Evidently Reapers didn't get nauseated, or had poor noses—they just wiped at the fluid in disgust.

All around, legworm digits twitched like fluttering eyelashes.

Valentine dropped the empty gun as he ran, pulling Gail along behind. Tons of legworm righted itself and he threw her under it, dove, rolled, felt its legs on his back as he made it to the other side. Snapping noises like garden shears came from the egg area.

Valentine drew his legworm goad, buried it in the back of one as it began to roll, and pulled Gail tight to him as they ended up on its back.

The earthen bowl writhed with searching legworms.

Valentine anchored one of his cargo hooks in the loose skin atop the legworm, and looped a chain around Gail. Her white fingers gripped it while the legworm's back rose and fell as it negotiated the lip of the crater.

A Reaper flew through the air. Well, half of one. Its waist and legs were still on the ground.

Another jumped atop the back of a moving legworm and ran toward them like the hero of a Western on top of a train, arms out and reaching.

Two legworm muzzles rose from either side, one catching it by the head and arms, the other by its waist.

"Make a wish," Valentine said. Gail shifted position so that she wasn't resting on her belly, and gasped at the scene behind her.

The Reaper parted messily.

More legworms carefully stabbed down with their muzzles, lifted them covered with black goo and shreds of black cloth, then stabbed down again.

"Help!" Gail screamed.

A bony, blue-veined Reaper hand gripped her leg, pulling her off the legworm.

She clutched at Valentine and the securing chain. He shifted his grip on his legworm goad. He brought down the crowbarlike shovel edge on the Reaper's head. Skin peeled back, revealing a black, goo-smeared skull.

The Reaper made a sideways climb, more like a spider than a man, still pulling at Gail so hard that Valentine feared both she and the baby would be divided between the antagonists in Solomonic fashion.

Valentine crossed the shimmying legworm back, jumping as the Reaper swung its free arm. He buried the goad in the forearm holding Gail, and the Reaper released its grip.

Stars—a ringing sound—pain.

The Reaper had struck him backhand across the jaw. Something felt horribly loose on the left side of his head; bone held only by skin sagged at the side of his face. Valentine blindly swung with the goad as he backpedaled, then lost his balance. This time Gail screamed as he clutched at her to keep from falling off.

Valentine's vision cleared and he saw, and worse, felt, the Reaper straddling him. The goad was gone, his pistol was gone. He put up a hand against the tongue already licking out of the Reaper's mouth. It pulled his shirt open.

Valentine groped at his belt. He had another cargo hook. . . .

Gail struck the Reaper across the back of its neck with her hands interlocked, but it ignored her the way it would a butterfly alighting.

Valentine brought up the cargo hook—feeling the pointed tongue probe at his collarbone—and buried the hook into the Reaper's jaw, returning pain for pain. He pulled, desperate, and the black-fanged mouth closed on its own tongue.

The Reaper's eyes widened in surprise and the tongue was severed. The cut-off end twitched on Valentine's bare chest. Valentine slid and gripped the Reaper by its waist with his legs. It brought up its bad arm to try to pull the hook out, fumbling with the chain.

Valentine pulled, hard, putting his back muscles into the effort, straining—God, how his jaw hurt as he gritted his teeth—the Reaper looking oddly like a hooked bass with eyes glazed and confused—*hurt it bad enough and the Kurian shuts down the connection?*—and the Reaper's jaw came free in a splatter of blood. The Reaper swung at his eyes but Valentine got a shoulder up. He punched, hard, into the open wound at the bottom of its head and groped with his hand wrist-deep in slimy flesh. He dug with fingers up the soft palate.

The Reaper's eyes rolled back into its skull as he squeezed the base of its brain like a sponge.

Gail whacked it again and it toppled off the back of the legworm. Valentine sucked in air and pain with each breath.

"You look funny," Gail said.

"I bet I do," Valentine said, though it hit his ears as "I et I oo." Valentine examined his chest. The tiny wound from the Reaper's tongue had a splattering of Reaper blood all around it. It itched. He tore up some of the fiberglass-like legworm skin and blotted the tarry substance away.

The legworm they rode waved its snout in the air as it hurried around the perimeter of the pushed-up earth. When it slowed to redescend into the pit, Valentine removed his first cargo hook, used it to lower Gail, and dropped off himself. He retrieved his goad and the other cargo hook.

This time she clung to him as he carried her, running for the telephone poles.

Valentine heard voices, and turned toward the sound.

"I can't believe you used me as bait," Thatcher said.

"I got it, didn't I?" Duvalier chided.

"A second later and it would have popped my head off."

"Uh-uh. I never leave less than a second and a half to chance, sweetie. Wait—"

The last was at the sound of Valentine setting Gail on her feet again.

"It's us," Valentine said, holding his jaw. He came into what might pass for a clearing—thick grasses rather than trees—around an old barn. The telephone poles lined a road like the Roman crucifixes on the Via Appia.

Duvalier knelt down, working.

Valentine stepped up and found what he expected, a headless Reaper.

"Hell, Val," Duvalier said.

"Uf igh," Valentine tried. "Rluff nigh."

Thatcher seemed lost in his own thoughts as he stared at the Reaper corpse. "You should have seen it—the Reaper was coming for me. I tried to fire but my gun was on safety, and before I could even flick off it reached, and there she was behind it."

"Big tactic," Duvalier said, examining the robe she had stripped off the Reaper for black—and poisonous—subcutaneous fluid. "Lying in the grass like a snake."

"You're one of those . . . one of those Hunter-things," Thatcher said.

"You have a problem with that?" Duvalier asked.

"Offerz," Valentine garbled. "Oturs."

"The others?" Duvalier said. "I dunno. I didn't hear any screams."

"Are there any more around?" Thatcher asked.

"Ope nog," Valentine said.

Thatcher took a better grip on his gun and looked warily around. "How do you know?"

"He knows," Duvalier said. "He just knows. Leave it at that." She gave him his rifle back, as though glad to give up an unpleasant burden.

"Can we sleep soon? How about in that barn?" Gail asked.

Valentine waved tiredly. "Attitude, Gail," Duvalier said.

"Stick the attitude. My feet are killing me," she said hotly.

"I think she's getting better," Thatcher said.

It took them a while to find the trail of Dr. Boothe and Pepsa. Valentine found their marks in the long grasses. They'd cut over to a legworm trail and followed it up the hillside.

"What are they going back in that direction for?" Thatcher asked.

Valentine shrugged, resolved to communicate with hand signals. Gail groaned as they started up the hill.

They caught up to the pair, Boothe hiking along behind Pepsa carrying the gun in one hand, her medical bag slung.

Valentine elbowed Duvalier, pointed, and made a T with his hands. She nodded and slipped into the bushes, gripping her walking stick like an alert samurai carrying his sword.

"What's the matter?" Thatcher asked, keeping his voice low.

Valentine found he could whisper coherently. He spoke into Duvalier's ear.

"Something's wrong," she said. "Somebody's been giving us away."

Back in the legworm valley, Valentine heard hoofbeats. Two legworms and perhaps a dozen men on horseback were investigating events in the pit. They looked like native Kentuckians intermingled with Grogs.

"Let's catch up," Duvalier said.

They went up the hill as quickly as Gail's weary, unsteady legs would allow.

The vets must have heard them coming. Both turned around. Pepsa looked frightened.

Boothe brought up the pistol and pointed it between them.

Shit. Guessed wrong. Why didn't I just shoot the pair of them?

Because they might not be in it together.

"Hey, Doc, it's us," Thatcher said.

"Guns! Drop them," Boothe said. The gun shook in her hands as she pointed. Tears streamed down her face.

Tears? Why would a Kurian agent cry?

"Epsah!" Valentine shouted, shouldering his rifle, sighting on the first Kurian agent he had ever looked upon.

The U-gun burned. Its stock burned him, the trigger guard; he felt the flesh on his hands cook; the agony of the steam in the Kurian Tower redoubled and poured through his nervous system. Drop it, all he could do was drop the gun.

Don't~think~so, a voice in his head said.

Thatcher brought up his rifle—*what the hell?*—the burning agony left, relief and wonder at freedom from pain but why was Thatcher shouldering his rifle with the barrel pressed to his collarbone and the butt pointed at Pepsa

Krrak!

Blood and bone flew from Thatcher's shoulder, the gun fell, the spent cartridge casing spun

and before it completed its parabola Duvalier was out of the Kentucky grass, sword held up and ready

Stupid~bitch!

Duvalier screamed, dropped her sword, jumped back from it as though it were a snake striking—

Valentine grabbed his short legworm pick, lunged up the hill

Boothe turned her gun at Pepsa, no, not at her, at a patch of dark shortleaf pine behind her, and fired.

Behind him Thatcher screamed. Valentine was still three strides away, the pain came, the legworm pick lightning in his hands . . . no, fire, hot blue flame that burned—

Lies. They fight with lies. Lies can't change steel to flame.

He raised the pick, screaming in agony, fighting the pain with sound.

You~dumbfuck~terrorists, Pepsa said between his ears.

And he threw, sent the pick spinning at her, watched it hit, saw the point bury itself in one fleshy breast, a gurgle, went to Boothe, took the hot gun from her shaking hand, pointed and fired

Where~are~you~lord?

Another shot, HEEELP~the~burn! the gun clicked empty, even as she toppled over he straddled her, hitting her with the pistol butt, silencing the screaming from between his ears by caving in her skull and the awful warble of her tongueless mouth, but nothingness yawned beneath him like a chasm, he felt himself tottering at the edge of an abyss.

Duvalier picked him up off her corpse, pulled him out of the darkness. Hoofbeats. The loom of riders in the darkness. Words, Boothe bending over Thatcher, applying pressure as Duvalier waved the riders over. Finally the strange emptiness in his head left, and he could distinguish faces again.

"Haloo, Bulletproof. You're far from home. What hospitality can fellow tribesmen offer?"

They bartered the Reaper's robe for transport and found their way back to the Bulletproof. In a few days they again knew Kentucky hospitality in a chilly, Z-shaped valley fed by artesian springs, his jaw braced and bandaged with baling wire by Boothe. Valentine learned to appreciate smashed cubes of legworm flesh, slathered in barbecue sauce sucked through a straw. He also got mashed squash, pumpkin, and corn, eating out of the same pot as the resident babies.

A giggling nursing mother offered him a spare teat after feeding her daughter. It hurt to laugh.

Once his jaw knit he borrowed an old-fashioned horse, loaded up a second with grain and dried meat, and rode out to where he had last seen Ahn-Kha. He left a stoppered bottle of Bulletproof bourbon at Grog-eye level with a note to his friend, telling him where they were wintering until warmth allowed travel again. He tried to learn what had happened to Ahn-Kha and his pursuing column, but only found some shattered glass and debris that might have been from a motorcycle eight miles away.

The fruitless search left him moody and depressed. His tender mouth troubled him every time he spoke and ate, and a fragment of mirror showed that his jawline now had an uneven balance to it thanks to the break. The only bright spot was Gail Foster's transformation into a convivial, charming woman, though she remained a little pallid, even on the hearty Bulletproof cooking. She looked as though she were about to have twins. He couldn't remember the last time he'd seen a woman with such a wide belly after the baby dropped.

The baby came on December 22.

Duvalier woke Valentine and passed him a hot cup of grassy-tasting tea. "Gail's water broke. Our vet is attending. Suki's there too."

She brought him to a modest, pellet-stove-heated home that served as a sickroom for the local Bulletproof.

Suki was a Bulletproof midwife. She was young, perhaps a year or two older than Valentine, but had a calming effect on Gail brought about by nothing more than her quiet voice and cups of the honey-filled silvery cinqefoil tea she brewed. Gail had given birth once before, but remembered nothing of the event but gauzy business on the other side of her screened lap.

Valentine went in and saw Gail lying on her side with her knees drawn up and buttocks at the edge of the hammocklike "birthing bed." He gripped her hand through a contraction, sponging the sweat from her forehead when it was over. She'd soaked through her shirt even in the winter cool.

"I wish Will was here," she gasped. "He always . . ." The words trailed off.

Valentine wrung out the sponge. "Will never forgot about you for a moment. Your husband wasn't the man you thought. Or he was. You'll understand when you see him again."

She smiled and nodded.

"First we have to get your baby into the world. Can do?"

"Can do," she agreed.

But you can't be there to see it. This trip, the risks. You'll never see a payoff. You could just as well have driven away with Ahn-Kha. You can never walk down an Ozark highway again. You're condemned by your own actions, an exile.

"She's quit dilating," Boothe said, bringing Valentine out of his thoughts with a flash of guilt over what Gail must be experiencing. She had a short flashlight attached to her forehead: a medical unicorn. "I'm going to C-section. Pe—Suki, get me the tray I laid out in the kitchen."

Valentine got out of the way as the midwife came in with the tray.

"Suki, keep her chin up."

Boothe poured a shot glass full of Bulletproof, then added a couple of drops of ether to it. She tipped it into a fist-sized wad of cotton.

"Have her breathe this," she said, handing the mask to Suki. Gail inhaled the mixture.

"Christmas baby. You were almost a Christmas baby," Gail said as the ether took effect.

"Enough," Dr. Boothe told Suki. "Gail, keep looking at the ceiling. Over before you know it." Valentine watched her focus on Gail's belly, steadying the scalpel.

Valentine watched, relieved and fascinated at the same time, as the scalpel opened Gail just above the pelvis.

"Coming now. Your baby's doing fine," Boothe said.

Valentine couldn't help but think about Malia. What had Amalee's birth been like? The sweet, burning scent of ether in the air, along with blood, sweat, and amniotic fluid?

God, do they all look like that?

Boothe pulled out a froglike creature, narrow, legs drawn up tight, arms folded like a dead insect's, brachycephalic skull all the more unreal as the doctor held it upside down. "Oh, Christ."

A baleful yellow eye, slit-pupiled, peered at him from a face pinched by internal agony. It hissed, fought for breath.

Gail Foster Post had given birth to a Reaper.

Suki backed away, hand over her mouth.

"Boy or a girl?" Gail said, then, when there was no reply, "What? What?"

Boothe showed her.

"Get it away from me!" Gail screamed. "Bastards! Lying bastards!" Her words trailed off into sobs.

"Stay still," Boothe ordered. "Suki, put three more drops in another shot glass."

"Give it to me," Valentine said, extending a towel. He took the struggling infant—cleaned its sexless body.

"What a mess. Tearing everywhere in the uterus," Boothe said. "I hope I can fix this." She turned her light on Valentine. "Just pinch its nose and mouth shut. Bury it outside."

Valentine took the infant out into the December air, instinctively holding it close against the chill. He looked at the blood-smeared face, purple and green and blue, crisscrossed with veins, horror in miniature. Black nails, impossibly tiny, gleamed wetly as it moved its hand.

The future death machine coughed.

Did yellow eyes make you evil? A pointed tongue?

"Do you have a soul?" someone asked, using his larynx, tongue, and mouth.

Valentine wondered if he'd directed the question to the newborn or to himself. Tiny nostrils, long little jaw; he could smother it one-handed.

My DNA is 98% identical to a chimpanzee. How much code do I share with you?

However much, a tiny amount of it was Kurian. Evil.

Or Lifeweaver. The *Dau'weem* and *Dau'wa* shared however many gene pairs they possessed, thirty thousand or three million. They differed only in their opposition over vampirism.

Could he say a creature fresh from the womb deserved to die, thanks to its appearance?

Not appearance, design.

A newborn, innocence embodied in what felt like ten pounds of sugar. Harmless. But experience told him otherwise.

Songs of Innocence and Experience. William Blake.

Did he who made the Lamb make thee?

Valentine closed up the towel, protecting the newborn tyger against the chill. The Reaper's head turned, sensing something it liked in Valentine's wrist.

Valentine pushed his pulse point a little closer, offering.

Its mouth opened, latched on, and Valentine felt the prick of the sharp tongue. The penetration only hurt a little.

Softly, the Reaper fed.

VALENTINE'S RESOLVE

In memory of Don and Rita,
who always had smiles on their faces, jokes on their lips,
and a cold beer in their fridge.

Acknowledgments

Liz for her patience and understanding; John for his guidance; Howard for his perception; Mike for his research, ideas, and experience earned in Laos; my parents for the family vacations to Washington; and Stephanie for her love.

There are some remedies worse than the disease.

—Publilius Syrus,
Maxim 301

One

Weathercut Manse, Iowa, November, the fifty-second year of the Kurian Order: A Hawkeye from the first quarter of the twenty-first century would hardly recognize his state in the snow-dusted fall of that year. The corn and soybeans, yes, the birches and willows claiming soggy land rimming the streams and lakes, and the majestic oaks, elms, and cottonwoods, the slopes and crests of the low rolling hills around the river basins, certainly.

The beef cattle in the fields give some hint that times have changed. They are undersized compared with the big steers of better times. A few cough; others have the strained look of an animal who has picked up a bit of wire or a piece of a can.

It's the architecture that's changed most, the roads and bridges and little towns in between. A well-traveled or imaginative Iowan might think himself in some quiet stretch of French or English countryside.

Instead of four-lane towns surrounded by farms with frame homes, barns, and silos rising nearby, or sometimes the newer Wal-Mart blisters girdled by parking lots and fast-food stops and sprawling exurb, the new centers of public life are the Great Homes.

Like the French villas and English manses of old, the Kurian Order Great Homes are built to impress. Some are vaguely Alpine, with high-peaked roofs, elaborate woodwork on the overhangs, and two or three stories of glass window broken only by balconies; others mimic the heavy beams and plasters of Tudor dignity; a few seem to be almost brick-by-brick re-creations out of a Jane Austen movie. But the most popular style might be called French modern.

Weathercut Manse is an example of the last style. A big, bold front of limestone and picture windows, shielded from the elements by a tall slate roof, grows a stablelike garage looking out over the gravel turnaround to the right, and a turret like a miniature castle keep to the left. The off-balance arrangement is pleasing in the daylight, when the sun lights the flower bed in the center of the turnaround, so that the manse seems to be reaching out to embrace visitors and present a bouquet in the day. However, at night the lanes resemble the arms of a boxer dropping into a defensive stance.

Around behind is a smallish patio, reached by French doors, flanked by the glassy refuge of the marbled indoor spa, and topped by a private balcony outside the master's bedroom, and the aviary-greenhouse locally famous for its lemons and year-round supply of plum tomatoes.

Gardens, wilder woods, and a nine-hole golf course surround the house. It is only once you get beyond the thick hedge to the east, the three rails of white fencing to the west, or the stone wall with iron gate running the road to the south that you reach the working part of the estate, a seventy-acre horse farm. There's housing on the grounds for the pigs and chickens, and a New Universal Church parsonage. A thick wood separates the Kurian churchman from a little square of prefabricated trailer homes, a repair garage, and a gas pump.

The Mansion is the pleasant face of the estate, the parsonage its conscience, and the barns and tenant homes its muscle. But next to the gate, built into that dignified wall, are a small stone house and garage that are the lizard brain of the estate, the security center. The workers check in here each day and pick up a radiolocator watch that can be fixed to a beltloop; all traffic into or out of the estate must first pass through security, a sodium-vapor-lit double-basketball-court-sized stretch of pavement surrounded by chain-link fencing, where vehicles can be parked while their contents are searched and inspected.

The guards walk with a bit of a swagger in their camouflage and winter fur hats (in the summer they wear black pith helmets), carbines with telescopic sights and bayonets mounted as if to warn visitors that they are ready to deal with trouble, either at a distance or up close and personal. They defer only to the master with his brass ring, and the parson with his white clerical collar, as they patrol the grounds on ATVs or, for the romantically minded security chief, an ox-eyed Arab gelding and a silver-tipped riding crop that he uses as a pointer.

Not that there's much trouble in this quiet corner of northeastern Iowa, far from the troublesome Grogs of the Missouri valley or the noisome guerrilla band that has recently sprung up in the Indian-head territory of Wisconsin. The security guards can joust on their ATVs with cattle prods—also used as nonlethal inducements for the tramps and "mexicretins" to move on down the road without applying for work or largesse at the manse.

Just that morning, as a new wind came along to kick up the remains of the previous night's snow, the security team rousted a tramp from his shelter in the rusted, weed-grown hulk of a sport utility, tireless remains in the woods where it had broken down in 2022. They woke him with a cattle prod and sent him on his way, after a cursory search of the grubby little odds and ends he shouldered in edge-worn bags. He carried a Wisconsin work card indicating that he'd last been employed a year ago, and swore he planned to return to his home province of Eau Claire. A request for food brought the cattle prod up again and instructions on how to reach the nearest New Universal Church hostel eighteen miles away—the manse parsonage serving only the Weathercut grounds and its tenants.

Now the tramp hobbles down the road in that toe-in, footsore fashion of a man who has gone too far on bad shoes. He wears a buttonless shirt held shut with stock twine wound round his waist crisscrossing his chest. His face, under a greasy thatch of tangled black hair, has a thick layer of dirt in permanent residence, and little can be read in his brown eyes, permanently downcast. It's a face that has seen its share of hardship; an old scar runs down from the right eye, and the jaw is a little off-kilter, though it gives his face a humorous set, as though he's turning up the corner of his mouth at a private joke.

The only piece of gear on him that might attract interest is his short walking stick, used to help mitigate the effects of his obvious limp. The twisting wood has a good steel cap where it strikes the road, a leather wrist loop, and a short handle projecting out of the knobby top.

One of the guards who questioned him looked like he was thinking of confiscating it, but the tramp told a convincing story of it being awarded to him after he was wounded fighting for the TMCC in Little Rock during Solon's brief tenure. The back of his ID card did have a half-peeled old shining service star—the sort of thing elementary school teachers used to put on spelling tests—and a discharge stamp, and at a glare from the senior guard, himself a TMCC veteran, the stick was returned.

The road wanders up a little treelined hill—only a technically minded surveyor would call it a ridge—as it reaches the edge of Weathercut's lands, then down and over a stream.

The tramp checks a litter-filled hole in the bridge's armpit—the bundle is still there, and the little piece of paper set to dislodge if it's moved is still pinned to the bridge's concrete by the pack—and then takes a long drink from the stream, lowering his face to the water as though he were one of the manse's horses, before settling down for a nap.

Had one of the guards followed to observe the tramp until he was off the grounds, he would have thought the last very strange. Travelers, especially vagrants, take care to travel only during daylight and hide deep and dark once the sun sets. Kurian Towers are few and far between in this part of Iowa, but their avatar Reapers use the roads as they go about their affairs, and are only too happy to remove a human mote like the tramp from the picturesque dells of this corner of Iowa.

David Valentine didn't rest under the bridge long. He got to his feet again well before dark, but not before he exchanged the flap-heeled road shoes for a pair of soft buckskin moccasins.

He was tempted to take one or two of the weapons from the cache under the bridge, but there was still a chance that he'd be observed sneaking through the estate's orchards. He could talk his way around a few pilfered late apples, but not a pistol.

Valentine carefully cut upstream toward the manse.

This was not his first visit to Weathercut Manse; he'd been on and off the lands a dozen or more times that November, getting a feel for the rhythms of the estate and its personnel. Taking your time with this sort of thing made the results exponentially surer.

This being a Wednesday, F. A. James, late of the TMCC but now enjoying a comfortable sinecure courtesy of Crossfire Security and the Ringwearer of Weathercut, would be on the east side of the grounds from eight to twelve, after which he'd put in four more hours at the gatehouse, then sixteen in ready reserve in the security apartments next to the utility garage.

Not that Valentine intended for him to finish the shift.

Sometimes the captain or one of the older hands would accompany F. A. James on the field patrols, but tonight would be cold. He'd probably be alone, driving his ATV from point to point, possibly with a dog riding in the back, as he checked the fields and fencing, warming his hands over the engine whenever he paused.

Valentine had picked out the spot a week ago, spent two long cold nights, one watching it to get the lie of the ground and the guard routine down, especially where the headlights of the ATV would shine.

The east side of the estate ran down into a soggy streambed, rough and dimpled and thick with birches and poplars and a drowned oak that had fallen. The estate fence ran down into the bottom, probably to protect the pheasants that nested there.

The fence wasn't very formidable at this point: a chain-link barrier with razor wire strung atop in a Slinky-like tangle, a final fence for the estate's livestock and a serious warning to anyone else. But whoever had built it didn't account for smaller-animal activity, or simply didn't care. Prowling raccoons had dug under it and a dog or two might have expanded it, chasing the raccoons, for all Valentine knew. He'd opened it still farther on one of his scouts.

He looked at the fence one more time, and checked the distinctly nontrampish timepiece he kept in a tobacco pouch in his pocket. Made of steel thick enough to cause sparks if struck against flint, it was a soldier's wristwatch long bereft of band; it had a magnified bezel so the big white-painted numerals and hands could be easily read at night.

Stalking makes one feel alive and focused, yet it is oddly calming in the stretches of idleness. This night provided a little extra frisson of excitement for Valentine. F. A. James would be the last. He didn't know what he'd do after this one.

Tomorrow would take care of itself.

He took a breath and extracted the red balloon he'd found near Carbondale, Illinois, and carried around knowing he'd find a use for it sooner or later. He'd slipped a rolled-up piece of paper into a tiny white-capped orange plastic container, the kind Kurian-issued aphrodisiacs and fertility enhancers usually came in, and attached it to the lip of the balloon with a bit of wire. He put just enough breath in it to make it look like it was on its last legs, then added a knot in the bottom. Then he reached up to hang it on the razor wire where he was sure the ATV's light would hit it as James turned along the path.

He examined the ground around the thick oak on the manse side of the fence, picked up a few twigs, and tossed them back over the fence. No telling just where he'd have to drop and how far he might have to run.

Valentine patted the small knife in the sleeve sheath on his forearm and gripped the legworm-leather handle of his hatchet-pick. It was a handy little tool of stainless steel used by the legworm riders of Kentucky to mount their forty-foot-long beasts. This one had a pry blade at the other end of the slightly curved pick with its nasty fishhook barb, great for popping small locks and a hundred other uses, urban and rural.

Including lifting yourself up into an oak.

Valentine hooked a limb and swung his legs up, crossed his ankles around the branch, and was in the leaves and branches as neatly as a retreating cat. In his last scout he'd even found the branch he wanted to rest upon.

He passed the time thinking about Mary Carlson with her currycomb, or giggling at the dinner table.

He didn't doze, but fell into a mental state that lowered his lifesign, a form of self-hypnosis. He doubted there would be any Reapers prowling the estate; they were scarce in this bit of brass-ring-thick Iowa outside the bigger towns, but it was still good to stay in practice. Even if the fleas and ticks on his body helped obscure the signal humans gave off.

The blat of the ATV lifted him half out of his trance, the way a mouse's tread might cause a rattler to open an eye even as the rest of it remained quiescent.

Valentine tensed. There was always the chance that F. A. James wouldn't see the balloon. Then he'd have to drop off the tree and knock him from the saddle with a body blow, and that could be chancy if James was alert.

No dog in the back of the minibed. A bit of his neck relaxed. He hated killing dogs, even when famished.

James directed his ATV slowly along the fence. Part of his job was to check its condition. Cattle rustling was not unheard of in Iowa even among the estates; an ambitious young Grog could easily lope off with a couple of prime calves or a young bull tied across his shoulders and paddle them back to the Missouri valley in a canoe.

And at the back of the estate owner's mind there would be old sins, walled out of the manse but still lurking there like Poe's telltale heart. Most Ringwearers had made enemies on their way up. The fence was Weathercut Manse's outermost layer of skin protecting the vitals at the great house.

Unfortunately for F. A. James, the skin could be easily gouged if that's all an intruder wanted. He was protecting the house and its lands. Nothing but a handlebar-hung shotgun and a cattle prod at his waist protected James.

F. A. James must have seen the balloon as soon as his headlights hit it. He slowed and then stopped his ATV.

He turned off the motor and Valentine silently swore. The idling engine would have covered his footsteps. James warmed his hands on the engine and climbed off.

F. A. James' fur hat, its security badge at the front glowing dully like a third eye, tilted upward as he examined the balloon. A message in a tiny plastic jar—the old prescription label had been stripped off so the paper curled within could be more easily read—would be tempting. It was traditional in Iowa for brides and grooms to loose balloons on their wedding day, usually with messages of good wishes—"sky cheer" was the phrase—but it was always customary to send one off with a large-denomination bill inside.

What's given up to the world is returned hundredfold, read the New Universal Church bible.

For the past two years Valentine had been in the karma business. After tonight he'd close up shop.

He tightened his grip on the hatchet-pick.

Valentine dropped out of the tree when he saw James yank on the pill container, popping the balloon not quite at the moment his feet hit the ground. Valentine softened the landing with a roll, came lightly to his feet, and took two quick steps to the ATV's saddle.

The shotgun was locked to its bracket, so he sprang up on the saddle and used it to vault toward James, who'd finally reacted to the noise behind and turned to be struck across the head with the blunt side of Valentine's climbing pick.

Valentine cuffed his prey and gagged him with a bit of his hat, so that this quiet corner of Iowa might remain so.

He checked the stout laces on F. A. James' tall combat boots and wondered how best to secure his captive to the cargo basket of the ATV.

Empty silos are not difficult to find in Iowa.

Empty, of course, as in "not containing corn or feed." Nature abhors a vacuum, especially when that vacuum cuts the wind and keeps out the snow, so the silo Valentine had chosen a week ago contained a good many creepers, spiders who ate the creepers, mice who ate the spiders, and barn owls who ate the mice.

And bats. Their guano added a fragrant decoupage atop the rusting chute gear and old feed sacks at the base of the silo.

F. A. James hung upside down by a single line of nylon cord, dangling from rigging far above in the black top of the silo. His slightest movement caused him to swing extravagantly, like the pendulum in a grandfather clock.

Valentine squatted atop the rusty mechanical rubbish, sharpening a short, thick, curved blade with a sturdy handle.

The security man's features were hidden under a white pillowcase, tightened about his head with a bit of the same nylon cord. Inked-in eyes and mouth made him look as though he were wearing an abbreviated Halloween costume. The effect was more for those who would find the body than for the benefit of the pair in the silo.

"Gate codes," F. A. James said, his voice stressed and cracking. "Is that what you want?"

Valentine kept sharpening the knife.

"There's a spare back-door key—"

"I don't want access to Weathercut," Valentine said, deciding the knife was sharp enough. "I wanted you out of it, Franklin."

"But I'm nobody important," F. A. James squeaked. "I don't even have my own room."

"That's the problem with being a Nobody Important. Someone might decide you're disposable. Kind of like that teenage girl back in Arkansas. The one you, Bernardo Guittierez, Tom Cray, and Sergeant Heath Hopkins raped and then killed."

Valentine smelled urine leaking.

"No! I mean, you've got the wrong guy."

Valentine was a little relieved that F. A. James kept talking. He hated the ones who just blubbered at the end. Cray had spent the last five minutes screaming for his mother.

"Her name was Mary Carlson. Ever catch her name? Bother to remember it? You must remember her face. What did it look like at the end? Now, I figure four guys, maybe ten minutes each—that was a long forty minutes at the end of her life. About as long as the next forty minutes are going to be for you."

James was panting now, and the pillowcase went in and out of his mouth like a flutter valve.

"Mary was into horses. Loved them to death—good at taking care of them too, once she learned what was expected."

Valentine drew the blade across the whetstone. The sound echoed off the cobweb-strung walls of the silo like a cat spitting. "This is a hoof knife," Valentine explained. "Horse hooves are tough to cut, and you need a short, strong blade to get through them. Hoof is way tougher than, say . . . the cartilage in your nose and ears, Franklin."

James spoke again from beneath the ghost mask: "Captain Coltrane over in Yaseda, he's got a whole jar full of ring fingers off of girls he collected for the Reapers. You should be going after him."

"I never knew the owners of those fingers."

"I didn't even come. I just did it 'cause the others did, and Hop killed her before I knew he'd drawn his pistol."

F. A. James' story didn't quite jibe with what the others had said. According to Guittierez, the corporal had demanded that the girl be "flipped over" to escape the indignity of "sloppy seconds," then made her—

But Valentine didn't care about the details anymore. The investigation and hunt were over. Now there was just duty to Mary Carlson.

"You see a white collar? The time to confess passed with the investigation. I read the documents. Consul Solon, for all his faults, didn't like civilians mistreated. You could have admitted it. You would have gone to prison, probably, but you wouldn't be hanging here now."

Valentine selected a spot for the first knife cut.

"This is just to scare me, right? You're done—I'm scared. What do you want? What do you *want*?"

Valentine never remembered much else that F. A. James said during his final moments, cut short, as they always were, because the screaming got to him. Part of him was distracted, puzzled by that last question.

Two

Hobarth's Truckstart and Trading Post, Missouri, February, the fifty-third year of the Kurian Order: The days of long-haul trucking are all but over.

Nevertheless a few overland "runs" still exist. The Atlanta-Chattanooga-Nashville artery still trickles, as does the old interstate between Baltimore and Boston. The Vegas-Phoenix–Los Angeles triangle is the scene of the yearly "Diamondback Run," where supercharged muscle cars roar from the coast to Vegas, where the crews switch to off-road vehicles for a trip to Phoenix, then make a final leg in tractor-trailers running loads back to Los Angeles, something of an indulgence for certain wealthy or engine-obsessed Quislings.

Dashboard cameras record the experience, and sometimes the final words of the drivers.

But the longest of the "hauls" still in existence is that from Chicago to Los Angeles, much of which runs along the old lines of fabled Route 66, even if the end point at the Sunset Strip meets the ocean rather more abruptly than it did a century ago.

The veterans of the "Devil's Dietary Tract," as the route is known, make fortunes hauling art, rare firearms, expensive clothing, and particularly electronics from point to point, liquor and consumables flowing west, finished products imported from the rest of the Pacific Rim back east. The Kurian Order shrugs at such baubles for their human herds, or perhaps believes that physical and mental energy expended acquiring a Picasso, a pristine set of golf clubs, or a vintage Remington 700 is activity that isn't being spent resisting the regime. Black marketers are given a wrist slap in most instances. The security services of the great rail companies make sure nothing that can't be hid-

den in a purse or backpack moves cross-country on the rails—at least without a substantial bribe. That leaves internal combustion engine or pack animal for the traders and smugglers who want to move larger loads.

Some say that the "independents"—as the nonrail transportation companies are known—are riddled with Kurian informers. Any firm that helps the burgeoning resistance is quickly seized, its durable goods auctioned and personnel packed off to the Reapers.

Trucks need fuel, tires, and spare parts to run, and of course the crews need food and rest. So on the fringes of the Kurian Order, or within Grog-held territory, there are "starts," where men and machines can be reconditioned for the next leg of the run.

Hobarth's is a typical example of a fortress truckstart, encircled by wire and then an inner wall of broken tires wired together and filled with dirt, a tiny human settlement deep within the Grog territory of mid-Missouri. There's a substantial warehouse devoted to trade with the Grogs, cavernous aluminum barns for the repair of vehicles and the storage of spares. Behind it rusts a junkyard covering a dozen-odd acres guarded by rifles and half-savage dogs. The penalty for unauthorized scavenging is a bullet.

But for the tired, broken-down, and road-weary there's safety within. Even for those without the price of a cup of coffee, the Hobarth staff will feed, wash, and accommodate the most destitute—"three days of a month, three months of a year." "Christian duty," the staff calls it.

Others are welcome to buy, sell, or trade at Hobarth's store or the stalls of mechanics and craftsmen. There's even a small jeweler under the old three-orb sign, who also acts as a currency exchange, able to deal in most of the Kurian scrips of the Midwest. The local Grogs have become adept at extracting and reconditioning everything from wheel rims to timing belts and spark plugs, bringing them in to trade for bullets or sealable plastic storage containers, which the Grogs prize for a well-appointed, bug-free hut.

Three high-clearance flatbed tow trucks, armored and armed with machine guns, compose the toughest salvage team an overnight drive in any direction. Two of the team, the front one prowed in such a way that it resembles a vehicular battering ram, fling gravel as they turn in to the main gate, bringing in a rusted cab-over. Once inside the compound and behind the main building, long and flat as Dakota prairie, the crews elbow one another and point at a smallish legworm contentedly pulling up leafless kudzu near the tire wall. A steel-framed ergonomic office chair, complete with ottoman, folding umbrella, and movable windscreen, sits stapled and chained to its spongy, segmented back.

"Argent's in," the green-hatted driver of the battering-ram wrecker announces, opening a tow truck door with DRIVER CARRIES NO CASH, LOTS OF LEAD *stenciled on the side.*

David Valentine, reading a book as he drank his coffee in the four-table "café," recognized Tim Hobarth's step behind—the tow truck driver wore steel-heeled boots, which rapped distinctively on the boarding.

"What's the crawl, Max?" Hobarth asked.

Valentine, who'd left his name in the shambles of a wrecked career in the United Free Republic, drew his cup and book a little closer, making room for the big driver. He'd just as soon continue reading his book with the brew, though the bitter mélange that the Kurians labeled coffee insulted the palate of someone who'd had the real stuff in Jamaica.

"Omaha's getting set for a fight," Valentine said. To the families who worked Hobarth's, he was just a wandering Grog trader blessed with unusual luck in avoiding the Reapers. Valentine had stopped and visited the Golden Ones, in the fading hope that his old friend Ahn-Kha had wandered home with an epic story of escapades from the Kentucky foothills to Nebraska's far horizons.

"Kur needs those rail lines out of Omaha badly, now that so much south of Missouri is cut and Tulsa's been burned to the ground. The Golden Ones are great fighters, but if they put some big guns into Council Bluffs . . ."

"Poor dumb Grogs," Hobarth said. The sympathy in his voice belied his words.

Valentine liked Hobarth. He possessed some feeling for the creatures Kur had brought from other worlds to help subjugate humanity. Some of the tribes found themselves in wrecked and poisoned lands after the fighting was over, and a few, like the Golden Ones, had turned against the Kurians.

"The Golden Ones are a long way from dumb," Valentine said. "And they know engineering. They've got a network of tunnels under Omaha you wouldn't believe if you didn't see it, and they've rigged a few likely buildings to collapse. I wouldn't want to be part of the Omaha garrison, assuming the Iowa Guard takes it. They're recruiting out of the scrub-country clans again, looking for tribal support. Doubt they'll get it."

"How's business otherwise?" Hobarth asked.

"Lean. Omaha just wants optics and precision tools." It had been so long since he'd talked to another man that Valentine felt his mouth running on of its own accord. "Those are tough to come by, especially when they don't offer much in return. Leatherwork I can sometimes sell, but pottery? Oh, that reminds me. I might have a connection in Springfield for you for tires. That Grog molasses tobacco is getting popular in Chicago."

"Wonderful. Hey, I talked to Gramps again about you. He's upped the offer to a full family share if you join up."

"I told you before: I'm a crap driver."

"You'll learn, Argent. We could use you and that freaky hair of yours." Valentine had once explained that a nearby Reaper had caused his hair to stand on end. "The spring run to the coast is gearing up. See the world, you know?"

"Tourism through scratched-up goggles at the trigger ring? Not my way to see the country."

"Oh, I'm not talking hired-gun stuff. Scout salvage. You have a knack for getting in and out of places none of our clan come within a Reaper's run of."

Hobarth's was a great place to take respite, but Valentine wondered about settling down there. If he joined up, the next thing they'd expect was for him to marry—and there were a couple of widows near his age attached to the truckstart. Lora, who worked in the garage, never failed to do her hair and put on her best when he visited. Problem was, her conversation was limited to engine blocks, fuel injection, and ethanol when she wasn't parroting the New Universal Church propaganda she'd learned as a child.

"I'll think about it. Promise," Valentine said.

Hobarth was canny. He knew "Max Argent" well enough to know that if he wanted something, he jumped at a chance, whether it was a night on clean sheets or a volume in the little library that existed in the Hobarth attic.

"Reading again? *Confed . . .*" Hobarth knew parts manuals and truck manufacturers, but preferred the pool table and old pinball machines of the family rec room when it came time to unwind.

"Confederacy of Dunces," Valentine supplied.

"Sounds like the ministers in Kansas City. I hear there's cholera. Both sides of the river."

Kansas was bleeding again, and much on the mind of the whole Hobarth clan. She had broken into warring factions, supported by the UFR in the east and the powerful Kurians of the Southwest on the other side of the Arkansas River. "Route 666" had become tougher than ever.

Valentine contemplated his tea. “One of them will get bled. The Kurians don’t like people dying without orders and proper processing.”

Hobarth stiffened a little. It didn’t do to say such things, even deep in the relatively neutral Grog lands.

Valentine changed the subject. “I’m about done with this. Can I get up in the book attic? I want to look up an item or two.”

“Look something up? It’s not an archive. It’s a paper junk heap. Most of the stuff’s falling apart.”

“I saw a book there last trip. I just want to read up on it a little more.”

“Wonderful. Do us a favor and clean up a few cobwebs while you’re up there, okay?”

“Gladly.”

“You accommodated?”

“Yes. Don’t worry, the Dragon Lady’s charging contractor rates. I had some Iowa scrip I wanted to dump anyway.”

Hobarth smiled at the use of his aunt’s nickname. “I’ll tell everyone to be extra nice. You staying long?”

“Maybe a week. My worm needs a few days of feeding.”

“You could use all that in-wall time to take a bath, you know. You could read in the tub.”

“What, and lose my camouflage? The critters confuse the Reapers, you know.”

“Wonderful. Something about you’s just a bit out of alignment, you know that, Argent? And I don’t mean that busted-up face of yours either.”

Valentine didn’t enjoy exercise. He’d rather heat his muscles chopping wood, or even digging a latrine ditch or picking apples, so something might be gained out of the calorie loss. He looked on exercise as a routine maintenance activity, like adjusting straps, darning socks, or sharpening and oiling a blade. It was not an end unto itself, but preparation so his body would be ready when called upon.

But he could combine it with a more interesting activity, like fishing.

So during his stay at the truckstart, every morning he’d sling his tackle on the legworm’s harness and goad it out to one of the ponds or creeks, provided there wasn’t a winter fog or cold rain. The Reapers sometimes prowled in daylight if the overcast was heavy enough.

So with a clear morning and in hope of a torpid catfish he’d prod his legworm out, where it could pull up bush in peace while he fished. On the way there and back he jogged from one side of the legworm to the other, practiced leaping on its back or mounting it using low tree limbs to swing himself up, until his breath came hard and fast and his bad leg ached. If the fish weren't biting, he'd practice with his battle rifle—a few cartridges now and again could be replaced, and there was no such thing as a wasted shot if it kept you in practice. The time might come when being able to eat, or draw one more breath, would depend on a single bullet.

Besides, the women at the truckstart believed the smell of gun smoke to be an improvement.

Evenings he'd spend in the attic library, unless a truck came in. Then he'd join the rest of the Hobarth's gang and listen to the latest news, reports of road conditions, and shortages, always shortages. Valentine would borrow any kind of printed material—even Kurian leaflets sometimes carried clues as to the progress of the UFR. He read them with the mixed emotions of an estranged relative catching up on family events.

He lingered at the truckstart until he found a driver Tim Hobarth recommended who was heading south into the UFR. He entrusted the woman, a wispy-haired piece of leather who went sleeveless even on a cold day and drove an ancient diesel pickup pulling a high-clearance trailer, with a letter and coin for postage. He'd addressed the wax-paper packet to "William and Gail Post."

Post would make sure his information about the Iowa Guard's movements got into the right hands. A few Bear teams and some Wolves inserted into Omaha would make a world of difference.

Valentine spent the rest of the afternoon and evening moody and anxious to be off. He'd staved off the empty feeling by composing his letter to Southern Command and seeing it sent on. With that done, the guilty memories marched right back into his forebrain and set up residence. Finishing with Mary Carlson's murderers had left him empty and with too much time to think. Now free to get back to St. Louis, conscience partially cleared by his plea for help for the Golden Ones . . .

He spent his last evening at Hobarth's wandering the acres filled with wrecks, getting glimpses of the old world through faded bumper and window stickers and business information printed on car doors and rear windows.

WARNING: FREQUENT STOPS AT GARAGE SALES
GET ANY CLOSER AND YOU'D BETTER
BE WEARING A CONDOM
IN THE EVENT OF RAPTURE THIS VEHICLE WILL
BE EMPTY

It was empty, unless you counted mice and spiders.

They weren't all pre-2022. Valentine saw one that he'd been told was popular in the early years of the Kurian Order. A smooth-sided luxury sedan with the half-sun, half-moon logo of the short-lived New World Fiber Network sat there, slowly hollowing like a rotten tooth as pieces fell away. Its rear-door sticker placed it firmly in the post-'22 generation:

I DON'T FEAR THE REAPER

Valentine heard a dull growl and turned, expecting to see one of the Hobarth dog pack. One good stare and they usually calmed down enough to make friends, animal to animal.

But he saw a quivering black-and-tan dog standing between the rows of creeper-covered cars, looking through the gap toward the next row. Valentine had time to see a barrel move before he heard a quick hiss and felt a firm tap just behind the neck.

He started to crouch, but the world turned gummy, and his defensive stance loosened into a kneel. Then he felt grass against his cheek and dirt in his eye, but that didn't matter. A pleasant, dark warmth beckoned and he gladly slid down the hill toward it.

Motion, and the smell of corn.

The corn came from fabric covering his face, probably a feed sack over his eyes. A cloying, wet mess in his pants. He tried to rise, but handcuffs held his wrists together behind him. *Fight it fight it fight it.*

"Hey, he's coming out of it already," a husky voice said. The words were being bent and twisted in his ear, where a surflike roar fought with a deep thrumming reminiscent of the old *Thunderbolt*'s engines at high revolutions.

A little higher-pitched whine: "The doc said out for twelve hours for sure. Nothing like that, nothing near."

"Knowing his system, he probably just had a nice nap," a female voice added. She cleared her throat. "Get him inside and sit him up. I'll get the others."

Nice nap, indeed. Valentine flexed, tried to clear the creosote someone had substituted for blood in his limbs. They settled him into a chair and he felt a distasteful squish in his underwear.

A needle went into his arm. This time he stayed awake.

Sort of.

Hard to tell if time was passing or not. He swore, but it came out as a dry-throated moan. It seemed the first part of his brain that was willing to try to work his mouth had a vocabulary limited to profanity.

More words, but they didn't make sense.

Then he was awake, only now the fabric over his face was wet; so were his chest and shoulders.

"Up and at 'em, Valentine," the husky voice said, more intelligibly this time.

They know my name. This can't be good.

Husky voice again: "You reading me?"

Valentine needed time to think, but more water came.

"Anyone want to work him over with a bar of soap? He really needs it," a faraway female voice said. Hard to tell if it was the same one he'd heard before; the earlier conversation came back vague as a dream.

Another voice, female, nearer: "David S. Valentine, former major with Southern Command, we meet at last."

"Mutfurker," Valentine croaked.

"I suppose you know you've made a lot of powerful enemies. Someone gets to be too big a thorn, it gets pulled out and snapped." A throat clearing followed by a soft cough. This voice was the same as the one in the car.

"Death teams, man," the husky voice said. "You got death teams on your ass. Just like the one that got your folks. Just like the one that has you now."

"He's awake now, I saw his head jerk," the faraway female voice said.

So that's it, Valentine thought. *I wonder if they'll leave me strung up like F. A. James in Iowa. No, some Kurian will get me.*

Husky voice: "Big reward. All we have to do is take you north of the Missouri. We'll all be rich."

"Spend it right away, you pricks," Valentine said. The words were slurred but sounded intelligible enough to him. "There's some Bears and a Cat who'll get you in turn."

Valentine heard light footsteps and the bag came off his face—a little painfully, it took a scab on his chin with it.

Alessa Duvalier stood in front of him, holding the feed sack. Her freckles had faded with the season and she had a fresh bandage on her hand. A long, tattered coat hung off her thin shoulders. "If I'm s'posed to be the Cat, I wouldn't be so sure, Val," she said. "I still remember the tap you gave me in St. Louis. The cut inside my mouth took forever to heal."

Confused relief flooded Valentine. He tried to form words, but they wouldn't come. His eyes went wet.

"Get him some water, Roberts," a woman in uniform said from the other side of the room. The air smelled like mold and termites. She had her back to him, and was studying a series of wedding pictures on the wall. It had peeling paper and old, dust-covered fixtures that at one time had thrown light on the pictures. A few pieces of furniture with the cushions long removed had been pushed against the walls, and Valentine noted that he sat at one end of an oval dinner table, once a fine piece of work but now scratched and water warped. A single fat white candle leaned at the center of the table, providing the only illumination in the room.

A short, wiry man with horn-rimmed glasses in a Southern Command uniform offered the mouth of a canteen. Valentine noticed a corporal's chevron on his arm. "Just water," he said, in a surprisingly deep voice for his slender frame. Valentine drank, marking another man in Wolf leathers snoring on the bare spring bed of a sofa, oblivious to the conversation.

"So I've been recaptured by Southern Command?" Valentine said.

"For the record: name, place of birth, most recent rank?" the female with her back to him said.

"David Stuart Valentine, unincorporated Minnesota, major," Valentine supplied.

"He's sensible enough," Duvalier said. "Hungry, Valentine?"

"I'll eat." Valentine was shocked to see Moira Styachowski step in from another room. His artillery officer from the fight for Big Rock Hill on the banks of the Arkansas had put on a little weight since last he saw her, but her face still looked pale and her eyes tired.

"Quite a reunion," Valentine said as Duvalier slid flatbread and a jar that smelled like fatted bean paste across the table.

"More than you know," the woman studying the photos said. She turned. A trim, neatly attired woman with a colonel's bird on her tightly buttoned collar regarded him with sparkling eyes.

Valentine felt a little like a hog at a county fair set before a judge. Sharp chin to match the eyes . . .

"Dots," Valentine said.

"For my sins, Colonel Lambert now," she said, her words cold and hard.

"Excuse me for not saluting," Valentine said. "I'm cuffed."

"Val, don't be difficult," Duvalier said.

"It's a private joke, Smoke," Lambert said. "I remember he once told me that he'd be saluting me someday, back when he was at the War College."

Duvalier, now sitting at the table, raised an intrigued eyebrow at him and he shook his head.

"Can I clean myself up?" Valentine asked.

"Please," Duvalier said.

"Roberts, take off the cuffs and show him his things," Lambert said.

The corporal led him to what had once been the house's kitchen. A ten-gallon jug of water sat on the counter; soap, towel, razor, and washcloth rested in a bucket.

Valentine saw packs and a duffel. The corporal extracted a set of Southern Command fatigues from one of them. Valentine recognized his old cammies from his stint as operations officer in the ad hoc regiment known as the Razors. His nose detected mothballs, though someone had made an effort to freshen up the uniform by packing it with acacia buds.

Valentine cleaned himself up, passed a forefinger over the thick fabric of the battle dress. Clever of Lambert. Once he was in uniform, sitting across the table from others in similar dress, old dutiful habits would naturally follow the way phrases come back when an adult who has long been in foreign lands speaks the language of home.

But Southern Command had made it amply clear that he was disposable. Valentine eschewed the uniform.

He heard a murmur from the other room and hardened his ears, but the exchange stopped almost as soon as it started. He returned to the table, the pleasant scent of clean women a welcome change in his nostrils.

Lambert watched him approach with steady eyes, a battered leather courier bag open in front of her. Styachowski was smearing peanut butter on a hard roll. Duvalier had taken off her duster and piled a small revolver, knives, and her old sword-cane on the seat next to her.

Valentine sat, the three women at the other end of the table making him feel like Macbeth looking across the cauldron at his witches.

"By the pricking of my thumbs, something wicked this way comes," he said.

Styachowski paused, the roll halfway to her mouth. Duvalier's nose twitched, but perhaps Lambert recognized the allusion. Her eyes warmed a trifle.

Valentine waited to hear it, playing with refusals ranging from polite to obscene.

"By now you've guessed we're not here to haul you back to the Nut," Styachowski said.

"I'll listen," Valentine said. "Right up until you slide the pardon across the table. I'm working up saliva."

"You can walk out that door, Valentine," Lambert said. "How long you can keep walking is the question you should ask yourself. The little drama we acted out could have been true. Kurian hit teams have you on their list. You do something traceable and they'll hunt you down."

"They just missed you in Iowa," Duvalier said. "I caught one of their sniffers drunk in a bar outside Garrison Nine."

"Suppose they do catch up. What's it to you?"

"You used to be one of the best young talents in Southern Command," Lambert said.

"I used to be a lot of things. Now I'm just tired."

Duvalier poked him with her toe. "Quit the burnout talk."

"You sure you want him, Moira?" Lambert asked.

Styachowski nodded.

"How's life treating you, Wildcard?" Valentine asked. "I never thanked you for visiting me in the Nut."

"Valentine, I need your help," Styachowski said. "I'm putting together a new unit."

"A force of condemned men for suicide missions, right? Not interested."

"You used to wait until you knew what you were talking about to open your mouth," Styachowski said, stiffening. "I liked that about you."

Lambert picked up her attaché. "Wasted flight."

"You flew here?" Valentine said.

"Once your old partner located you, yes," Lambert said. "Uncomfortable, cold, and loud."

Valentine knew that Southern Command had few air assets. Even generals traveled by train and car. Lambert must be a very big bug to have an airplane at her disposal.

"So Smoke tracks me down and Styachowski offers me the job. How do you fit in?"

Lambert tapped her courier bag. "I'm the answer girl, just like at the War College, Valentine."

"Young for a colonel," Valentine said.

"It looks better on the letterhead," Lambert said. "I had a staff position, really unimportant a few years back, 'cooperative commands operations director.' If something was happening in New England or Europe or South America that the staff needed to know about, I summarized and passed it on. Once in a great while we'd get a liaison visit from Denver or Quebec City and I'd arrange briefings.

"Then Archangel hit and suddenly we were plunged into joint operations with the Texans. I had all the old responsibilities, but suddenly ten times the information was coming in, and we had to coordinate our movements with theirs, work out shared-supply issues, ad hoc attachments of Southern Command and Texas forces. Am I boring you, Valentine?"

Valentine looked up from his hands. "Not at all. I owe you a thank-you. You helped save the Razors."

"Texan enthusiasm saved the Razors. Once they started rolling I got out of their way. I just found them a few tugs."

The emotions of seeing the fleet of little boats come down the Arkansas River came back. Even the pain from the burns on his back and legs throbbed anew with the memory.

"What is my old friend General Martinez up to these days?"

Styachowski glanced at Lambert and shook her head, but Lambert spoke anyway: "Inspector general. It suits him. He keeps to the rear areas, getting expensive dinners and cigars as he makes his rounds. I can't deny he's popular. He sees to it that the food and comforts improve whenever he visits a post."

"Which reminds me," Duvalier said. "I've got a letter for you from Will and Gail. Over a year old now, but you haven't been leaving forwarding addresses." She dug in her duster and produced a wrinkled, grease-stained envelope. The letter smelled like turned bacon, but Valentine accepted it gratefully.

"So much for the past," Valentine said. "What do you have in mind for my future?"

"What I'm about to tell you is about as secret as anything can get, Valentine. Does your disenchantment with the Cause extend to materially hurting its efforts?"

"If anyone asks about this meeting, I'll assure them it was purely sexual."

Duvalier rolled her eyes. "Dream on, Valentine."

"C'mon, Major," Styachowski said.

"I don't have anyone to talk to, unless you count my legworm. If Kur does get its hands on me, there's no keeping secrets from them." Valentine had been questioned under drugs before.

"This is more of a morale matter for our side. Our Lifeweavers have disappeared."

"Still?" Valentine remembered that after Solon's brief occupation of the Ozarks the Lifeweavers had fled, but he'd assumed they would return. *Assuming makes an ass out of—*

"Almost," Styachowski said. "Your Old Father Wolf has been located in the Sierras in Mexico. We're working on getting him back up here. Ryu and the Bearclaw are thought to be dead. There were a couple others in Southern Command, staff-level advisers, also gone. With no Lifeweavers . . ."

"No more Hunters," Valentine supplied, so lost in his thoughts that he brought up what was obvious to all of them.

"Our regulars are a match for theirs any day," Lambert said. "Unless they get the bulge on us with artillery. We can even handle the Grogs, most of the time. But when the Reapers show up—"

Valentine knew all this. "I'm supposed to locate some, right?"

"No, the locating's been done. We want you to get a message through to them. Maybe even try to bring a few back."

"They're not just across the Missouri somewhere, I take it."

"Seattle."

Valentine managed to blink.

"You got one out of the Zoo in Chicago," Styachowski said.

"His body, you mean. I came upon Rho by accident, and he died during the escape."

Lambert had clean nails. Valentine got a chance to examine them when she placed her hand, palm down, near his. "This isn't a case of going into a Kurian Zone and breaking one out. You'll simply travel to the resistance in the Cascades, meet one, and let it know our need."

"Simply? It must be fifteen hundred miles. One way."

"You've been traveling the Kurian Zone for years."

"You don't know that."

Three sets of eyeballs exchanged glances. "We just assumed—"

There was that word again.

Valentine let out a breath. "It's not worth arguing. I'm not interesting in slogging over who knows how many mountain ranges, sorry. Send a radiogram."

"You haven't heard what we're offering," Lambert said.

"Some kind of pardon."

"Not for you. You know that baby Reaper you brought out of Kentucky—"

"He has a name."

"How can you tell it's a he?" Duvalier asked. Reapers had no vulnerable reproductive organs sharing space with their simple elimination system.

"Calling him 'it' won't—"

"You've been good enough to let the researchers at the Miskatonic take a look at him a couple of times," Lambert interrupted.

"Until he broke two fingers and the wrist of the nurse subjecting him to ultrasonics," Duvalier said.

"They were hurting him," Valentine said, heating at the memory.

Lambert smiled. "The Kurians are very interested in your little Reaper. Their agents have offered substantial bribes for information up and down the Free Territory as to his whereabouts. They think we've got him in a lab someplace."

"Of course," Valentine said.

"Even I don't know where you've got him stashed, 'zactly," Duvalier said. "You always meet the Miskatonic people in the Groglands around St. Louis."

Lambert ignored her. "They think we've got him hidden in the deepest, darkest hole in the Ozarks and they're trying to find it. Sooner or later they'll learn the truth."

Valentine remained silent, waiting for it.

"Or," Lambert said, "I can make sure that every record, every test, every note, and every photograph disappears. We've mocked up a pretty convincing skeleton out of bits and pieces of other Reapers. He'll be listed as dead, killed during testing, the bones archived, some tissue samples dropped into formaldehyde, and everything but abstracts of the research will be destroyed."

How did they know the chink in his armor? Duvalier, probably. At times it seemed she knew him better than he knew himself. She was a sound judge, not just of risk, but of character, vulnerabilities—it made her a better assassin. Save for the bloodlust that sometimes came over her when a Quisling touched her—if she'd had an education beyond the sham of her early years in the Great Plains Gulag, she could have . . .

Keen judge of character. She picked you to train.

Valentine didn't know whether to hate the trio or admire them. He'd gotten careless with the last of Mary's murderers gone. Part of him was itching for something to do anyway. How much of his unwillingness was an act?

"There's got to be more to this," Valentine said. "Why not just contact the Pacific Northwest by regular channels? Southern Command must have some kind of communication route."

Styachowski suddenly became interested in a frayed cuff.

Lambert spoke again: "The Cause up there is in the hands of a genius. But like many geniuses, he's got his own ways."

"Friends and enemies both call him 'Mr. Adler,'" Styachowski said. "They say he came out of Seattle, originally. Didn't know one end of a gun from another when he showed up barefoot to volunteer, but he carried sixteen tons of grudge. He took a bunch of guerrillas starving in the mountains and fighting each other as much as they did the Kurians, and turned them into the Terrors of the Cascades. They appear and disappear like a fog, always somewhere the Quislings are weak. He's putting a headlock on the most powerful Kurian in the western half of the United States, Seattle himself. The Big Wheel."

"Him I've heard of," Valentine said. "Wasn't he trying to absorb the whole West Coast?"

"We were both at the War College then," Lambert said. "It was all the talk among the higher-ups, worries that Seattle would be running the whole coast, knock Denver out, then come after us. I suppose it could still happen, if the forces in the Cascades fall apart."

"All the more reason to set up liaisons," Valentine said.

Lambert shook her head. "It's been tried. One mission came back saying this Adler had no time for any war but the one he was waging against Seattle. The next mission we sent quit Southern Command and started singing his praises as the savior of the human race. The third never even made it there."

"Lifeweavers don't exactly advertise their whereabouts," Valentine said. "I don't see how I can find any without this genius' permission."

Styachowski opened her mouth to speak but lost her words in a cough.

"Ahh, but that's your specialty, Val," Duvalier said. "You're going to show up and volunteer."

Styachowski glared at her.

"Barefoot?" Valentine asked.

"I don't think that's necessary," Styachowski said. "You're talented. An ex-Cat of Southern Command. Hero of Big Rock Hill. You're bound to end up in Pacific Command's version of the Hunters."

Their faces stood out against the dark uniforms and the shadows beyond the table. Odd that all three were approximately the same height when seated. Three witches, telling him his future over a dirty table with finish bubbled and cracked.

"And if I make contact with a Lifeweaver?"

"Simple message. Southern Command needs their help. Badly. Or we're finished."

"That dicey, is it?"

"We're running out of Hunters," Lambert said. "The lieutenant I used to admire would have known what that meant, and been the first to volunteer. We've sent calls for help north, east, and south. We want you to be west."

The lieutenant Dots used to admire would have been so startled at the news of her admiration that he would have been able to think about little else. Valentine just noted it as an interesting detail.

Duvalier, eyes raised to heaven, and mouth like she'd just swallowed a spoonful of castor oil, muttered something about "Ghost" being the wrong clan nickname.

"Have you told me everything?"

"Everything," Styachowski said. "Trust me, Val. You did at one time."

"There is one more thing," Lambert said. "It's not an important detail. But it might mean something to you. The third mission, the one that disappeared, was led by your old CO from Zulu Company. LeHavre."

Lots of things could happen on the trail. Even to a man as experienced as LeHavre.

"I don't suppose Ahn-Kha has wandered in from across the Mississippi? He'd be invaluable."

"Sorry, Val," Duvalier said, her voice soft for the first time that evening. "He'd be sitting here if he had."

Styachowski smiled, but Lambert leaned forward. "Does that mean you're going?"

"I haven't spoken to a Lifeweaver in years," Valentine said. "I've gathered quite a list of questions."

"Great. We can get you as far as Denver," Styachowski said. "They can—"

"No. Sounds like your pipeline's got leaks, if LeHavre couldn't get through. I'm going as David Valentine, ex–Southern Command. He'd have to figure out his own way there. I'll have to write up a list of gear I need, though. Gold will be on it."

"Give it to Moira," Lambert said, suddenly informal. "Where do you want it delivered?"

"Do you know Nancy's?"

"I know Nancy's," Duvalier said. "Used to be the best safe house between Kansas City and the Rockies. Practically in Free Territory these days."

"I'll meet you there in three weeks."

"Thanks for rejoining the team, Valentine," Lambert said.

Valentine felt a little warmth in the look they exchanged. A bad use of a football-coach metaphor made her fallible—and therefore human.

"Will I have a contact I can trust out there?" Valentine asked. "I might need backup. Supplies or gear."

"I'll catch up to you at Nancy's," Styachowski said.

"Good to see you again, Valentine," Lambert said. "From this day on, your little charge is history. On paper, anyway."

Duvalier was the last to leave and ran her tongue obscenely against her lips as they said good-bye. "Even Queen Balance Sheet folds at last," she said quietly. "I'll buy you a drink at Hob's to make up. I'm guessing that ego of yours needs some soothing after getting shaded by a woman half your size."

"I'll have to chit that. If I'm going to be back at Nancy's in twenty days, I have to get that list to Styachowski and get my worm rigged."

The corner of Duvalier's mouth went up, but she ignored the opportunity for another raunchy joke. "Be careful, sweet David. May flights of angels sing thee to thy rest."

First *Macbeth*, now *Hamlet*. He wondered where Duvalier had even picked up the line. He kissed her on the cheek. "I will."

Three

St. Louis, Missouri: The mighty river-flanked city has again grown to be one of the most crowded civic centers in the Midwest, second only to Kurian-held Chicago, almost bursting at the bluffs when set against the mile-high vistas of the thinly populated Denver Freehold.

Except that the population is mostly nonhuman.

The Missouri River valley from St. Louis to Omaha belongs to the sentient bipeds—"Grogs" in the highly unspecific vernacular. In some of the Zones, they still serve their original purpose, acting as a military caste between the Kurian overlords and the human populace. Other Grog clans and tribes took land grants after their twelve-years service (Grog tradition holds that there are five twelve-year periods to a full life, and the Grog who makes it past his fifth age is revered indeed). The Kurians settled them as bulwarks against the few areas not under their control.

The reason the Kurians left such backwaters held by enemies or unreliable transplants is still a subject of no little debate.

Grog custom makes warfare a way of life and a path to status; theft entrepreneurship and slave-taking are the twenty-first-century version of human resource management. While the "Gray One" clans and tribes that inhabit the valley consider herding a noble and respectable duty, the dirt digging of agricultural work is left to their slaves of the human caste, not quite despised, but only rarely admitted into Grog homes on an equal basis.

Free humans live among the Grogs, wearing hatbands or wrist tokens that serve as proof that "foot pass" (as the term is translated) has been paid to the admitting tribe. "Looie" is a refuge from both the terror of the Reapers and the justice of the embattled United Free Republic to the south, and humanity there has carved out niches that many would consider enviable. They perform for Grog audiences under the Oriental decor of the Fox Theatre, sweep the streets of the Hill, operate specialized workshops, breweries, and distilleries in Carondelet, or keep trading posts stocked with goods imported from both Kurian Zone and Freehold. A small cadre of experienced arms men even teaches at the old City Museum. The best of the Grog child warriors are sent there by their tribes to improve their warcraftiness and learn from others.

Churches educate, heal, and minister to both human and the rare Grog desperate enough to seek succor outside his clan, under generous land grants from tribal leaders who otherwise would have fewer men to serve them. An entire human ghetto has grown up around the Basilica of St. Louis, catering to human needs, including that of a surprisingly well-equipped hospital and small school. The orderlies drink and the students study nearby at that eternal mark of urban culture: a café looking out on the sugar-beet gardens of the Jefferson National Expansion Memorial.

But everyone is careful to always have a foot-pass token on display: a red wooden bracelet with copper pennies inlaid for the Headstriker Tribe, a decoupage of old postage stamps set on a wooden tongue depressor for the Sharpeyes, a battered bit of embossed black leather with white stitching for the Startold. . . .

David Valentine stepped out of the confessional, still able to sense the anxious sweat on the priest who remained in his stuffy little booth. The cathedral, lit by candles, arched overhead like a vast cave and echoed the noises of the few who remained after evening services. Janitors were putting out the oil lamps.

"Father Dahl might need a moment," he told the three people waiting. It had been a long and busy year since he'd last knelt next to a priest. The ritual always made him feel better, thanks to its tiny, tenuous connection to his upbringing in the schoolhouse of Father Max.

The priests and nuns also liked you to set an example. He'd happily swallow his doubts and buy some new rosary beads and show up for a few masses for Blake's sake.

He checked his tribal city pass as he left the church by the public side door. He wore it around his neck on a shoelace tether: a cardboard emblem the size of a bar coaster emblazoned with a two-color circle of blue and white copied from the BMW logo. The Grogs of the Waterway Guides had a knack for picking up on designs of deep spiritual significance. He shared a hobbyist's enthusiasm for fishing with a clan chief and they gave him his Looie foot pass at a steep discount.

The well-maintained shotgun formerly of F. A. James greased the transaction, of course. Offering up the weapons of a killed enemy transferred spiritual power to the Waterway. Valentine had been glad to be rid of its weight and associate memories.

Just across the corner from the cathedral was the dormitory and school. Even his limp became a little less pronounced as he bounced up the steps and signed in with the desk warden. She wore her foot pass in the form of an oversized earring, which swung as she pulled on a bell cord.

"He's still downstairs?" Valentine asked when Monsignor Cutcher welcomed him back.

"And thriving like a mushroom," the bristle-haired Jesuit said. He spoke with a faint accent, indefinite but distinctly European when compared with the usual Midwestern drawl of the Looies, and sometimes chose odd similes. Cutcher was the most well-traveled man Valentine had ever met, and had come all the way from Malta to assist with Blake, though he spoke of Cape Town and Kyushu with equal ease.

Cutcher took him to an alcove with a discreetly placed, heavy wooden door. "He gets the playground all to himself every night," Cutcher said. "We had a dark episode with a squirrel he'd been offering tidy-bits. He gained its trust and then attacked the poor rodent. Just like with the pigeons. He always obeys a warning for a few minutes but forgets unless frequently reminded. Tiresome."

"We may have to move him," Valentine said.

Cutcher paused at the bottom of the stairs. "Oh?"

"I've been informed that *they* are hunting him. The Freehold is going to fake his death in the documents. I'd like to make sure the trail dead-ends here at the same time."

"There is a small mission in La Crosse. But it may perhaps be easier to hide him somewhere else in this city. Strangers are noticed here—someone snooping around is sure to draw attention of the tribes."

They descended to what had probably once been preparation and scullery rooms for kitchens, judging from the number of sinks. Wooden partitions filled one whole wall, storage space and dormitories for the worst of the summer heat. Valentine's odds and ends filled one; the more permanent trunks of the Bloch brothers rested open in another. Behavioral biologists from the Miskatonic in Pine Bluff, they studied Blake's every intake and excrete, and gave him an occasional medical examination—and then only under supervision Valentine trusted. Getting Narcisse out of Southern Command had been easier than he'd thought: They'd put her to make-work in a convalescent home and treated her more like a patient than a skilled nurse or cook. Will Post had presented her with his offer and arranged to relocate her to a border town where they could be reunited.

Valentine looked forward to giving the Miskatonic fellows their walking papers. Their faces would drop lower than the muddy bottom of the nearby Mississippi.

Valentine smelled food cooking. The Blochs were probably at breakfast. Blake was mostly nocturnal, and they'd adapted their schedules to his.

A squeak of rubber turning on linoleum sounded from the darkness of a corridor ahead.

"I heard your step on the stairs, Daveed," Narcisse said, coming into the dim light reflected from the dirty tile.

Valentine's old guide from Haiti smiled up at him from beneath one of her colorful bandannas. Her face had a few more lines, a few more liver-colored blotches.

"Hello, Sissy."

"You look tired. Rest and eat. Let me pour a bowl of soup for you. There is bread. Olive oil too, from some raid or other. It gives the gray folk the runs something terrible, so they give it to us."

"I'd like to see Blake first."

"Of course."

"I'll say good-bye to you two," Cutcher said. "Feel free to hop up and talk, David, if you have any concerns regarding Blake."

"Will do, Monsignor."

She led him down the hall. They'd mounted a first-aid kit the size of a briefcase on the wall since he'd last been there; Valentine wondered if there'd been worse trouble than with squirrels and pigeons. They entered the incinerator room that now served as the young Reaper's bedroom.

An aged nun with a face like a raisin watched him as he slept, a crack in the basement window admitting a shaft of sleep light.

"David Valentine, we see you again at last," she whispered as she hugged him. "Such a blessing."

Blake had grown like Iowa corn in a hot, thundery summer. Valentine felt the old pain, looked at his wrists, both of which still bore a faint track or two, like needle marks on the addicts he'd seen in Chicago's Zoo. He remembered the exhausting first months with Blake, shuffling him from Nomansland hole to Nomansland hole under cover of darkness, feeding him when there wasn't livestock to be had. He'd looked in a mirror once and thought he was staring at his own ghost.

"Blake," Valentine said from across the room. He could sometimes lash out like a wild animal if he was touched in sleep.

Yellow, slit-pupil eyes opened. The small figure sat up, wearing an old pajama top with characters that Valentine recognized as Ernie and Bert.

"papa," Blake said in his tiny, breathy voice. He sprang out of bed, crossing a meter or more in a clumsy jump.

"Jumping," Narcisse warned, and the obsidian-toothed mouth formed a regretful *"o."*

Valentine took Blake up, turned the child's head up and away from his breast—no sense taking chances, and besides, he wanted a good look at the growing face. He was shocked at the weight gain. At two years and three months, Blake was a good deal heavier than a human child his size, perhaps the weight of a five- or six-year-old. *"papa bek. papa bek see bwaykh!"*

"Yes, I'm back." Valentine's wary ears picked up a faint thump from beneath the cot and a little terrier mix appeared, wiggling as it scooted out.

"That's Wobble," Narcisse said. "Blake got heem as a puppy."

"wobbow not for eat," Blake informed Valentine, his blue-veined face going serious.

Wobble had a bare patch on his back and a tiny ridge of scar tissue, and a bit of a limp. Valentine wondered how many close calls Wobble had survived before Blake had finally learned.

"Of course he's not for eating," Valentine said, going down cross-legged—with a twinge from his bad left leg—so he could set Blake's formidable weight down and pet the squirmy dog. Of course when he'd run with Southern Command's Wolves he'd learned to dine on dog and had eaten them innumerable times since, but what was civilization but a lengthy set of agreed-upon tribal taboos?

Despite his change in size, Blake's grip on his arm and shoulder was a good deal more gentle than he remembered. What accidental pains Narcisse had suffered to her shattered body as Blake's nursemaid Valentine couldn't imagine.

Blake began to produce his favorite toys.

Which reminded Valentine. "I had a letter from Will and Gail. Ali tracked me down."

"A letter!" Narcisse said. The St. Louis Grogs weren't on any postal network. "What it said?"

Valentine handed her the grease-stained envelope, spiderwebbed with creases. "You can read it." Valentine went back to helping Blake work a spinning top made out of an old office-chair caster.

William Post, the former Quisling Coastal Marine who'd helped Valentine while crossing the Caribbean in the old *Thunderbolt*, had been given a sinecure with Southern Command. With some reading between the lines Valentine determined that Post had made himself indispensable with his usual efficient intelligence. He'd been given a minor position cataloging captured documentation from the Gulf Coast area and the Mississippi River valley, and had started making educated guesses based on everything from shipping manifests to maintenance logs.

His evaluations, thanks to his years of experience in the area, won him a position in the staff's Threat Assessment Bureau. TAB was charged with ensuring that Southern Command wouldn't get surprised again by the kind of coordinated attack that had allowed Consul Solon to roll up Missouri and Arkansas.

The news contained in the letter was good. Post knew that someone working the Kurian Zone would just as soon hear nothing but cheer. He and Gail were settled in Fort Scott, a trolley ride from his air-conditioned office. Hank Smalls was getting good marks in school and had a place as top starting pitcher on the academy's baseball team. His fastball was already attracting local fans.

Valentine could almost recite it word for word, especially one tantalizing paragraph:

> *I'm breaking security with this, Dave, but it's nothing the KZ isn't aware of anyway. Thought you'd like to know there's been a spike of action up and down the Appalachians, mostly in the Virginias and Kentucky. Only info on it is from secondary sources, but it's all the same story: guerrillas on legworms, popping in and out of valleys, and the K aren't having much luck with their whack-a-mole mallets. The coal mines are caught up in it, too. Here's the interesting bit: Supposedly some huge Grog's leading the revolt, bat ears and fur described as being either straw-colored or white. If we weren't SO short, we'd send a mission to help and I'd know for sure. It's been ugly.*

Valentine had been tempted to tell Styachowski to let Mr. Adler remain mysterious and take the first slow barge up the Ohio. Post's mention that Southern Command was short on "Special Operations"—Wolves or Cats and Bears in the latest military parlance—put him back on the leash.

Of course, it wouldn't be above Moira Styachowski to ask Post to slip in a mention from someone Valentine trusted as a clincher. Styachowski and Post were both veterans of Big Rock Hill. She might ask a favor.

And so what if she had? They're your friends, man. Been in the Zone too much. They've given you a taxing but not particularly dangerous job to bring you back into the fold. Be grateful. And stop talking to yourself.

Narcisse waited until Blake was lost in the spinning, clattering, multicolored wheel from the old Life game to speak again.

"If Ali found you, that means they needed you to be found. Are you going off again?"

"Afraid so, Sissy," Valentine said. The wheel spun again and Blake pointed to the new number. Wobble chased his tail, imitating the whirling toy.

"You have so little time. He misses you, you know. He's human enough to pine. Too young to understand."

Valentine wondered how Narcisse had tipped to that. Of course he'd been interested in the challenge of the journey. But what was his absence doing to Blake? Was he cocking this up, along with everything else in his life? *Wait, Val, you made a bargain with the past four years ago. Let it be.* "Ten days. I'll stay here ten days. I need to fatten up on your cooking."

The wheel came off its mount. Blake picked up the wheel and offered it to Valentine. *"papa help bwaykh!"*

"You can do it yourself. See? Circle in the circle?"

Blake's bony features screwed up in thought. He put the spinner back in the little green dish of plastic. But he didn't align it and settle it on the pin. Valentine reached, but Blake gave it an experimental spin and sent it skittering across the floor.

"bwoke!" Blake said, smashing his fist onto the green cradle. The green plastic shattered and Wobble froze. Blake made a gurgling sound.

"Now it is," Valentine said. Narcisse stroked the back of Blake's neck with her intact hand.

"sowwy," Blake said in his faint, breathy voice. *"vewy sowwy, papa."*

Valentine picked him up again. "We'll make a new one." A piece of planking and a small, dulled nail would do. "Together."

Blake liked the sound of that. He showed all his fangs.

The days passed like the cars of a speed freight. Valentine contrived to take Blake on a fishing trip. Sufficient dirt, an oversized droopy boat hat, and some baggy clothes made him into a lean boy whose arms and legs were finishing up a growth spurt. The fish were biting, but any sort of motion, from a frog's leap to a rabbit's careful hop, made him drop his rod and investigate.

On his own, Valentine visited a little shrine near the old arch that he'd found on his first trip to the city. Years ago his father had eliminated the Kurians from St. Louis—he learned this not from his father but from some men who had served with him—and the Grogs set up their form of memorial in the lobby of what had been an elevator to the top of the monument. Some bits and pieces laid out in an arch of parachute "silk" that imitated the one above—bullet casings, a canteen, a K-bar-style knife, a climbing glove, and some nylon rope he understood, but there was also a fox tail, a bunch of oddly shaped dice in a clear plastic tube, and a stoppered bottle of what looked like salad oil.

The mementos were meticulously dusted. Maybe at festivals a storyteller hopped up on the display (did the Grogs believe that putting the items behind glass detracted from their power?) and used the props. Or perhaps there were bodies buried behind the access door the heavy case blocked; the Grogs often put mementos outside grave sites. It wasn't even taboo for a Grog to take them up for a moment's examination or obeisance, provided they were returned when the task was done.

He was tempted to take the glove. Though it was larger than his own hand it still seemed small when compared with his memories of his father's huge, capable ones, but the aging Grogs clustered at the doorstep were already snorting and huffing when he bent too close to the display.

Cutcher took him up to the riverbank bluffs and showed him a house with a rambling basement cut into the limestone, lately occupied by a river trader who owned a wharf-side sawmill and a bone-wracking tubercular cough. In a fit of anxiety about his approaching death, he'd donated the property entire and its furnishings to the church.

"One last trade, this time with God," Cutcher chuckled. "May his bargain pay off."

They planned to move Blake as soon as the researchers from the Miskatonic did their last set of visual-acuity tests. He'd have room to explore up there, in the moonless darkness under the trees. Cutcher said that keeping up with him would be good for his cardiovascular health.

It felt wrong to say good-bye in a basement. Good-byes were for front yards, garden gates, train platforms, and bus pick-up corners, not shuttered basements that smelled like soaking diapers.

"If you need more money—," Valentine said to Narcisse.

"Monsignor Cutcher has ample sources. We want for nothing."

"Except the sight of one of those big palms."

"Royal palms," Narcisse said, nodding. "I do miss them, and the smell of morning wind off the sea."

"I want to thank you again for—"

She poked him in his good thigh. "Daveed, please. I am old, and have learned the difference between needed and used. Here I am needed. Here I talk long through the nights with our fine priest as we watch. A deep, kind man with the magic of the right hand. I have known only two or three others like him."

"I wish I'd had time to find Blake some blocks. And some early-reader books."

"I will find or paint some Scrabble pieces. Like the ratbits had. He will learn ABC's when he is ready. He learns, but his mind has not yet caught up to his body."

Valentine regretted the lost mah-jongg pieces. Blake would probably enjoy the colors and intricate designs. Valentine's last reminder of the good days with Malia Carrasca were in some prison warehouse deep in the Nut, probably.

Narcisse gave him a bag of dried-meat sticks, a bag of glazed biscuits, and some nuts mixed with oats and corn-bread crumbs—the Grog version of trail mix. He rolled one of the cheroot-sized tubes of meat and sniffed the greasy, peppery coating. Narcisse could make even the spongiest legworm flesh taste like tenderloin medallions in a sauce, but he suspected this was pork.

"You must not leave yet," she said. "I must press one last hug on you."

He knelt down so she could hug him. Those mauled limbs that had first met around his neck on a sunbaked Haitian street pressed at either temple, pressed hard, as though trying to meet somewhere in his corpus callosum. She closed her eyes and spoke in her Creole, sliding the words together so fast and low he didn't have a hope of understanding with his mother's Quebecois French. It went on for some moments and his pressed skin began to tingle.

Finally she stopped.

"What was that all about?" he asked.

"I asked heem to put honeycombs in your path, so your journey is sweet. There is too much bitter in you, Daveed, and it finds its way out."

Narcisse had a talent for cryptic expression that sometimes rivaled that of the Lifeweavers. Valentine wondered if he'd been cross with Blake, or the Bloch brothers from the Miskatonic when he gave them their marching orders. "If only you could add a little molasses to me, the way you do to the spoon bread."

Narcisse pursed her lips, then poked him in the breastbone with her maimed arm. "You already look better. Go now, or I cry some. Maybe I cry some anyway, but I don't want you around for that."

Valentine made Nancy's north of Tulsa in three days of round-the-clock legworm travel, arriving on the eve of the promised rendezvous. He'd made a deal with a driver from the Rabbit's Foot clan whom he silently called "Tic-tac" because the Grog's back-hide scars looked like a couple of drunks had started playing tic-tac-toe on it with hot knives.

Which wasn't out of the realm of possibility. Captured Grogs were sometimes cruelly treated to put the "fear of Man" in them before they were released. Of course captured men were often eaten when not enslaved, so cruelty was a matter of perspective.

They took turns driving the beast through day and night, skirting the UFR. Valentine hoped that the unofficial truce of the Missouri brush that had settled in when he'd first become a Cat was still holding, and that no wide-ranging patrols would risk a flare-up by potting what looked like a human small trader and his driver.

Difficulty showed itself in a six-man patrol. Three challenged him, and three more waited, kneeling in the brush. Five kids and a senior NCO. The kids were too young and the NCO was grizzled right to the hair growing out of his ears.

Valentine felt for the oldster, riding herd on a bunch of downy cheeks too young to know how easily they could die. But the Missouri bushwhack country would lend itself to giving the kids some experience without the risks that went with the swamps around New Orleans, the open plains to the west, or the alley between Crowley's Ridge and Memphis.

Valentine watched the rifles and picked out an escape route through the brush. If things looked bad, he'd topple off the legworm and run like a rabbit, twisting and turning across the mud through first spring flowers of the blackberry bramble.

"Hey, Freebies," Valentine called. "You boys looking for a little joy juice to keep out the nightly chill?"

"Check out that chair. Quite a ride he has on that legworm," one of the kids in the brush remarked to his fellows.

The NCO's rifle dangled in its sling, but the officer kept his hand hooked casually in his ALICE belt, close to the butt of his sidearm. "Just a friendly warning, Wally," the NCO said, using the Missouri slang for a trader who bartered with the Grogs. Valentine had been called worse. "You're about ten miles out of a UFR settlement. They'll panic at the sight of a worm and open up on you."

"Like a bunch of potato diggers could hit a legworm if it were on top of them," one of the kids in the brush said. The two backing up the NCO knew better than to add comment, but one kept swinging his rifle muzzle back and forth, making little figure eights in the air.

"Where you bound for?" the NCO asked, looking at the packs and accoutrements dangling from both sides of the legworm.

"South of Kansas City, Kansas."

"Top, he's traveling with a stoop—that puts him under suspicion," the twitchy kid said. "Stop and question."

"Question away, I'd like an excuse to get off this damn worm," Valentine said. "It's Tic-tac here who is on tribal-conference business. I just own the worm."

Tic-tac rocked nervously in his saddle, his anxiety evident, but kept his hands away from his long, single-shot varmint gun. Valentine doubted he even had any bullets for it. Instead he had a grip on his sharp-hooked worm goad. Valentine hoped Tic-tac wasn't getting any ideas about the worth of the kid's rifles and hair at the next tribal bragging session. If the kids knew just how quickly a Grog could throw a balanced utility ax like the one dangling from its leather thong on the saddle hook, they'd be back another ten yards or so.

Valentine tried to will the kid into slinging the gun and losing interest in the encounter, but the boy had either imagination or a grudge against men out of the Groglands.

"That's maybe a Kurian agent," the kid insisted. "He should be put under arrest."

"Not another word, Cadet," the NCO said. "If that Grog is a messenger, he'll die before he'll come out of that saddle. Then we'll have a feud with Rabbit's Foot and their allies."

Valentine's stomach sank. The kid was an officer candidate, looking to establish his record for initiative.

"Bury and buckle up, Top. C'mon," one of the kids quietly urged from the brush.

"And if he were a Kurian agent, we'd all be running to check out the sound of seventy legworms passing north of here, or shooting at each other," the NCO added.

Valentine felt a gurgle in his stomach, and took the opportunity to lean to his right and bounce a loud fart off his chair.

"Never could handle those Grog mushrooms," he said.

The NCO chuckled and the quieter of his two charges laughed.

"Pass wind, friend," the NCO said, stepping aside and gesturing with his hand to the west. The cadet glared at him.

"Don't worry, we'll be out of UFR lands by nightfall," Valentine said as they goaded the legworm into its rippling motion again.

The NCO pulled the boys out of the way of the legworm's antennae and nodded to Valentine as they passed. Valentine considered that the peacefully concluded meeting was an example of the differences between the Free Territory and the Kurian Zone. In the Free Territory an NCO could use his judgment. In the KZ they'd be kept waiting while the NCO called his officer, who called a higher officer, who would order them searched and then, when they found nothing of interest, would call a higher officer still, who would ask "Why are you bothering me with this?" and order them released anyway, provided there wasn't a Reaper breathing down his neck with an appetite that made starting a feud with a Grog tribe over a single wanderer's aura worth it.

The kids who were covering from ambush stood up as they passed, and gaped.

There was a time when the whole check in the Nomansland between would have been done by Wolves, who would probably have just observed them from cover and tracked them to see what they were up to, unseen and unheard unless the patrol leader decided they constituted a threat. Then Tic-tac would have been dead and Valentine roped and cuffed in about the stopwatch time it takes a rodeo champ to bring down a calf.

It was a good thing for the UFR that Missouri was so quiet these days.

On the third day it took both of them together to keep their mount going—legworms had astonishing reserves, but eventually even the digging goads would have no effect.

Valentine let the Grog have his legworm and rig with many thanks and a swapping of Tic-tac's delicately carved ear-grooming stick for a half-empty tin of Valentine's foot powder. He felt no particular sympathy with Tic-tac, but if this wasn't the longest trip the Grog had ever been on, it was close, and he'd want something to point to when telling the story.

Valentine walked into Nancy's oddly peaked roofs—they always reminded him of old Pizza Huts—under his own steam, taking the first of many steps westward.

Four

Nancy's, March: David Valentine first learned of Nancy's from his old tent mate Lieutenant Caltagirone of Foxtrot Company.

Nancy's had been a retirement home for Tulsa's well-to-do who were unwilling to quit the rolling hill-country of eastern Oklahoma. Its single-story, vaguely Prairie-school architecture was spread out over several acres, with a central hub and an outbuilding or two. In the Kurian Zone people were "retired" in much the same manner as an old, worn-out tire, with the Reapers serving as mechanics, but its layout made it a convenient rehabilitation center for Quisling veterans. Nancy herself was something of a legend in the Nebraska Guard for her devotion to the maimed and shattered.

She kept her charges busy with arts and crafts, which she sold in Tulsa at Kurian patriotic festivals to buy a few luxuries. The "Nancy's" sticker became so famous that an art colony of sorts had sprung up in the area, with workers of metal, leather, wood, ceramics, and paint adding to the trade.

Nancy's also had the best food in three states. Kurian Order and New Universal Church dignitaries often spent long weekends visiting the "home" and enjoying the cuisine as they got their picture taken shaking hands with the more photogenic of the wounded.

It seemed the last place one would expect to be a warehouse for the resistance. When the Kurians heard the occasional whisper or screamed confession that Nancy's had been the place guerrillas got their explosives, they assumed that their prisoners had been coached into fingering the establishment in the hope that the whole staff would be swept up in a purge. The routine searches revealed nothing.

Of course, they didn't remove the wounded from their thick, comfortable, bleach-scented bedding, pillowcases lined with gleaming rows of decorations. Only the laundry staff, under careful supervision of senior nurses, ever changed the bedding.

Nancy's had grown since the last time Valentine visited, as a tired and hungry lieutenant trying to supply his men scouting the Kurian Zone.

The "Kurian Pillar" he remembered, breaking the horizon like a white needle, now had a cross openly displayed upon it, and the trees had spread their shade over the windows and doors. The vegetable gardens and stands of tomato vines had multiplied and spread to both sides of the road that met the old interstate a couple of miles south. New houses, mostly two- or three-room shotgun shacks built around a common well pump, circled the grounds like campers keeping warm at a fire. A red-painted market that Valentine had remembered being a livestock barn, promised FUEL * FOOD * LODGING thanks to a blue and white sign salvaged from the interstate. To the southwest, behind a small hill, birds circled the community trash heap. No distance seemed too great for gulls to travel in search of garbage.

A few hardy souls were out on the blustery day, mostly working in the vegetable patches or trying to dry laundry under the eaves. Some muddy kids and dogs chased one another through the culverts at the roadside.

Valentine paused at a roadside tap for water, tried to get some of the caked-up grime off his face and hands, and then turned up toward the main entrance of the hub.

WE'RE FULL

a repainted folding yellow caution sign told him.

Valentine ignored it and paused in the entry vestibule. A six-foot panel of plywood served as a local notice board. Along with advertisements for watchdogs ("Garanteed to bark at Hoods") and ironmongery and the weekly swap meet and different flavors of Bible study were dozens of messages giving names and destinations, probably of refugees from the destruction in Tulsa. Valentine scanned them until he found what he wanted.

Black—
I'm in Comfort 18.
—Red

Ali had written their old nicknames from the trip across Tennessee and Kentucky. A faint pang of regret at their parting—she'd insisted he was crazy for harboring Blake. . . .

Jury's still out on that one.

Valentine stepped into the old reception area of the nursing home. The limestone of the outside gave way to cool, homey brick within. Two armed men wearing five-pointed stars played cards at a round wooden table, rifles and shotguns placed across a pair of ottomans with a snoring mutt between. A wide reception window looked out on the doors and waiting area, and behind it, a disarmingly young teenage girl sat writing on a pad.

Something about Valentine caused the security's antennae to twitch, and they gave him a long, careful look as he inquired of the girl. She directed Valentine to the appropriate room.

"Much obliged," Valentine said, and gave a friendly nod to the constabulary. He risked a glance back as he found the appropriate hall, and noted that they'd left their cards to watch him.

Valentine smelled barbecue and laundry soap and disinfectants—sharp odors of chlorine and borax. A New Universal Church hostel smelled much the same, albeit with potatoes and cabbage substituted for the barbecue. Someone had brought in bluebonnets and redbud for the vases at the hallway intersections, adding color and aroma. He thought them a nice touch. Four-color propaganda posters provided the only color in NUC lodgings.

The halls were wide for the accommodation of hospital gurneys. Now spare cots stood in the halls and the little social rooms used by the patients. A TV or two blared old digital recordings in all their sound and spectacle—pre-'22 titles were much sought after, as the message-riddled Kurian productions had all the artistry and interest of an appliance manufacturer's instruction manual. More children played in the halls, racing toys on the smooth flooring or hard at work with blocks, LEGOs, and Tinkertoys.

Valentine found Duvalier's room. Its door stood open.

He knocked at the bathroom just to be sure.

He heard a step in the hallway. A matronly woman in one of the cheery, embroidered staff aprons chewed on the inside of her cheek for a moment as she looked him over. He noted the frame of a cart behind. "The young ladies in this room are either at the clothes swap or the"—she lowered her voice—"bar. There's gaming and music and storytelling for those who like wasting good daylight."

"Thank you."

"They said a tall man with straight black hair would be coming.

You shining on one of those gals, or are you already married up?" She fiddled with a scissors in her apron and Valentine wondered if he were being measured up for a trim.

"Not exactly."

The honey in her voice turned sticky. "Then there's something wrong with you. Sweet things. They shouldn't be unprotected."

If the other "sweet thing" was Moira Styachowski, the pair needed as much protection as a pair of ornery wolverines.

"Thank you. Clothing swap—"

"The big green aluminum barn to the north," she supplied.

"Right. Or bar."

"It's not on Nancy's property. I never met a man who couldn't find a bar hissownself. The owner's name is Trumpet."

"Trumpet. Thank you, ma'am."

"You can thank me by handing me that water pitcher. The stuff from the tap is strictly wash water unless you're a local and used to it."

Valentine held it for her while she filled it from a set of big plastic jugs on her cart, and replaced it on its aluminum tray.

He wandered to the clothing swap first, and found the cavernous barn filled with odds and ends from darned socks to snappy but stained felt hats. A giant iron-bottomed laundry pot bubbled over charcoal and filled the whole barn with a faint smell of lye. More women and children sat on folding chairs or fruit boxes, talking and sewing.

"Offering, trading, or needing?" a bored teenage boy asked. He carried a plastic hamper.

"Looking," Valentine said.

He hadn't seen a bar coming into Nancy's, so he made for the other end of her property. Sure enough, some entrepreneur had taken an old buffet franchise resting just on the other side of the hill from the garbage pit and turned it into a sawdust-and-fat-lamp saloon. A tarnished trumpet hung from the sign outside. A few biodiesel pickups, several bicycles, and some wagon teams were arranged outside, with shade given to the animal transport and proximity to the door taken by the bikes. The pickup trucks were parked facing the road to give passersby a good look. One driver had even popped his hood to show off chrome exhaust pipes and a supercharger.

Valentine entered through the door cover, a carpet-remnant strip that acted as a windbreak.

Under the light of the front windows a guitar and banjo were keeping each other company, with bootheel syncopation as percussion.

Valentine smelled fryer oil and kidney-filtered beer. As soon as his eyes adjusted he picked out Duvalier in what would have been a crowd if everyone weren't spread out as though trying to keep out of one another's business. He walked past tables with cards and dominoes and guns being examined for trade or sale. A pair of women worked behind the bar, serving drinks and making sandwiches.

Lounging in a wooden, high-walled booth, Duvalier was in her usual earth-toned Free Territory clothing. Her knife-cut red hair dirty and disarranged, she'd put a good deal of effort into making herself look less attractive than she was, wrapped up in the duster that hid her body from the neck down. Valentine didn't recognize the young woman with her, noted only that she was blond with a longish face and nose. Duvalier pointed for the benefit of her companion, and Valentine took in the blonde's wide-set, steady eyes.

Then she blushed and dropped her gaze.

"Blackie, this is Jules. Be nice, she's like a sister to me."

Public code for another Cat. Valentine wondered what her real name was.

"Max Argent," Valentine said.

Duvalier waved over one of the bartenders and ordered three ciders.

"Bad news, looks like," Duvalier said. "Your shipment's delayed. Em is still getting it together."

Valentine wondered at that. Lambert could take a plane for a rendezvous with a potential operative, but they couldn't get a footlocker of gear to the edge of what amounted to the Free Territory?

United Free Republic, he reminded himself.

Jules spoke. "I hope you weren't planning to meet a train." Valentine wondered at her voice; there was a bit of Eastern giddyup to it. She must not have operated in the KZ much or she would know to smother the accent; it attracted too much attention.

"No. I dropped word at Hobarth's that I'm looking to pass west."

"Not as driver, I hope," Duvalier said. Most of Valentine's efforts behind a wheel were ill-fated.

"Scout work, security, maintenance, whatever they need. There'll be westbound convoys for a month or two."

"I'll leave tonight to let Em know you've arrived," Duvalier said. "You can have my bed."

Valentine waited for a remark about staying in it; Duvalier treated his cocksmanship as something of a joke—which it was, considering the results.

"Traveling at night?" Valentine asked.

"It's almost as quiet as the Ozarks around here nowadays. Nearest organized Kurians are a hundred miles away west and north."

"Diddo-dish," Jules said, using Iowa slang for something easily accomplished.

In the last three years the Great Plains had been transformed into a bloody quilt of territories in revolt and those still under the Kurians. Grogs and mercenaries from as far away as inland China were holding on to North America's breadbasket.

The ciders came and Duvalier paid in cigarettes, one of the lower denominations in a ranking that went thus: gold, batteries, whiskey, ammunition, tobacco. Lesser necessities like darning thread, pens, gloves, and toothbrushes also served as unofficial currency in booze boxes from Kurian Zone to Freehold and back again, if someone was running short and could be talked into a swap.

Between songs, they made small talk about the weather and the food. When the guitar and banjo made enough noise to cover conversation, Valentine learned that Jules hailed from a privileged family in Iowa—her father owned an estate that sounded similar to the one he'd visited in search of F. A. James. She'd spent her teenage years "out East" at school and returned to the usual privileged child's choice of military, church, or management career. She ran away just in time to get caught up in Consul Solon's bid to put the Trans-Mississipi under the Kurians.

"I tried to join the guerrillas, but since I wasn't anybody's cousin or sister-in-law I couldn't find out anything about where they were hiding. When the 'strike' speech came," she said, "I didn't get to hear it but saw it on a leaflet—I didn't know what else to do, so I started a fire in a tire pile outside a TMCC garage. Some janitors were executed for it."

"Don't put it like that," Valentine said. "The Kurian Order executed them, not you."

Valentine waited for her mind to leave memories of strung-up bodies and return to Oklahoma. "I did a bunch of other stuff," she continued. "Punctured tires at night. I learned how to cut a hot electrical wire. Stuff where I could do a little damage quietly and then run away."

"A girl after my own heart," Duvalier said.

"I take it she never went through our little ceremony." Valentine looked at the scar on his palm, barely distinguishable from legworm-hook-hardened skin.

"No," Duvalier said, and Jules looked down, hiding under her hair. What did the girl have to be ashamed of? It wasn't her fault the Lifeweavers had disappeared.

For one awful second Valentine wondered if she was a Kurian agent, slowly digging her way into Southern Command. No, Duvalier was a good judge of character. You didn't walk up and apply to be a Cat; the Cats found you.

After the evening meal Duvalier disappeared. In all the time he'd known her she'd rarely been an initiator of good-byes—like a careful extra in a stage play she liked to make unobtrusive appearances and disappearances.

Probably why she still had blood in her veins after all these years in and out of the Kurian Zone.

Valentine explored Nancy's. It still housed dozens of crippled Quislings, pitiful objects limited to bed and wheelchair. They'd taught him in his Southern Command lectures that the Kurians consumed cripples, even those wounded in defense of their Order, save for a few to be trotted out at rallies and blood drives. Whether the soldiers still lived because of some shell game of Nancy's, or the sudden turnover of territory spared them, or he'd even been given a spoonful or two of medicinal propaganda, he didn't attempt to determine.

He saw Nancy herself, behind a wide nurses' counter, speaking to what looked like doctors. Her face drooped like a bulldog's. Hair that could be mistaken for a hawk's pole-top nest gave her a bit of a madwoman's air, but even the medical men listened to her speak.

As night fell people filtered back into the connected buildings and gathered around the tiny charcoal stoves on the grounds that provided heat for cooking and boiling laundry.

The talkative in the refuge discussed either Tulsa—when it would finally be cleared so people could return to see what was left of their lives—or the possibilities of finding work far from the fighting in Texas or Arkansas.

Then there were the doomsayers: "They'll be back," one man said, shirtless and with Kurian service pins on his suspenders. "No such thing as 'safe.' 'Scorched earth,' the order said, and just because the flame ain't touched you yet, doesn't mean it's not burning."

Even in the facility's new role as improvised refugee squat, Valentine had to admire the cleanliness of the rooms, painted in an institutional color he called "muted lime." The medicine cabinet in the shared bathroom held a couple of tonics for Duvalier's on-again, off-again stomach problems, antiseptic ointments, and a thermometer. The only disappointment was the ashy-tasting toothpaste.

They went to their individual beds with lights out—Nancy's had its own generators, but fuel for them had to be conserved. Valentine hid under a sheet, a little ashamed of the state of his underclothes. *Maybe a visit to the swap is in order after all.* Jules produced a bottle of Kurian rum and they passed it back and forth. Valentine refused more than two swigs.

"You need to be careful with alcohol in the KZ," Valentine said. "They say a little helps cut lifesign by relaxing you. Whether it's true or no, I'd rather be alert."

"This isn't the Kurian Zone. Not anymore."

Though she asked, he didn't want to talk about the rising in Little Rock. Instead he shifted the conversation to their childhoods. He told her a little about growing up in Minnesota—to an Iowan, nothing but hairy, thick-blooded barbarians lived north of Rochester—and in between swallows she painted a picture of the privileged life of a Ringwinner's daughter.

"I was supposed to go into the church," came the voice from the darkness. If anything, her diction became more precise as she drank. "I was a youth-vanguard leader, of course. Then it was army, church, or industry. Since Ving Junior went army, and Kirbee got her master's in production, we had that dried-up old prune of an priest sitting me down for improvement, effort, humility, care, and acceptance." Valentine's ears picked up movement in the darkness as she listed the church's virtues. You were supposed to touch forehead, right shoulder, right hip, left hip, and finally left shoulder as you said them. Her words faded as she spoke. "Man in his unnatural state. Spiritual recycle. Can't believe how much of that crap I remember. Didn't even try to learn it, but I can still recite the Truths word for word."

Valentine listened to her breathing until he too drifted away.

He woke, a little, when she got up to use the bathroom. He woke further when she returned and slipped into his bed. She nuzzled his ear.

"Object?" she asked.

Her clean-smelling skin enticed, and her hand knew what it was doing. He felt an erect nipple against his tricep. "Ask a silly question . . . ," he said.

She tested him with her grip. "Nice answer. Not a bit silly. Drop in."

He recognized another Iowaism, but one Valentine had never heard breathed in his ear, only secondhand from guy talk over beers.

"Not so fast," Valentine said, beginning a series of kisses down her neck. He hadn't touched a woman in over a year. Might as well enjoy the opportunity.

Spent, aroused, and spent again, he slept deep and hard in the sweat and slickness of their lovemaking after she retreated to her bed.

Gunfire and screams woke him. For three terrible seconds he was back on Big Rock Hill the night the Reapers dropped from the sky. *Waking from a dream, or waking into another nightmare?*

Jules sat up in her bed, the flush of lovemaking replaced by an awful pallor.

"Reapers!" came a shout from the hallway.

Her eyes, searchlights of fear, turned to him.

Valentine felt them. His old comrades in the Wolves called it the "Valentingle" and trusted it more than Valentine did. Sometimes he could detect a Reaper with pinpoint accuracy; other times he could walk right over one without sensing it. Now they seemed to fill his whole mental horizon, could be a dozen or more.

"Might mean nothing," he lied. "Every time there's confusion in the dark, someone shouts 'Reapers.' You have a weapon?"

"Beretta. Bag on the chair."

"Get it." She moved for her pants. "No, get it first, then get dressed."

Valentine retrieved his .45 ACP, the weight a calming comfort in his hand. Two more shots, this time from the front of the building where he'd passed the tin stars. "Drop lifesign and—"

"I don't know how!" she said, her words half-strangled with fear.

Jesus, Duvalier—

Reapers hunted using lifesign, an energy created by the vital aura their masters desired. Humans produced more than livestock; livestock produced more than crops. . . .

He checked the window, saw a family hightailing it across the fields, each holding a child over a shoulder as they ran, a dog keeping worried circles.

Over by the barn, a woman ran in the same direction. A shadow, moving so fast it seemed a trick of the eye, followed her across the field and engulfed her.

Or did it?

"Crouch, both hands on the floor," he told her, shutting and locking the doors to the hallway and shared bathroom. She complied quickly enough. He'd been told contact with the earth acted like the ground on a lightning rod, but he suspected it was bullshit. But it was a relaxing pose, you didn't feel as vulnerable as you would lying down, and there's the tendency to shift nervously when standing.

"Picture your whole life folding up, into a box," he said, hard ears searching the building. Still no destructive noises, but a lot of consternation in the halls, a confused babble.

"They'll locate. They sense pregnant women best!"

A beeping racket from a few crackly loudspeakers made her jump. "Emergency Alert Code Black Multiple. Code Black Multiple."

That doesn't sound good.

"What's that?" Jules said.

"Never mind. Fold up pictures of your family, friends, memories, whatever, and put it in a mental box," Valentine said.

The loudspeakers shrieked one final "Stop!" and went dead.

"I don't see—"

"Keep your eyes shut! What kind of flower do you like?"

"Flower?"

"Picture your favorite flower."

"Daisy," she said.

"Great, a daisy. There's just a daisy, nothing else, blackness and a daisy. It's a big one. You're keeping your eyes on the yellow center."

"Yes," she said, sounding a little better.

"Now it starts to spin slowly, like a windmill. Oh so slowly."

"Yes," she said.

Screams and a crash from the center of the building.

"Never mind that." Valentine lowered his own lifesign and tried to open the window. It had been painted recently and was sticky.

"Speed the daisy up. It's spinning faster now."

She didn't respond.

"Slow it down now. Slower and slower and slower." He lowered his voice. "Slower than that windmill, slower than a second hand on a watch, slow it so it's moving like a minute hand. You can barely see it, it's moving so slowly." More screams, this time female. The deep blast of a shotgun and running feet in the hall.

He unwrapped a souvenir from his time with the Kentucky worm riders. It was a short, stout hand ax, blade tapering into a legworm hook. He pulled on his pants and laced his boots.

For Valentine, lowering lifesign meant taking a big, bright blue ball that represented his consciousness and slowly shrinking it to a point like a star, which he watched with all the concentration of an astronomer at a telescope eyepiece.

"Keep watching the petals turn," he whispered. He reached up and gripped a chamois-wrapped handle from beneath his pillow and drew it close beside.

A heavy tread in the hall and she groped for his hand.

"Turning," he whispered.

A door torn open with a sharp metallic cry. Another scream.

"Turning," he repeated. He tried a fearful whining sound in his throat, trying to imitate a whimpering dog.

Something jiggled the doorknob.

More shots from the hall, and heavy, pounding footsteps as the Reaper ran toward the door . . .

"Turning," Valentine whispered.

Five minutes later the noises faded into a last distant scream.

"Safe?" Jules asked.

"We are. They're not . . ."

The old Cat Everready got to be an old Cat by hunting Reapers only in the daylight, when their connection to their master was weakest, or after they fed, when they, or more accurately the master Kurian animating them, got dopey from the aura feed.

The Valentingle weakened and diffused, throbbing on and off in his head like a bulb on fading current.

He stepped into the hall.

Carnage was the only word for it. Bodies, some still dripping and twitching, lay in the hallway, or had been flung across gurneys. Crushed necks and heads mostly. Some bore wet blossoms on their shirts from punches that had caved in rib cages.

Valentine followed the pointy, bloody boot prints down the hall, found the corpse of the person that had saved him with gunfire. The teenage girl who'd checked him in at the desk was folded around her broken ArmaLite, her auburn hair bound up with a cheerful, polka-dot scrunchie. She had a hole at the base of her throat, paying for the insult of her .223 shells with coin drawn straight from the aorta.

Valentine shut her glassy eyes, turned her on her back, and straightened her, tenderly placed her heels together and her palms at her side, put her riven weapon on her chest, and covered her with a bedsheet from one of the gurneys.

He walked out the exit door at the end of the hall. The walk turned into a trot, which turned into a run, which turned into a sprint, ax held like a runner's baton in his left hand, pistol in his right.

The cool night air hit him like a slap, and like a slap, it brought him out of the moment's madness.

These weren't "wild" Reapers, sometimes sent into the Free Territory to brutalize and maul, little dandelion seeds of chaos drifting where instinct took them. These Reapers had gone through Nancy's quickly and methodically, trying to cram as much death into a given number of minutes as possible.

Which probably meant they had a long trip back. Perhaps as far as Tulsa?

Valentine's cat-sharp eyes picked out motion at the outbuildings. A

Reaper, moving south, hopping from rooftop to rooftop as it tried to sense if any beings hid within.

He pulled back the hammer on his gun, then dropped it and the pickax on the ground. He sank so his knees hid them.

"Why?" he bawled. Not much acting required for this. He searched the low spring clouds. "Why us?" He covered his eyes, decided not to sob—there was such a thing as overdoing it.

The Reaper didn't even bother to cut back so it could approach him from behind. It approached a little off kilter, shifting this way and that, reaching too far with its lower limbs stepping toward ten and two rather than straight ahead.

Valentine smelled the cordite on it. He hoped this particular one had killed the girl. Dots of blood decorated its face, a sticky pox. Old Father Wolf was proved right again: Enough hate and you felt no fear, just nervous anticipation.

It planted itself in front of him.

"some prayers are answered," it said, sibilants sliding out of its mouth like a snake's. *"look up and see."*

Valentine knew better than to meet its eyes. He waited for the knees to bend and rolled sideways, shoved the gun almost into the folds of its robe, and fired.

Bullets wouldn't kill it, but the kinetic energy could sometimes stagger Reapers. Even with the powerful handgun cartridges slamming into it, it still reacted aggressively, swung at his head with a scooping motion that would have sent his skull spinning like a field goal kick.

Except Valentine was already behind it.

He buried the pick end of his hand ax into its upper back, where the nerve trunks gathered on their way to the armored brain case. He got lung instead, heard a sucking sound as flesh closed around the point.

It spun, jerking the handle of his pick out of his hands, and both opponents lurched off-balance. Its elbows clicked backward and its arms reversed themselves in a ghastly fashion as it sought the pick.

Valentine restored his equilibrium first, dropped, and sighted under the jawline. He put his remaining bullets into the underside of its chin.

The Reaper went mad, tore the pick free, and took off running, a blind flight with its hand held in front of it and the other holding its jaw on.

Valentine reloaded, retrieved his pickax, and trotted after it. It dived into the culvert beside the road and began to slither south at a pace he could just keep up with if he ran.

The Kurian clearly wanted his puppet back, even with a string or two cut. Had it been willing to sacrifice its avatar, it could have chased him down and killed him, hunting by heartbeat if nothing else. He paused in a tomato garden and calmed himself, tried to sense the emanations from the Reapers, caught a flicker off in the direction of the settlement garbage heap.

Valentine picked out a line of trees and used them as cover for an approach, hoping there wasn't a sniper or two guarding the gathering. He heard engines and movement, and risked a run.

He broke for the top of the low hill that kept the dump's sight and smell away from Nancy's, got up just in time to see a truck pulling a horse trailer, turning onto a brush-choked access road. A cut-down Humvee with a toothy brush cutter on the front and a winged Southern Command battle star painted on its side led it down the road.

You could pack a lot of Reapers in that trailer. An unpleasant surprise for the soldier who opened the door to check inside.

The vehicles, driving without lights—if they still worked—disappeared.

A roadblock would be helpful somewhere down that overgrown alley, but the false-flagged Hummer could just pull a disabled—

A blatting broke out from the garbage heap and Valentine saw a man in cammies with a scoped rifle slung across the handlebars of a dirt bike take off after the vehicles up the road. A cold wave passed over Valentine. Probably the sniper, tired and anxious after the operation and listening to the sounds of his buddies driving off, hadn't been searching the hill line or the trees in the direction of Nancy's through his night sight.

Had anyone in Nancy's called for help as the Reapers attacked?

They arrived within a couple of hours, a thin string of cavalry on horseback, followed by more troops on mountain bikes, riding in a pair of lines on either side of the road. He watched them the way a rancher might watch a cattle drive—making guesses as to health, morale, and training from everything from the condition of their bootheels to how they shaved their sideburns. Someone in Southern Command knew his business. Valentine guessed this to be a garrison from one of the supply depots supporting operations west of Tulsa.

He sent Jules over to tell the captain in charge. They could radio to scouts around Tulsa. Even if the vehicles couldn't be intercepted, the scouts might be able to track them to whatever hidey-hole they sought. The woman possessed an agile enough mind, and he could forgive a panic attack with a Reaper scratching at the door.

Valentine helped collect bodies. The Reapers had struck hard and fast, over a hundred deaths and a handful more wounded who would probably die in the coming hours from assorted traumas.

He mopped his brow after lifting one of the starred lawmen into an awning-draped wagon. He was happy to take part in the gory work; nothing quite took the spirit out of a man than having to pile the bodies of friends like cordwood, and as a stranger here he didn't know faces or names. The nasty business had to be taken care of both hastily and reverently.

Shadows on the road. Valentine looked up, saw the captain with a corporal and three soldiers trailing behind, Jules bringing up the rear, probably going inside to find Nancy. He lifted the camphor-dipped bandanna he kept over his face while moving bodies, and covered his features, wishing he'd grabbed a hat.

They turned for him. *The hell?*

Jules looked anxious. Was the captain going to get another paragraph added to his Q-file by bringing in an outlaw? Valentine went around to the other side of the cart and stuck a stiffened arm back under the awning.

"Excuse me, Mister," the captain said, a little Kansas twang in his voice. He smelled like horse sweat and service aftershave.

"Yes, Cap?" Valentine said.

"Major Valentine," a man with corporal stripes said, saluting. His hedgerow eyebrows had collected some road dust. "Sorry to disturb, I'm—"

"Tonley, from the Razors. Corporal Tonley now, by the look of it."

"Recognized your walk, sir. Saw you goin' up toward the buildings."

"Glad to see you again, and well. Or should I be?"

"No, Major," the captain cut in. "Nothing like that. I just wanted a chance to shake your hand."

Jules let out a deep breath.

"Glad it's that way." Valentine toweled off assorted flavors of filth and shook hands all around.

"Oh, you thought—," Tonley said.

"Hell no. Hell no, sir!" an unfamiliar private added. "Any sooner tries that, he'll have to walk back to the depot with his bike shoved up his ass."

"I beg your pardon," Valentine said. "Sooner?"

Tonley chuckled. "Oklahoma mounted. Mounted on bikes, that is. Get there sooner than the next guy and all that."

Tonley kept looking at his jaw as he explained the term and Valentine tapped the fracture point and said, "A nasty left hook." Unsaid was that the pugilist had been a Reaper, hunting him and Gail Post in the hills of Kentucky.

Valentine was invited to offer an opinion on tracking the Reaper-bearing vehicles, and the captain broke out his map. The party broke up within minutes, leaving Valentine with the feeling that he'd just got up from a long meal with old friends. Such was the nature of Southern Command's terrible, tasking comradeship.

"Sorry about that," Jules said. "I tried to tell them it was some big mistake, but they insisted on talking to you. They told me they just wanted to shake hands, but Duvalier said—"

"It turned out all right. But you needn't have worried, even if it hadn't. I would have gone quietly. They're Southern Command's boys."

"Meal break?"

"I won't feel like eating till tonight," Valentine said.

"Oh. Of course."

"Mind if I ask you something, though?"

She blanked her face, wary. "You bet."

"What was that about pregnancy last night? You're not expecting, are you?"

She glanced around, as though searching for an escape. "I was scared. I had a close call a little while ago."

"If I'd known you weren't on the pill," Valentine said. "Dumb chance to take last night."

"It's a chance, all right," she said.

"I'm used to riddles from the Lifeweavers, or in the Kurian Zone. But not from fellow Cats."

Her shoulders sagged. "Can we go somewhere and talk?"

All the music and liveliness had vanished from the bar. Its door had been torn from the hinges. One of the bartender girls scrubbed a stain on the floor, and the other's eyes were downcast and red.

They had free Lemonclear, a sour concoction posing as lemonade, thanks to the soldiers. Southern Command's forces were departing, the bikers down the road and the horsemen cross-country. Before they'd left they'd put tabs of Lemonclear in five-gallon plastic jugs of the local water. The medicine both killed bacteria and water parasites and gave it a mild flavor.

They found a quiet corner out of hearing of the bartenders. Valentine skipped the polite talk. "Get it out. You'll feel better."

Jules' hands went to her kneecaps. "It's like this. You know we can't find the Lifeweavers, right?"

"I've heard rumors," Valentine said. No reason for her to know his mission.

"I feel like a creep. We should have just told you, but Ali said you'd have more fun the other way."

She expected a "Told me what?" so Valentine offered it.

"It's my way of, hopefully, becoming a Cat. I know the Lifeweavers do something to us, change our physical makeup somehow. They trigger a switch that's already inside us. That's the way it was explained to me, anyway."

"I don't think anyone really knows," Valentine said.

"Like blood from Bears, a transfusion heals stuff, practically makes a miracle. Or the way a couple of Wolves have sex and their baby turns out able to smell really well. Seems like if Southern Command wants more Hunters, it's up to the Hunters to make them."

Jesus, we're being bred like foxhounds, Valentine thought.

"There's also the Dulcimet effect," Jules said.

"I've never heard of that," Valentine said.

"This doc, Dulcimet, with the Miskatonic discovered it. He did this study on a Cat from the Yazoo Delta who got a couple of teenage girls pregnant. Women make better Cats, generally, just like men make better Bears. It turns out that when a woman is carrying a Hunter's baby, sometimes it has an effect on the mother, since she and the baby sort of exchange blood while she's carrying. That's the Dulcimet effect."

"So the idea is, I get you pregnant, maybe you turn Cat, and Southern Command gets another potential Hunter in nine months. What do they do with the baby?"

"Secret. They have to guard them from the Kurians."

Valentine sighed. At least he'd had a choice when he became a Wolf. Or had he?

"Anyway," she continued. "There are only a couple of male Cats. They've been looking for you for a while now, hoping that you'd get one of the volunteers pregnant."

She laid the tiniest extra stress on the word "volunteer."

"Was it real volunteering, or are you being a good soldier?" Valentine asked.

"Oh, it was real. Ali had me meet Stykes . . . er, Major Styachowski. She painted quite a picture. Also, your rendezvous here was right for my cycle. They're keeping close track of that."

"I suppose they have to," Valentine said, feeling a bit like the butt of a cosmic joke.

"It's been almost a day. Maybe we should give it another go. The more sperm, the better."

They tried again. But Duvalier had been right: Knowing took a lot of the fun out of it.

Duvalier returned two days later with Styachowski and another fit-looking young woman wearing Southern Command Labor Corps fatigues and teardrop sunglasses. The last served as driver for a post-'22 flatbed, a high-axled transport vehicle made out of the odds and ends of other heavy-duty diesels. They were bringing a new generator and another radio set to replace equipment smashed in the Reaper raid.

A footlocker strapped to the rear seat held the gear Valentine requested. Styachowski carried a waterproof file folder with maps and basic information about his destination.

Duvalier hopped down from the webbing holding the generator, where she'd ridden, using the straps as a combination hammock and harness. She looked like a hungry, road-weary hitchhiker, but her eyes were as bright as ever.

"Heard about the trouble," she said.

"Jules and I came through for the team," Valentine said. In other circumstances he would have added an exaggerated wink, but Nancy's was almost a ghost town now. Many of the survivors of the raid had fled east after the dead were buried in their common grave. Some of those buried had been decorated Quislings, killed in some final fit of pique from the almost-vanquished Kurians of Tulsa.

Styachowski slicked back her moon white hair, impatient.

Duvalier twirled her sword-stick on its leather thong. "They think they've got it tracked down to central Tulsa. Storm sewers maybe. I'm going to go poke around a little. Be nice to get at least one before it has a chance to bolt."

The Kurians were near-legendary escape artists.

"When are you heading west, Val?" Styachowski asked.

"When the right convoy comes through."

"Spare me a couple more days?"

"Sure."

"Val, this is Darlene," Styachowski said, introducing the slim-hipped, curly-haired driver. "She's been selected as a potential, an aspirant for either Wolf or Cat. We were hoping you could find time to take her into the field for a couple of days, up toward the Zone but not in it. Teach her a little. Then we'd like your opinion."

"'Lina' for short," Darlene said.

Valentine wondered what kind of eyes waited behind the driver's sunglasses, and if she'd been counting the days since the beginning of her last menstrual cycle. "Glad to be of service. As a favor to you and Ali."

Five

Borders, Barters, and Bandits, April: Because the Free Territory and Kurian Zone find their lands subject to change of ownership, and the occasional proposal to sit down and draw up peace plans meets only with ridicule, there are few well-defined borders. Even a widely acknowledged geographic obstacle such as the Mississippi River, serving as the unofficial eastern border of the UFR, is rather porous to penetration by small parties. David Valentine crossed it a number of times in the course of his duties as a Wolf or Cat.

In the flats of the high, dry country around the Oklahoma Panhandle there's no such divider. Only a depopulated strip, perhaps fifty miles wide, where farming settlements emptied over the summer of 2074, once the locals learned that the UFR would advance no farther.

Some say the dry, flat plains unsettled soldiers used to bushwhacking their enemies from hilltop and timber. Others insist that the Kurians of the old USA's Southwest, one of the better-organized and more cooperative collections of the New Order, saw the coming threat and launched a Grog-led counterattack that sent the Texas and Ozark natives tumbling back. Still others say Southern Command ran out of plan and logistics, growing fearful at the decidedly mixed results of the revolts between the Platte and Red rivers, which their assault was supposed to support.

Historical bickering aside, the region between the Kurian and UFR watch points is the home of rabbit, coyotes, and hawks, surveyed by high-flying Gargoyles during the day and aura-sensing Reapers at night. Remnants of the cash crops of the region—wheat, soy, sorghum, and barley—can still be found growing wild, sometimes grazed down by small herds of wild sheep and wily, testy goats.

The old interstate, shooting east-west through the flat with a bend here and there placed by engineers to keep motorists from growing hypnotized by the road, still sees a convoy every week or so. The Kurians allow the traffic so that their favored supporters might have luxuries brought in from far away, with the thrilling but harmless taint of black market goods, and the Free Territory needs the gear and medicines the inevitable smuggling compartments contain. The third winner in the arrangement is the road patrols, who inevitably take away a bottle of liquor or a carton of cigarettes as they carry out everything from fugitive searches to safety inspections on the road traffic.

David Valentine waited quietly in the backseat of the Land Rover, watching the checkpoint soldiers inspect the convoy behind.

The convoy had pulled off the road in the vast, empty plains at a watchtower-flanked checkpoint, the first and most important on their ride through the Southwest, according to the driver. A slight ridge, thick with spring prairie flowers, was noticeable only because the rest of the topography was so flat.

His "overwatch car" was the second of the string of nineteen vehicles in the convoy, not counting the motorcycles riding at the head and tail. Road Chief Lautenberg, a good friend of the Hobarth clan, signed on "Max Argent" when his convoy stopped for an overnight at Nancy's. The stolid Lautenberg, so phlegmatic he might be mistaken for one of the uniformed dummies that filled out the real warriors in the big army truck at the center of the convoy, had looked him up and down with his one good eye, and assigned him to one of the combat teams.

It had taken Valentine some weeks to find a ride, spending hours reading and waiting at Nancy's. Though he kept himself clean-shaven, his legworm leathers and their armored plates polished, and his boots beyond even a labor-corps fatigue sergeant's reproach, several smaller convoys weren't willing to take on a stranger.

When a big convoy finally arrived it was bound for Central America, and the second, riding in a series of converted school buses, gave him the willies. They purported to be musicians and dancers who sold protein powder and water filters during the day and performed for tips at night. Despite their promises of a substantial reward in the payout end of the trip in exchange for light guard work, Valentine wondered if they weren't "headhunters," especially after he heard the quiet rattle of chains beneath the seats of their vehicles. A man could get rich bringing warm bodies to the Kurians, and Valentine guessed that the attractive slatterns who rode in the front minivan served as bait for the unwary. The whole group had a quiet, dangerous air that put him off.

The next had a desperate, last-chance feel to it, and the owner and all the drivers looked hungry. Valentine began to feel like Goldilocks, unable to find a convoy that was just right. Then Lautenberg came in like a thunderstorm of diesel exhaust and rubber.

At first Valentine rode guard with the "back team," a group of drivers in an armored minibus who slept or played cards while they waited to replace others when they came off shift. After he brought down a buck grazing in a field from 250 yards at dawn, Lautenberg transferred him to the overwatch "Rover."

The "Rover" was a high-clearance four-wheel drive, panels long since replaced by welded corrugated aluminum and old bulletproof vests. It had thick off-road tires, spotlights, a winch, and a cupola complete with bullet shield and a venerable heavy machine gun called the poker.

Its sights were made of carved Reaper teeth and wire.

Valentine patted his gun in its bracket on the back of the driver's seat. Styachowski had answered his request for a reliable, accurate, but not threatening-looking carbine with her usual precision. She'd shown up with a Steyr Scout "Viper," a deadly little killer with a forward-mounted 2.5× sight, flash suppressor, and eighteen-round minidrum feeding the oversized bolt action.

Valentine especially admired the scope. Your eye could wander to find the target, and then—as you aimed—your eye glided into the magnified image as if drawn there, with the weapon already lined up.

They'd supplied him with four boxes of ammunition for it, and a special little five-bullet leather holder. A note accompanied them, from a weapons researcher at the Miskatonic. He explained that the five shells were a new, experimental delivery method for Quickwood, suspending a distillate of the sap in a capsule that would be broken as the armor-piercing bullet fragmented, hopefully inside a Reaper. "Write me and let me know results, good or bad," the note ended.

Valentine wondered at that. If the results were bad, he probably wouldn't live to write the note.

New steel-tipped hiking boots, a hard-frame pack, thermal underwear, a bamboo sleeping mat, a thick wool scarf, leather gloves, mittens, a compass, and survival gear filled out the rest of the footlocker she'd brought. She also provided him with a thick nylon laborer's girdle that could be popped open to reveal two dozen gold coins. Resting in sawdust padding were six bottles of bourbon, and a minitelescope. Nothing had any tagging or labeling to identify it as originating with Southern Command. Even his ammunition was in Kansas City's Zero-load boxes, one of the biggest armorers in the Midwest.

Best of all, she'd found his sword. He'd asked for a similar blade to the one he'd carried on his first mission as a Cat, never expecting for his original to show up, sharpened and in a new stiffened black leather sheath.

Who knew what warehouse it had rested in since the day he, Duvalier, and Ahn-Kha left for his long mission into the Kurian Zone in search of a half-legendary weapon to defeat the Reapers that turned out to be Quickwood? Duvalier guessed that Dix Welles had buried it along with the other Cats' left possessions when Solon took over. The cache had evidently been recovered since then, and probably sat in some warehouse with his books and a few other personal items, a curiosity on some long inventory list.

Valentine watched the Quislings bearing ROAD RANGER patches on their shoulders conduct their inspection. Ostensibly the convoy carried pumping equipment, high-voltage cable, machine tools, and a dozen other industrial necessities. But behind the heavy equipment that required a forklift or crane rested cases of sealed black-label bourbon, boxes of chocolate, jewelry, furs, and precision optics.

The Quislings at the checkpoint wore dark khaki uniforms and bandannas. Most had cheap plastic sand-and-sun goggles. High observation towers and earthworks bristling with machine guns and 20mm cannon covered the inspection siding.

An officer with a red pillbox hat, thick with Kurian service pins, stuck his head in the window, examining Valentine's profile.

"I need that man out, please," Pillbox Hat told the driver. He pointed at Valentine. "Cuff him for now."

Valentine's back went clammy. Had a wanted poster made it into the Southwest? He could confuse the issue for a few days with his false IDs, but capture would mean—

"Okay, boss," the driver said as the man in the shotgun seat pressed a button three times on his belt walkie-talkie. "Get out, Max. The girls here want to look into those pretty brown eyes."

Valentine complied, leaving his weapons in their brackets, and as they snapped the cuffs on and patted him down, more Quislings gathered to watch.

"You ever go by the name David Valentine, chief?" Pillbox Hat asked.

Valentine just breathed, centering himself, pulling in lifesign. It kept the Reapers away, but it was also calming. "No, sir, don't know him."

"I didn't say if you knew him."

"Sorry, sir."

Lautenberg walked up, moving at a pace just short of a trot, his lead rig driver just behind. He approached the officer in the pillbox hat. "What now, Hopgood?"

"We're detaining one of your men so we can run some prints. He fits a description. Indianish, black hair, scarred, 'bout the right height and weight."

"Detain? How long's that going to take?"

"A day or two at most. You can move on."

"Argent, you wanted for something?" Lautenberg said.

"Some guy named Valentine," Valentine said, hoping he could still brazen it out. "All red man heap look alike, Road Chief."

Lautenberg planted his feet and crossed his arms. "This convoy isn't leaving a man behind."

A sergeant passed Valentine's papers over to Hopgood with a shrug.

"Up to you," Hopgood said. "Bring the wagon," he yelled across the gravel to his idling men. "We'll take him to Blackwater Holing."

"The hell you are," Lautenberg said. "Hopgood, I've been easy on you because you're new, and I don't like making enemies. But wouldn't it be kinda dumb for some fugitive to pass right through one spot he's sure to be looked at?"

"This guy's clever. He took out a whole regiment of TMCC and blew that big Mississippi Grog cannon into orbit."

"Be news to his mother," Lautenberg said. "Until she passed, Max here was taking care of her every day of his life. Kansas militia trusted him with a gun, I know that. My Ingrid's married to Tom Stormcloud over in Topeka. He's Stormcloud's cousin."

Valentine had no idea what spring this torrent of bullshit was coming from, but it fitted his faked papers like a jigsaw piece. Lautenberg had just glanced at them briefly back at Nancy's.

"Now, you can detain this kid," Lautenberg said. "I can wait here, getting madder and madder every hour. And when General Cox in Albuquerque runs out of black-label bourbon and has to listen to those three coochies of his bitch about how they're all outta lipstick and undies, well, I might just call you a bad name or two when he asks what was keeping me. You ever talked to Cox when he's bone-dry on whiskey?"

Hopgood looked from his thick sheaf of wanted posters at Valentine, then at Lautenberg, and back again.

Lautenberg patted his hip pocket. "Lord, Corporal Guadalco, you smoked three cigarettes with Max here last October. You showed him a picture of your kids."

"Oh yes, I remember, remember very well," a corporal in a non-regulation straw hat spoke up.

Hopgood wilted. "I'll cut him loose this time, Lautenberg. But your reputation's riding on this."

"My reputation's riding on about three hundred tires," Lautenberg said. "I just want them spinning again."

Valentine felt the cuffs come off, and showed his relief.

"Thank you, sir," he said to Hopgood.

"Smile, Hoppy, and have a cigar," Lautenberg said, extracting a gleaming silver case. "You road rangers know I'm just trying to get from A to B and back to A. Smuggling fugitives doesn't come between A and B. Or A and Z for that matter—it's a whole 'nother alphabet."

As the groups parted, Lautenberg offered Valentine a wink, and slipped something into Guadalco's hand as they shook.

And with that, the convoy got moving again. The scout cycles blatted out first, then the combat craft; the big tow trucks, capable of pulling a disabled truck or moving an unexpected obstacle with their thick cable winches; Lautenberg's Winnebago office on wheels; the "money trucks" with the tanker and "chuck wagon" RV guarded by a truck full of dummy soldiers; a few "gypsy" vans traveling with the convoy for protection like pilot fish hovering close to a shark; more cargo trucks; then the rear guard: the "remount" truck and more cycles.

"The Spikes must really have it in for that Valentine fella," the heavyset commander of the overwatch car said. By "Spikes" he meant the Kurians; their towers did look a little like spikes, glimpsed from a distance.

He had thoughtful eyes and a patchy beard. The rest of the car, Zuniga at the wheel and Swell at the ring gun, called their commander "Salsa." He spread hot sauce from an endless supply of tiny red bottles he kept in a machine-gun belt case on everything he ate, save fruit.

"Nice of the road chief to stand up for me. I was in a cell once before. Thought I'd cashed out."

"What were you in for?"

"Fighting and public drunkenness."

"That where you got your face rearranged?" Zuniga asked.

"Yes," Valentine said, which was almost true.

"What you guys talking about?" Swell called down from the ring gun. Swell loved riding in the wind, leaning on the canvas-covered poker, but always wanted details of in-cab conversations shouted up to him.

"We're talkin' about how your mother undercuts all the other whores," Salsa shouted up. Then to the others: "I swear to God, I should make him drive so he doesn't miss nuthin'."

"Except he bitches about how he feels cooped up in here," Zuniga said, leaning over to pass gas at a volume that rivaled that of the motorcycle sixty meters ahead.

"Phew, Max, I think this kid could drop a Hood with that," Salsa said.

"What's that?" Swell shouted.

Valentine winked at Salsa as he tied Swell's shoelaces together.

And with that, David Valentine passed out of Oklahoma.

Brief thunderstorms drenched the convoy.

"If you make this a habit, you'll learn that this is the best time of year Southwest," Salsa said.

Valentine had to agree. The forests, whose trees felt spaced out and airy compared with the thickets of the Ozarks, were cool and breezy and the dry grasses of the range country were bright with flowers, yellows and pinks and blues that attracted butterflies. Sadly, many of the latter ended up in gooey, colorful pieces on the windshield and grille of the 4×4.

Valentine, with little to do except watch the terrain roll under their wheels, enjoyed the trip. Except for train travel, this was the fastest he'd ever eaten miles.

There were stops, of course, for meals and refueling, and long detours around Kurian Zones or demolished bridges and culverts. He trotted around the vehicles, exercising his unused legs, marveling at the distance they'd come in a few short days.

At the overnights the convoy pulled off into lonely road stops, throwing a wide circle around Albuquerque, where Kurians who were at odds with the rest of the Aztlan Confederation were famous for letting strangers enter, but not leave. The road chief avoided towns as they crossed New Mexico. Towns brought local police to the vehicles like thirsty ticks looking for blood. New Universal Church missions and *monastis* provided safety of another sort, but the churchmen in their tube-steel clerical collars (grades of metal differentiated just what the ascetics had given up to more fully devote themselves to the betterment of mankind) were a more hygienic and annoying version of the lawmen. At least the lawmen didn't subject one to lectures about reproductive responsibilities as they took their graft.

"A tree must be rooted to grow strong in safety!" one wild-haired monk intoned as the maintenance teams replaced lost tires in the Cíbola foothills. He climbed a light pole to be better heard. His monastery had a patchwork look to it; this station was probably an exile for the head cases of the church. "Wandering seed is lost in the wind."

"Or lost in the joy girls in Los Angeles," a truck driver muttered to Valentine. He spit a mouthful of tobacco in the direction of the Easter Island–like Reaper-face set looking down on the monastery's wash well. "Ever hear about the Honeypot, pickup?" the driver asked.

"We have to get there first," Salsa said, interrupting. "Scouts are reporting some burned rigs in Holloweye Valley."

"We're too big for the Jaguars to try."

"I hope they know it as well as you," Salsa said. He turned and Valentine followed.

"Jaguars?"

"They wear bits of fur," Salsa said. "The big medicine guys wear spots. A successful warrior gets mountain lion skin, or wolf. The low-lifes have to make do with coyote. They're half-wild, worship those Reaper monoliths you see in this part of the country. They ain't after our gear or cargo, just our giblets. They think if they take lives, drink blood, they become as strong as the Reapers. Or turn into them."

Valentine searched the copper-dusted mountains of the Mogollon Rim ahead. The dry air gave the horizon a clarity that seemed to expand his personal patch of earth as it reduced his place in it. He felt rather like one of the valley butterflies, perhaps determinedly unaware of an approaching windshield.

"Will they keep off us?" Valentine asked.

"Depends. Some of the young men might be feeling their oats. Wish I could tell you more. All we got to go on is rumor. No one's lived in Holloweye Valley long enough to do any social studies."

"I didn't see that on the road map."

"It's unofficial, like Checkpoint Circlejerk back there. The valley's not a problem. It's the passes you have to watch. They'll roll a wreck down and try to cause an accident."

"Why Holloweye?"

Salsa probed an ear. "Let's hope we don't find out."

The bikers, skin almost as dark as their faded leathers, reported back as the convoy paused on a long turn looking down into the valley. While they refueled stomachs and tanks from chuck wagon and bowser, Road Chief Lautenberg held a meeting.

Salsa returned and put his crew back in the overwatch vehicle. "We're going to go clear the road while we still have daylight," he told his crew. Swell wiped his palm on his jeans as Salsa described their operation.

"The Jaguars have the road blocked good with wrecks. They ain't manning the barricade, but somebody launched off slingstones at the bikers while they checked for survivors. We're going to go in and cover the wreckers while they clear the road."

"Could they tell how they took out the wrecks?" Zuniga asked.

Salsa shrugged. "Looked like a big road accident, they said. No question, one vehicle blew up. I had dynamite lobbed at me a couple runs back when I was driving the tanker. Maybe they got lucky with a toss. Any more questions?"

"How many dead?" Valentine asked.

"They said it was a dozen at least. They're not even dried out yet."

Zuniga shook his head slowly. Salsa continued: "Yeah. They were about to cut the bodies down when the slingstones hit."

With two motorcycles riding scout, flanking the operation like prowling dogs under the perfect yellow of an Arizona sun, the two wreckers and Salsa's armed 4×4 approached the blockade at a creep. Valentine hung out one door by a safety strap, searching the road for signs of mining. Salsa did the same, from a slightly more conventional position in the passenger window.

The expedition stopped fifty yards from the blockade. Valentine smelled burning tire.

Vultures rose from the wrecks when Zuniga blasted the Rover's horn.

"Okay, Argent, go earn your coin," Salsa said as the vehicles halted.

"Seen-yority," Swell said, swinging the now-uncovered gun to cover the wrecks. "It's got its privileges."

Valentine trotted up the median of the highway with carbine held ready against his shoulder—there was precious little cover on the road itself, and if he had to go to ground, he at least wanted the dry-looking brush in between him and the Jaguars.

The eight bodies were laid out between the wrecks in a pattern that might have been trying to be a flower, or a boat propeller. All were hollow-socketed and opened at the rib cage. Valentine guessed that the heart and liver were missing at least, along with more obvious extractions of eyes, noses, and tongues. Taking a deep breath, he knelt beside one sandy-haired corpse and looked in the nose.

They'd spooned out a good deal of brain as well.

Valentine heard a flutter and whirled, but it was just a crow. The black bird opened its mouth, an angry *Kaww!* contesting the bodies.

Valentine paid it no attention and did a fast search of the trucks and vans. He found three more bodies, similarly picked at but not arranged in any fashion save what was needed for a quick extraction of organ meat.

He heard a chatter of machine-gun fire and the sudden gunning of a motorcycle. He hopped up in a pickup bed—the contents had been stripped as hastily and messily as the bodies—and saw one of the bikers taking off against a running, sun-browned figure. The runner had a bad limp, with blood and dirt caked on his leg.

The biker stopped his bike, lifted an oddly thick rifle, pumped its action three times, and fired. Valentine saw a thick dart blossom in the back of the runner, who flopped over again.

The biker answered a hoot from one of the wreckers with a wave of his leather cap, and turned his bike back for the road.

Somehow the Jaguar rose again, a thin spear lodged in a grooved thrower. Valentine brought up the Steyr and sighted on the dark blotch of armpit hair under the Jaguar's raised right arm. The gun boomed, startling more crows.

Valentine didn't watch the effect of his shot. Instead he scanned for more threats.

Valentine watched the misthrown spear change trajectory, from straight up to straight down. The biker glanced over his shoulder, turned his bike again, and made for the spot where the Jaguar fell. He raised himself in the saddle and bumped over the body in a figure-eight pattern, making sure this time. Valentine scanned the countryside, wondering if the wounded warrior had been sacrificed to draw the biker into a trap, but no other threats emerged from the brush and cacti.

With the killing that couldn't quite be labeled a skirmish over, Valentine waved the Rover forward, and Salsa gave the okay for the wreckers to come up.

Valentine grabbed a bungee cord and a shovel off a bracket on the back hatch of the Rover. Using the bungee around the ankles, he pulled the bodies one by one off the road, lining them up in the median. When the corpses were lined up, he loosened some soil with the pick end of his worm hook and threw loose dirt over the butchered collection.

Swell rinsed his mouth out with a canteen and spit onto the front windscreen. Zuniga activated the wipers. "You don't mean to bury all those bodies?"

"I do," Valentine said.

The bikers roared up, curious. "Hell, man, the birds and coyotes will take care of them with a lot less sweat," the fat one with the beard said.

Valentine ignored him.

The one who had chased after the Jaguar, a lean, greasy-haired man who looked as though he'd crossed New Mexico dragged by the bike rather than in the saddle, put his bike on its stand. "Coot, be a mensch for once," he growled. "Have a little respect."

The biker slid into the median and took up the pick. "Name's Loring," he said. "Zeb Loring."

"Max Argent," Valentine said. *"Mucho gusto."*

"Aye-yup," Loring said.

"Never met a Zeb before," Valentine said. "That short for Zebulon?"

Loring had his share of scars. His leathers were carefully stitched up, his face much less so. "My father never made it much past Genesis in the Bible. Mom was a rabbi outta New York. It was a compromise."

They moved on to another body. Valentine rolled a rock using his shovel as a lever. "You're a long way from the East."

"Aye-yup. You too, looks like. Those are Kentucky legworm leathers."

"That they are."

"Always thought those beasties were grand. You don't have to feed them gas and oil."

"Ever rode one?" Valentine asked.

"Naw. Too slow. I like to be on something that can outrun those damn golems."

Valentine grunted agreement. "Hey, lookit that," Loring said. He leaned the pickax against his knee and pointed up.

Valentine saw aircraft, in three groups, flying high toward the southwest.

"I bet Denver got hit again. That's the Flying Circus. They range all over the Southwest, set up temporary airfields on old roads."

"Pyp's Flying Circus?" Valentine asked, shading his eyes to take a look at the craft. He guessed they were at above ten thousand feet.

"That's what they're called. I saw a couple of them in their fancy leathers in a bar in Nogales once. Aye-yup. They're not ones for staying put either."

"What are you going to do when we hit LA?" Valentine asked.

"Celebrate. Then we might head up the valley to wine country. They do a few runs a year over the mountains to the Missouri and Arkansas riverheads. Good money guarding wine, and a flask out of the supply cask really makes dinner an experience." He mumbled a few words as Valentine covered a corpse with a thin layer of dirt. Valentine stood silent.

"I like the old words, don't you?" Loring said.

"Yes. Thanks for the help."

"Mucho gusto," Loring said.

With the wrecks out of the way, and their remaining fuel safely stowed in the tanks and drums of the bikes and wreckers, the vehicles reassembled in the formation they'd used as they approached the blockade. Valentine, sweaty from his exertions and moody because of the bodies, ate a salted hard-boiled egg after carefully washing his hands.

"You feel better?" Salsa asked.

"Pardon?"

Salsa threw his arm over the seat. "You feel better now that those bodies are buried? 'Cause it sure makes no difference to them."

"Nothing in my contract about leaving bodies in the sun," Valentine said.

"Coyotes will probably have them dug up by midnight," Zuniga said.

"What's that?" Swell shouted from the gun.

"Oh, for Kur's dark asshole," Salsa said. He poked his head out the window. "You're at the wheel next—hey!"

Valentine heard it too. A sputtering engine sounded overhead and Valentine marked a twin-engine plane, a dirty-clay color with a red stripe going up the tail like a hockey stick; it spewed white vapor from one engine and faint black puffs from the other as it passed overhead. The engine sounded stronger for a moment and the plane gained altitude, trying for the mountains to the west. Valentine watched as it shrank to a cross in the distance. Then it plunged, leveled off, and disappeared into the valley floor.

"That poor dumb bastard," Salsa said. "He should have set it down in the road by us."

Valentine, meanwhile, searched his map of the Southwest.

"He was trying to make it to his home airfield," Zuniga said.

"Are those the guys with the reward message on the backs of their jackets?" Valentine asked.

"Tempting, isn't it?" Salsa said. "But forget it, the Jaguars will have him by dark."

"How long would it take us to get to where he landed?" Valentine asked.

"I ain't even guesstimating. We're not risking the Rover."

"Then stop, please," Valentine said, feeling light-headed. "I'll go on foot."

"You're nuts," Swell shouted down from the gun.

"Now he can hear," Salsa said. "What about your contract, Argent?"

"I've got the option of breaking it. Please, stop the car."

Zuniga honked and the vehicles slowed, then stopped.

"You don't get paid, then," Salsa said.

"I'd appreciate an extra canteen and some of the freeze-dry," Valentine said.

"Hey, if this is about those bodies, I didn't mean to step on any religious practices. Running my mouth is just how I get to know a man. Nothing to kill yourself over."

Valentine got his gun, sword, and pack and tucked a few extra odds and ends in from the Rover's supplies: freeze-dried veggie packs—about as appetizing as a bathroom mat but full of vitamins—beef sticks, dried fruit. . . .

"Guy's nuts," Swell called to a grizzled mechanic leaning out of a tow truck window to watch. "He's going to go rescue that cloud jumper. Wants the ten grand in gold."

"Big money isn't worth getting dead over, kid," the mechanic advised.

Been a long time since anyone's called me kid, Valentine thought. But the strange clarity that came over him sometimes, the one that infected him when he went into Chicago after Molly, or struck off into the Nebraska sandhills to warn the trekkers against the general, or pushed him to save a wounded Grog who would become his best friend—Valentine felt his eyes go wet at the memory of Ahn-Kha—told him he was doing the right thing.

Sergeant Patel used to talk about a third eye capable of perceiving the invisible. Valentine wondered if there was a third ear, hearing the whispers of guardian angels.

A motorcycle engine blatted and Loring sat his bike next to him as Valentine marked a reference point for the fallen aircraft. The bike growled like a threatening watchdog.

"You're not," Loring said.

"I am. Interested in making a Troy?"

"I'm not parking three butts on my bike for an off-road trip to Neverland."

"I just want you to get me to that airplane."

Loring looked at the sun. "Let's see the color of your gold."

Valentine reached into his belt and palmed one of his coins. He passed it over.

"That thing with the bodies wasn't an act, I hope. If this is some fancy plan to get me out so you can debit my bike—"

Valentine checked the buckles on his pack and the strap fixing his legworm pickax. "I arranged for the plane to go down just so I could get your ride?"

"Right. Sorry. Paranoid is the best way to stay alive when you road it for a living."

"No offense."

"Give my regards to Lautenberg," Valentine told Salsa. "I'll either meet you guys tomorrow when you run the valley or dog southwest."

"You a crusader, Argent, or just greedy?"

"A little of both," Valentine said.

Loring exchanged knuckles with his fellow biker, and edged forward on his seat. "Hang your pack there," he said, indicating a little backrest just above the taillight. "You can put the gun and the giblet prodder on the front rack, if you like."

Quick-release plastic snaps secured the gear there. With that, Valentine climbed on and they were off, back into the once-fertile valley.

Loring gave him a quick lesson on how and when to lean in turns, where to put his feet when they stopped the bike, and what to do in case of attack: "Hug me like an ass bandit. You come off, I'm not turning round."

They stopped once while still on the highway to reconnoiter from a slight hill, and Valentine pointed to where he marked the crash site.

"If you want to take a leak, do it now. It's going to be bumpy for a while," Loring advised.

After a companionable release—Loring loosed a long, satisfied "Aye-yup" along with his bladder—they bumped off into the Arizona dirt, crossing through stands of cacti and waxy succulents.

Loring negotiated the big, woolly bushes and dry washes with a good deal of skill. All they disturbed were rabbit, whose Ping-Pong ball tails bounced away from the bike's noisy exhaust, and roadrunners.

"Practically ringing the dinner bell for the Jaguars, you know," Loring said, at a stop where Valentine mounted a rock to recheck their bearings.

They reached the crash site perhaps two hours after the pilot had set down. Judging from the tire tracks, he'd made a good job of the landing, snapping off a few taller cacti, until the right under-engine landing gear hit a rock. The gear hadn't broken, but it bounced the plane up, and the right wingtip caught and spun it, and once the nose struck it was all over. The rugged frame of the aircraft, though thick with patched bullet holes, had stood up to even the pancake. Wings and tail were still intact.

They made a slow circle of the wreck. Valentine cocked his head to admire the nose art: A girl in an abbreviated red uniform, fighting to keep the front of her skirt down, rode a rocket pointed toward the nose gear. Valentine retrieved his weapons and gear from the bike.

"Wonder if they got him already," Loring said.

"I don't see any tracks." Valentine looked at the upside-down craft. "Anyone in there?"

Loring switched off his motor so Valentine could listen. He saw a pair of bloody fingerprints below one of the windows, upside-down letters reading

MILKMAN

He stuck his head in and looked at the field of gauges and controls. He smelled blood, strong now.

Cargo netting filled the rear of the plane, mostly empty save for a couple of battered crates and strewn duffel bags. He smelled a sweet odor, and traced it to a broken jar of preserved plums in syrup resting against a big water bottle and a mouth tube. An open camera case with a body and a long lens inside rested on the roof. "There are some bags of cargo here. And a camera. You want to check for salvage?"

"Rocket rails," Loring said, still firmly in his saddle, bike pointed for a quick exit.

"Hmmm?" Valentine asked. He pulled the camera case out and inspected the prize. It looked quite valuable.

"On the bottom of the wings. This thing's built to carry rockets, and they've been fired a lot. Let's get out of here. Let the colab choke out here."

Valentine made a slow circuit of the plane. The ground was rocky and—

Blood on the air.

The pilot's keeping close to his ship, but hiding. Sensible, if his friends come looking for him.

Valentine approached the bike. "He's still in the area," he said quietly.

Loring watched the sun, now touching the mountains. "If you say so. I'm dusting off. You coming?"

"I want to meet this guy," Valentine said.

"Shit. You said there were bags of stuff?"

"Yes."

"Gimme one." Loring unwrapped a bungee cord from his handlebar.

Valentine retrieved an ordinary-looking service duffel. It contained a rolled-up sleeping mat and spare blankets. He watched while Loring took off his leather jacket, zipped it on the upright duffel, then placed it in the saddle behind him. He whipped the bungee around it and fixed it at his belly button.

"From a distance it'll look like we're still riding together. Maybe the Jaguars will chase me instead of hunt you up. Pyp's gold isn't worth your life, Max."

"No," Valentine agreed.

"Hope you make it back to the road, then, Samaritan."

"Ride free," Valentine said, summoning his one piece of biker slang. He handed over the camera case. "Give this to Lautenberg. Maybe you and he can split the proceeds of the sale. A thank-you from me."

"Aye-yup," Loring agreed. "Keep on God's good side." He winked and started up his bike.

Valentine ducked back into the shadow of the plane and watched Loring bump off. He dropped into a crouch, and began to hunt.

Valentine followed his nose uphill, found a telltale drop of blood or two, and finally heard rather wheezy breathing from a thick stand of barrel-shaped cacti. Wild sheep dotted the mountain slopes above, feeding on the grasses in the wind-sheltered washes.

The flier had chosen his vantage well. It offered a good view of the wreck and the mountainside.

Valentine sat down on a flat-topped rock about ten feet away from the cactus and opened a bag of dried fruit, listened to the breathing. He rinsed his mouth out, then extracted a couple of apple chips and crunched them down. "You want some?"

The cactus stand didn't say anything. Whoever was within held his breath.

"This is a nasty patch of ground, flyboy. You're not going to like the natives."

Valentine took a swallow of water.

"On the other hand," Valentine said, "they're going to be happy as hell to meet you. What I can't figure out is what they do with the eyes. Eyes don't keep. Do they eat them as soon as they pull them out, maybe with a little salt like a hard-boiled egg, or do they carry around a jug of brine—"

The cactus stand let out a cough and went silent.

"Option three is me," Valentine said. "I'm just interested in that reward on the back of your jacket. I'm sure you know the wording by heart. It's a win for both of us: You get to be alive, and I get my money."

"Ya-hey," the cactus stand said. A man stood up, a bloody bandage on his hand and a good-sized swelling on his head. He had the blond good looks of an old magazine cover model. Powerful shoulders tested the limits of his jumpsuit, and a brown leather jacket of the type Valentine had last seen outside Dallas was tied around his waist. "You could have said so to begin. Navajo or Apache?"

"Neither," Valentine said. "Max Argent."

"Equality Hornbreed."

Valentine wasn't sure he'd heard correctly.

"First name was good politics," Hornbreed said. He blew his nose into a silk handkerchief, coughed again. "My genitors were all about good politics."

"Your ribs intact?" Valentine asked.

"It's the pollen. Spring allergies. I can walk all night if I have to. Got a headache that about has me cross-eyed is all."

"I think I've got some aspirin—"

"Took a couple, thanks. Grabbed the medical kit first thing."

"Your friends know you went down?"

He took a handful of dried fruit. "They do. Everyone was low on fuel—end of the leg. Guess no one had the guts to try a setdown to pick me up—strict rules about that, we lose too many ships. The strip we're heading for is just a temp, though, no pickup helicopter. There's a couple parked at Yuma, so I might be on my own until tomorrow."

"Hurt the hand on landing?"

"No. Planted it on some broken glass, otherwise I'd offer you a candied plum. Didn't look when I unhooked. I smelled smoke and was worried I was on fire."

"You armed?"

"Pistol and my flare gun. Want me to turn them over to you?"

He was oddly accommodating.

"Can I look at the offer on the jacket again?"

The wording hadn't changed, nor had the logo of a rattlesnake with dragon wings flying openmouthed toward the viewer. Colorful mission patches and squadron insignia—a hairy pirate face with a classic skull-and-bones cap appealed—decorated the sleeves and pockets.

Valentine joined him in the cacti, saw a blanket spread out with a big water jug, a signaling mirror with a hole in the center, and a fire starter. He uncased his binoculars and made a slow survey of the valley below them from cover. Nothing. Of course, that didn't mean the Jaguars weren't approaching. There was ample cover in the dry washes and brush.

"You picked a good spot." Valentine broke out the preserved chow.

"I've had to set down before. Never flipped my bird, though. I'm sure the squadron's having a good laugh. That's a nice rifle."

"Steyr Scout," Valentine said.

Hornbreed checked his wounded hand. "Hope I don't have to see it in action."

"We've got two options, Equality," Valentine said. "Wait for your friends to show, or try to make it to the interstate you passed over. There's a convoy that'll be passing through at first light tomorrow. We can hitch up with them and drop off at the next crossroads and make for Yuma."

"We'll be easier to pick out if we move. I'm supposed to stay with my ship unless I have to evade."

"The Jaguars—"

"There are Jaguars in this valley? I thought they'd cleared out."

"Change your mind?" Valentine asked.

Hornbreed searched the skies. "No. Generally it's best to wait for help to arrive."

Valentine moved to the other side of the cactus-shrouded enclosure. "I'm not one for waiting. But you know your fliers."

"There are more pilots than there are operational ships. But I'm a wing leader. My pilots will come."

Valentine scanned the ground around the overturned plane again. Was there a new shadow next to the brush in front of the engine?

"I like your confidence," Valentine said.

"Stay put and wait," Hornbreed said. "I was a Youth Vanguard leader up Provo way. Worked my way up from larva to scout ant to warrior-guard. We'd go out on squat clearance, burning old homes and buildings outside of town, finding hidden livestock and fields. One time we came on—sheesh, I don't know what to call it. I guess a pilgrimage. Thousand people or more on foot heading for California, hauling stuff on bicycles and handcarts. Our leader decided to follow 'em, see what they were up to. We just walked up and asked where they were going. They got rounded up, of course, and boy, did we hear it from the Churchmen when they found us dogging the column. They kicked the leader right out of the Vanguard. Worked out for me, though, I was the one who argued that we'd been told to burn down houses and we shouldn't go mixing with deadfeets. Were you in the Vanguard?"

"I grew up off the grid, more or less," Valentine said, still scanning. "I did help teach in a Churchman's one-room schoolhouse." His eyes caught a brief flurry of bouncing brown balls. By the time he got his glasses up and located, the might-bes had vanished into an arroyo.

But the heads were on course for the wreck.

Hornbreed let out a little gasp. "*Huff.* I always fell asleep somewhere between collective rights and mankind's atrocity catechism."

Definite movement at the wreck now. Through field glasses Valentine watched a scout explore.

"Well, the Jaguars are at your wreck," Valentine said.

Hornbreed shrugged.

The scout entered the overturned craft, which tipped a little as his weight changed its center of balance. A minute later he emerged again, eating from the broken jar of plums. With the sun now fully behind the mountains the desert flats turned blue. The clouds above warmed into reds, golds, and pinks and purples.

Valentine decided he could get used to desert-country sunsets, but he kept his attention on the wreck. More Jaguars had shown up and were now tearing the little ship apart, salvaging everything from bits of wire to the seat covers. Hornbreed took one brief look and handed the glasses back. "Savages. I can't watch any more."

A Jaguar in much longer furs, cut about his shoulders like a cape made of animal tails, with a spotted headband around his forehead and furry-trimmed sandals, began a rampage. With a good deal of gesturing toward the mountains behind Valentine he gave his tribesmen a dressing-down, put them in a staggered line like a top sergeant with well-trained recruits, and hustled them away with a glance or two behind.

Valentine couldn't help but turn and look at the darkening peaks behind.

"What do you know about these mountains?" Valentine asked Hornbreed.

"Some farms and ranches on the other side. Pretty well organized, typical Aztlan stuff. There are collar towers below the ridgeline—they're easy to spot from the air."

"Collar towers?"

"Keeps the peons on their ranchos. The collars tighten if they start to stray. Top-quality Korean electronics."

"What about this side?"

"Sheep. Mud pueblos."

Had these mountains turned into a choking, deathly place according to local legend? Then why did the medicine man have to remind his tribesmen?

Hornbreed stretched out, pulled his reflective survival blanket up. "Long, bad day. I'm going to try to sleep off this headache."

"Should we set a watch?"

"You're my rescuer. If anything's going to happen, it'll happen whether we set a watch or not. They outnumber us twenty to two." He blew his nose again. "You wouldn't know it to hear me, but I am a healthy specimen. Just spring air."

Valentine watched the valley until darkness made it impossible, then admired the stars and planets. He hadn't seen them so bright since he'd been at sea in the Caribbean.

The memories that evoked turned him sour and gloomy. He slipped out of the cactus thatch—his old Wolf habit of changing positions after darkness was so deeply ingrained he did it even if it was only a shift of twenty feet or so—and listened. A distant coyote howled in the valley. Others took up the chorus, but none called from the mountains he and Hornbreed rested against.

Too uneasy to really sleep, he dozed, sitting cross-legged with his rifle against his lap, small of his back pressed up against a sun-heated rock. The air had turned cold with astonishing speed, a desert feature he was still getting used to. . . . The moon came up, so bright it looked as though an artist had painted it on the sky with radium.

He heard Hornbreed come out of the cacti, mumble something about *pinching a deuce*. Valentine saw him move off into the bushes, heard him stumble, curse, right himself.

Seemingly moments later, Valentine came fully awake, though he couldn't say why. How long had it been since Hornbreed had stepped behind the bushes?

"Hornbreed?" he said quietly. He raised the gun to his shoulder and came up to one knee.

"Hornbreed?" Louder this time.

The bushes didn't answer.

Valentine touched the sword at his back, tested the slide of the blade in its sheath.

"Hornbreed!" Valentine said, coming up to a crouch.

He advanced, well clear of the bushes.

No sign of the pilot. A white packet shone in the moonlight. Hornbreed had picked a sandy spot for easier burial. Valentine studied Hornbreed's footprints, placed in the expected position to either side of his—well, with a mule deer it would be called "spoor." The white packet was a little cardboard-banded issue of "field hygiene paper" courtesy of High Sierra Paper Products.

No body. No sign of the Jaguars. And no Reaper.

Strange divots stood out in the sand here and there, like little craters. Near-perfect circles. If they were tracks, only an unusually hard-stepping big cat like a mountain lion would make them. But there were no drag marks away from the bootheels and TP.

Ten thousand dollars in gold—and more importantly, a key to the mercenary pilots of Pyp's Flying Circus—had been spirited away without a sound or a cry of distress.

Valentine felt a cold sweat that had nothing to do with the Arizona night. It occurred to him that he'd been meaning to ask Hornbreed why they called him milkman.

Something glittered in the night a few feet away. Valentine knelt, saw loose coins scattered in the rocks and sand. Valentine picked one up, a "five-dollar" piece marked AZT-CON. He'd seen them before, in plastic Baggies holding Texas Quisling prisoners' possessions. He'd been told the coin was good over much of the Southwest and northern Mexico.

Valentine guessed that Hornbreed, literally taken with his pants down, had lost whatever change was rattling around in his pants. At least now he could guess in which direction the mysterious tracks went.

The lack of blood gave him some hope.

As he followed the tracks there were other signs—the creature must have been of some size, at least that of a small tractor. It had snapped off cactus stems in several spots over two meters apart.

It also left an odor, vaguely musty and yet ammoniacal. He traced the source of the smell, an object that looked a little like a hollow-reed thorn, in a vaguely green brown polished-turtle-shell color. Some sticky material coated one end, and Valentine hazarded a guess that it was a quill or spine.

Had a giant Arizona porcupine made off with Hornbreed?

The trail led up into the mountains. The mystery of the Jaguar leader's imprecations against hanging about the wreck had been explained. Anything big enough to approach and then make off with a sizable man in silence was a foe to be feared.

The musty-ammonia smell grew stronger, and Valentine realized that the dark of the mountainside had a darker spot. A cave opening, shaped like one of the little lateen sails he'd seen on fishing boats in the Caribbean. Valentine looked around, got his bearings, and listened to the cave mouth. A bat fluttered somewhere above.

A metallic *clang* sounded from the cave mouth and Valentine went flat, his senses sparking like a downed line. Valentine heard low snorts and growls and watched three Grogs emerge from the cave, heavy sacks across their shoulders. They waited, standing back-to-back, and Valentine felt a fresh chill. A Reaper emerged from the shadows, carrying a long staff that made the robed figure a scarecrow caricature of a desert prophet. It hissed at the Grogs and followed them on a westward-leading path.

The sensible thing to do would be to hotfoot it back to the convoy, leave these mountains crawling with assorted enemies, and let fate have its way with the fatalistic Hornbreed. Duvalier, had she been with him this trip, would no doubt be resting in some hidey-hole with a good view of the interstate, waiting for the roar of truck engines and the rumble of tires.

But dammit, he needed Hornbreed—and the promised reward, provided Flying Circus would be willing to negotiate, not amount, but kind. He slipped off his backpack, extracting a small, tough flashlight with a clip that allowed him to hang it on a pocket or attach it to the underside of his gun. Something in him had to know. He fixed the light to his carbine, coaxing himself into making the attempt by getting his gear ready. If he squatted here much longer, he'd freeze up and come up with more reasons not to try it. . . .

Valentine stepped into the ammonia smell.

A big metal locker, whose door was the source of the clanging sound, he guessed, stood just inside the cave. Electrical cable ran down the top of the cave and into it. The locker was fixed by a simple bolt. Valentine drew it back and opened the locker, smelling Grog sweat.

Long objects like fishing poles rested there, six of them, thick handles fitted into sockets and a battery case where the reel normally stood. Valentine read the pictograms on the poles, saw the electrical insulation. They were like overlong cattle prods. Valentine lifted one up and blue LED bulbs lit up at the end. They offered just enough light for him to see a few feet into the cave, which sloped down precipitously. Someone had tacked down rubber mats to improve the footing.

Valentine guessed what the big red plastic switch at the "reel" end was. He turned it on and touched the end to a rock. A spark like a photo strobe jumped and Valentine smelled ozone. Capacitors whined faintly as they recharged.

Cattle prod.

Valentine slung his rifle and took two from the green-lit sockets, wondered if the Miskatonic had tested electricity on a live Reaper. Of course, had someone suggested they try it on Blake . . .

Movement behind and Valentine whirled.

An arachnophobe's nightmare stood framed by the desert stars, brighter than ever when contrasted with the cave mouth. Shock turned it into a Picasso sketch of limbs and stingers and spines, and Valentine found himself backpedaling, throwing the steel bulk of the locker between himself and the creature, his illuminated prods waving in front of him like drunken fireflies—

It paid him no more attention than it did the locker next to him and clattered down the hole. It had six spiny legs, three to a side, and two "arms"—though perhaps they were vestigial wings, as they swept up and out, folded, and were tipped with a sharp curved point. Its head—Valentine didn't know what else to call the front end—resembled a big tongue more than anything, and held a limp, white-eyed sheep in thousands of mushroomlike organs coating its underside, a carpet of organic Velcro.

Whatever it was, it didn't have a strong "defend the nest" instinct. Valentine wondered if the result would have been different if it weren't already carrying a sheep. Were these some big version of the sand bugs the Kurians used to kill the trekkers' cattle in Nebraska?

Valentine said the kind of prayer typically uttered in atheist-free foxholes and followed it down. It didn't have much of an abdomen—usually the largest segment in a terrestrial insect—just a rutted organ that reminded him a little of an oversized, rotting cucumber. The motion of its legs fascinated him as it negotiated the slope with ease, using the tiniest of projections from the cave wall as steps.

The tricky down shaft lasted only fifteen meters or so. Valentine found himself on an easier-to-negotiate downslope. He wondered where he would hide in the narrow space if another bug showed up, and smelled the bat feces littered about. Maybe the ammonia smell came from bat droppings accidentally picked up here. The cave ceiling came down low enough that Valentine had to crouch.

Red glinted in the dim light of the LEDs on the cattle prods. What Valentine's brain identified as a big rat turned into a little six-legged creeper, shooting out of a crack toward him, wing limbs telegraphing a code he couldn't begin to understand. Valentine put his prod between himself and the explorer and it scurried off.

The cavern opened up, and there was dim electrical lighting ahead, or perhaps an opening to the moon and stars. Valentine found himself crouching in a much larger cavern, curving off into darkness and other chambers like a cow's stomach, lit here and there by panels that gave off a faint yellow glow from behind thick screens.

He scooted out of the low passage, not wanting to block access for the hunter-gatherers. A small horde of the little ratlike creepy-crawlies were massed under a sheep, holding it in their collected top arms, bringing it to the ceiling of the cavern.

Valentine heard—worse yet, felt—a presence overhead. He saw dozens of sacks hanging there, reminding him of a laundry he'd patronized in New Orleans with its rows of canvas bags hanging from the conveyors. Valentine saw a sheep hoof sticking out of one, an emaciated human hand hanging from another. Some of the bags hung from long stems, others shorter, and the scientific bit of Valentine's mind observed that the shape of the sacks turned into a more regular teardrop the closer they got to the floor. Fat, white wormlike creatures fixed their mouths to the lowest-hanging bags and suckled there.

Something vast, glistening, and dark moved among the bags at the ceiling.

Valentine took three cautious steps, careful of where he placed his feet, and found a shriveled teardrop of a bag. It was next to another empty stem, cut neatly off. A faint, sweet corruptive odor came from the bag, but it wasn't the smell that fascinated him—it was the curious, shiny weave of the bag.

He touched it to make sure. Reaper cloth! These creatures produced—wove, even—a rough version of the fabric.

Valentine was tempted to chop off the nearly empty teardrop. But he had to find Hornbreed.

Valentine searched the walls and ceiling, waving the LEDs at the end of his prods, probing corners. He explored deeper into the cave, felt one of the worm things nudge his foot.

He jumped, and came face-to-face with Hornbreed's upturned face. Dozens of the smaller creepy-crawlies were passing the pilot up a living conveyor belt to the ceiling, where the shadowed mass rubbed its limbs against one another expectantly. Sightless eyes looked past him into darkness, but Valentine heard the faint wheeze of Hornbreed's lungs, and drool ran out of the corner of his mouth.

"Sorry, Equality," Valentine said. He reached and struck Hornbreed in the buttock with the cattle prod.

Flash-*tzzap*! The body convulsed, broke away, and fell as its handlers broke contact, or had their pincers torn loose by the muscle spasms. The thud of Hornbreed hitting the cavern floor sent the white larvae humping away.

A rattling like dry bones falling from a crypt crèche, and Valentine looked insectoid death in the not-face. Eyes like gemstones glittered in the reflections of the LEDs on his prods.

"Noogh . . . enoogh . . . havin' a heart attack," Hornbreed bubbled.

The two upper front limbs on the hunter-gatherer struck down and forward. Barbed stingers missed as Valentine dived out of the way, lunging with his prods, but the hunter-gatherer matched him in their dance, keeping the eye clusters toward him. The red tip of the tongue-carrier retreated farther into its forebody.

Valentine lunged for the red mark like a dueling Musketeer, scored a palpable hit. Flash-*tzzap*!

The hunter-gatherer collapsed, legs twitching. Valentine's world whirled as he was jerked off his feet by jointed arms that enfolded him in a firm, irresistible, yet gentle embrace. Twin stingers pinched him at his chest, but couldn't penetrate, emptying themselves uselessly on his leathers. The prod he'd just used fell where his feet had been a second before.

Valentine struck wildly behind with his other prod, convulsed as the current traveled up the hunter-gatherer's limbs and across his chest. Heart stalled, then pounding in shock, he fell to the ground, suddenly at war with his body. None of his limbs seemed to remember how to function.

The hunter-gatherer who'd got him from behind batted at him with one of its legs, but it was just a reaction to the charge. Valentine managed a roll toward Hornbreed.

"What the Kur's this?" Hornbreed gasped, batting weakly at the smaller, rat-sized bugs. Every move brought a wince.

Some of the Christmas tree ornaments above rocked as the roof creature shifted.

Valentine managed to slow his heart, retrieve his rifle. "Can you walk?"

"Lookit my back. It feels like there's about two kilos of flesh ripped out." Hornbreed came to one knee, turning.

Valentine saw a purpurant swelling at Hornbreed's right shoulder blade. He guessed that the welt was the size of a dinner plate.

"You got stung by one of these bastards." Valentine's body was back under control and he felt strangely calm and placid. The bugs weren't so bad, just little machines doing their jobs.

Or very big machines, like the one above . . .

. . . and coming down.

Christ, it's as big as a whale.

Valentine flicked on the gun light, saw ring after ring of arms around a lipless, spiny orifice, a zeppelin of a body behind, long thin arms that couldn't possibly support that mass, froze up until his eye and trigger finger, acting perhaps for their individual preservation against an overwhelmed brain, fired up into it.

It accepted the bullets in silence. A few of the arms around the central orifice stiffened—

Before the cartridge casings even finished their tinny bounces Valentine grabbed Hornbreed by the shoulder, pulled him up and along, when he wasn't moving right got under the pilot's armpit, and half carried him in a stumble toward the exit, carbine in its sling bouncing against his plated leathers. Hornbreed screamed out his agony like a police siren.

Another hunter-gatherer entered, a coyote borne in its tonguelike front appendage, ignoring them and the chaos within. Valentine regretted the dropped prods, grabbed Hornbreed by the collar, and dragged him, shrieking in pain, like a resisting dog, through the low entrance aperture.

A hunter-gatherer's captured limbs darted into the crack, and closed on Hornbreed's leg. Valentine found the carbine's trigger and sent four bullets to the source of the limbs with the serene, observant corner of his mind trying to remember just how many rounds the little minidrum at the bottom of the carbine carried. But the legs let go.

Hornbreed was crying, blubbering to be left in peace, but Valentine got him up the shaft of near-vertical stairs, pushing from behind the whole way. He made it to the locker and retrieved another prod and was tempted to use it on Hornbreed to calm the pilot down. Instead he half carried him out of the cave and to his pack.

The cold night air and open sky acted on Valentine like a refreshing dip in a pool. His limbs tingled and his skin felt delightfully alive.

"My whole friggin' body's throbbing," Hornbreed gasped. "Sears like a hot frying pan. Put a bullet through my head, for Kur's sake."

Valentine retrieved his little razor-edged kidney puncher of a knife from his boot sheath and opened Hornbreed's bulging flight suit, a splotch of red marking the center of the bulge like a misplaced nipple. He tore open the cloth and took a breath at the blister the hunter-gatherer's venom had raised.

"You could be worse. Those things have two stingers. Hold on now."

A lot of liquid was trying to get out. Valentine held the sagging Hornbreed down with his knee and nicked the blister, eliciting a gasp from Hornbreed. Valentine squeezed hot, clear fluid from the wound, then dusted with antibiotic powder.

He gave Hornbreed two pain pills from the first-aid kit. Valentine recognized the odd little hexagonal shapes from his wisdom-teeth extraction courtesy of a Southern Command dentist, and wished he'd gotten morphine instead.

"Doesn't burn so bad," Hornbreed said, catching his breath as Valentine applied butterfly bandages.

They exchanged Valentine's canteen a couple of times. Valentine kept an eye on the cave mouth, wondering when the next hunter-gatherer was due to appear.

"I think we should get going," Valentine said. "Still want to be left to your fate?"

"I want a long, cool drink at the Mezcal," Hornbreed said. "Ice. A whole bagful."

"Better get back to the cactus stand."

About halfway down the mountain it occurred to Valentine that there'd been a yellow rubberized box or two in the locker at the cave mouth that he hadn't investigated. For all he knew, they contained electrical tools, but if the Kurians had some kind of antivenom, that would be the place to store it. But then it might be dosed for those big mountain Grogs. . . .

Bug prod ready against another appearance of a hunter-gatherer, Valentine traced a route that carried them well away from stands of bush and sandy washes (in Nebraska's cattle country he'd once been stung by a smaller creature that could dig, and he still wasn't sure exactly how the beasties hunted).

When they reached the cactus stand Hornbreed collapsed atop his survival blanket. "Enough . . . enough . . . I'm done," he said.

"I want to get farther away from that cave," Valentine said. He stomped hard next to a wandering scorpion, sent it scurrying back into the thorns. "Fifteen minutes, then we'll pick up and move on."

Hornbreed's breath left a moist wing on the reflective surface of the blanket. Valentine decided it was safe to reload, opened a box of shells, and fed them into the magazine. He decided to give Hornbreed a few more minutes and cleaned the barrel.

"C'mon, bud. Up," Valentine said.

Hornbreed moaned. He looked like a deboned fish, sweating and gasping. "Can't. Muscles won't work." He managed to drag an arm under himself.

Valentine sorted through Hornbreed's gear, took medical supplies and water, the flare pistol and signaling mirror. The rest he buried.

Hornbreed was a big man. Valentine could carry him, but he would have to stop and rest frequently, and a few hours would exhaust him utterly. His bad leg started up a preemptive ache at the thought. They'd never make the highway.

A drag might be possible, if—

The wreck!

Valentine felt the flier's pulse, which was regular but fast, picked Hornbreed up in a fireman's carry, and thanked creation that they'd be going downhill. He placed Hornbreed inside the rear cabin of the plane, closed the door, and went back for his pack.

With that done, he looked around the wreck site.

The fuselage was intact—if only one of the rear wings had come off, it would make a good sled.

Doors! The hinges were designed to come apart easily; all you had to do was pull a pin. Even better, a broken piece of landing gear could be used in an improvised wheelbarrow.

He tore up some cargo netting, clipped his light to the higher of the two wings, and went to work, careful to keep the Steyr within reach.

It was in the deep night of predawn by the time he finished. He dragged Hornbreed back out of the aircraft and tried him on the improvised wheelbarrow.

"It works!" Valentine said, though the balance left a lot to be desired. Hornbreed, wheezing and whimpering, managed a nod. Valentine lowered him gently and put the canteen to his lips. "We're out of here, Hornbreed."

It would be a race against the sun.

Valentine never got to test his contraption any further. He caught a whiff of the telltale ammonia smell on the clean night breeze and reached for the Steyr.

The hunter-gatherer rushed out of the night, grasping arms up and ready. Valentine had no idea where the vital spots were, so he settled for sending shot after shot straight down its centerline, trusting that the big-game 7.62mm shells would find something important.

The bug collapsed, flipped forward in a weird imitation of the downed aircraft, continued to twitch with the three legs and the pinioned arm on one side of its body. Valentine reached for the bug prod, held the rifle at his hip in his right hand and the prod with his left.

The shots roused Hornbreed, though he grasped the flare gun rather than his pistol.

"Most-heeeeee!" a voice shrieked from the darkness.

Others took up the chorus. *"Most-heeeee!"*

A fast metallic rattle, either an imitation of a snare drum on some piece of aluminum or an attempt to re-create a rattlesnake's warning, broke out in the desert predawn.

"That can't be good," Hornbreed said, and managed to rise to his feet using the fuselage for support.

"I think I just committed blasphemy," Valentine said.

Something whizzed nearby and the fuselage popped near his ear. Stones!

"Inside," Valentine said, shoving the pilot toward the rear door.

Stones didn't leave a telltale muzzle flash to shoot back at. Valentine fired twice more into the darkness. He helped Hornbreed in, felt a sudden pain as a stone struck him in the leathers just below the shoulder blade. Valentine dived inside.

Stones and thrown spears rattled against the fuselage like a dying hailstorm. More yips and coyote howls broke out around the aircraft, along with a deeper drumming.

The banging grew louder. Voices just outside the fuselage shouted, and the clattering redoubled as the Jaguars banged on the overturned plane with hand weapons.

Valentine checked the lock on the rear cargo door, crept to the missing front door. A shadow loomed outside; Valentine marked a tangle of dirty hair held in place by a broad headband. He fired and the head disappeared.

"Fhway! Fhway! Fhway!" a voice shouted outside from just beneath the pilot's seat.

Valentine smelled woodsmoke. He went to the copilot window, saw a figure with a flaming torch, and opened the window, but a hand grabbed the muzzle of his gun. Valentine jerked it back violently, shot through the fuselage at where the grabber must have been standing, then found his torch target was gone.

Hornbreed said something, but his words were lost in the hammering on the fuselage. They might as well have tried to converse on the inside of a giant drum. Valentine smelled more smoke, unsheathed his sword; there was nothing to do but go out the missing door. Otherwise they'd cook.

Hornbreed suddenly opened the door, stuck his flare gun up.

"No," Valentine shouted.

A knife blade stabbed in, glinting on the sudden illumination of the flare. Hornbreed fell back from it. Valentine brought the handy little carbine around and fired through the fuselage again. A hand appeared as one of the Jaguars tried to hoist himself in. Valentine discouraged it by severing a couple of fingers with the sword. He shouldered his gun again.

Thunderous pounding outside—*How the hell are they making that noise?* Then Valentine realized he was hearing the beating rotors of a helicopter.

Tracer lit up the pinkening dawn, bright shards of yellow rain from the sky. The hammering on the fuselage let off and Valentine saw the warriors scatter.

"It's the pickup chopper!" Hornbreed almost shouted. Hope had given him new strength.

Valentine looked outside, saw a big bulbous desert-tan fuselage, a greenhouse of glass at the front, red and green running lights, a uniformed gunner at an oversized door at the side. Valentine grabbed his clip light and used the signaling switch to blink three times at the craft. Three times again, three times again. They might not know the old

Quisling Coastal Marine distress code, but the gunner swerved his crosshairs away from the flipped aircraft.

The faint popping of small-arms fire sounded. Hornbreed crawled to the rear cabin door and waved. Men tumbled out of the helicopter. Valentine saw another prop plane roar overhead, turning tight circles around the crash site.

Hornbreed waved Valentine out the door. Valentine surrendered his gun, sword, and pack to a corporal. Another soldier, a businesslike submachine gun in his grasp, eyed Valentine. Three soldiers and a medic assisted the noncom, one of them openly gaping at the hunter-gatherer, still twitching at the extremities. Valentine heard one of the soldiers shouting something about a "salvage bird" into a headset.

"Rough night," Hornbreed wheezed at the medic, who helped him out the door and toward a litter. "Forget that. I want to get in the chopper with him."

He held out an arm to Valentine, and accepted a lift. "Max, help me on the bird of paradise. We'll be in Yuma in time for cocktails."

Six

Pyp's Flying Circus, Yuma, Arizona: The old Colorado River steamboat stop grew up under three flags, Spanish, Mexican, and finally the Stars and Stripes after the territory was acquired in the Gadsden Purchase. Famous after the Civil War mostly for its territorial prison, it became an important military hub and storage center thanks to its dry climate, ideal for testing and storing hardware of various kinds, and the premier Marine Corps pilot training center.

Under the Aztlan Kur, an association of like-minded Kurians covering northern Mexico and the Southwestern United States called the "Confederation" by the locals, it's still a city that breeds pilots. The more mundane Aztlan Air Carriers shuttle Quisling dignitaries and churchmen from post to post and fly police patrols, but the much more colorful "Flying Circus" of airborne mercenaries, with their distinctive winged-rattlesnake insignia, is what people usually refer to when speaking of the fliers of the Southwest.

In typical Kurian fashion Pyp's Flying Circus is divided into three centers for better control. Most of the fliers and their families live in Yuma, in well-guarded gated communities. Their amenities are so plentiful that it's hard to recognize them as hostages to their good behavior. Airplane storage and maintenance is located at the famous aircraft graveyard at the old Davis-Monthan Air Force Base, now just called "Lucky Field" by the ground staff, thanks to the job security it affords, and "DM" by the fliers. Pyp's operational headquarters is in Tempe, where orders are received from the Kurians and planes are armed and staged for their various missions. No one group of officers, and no one Kurian, really commands the Circus, though all think of their titular figurehead commander as the unit's boss.

There's an air of ringmaster flamboyance to their beloved "Pyp." Patrick Yenez-Powell is the sort of man who stands out in a crowd, not always an advantage that leads to survival in the Kurian Order. With his round-brimmed, black felt Navajo hat, river-guide sandals, gold earring and necklaces, often grease-stained denim flight suit, and elaborately beaded shoulder rig for his ivory-handled peacemaker, he's easy to pick out in a crowd. Though on the ugly side of fifty, he still moves with a spring in his step, and he's hard to follow, as he changes direction the instant he spots anything from flaking paint to litter to a misplaced tool; an adjutant usually carries a bag for such trash that blows across Pyp's transom, which will then be upended on some unfortunate lieutenant's desk.

David Valentine met the mind behind the odd wardrobe and energetic body on a hot April afternoon in Yuma.

The long trip, begun in the noisy vibration of the helicopter, was briefly suspended at a refueling stop at a service strip, where they shoveled down a quick meal of eggs and sausage. After breakfast they were both dusted with some kind of disinfectant/insecticide. Then it was back in the beater until another landing at the sprawling air base in Tucson, where they switched to a tiny, cramped prop plane for the final leg, which left Valentine tired and disoriented. Other than his astonishment over the distance they'd traveled in just a few hours, he also felt nauseous with fatigue.

He wanted cool and darkness when they arrived at Yuma. The soldiers threw their dunnage in a propane-powered flatbed and whisked Hornbreed, Valentine, and the medic with a clipboard full of notes off to a white building with the traditional red cross painted on its roof and walls. Valentine surrendered his weapons again to a pair of desert-camouflaged men with sidearms and blue-banded helmets. Hornbreed whispered into one of the military policemen's ears, but said little else until they reached the triage room, where he refused any attention until the MPs showed up again and looped a laminated ID card around Valentine's neck. Then Hornbreed allowed himself to be put in a wheelchair and taken to an operating room.

Valentine fell asleep on the paper-covered table of an examining room. A thin woman who looked like a hat tree in a lab coat, stethoscope over her shoulder, woke him and checked his eyes, lymph nodes, pulse, and temperature. She asked him how he felt and where he'd traveled in the last month and he answered honestly.

"Drink lots of water," she advised, and turned on the tap in the washbasin. "If you want to get cleaned up, you can use the showers in

'E' corridor—just follow the signs. You can read, right? Wear your ID at all times, even in the shower. There's a staff commissary in that wing too—eat a couple of bananas." She signed a piece of paper and handed it to him. "You're on unlimited rations for three days, so enjoy. Don't skimp on the veggies."

She went to an intercom by the door. "Room three is cleared," she said.

"What about Equality?" Valentine asked.

"Wing Leader Hornbreed's doing fine. He's staying here for observation overnight. Check with the base security by the admitting door and they'll find you a bunk. You'll probably be here until we release the wing leader."

Valentine cleaned himself up using the washbasin, and felt better but still bleary when he presented himself to a potbellied example of base security. They looked him over as though wanting to arrest him on general principles, but eventually informed him that his reward was being arranged.

"Old Pyp's on the way," the corporal explained. "He wants to see you and the wing leader."

Valentine wondered if there was a "Young Pyp," or if the phrase, with its poetic evocation of *Tempus fugit,* indicated some measure of endearment.

"Mind if I grab a meal first?"

"Just don't be long about it," the desk sergeant barked. "He's a busy man and we don't want to be running around looking for you."

The corporal took him to the cafeteria, whistled at the food prescription. "Enjoy. We've been on ration cards for over a year."

Valentine winced. "I know what that's like."

He piled a tray with some dubious-looking meat in gravy, potatoes, fruit, and rice buns. The servers examined his piece of paper at each station, even the woman who poured him a glass of juice.

The corporal settled for a thick slice of bread smeared with "protein paste," and water.

"Hope that tastes better than it looks," Valentine said.

The corporal rolled his eyes. "They say it's refried beans. Tastes like they scraped it off a Dumpster."

"Dig into mine," Valentine said.

"You're a real *guapo* . . . uh, Mr. Argent." He hunched over the table and worked a chunk of Valentine's steak free from bone and gristle.

"Why the food shortage?" Valentine asked.

"Troubles out east," the corporal said, shoveling food and looking over his shoulder. "We just took a bunch of California farmland, thanks to the Circus, but it's taking time to get organized. Headhunters down south are having a tougher time finding peons to work the land. This territory used to be Frolic City—Pyp's Circus brought in a lot of in-kind trade from the Gulag. Now we're fighting to hold our own."

"Here's to better days," Valentine said, swallowing some watery juice.

The corporal removed some gravy with his heel of bread. "If you're looking to set up an establishment somewhere comfy with your reward—"

Valentine picked up his wiped-clean tray. "Haven't thought that far ahead, friend."

Hornbreed was on the telephone when they entered the room. The corporal pulled up a chair outside.

"No," Hornbreed said, wincing a little at the effort. "No. Let's get *Bettie Page* stripped. Put *Tigress* and *Zorro* into reserve, and *Brunhilda* in for a complete overhaul. Let me know the status of *Rockette* as soon as the salvagers bring her in. Yeah, I flipped her. Tell them at least a week for the wing to reorganize. Colorado tore us a new one."

He paused. Then: "Kur! I don't care. We'll lose half the wing if we go into action now. Yes, I'll take the responsibility."

Valentine listened to another call to someone named "Lo," full of many reassurances as to his condition. He went to the window, watched the quiet airfield. Gliders circled far above, featherless hawks on the air currents. Valentine watched a new string of gliders take off, a twin-engine prop with five fiberglass baby planes in tow.

Hornbreed returned the phone to its cradle and rubbed his eyes.

"What are all the gliders for?" Valentine asked.

"Pilot training. You learn most of the principles of flight, and it saves a lot of gas."

"Looks fun," Valentine said, and meant it.

"Just say the word and—"

The corporal's chair in the hallway scraped and Valentine heard him come to his feet. Boots squeaked on the linoleum.

Patrick Yenez-Powell had darkish but freckled skin, a boxer's squashed nose, and ears like a pair of beat-up trash can lids. Valentine didn't know what to make of the variegated uniform. The gold necklace, dungaree overalls, and shoulder holster made him look like a motor-pool inventory guard called away from a good card game, but the round, black felt hat added a serious note.

Valentine envied the sandals, though. They looked cool and comfortable.

"Knock knock," Pyp said. "Got a minute, Horny?" His voice flowed low, musical, and a little sad. If basset hounds could talk, they'd sound like Yenez-Powell.

"Always," Hornbreed said.

Valentine saw a pair of adjutants, male and female so alike that they looked like brother and sister, peering in from the doorway.

Pyp strode in, holding his left arm behind.

"You dumb sonofabitch. I told you *Rockette* wasn't fit to get home. You had to be a hero and make it or go down with the ship."

"Got her in range of the salvage bird," Hornbreed said.

"We'll have to invent a new medal for you—you got all the others. Just park it for now. I brought you a present. Fresh from the Cali Dairy," Pyp said, revealing a big bottle of white liquid Valentine guessed to be milk. "Still a little warm from the cow."

Hornbreed produced one of his little gasps. "*Huff.* Thanks, sir. You're a wonder." He twisted off the cap and tried a swallow.

"Milkman," Valentine said quietly.

"Is this our stray herder?" Pyp asked, turning to Valentine.

"He got me out of a dark hole," Hornbreed said. "Almost punched out doing it."

"Thank you, young man." He offered his hand. "Call me Pyp."

Valentine shook his hand. "Max."

"Good with his gun and cool in a hotbox," Hornbreed said. "We could sure use him."

Valentine shrugged. "I'm flattered, but I'm more interested in the reward."

Pyp sucked air through his teeth. "Sorry to hear that. But don't worry, you'll get it in full."

"Your jackets say the reward is nonnegotiable," Valentine said. "Is that firm?"

Both the pilots exchanged looks and frowns. "Hey, Max—," Hornbreed started.

"Son, most of the fellers who want to haggle don't hand over the pilot first," Pyp said. "You're either dumb or impractical."

"I didn't mean the amount," Valentine said. "I meant the type. Does it have to be gold?"

"What, you want something lighter? We can look into gems," Pyp said.

Valentine held up a hand. "Oh, nothing like that. I was wondering if I could trade the reward for a ride in one of your planes."

This time the pilots exchanged furrowed brows.

"Where you wanna go, Japan?" Pyp said. "You're screwing yourself, son."

"Gold just brings trouble. I've got family on a patch of land up toward Canada. I'd like a ride up there."

Pyp tipped his hat up and forward, scratched his stubbled head. "Easily done. We've got a friendly field in northern Utah."

"Thanks."

"You'll find a little gratitude goes a long way," Pyp said. "We'll put you in the VIP jet if you like."

"Throw in some flying lessons and we'll call it a deal," Valentine said.

"Not sure a man who turns down mint gold should be working a stick and rudder, but we'll oblige," Pyp said. "Horny, you tell Alvarez to arrange some privates."

"I'll take him up myself," Hornbreed said, setting down his almost-empty quart of milk. "The wing's going to be down for a while anyway."

"That's the other thing," Pyp said. "We're going to have to dummy up for a week or so and make you look operational. There's a purification drive."

"Huff . . ." Hornbreed lost some of his color. "Oh hell."

Valentine wanted to ask what a "purification drive" was, but Hornbreed read his face. "Looks like you haven't spent much time in the Confederation."

"They could show any day," Pyp said.

Hornbreed swung his legs out of the bed, took a deep, wheezy breath. "Get my boots, huh?"

They put Valentine in a comfortable little house in a no-man's-land of fencing that wasn't on the airfield, but rather grew out beside the main gate in a dogleg shape. More houses, a little school with thick bars around it, and some rows of two-story apartments surrounded an empty pool that someone had turned into the world's biggest sandbox for the kids. A driving range/putting green ran in a green carpet out to the fencing. As if to make up for the missing pool, housing management turned a big sprinkler on every afternoon, watering the putting green, and the base kids shrieked as they ran in and out of it.

Runoff fed a vegetable garden, and served as a birdbath. The birds looked every bit as happy as the kids.

Skinny, shoeless, half-naked kids watched from the other side of the wire, sticking their arms through the fencing and begging food, alternating pleas in Spanish and English.

Valentine took a short joyride his first evening. A young instructor named Starguide offered him the chance to watch a sunset from just beneath the clouds. Valentine gazed down on the rooftops of Yuma, spotted a few antlike vehicles on the wide roads, saw the Colorado and Yuma rivers running muddily beneath, along with the old, perforated border fences and trenches dividing Arizona from Mexico. And of course the sun, turning everything shades of red and copper.

I see why, Dad. But how did you ever give this up?

"Ready to take over?" Starguide asked

Valentine wiped the tears out of his eyes.

"Like with most everything, first time's the best," Starguide said. "Pick a spot on the horizon and keep her level. Don't be afraid—I'm here. Small, gentle movements. You'll just have her for a few minutes—it's getting dark."

Valentine took the controls. The plane waggled a little and settled down.

"You've got good hands for this, Argent," Starguide said.

"I bet you say that to all the boys," Valentine said.

"Dude, don't even joke about it. You don't want a rep as a rainbow chaser. Pilot culture is *muy* macho."

After the exhilaration of a night landing, with the airfield lights changing speed and perspective until they touched down with the softest of bumps, Starguide filled out some paperwork. He then took Valentine toward Yuma on a spring-worn shuttle bus. They stopped well outside of town at a cavernous wooden restaurant, where Hornbreed watched while some musicians set up. A petite, caramel-skinned woman with cheekbones and jawline as sharp as a hunting arrow sat beside Hornbreed, resting her hand on his arm, loving but not overly demonstrative.

"Any news?" Starguide asked.

"No sign of 'em yet," Hornbreed said. "Maybe they'll skip us and concentrate on the out-there."

Starguide didn't say anything, but he didn't have to. His face said "That'll be the day."

Valentine looked around the place. A big U of a room, with pillars where he guessed dividing walls once stood, surrounded the bar. Doors to the kitchen were on one side, to the washrooms on another. A stairway at the side had a blue neon arrow zigzagging up and the legend WILD BLUE YONDER in cloud-scrolled letters.

"Welcome to the Mezcal," Hornbreed said, pulling out a chair at a table with a good view of the band. "Best liquor and music between the LA Slimepits and Austin Holdout. This is my wife, Louisa."

"I am, jusslike, so grateful to you," the caramel-skinned woman said, her voice oddly nasal.

"That's the sound of California class," Hornbreed said. "But she fell for a dashing pilot and joined me in the wasteland."

"Jusslike the movies," Louisa agreed.

Hornbreed gave her a kiss on the temple. A waitress approached them. "Buy you a drink?"

"Whatever you're having."

"It's milk. I don't drink."

"Milk, then," Valentine said.

"Struth, not another one," Starguide said. "Hey, he needs his wings."

Starguide went to the bar and yanked a piece of plastic off a peg. He returned just as the milks and drinks arrived, set it on Valentine's head, and fixed a thin bungee under his chin. It was a kid's toy hat, spray-painted silver, with wings that swept up and back.

A trio in leather jackets, parked at the end of the bar and chatting with a buxom bartender, whistled and raised their glasses to Valentine.

Valentine, Hornbreed, and Starguide clinked glasses. Valentine's milk slopped out a little.

"Why the milk?" Valentine asked.

"My folks were sort of fitness fanatics," Hornbreed said.

Valentine knew better than to inquire further about their health. One never asked about relatives in the Kurian Zone, especially when the past tense was employed. Instead he watched customers stream in. Some pointed to his funny little silver hat, and a pilot or two broke away from their friends and came up to clap him on the back.

"Kick it, Ge-arge," a bandsman with a guitar said. Ge-arge raised his sticks above his head and clacked them together three times, *tchk tchk tchk*—Valentine jumped a little. The sound reminded him of the hunter-gatherers.

A fusion of salsa and Western coursed through the bar.

"Place is gonna be full tonight," Louisa predicted. "Everyone's nervous."

Valentine raised an eyebrow at Hornbreed, who shook his head. A few couples left the bar and began to dance. Valentine recognized one of the pilots from the rescue helicopter, stomping away in elaborately stitched pointed-toe boots.

The band took a quick break. Hornbreed used the silence to tell an abbreviated version of the hunter-gatherers story, attracting a small crowd. "I've seen their tracks, on mule patrol up Goner Ridge," a woman put in. "He's not exaggerating."

Hornbreed left out his injury, and embellished a little, saying Valentine had carried him halfway down a mountain, plinking at bugs the whole way.

When the band started up again they were joined by a zebra-haired singer. She performed in a silver mesh bikini and matching strappy cork-heeled sandals, rattlesnake tattoos winding down each arm and a Chinese ideograph on her back. She'd applied makeup with an airbrush, giving her bright, intense eyes wings like a pit viper's:

"Take one take two take three take me
Bled out in an attic so's nobody sees"

The dancers were limp in one another's arms as they moved, shambling like ravies cases about to keel over. The singer's arms waved hypnotically as she passed the microphone first to one hand, then the other. Valentine looked around, a little shocked at the explicit lyrics, but maybe musicians could sing what no one dared say.

"Hiya, cherry," a female voice twanged in his ear.

A girl in fishnets and feathers, a swan-shaped black bottle nestled under one netted breast, put down a shot glass in front of him. "Jolt of Swan Neck? On the house."

"I'm not drinking," Valentine said.

"He's already at half-staff," Louisa said. "No assistance required."

The woman planted the bottle at the center of the table, put a hand on each of Valentine's shoulders, and did a brief bump and grind. "You wanna go upstairs? Ready, willing, and free of charge."

"No thanks."

"Ah, the follies of youth," Hornbreed said, though Valentine guessed the wing leader had only half a decade on him. "You should take advantage of the newbie's wings. One night only."

"What was the fighting up in Colorado about?" Valentine asked.

"Those jokers are trying to starve us by cutting off the Colorado River. We took out the dams."

"Must have been big bombs."

"No, demolition teams. It was more an airmobile operation. Ever since that fiasco in Fifty we use our own troops on the ground if we have to land anything. Damn Grogs flapped off as soon as things got a little hot."

Valentine wondered if the Kurian Year Fifty "fiasco" was the operation at Love Field in Dallas. His old regiment, the Razors, had been so battered by the aerial pounding, Southern Command had broken it up—but he wasn't about to make Hornbreed feel better by saying so. Odd that he felt more like shaking the man's hand than ever. The aerial assault had been well coordinated and deadly.

"Don't let the rationing fool you," Starguide added. "This is a profound crèche. You never hear a Hisser, unless you're riding a desk at GHQ. We run our own lives. We get—"

A rattlesnake-decorated arm cut him off as the singer wrapped herself around Valentine's back.

"We've got a first timer here tonight, named—"

"Max," Hornbreed supplied.

She hopped up and planted her thong-divided buttocks on the bar table, planting her sandaled foot firmly on Valentine's crotch. Valentine watched her eyeballs rattle around and decided she was a little stoned. "Let's rass it for the Circus' newest hero, Max.

"From the rigs of Catalina
To the shoals of Mississippi
We shall fight for mankind's uplift
To Earth's glorious destiny

"In our fight for truth and justice
And to keep our conscience clean
We will always follow orders
of the Saviors of Our Dream."

Cheering broke out at the end of the song and Valentine reached up for a kiss, lifting her leg out of the way. He used the leverage to throw her slight body over his shoulder.

"I'm taking her up," he called to the crowd, heading for the stairs.

"Hit that silk hard!" a drunk in the crowd shouted.

"My set's not over, you bastard," the singer yelled, punching him in the small of the back.

Two pipeline-armed men in leather vests, probably bouncers, appeared at the front of the crowd, but no call for assistance came.

He slapped one tan buttock in return. "She'll be back after a brief intermission," Valentine said as he took the first steps, to cheering approval.

He paused at the top of the stairs. A hallway led to a marked washroom and several doors. He tried the nearest door; it wasn't locked.

A big, cushioned wooden lounge chair and a double bed almost filled the little paneled room. Sponge-painted clouds gave the room a nursery feel. He found a light switch. A single bulb in an orange and blue Chinese lantern gave the room a grotto glow. There was a rag rug on the floor, and a pair of towels next to a washbasin and an empty pitcher on a little shelf.

The band had already transitioned into a dance number. Muffled percussion and guitar rose through the floor.

"Classy," Valentine said. He dumped the singer on the bed.

"Fucker!" she protested. "You could ask a—"

"I will," Valentine said. "What's your name?"

She sat up and kicked off her sandals. "Gide. Be careful with my face, okay? Rough stuff will mess up the makeup." She took off the bikini top. "I know it's traditional to keep the pants as a souvenir, but these were—"

"Gide, you can keep them on." Valentine sat in the chair. "I just want to talk."

She flopped back against the wall, extracted a hand-rolled from her hairdo. "What, like dirty?"

"No. One of those songs, the one about the attic, it struck me as odd. Aren't you afraid of saying stuff like that?"

"Got a light?"

"I don't smoke."

"Shit." She felt around under the mattress, peeked under the bed. "They sneak in condoms all the time, but can they leave a match? Dream deferred." She reattached the cigarette, or joint, to a hairpin and put it back in her tangle of hair.

"You wrote that song?"

"Yeah. You hot shits could use a bite of reality. It got a response, you saw."

"What's a purification?" Valentine asked.

Some of the hard edge came off. "It's—it's not my place."

"Please. I'm new here. Call me Max, if you like. I brought in Wing Leader Hornbreed. I'm wondering if I should grab my reward and run while the getting's good."

"You got your gold yet?"

"Working on it. I'm trading most of it for a trip far away."

"Purification's head-count reduction," she said. "Lotta times it makes no sense, who gets chosen."

"Who does it, Churchmen?" Valentine asked.

"Yeah, the church handles it."

"Ever worry that your songs might get you purified?"

"Fuck no. I think they like having me around. They need a place for the zips to let off a little steam. The Mezcal's sort of cathartic."

"Sort of what?" Valentine asked.

"Catharsis. Healthy elimination of emotion. Like a big bawlin' shit into the toilet of life."

"Singer *and* philosopher."

"My old man was a cowhand, but that doesn't mean he was dumb. Always had a book or two tucked away and he read to me a lot. I grew up in the saddle with a rifle instead of a doll. Killed a mountain lion when I was eight."

"If you can shoot, why didn't you join the service?" Valentine studied her tattoos. The snakes were posed differently. The left arm seemed to be striking; the right wrapped itself protectively around her upper arm and watched the world from the soft spot on her forearm.

"I'd be tempted to pull the trigger with the gun pointed the other way. How far away from here are you going?"

"About a thousand miles north."

Her fingers tightened on the stained bedding. "Take me with? I can work off my expenses. Or we can arrange something. I ain't exactly a virgin, but I'm healthy and horny on my own account, not just to keep my job. I'll fuck you like Scheherazade, not some high-mileage brothel cunt."

"I'm tempted just for the conversation."

She tipped back into the bed. "Make fun. Who are you to talk to me like that?"

"I was hoping to figure that out on this trip. How do you survive a purification?"

"No telling what sets them off. But I'd cover that limp if I were you. Life is precarious for the lame and halt. I don't suppose you're a big shot somewhere, and you're just keeping your brass ring hid?"

"No such luck," Valentine said. "How can I get in touch with you?"

"I live above Ling's market in Yuma. I help him stock after a gig. Then I sleep out the day. But don't be afraid to wake me up, know what I mean?"

"I look forward to the rest of your set."

"Wait," she said, standing. "Undo your hair."

Valentine unwound the thick rubber band that kept his hair out of the way. Gide reached up and ran her metallic-nailed fingers through his hair, tousling it.

"You've got three gray hairs," she said, and kissed him. Her lips traveled down his neck. "Just a little lipstick smear. Someone might wonder why you carried me up here to talk. Though I ought to give you a black eye."

"Thanks for the advice, Gide."

"What about my offer?"

"Under consideration. But if I bring you, it'll be for your trigger finger, not the thousand and one nights."

She blinked. "You've done some reading too."

"Haven't had the time lately." Valentine put his hand flat against the small of her back and gave her lips a quick brush with his own.

"And what was that for? My makeup's already fucked."

"Gratitude. Lone man's dilemma. I was beginning to think all these flyboys were the sane ones and I was the nut."

Valentine took the stairs quietly, noticing on his way down that the crowd had grown. Masses of people and noise made him tense and headachy, so he joined some of the smokers outside. People sat on old car seats and lawn chairs, drinking and smoking and looking at the stars. In the shadows, couples kissed.

Cigarette smoke, stars, and the occasional eager moan turned above Valentine as he stargazed. Were women aware of their strange healing power? He felt the wounds begin to close, but nothing, not Gide, not Blake, not even the satisfaction that would come with a successful assignment, could replace his daughter.

"Never should have made that trip," he said.

"How's that, Max? You regretting popping off into the sage to get me back?" Hornbreed said from behind.

"Didn't see you," Valentine said. "No, different trip, two years ago. Just as soon not talk about it."

"Suit yourself. How'd you like your flight?"

"Loved it, but I still want my reward."

"We're always short planes, but it'll be arranged. You'll go fast and in style. We'll tack on an extra day or two to maintenance and put the fuel use down to testing. Tomorrow I'll set you down with some workbooks—you need to learn a few principles—and then maybe you'll go up in a two-seat glider."

"You worried about some 'purifiers' showing up?"

"I keep my nose clean. Worst thing you can do is get all nervous about it. They see you stammering and sweating, they figure a guilty conscience is showing itself."

"I know what you mean," Valentine said, prickling at Hornbreed's blasé attitude. Did they put something in the water here? Suppose they carted Louisa off?

"They might not even show. The higher-ups are more worried about the food situation. They'll probably concentrate on agro in California and Mexico."

"I'd just as soon get going."

"We're still going to give you a couple thousand in gold, you know. That's got to be arranged for."

Valentine wondered if a stall was on. "How you feeling?"

"Better. Whatever juice the bugs put in me, I think it's about worked its way out. Just sore as hell. You're bunking in our house tonight, by the way. Let's go over to the hospital and sign for your gear. It sits there too long, someone might decide to sell it."

"I'm ready to go."

They took a little Volkswagen ("The Mexicans changed the name for a couple years, but people quit buying them," Hornbreed explained). Hornbreed's house was just shy of some of the estates in Iowa. The imposing, Spanish-style house lacked only the expansive grounds to be a true manor. Instead it sat on a small plot of land in a gated community filled with other equally impressive houses. Louisa gave Valentine a pleasant little room of his own on a central courtyard—its fountain made a pleasing sound—where he could look up at the master suite's second-floor balcony.

He startled awake, reaching for the sword under the pillows, but it was only a pretty Asian teenage girl in an apron bringing morning coffee—real coffee, at that.

"Breakfast in kitchen," she said.

After the strictly portioned meal Hornbreed showed him "the neighborhood." There was a swimming pool, a school, and a small golf course, a private store, and a common garage where the favored families "checked out" vehicles. Hornbreed explained that most of the residents rarely went beyond the gates. Necessities were brought to them.

There was a small playground but only a few children, in simple clothes that looked homemade. They shrieked and chased each other, shouting in a Spanish-English patois that sounded like it had a little Chinese thrown in for flavor. "Staff children," Hornbreed said. "They're really not supposed to be there, but no one complains."

"What about the kids who are supposed to be using it?"

"Most of our kids go to church school, or private academies. Class all morning, sports in the afternoon, and tutoring or apprenticeships at night. Really first-class schooling. Tumlo next door has a daughter already beginning medical training, and she's only fifteen. We got to get to the field. But we're making one more stop. I've got something to show you."

He said no more until they took the Volkswagen out to one of the more remote hangars on the big airfield. Hornbreed maneuvered it around piles of junk, engines hanging from chains, and racks of assorted rusting spares. It was half-junkyard, half-machine-shop, worked by men with overalls and close-cropped hair in their last days.

Hornbreed parked in the shade inside the hangar. A radio hanging from a cord played cheerful NUC choir music as it spun in the dry desert breeze.

"This is sort of a private workshop. The men here aren't paid by the Circus or AAC. The pilots keep them to work on their private craft. Hey, Jimmy."

The man who'd trotted up to get the door liked to chew tobacco. His hands had a fascinating patina; the oil had worked itself into every crevice. He wiped them on a rag before shaking hands with Hornbreed.

"This the bounty man?" Jimmy asked, looking at Valentine's ID card. An aluminum can with a rubber lid hung around his neck.

"Max Argent," Valentine said, extending his hand.

Jimmy didn't shake it. "You got a lift all the way back to Yuma. Sure didn't do much for that gold. I could've done that."

"You didn't face down ten-foot scorpions," Hornbreed said. "He did. Where's the crate, Jimmy? Hope you haven't put it in the same spot as your manners."

"Just speakin' my mind, sir. Pat's just over here."

Jimmy led them past a couple of fixed-gear prop planes and to a little contraption in the bright colors of a yellow jacket that looked like a wheeled two-man bobsled under an oversized beach umbrella missing its fabric. It had a big prop sticking out the back.

"This is a Personal Advanced Aerial Transport. It's an autogyro, Max. Just about my favorite toy for flying out over the dunes. Seats two and some personal cargo. She's a fun little ship, and can run on ordinary high-octane gasoline. Twin rudders. Pretty safe, as long as you watch the weather, and if you stow your gear in to balance the load. Can take off from a cleared field and if the engine conks out, you just rotate back down."

"What works the rotors? All I see is a control mechanism. Or is there an axle hidden in there?"

"Forward velocity. Air resistance keeps the rotors spinning, and they give lift. That's where it's different from a helicopter—you can't hover, and you need takeoff room. Engine's a hundred ten horsepower, and you can engage a driver that works the wheels so it's a motorized tricycle too. There's pretty good ground clearance. This thing was the range model."

"All yours?" Valentine asked.

"No. She's yours now."

Jimmy popped the lid and spit into the aluminum can.

"You're kidding."

"No. It's a thank-you for going into that hole after me. Most men wouldn't have."

"Most men don't like seeing an Archon's ransom disappearing down a big rat hole either."

Hornbreed shrugged. "Maybe. Maybe not."

"Don't know how to thank you," Valentine said.

"I still got my Air Ranger, Argent. You're getting the kiddie toy."

Valentine gave in to his pleasure at the gift. "What are we waiting for? Let's take her up."

"Duty calls. And you've got some workbooks to get through. I'll be checking your math at lunch."

There were anxious faces all over the utilitarian command building and the sound of steel doors opening and shutting as people hurried from office to office.

"They're at the tower now," an airman said.

"That just means they'll be gone by lunch," Hornbreed countered calmly.

Hornbreed's office had pictures of aircraft, glossy pre-'22 images and simpler black-and-whites of younger versions of himself in a neat school uniform and flight suits standing in groups in front of various craft. Manila envelopes and folders were piled on his desk. Assorted pilots were gathered outside, seeking an opportunity to take their planes up. Hornbreed checked off flight card after flight card.

"*Huff.* We'll look busy today, that's for sure."

Hornbreed whistled tunelessly as he got out a clipped stack of paper titled "Basic Principles of Aviation" and handed it to Valentine. "Grab a pencil off my desk if you like. There's an empty classroom at the end of the hall, if you want somewhere quiet to work, but you should shut the curtains or it'll get hot."

"I'll just grab a chair in here."

"Be my guest."

Valentine dived into equations about lift. Some of them brought back memories of the book-walled little room in Father Max's house. He'd read some about flying in the lonely days after he lost his parents and siblings, suddenly wanting to know about his father only after he was cold in his grave.

Three times Circus personnel popped their heads into the office to tell him about the "purifiers." Each time Hornbreed waved them off.

"They said we lost too many ships in Colorado!" one nervous, pimpled young airman said. "They already took two out of the tower."

"We got the water flowing again," Hornbreed said. "Tell you what, I'm out of copier toner. I'll give you a warrant to run into Yuma and pick up some more. Grab a lunch while you're there, Daw."

"You know Ling's market?" Valentine said as the young man stood first on one foot, then the other, waiting for the purchase order and pass.

"Sure," the kid said.

"You need something?" Hornbreed asked.

"I might take up your milk habit. But give a message to this girl Gide. She lives above Ling's. Tell her Max would like to see her again."

"Max would like to see her again," the kid repeated.

"That oddball?" Hornbreed asked.

"I like the tattoos," Valentine said.

"This I have to hear. Let's take a coffee break."

"While the purifiers are here?" Daw squeaked. Hornbreed passed him the paperwork.

"Why not? Coming, Argent?"

They took some stairs down to a cafeteria, where the workers were frantically cooking, cleaning, and polishing. Valentine smelled cleanser and wet mops.

"Gide, huh," Hornbreed said, buying them some coffee with his ID. "I don't think she's all there. Though I'll admit what there is of her was expertly assembled."

"I like a challenge," Valentine said.

"If it'll plant you here, then I'm happy. Tumbleweeds have a way of disappearing. You could do a lot worse than the Circus, you know."

"I know," Valentine said, and meant it. He'd seen less comfortable cages.

A hubbub broke out in the hall, and a party entered.

"*Huff.* Oh hell," Hornbreed said. He stood and faced them.

Valentine did likewise, trying not to gape, but it was a strange procession that strode into the cafeteria.

Two teenagers led it, a handsome Hispanic boy and a blond girl with prom-queen hair. They wore impossibly clean white robes that might have been martial arts uniforms had the coats been a little shorter. Neither of the youths could have been over seventeen or eighteen.

Behind them a New Universal Church Youth Vanguard warden carried a big briefcase handcuffed to his wrist.

Then came the muscle. A pair of men in combat vests, burnished pistols holstered low on their thighs, might have been watching him from behind dark sunglasses. It was hard to tell—they kept their noses pointed straight ahead.

Hovering at the edge of the mass was Pyp himself, hatless and complaining. His stray hair gave him a desperate look.

"Wildlife's one of my best radarmen. He lost that arm in action, you know."

"He seemed insolent," the boy said. His voice was that of a man's, but nevertheless a little high-pitched. Sergeant Patel would tell him to "talk like you've got a pair, boy."

"Uh-huh. Or maybe he was just trying to make sure that those planes taking off didn't crash into each other."

"Who's this?" the girl asked, staring at Valentine.

"Follow your heart, Ariel," the warden advised. He opened his briefcase.

"You don't have paper on him," Pyp said. "He brought in the wing leader, here. Saved his life in tribe country."

"No doubt seeking the reward. Greedy," the young man said.

"Is that how you spend your life?" the girl asked. "Chasing money? Flesh for gold?"

"Shut up, Ariel," Hornbreed said. He placed the slightest extra stress on the name, perhaps mocking it. "You don't know what you're talking about."

The teens stood up, almost crackling like charged hair.

The warden shuffled through his folder. He handed a sheet to the young man.

Pyp put himself between the purification team and his wing leader. "You don't let men who bring in our pilots claim their reward in peace, that'll be it for anyone who goes down."

"That's the problem, isn't it? They keep going down," the boy said. "There's sabotage among the mechanics, certainly."

"If we could trade for real spares instead of modifying stuff from the boneyards," Pyp said.

"Do you think you're immune, old man?" Ariel asked. "One word from me and you'll be off with the others. There's more than a whiff of personal corruption about you." She glanced at his feet. "Too lazy to wash your own socks and shine your own shoes?"

Valentine recognized a couple of the phrases from the New Universal Church *Guidon,* while the rest of him was tensing as he evaluated the muscle. How much was show and how much was go?

"You take him and you'll never see three-quarters of the pilots again," Hornbreed said.

The young man consulted the sheet the warden had handed him. "A man who crashed on his last flight might be worried about his own fate."

"Crashed?" Ariel cut in.

"Wipe that sneer off your face or I'll do it for you," Hornbreed said.

"He was trying to get a lame bird back," Pyp said. "I'd ordered the ship destroyed at the forward field, but he insisted he could get it back. He almost did. She's been salvaged and is being repaired now. He's a damn hero."

"This is the real test, Ariel," the warden said.

"He's going," she said, glaring at Hornbreed. One of the security talked into the mini-walkie-talkie clipped to his epaulet.

Hornbreed shook his head, a sad smile on his face. "You'll think about today. Later."

"Lack of humility. Willfulness," the youth said to no one in particular, but the warden checked off ticks on a pad. "Disparagement. What's the phrase? 'Three strikes and you're cut'?"

"Out," Valentine corrected, watching two men, one with a baton in his hand and the other with cuffs and leg-irons, step inside.

"Max, be quiet. Looks like someone else will have to check your equations at lunch." Hornbreed wore the same bland fatalism Valentine had first met in the desert.

Valentine's hand convulsed over the sword hilt that wasn't there. If he angled it just right, he could open both sets of carotid arteries with a single sweep. Make a red mess of the spotless white robes.

Hornbreed turned toward the girl, chuckled. "One day it will be your turn. . . . I wonder how you'll take the news."

"Our generation will not be tainted," the youth said. Pyp fought with his hands, which were balling up into fists.

"Tell Louisa I'm sorry," Hornbreed said to Pyp as they shackled him. The wing leader was shaking, just a little. Valentine looked away, embarrassed. Just another Quisling, getting what's coming to him from the blood-greased machine he kept moving, he told himself. "I know she loves that house," Hornbreed said as they led him toward the door, where a woman and two other men waited, chained together. "It's gonna kill her to leave it."

"Let's see how clean that kitchen is," Ariel said, looking past Hornbreed. Did she have a tear in her eye? The kids led the procession away. One of the guards didn't like the look of Valentine, and watched him.

"Argent, wait for me in his office," Pyp said. Valentine listened as they walked toward the kitchen. "Last chance, you two. I'm going to fight to get this commuted to a labor term in California. You resist me on it, and, well, I've got old friends in the church, right up to the Archon. I'll make sure there's a set of eyes on you both every time you draw a breath. You so much as yawn during services . . ."

Valentine hoped for Hornbreed's sake that Pyp could get it done. He returned to the office.

He could still smell Hornbreed's aftershave on the chair. Valentine found the rest of the math impossible.

Pyp didn't return until after 1500, according to the twenty-four-hour clock on the wall. Valentine spent the time looking at the photos around the office, and didn't like what he saw.

"I'm so tired," Pyp said, sinking into Hornbreed's chair.

"Who was that Ariel to Equality?" Valentine asked.

"How'd you work that?"

"There's a picture of them on the shelf next to the running trophy."

Pyp looked up. "I see. She's his sister. He half raised her after their father disappeared. His mother was useless, from what I know about her. I need some food, or I'm going to upchuck."

"I'm not sure that I want to go back to the cafeteria," Valentine said.

"I know," Pyp said. "Let's go down to the ready room. They have a pizza oven."

The ready room was mostly maps on the walls and old books and magazines on the chairs and chipped tables. A shower hissed down a hall that was marked HYGIENE. Comfortable armchairs and recliners were grouped around a somnolent television, where *Noonside Passions* played out the melodrama. Valentine noted that the aging Rebeccah had a new, matronly hairstyle and a church ribbon around her neck. With a better angle Valentine recognized one of the pilots from the rescue helicopter, reading his *Guidon*. Maybe he was resolving to be a better example of mankind's evolution toward the communal spirit. Or maybe he was just memorizing a phrase or two to trot out to the next purifiers.

They found some congealed pizza and warmed it in the oven.

"Want a milk?" Pyp asked. "I'm having one."

"Sure."

They sat. Pyp lifted his carton, held it up until Valentine did likewise. "A good man."

"A good man," Valentine repeated.

The milk didn't do much for the greasy pizza. Both men ate mechanically. Another pilot came in and turned up the volume on *Passions*.

"Crap, a repeat," he said to the reading man, but sat down to watch it anyway.

With some noise cover Valentine finally spoke.

"What the hell was that?"

"Fair question, son," Pyp said, taking some napkins from a metal dispenser and wiping his hands. "It's just how they keep us on our toes.

I spent some time researching it, if you want to hear. Pretty clever. You interested in mass psychology?"

"I'll take the short version."

"I think it started in the early years of the Redemption," Pyp said, setting his elbows on the table and leaning close. "In the Southeastern United States the Kurians started using pretty, teenage girls as spokespeople every time they opened a new medical center or fair-housing block.

"They find some young folks useful. They're good at picking out an elite, grooming them. Pretty soon the young and the beautiful were acting as spokespeople, passing news, bad usually. Up in the Northeast they were using kids as informers. If they turned in a ring of renegades, saboteurs, terrorists, whatever, the kids got rewarded pretty handsomely, positions in the church and whatnot.

"Practice spread. Down South, where they were having a lot of trouble with the old faiths, they started having the kids of a 'purer generation' rooting out those who didn't have their minds right. Our leaders adopted it. Having a couple kids go around picking out the wild hairs focused the resentment somewheres besides up."

"How do they get the kids to do it?" Valentine asked. "Turning in your own brother, even if he hasn't committed a real crime."

"The real crimes take place up here," Pyp said, tapping his temple. "The kids are actually pretty good at picking out those who have some kind of resentment. Good antennae for picking out those who don't fit in."

"Or maybe less empathy," Valentine said.

"You have kids?"

Valentine shrugged. *Depends on the definition.*

"Me neither," Pyp said. "Not that there haven't been women who've tempted me to settle. No. Some little shit telling his teacher who visits me in my own home at night."

"Why the interest in the purification, then?"

Pyp looked around without moving his head—a skill most older people in the Kurian Zone possessed. He used the shiny side of the napkin dispenser like a rearview mirror. "I was one. One of them. Raised in a church orphanage. I led up the first purification in Aztlan. Mind spotless as an Archon's bedsheets. Zealotry comes easy at that age. They used fine words on us, oh, yes. We were a new generation who'd tear down all the old injustices, the old prejudices, the corruption. But twenty years passed and then it was our turn to be judged corrupt."

Valentine decided to probe: "Ever think about putting your planes in the air and blowing up some of those towers?"

"You're kidding, right? I thought you were a traveling man. You know the teams, I'm sure. We got it better here than ninety percent of the world."

"You're on tight rations."

"Ahh, that'll pass. Same thing happened back during the Lincoln-Grande War. They'll swap a couple hundred square miles and it'll be put right."

"They're having a tough time containing Texas, now that they're linked up with the Ozarks. Suppose Denver throws in with them, or with that fellow up in the far Northwest, what's-his—"

"They'll just drop some new virus on 'em and that'll be the end of it. Now, Argent, listen. You seem bright enough. I know the towers give you the twitch. They do everyone. But that doesn't mean you can't do well in the shade of 'em. Learn a vital skill. Purifications don't come about closer together than six or eight years, and I've got a good chance of getting Hornbreed sprung."

"Seems to me no purifications would be better."

"That kind of operation would take weeks, hundreds and hundreds of sorties. We'd land and get throttled by—"

"So you have thought about it," Valentine said.

Pyp drew back. "Don't think you're going to inform—"

"I'm no rat," Valentine said. "Just heard someone say something about, if given a gun, they'd be tempted to point it in the other direction."

"I've been on Internal Security work groups. Renegade pilots are rare, but it's happened. They have contingencies. I'm sure there are contingencies I don't even know about. I'll tell you this: There are tunnels under this base, under the housing areas. Not sure what's down there. I don't want to find out."

A jet engine rattled the airfield with the noise of its passage.

"They have long memories," Pyp continued. "You do them enough damage, they'll get rid of you one way or another. Even if you flee to the rebels. Assuming you survive touchdown. They chop men like me up, one joint at a time."

Frustrated, Valentine sat back and pushed away the crumbs of the pizza. The man was just as right as he was wrong.

"Anyway," Pyp said. "Pressure's off now. I can arrange your trip north anytime."

"Speaking of valuable skills—I'd like a couple more flying lessons," Valentine said. "Equality gave me an ultralight, I think he called it." *Was that just this morning?* "I'd like to know more about it."

"So you did listen. Good man. I need to get out of here anyway. Think I'll take you up myself."

Seven

Southern Washington, May: Most people think of the Pacific Northwest as a cloudy, rainy woodland, fragrant with the moldy, rotting-pine smell of a temperate rainforest. But beyond the rain-catching Cascades, the eastern plains of Washington have more in common with the high plains of the Midwest than the foggy harbors of salmon fleet and crab boat.

Wolves trot through the open country in the summer, pursuing the prolific western antelope, retreating to the river-hugging woods when winter comes.

The former ranching and orchard country of the dry half of Washington is sparsely inhabited but frequently patrolled for reasons unique to this part of the country. A few Kurian outposts, fed by rail lines running up from Utah and Oregon or in from Idaho, circle their lands with towers like teeth, easily visible from the air thanks to the irrigation technology still in use. But these are the terminal ends, for nothing but one Grog-guarded set of rail and highway line runs up the Pacific coast, thanks to the highly effective, organized guerrilla army under their "Mr. Adler."

The Osprey-style jump jet touched down on an empty stretch of highway, cutting over a high, dry plateau. The Cascades ran in a blue line in the distance, darkening as the sun descended to meet them. Valentine, ears popping in the change of pressure, drank a final pint of milk in memorial to Hornbreed.

It felt like a long flight, and ended with several low passes to find a suitable stretch of road for landing. Valentine had grown used to short training hops in his time with the autogyro, gliders, and small training craft. The jet, a courier craft for high-level Quislings, was plushly appointed beyond anything Valentine had ever experienced and had ample space in the cargo bay for the autogyro, with its rotators folded away. He rode in the cockpit for an hour or two, listening to Starguide's stories of Utah and Nevada.

"That's right, a big chunk of the Salt Lake City folks just disappeared, almost overnight. Some say they all marched up a mountain and killed themselves. Others say they went to another world. I think it's kinda both—Mormons always were weird," he said as they viewed the Great Salt Lake from fifteen thousand feet.

After a refueling stop at a combination armory and coal-processing plant, featuring the first Grogs Valentine had seen since coming West, they took the rest of the hop up to Washington. The jet had enough in its tanks to make it back to Utah.

"I don't believe it. We're out," Gide said. She'd regained the color she'd lost when they hit turbulence leaving Utah.

Much of the past few weeks had been occupied with Gide's "Exit Authority," a polite term for a sheaf of papers representing a series of undercover transactions that allowed her to leave the Confederation. It wasn't difficult for Valentine to convince Pyp that he'd fallen hard for the girl and wanted her up on the family land in Washington. An allied Kurian enclave in northern Utah agreed to buy her, in exchange for three children—one partially deaf and another in a foot brace—who were to be apprenticed to the New Universal Church in Tempe. The Circus arranged for her Utah paperwork to be "misfiled" using some of Valentine's reward.

She stood well clear of the plane now, lost in a heavy military jacket and knee boots, her dark-and-light-pleated hair bound up atop her head like a swirl ice-cream cone.

His pilot instructor, Starguide, helped Valentine take the ultralight from the cargo hold and give it a final flight check.

"What do your people raise, anyway?" Starguide asked, helping Valentine roll out the autogyro from the cargo bay doors.

"Pigs," Valentine said. "There's a catfish hatchery too. That's where spare feed and pig shit goes."

"You must really love him," Starguide hollered over to Gide.

With that, he closed the cargo hatch with a hydraulic whine. "Well, Argent, I still say you might make a good pilot someday. Come back if you get tired of slopping the hogs."

"I just want to be far away from everything," Valentine said.

"The sky doesn't qualify?"

Valentine shrugged, already composing the part of his report about the Flying Circus. Like the sailors on the *Thunderbolt*, at least part of the Circus took to the sky to be free of the Kurians, if only temporarily.

He and Gide stood well clear of the jet as it turned around, plugging their ears against the thunder of its exhaust. Starguide used a more fuel-efficient, traditional takeoff. When the Osprey took its running start back into the brassy late-spring sky, they were alone with the wind.

"We're out," Gide repeated. She hugged him. "Fuckin'-A."

"Feels good, doesn't it?" Valentine asked.

"I'll say. Let's take our clothes off. Like little kids in the sun. I'm so in the mood for a frolic 'n' fuck."

"I think we should get going. That jet might have drawn attention."

She broke contact. "You're a torqued kite, Max."

Valentine considered telling her his real name now, and his destination—though not his purpose. Travel was a lot safer with a companion in case of illness or injury, he rationalized. "How's that?" he asked instead.

"Never taking a run at me. Queer?"

"No."

"Balls blown off?"

"No."

"What, then?"

"Don't have much luck with women," he finally said.

"Just sex, you know. It's healthy. Might get that stick out of your ass."

Valentine opened the autogyro's canopy, revealing the twin seats, the passenger above and behind the pilot. He grabbed the steering-wheel-style stick and turned it so the little ship was pointed down the road, and opened the tool pouch. His nose detected something rotten in the right cargo compartment. Sure enough, Jimmy had left him a dead rat as a going-away present. Valentine extracted it and flung it into the dry, weed-pocked soil beside the road. "Wouldn't work that way with you," Valentine said.

"How's that?"

"I like you."

She stared at him for a moment, her upper lip working back and forth, then tousled his hair. "I know you do. Otherwise you wouldn't have gotten me out."

"I'd like to think I'd still have tried even if I didn't."

"You hide behind a lot of ifs, Max. I know you're a pretty good card player. That's about it."

"Let's change the subject. What's next for you?"

She squatted beside him and lowered her voice, even though there was no one to overhear them but the grasshoppers. "I'm joining up."

"Joining what?"

Her eyes brightened. "The resistance. There's a big army up here, out in the mountains to the west. The flyboys tell me they're tearing assholes out of the KO. I'm gonna join them. I didn't tell you before because . . . because I didn't want you to be an accessory. Just in case they picked me up or something."

"Or in case I was some kind of informer."

She shrugged. "I suppose anything's possible."

"How do you know they'll take you?"

"Can I fire off a couple from your gun?"

"Help me get this thing ready first. I want to be able to take off quickly if we need to."

She helped him stow their gear intelligently enough. "You keeping this thing, or you going to trade it?"

Valentine sat down and tested the simple cable controls. "I'm wondering how easy it'll be to find fuel. I'm more of a horse-and-pack-mule person, most of the time."

"Thought you were a biker, with those leathers."

Load balanced in the little cargo spaces to either side of the chute-like cabin, they were ready to go. "I think it's time to come clean with you, Gide. I'm aiming on the resistance up here too. I just had a few hundred more miles to come."

"Fuckin'-A!"

"If you like, I'll give you a lift to the mountains. Safer for two to travel together."

"You're this gal's knight in shining armor, Max."

"With a motorcycle engine attached to an oversized food processor as a mount."

"So how were you going to get all the way up here without the flyboys?" she asked.

"I've had some experience with ships and boats. Thought I'd get to LA by hiring on with a convoy, then work north up the coast. But an opportunity presented itself, and I always wanted to know more about the Circus."

"Seen them buzzing around?"

"Something like that."

"I'd still like to try that gun. I've only ever shot over open sights since I was little."

Valentine showed her the points of the rifle. "You cock the first with the bolt. Crosshairs are zeroed for one hundred yards."

"Regular 7.62?"

Valentine nodded. She sighted on an old wooden post perhaps seventy yards away, peeping like an owl from a patch of brush next to the road, and fired. They walked over and inspected her shot. She'd almost centered the post.

"Again?"

Valentine decided that ammunition used in practice wasn't really wasted, and he wanted to test the stuff he'd picked up in Yuma anyway.

He fashioned targets by inking a couple of pieces of toilet tissue and fixed them to a tree trunk back toward the autogyro. She was an even better shot than he was at two hundred yards, using the stabilizing built-in bipod.

The only thing they disturbed with the gunfire was the birds.

"I'm convinced," he said.

"The old man sent me to bed hungry if I missed with my bullet," she said. "One shot, meat and all that."

Valentine examined the road. It had been used recently, light trucks by the look of the tread. Someone was taking care of the primary roads out here. He unrolled and studied his map of Washington State.

This could be one of the highways that communicated between the forces in the Cascades and Mount Omega—which wasn't really a mountain, of course. Strange that over all these years the Kurians had never located it. His contact with Southern Command was there. He hoped he'd have reason to visit.

Valentine cleaned and stowed the gun and they climbed into the autogyro. Valentine had flown it tandem before while learning, but never with his food, weapons and accoutrements, blankets and bamboo sleeping mat, and spare clothes aboard.

He worked the throttle and opened the engine all the way up. The autogyro ate highway as it sped up, and finally jumped into the air. Gide let out a gasp.

Valentine brought it up to about a thousand feet.

Flying in an autogyro is noisy and busy. The lift from the rotors makes it sway and bob like a cork in a choppy water.

"Oh shit. Land again. Land again," Gide gasped.

"Are you—"

A loud retching sound from above and behind answered his question. The smell filled the cabin, half-digested bologna-and-cheese sandwiches giving off a beery odor. Valentine fought his own gorge, rising in sympathy.

Gide cracked a little panel window, letting in even more of the engine's roar. "You can set it down, Max. I think I'd rather walk."

"Give it an hour," Valentine said, watching the falling sun and wondering if he could stand an hour with the vomit smell. "Fix your eyes on the mountains. That's where we're heading."

Twenty minutes of groaning later Valentine spotted a strange bare patch of earth below, a short hike away from a treelined pond. It was too good an opportunity to pass up. He passed low over the cleared oval of ground and sent small, chickenlike birds on short hop-flights.

He landed with a bad bounce.

"Thank Christ," Gide said as they halted.

"Let's clean out the ship," Valentine said. He extracted a collapsed plastic jug and passed it to Gide. "Your spew. You can carry the water."

She looked at the cleared ground, frowning. "What did this? Helicopters?"

"Don't think so. With luck, you'll see tomorrow morning."

Woodpeckers, always up and hard at work even before the roosters cry or the larks rise, woke them. As the sun came up Gide got to see a prairie chicken dance.

The birds, mating in the late northern spring, gathered together at the tramped-down earth and began to jump up and down in front of one another, in wild displays of feathery athleticism.

"Looks like the dance floor at the old Mezcal on a Saturday night," Gide said. "Except no music."

"They're resourceful little birds," Valentine said. "When the snow comes they dive right into a drift and wiggle down deep, making a little igloo. Coyotes and foxes can't smell them under the snow."

"What's an igloo?" Gide asked.

Valentine explained the principle.

"I wonder what the winters are like up here," Valentine said.

"We've got some time to get acclimated. But you don't talk like an Aztlan. Or a Texican, or a Cali, or a Yute. You're hard to place."

"I was born in Minnesota. At least I think I was. I spent my childhood there, anyway."

"That's like Canada, right?"

"Next to it."

Valentine carefully took out his surgical-tube sling, fixed it to his wrist, and put a rounded stone in the leather cup. He sighted on a male at the edge of the fracas, making halfhearted little hops.

"Oh, no, don't spoil their fun," Gide said.

"I don't like to dip into my preserved food unless I have to," Valentine said. "Hickory-and-sage-smoked prairie chicken's good eating."

Valentine knocked the oldster off his feet, scattered dancing chickens as he got up and ran to finish the job with a quick twist. He bled the bird into a cup and dressed it quickly.

"There goes your invitation to the next church cotillion," Gide said as Valentine dropped it in hot water to soften the feathers for plucking. He lifted the cup. "You're not really going to drink warm blood, are you?"

"Can't afford to waste anything. It's like a multivitamin," Valentine said.

"Give me a sip. Might as well start the mountain-man stuff now." He passed her the cup and she made a face as she sipped. "Fuck, that's rude! Like having a bloody nose."

"Your dad never had you drink blood?"

"We liked our food cooked. Haven't you ever heard of salmonella, Mr. Igloo?"

"Who did the cooking? Your mom?"

Gide worked her upper lip again, this time tightening it against her teeth. "She died having me. There wasn't a midwife or anything, just my dad."

"I'm sorry," Valentine said.

"Kids always get along better with the opposite-sex parent, ever notice that?" she asked.

Valentine accepted the change of subject. "I guess you're right." He'd not had the time to experience it with Amalee. Circumstances had changed.

"I'd better see about that bird. Thought I smelled some wild onions down by the pond. We can have a nice fry-up, then wash while it digests."

Gide kept her food down on the next hop. Valentine argued with himself over what to do with the autogyro. Aircraft of any kind were valuable enough that the guerrillas would probably seize it outright. But on the other hand, it might allow him to make more of an impressive entrance.

He opted for showmanship.

What he guessed to be Mount Rainier loomed in the distance. He passed over valleys under thickening clouds, watching his fuel gauge sink toward E.

Apart from herds of goats, sheep, and cattle, and the attendant fires in the shepherds' bunkhouses, he saw little sign of habitation. But then a good guerrilla army wouldn't advertise its presence.

Then he passed over another town, built around a bridge and its patched-over road in a boomerang-shaped valley, and saw what he suspected was mortar pits in the hill above, looking out over the reduced hills to the east. Camouflage-painted four-wheelers were parked in a line like suckling piglets in front of a redbrick building in town, and there were well-used paddocks behind the line of buildings and what looked like houses converted to stables. He marked freshly sheared sheep.

Best of all, a limp American flag hung from a flagpole in front of what looked like the town post office. No Quisling force Valentine had ever heard of flew the despised Stars and Stripes, a symbol of racism and greed according to the histories of the New Order.

Valentine swooped around again, enjoying the feel of the tight turn. Men in civilian clothes and uniform were coming out onto the street now to watch the acrobatics.

"Gide," Valentine said, almost shouted. "This looks like the guerrillas. One thing you should know."

"Yeah?" she said, eyes closed, sounding like she was fighting with her stomach again.

"My name's not Max Argent. It's Valentine, David Valentine. I travel under a false name."

"Okay," she burped. "Land, all right?"

Valentine set the gyro down on the other side of the bridge from the town, where the road widened outside the bridge. He engaged the wheel drive and motored toward town. The road was badly pocked, and they bounced a good deal.

Some armed men in timberland camouflage were walking up the road.

"Ma—David, whatever. Open up!" Gide said.

Valentine popped the hatch as he applied the brakes. Gide jumped out and fell to her knees, bringing up a mostly liquid mess.

Valentine jumped out to aid her, but his bad left leg betrayed him and he stumbled. As he caught himself, his foot slipped in a pothole and he felt something in his ankle give. He sprawled.

Gide turned her head, wiped saliva from her mouth.

Valentine rolled over and probed his ankle. *Great, a sprain. So much for showmanship.*

"Here they come," Gide said.

A brown-haired man under a wide-brimmed black hat with yellow cording halted the others about ten yards away. He had a long, thick mustache that covered his upper lip.

"I hope you two have good reason to buzz us like that," he said. "Otherwise, your welcome to Brantley's Bridge will end with you hanging from it."

Valentine sat up. "We're not spies. We're here to join up. Can you put me in touch with a recruiting officer?" He tried to rise, but the ankle hurt too much. He ended up balancing unsteadily on his bad leg.

Gide got to her feet, parked herself under his armpit. "That's right."

"Shit," one of the men behind, a shotgun held professionally but pointed down, commented. "We should just make heroes out of them now. Save a lot of trouble."

"Recruiting officer, huh?" the man with the mustache said. "I don't know that we have any of those. Least not at this depot."

"What do you suggest for recruits, then?"

"You want to die under ol' Adler, we can assist." It began to drizzle. The officer lifted his face to the rain, took off his hat, and wiped his forehead before returning his cover to its place. "First we have to detick you. Then you get questioned. You out of Sea-Tac?"

"No. Opposite direction. We came across the Rockies. The last KZ I was in was the Aztlan Confederation."

"Long trip in that little eggbeater."

"You'll hear the whole story, if you want," Valentine said.

"Tell you what, Mister, we support some garrison militia right here in town. I'm going to hold you here for now, warm and cozy, but we have to keep you to visitors' quarters. We'll turn you over to them and they'll feed you until someone from Pacific Command can get down here. Hope that goes well for you—the alternative isn't pleasant."

After a warm disinfectant shower and a quick physical, the captain put them in a rather moldy house. They had running water, though it was cold. Tallow dips offered smelly light at night, and there were some old books to read.

The windows and door were barred from the outside. Valentine watched off-duty men inspect the autogyro, everything from the still-smelly cockpit to the tail rotor. Valentine's weapons and gear were all locked up in the "armory," what had formerly been the modest post office in the middle of town.

Gide silently fretted. Being locked up, in her experience in the Kurian Zone, meant doom.

"They're just being careful," Valentine said.

Finally a tired-looking young lieutenant driven by a heavyset sergeant with a maimed right hand pulled up in a two-horse carriage and visited the redbrick headquarters building.

In a few moments they emerged, accompanied by the mustachioed Captain Clarke and the militia staff sergeant, who inspected their lodgings daily for signs of damage or mischief.

Clarke knocked and entered without waiting for a response: "You two got a visitor. He'll figure out what the hell to make outta you."

The captain and the militia sergeant waited outside the locked door while the newly arrived lieutenant sat down and opened a folding notebook. He had ink stains on his fingers thanks to a problematic pen, and the frames of his thick glasses looked like they'd originally been intended for a woman.

"My name is Lieutenant Walker. This is Sergeant Coombs. You are . . . ahh, David Valentine, I take it?" he asked, looking through the bottle-bottom lenses.

"Yes," Valentine said.

"So you're Gide. No other name?"

"I've been called lots of names," she said. "But I wouldn't want them written down."

The sergeant assisting licked his lips as he looked at her. She'd found a thick flannel shirt in one of the closets, and pulled her hair back into a tight ponytail, but she still exuded her aggressive sensuality.

"Have you been treated well since you arrived? You can be honest—I report to a whole separate chain of command. Plenty of food? Wash water? Medical care?"

Valentine plucked at the elastic bandage on his ankle. It had healed with its usual alacrity. "They've been generous with everything," Valentine said.

"Good. Place of birth?"

"Boundary Waters, Minnesota," Valentine said.

"Choa Flats, Arizona," Gide supplied.

"Freeborn?"

"Meaning?" Valentine asked.

"Not born into slavery, on an estate or whatever."

"No," Valentine said. " 'Freeborn.' "

"I was born in the Confederation, obviously," Gide said.

"Military experience? Someone must have taught you to fly, David. Should we start with that?"

Valentine put his hands on his knees. "Have to go back a few more years. I first joined Southern Command in May of 2061, when a Wolf patrol came through our area. . . ."

The rest took about twenty minutes. Valentine just skimmed his wanderings after his adoption of Blake.

Lieutenant Walker's pen ran out when Valentine described the bounty he'd claimed. "Damn," he muttered. "Look, ummm, Major Valentine, this is a bit more than I expected. If I can ask you, though, sir, what did you come here to do?"

"I want our side to win," Valentine said. "Your general's fame has crossed the mountains."

"He doesn't claim any rank, actually," Walker said. "Technically, he's still a civilian. But he's kind of like the president to us. Sometimes he's called the Old Man."

"Just say ol' Adler and everyone knows who you're talking about," Sergeant Coombs added.

Walker fiddled with his pen and inkwell. "I'm going to have to refer your case to higher command. Do you want to stay here, or come back with me to my station?"

"If that would save travel time," Valentine said.

"We'll try to accommodate you," Walker said, looking over his shoulder at the sergeant, who straightened up a little in his lean against the wall.

Walker turned up a new page. "Now, Gide, are you going to tell me you sank the Eisenhower Floating Fortress?"

She was looking fixedly at Valentine, as if trying to decide what the symptoms of delusions of grandeur looked like.

"No. I can ride. I can shoot. I'm healthy," she said.

" 'Can shoot' doesn't do it justice," Valentine said.

Walker spent some time questioning Gide, but Valentine could see he was preoccupied. He was a good interrogator, and for all Valentine knew, the thick glasses and cranky pen were props to put people off their guard. He was good at an interrogator's first job, which was just to get people talking by asking questions that were pleasant to answer.

What assistance Sergeant Coombs offered wasn't clear to Valentine. Maybe he just had a good eye for liars.

They broke for lunch, a mutton stew and applesauce. Then the militiamen packed up a box of wax-paper-wrapped sandwiches and thermoses.

"We'll be there by midnight or so if we get moving," Walker said. He wrote out an order sheet for the gyrocopter to be moved, and handed it to the captain.

"You travel at night?" Valentine asked.

"We don't go fast enough so it's dangerous," Walker said.

"I take it the Reapers don't get this far into the mountains, then?"

"No. We give them too much to worry about in the basin. The tower's men are the ones who fear the night. Not us."

Valentine couldn't tell if this was just rear-area bravado, propaganda, or confidence born of experience.

"I don't suppose I can have my carbine back."

"Sergeant Coombs, what do you think?"

"If he's who he says he is, he doesn't need a gun to kill us."

Walker giggled. "The sergeant has a dark streak like the Columbia River. But let me keep the hardware for now. It'll save questions at the stops, as you don't have so much as a militia cap."

Their gear stowed beneath the seats, Valentine helped Gide up into the open carriage, then climbed up himself. It had iron-rimmed wheels and a camouflage-netting top.

"Sorry for the rickety transport," Walker said. "As a lowly lieutenant, I don't rate a gasoline ration for my duties. Our supply line for fossils stretches way up into Canada, and it's not altogether reliable." He took off his glasses and nodded to the sergeant, who set off.

They stopped three times on the journey, twice at checkpoints outside of settlements and once for an exchange of horses. Passwords were swapped and orders and identification examined. The fresh horses made a difference, and they creaked and rattled on the iron rims into an electrically lit military camp a good half hour before the lieutenant's prediction.

Gide sneezed a few times on the ride.

The sign read CAMP DEW, and the town looked to be built around an old high school. There was a hospital just down the highway, and many of the houses had electrical lights.

"Back to civilization," Walker said. "We'll put you in the Lodgepole Motel for now. I'm afraid you'll have to stay under guard."

"For the gal's cold," Sergeant Coombs said, slipping a flattened bottle into Valentine's pocket as he waved over help with the horses and luggage.

Valentine surreptitiously examined the quarter-full bottle. It was hard to tell the color of the liquid in the dark, but Valentine smelled whiskey.

"Nice of you, Sergeant, but I'm trying temperance until I find my feet here."

"I'm not," Gide said, and Coombs passed her the bottle.

As they got settled in, Walker showed up with a camera and took their pictures, both from the front and in profile. Two more days passed while various orders wandered up and down the chains of command. Gide's face turned red from her cold, or maybe the back-mountain whiskey, and they got sick of washing their clothes and darning socks.

The motel had a water heater that they kept fired up from six until nine in the morning, so Valentine enjoyed hot showers every day. They "exercised" for two hours in the afternoon on a chain-link-fenced basketball court that had replaced the motel's pool, bringing back uncomfortable memories of his time in the Nut. The rest of the time they filled in companionable silence. Though Gide relished stories of his travels and descriptions of the effect Quickwood had on Reapers, Valentine had turned moody and taciturn when not even Walker visited on the second day; he wondered if he'd be sentenced in Washington for crimes committed in Arkansas.

"It's not fun, you know," Valentine said when she asked about the Wolves, and how many women made it into the ranks. "You'll be tired and bored most of the time. Then there's a lot of noise, and you'll look around with your ears ringing and realize half the people you know are dead."

"I don't expect this to be fun," she said. "I just want a chance at them. I'm sick of standing around watching it happen. I can hack it."

"A couple of tattoos don't make you hard," Valentine said, and instantly regretted it.

She crossed her arms and turned away, looked out at a patch of blue sky through the barred window from the front chairs.

"I'm sorry, Gide."

She studied the street. "Whatever."

"Being cooped up with nothing to do gets on my nerves."

"I've killed a man, you know. Two men," she said.

"Sorry to hear that," Valentine said.

"My dad was drinking a lot as he got older. He got scared of going into towns to get work. Thought they'd pick him up, you know? Finally . . . I'd just turned fifteen. He tried to sell me. For sex, you know, I was a virgin and all. Some rich guy from Tempe and his manservant came for me. The servant washed me up and combed out my hair and told me how I shouldn't be afraid.

"He got sick of me after about a week or so and sent me back to Pa. But I learned the ins and outs of his house, and knew when the servant door in the wall was unlocked. I got me a couple of mean rattlesnakes and chopped off their rattlers. He had this little toilet room with a phone in it. Always went in there first thing in the morning. I cut the wires, broke the bulb, and put them in there.

"The snakes got him, sure enough, and he started hollering. The servant came and put down this big cut-down shotgun to drag him away from the snakes, I suppose so he could shoot them without blowing his master's leg off. I snuck up and got the gun, shot them both in the face. One barrel each.

"Funny thing is, the guy was nice enough. Really loving and gentle with me, and he gave me some kind of pill when it was over that flushed me out, made sure I got my period. The one I wanted to shoot was my father. Maybe not in the face, in the foot or knee or something. I heard later they hauled off the servants, the ones who worked there during the day, and that seemed the most unfair thing of all. A cook, a gardener, and a housekeeper, who all lived miles away and had to take a broken-down old bus even to get there. Up until then everything about the Order was scary, but in this theoretical sense. When I saw it in practice, it changed me more than getting poked by that old guy.

"I ran for Yuma, wanting to get across to Cali, and made it. But I met a nice kid in Yuma, working part-time at the store while he apprenticed at the airfield in electronics. He got purified, though, my first year there."

Valentine waited until he was sure she'd stopped talking. "What happened to your dad?"

"Dunno. I should have gotten a job in town, kept him somewhere out of the way. He wasn't on any sets of official books, I don't think—no one would have looked for him. Stupid old drunk."

"You are tough," Valentine said.

"Only on the outside. Like a bug."

Valentine nodded. "I know what you mean."

A thunderstorm rumbled outside when higher authority called for them. Valentine put on a pair of moleskin trousers they'd given him and his only shirt with a collar, a field turtleneck.

They took them down the road to the echoing halls of the high school, where maybe thirty or forty people worked in classrooms in a school built to hold a thousand. Patched cracks from earthquake damage ran across the floors and up the walls.

It had been a long parade of death since the "turnover" of 2022, when mankind relinquished its throne at the top of the food chain. . . .

Valentine guessed the room they brought them to had been devoted to science. A yellowing periodic table hung on the wall, and all the tables had a thick, black, chemically resistant covering. Cabinets on the wall held binders rather than test tubes and Bunsen burners. A preserved Reaper head sat in a jar on the counter, next to glass-covered trays holding molds of Grog tracks and recovered teeth.

A rather sad-looking elderly man, lost in his green uniform collar, sat on a stool, resting his back against a whiteboard. Another man, bald with a lightning-bolt-like zigzag tattooed on each temple, wore a smart steely gray uniform. Blued-steel collar tabs and matching arrowheads on his epaulets gleamed like a polished piano top as he stood talking to Walker.

The guard halted Gide outside, offered her a chair.

"She's my aspirant, Walker," Valentine protested as the other guard led him into the office/classroom.

The older man pulled at his ear. "Hmmmm . . . can't say. Can't really say, maybe around the eyes."

"Major Valentine," the bald man said. "My name's Thunderbird. You know Walker, of course, and this is Colonel Kubishev. Colonel Kubishev is semiretired. He came down as a favor to me."

"Sorry, I'm afraid I bunged things up and delayed you a day," Colonel Kubishev said. He had a faint accent. "They asked me to take a look at you. I worked with your father, briefly, in Montana. Calgary Alliance. They asked me about the name and I wanted to see for myself."

None of that meant much. Valentine vaguely remembered the Calgary Alliance being mentioned in War College; it was a short-lived Freehold that collapsed under the Black Summer Famines of the forties.

"I'm honored, sir," Valentine said.

"How is he?"

"He's dead," Valentine said.

"Oh, I am sorry. I am sorry. My wife and I will remember him."

"Thank you, sir."

"You wouldn't know whatever happened to Helen St. Croix, I don't suppose," Kubishev asked.

"He married her," Valentine said. "She's my mother. She died at the same time."

"That's it! He has her hair, exactly," Kubishev said, as though the observation relieved him of a burden. "That is good. That is very good. Died at the same time?"

"Yes."

"I'm glad you were spared."

"I was eleven. Some distance away at the time."

"Major Valentine, I'm sorry to hear that," Thunderbird said. "Were you aware that your Q-file with Southern Command lists your father as J. D. Valentine and your mother as H. Argent?"

"Argent?"

"Yes, the same as that excellent set of fake Oklahoma papers you had."

Valentine stared. "I couldn't say why that's the case. When I filled out my enlistment paperwork I put down the correct names."

"I don't have that—this is just a short version—but it does list parentage and place of birth. Oh, your birthplace is listed as Rapid City, South Dakota. Strangely coincidental error, still."

"Maximilian Argent was a family friend," Valentine said.

"We don't doubt that the man in this file is you," Thunderbird said.

"I'm glad to hear it, ummm . . ."

"Colonel. The insignia for Delta Group is somewhat esoteric. I mean for you to learn it, though. I'd like to have you under my command."

"Delta Group?"

"Lifeweaver Enhanced. Delta is a symbol of change. We're mostly all Bears up here. I'm not sure if it's a regional affinity, or just that we know right where the Fangs are and we don't need Wolves and Cats and whatnot to locate them."

"I've worked with Bears," Valentine said. "If you want me to become one—"

Thunderbird clacked his tongue against the roof of his mouth, thinking. "I don't think I have a slot for you at your former rank. But we might find a job for you and that gizmo you flew in on."

"As you wish," Valentine said. "It'll be good to be back on a team again."

"Then you can satisfy my curiosity, Valentine. Why did you come all the way here? You could have made yourself useful in Denver, Wyoming, even the Caribbean, and saved yourself a lot of mileage. Why us?"

"You're winning," Valentine said.

"Damn right we are," Walker put in. "And we'll keep winning, as long as the Lord sees fit."

The old man bowed his head, and Valentine saw his lips moving silently.

"We'll give you an orientation later. I want a detailed debriefing first."

They sat down and Walker brought in coffee. For forty-five minutes or so they talked, much more conversational than interrogatory. They were especially interested in his trips to the Caribbean and the exact circumstances of his court-martial and conviction under the Fugitive Law. "Typical," Thunderbird said. "They want victory. Just don't like the color of the coin that'll pay for it." Afterward they took a short break, and Valentine saw Thunderbird pick up the phone.

Later they talked to Gide, and Valentine idled in the hall. Her interview was much shorter.

"Term in the militia," she said. "I guess it's a start for us."

Valentine went back into the classroom, where Thunderbird was on the phone again. "Yeah, that's right. I want everything north of Woodinville Road cleared. They think Redmond's next, but we'll pull back and slide the Action Group north." He looked at Valentine. "Yes?"

"My friend Gide. I was hoping we'd be able to stay together."

"We'll pick this up in ten," Thunderbird said into the phone. He hung it up. "She's a natural. And a woman besides. No room for her with the Bears of Delta Group."

"She and I—"

Tok tok, his tongue sounded. "Something warm to come home to?"

"More like mutual affinity."

"Better check the true-love meter again. She sounds eager to serve, with or without you. If you want a slice of something juicy, Delta Group gets their pick, believe me. Tell you what, I'll get her posted near our operations HQ. She'd just be a short walk away. Fair enough?"

"More than," Valentine said, wondering why his stomach was going sour.

He picked up the phone. "See you on the other side of the mountains, Valentine."

Eight

Fort Grizzly, overlooking the outer suburbs of Seattle, Washington: The men call it either "Fort Gristle" or "Fort Drizzly" depending on whether the barrack-room conversation revolves around the food or the weather. Valentine was seeing the Seattle basin in its finest month.

Grizzly is settled on the east-facing slope of a ridge, at an old mine and quarry complex with a network of tunnels dug as though designed to be confusing—which it was. The "rabbit warren" underground works of Fort Grizzly serves as armory, bomb shelter, garage, and warehouse, and, most importantly, staging area for operations against Seattle.

Mining equipment chatters away all day, slowly expanding the works, serving as exercise for men with nothing better to do, adding background noise to all conversations except those in the deeper caves. At night blessed silence reigns, broken by the sounds of training, for the Bears of Fort Grizzly operate under the cover of darkness up and down the western slopes of the Cascades, daring the Reapers to face them when their powers are at their height.

Three-foot-high letters at the entrance tunnels exhort and warn: *WE DO OR DIE FOR THE FUTURE; ANYONE CAN BE A HERO; WE'LL HAVE THEIR THANKS AFTER THE VICTORY; PEACE IS FOR GRAVEYARDS.*

The warren is surprisingly light and airy. Masonry walls exist in many places, cheerfully painted in soft greens and yellows. It's comfortably furnished with items taken from old houses; indeed, in some places it seems more like a furniture showroom than a bunker. There is running water in some of the caverns and electricity in all but the blind alleys and undercuts designed to fool intruders. To reach any of the high-priority caves, one has to travel through darkness, then approach checkpoints blinded by spotlights. Almost no amount of shelling would do much but close up a few of the entrances, and an assault on the complex would be akin to bearding a horde of grizzlies in their dens.

". . . to never doubt, never surrender, and never relent until our future is our own again," Valentine repeated with Gide, right hand held in the direction of the Stars and Stripes and a totem pole of the faces from assorted monetary denominations that depicted American presidents, left hand next to Gide's atop a black Reaper skull on a wooden pedestal. "I will obey the orders of my lawful superiors until victory, death, or honorable release."

The wording had a tang of blood and iron to Valentine. The oath he'd taken on joining Southern Command, administered very informally by an old Wolf sergeant holding a dog-eared Bible after his first week on the march south from Minnesota, used one similar phrase—"obey the lawful orders of my superiors"—and to Valentine, who turned the words over in his mind afterward, there could be worlds of interpretation separating the two.

He took the oath at Fort Grizzly with Gide, a final sop to their friendship, at the base of the eastern slope of "Grizzly Ridge" with the sun shining above and the pines of the western mountains blue in the sunshine.

"Smallest swearing-in I've ever attended," Thunderbird said, waving a private forward with a black bowling-ball bag for the Reaper skull. "But you're no ordinary recruit." A corporal on Thunderbird's staff named Wilson lit a cigarette and puffed eagerly.

Valentine felt Gide trembling next to him. Didn't Thunderbird recognize that this was an important moment in her life?

"You've done it, Gide," Valentine said. "Congratulations."

"Let's get you both into uniform, now that everything's legal," Thunderbird said. "Recruit Gide, they're expecting you at the fueling depot. You'll get your muster gear there. Get going."

"Salute," Valentine whispered.

"Thank you, sir," she said, saluting. He returned it.

"That entitles you to a drink on me," Valentine said. "Southern Command tradition. I'll call for you as soon as I can."

Tok tok. "This is Pacific Command, Valentine," Thunderbird said. But he smiled as he said it. "But we'll make sure you two keep your date.

"Valentine, let's get you out of that biker getup. Wilson, get Valentine over to the medical center for his capabilities physical, and see if the professor can spare an hour for a quick background lecture."

Valentine shook hands with Gide. She looked brisk and ready for anything, had been quick-witted enough to add the "sir," and she was capable enough. She'd be fine. Why this strange reluctance to let her go?

"My office is K-110, Valentine. The door is always open," Thunderbird said.

Wilson finished his cigarette with a long drag, stubbed the bright red remains out in his palm, and pocketed it. "No smoking in the warren."

"Doesn't that hurt?" Valentine said as he followed Wilson away.

"If it didn't, it wouldn't be much of a trick," Wilson said. "It'll be healed by tomorrow. Privileges of Bearhood."

The physical was more like an athletic contest against a stopwatch than a doctor's evaluation. First they tested day and night visual acuity, then color vision (he had trouble with reds and greens, as usual). Then they watched him climb a nearly vertical slope toward a red demolition flag. He ran laps and they took blood and had him breathe into a lung volume tube. He was measured for standing vertical jump (eleven feet, well short of his record of sixteen his first year as a Cat). Then they ran him through a maze of swinging tennis balls, waving back and forth at the end of various lengths of string. He had to roll, jump, and dodge at intervals measured in split seconds.

"Eighty-five percent," the doctor said as her assistant turned off the machine that agitated the wooden rigging. "You Cats are something."

"Are there any others here?" Valentine asked, watching her through the mass of waving lines and greenish balls.

"No. The last one disappeared in the KZ a couple years ago. There are some Wolves with the forward observers."

Then Wilson took him to the professor, Delta Group's archivist and resident historian, a sagging mass of a man with a neatly trimmed gray beard, who sat in an office with three humming dehumidifiers and piles of paper atop piles of file cabinets. After a short lament that he was forever being called away from the *History of the Establishment of the Kurian Order,* he briefed Valentine on Pacific Command's resurgence.

In the last dozen years or so they'd gone from being a shabby group of guerrillas hiding in the mountains to the Terrors of the Cascades, thanks to a single man. "Mr. Adler," now "the Old Man," walked out of the Kurian Zone, met a patrol under one of the few aggressive commanders in the "Seahawks" as they styled themselves, said something about his family being killed, and offered to guide the troops to an unattended depot where they could get better weapons and explosives, provided they'd use them on a Quisling named Doorward, who'd betrayed him. Doorward turned out to be a soldier in the Seattle Order and a recent Ringwinner. They ambushed him as he pulled into the garage of his mansion, then got away clean.

"He's one of those curious men who can sense when a Reaper's in the neighborhood," the professor explained. Valentine felt a prickle of recognition. Affinity, perhaps.

"Mr. Adler" never put on a uniform, but just directed to target after target. Success swelled their ranks, a Lifeweaver arrived to assist, and soon they were picking off isolated Kurian Towers.

"Same Lifeweaver still with th—us?" Valentine asked.

"Oh yes," the professor said. "He's an odd one, but he can make Bears, sure enough."

Then the "clearing" operations started—"Action Groups" of Bears who hit the Kurian Zone and caused so much damage their targets were unproductive for months or years to come.

"Hard on the poor SOBs under the Kurians. But that's the strength of the constrictor."

The "constrictor," as the professor explained it, was a steadily tightening ring around the Seattle area, denying resources to what had been one of the largest and best-organized Kurian Zones in North America. Now the Seattle KZ was a shadow of its former self, and the awful Chief Kurian at his refuge in the tower that dwarfed even the Space Needle was increasingly isolated. Thanks to the quick-moving and hard-hitting Action Groups, he'd been bereft of several of his key subordinate lords.

"They give up and relocate, if they get a chance. Mr. Adler's got a good sense for when one's getting set to bug out, that's for sure. He nudges them right along."

Valentine got his own room with a private toilet and shower, and eventually learned his way to the cafeteria, gymnasium, laundry, and underground range.

The Bears were a big, bluff collection. Canadians and Native Americans added their own accents and mannerisms. Several had tattoos that read DOER on their upper arms, sometimes pierced by a dripping dagger. They felt more a military machine than the atavistic Bears of Southern Command, but maybe it was because there were so many of them grouped together. They were proud of their position.

"Never thought I'd make it," one told him as they sat and sweated in the gym's wood-walled sauna. "First time out, I thought my heart would burst. But I'm used to it now."

"What have you been up against?" Valentine asked.

"Mostly Seattle Guard types. They run away when an Action Column roars into town. They've seeded the waters with some Grogs—you got to watch it around rivers and so on."

"Big mouths?" Valentine asked. He'd run into them in Chicago.

"We call them Sleekees. That's the noise they make when they're hopping around on land. *Slee-kee, slee-kee,*" he wheezed in imitation.

"What about the Reapers?"

"Not so much. Sure, they'll defend a tower or a hole, if their master's inside. I've heard it's bad going up against a bunker full of those dropedcocks, but Adler's all about Jew-Ginsu. Hit them where they ain't."

Valentine's gyro arrived and after some technicians partially took it apart to learn the design, he started doing practice flights over the backcountry. An overzealous Resistance machine gunner tried to take him down—Valentine dived behind the tree line to avoid the tracers and came home with brush in his landing gear, but refueling gave him a chance to catch up with Gide.

The militia just got issued green caps with yellow safety tape at the back, and the rest of her uniform consisted of a big green field jacket, construction trousers, and some sad-looking sneakers made out of tire tread.

"Someone swiped my boots," she said. "The women have a hell of a time with the footwear. The rifle's a joke. Worn-down barrel."

"Do your duty."

"I do," she said. "Your friends from the Holes have an interesting definition of duty, byways."

"Meaning?"

She shoved her hands in her pockets. "Taking it down pipes or up the chute for the team. It'd be one thing if we were in a bar in town, but I'm just trying to do my job."

Valentine didn't like the sound of that. He'd been in too many Kurian Zones where the soldiers exerted certain "prerogatives."

"Let's go into town. I'll buy you a beer." "Town" was a little row of saloons, a café, and two theaters, one that showed movies on an old presentation projector, and the other with little rooms playing pornography.

"Duty tonight."

"Breakfast at the Coffee Grinder, then."

"Sure. I should tell you, though, I'm asking for a transfer to one of the ranch towns. Being a pump jockey isn't my thing. And I don't like those guys from the Holes. They remind me of the Circus flyboys."

* * *

Tuesday nights there were political and social lectures about the miserable lives of those in the Kurian Zone. Valentine hadn't seen anything of the Seattle area, but it must be a hellhole in comparison with some of the most wretched corners of the Caribbean, so black did they paint the picture.

"Their only relief is death," Thunderbird boomed, backing up the mousy little refugee who gave that week's lecture. Foot-high letters painted on the wall under the ceiling read, *Are you a SHIRKER or a DOER?* "We'll pick this up in the conference room in fifteen for those who want to know more. Card tournament tonight, grand prize is a four-day weekend at the next quarter-moon party at the Outlook."

"What's the Outlook?" Valentine asked Thunderbird as the Bears rearranged their folding chairs to make room for the poker tables.

"That's a big resort in the mountains. Beautiful area. Sort of a retreat and conference center for the Free Territory. Sometimes we even get visits from the Old Feds at Mount Omega."

"I thought that was a myth," Valentine said, though he knew differently. The last refuge of the old United States government was part El Dorado, part Camelot, in Freehold urban legendry.

"No, it's real enough. Going there's a bit of a letdown, though. It's not as impressive as it sounds."

The poker tournament got going, a fairly basic game of five-card draw with jokers wild. Each player started out with small stakes, a hundred dollars in chips, and when he accumulated five hundred dollars he could move to the five-hundred-dollar table.

The "grand prize" table required a three-thousand-dollar buy-in. The laurels would go to whoever managed to reach the ten-thousand-dollar mark.

Valentine was lucky—first in betting and then in card strength—for his first two hands and shifted to the five-hundred-dollar table. Other men who'd abandoned the tables made sandwiches and passed out low-grade beer, apple ciders, and "Norridge Cross," a wine from some pocket in the Cascades. Valentine stuck to coffee.

The men at the five-hundred-dollar table were serious players, and Valentine languished there until after midnight, until he got a feel for their respiratory tells. Using the hearing he'd acquired as a Wolf gave him an unfair advantage, he supposed, but a card table knew no law but Hoyle.

He was the last of six seats to join the championship three-thousand-dollar table.

His luck returned the first two hands, thanks to three kings and then a dealt flush. After that promising start, he began to fight a long, slow, losing battle against a Bear named Rafferty, who called him on a bluff. Rafferty's black ringlet hair, long as a pirate's, brushed the felt-covered championship table as he gathered the lost chips.

Thunderbird checked in occasionally to offer a joke and console the losers, and then returned to the bull session in the corner of the conference room.

With a full house Valentine assayed forth, and Rafferty folded. Valentine played the next hand cautiously, and eked out a win with three of a kind, causing two others to drop out. Another Bear demolished all of them the next hand, and then retired to bed, yawning, as a winner in his own mind but unwilling to hang in for the grand prize.

The Bears ate, drank, played, ate, and drank some more. Bear metabolisms could tear through six thousand calories or so a day and still feel underfed.

Card playing provides its own kind of late-night tension, and Valentine gave in to it as the advantage shifted between him and Rafferty, both built up enough so that they could not hurt each other. The other two at the table just played along out of interest.

Valentine drew into a straight, judged Rafferty doubtful, gulped down the last of his second glass of wine, and went all in. Rafferty laid down four of a kind, plus a joker.

"Good night, David," Rafferty said, gathering the chips and draining a tankard of beer. "I'll give your regards to the Outlook." He whipped a thong off his wrist and gathered up his hair, then did the same with his chips.

"I don't know anyone there who can accept them."

Rafferty cocked his head. "Never been?"

"No."

"Oh hell, well, take the prize," he laughed. "You hear that, Thunderbucket? I'm offering up my poor winnings to our newcomer."

"Don't you always get thrown out after half an hour anyway, Riffraff?" Thunderbird called back. "But duly noted."

"Give me a ride in your whirlybird sometime, eh?" Rafferty said.

"Gladly," Valentine replied. "Interested in flight?"

"No. I want to take a crap over downtown Seattle from a whizzing great height."

"Spoken like a patriot," one of the losing Bears commented.

Valentine, with a routine established, felt the days fly by while tension mounted at the warren. Late one afternoon he watched an Action Group set out at the next full moon. Various hidden, revetment-shielded doors opened and belched men and machinery from the depths of the caverns. Armored cars led a long line of pickup trucks towing oversized horse trailers behind, followed by a few military trucks hauling light artillery.

Valentine watched, leaning on the empty mount of a machine-gun nest high on the ridgeline. He'd volunteered to go, but Thunderbird had declined. "It'll be a tough one. We want to start you out on something easier. Besides, I'm setting up something for you and your whirlybird."

So he had to watch.

"Make the poor dumb bastards die for their country!" a legless Bear who manned a communications relay shouted as they passed. His voice boomed over the sound of the engines.

A long arm and hand reached out from the cave mouth and patted him on the back. Long, scraggly hair dripped from it like Spanish moss.

A captive? The Lifeweaver?

Valentine hopped down the shaft leading up to the machine-gun nest, ignoring the iron rungs, and hurried down to the "Gathering Deck," as the extensive level at the valley floor was called. He took a wrong turn, and had to retrace his steps, and arrived at the right cave mouth only as the legless Bear wheeled himself back into the communication center at the cave mouth.

"Excuse me." Valentine fumbled the man's name. He turned and read the man's name tag. "Pop-Tart?"

"Yeeeees?" he said, holding a headset to his ear.

"I was above and saw someone pat you on the shoulder. Funny-looking arm."

"That's the old hairy-ass himself. Came up to see the guys off."

"I've just never met him."

"How'd you rate that uniform?"

"Import from Southern Command."

He put down the headset and looked at the gauges on the master radio relay. "Hairy-ass is the only one we got left. Our others disappeared after the big raid up Interstate Pass in 'sixty-one, where I earned these wheels. He lurks under a blanket of Bears ever since."

One Lifeweaver left. And from the sound of it, even he's not all there.

"Still like to meet him."

"Talk it over with T-bird when he gets back," Pop-Tart advised.

"Hey, Pops," an assistant called from the radio.

" 'Scuse me," Pop-Tart said.

Valentine went down to the reading room to await the Action Group's return.

They came back, almost unscarred. They'd lost one Bear to a booby trap, and another to "overexertion" (Valentine had once heard a story in Arkansas about a Bear dropping dead as he and his teammates worked themselves into a battle frenzy over a Bearfire) and still more suffered wounds and contusions Bear metabolisms would soon overcome. Valentine watched them eat before they even cleaned up.

They were a strangely taciturn bunch. Maybe it was the gloomy climate. A group of Southern Command Bears back from action chattered like magpies, though the conversation usually limited itself to light subjects, like unusual vehicles they'd seen or how much quality toilet paper they'd managed to loot.

Thunderbird, looking drawn, walked among them, passing out candy bars and bags of greasy peanuts.

"New-moon party this weekend," Thunderbird said. He had a fresh uniform on, but Valentine saw dried blood on his boots. "Have they issued you a dress uniform yet?"

"No."

"I'll make a call."

"What's a PB?" Valentine asked. He'd heard the acronym tossed around as the soldiers talked.

"Punishment Battalion or Brigade. We've got a Brigade, unfortunately. Two combat battalions and a short support."

"What, hard labor, that sort of thing?"

"More like Reaper fodder. They're our first line, out in pickets about three klicks west. Their commander's not a bad sort—they've really shaped up under him. They're criminals. There's some shady types in these mountains, preying on both sides. If they don't like the feel of the noose, they can opt to PB their term. Of course a lot try to desert as soon as they get their bearings. They get shot, of course."

"How did the fighting go?"

"Well. Adler was right, as usual. We caught them pulling back. Got a fair bit of booty—they dropped everything and ran when we showed up."

"I've never seen Bears operate in those numbers before. They're usually used at platoon strength at most where I come from. Accidents."

"They divide up pretty quick when we go into action, cuts down on the chances of two teams attacking each other. We're careful about getting them revved up and pushed into the redline. You'll see. Have a good hurrah up at the Outlook."

"I'd like to bring Gide. She could use a little cheering up."

"You're loyal. I like that. I'll authorize her transport, but she'll have to clear it with her militia duty."

Gide cleared it easily enough. Perhaps Thunderbird made an extra call or two. In any case, they hopped on a horse-wagon train bringing captured scrap for salvage or to be melted down and recast. It was bottom-of-the-barrel stuff, mostly cookware and gardening supplies for civilian use. Hardly worth hauling away.

"How's the transfer coming?" Valentine asked. The dress uniform hadn't shown up after all, so he cleaned and pressed his daily as best as he could.

Gide wore a summer-weight sweater and skirt. "Denied. They want me to spend at least a year," Gide said. "I think it might move along if I fucked old D. B., the militia chaplain. He can arrange about anything."

"Some chaplain," Valentine said.

"Back in Arizona I would have dropped my drawers in a heartbeat. But I don't want it to work that way here."

"Think you made a mistake?"

She rubbed the bottom of her nose. "Shit no. Free air, you know?"

"That's a good way to put it."

"I don't feel like I'm being watched all the time, except maybe through the peepholes in the showers. There's a rumor going around that I've got something exotic tattooed around the ol' chute, and everyone's trying to verify. Just fucked luck. I'll do my year. There's another girl there who isn't too bad—it's better if you've got someone to talk to."

Valentine nodded. She understood, and patted his hand. He squeezed in return.

The Outlook was beautiful under its sickle moon.

It hung out next to, and partly over, a waterfall. Two long blocks of rooms, two stories tall and covered with balconies, looking out over the spill. At the center a great A-framed prow of glass and rough-hewn timber arched like an eagle's head.

The carpeted inside was hunting lodge overlain on luxury hotel. Clean as an operating room, it even smelled like evergreens within. A small army of staff in jet black with immaculate white aprons scuttled around at the edges of the rooms and corridors.

A clerk in a neat, gold-buttoned black shirt and pants admitted them, verifying their presence on an old computer. Valentine tried not to stare. He couldn't imagine Southern Command wasting a functioning computer on a hotel. But then he hadn't spent much time in the higher-class social circles.

The clerk issued them alligator-clip name tags, with first names and designations. Gide's had her name in large letters and VOLUNTEER MILITIA in smaller type below. Valentine's read DAVID/DELTA GROUP.

He tried to decline having a porter carry their small bags, but when the clerk said, "It's his job, sir—he needs it," he relented.

Luckily the scrip he'd won on poker night was accepted at the Outlook. He overtipped the porter as the bags hit the floor of their room.

"King-sized," Gide commented with a smile.

Old beaver traps decorated the walls, and the lights were made to simulate ironmongery holding candlesticks. The candlesticks were topped with small but ordinary-looking bulbs. A painting of a farmhouse surrounded by wildflowers adorned the wall above the dresser; a nude of a strategically disrobed seated woman drinking hot coffee, looking out her window at ice and snow, hung next to the bed by the window. Another sleeping nude hung above the bed.

If it was a brothel, it was the plushest one he'd ever been in.

Valentine checked the view. The waterfall was obscured by a deck from their room, but he had a good view of the river running west. He tried to guess how high it went in the opening minicanyon below the falls in the spring flood, but even with Cat eyes it was hard to judge.

"Cocktails, dinner, dance party," Gide said, reading a schedule on the desk. "Looks like we missed cocktails and part of dinner. Tomorrow: breakfast, exercise, lecture on the glory of heroism, games, cocktails, dinner, party. Sunday: services, brunch, departure."

Valentine despaired at a grease stain on his uniform. He must have brushed against a greasy pot in the wagon. "Let's get cleaned up and eat."

There were two galleries showing movies on the biggest televisions Valentine had ever seen, colors impossibly bold and bright in the dimly lit rooms. A small casino added that special thick, nervous air unique to gambling dens, and some kind of art exhibition was going on in one of the lobbies, well-crafted patriotic pieces that Valentine liked better than the four-color slogan posters of Southern Command.

Attractively dressed women lounged in the bars and in front of a gallery autopiano, ready to talk or dance or be taken back to a room. Valentine watched one military-haircut man in civilian clothes head for the rooms, his hand resting lightly on his companion's buttock. Valentine examined her eyes as they passed. She'd popped or smoked something to get up for the evening.

Valentine suppressed a shudder. He kept expecting the maître d' from the Blue Dome to appear at his elbow.

Gide, now dressed in a borrowed little black dress and heels, eyeliner running up the backs of her legs to simulate stocking seams, tracked down a late-night buffet and they ate.

"I poked my head in the gift shop while you were looking at the pictures," she said. "Nice booze. Perfumes even."

"Bonded whiskey, but they can't get you a decent set of boots."

"Speaking of which, there's a shoe store on the gallery. If you'll loan me thirty bucks, I can sign for the rest. I have to hurry—they close in ten minutes."

Valentine gave her the cash.

He went out on the balcony and enjoyed the summer night, watched the roar of the fountain. He fell into a conversation with another falls gazer, an artist in an ill-fitting sport coat and trousers.

"My piece is called *Hope and Glory*," he said. "I won a new-moon party here with it."

Valentine quietly raked his memory. "The two rising—what are they, angels?"

He seemed pleased that Valentine had remembered. He started talking about the difficulty of getting good paints, when he looked up. "That's Adler. He gave a quick talk at the reception for the artists."

Valentine looked up at the peak of the A-frame. There was a small balcony, hanging over their own, and muted light glowed within. A man stood looking over the edge, his face in shadow thanks to the backlighting. He turned and leaned and Valentine got a better view.

Valentine liked the look of him. Tanned—maybe the altitude of the Outlook helped—and lean but not gaunt, with gray white hair that set off the tan, a father figure in the twilight of middle age stood looking at the western horizon beyond the foothills of the Cascades. He held a lit cigar in his hand.

Late-night diners trickled out of the dining room and joined in the waterfall watching. Gide returned, wearing low black-heeled shoes and real stockings.

Adler set down his cigar on the railing. It rolled and he stopped it with a digit.

"Liquor holding out?" he called down to those below. He had a clear, fast speaking voice, like a radio news announcer.

A few men raised their glasses. A couple applauded.

"I'm here for the night air, not a speech. Enjoy." He lifted his finger and the cigar rolled off the balcony rail. A muttonchopped officer in a black dress uniform grabbed it as it fell.

By the time Muttonchops was showing his trophy to his escort, a blonde who had the body of a seventeen-year-old and the eyes of thirty-five, Adler had vanished indoors.

"He's shy," the artist said. "I like that."

Valentine looked out into the clear night, wondering what the shy military genius had been looking for to the west. Sulfur-colored light painted the distant clouds above Seattle.

"I thought you were going to buy boots," Valentine said as they returned to their room. The bed had been turned down, and the room carried a floral, elegant fragrance.

"I did," she said, pointing to a box. "Socks too, lots of them. Great quality. I picked up a few pairs for Julia. She loaned me this dress I'm not really fitting."

"Who's Julia?" Valentine asked.

"My roomie. She takes a little getting used to—she was born a slave to some Grogs in Oregon. They caught her poking around in a larder and chopped off her nose with a set of tin snips. Though she's always joking about it . . . really a lolly person once you get to know her. When she goes out, she wears this silk veil and calls herself 'the Phantom.' The guy gave me a great deal on the shoes, because they were used. You can hardly tell."

Valentine looked at the label in the bottom, something in Italian, as he took off his tunic. It added to the air of fantasy in the lodge.

"Mmmmm, they spritzed the sheets with lavender water," Gide said.

"It's supposed to relax you," Valentine said.

"They had tabs of Horny in the gift shop, can you fuckin' believe it? KZ aphrodisiacs? Here?" She let her two-tone hair fall, though the roots were now coming in an even walnut brown, and flopped back on the bed, her hair spread out like a fan.

Valentine adored her for a moment. Her hard-bitten, tattooed beauty, her profanity, and the military acronym somehow complemented one another. But a moment was all he allowed himself. Much more and his self-control would go.

"I think I might take a walk before I shower," Valentine said.

"Going to buy some Horny?"

"You wish," Valentine said, and winked.

Her upper lip twitched rightward. "I'm not so sure anymore."

The cool, clear air took the lavender out of his nose and replaced it with the mountain smell of pine and cedar. Valentine walked out in front of the resort, where a winding road ended in a dark oil slick of the parking lot. In the distance the green light of the military checkpoint glowed. At one end of the lot by a couple of bright outdoor lights—insects flashed like shooting stars as they whizzed by—a drunken game of pickup basketball proceeded noisily. Valentine watched the players try to dribble with one hand and hold a beer with the other, then turned toward the river.

He caught a little music from the small dance club at one end of the Outlook, but even that was soon drowned out by the quick-flowing river, rushing out of the mountains in a white froth. Some kind of cable contraption hung over the waterfall downstream, a gondola basket providing both a crossing for the river and a unique way to view the spectacular falls. Valentine saw motion across the river, just a sentry out to have a look at him.

He returned to the patio.

Most of the parties had broken up. A few people still smoked, or chatted over hot drinks in the chilly air; Valentine had to remind himself it was June, as in the mountains it felt more like an Arkansas March.

Valentine couldn't shake the feeling that something bad loomed out there, watching the hotel. He turned over in his mind ways he might try to assault the place. There were sentries at the door, and Valentine suspected some kind of security reserve lurked in the basement, as he'd seen uniformed soldiers disappear into the doors marked SERVICE USE ONLY leading down.

Or was he just talking himself into a breakdown? *Not enough stress in this getaway, so you have to bring some along?*

Or are you scared of what's in that king-sized bed?

He undressed and got into bed quietly, the vast bed giving him a margin of error.

She rolled, faced him. "This is different," Gide murmured. "I'm glad you brought me."

"Nice to have a familiar face around," Valentine said.

She took a deep breath, closed her eyes. "Good to be just in bed with a man. Lavender and guy. Someone needs to bottle that."

"What did you mean when you said that you weren't so sure anymore?" Valentine asked, curiosity getting the better of him. Or maybe it was a game he was playing with himself, with her as the prize. Or the other way round.

She thought for a moment. "I used to just be able to . . . turn everything off and enjoy fucking. But I'm starting to know you better. There's a lot of stuff in there I think I like. That weird little smile you wear."

She touched the corner of his mouth.

What the hell.

He reached up, took her wrist, kissed her gently on the back of her hand, then turned it over and kissed the palm. He released it and she reached up to play with his hair.

"Shit, now I've done it," she said. She lunged across the bed as quickly as one of the snakes tattooed on her arms, kissed him.

The rest came in a frenzy of pent-up desire, effervescent as champagne and just as intoxicating.

Valentine woke with a start in the predawn.

Reapers!

He found he was sitting up listening in anxious silence. No . . . the strange cold place on his consciousness wasn't there, wasn't real; it was echoes of memory and nightmare.

"You okay?" Gide murmured.

"Cramp," Valentine lied.

"You're sweating."

"Yeah. I'll be right back."

He washed his face in the bathroom, still listening. Then he went out to the balcony, looked around at the darker-than-ever world under a pinkening sky. He heard someone sweeping on the balcony below, smelled fresh bread, the feminine musk of Gide on him.

He returned to bed and slept hard.

They spent the rest of the weekend mostly in the bedroom, trying something Valentine had never experienced before: room service.

Saturday passed in brilliant sun and wandering clouds, and they restored themselves from bouts of lovemaking with coffees and teas on the balcony, sitting on an old bench with one of the bed pillows cushioning their backs. Gide, like her father in his better days, was also a big reader and they poked through worn, yellow-paged books collected from the hotel's small library together. They dressed for dinner and later discovered a second night together more delectable than the first.

They hitched back west on Sunday, riding in the bed of a king-cab pickup carrying a trio of captains who reminded Valentine of one of the poker hands that brought him up.

Saying good-bye to Gide was hard. But like all such days pried from the routines of war, the brevity made the memories that much sweeter.

Four days later he saw his first action.

"Courier duty," they called it.

Valentine buzzed out over Seattle's waters in the dead night, low and slow as he dared. Any watching Reaper might mistake him at a distance for a fast-moving patrol boat.

They'd modified the exhaust of the PAAT to lower the noise and make its voice resemble the oversized motorcycle it was. Valentine sensed a slight loss of horsepower but it just meant he couldn't do much in the way of fancy climbing turns.

The entrance to Seattle's harbor now had two tall lights marking it, constructed from old radio masts. The north rose up from an island and the other was on the coast. Allegedly some poor bastards made the long climb to the top of each four times a day, keeping watch on the water approaches to the city.

He wondered if they'd mark him as a potential smuggler.

He kept well clear of the southern tower but used it as a waypoint. He picked up a little altitude over the southwestern peninsula, saw the three lights, one blue and two red, laid out in an equilateral triangle.

Two of the lights went out as he passed overhead, leaving only the blue. He banked the autogyro and made his approach.

Heart pounding, he set the craft down on the little field by the signal. He was on a grassy flat next to some manner of drainage canal. Foundations of cleared houses lay under a carpet of weeds, and young pines shielded him from a road. A man left two companions, one with a rifle, the other with a big sporting bow, and ran up to the craft.

Valentine popped the canopy.

"Stop," the man called, crouching.

"Light," Valentine responded.

The stranger hurried up, face concealed behind a scarf and a hat pulled down to his ears. Valentine reached around and took out the duffel bag. Whatever was inside didn't weigh much more than plastic. It rattled vaguely as he handed the sealed case over.

"There you go."

"Tell 'em not to worry, plenty of heroes on this side of the sound." He offered his hand.

They exchanged grips. "I'm sure there are."

He handed over a heavier case that probably contained radio equipment or explosives and the man hurried off.

Valentine checked his map again. His next waypoint was the old Sea-Tac Airport, but he was to keep well south of it; they had searchlights that could blind him and guns that could bring him down.

He shut the canopy and gunned the engine. As he bounced away across the field, the men were already picking up bicycles and hurrying to meet over the bag. He marked a little flag and some piled-up dirt at one end of the field, and rose in the air. A target on a post flapped in the sea breeze.

They'd met him on a rifle range.

The flashes of gunfire looked like sparks from the air. They left little ghosts on his retinas for a split second.

Valentine had never seen a battle from the air. The sporadic gunfire seemed to be coming from spots along a long, ragged line stretching over perhaps a mile and a half of ground. They were fighting in what looked like a residential zone, long lines of what he guessed to be post-'22 housing—from what he'd heard, a good deal of the southern areas of the city had suffered badly from earthquake and volcano damage.

He passed over a street filled with bodies, tightly packed, around a pair of buses. The Bears must have caught reinforcements arriving in a deadly ambush to have the corpses laid in windrows like that. . . .

No wonder the Seattle Guard didn't care to take on an Action Group.

Valentine's orders were to check in at the Action Group's field headquarters for the operation. He could evacuate up to two wounded on the stretcher fittings added onto either side of the PAAT. It would be a hard load to fly, because carrying one meant carrying two, or the unbalanced autogyro would crash on takeoff. He hoped that if he had to carry two, they'd be of similar weight, preferably both light.

The Action Group lit the road he was to land on with headlights from the reserve Armed Truck force. Two smaller dune-buggy-like craft, one with a recoilless rifle and the other a heavy machine gun, crouched at the intersection with the command Hummer pulled into a half-collapsed brick storefront. An observer and a temporary aerial had a precarious perch at the steeple.

Remember to refuel if you've got wounded. Remember to refuel if you've got wounded.

Of course the high-octane gasoline they were supposed to be carrying with the medical inflammables was probably misplaced.

He puttered the autogyro up to the command vehicle. At the other side of the half-collapsed building, the white medical bus idled, the men sheltering in a doorway.

Valentine popped the canopy and got out, the sweat on the back of his uniform turning cold in the night.

He did see a wounded man, his arm dressed and in a sling, waiting by the command vehicle. Valentine wondered if they'd demand that he be flown out, just to test the system. From the other direction soldiers herded a group of civilians into a dark recreation center, judging from the basketball courts and running track outside. They kept them jogging, despite the age of some of the men, several of whom were gasping for air and supporting themselves on the runner in front.

A sudden burst of gunfire sounded in the distance.

Valentine extracted his carbine and approached the command vehicle. He was waved in by the man with the long, night-sighted sniper rifle keeping watch on the road. He found Thunderbird there with some of his subofficers, talking intently to Rafferty with a noncom behind carrying two rifles. Rafferty had his helmet off, showing his ringlets bound up like a hairy handle sticking out of the back of his head.

Behind Thunderbird they'd set up an easel with a carefully drawn map. The radio reports were translated into visual form by putting red slashes over depictions of buildings. Some of the slashes had been turned into an *X*.

Two corporals relayed information over radio to the officers.

"Bravo block cleared, eighty-one."

"Bravo, eighty-one," a lieutenant said in a bit of a singsong, finishing an *X* on the easel.

The ruined building had once been a hair salon. The man with his arm in a sling tried leaning back and resting his head in a debris-filled washbasin.

"Scouts are reporting traffic on Five-One-Five southbound," one of the radiomen said in a loud but calm voice.

"Rafferty, we'll pick this up tomorrow," Thunderbird said. "You dumb bastard. I told you I'd court-martial you." He turned to the men at the radios, clicking his tongue in thought. "Sound recall to all teams. Delay red column if possible."

"Recall, repeat, recall," the men at the radios echoed.

"Tell the scouts to mine the roads and haul ass," Thunderbird added.

Valentine saw a camouflage-painted pickup truck roar up the road. Two soldiers in back sat in a sea of children. Baby carriers with squalling infants stood in a crash cage.

The sergeant marched Rafferty out. "Rape," the sergeant muttered to Valentine under his breath as he passed.

"Anything for me?" Valentine asked.

Thunderbird looked startled for a second. "Valentine. How was the drop?"

"Completed."

"No, we're good. You can get out of here."

A long rattle of gunfire from across the street dropped Valentine behind cover, but no bullets zipped the headquarters. Valentine saw the athletic building the civilians had been run into alight with the reflection of gun flashes.

The hell? Were they ambushed?

The men at the vehicles guarding the headquarters didn't so much as change the covered arc of their weapons.

"Gamma-Gamma, forty-four," one of the men at the radios said.

"Gamma-Gamma, forty-four," the singsong lieutenant repeated, drawing a big *X* on the map. Valentine blinked.

He'd just put an *X* through the athletic building. Yes, three concrete apartments around it in a U. *Jesus Christ!*

"What kind of op is this?" Valentine asked, knowing, not wanting to know.

"We're clearing this housing complex," Thunderbird said. "Dee Oh Ee Ar."

Valentine heard isolated shots as the executioners in the athletic building finished off the wounded.

"Team Kostwald is loaded and leaving," one of the radiomen said, and an officer made a note on a clipboard.

"Of what?" Valentine asked.

"Destruction of enemy resources," Thunderbird said. "Can't stand to actually see a DOER?"

Enemy resources. "Enemy resour—you mean the population?"

"Without a population to feed on, the Kurians pull out," one of the lieutenants said.

Valentine looked at the *X*s on the map.

"No objections, I hope," Thunderbird said. His subordinate officers tensed, and Valentine saw the man with the busted arm shift his rifle around.

"Objections? Hell yes! For starters—"

Tok tok tok. "Hop off that high horse, *Valentine.* Clearing operations work. Your old man invented 'em, after all."

Nine

The Lifeweavers: Discussions of the Lifeweavers easily grow heated, especially since they rarely present themselves to conduct their defense.

The schools of thought—or bull-session opinion—on the Lifeweavers fall into four groups, often blended and shaded into one another at the edges like paints on an artist's palette.

The mystics see the Lifeweavers as divine intervention on humanity's side, or evidence that whenever evil arises, karma will marshal good to the side of the righteous so that the universe might be kept in balance. Thus the Lifeweavers should be considered reverently, and their actions as a form of religious truth. When skeptics point out that raining holy destruction down on the Kurian Towers Sodom-and-Gomorrah-style would save a good deal of effort all around, the conversation usually shifts over to pure religion.

The utilitarians aren't interested in the motivations of the Lifeweavers, only their efficacy in aid of the struggle against Kur. Their opinion of the extraterrestrials rises and falls along with humanity's fortunes in war. They'd prefer a little less anxiety over how the Lifeweavers are using the naked ape, and a little more thought put into how mankind can make better use of the Lifeweavers. Another set of utilitarians calls for some kind of planetwide exodus (along the lines of the improbable story Valentine heard while passing over Utah) where the Lifeweavers guide mankind to another world that might be made impregnable against the Kurians.

The diplomatists wish to see the Lifeweavers exert themselves less in resisting the Kurians and more in arriving at a solution that would end the fratricide among both species. Visions of some sort of world-

wide strike, where mankind nonviolently refuses to aid either side until they solve their differences or take their war elsewhere, make for an attractive flight of Pegasus-winged pigs. But even among the diplomatists, arguments break out when specifics for a peaceful solution are brought up.

The conspiracists come in almost as many flavors as the mystics. Many maintain that the Kurians and Lifeweavers, being of the same species, are simply playing an elaborate game of good cop/bad cop with humanity, to better control them for their own nefarious ends. Others see the Lifeweavers as basically good, but using humans as cannon fodder to fight an ancient war that spilled over onto Earth, to mankind's misfortune.

In Valentine's opinion, the Lifeweaver lurking in the depths of the rabbit warren offered strong evidence that excluded two of the above schools of thought.

Valentine hadn't slept since he set off on his courier flight. *Thirty-six, no, forty hours now,* he corrected himself.

Someone knocked on his door. "Yeah?"

Thunderbird's voice through the steel: "You wanted your interview, you got it."

Valentine wondered if he should shave. No, the sooner the better. Shaving wouldn't make a difference one way or the other. He opened the door.

Thunderbird stood there with two of his bigger Bears.

The enmity that had sprung up between himself and Thunderbird had turned into a wary truce back in the warren. As there was nothing Valentine could do on a battlefield—or a multiblock killing floor, in his mind—without getting arrested at the very least, he'd followed orders and flown back to Grizzly Ridge. He took the precaution of landing at the fuel depot to refuel, found Gide, and had her guide him up into the hills above the motor pool to a vacant house with an even more vacant garage. She sensed that there was something wrong and asked him about it, but Valentine didn't want to explain, couldn't without following the cowardly urge to flee the Cascades entirely.

But flight wouldn't save any lives but their own.

He trotted back to Grizzly Ridge, explained that his engine was misfiring and being maintained back at the motor service yard. He had written up both a request to see the Lifeweaver and a letter of resignation from Delta Group by the time the column returned. He waited outside Thunderbird's office and told him that unless the request was immediately granted, the resignation would follow.

In all probability he'd resign anyway, but Valentine didn't add that. He needed the interview.

That rated six clucks of Thunderbird's tongue, then an order to return to his quarters and get cleaned up.

Thunderbird walked him to one of the big, gurney-sized two-door elevators that served the medical center. Shielding the control panel with his body, the colonel pressed buttons using both hands.

"I think we got off on the wrong foot," Thunderbird said as the elevator dropped. "I figured you knew about your old man's solution."

Valentine didn't want to ask the question on his mind, and luckily the elevator stopped, and he had a brief reprieve as they met two more Bears at a duty desk in a rough-hewn, unpainted tunnel. Under bare bulbs projecting from boxes linked by a conduit, Thunderbird handed over an order sheet and he and Valentine turned in their IDs. Thunderbird checked his sidearm and they submitted to a pat down and being wanded by a metal detector as one of the Bears spoke into a phone.

A woman in a medical uniform appeared. "He'll see them," she told the Bear at the duty desk.

"Pass nine-nine," the Bear shouted down the hallway.

"Pass nine-nine," a voice shouted back.

The big Bears sat down opposite the duty desk to wait. Thunderbird and Valentine walked down the darkening corridor, following the woman in white, the bulbs becoming less frequent and finally giving out. Valentine spotted an old hunk of armored vehicle crammed into a turn in the tunnel, a turreted gun that looked like a 30mm cannon covering the tunnel back toward the duty desk. Two layers of thick metal cage kept the Bears inside—Valentine guessed there were two, but it was hard to tell—at their station. Valentine saw a portable toilet between the layers of cage.

They turned the corner past the dug-in vehicle and came upon a set of bars worthy of a rhino cage, a small door in a heavy frame offering access to the other side. Valentine heard dripping. The medical officer fought down a yawn, took a key looped around her neck, and put it in a lock at the half door.

They crouched to pass through.

There was another turn ahead, and Valentine felt the space and light around the corner through the transmitted drippings.

"I want to see him alone," Valentine said.

"Don't try anything funny. If the medical staff calls, I'll come in and put an end to you."

"Maybe," Valentine said.

The medical officer looked to Thunderbird, who nodded. "Take him in," he said.

She looked Valentine up and down. "You look tired. Are you okay?"

"Fine."

"Don't be nervous—he's just a bit eccentric. Remember, he's not a human."

"I've met them before," Valentine said.

She took Valentine into a—grotto was the only word Valentine could use for it. It was warm and humid. Banks of what he guessed were grow lights fed thick ferns, palmettos, rhododendrons, and other plants Valentine hadn't seen since he'd been in the tropics. Off to one side a pool, fed by a sheet of water coming down the wall that most people would call a leak rather than a falls, moved quietly, stirred by some unknown current. The banks of plant boxes and platforms made something of a maze, but the medical officer guided him past the pool and into the center of the plant life.

"What's his name?" Valentine asked.

She led him past a bank of purple flowers. Valentine heard a bee buzz. Something was wrong with that, but he couldn't remember what. "He said we couldn't pronounce it. We just call him 'Sir.' It's quick and easy.

"Don't let his appearance throw you off. Remember, it's just a show," she said, coming to a gauzy tent. She lifted a flap.

"David Valentine to see you, Sir," she said.

Valentine saw a hairy mass and several sheet-covered floor mats within.

"Enter, sojourner," a slightly lisping voice said.

Valentine went into the tent. Enough light from the intense bulbs penetrated the thick white gauze to make him feel as though he were inside some kind of cottony womb.

The creature within made a startling contrast to the whites and pale greens of the sheets covering the mats on the floor. The Lifeweaver looked like a half daemon, half satyr, right down to thick hairy legs hinged like a goat's. Overlong fingers and toes with nails that weren't quite claws displayed delicately painted, mysterious glyphs. Pointed of ear, flat-nosed and slant-eyed, it was barrel-chested but thin-hipped, covered with limp, stringy, dirty hair and the odd bubo about the neck and groin. Valentine couldn't say whether he was faced with a combination of legends or nightmares.

"Sit," it said, with an artful wave of the wrist and overlong fingers. Valentine was reminded of an exhibition he'd once seen after his return from Nebraska where a martial artist showed how to use a war fan. "Cross-legged is best, for your kind." Valentine sat.

It reclined on one of the mats, lounging. "Speak your mind, sojourner."

"Why do you look like that, Sir?"

The medical officer brought in a wide, water-filled bowl. A candle and some flower petals floated within. She set a small stainless steel cup in front of Valentine.

"Suits the profession. Suits of the profession. War, famine, disease, and death. All I've known, watching these thousands of years. It's all that's left of me. I stayed on, you see, though others left after the old battles of your ancestors' time. I stayed and watched, for I loved and admired you. But I'm afraid it's driven me a bit mad."

He smiled, showing brown and green teeth. "Valhalla awaits, if you have the courage and survive your ordeal," Sir said, reaching out with arms that thinned as they extended. Valentine felt the greasy touch of its hands, the prick of its claws, as it cradled his head.

"You will be death, destroyer of worlds," Sir whispered in his ear, despite the fact that his head remained on the other side of the tent.

Valentine broke away from Sir's grasp. "Wait. I think there's a mistake. I'm not here to become a Bear."

The arms pulled back. "Not a Bear?"

"No, I need your help. I'm from Southern Command," Valentine said hurriedly, wondering just how much of this the nurse was hearing.

"A Wolf once, now a Cat, and more in your blood besides," Sir said.

Valentine didn't bother to ask for hows and whys. "They need the help of the *Dau'weem*."

"I never accepted that title. We were right, not backward," Sir said. The shape blurred and returned. "Southern Command, where is that again? Argentina?"

"The Ozarks, Texas, parts of Oklahoma now—"

"Mississippi River, oh yes, of course. Louisiana Purchase and all that. One of your better specimens, Jefferson, though I've only known him secondhand. I met Washington once. A good man and true. You're not fighting with the Britons again, are you? You've got to settle these squabbles yourselves or you'll never get anywhere as a people. All Rome's fault, of course—if they'd only stayed the course and not become addicted to slavery. It's like an opiate."

Valentine wondered how to drag Sir's mind back out of lost millennia.

"We need your help. I have to get in touch with the other Lifeweavers."

"That can be dangerous," Sir said. "Very dangerous indeed. I can't take that step without revealing myself in the process. Never mind the danger to you."

"I know it's a lot to ask," Valentine said.

"Do you ask?"

"Yes."

"No matter the consequences, the possible harm?"

"I would think that would be your decision. But it's important."

"Not my forte. Not my forte at all. But I'll try."

"Thank you."

Sir slipped out one side of the tent.

Valentine wondered if an all-out assault on Grizzly Ridge would be entirely a bad thing. The medical officer poked her head in. "You got him all stirred up."

"I hope that's all right," Valentine said, wondering if Thunderbird would bust in and start beating him to death with a shovel.

"He needs the activity. He lies around too much, not that we really know what's healthy for his kind. How do you feel? Hot yet? You should have another—"

"I'm fine," Valentine said. "Wait, I think there's been a mistake. I didn't come here for an Invocation."

She blinked. "No?" She knelt and looked in each of his ears, folding his lobes back to peer behind. "That's a relief. But that's all he really does for us. Just a moment." She disappeared.

"Success," Sir said, returning to the tent. He held a small, slightly curled rubber-tree leaf in his hand. Valentine saw a small green stone on the strange presentation leaf. "Took some time to find the right one. Ready?"

"For what?" Valentine said, warily.

"To speak to our kind. You needed to communicate with us, yes?"

"Yes," Valentine said.

"This will do the trick." He passed the leaf to Valentine, waddled around behind, and put his hands on Valentine's shoulders. The hands turned into tentacles, soft grasping veined leaves at the ends. "Just touch it with your fingertips."

Valentine looked at the shard of jade. Some kind of hieroglyph of a bird was carved on the side. "I'm ready, if your ka is," Sir said. "It's quite painless."

Valentine reached down and touched it.

It felt like ordinary jade, cool and smooth.

A roar, hundreds of voices in his head, the static noise of an excited crowd. It overwhelmed him, incendiary butterflies opened their full-spectrum wings in his mind, and he spun around, looking for a way out, but the voices—

He opened his eyes, found he was lying on one of the mats. The medical officer hovered anxiously, Thunderbird behind.

Sir looked at him, eyes narrow and calculating.

"Are you still with us, David Valentine?"

Valentine felt as though he were in another time and space. "I think so. What does that thing do again?"

"It's a touchstone. It opened up your mind."

"Nothing made sense," Valentine said.

"It takes a great mind to comprehend a touchstone on contact. But everything you need to know is—"

The medical officer put a hand to his cheek. "He's hot. Sir, is he entering up as a Bear?"

"No, I simply opened the channels. He shouldn't have the biological resour—wait. . . . Design help us! I forgot. Oh me! Oh me! Your father was a Bear, I believe."

"I think so."

Sir licked his lips with a pustule-coated tongue. "You may have had the talent passed down to you."

The medical officer looked at Thunderbird. "We'd better isolate."

Thunderbird nodded, hurried off out of the grotto. Valentine heard a plant crash to the floor.

"Oh, and he needs calm now more than anything. Oh me, oh me, I've been a fool. Careless! I expect he'll go mad. They said I was useless and they've been proven right again."

"Tell Thunderbird," Valentine said, feeling like he was floating away on a river. "Danger. Sir, you revealed yourself. Don't forget."

"We'll take care of it," the medical officer said. "What's that about?"

"He's confused," Sir said. "He must have thought . . . I had to take my true shape to guide him to the right part of the touchstone, make sure it didn't rush in all at once. I meant the danger was to him, not to me. Oh, this has been bunkum and confusion from the first."

"I'm going to sedate him," the medical officer said. She yanked a big white case from within a stand of ferns and opened it. The needle squirted something on Valentine as she positioned it above his arm. "I doubt it'll last—," Sir said.

"Long enough for him to get on the gurney."

Valentine, disoriented, half-awake, and anxious, didn't even feel the needle going in. . . .

"Don't let him get up. Don't let him up," someone was shouting. A weight pressed on his chest. Valentine saw lightbulbs passing above, one after the other, each leaving a snail trail glowing on his retinas. His heart began to hammer.

Something was in his mouth, he bit down, it snapped, a tooth gave way.

And then a convulsion. Even though he felt that he was lying on his back, someone still managed to clobber him across the small of his back with what felt like a baseball bat. His arms and legs forgot how they worked. He smelled eucalyptus.

"Zap him again!" a voice shouted.

The gurney's wheels chattered as they passed over the uneven surface below. Valentine felt calm and collected, even as his body jumped under another jolt. The world faded away, but whispered to him that it would be back, new and improved.

Madness, fighting in vain against tentacles, bludgeons, ropes, the world had turned crimson and black, shadows surrounded him, baying like a wolf pack. But above and behind it was singing, the most perfect singing he'd ever heard, an angelic choir majestic.

He sang along as he fought until he sagged in exhaustion.

He awoke to find himself in a dark room, his arms bound around his own waist as though he were mummified. No, straitjacket, it was a straitjacket, made out of thick leather. His legs were swathed in some kind of padding and buckled down flat. He sensed he was lying face-up, somewhere underground, but beyond that, he could tell nothing, except that he felt dirty all over, particularly itching and filthy between his legs.

"Hello?" he croaked.

Thirsty. So thirsty.

A presence at his side. He felt a plastic nozzle enter his mouth.

"Get ready to swallow, okay?" a voice said. Gide's, it was Gide.

He nodded, vaguely aware of tubes and wires connected to him. He suspected one of the wires could give him a jolt.

Water, just a tablespoon or two, went in his mouth, and he swallowed. So salty it tasted sweet. They repeated it. Twice.

"Good," the voice said. It wasn't Gide.

Valentine felt a gap in his teeth on the upper left side. He probed with his tongue, felt a missing tooth, or rather the stump of one. The other felt good and cracked.

The next day—at least they told him it was the next day—he could sit. The tubes were gone, but he still had wires running the length of his body, individual ends attached to forehead, Adam's apple, chest, stomach—a couple more on his back. They hung off the bed and met at a black box.

He had the run of a two-person berth on the hospital floor. It was in the "security" wing—the doors were solid steel, hinged on the outside and closed with what sounded like a heavy bar reinforced by bolts dug into stone beneath the linoleum. The man in civilian clothes sitting opposite, under two painted panels masquerading as windows, didn't have many answers.

His name was Wholmes, and thanks to burned and reconstructed skin, he looked like he'd been freeze-dried and rehydrated. He spelled it as he said it, though Valentine could read it on his ID card.

"How do you feel?" Wholmes asked.

"Better," Valentine said. "I had eggs and oatmeal for breakfast."

"You're on soft foods until those teeth get taken care of. Tomorrow or the next day."

"Has anyone figured out what went wrong?"

"Nicely put?"

"Clearly put."

"You were a pig who wandered into a bacon factory in hopes of speaking with the management. But when a pig visits a bacon plant, there are obvious hazards. Sir doesn't direct or guide or advise this freehold. He's used strictly for creating Bears."

"Who are you, Mr. Wholmes?"

"I help new Bears with their adjustments to transhumanism. You're an interesting case, though, Valentine."

"Why's that?"

"Sir didn't do anything to you. Well, anything much. To the Lifeweavers, the human body is like a big, locked-up factory with all the switches turned off. How we got that way—well, I'm not going into the various theories. I'll leave that to the philosophers."

Valentine felt a little jolt of recognition; Wholmes talked a little like the general who'd offered him a choice of death or the possibility of eternal life in service of the Kurians.

"Are you feeling all right?" Wholmes asked.

"Yes. Closed factory and all that."

"Now, throughout history a few individuals have managed to turn on bits of their factory on their own, transcending normal human limits, like some of the great athletes or, with mental discipline, astrophysicists and yogis and the odd musician and so on. Some combine the two; I'm told there were martial artists who could do the same sort of tricks you Cats can.

"Now, of course when the Lifeweavers go into the factory and turn on a couple of machines, sometimes it takes the mind a little while to catch up and learn to channel the new outputs. That's where I come in, and were you aware your crystal-spark-snorting mother sucked off drovers in station bars to get her fix?"

"When your old man wasn't beating her to it," Valentine said. "What's the deal?"

"That's the fascinating thing." Wholmes reached under Valentine's bed by the black box and tore off a piece of paper covered with squiggles. "A little stress peak when I questioned humanity's origins. A bigger one, a good deal bigger, when I insulted your mother. Another Bear, fresh from his Invocation, would have jumped out of the bed and started pounding me."

"I take it your job has a comprehensive benefits package."

Wholmes chuckled. "Like you, I'm a fast healer. Plus they learn an important lesson when they calm down, and it sticks, and they become more receptive to my training." He lifted an object that looked like a flashlight held backward, with two small silver prongs. "Besides, a quick jolt calms you down.

"But you, you've been controlling yourself and your reactions since childhood, I'm guessing. You've got straight pipes, so to speak, in the brain-body connection, but you've managed to install a muffler yourself. I wish we knew more of your early childhood."

"I remember fighting a lot with my sister."

"Did you ever hurt her?"

"I—I can't remember exactly. Just kid stuff. She'd start swinging—but since she was littler I had to take it. Mom was always separating us. She'd sing to calm us down." Memories returned vague yet powerful blasts, Mother's leonine bronze face as she held him down, blood on her upper arm. . . . "She'd sing to calm me down."

"Whoa there, Valentine, you're spiking again. And—it's gone. Remarkable. A ramp like that should lead to a redline, and you pull yourself back each time. Your father was—and there's another spike. Perhaps I should leave off your family for a bit."

"What about the—the touchstone?"

Wholmes tapped his thigh with a scar-covered hand. "We don't know."

"Does Sir?"

"Depends on the state of his mind when you speak to him. I understand at one time he was one of the Lifeweavers' leading lights on the study of humanity, followed our civilizations very closely. But he's old now, very old, and he's slipping."

"How did he end up here?"

"In the mess of 2022 he and a few other Lifeweavers revealed themselves to the government. They went to a 'secure area' at Mount Omega, but weren't of much practical help—meaning they couldn't deliver on the magic bullet everyone keeps thinking will get rid of the Kurians."

"There's stuff that helps. Like Quickwood."

"Somebody showed up with a couple seeds of that stuff. I've no idea where it's growing, big secret."

"So did the other Lifeweavers leave?"

"Seems like. I'm told they kept trying to pick up stakes and go elsewhere. They ended up breaking out somehow, oh, about the time I was born. All but Sir, and no one really knows what happened next. The other Lifeweavers had vanished. But I wonder. About the time they disappeared was when we first started hearing about this über-Kurian in Seattle. Some people say they defected."

"Defected?"

"I think it's bunk myself. Adler says he thinks they were captured, and the old King of the Tower used them to increase his power."

Valentine felt exhausted, but he forced a few more words out. "How does he do that?"

"We're still working on figuring out how Bears can grow a new lung back, but not a hand. Ever seen a grown-back Bear limb? Looks kinda like a flipper. Some of the guys have doctors tie the nub off so nothing weird grows back."

Valentine sagged back into his pillow.

"You need some food. I can tell. I'll get someone to bring you a tray."

He saw the dentist, a chattering type who covered all the discomfort with a steady stream of talk. He offered to cap his teeth with ground-down Reaper fangs, a popular option for Delta Group's Bears. One soldier, who had lost his upper lip and a good chunk of gum line, replaced all his uppers with Reaper fangs. Valentine declined.

Nights passed in weirdly vivid dreams, swirling mists that formed into wells and towers only to dissolve a moment later like a sand castle falling to a tide.

"Think I might get a little fresh air today?" he asked Wholmes, who was now dividing his time between Valentine and two fresh Bears in a cell next door. Valentine heard a good deal of screamed profanity, not quite as eloquent as that of the engineering crew on the old *Thunderbolt*, who had practically cursed in iambic pentameter as they overhauled an engine, but a good deal louder.

"It would do you good. Colonel Thunderbird will probably send a couple of men to keep an eye on you."

Valentine was interested to hear a rank used. In Delta Group ranks were for outsiders, rear-zone lurkers, or Pacific Command apparatchiks. Perhaps Wholmes didn't like Thunderbird.

When he went next door Valentine hopped out of bed, tried a few stretches and push-ups. His old leg wound gave him hardly a twinge, though usually a long spell in bed left it more sore than ever when he used it again.

But even that small amount of exercise left him ravenously hungry. He called for food and a nurse gave him a heaping plate of brown rice and dark beer, pushing it through a notch under the door.

He scraped his plate down to the last rice husk, listening to Wholmes encouraging the Bears to calm themselves by mantra. In this case, the old "Itsy-bitsy Spider" song every child picks up somehow or other. Hearing snarly voices talking about spiders traveling up and down waterspouts got him thinking. . . .

Wholmes must have given him an enthusiastic recommendation, because they released him the next day into the charge of a stiff-legged old Bear named Yarborough.

"Machine-gun bullets, both legs," Yarborough said, easing his way down the corridor with a cane carved from Reaper femur.

Yarborough took him up to the Bear cafeteria and watched Valentine consume a vast meal of potato-heavy stew. "Tired. Very tired," Valentine said, wiping up the plate with a heel of warm bread. He was only half paying attention to Yarborough; his mind was on the layout of the elevator, in particular the bumper at gurney level.

"You'll get used to it." Yarborough winced as he rose. "A little exercise helps. Want to throw some pins around?"

"Maybe a walk outside."

Yarborough looked doubtful. "I was nervous as a colt my first time out of doors. You might panic and try to take down a truck."

"I've got it under—"

"Boo!" Yarborough ejaculated, lunging with both hands across the trays.

Valentine found himself six inches backward, heart thudding away, and nonplussed.

"Um . . . grrrrr?" Valentine said back.

They both laughed. "I think Sir's slipping," Yarborough said. "Even a week after my Invocation, I would have been trying to open my head like an M-22 if I were you."

"Can I ask a question, Yarborough?"

"Fire away."

"What happens to the little kids?"

Yarborough's brow came down like a guillotine. "What do you mean?"

"I saw a truck full of little kids, too young for school, babies, pulling out after the last clearing operation. What happens to them?"

"They go to orphanages, poor souls. Some up to Canada, some out East or the other side of Rainier. You know Eagle, right? He came out of one of the orphanages, went in older than most even, ten, I think he said."

Valentine didn't know Eagle, but relaxed. He'd been worried they were used as Reaper bait. Or worse.

"How about that walk?"

"Sure."

The cafeteria was starting to fill up with the lunch crowd. Bears hurried to pile their trays with rice-flour bread and mulligan stew. Thunderbird and an adjutant came walking in as they approached the door.

"Valentine, a new man, I see," Thunderbird said.

"Tired as an old one," Valentine said. "But I'm going to try a walk aboveground, if that's okay."

Thunderbird clucked his tongue. "Sure. Be good for you. Stop by my office when you feel yourself again."

"How about tomorrow instead?" Valentine couldn't say whether he'd ever be himself again, after witnessing Pacific Command's Bears in action.

"Anytime. Door's always open, you'll remember."

Valentine took his walk on the flattened valley floor at the foot of the ridge. He tried balancing on one of the train rails that led to the big unloading station in the tunnellike terminal, though he'd never seen or heard a train come in. The breeze felt good on his face, but clouds screened the sun.

Yarborough watched him from the bench at the headquarters shuttle pickup.

Valentine took a short run about a third of the way up the hill, and

Yarborough opened a box marked with the network-phone squiggle. Puffing a little, Valentine reached the halfway mark on the ridge and hurried back down.

His bad leg twinged, but stayed steady on even the steep slope of the warren. He ran to the train-cave mouth, saw a big wire gate inside, and ran back again.

"Good to get some air." Yarborough nodded in agreement.

An engine started up, and Valentine saw a flag-draped coffin inside a black horse-drawn station wagon pull out of one of the tunnels. A big plastic wreath was propped up in the empty, hoodless engine compartment, and the driver steered the horses through a missing windshield, but otherwise the wagon was black and polished right down to the tires, which gleamed and smelled like gun oil. The engine noise came from an honor guard riding behind, rows facing each other on benches in the back of an open pickup.

"One of the new Bears. Poor kid burst his heart," Yarborough said, standing up. "Doctors don't catch everything."

Valentine lined himself up next to Yarborough and followed form as he saluted as the station-wagon hearse passed. It was just about the first salute he'd seen since coming to the warren.

"They dye the horses black," Yarborough said after the escort passed, grinding along in bottom gear. "Don't see what difference the color of the horses makes, when you're standing before that Golden Throne getting judged."

"I'm worn through," Valentine said, sitting down.

"Keep drinking water. Lots of water helps," Yarborough advised. "Let's head down."

Yarborough dropped Valentine in his original room, told him that he looked healthy as a horse, then went doubtful as he remembered that the last horses they'd seen had been drawing a hearse.

"I'm going to sleep. If you're supposed to escort me to dinner, give me a break and knock softly," Valentine said.

Valentine hadn't been back since his appointment with Sir. He checked his weapons, which were all still there, along with his ammunition. Someone had picked up his rifle, and accidentally snapped shut both buckles on his pack rather than the one.

He took out his razor-edged boot knife and opened the seam on his mattress, tilted it up, and shook it. He felt around through the hole, came up with his coin belt. More to give himself something to do than out of guilt at the vandalism, he closed up the seam for the second time with needle and thread from his sewing kit. Then he turned out his lights and rested.

The soft knock woke him, but he didn't answer. Yarborough was right, though—he was thirsty. He drank, and whiled away the hours dozing on and off. In the bustle of sentry shift change at eleven p.m. he slipped out the door, gear crammed into an enormous Pacific Command duffel with his bedding peeking out at the top. He went down to the laundry, checked in with the attendant and got tokens for the machine, and put his sheets in. He wandered, grabbed a couple of pieces of fruit from an elegant porcelain bowl resting in the small library on the same floor as the laundry, and returned to put his sheets in the dryer.

Someone else would have to take them out of the dryer.

The attendant didn't notice him extract his duffel from between a couple of machines and exit again. He ducked into the library again and took off his boots.

He went to the elevator bank and was momentarily frustrated when he found it occupied by a couple of bored technicians carrying toolboxes. If they noticed his socks, they didn't say anything. He got off at his own floor and then idled, waited for another. This one was empty.

He punched the button for the second-to-the-top floor, climbed up to the rail, and hung on in the corner using his toes. He opened the service access on the roof, picking the lock with his hairpinlike jimmies, praying that the elevator wouldn't stop on its upward trip.

He tossed the duffel up through the gap and made it to the elevator roof. The rolling gears and cables pulled steadily, their companions to the counterweight on the other side vibrating.

Valentine didn't want the elevator to stop at the top floor; a bell sounded in the corridor whenever the elevator arrived to alert the sentries that someone was coming up.

He climbed to the next level easily enough; rungs were built into the shaft for workmen, firefighting, or a loss of power. Using his gun flashlight, he examined the top-level door, found the trip for the bell. He lifted the latch on the door at the top level, and just cracked the door so he could slip through.

Valentine tucked his stiletto into his sleeve and listened, checking down the corridor toward the machine-gun-post exit. A sentry sat at a junction of rough-hewn tunnels, reading a book.

Nothing to do but bluff. Valentine strode down the corridor. The sentry lowered his book.

"B aerial crapped out," Valentine said. "I'm checking the connection before making a big issue with service." Valentine didn't know if there was such a thing as a B aerial, but it was quite possible the sentry wouldn't either.

The sentry stood, didn't reach for his rifle, but put his hand on his pistol holster. "We need a—"

Valentine jumped, and drove the outer edge of his boot into the sentry's midsection. The breath left the sentry's lungs with a whoosh and Valentine put a foot on his wrist and a knee on his neck, bearing down hard. He dropped his knife out of his sleeve and poked the sentry hard under the chin.

"Last thing I want to do is hurt you, friend," Valentine said. "You make me open up your carotids, it's going to bother me for days."

"Mrfph," the sentry agreed.

Valentine relieved him of his pistol, was happy to see a pair of handcuffs on his belt and a Taser. "Stay flat on your face, spread-eagle. I just got invoked a couple days ago, and I'm twitchy as hell. What's your name?"

"Appleton."

Valentine gave Appleton careful instructions, and in three minutes he was handcuffed and stuck in the big duffel bag, with his bootlaces tied together and threaded through the grommets.

"I'm going to leave your rifle with the handcuff key near the exit. You can work your way out of this pretty easily, I should think."

The sentry was breathing a little steadier now, listening.

"I'm going to be looking around for a while from the exit. Any booby traps I need to know about?"

"No."

"While I'm looking around, if I hear you moving around, I'll come back and taze you.

"Way I see it, you've got two options, Appleton. You can be a good soldier and work your way out of the bag and ring every alarm in the warren. Someone might ask why you didn't hear the elevator bell, how I caught you unprepared and got the drop on you."

"There are patrols outside," Appleton said. "They shoot on sight, you try going down the west side of the ridge."

"Don't worry about that. Your other option is to ditch the bag and play dumb. I hear alarms going off and they catch me, well, I'm just going to have to tell them I caught you jerking off with your belt around your ankles."

"I wasn't—"

"I know you weren't. But I'm a good liar. Think they'd send you to the Punishment Brigade for that?"

"Don't forget the alarm on the hatch. It's just a switch on the side of the battery," Appleton suggested.

"If I were you, I'd get out of the bag, inch my way down the hall, uncuff myself, and go back to my book. But, then, I'm a deserter."

Valentine remembered the alarm, gave Appleton a little bit of a poser by sliding the handcuff key down the rifle barrel, and cracked the hatch to the air-defense post.

A drizzle that fell like it was too tired to work up into actual rain slicked on his face and hair as he negotiated the warren's slopes, making off down the eastern side.

He marked no activity on the road-rail terminus—the warren might as well have been a graveyard—but that didn't mean eyes weren't watching from doors and sentry posts. Valentine made a long, elbow- and knee-battering crawl to the bottom of the slope. A garbage pit gaped fifty or sixty meters away; one of the more common punishments for minor infractions was a spell either digging new space for garbage or covering up whatever the scavengers—human, rodent, or insect—left.

A dog barked, freezing him, but it was a distant warning from the southwestern side of the ridge.

He rested and waited. Headlights glowed; then engine noise sounded from the road winding down from the western foothills. A motorbike leading a car approached the checkpoint, and Valentine took the opportunity to make a dash for the garbage pit. Half expecting a warning shot if not another bullet through the thigh, he was there by the time the vehicles reached the gate.

On the other side of the garbage pit the woods began. A fence ran through it, patrolled, but it was militia backed up by a few Bears. But the fence was little more than a polite warning, and the patrols were a training exercise, and Valentine had heard stories of paths to sneak out and go into town for a little fun. The tough part was getting out of the warren.

Valentine crept up on Gide's fueling station and motor pool, having gone over another fence. There were a couple of guards at the gate, but the rest of the buildings were locked up tight. Valentine rejoiced in his luck when he saw a woman Gide's size work a crank, pumping fuel from an underground reservoir into a fifty-gallon drum. Then she turned. The woman's profile was a straight horizontal line, flat as a building.

"Julia," he hissed from the shadows.

She stepped away from the pump and reached for her sidearm. "Who's there?"

"David. I'm a friend of Gide's."

"*The* David," she said, reaching for something at her throat. She pulled up a plastic nose and a surgical mask.

Valentine walked up and shook her hand. "You make me sound like a statue."

"Umm . . . sorry? Gide's not on duty until seven."

"Can you get her, please? It's really important."

"Ah, love," she said. "Where are you storing your white horse?"

"It's desert tan, and that's what I needed to see her about."

"Burb," she said, employing the local slang for "be right back," and went off toward a long building that looked like two separate pre-'22 houses that had been enlarged toward each other until they joined.

She returned alone, as though from a trip to the bathroom. "Meet her in the tomato stands. Far end of the garden."

Valentine found her crouched in the tomato patch under an oversized umbrella. She'd brought a blanket and smelled like freshly applied scent.

"Lousy night for this, you know, it's damp. You could have given—," she said.

"Sorry, it's not that," Valentine said, squatting down beside her, hedged by ripening tomatoes. "I do mean sorry. Gide, I'm getting out of here."

"Huh?" She sat up.

"This place is poison."

"What, sodomy and the lash back in the Holes too? And you an officer and all."

"No. They're fighting . . . they're squeezing the Kurians in Seattle by getting rid of the population. And I mean getting rid of, not relocating."

"Cheezus. Poor bastards."

"I've done what I needed to do here, sorta, and I'm getting away."

"David, you're creeping me out here. Those sheeple are going to get it one way or another. Might as well make sure the towers don't have 'em."

"Don't tell me you knew too?"

"No, you just told me now. But—fuck!—it makes sense. We're what they need, right? Why let the bloodsuckers have what they need?"

Valentine felt his cheeks go hot. "You used to live under them. Your whole life, pretty much."

"Yeah, and I'd rather've been shot or hung or whatever they do than let some fuckin' Hisser get his hook into me."

If she could just see it, see it as it took place . . .

"I'm getting out. I'm going to report to my contact. Maybe . . . maybe change something, I dunno."

"Good luck with that. Me, I'm bucking for the regulars. There's a shooting tournament soon—you can win a monthlong trip up to the wilds for some hunting and training. It's a great way to get noticed." There was an edge to her voice, but she blinked hard, several times.

"Then this is good-bye," Valentine said. He gave her his Steyr. "Maybe this'll help you win the competition."

She cradled the gun, on her knees, the oversized uniform shirt making her look like a beautiful but well-armed garden gnome. "Can't you . . . can't we sleep on it? Maybe it'll look different in the morning. We can talk. You're smart enough to see reason—"

The last thing Valentine wanted to do was kiss her, but he found it happening all on its own. "They'll come looking for me, and yours is the first bed they'll check. If they ask about the gyro, play dumb. I need to steal some high-octane gas off you."

"Let me put my boots back on," she said. A lace broke as she tied it. "Fuck! I'm supposed to be tough. I've been through . . . but you drop your guard just a little bit and it's like you never learned in the first place." She wiped her eyes, buckled her belt. "I'll help you get the cans over the fence."

Ten

Mount Omega: So many legends have grown up around Mount Omega that even its mention lays a shadow of doubt over any narrative featuring it.

Certain facts are not in dispute. Mount Omega had its genesis in "Fitzhugh's Folly," when the asteroid ZL-624 had its near-Earth encounter. Poor Dr. Donald Fitzhugh—while two other astronomers actually presented the case at the secret government briefing with him, their names weren't quite as euphonious with "folly," so they dropped out of history and the high-level panic surrounding ZL-624's approach. It was predicted to strike early in the second decade of the twenty-first century somewhere between the Mississippi River and the Azores, and Mount Omega was hastily constructed with equipment from the nuclear-waste storage facility in Nevada.

Even after fresh tracking data predicted a near miss, Mount Omega construction continued. It was a massive, well-funded project already under way, employing thousands and thousands of highly paid, security-clearance construction workers and technicians across rural Washington and northern Oregon. An eleven-month, money-is-no-object crash project stretched out into its second decade. Mount Omega eventually worked its way into the defense budget as a secure location for government officials in case of a catastrophic terrorist strike on Washington DC. Work on it never ceased.

Had it ever been finished, it would have been a wonder of the world. Nuclear power, state-of-the-art hydroponics, air- and water-filtration systems supporting office space and housing larger than the Vatican, the Kremlin, and the Forbidden Palace combined (with the

Mall of America thrown in as a cherry on top), from the golf course on the surface to the deepest geothermal heat pump, it would have had space to rival a small city.

But the project was never really completed.

The Kurian onslaught of 2022, with the civilization-shattering mix of seismic activity and the ravies virus, led a skeleton crew of key elected officials, staff, and support personnel to receive their orders to relocate to Mount Omega. As the disaster grew, a stampede to the lifeboat Mount Omega represented began, and only after the shootdown of flight 5X03 did planes cease landing at its little emergency strip of blockaded, reinforced-concrete highway.

And there, guarded by the best the army, navy, air force, and marines had to give under General Roma, they buttoned up.

This narrative will not attempt to answer the question of why the Kurians never attempted to take over Mount Omega. Of course it would have required launching an operation of the scope of the Grog-versus-human battle that took place in Indianapolis now recorded as Congress' Last Stand. There were certainly enough organized Grogs on Oregon's Pacific coast in the years following 2022, after they swept up through Mexico and into California. Perhaps Fort Roma's inarguably passive role in resisting the Kurians led to it being spared. Cynical humor holds that there weren't enough uncompromised human souls buttoned up in the underground refuge to make the game worth the candle, but the fact remains that a number of senators and congressmen indisputably left Mount Omega to make it back to their constituents and share their fate. Only a handful ultimately lent their names and voices to the Kurian Order, and those black names are recorded elsewhere.

Mount Omega was neither a sybaritic paradise where champagne was lapped from silicone-enhanced cleavage between banquets with Kurian diplomats nor a monastery to Truth, Justice, and the American Way where senators and cabinet officials wore sackcloth and ashes and debated the finer points of federalism by the light of candles, all the while making hand copies of the Constitution and Bill of Rights.

A social scientist or a psychiatrist might make sense of some of the oddities David Valentine saw on his brief visit to Mount Omega, but if any did, their observations aren't easily found. Self-enclosed populations, as Darwin noted on his trip to the Galápagos, lead to a strange selection of attributes. Valentine himself, when asked his opinion of Mount Omega, always shrugged and said, "Three generations of cabin fever."

* * *

"That is one darling little helicopter," the corporal said.

Valentine didn't bother with the lecture on the difference between an autogyro and a helicopter.

He'd made Fort Omega in one long, exhausting flight with only a brief stop for refueling and sanitary purposes. The autogyro's stomach-tossing, bobbing motion left him feeling the same way he'd felt when climbing off the old *Thunderbolt* onto dry land—the odd sensation that the ground was swaying.

Mount Omega wasn't on any map; indeed, its "undisclosed location" wasn't even a mountain, more of a sheep-littered ridge on the grounds of an old army training base, a little west of an old, spent nuclear-fuel repository. Valentine simply skimmed the surface until he saw the skeletons of some stripped commercial jets beside a wide patch of concrete highway with a big Day-Glo *X* painted on either end, and then landed and waited for someone to come point a gun at him.

Several someones did, displaying admirable handling of their old, but immaculately maintained, weapons. Of course "old" was a bit of a misnomer, as they looked lighter and of better quality than even the products of the Atlanta Gunworks, with combat zoom sights, lasers, and 20mm integral support cannon. Leather and plastic knee and elbow pads were fixed over outer shells made from old ponchos. Wash-worn uniforms beneath showed signs of heavy patching and repair, but they were still men Valentine would have been proud to line up in front of one of Southern Command's staff inspectors.

They ordered Valentine to lie down on his face, and he complied.

He tried to speak, but they told him to "shut up" until they fixed his hands in what felt like plastic wire, perhaps ripped from one of the airliner carcasses lying by the side of the road.

"Let's have it," a lieutenant said. "Why did you not acknowledge radio signal and land without permission?"

"First, the radio's a piece of crap that's preset to only receive three Quisling frequencies. Second, I'm on Southern Command orders, Hunter comma Cat, precleared to contact civilian authority. I have a verification code that I will supply to anyone with the prefix."

"Shit. Let me get someone from liaison, sir. I'm afraid you have to stay under restraints and guard for now." He gave orders to a messenger, who double-timed off toward one of the grounded planes and disappeared up a nose ladder.

"If it's going to be much of a wait, I need a trip to the john. And I could really use a hot meal." Valentine couldn't remember when he'd last been so hungry, and wondered if Sir had permanently accelerated his metabolism or if he'd adjust in time.

"Understood, sir. We'll have to watch you, though. As to a meal, if you get taken Inside, the food's better than what we can give you out here."

After seeing to his comfort, they started making small talk about the gyro. A five-stripe came out to observe.

Valentine heard bicycle tires and a driving chain. A tall pipe cleaner of a man in civilian clothes, brown wool trousers topped by a khaki shirt, pulled up and removed his helmet and hung it on a hook on his belt. He took a courier bag off the bike's handlebars and trotted up to the soldiers, a holster bobbing at his hip.

"My name's Patterson," the man said, kneeling so his eyes were level with Valentine's.

"Valentine," Valentine replied.

Patterson took out a neatly printed card. "I'm your Professional Military Surrender Resource. I'm completely outside their chain of command, and my only concern is for your behalf. I'm here to see that you get food, medical care, legal representation, and religious or social comfort between now and your release or execution. Do you understand?"

Valentine wondered how the title looked on the paperwork and smiled. "I just need to speak to the liaison officer."

"You should see him do this with Grogs," one of the older waiting soldiers told another, sotto voce. "*Oook*s and bobs his head and rattles beads until they head-butt him."

Patterson ran through a flow chart of questions regarding his treatment. Valentine denied being harmed or humiliated after his surrender.

"Captain Sagamoto is on his way," the lieutenant reported. "He'll verify your credentials and then we'll be done with you. Hope you're telling the truth, because otherwise—"

"Lieutenant, don't terrify the prisoner," Patterson cut in. "I'll have to log that."

"Beg your pardon," the lieutenant said, whether to him or Patterson Valentine couldn't tell. He backed off, and a five-striper nudged him.

"Don't let it bother you, sir. Just a bunch of papers."

Patterson had the lieutenant sign a piece of paper, and while they were so occupied the sergeant knelt down behind Valentine and checked his bonds.

"Inside, ifs they asks you where you comes from, say Canada. Make up some small place nobody's ever heards of like Moose Dick or Fragileoshus," the sergeant whispered.

The sergeant stood up as soon as the officers turned. "Just making sure I could wiggle a finger through," he said to them.

Valentine's ears picked up a faint whine and wheels turning on the landing strip. A golf-cart-like vehicle emerged from between two fuselages and joined the party, parking next to the autogyro. Like Patterson, the driver was on the lean side. His margarine clothes were thin and seemed hardly enough to keep out the dry wind. They reminded Valentine of the hospital gowns he'd seen at Xanadu.

He had faintly Eurasian features and a growth of beard that made him look like a model from one of the old magazines trying to look rugged and fresh off a mountain.

"I'm Captain Sagamoto," he said. He nodded to the lieutenant. "Patterson, I don't think this'll concern you. Can the newcomer and I have a moment?" He squatted down opposite Valentine as the others moved away. Valentine ran through the signs and countersigns he'd memorized back at Nancy's in his head.

"Red to blue?" Sagamoto finally asked, extending his left fist.

"Negative negative negative," Valentine said. "Sorry I can't lock knuckles."

Sagamoto smiled. "I can see that. Prefix two oh nine."

"Suffix V April twenty-seven. I'm here to see Senator Bey from the illustrious state of Oklahoma."

Sagamoto stood. "Lieutenant, he's cleared. I'm going to ask you to use your comset. I'm taking him to the Inside. Patterson, aren't you needed in the marshes? I heard a team of Grogs got captured after the fighting. You pedal hard, you'll be there to make sure they're tucked in tonight and get properly exchanged. Might win you that promotion back to the Inside."

"Barbarians," Patterson said.

The sergeant cut Valentine's bonds and he and the corporal lifted him. Everyone watched Patterson bike away.

"I didn't knows about no fighting in the marshes," the sergeant said.

"I could have heard wrong," Sagamoto said. "You know how rumors fly in there."

It was a fifteen-minute trip to the ridge that sheltered Mount Omega. They drove around a depressed-looking golf course that kept a single hole mowed, plus a putting green. "They cut back and start watering a new hole every couple of months just for variety. Of course even going out to golf is a privilege, Constitution-level officials only."

Sagamoto took his time driving, enjoying the clean, open air and the sunshine. Valentine found it was a relief from the gloom of the Seattle basin too, though hunger still gnawed at him.

The electric car zigzagged around a small, sloping mountain of brush-covered dirt and came to a wide steel door that looked like it was built to keep in King Kong. It was open wide enough to allow two of the little electric golf carts to pass. Part of it was filled with a trestle of closely packed rollers. Men were taking bins of potatoes and onions off of a beat-up farm truck and its companion trailer and sending them rolling down the track. The hundreds of little wheels spun on their bearings as load after load of produce disappeared Inside, sounding like a cave full of angry rattlesnakes.

Sagamoto beeped the friendly-sounding horn on the golf cart twice and passed through the formidable doors. He showed ID to a trio of bored, blue-uniformed police who intercepted them. There seemed to be two ways into the mountain, an express lane for those who lived and worked within, and a serpentine of desks and examining areas. The only other person being processed in the serpentine was a shaggy-looking man with a big netting bag filled with dead pheasant and chickens. They waved Valentine over to a brightly lit alcove. They let Valentine keep his pistol but put a trigger lock on it.

As they patted him down, Valentine looked down the vast tunnel, big enough for a freight train or a couple of tractor-trailers to pass into the mountain abreast. There were tracks built into the ground, as a matter of fact, and the vegetables were being loaded onto a flatcar.

"What about the damn sword?" the police officer searching Valentine asked as he stood with a thermometer in his mouth while a medical officer checked his blood pressure. "Bells, he's got a knife on him too. You from the bad side of the mountains or what?"

A gray-hair in a wheelchair supervising from a duty desk, an old leather jacket with a CAPITOL POLICE patch draped over his shoulders, glanced at Valentine. "Locker all his gear. Locker, dummies!"

The medical officer stamped his hand with blue dye. After that, they inked his thumb and pressed it on a set of cards. Sagamoto got something stamped at the desk and returned with a temporary ID bearing his name and thumbprint.

By the time the carload of vegetables was on its way into the mountain, Valentine had the slip for his gear in the locker. Two more officials, in black paper clothing that made their skin look even more pale, met him at the next desk.

"General Accounts and Revenue," Sagamoto whispered. Then to the woman: "Visitor, let's get him a card for two days of food."

"What'll that be, an ear tag?" Valentine asked.

The woman at the desk unlocked a big paybox, but the man glared at Valentine. "State of birth, United States designation?"

"I'm Canadian," Valentine said, wondering if he should try to imitate the accents he'd heard on the White Banner Fleet in the Great Lakes.

This made the official even madder. He pushed a yellow card at Valentine and passed over the stub of a dull pencil. "We'll be checking that."

Valentine filled out the yellow card, no easy task with a pencil under an inch long. He gave his correct date of birth and listed his birthplace as "Fat Log, Saskatchewan."

"Two days' visitor rations, six hundred seventy-one dollars," the woman said.

"You must run a hell of a cafeteria," Valentine said. The woman tapped a laminated statement on the desk that showed the daily prices along with various taxes, duties, fees, and environmental-impact charges. He reached for his coin belt.

"Keep it. Guest of Senator Bey," Sagamoto said.

"We'll have to clear it with his office," the GAR man said, reaching for a phone.

"An aide is on his way up," Sagamoto said. "I'll sign and put my sosh." Sagamoto didn't wait for approval; he scrawled a signature on Valentine's yellow card.

"I should tear that up in front of you," the GAR man said.

"Want your bulletproof vest back? You do and I'll have the GAO and the AG on you tonight. You'll be out riding a motorcycle in the boonies, collecting Patriotic War Duties."

"Table it, Barry," the woman said, tearing off a preperforated card from the yellow sheet and handing it to Valentine. "Sag here is engaged to a guy on the AG's staff." She stamped it and handed it to Valentine.

The last checkpoint was a velvet-rope serpentine. Sagamoto lifted a latch and they cut through the empty switchback alleys, and came to a pert, attractive woman in a thick blue blazer with a red, white, and blue scarf. Her smile was almost as bright as the sodium floodlights at the top of the tunnel. She checked Valentine's ID.

"Welcome to Mount Omega," she said, handing him a small, dog-eared book held together with a rubber band. "If you have any questions, this guidebook may assist you. Issuing the guidebook is not an implied contract to provide services. Acceptance of the guidebook places you under all the provisions of the Visitor Security Act."

"Take it. Don't worry," Sagamoto said.

Valentine accepted it and the woman recorded his ID number on a clipboard. Her smile brightened by another couple of watts. "Thank you. There is a FAQ and a list of security restrictions in the guidebook. Failure to comply with speech codes on page three will result in loss of

Inside privileges. Mount Omega is a discrimination-free zone. Mount Omega is smoke-free since 2024. Mount Omega is proud to be Working for Victory under VO-2011 protocols under the Just Human Rights and the Resistance Acts. For more information on any of these initiatives, consult your selected representative."

Valentine felt air moving, like a fresh breeze outside. The strong air currents indoors weren't exactly disturbing, but they lent an unreality to the cavernous underground.

"We call this level Grand Central," Sagamoto said, pulling Valentine out of the way of a platoon of soldiers with Marine Corps insignia walking toward the entrance, two navy officers in timber stripes trailing behind, one carrying a camera with a long telephoto lens. "Sometimes people come up here just for the chance of seeing a fresh face. Above this level is the atrium, and there are greenhouses that are the next best thing to going outside on your vacation. Getting to be Outside again is a big recruiting incentive for the military, but people generally find out it's not all it's cracked up to be."

"That why you signed up?"

"Wanted to go out and change the world. Felt like it for a while—I was helping refugees relocate."

"Same here," Valentine said.

Sagamoto pulled the string on his paperlike pants and he opened his waistband, as though they were two little boys comparing genitals. Valentine saw a wide plastic tube emerging from a fleshy hole just above his line of pubic hair. "My first battle didn't quite work out the way I thought. Have to stick close to medical care now."

They stepped under a big electronic board, above a guarded alcove with four banks of elevators, where LED lights spelled out activity on different levels. Congress was in session, and various cases were being heard in courts, including the Supreme Court.

"You heard of that butterfly's wings stuff?" Valentine said.

"When there's no lower intestine left to stitch—"

"No, it's this theory—a butterfly flaps its wings in China and you get snow in Virginia. Little, imperceptible events have big repercussions later. Maybe you caused two people to meet out there, and their kid grows up to be the next George Washington."

"I heard that kind of thing from the rehab team. They don't have to wash out colostomy bags—look, Valentine, I'm not challenging. You were trying to be nice." He took a deep breath. "Sure. You never know. At least I tried. I'm still trying, just in a different way. Looks like you've had a near retirement or two yourself."

Valentine opened the guidebook. The map of Mount Omega was a combination of a cross section of the decks of a ship and a subway chart. He tried to find their location on Grand Central.

Sagamoto pulled it out of his hands, snapped the rubber band back on, and shoved it in Valentine's pocket. "That thing's useless. The map makes a lot of sense once you already pretty much know your way around. As for all the rules—just be polite and wait your turn in line, and if the police tell you to do something, do it. Just a second, I'm going to use one of the phones and get in touch with the senator's office.

"As a visitor, you really just need to know about the Mall, the Hill, the Point, and the George. The Mall's just below Grand Central—there are a couple of escalators just ahead there. The Hill's at the end of the Mall—it's an old indoor arena the reps and senators use for Congress. Point is above us—it's pure military. The George is where guests stay—it's also off Grand Central here. Of course there are archives and sewage treatments and waste and workshops and everything we need to keep going, plus the housing levels. The vice president and Speaker and chief justice all get windows and patios. The rest of us make do with twenty minutes in the UV rooms every day." An elevator opened and a small throng emerged. "And I think this is your aide."

A woman with wide eyes and tired hair, but almost glamorous thanks to her choice of scarf and gloves and satchel, broke away from the group leaving the elevator. She had an ID printed on a half-Capitol-dome, half-eagle-wing design, her picture and a thumbprint superimposed.

"Hello, Captain," the aide said. "Good to see you again. Is this our contact?"

Valentine extended a hand: "David Valentine. Southern Command, and lately Pacific Command."

She shook it: "Daphne Trott-Diefenbach, Senator Bey's chief military aide. I bet you're hungry."

More than half the people walking the wide corridor of Grand Central looked hungry to Valentine. "I'm all right."

"Well, I could use a bite. Captain, join us?"

Sagamoto took a step back. "No. I've got to log paperwork on the fresh face here."

"Thank you, Captain," Valentine said.

"Just doing my bit. Ma'am," Sagamoto said, turning.

"Then it's us. I'll take you down to the Mall—it's worth seeing," she said. "Can I call you David, or do you do Dave?"

"Most people just use Val," Valentine said.

"I'm Ducks, then."

"Ducks?"

She jerked her head down the tunnel, and they headed farther in, Valentine unconsciously falling into step. "They used to call me Daffy in school. Daffy Duck sometimes. I liked the Duck bit."

She took him down a worn old escalator. The new tunnel was even higher and wider than Grand Central. It was arched at the top, like a cathedral, and twin banks of lights shone down on small trees and grass running the length of the Mall. Valentine heard a fountain roaring somewhere. Bars, eateries, shops, movie booths, even a massive gallery piled with used books, lined the Mall. Valentine heard a pounding and hard breathing, looked up, and saw a walkway running above at treetop level, its railing thick with plant boxes. Joggers were running up there.

"I use the pool, myself. Warm as a summer lake, not that I've had a chance to swim in one. Let's break in John Bull's."

Valentine guessed it was an English-style pub, as there was a picture of Winston Churchill he recognized on the wall, and some black-and-whites of Congress being addressed. Behind the bar in a place of honor was a high blue helmet that reminded Valentine of an oversized egg.

"Two fry-ups and two shakes, Walther," she told the barkeep. She led Valentine to a back booth. His strange clothing was drawing stares from the Omegans in their scrublike paper clothing.

"Beer, Ducks?"

"No."

A server wiped their already-clean table and they sat.

"I'm just so eager for news of Outside. Tell me anything and everything," Ducks said.

"Ummm—where should I start?"

"How about Operation Archangel?" she asked.

Valentine took strange comfort in the fact that she'd heard of it. "I didn't see much of it."

"We had—I can't remember exactly how many, but several all-night sessions. Had this whole place buzzing like a beehive. Not that I've seen one."

"Really? Go up to the old airfield. I heard a bunch in the engine housing of one of those big jets."

"I guess they keep bees in some of the agro areas Outside, but on my vacations I usually just go to the river."

"Why were there all-night sessions? Trying to get other areas to join in?"

"State handles that. No, we were upholding the legality of the operation pending."

"Pending what?"

"Restoration of constitutional civilian authority."

The meal arrived, a couple of fried, sliced tomatoes, a few French fries, and a breaded something about the size of a small sausage. Two big pint glasses came with it, thick with something that looked like a strawberry milk shake.

"Here's to it," Valentine said, lifting a glass. He tried a sip. It tasted like someone had tossed ice and old newspapers into a blender, then added a little syrup.

"Takes some getting used to. I'm told the flavoring is strawberry."

Valentine waited for the "Not that I ever had one," but it never came.

The server was already long gone, arguing at another table that Representative Mowbrarun's credit wouldn't buy a shot of pickling juice.

"What's really in it?"

"Mostly fiber-powdered vitamin supplement. It leaves you feeling full, anyway."

Valentine tried the fried whatever, mostly ground-up bean paste and gristle, he guessed. Ducks went on: "I never get invited to the good parties anymore because I still support the military, as does the senator."

"Who else is going to get rid of the Kurians?"

"Oh, I don't mean the *Resistance*. Everyone supports that, especially Senator Bey. Well, almost. Our military. They're supposed to be out there getting food for us, but a lot of people think they're keeping it for themselves."

"Speaking of the senator—"

"Oh, just a second. We can't talk about him or your operations just yet. I was hoping you might have a valuable or two up in your locker you could donate to the Winter Harvest fund. Also, Senator Bey has a reelection court date coming up, and lawyers are expensive. Even a small donation will help him win his case and keep supporting the people of Oklahoma in their struggle."

Valentine knew a demand for a bribe when he heard one. At least the fries were tasty, thanks to the salt.

"What's the senator like?"

"He's wonderful. A real American success story out of the good old days, you know? Bunting and John Philip Sousa and all that. A son of one of the tunneling engineers. But he broke out of the father's-footsteps stuff and started standing for selections young. He represented himself at his first selection and the judge was so impressed by his rhetoric, he became a representative from Third District. He caught the eye of the SecDef, and got a position on the Resistance Approbation staff. His press conferences were really something, I think I was nine when—"

"There's a press here?"

"Of course. All the big newspapers still exist—of course they only come out on Tuesdays, which is good news, Fridays, which is bad, and Sundays, which is all analysis. I've got a copy of the *Times* here. . . ."

She extracted a single sheet of folded newsprint. Four "pages" of close-set type under a banner, front-page headline:

PALMETTO-BERGSTROM
INVESTIGATION WIDENS

POSSIBLE CABINET INVOLVEMENT

VICE PRESIDENT DECLINES COMMENT

"WILL BLADES CUT HUD STAFFER'S THROAT?"

Valentine scanned a couple of paragraphs. Evidently a judge's clerk named Palmetto was caught sharing a portable walkie-talkie phone with a congressional aide named Bergstrom, violating Separation of Powers practice. The "new evidence" was from the Housing and Urban Development chief of staff, who admitted to Justice Department investigators that he tried to call Bergstrom, got Palmetto, and mentioned that a fresh supply of razor blades had come in.

"What an unwise," Ducks said. "All I can think is she didn't know who Palmetto was. They're just making a meal out of it because right now the VP and Donovan Baltrout are both in Majoritarian. So what about that contribution?"

"This shake is going right through me. I'll be right back," Valentine said. He went to the washroom, festooned with NO SMOKING and WATER NONDRINKABLE signs, took out two of his gold coins—the belt was now well over half-empty—and returned to their booth.

"Okay, I've got—"

"Oh good God, don't give it to me," Ducks said, sliding so far away from him she almost fell out of the booth. "Are you out of your mind? We'll swing by the Fair Politics booth and you'll fill out an envelope, one for Winter Harvest and a separate one for the senator's campaign. You'll have to do a lot of paperwork for the latter. Then they'll give me the envelopes."

"Uh-huh."

"The senator is on the anticorruption committee, you know. We're not going to be caught out."

She put the meal on the senator's account and they went through the paperwork at the busy booths off the Mall, which had an entire section of tunnel devoted to them.

Clusters of people with placards, pamphlets, cups, jugs, and purses filled the hall, swirling around those traveling to and from the booths. "Support Booth-Ramierez!" "Bring America Back needs you!" "Volunteer labor needed for Food for Thought, one free meal per day!" "Stop the Midwestern Senatorial Junta before they stop you!"

Ducks used her satchel like the prow of an icebreaker, holding it in front of her and forcing her way through the throng.

"Unpleasant."

Valentine pressed tightly behind her. People were shoving flyers in his collar, his boot, his empty holster, anything they could reach. They made it to a police officer, who put them in line for the next available federal bursar.

Valentine watched people step up to the glass booths. He'd seen rations doled out at old currency exchanges in the KZ and the setup reminded him of a clean, well-lit version of that. They only had a ten-minute wait, and Valentine's stomach gurgled as it tried to figure out what to do with the pub shake. Valentine extracted folded flyers from his clothing. Most featured drawings of ragged, starving children or trios of heroic-looking soldiers, two healthy supporting a wounded comrade.

Ducks' eyes lit up when she saw the gold coins. She helped him with the paperwork under the bored eye of the woman behind the glass. The bursar gave her a receipt for the Winter Harvest contribution, and the coin for the campaign went into a concealed neck pouch under Ducks' thin clothes.

The rigmarole left Valentine nonplussed. But all the careful record keeping gave the people in here something to do.

"You just made my day, Val," she said, pushing her way through the donation seekers again.

They emerged from the crowd, where another policeman made sure the donation seekers didn't step out into the "sidewalks" and grass of the Mall.

"When can I see the senator?" Valentine asked.

She consulted a clock projecting from the wall ahead. "They're in session for another hour. Want to watch from the senatorial gallery?"

Valentine shrugged. "I could use a shower."

"You can use the one off my unit. Staffers have to share bathrooms, though."

They passed an overlarge team of gardeners taking care of a set of trees and she took him to another elevator bank. She showed her card to the operator inside, who punched a button for 26 and the elevator descended.

The tunnel level 26 was a good deal rougher, about fourteen feet high and still circular, painted in a cheery soft yellow that had gone dingy, with exposed conduits and pipes running the ceiling. This part was not as well lit; only one light in three even had a bulb. It snaked along in a long bend of about three degrees, Valentine guessed. Seven-foot-high blue cubicle separators closed off by shower curtains divided the tunnel on either side. Some had "roofs"; others were open to the tunnel ceiling.

The cubicle panels were decorated with family pictures, cartoons, even old pictures taken from what Valentine guessed to be calendars.

"This is mine," she said, stopping at a roofless cubicle. Her "door" was a quilt of old materials, mostly faded logos from T-shirts. A Rodgers and Hammerstein *Oklahoma!* poster decorated the outside, a 2016 Broadway production with the cast either rootin' or tootin' energetically in splashy colors. She also had a semifamous black-and-white photo of a tired-looking guerrilla, his back to an old oak, keeping watch while an old man, a woman, and two kids slept in a huddle.

"Hope you live here alone," Valentine said.

"I do, unfortunately. Marrieds and cohabitants get more space—families even get their own toilet. But this is really pretty nice. Downstairs the service staff really just gets a barrack bed with some privacy curtains hanging down. Yeah, the cubicle paneling smells musty, but it absorbs noise like a sponge. I could never sleep in a barrack."

"Consider the criticism withdrawn," Valentine said.

"Let me just grab you a towel and some soap." She ducked into her cube.

It was hard to say which was rougher, the towel or the grainy soap, but Valentine made use of them in the common shower room, a tiled-wall area in a dimple off the main passage. At least the water was deliciously hot. She gave him a tour of the rest of "her" level. They passed other dimples along the way—one had a television and four battered lounge chairs. Valentine was shocked to recognize Kurian Zone programming.

"Actually, their stuff's popular, not that any of us have much to compare it to. We do our own news, of course. Majoritarian news at five and nine, Minoritarian at five thirty and nine thirty. Every now and then they show a movie or a TV series from the Old World, but I don't like to watch those. Shallow, stupid stuff. The real old movies are better. Have you ever seen *Gone with the Wind*?"

"I like it. Don't knock shallow. Any culture that can put that much effort into entertainment about who is dating whom has all the big Maslow-sized problems pretty much solved."

She pointed to an old magazine cover on a staffer's cubicle. "Everyone was so pretty back then. About the only way we look like them is thin. Thin we can do."

They traveled back up in another elevator with a yawning attendant and she took him to the end of the Mall. After another ID check and search they went up another escalator to a sports and meeting arena, a vast open area under reinforcing girders.

The Senate held court from a ring of upholstered club chairs circling a wooden floor with old basketball markings. Little groups of three and four people down on the first level sat together, talking or listening to the senator addressing chambers from a round platform in the center with a podium that slowly rotated. The nonsenatorial watched from the old plastic chairs; every now and then one was missing in the rows, giving the audience area a gap-toothed look compared with the last arena Valentine had been in, the horror show under the Pyramid in Memphis.

The senators had real clothing, it looked like, complete with ties and shined leather shoes.

"One faction in the House wants to set up basketball league play again," Ducks said quietly. "The Senate keeps killing it, says having the Senate break for a game would destroy the dignity of the chamber."

"They're just scared because basketball would draw a bigger crowd," a man a couple of rows behind said.

"Mount Omega can't raise chickens for anything, but we can sure breed cynics," she muttered.

Valentine tried to catch the thread of the speech. The young man kept pausing and saying "hummmm," from beneath a generous overbite.

"McCaffee isn't much of a speaker," Ducks said. "But he is a third-generation senator, and half the Majoritarians owe his family favors."

"So those are senators in the big chairs?" Valentine asked. "They're not thin."

"Privileges of constitutional office."

"I see," Valentine said. "Sounds like he's done."

"New Hampshire is next. Now she can talk."

"Has she ever been to New Hampshire?" Valentine asked.

"Of course not. Senators argue their elections in front of the Supreme Court, so you can be sure she represents their values. She's flinty, tough, practical."

"And married to the head of the Unified Journalism Network," the man from behind said.

"That's Senator Bey there, in the leather chair with the bull horns at the top."

Whatever remained of the miner in the graying body was in the set of the shoulders and head. Senator Bey leaned forward in his chair, chin up and out and fist set on his knee, as if ready to rush the podium and tackle the speaker.

Valentine tried to follow the debate. The "distinguished senator from New Hampshire" was defending the credentials of a new director for the Law College.

"There's a college here?"

"Of a sort. They feed the specialty schools: Military, Law, and Social Support or Revealed Religion, plus a special technical school for the people who keep the juice and water running. Most of the learning is computerized up until tenth grade. Then you get teachers, most of whom are studying at the college at the same time—it's how they pay their tuition. College is tough. I only barely made it. Try going four years on nothing but study naps."

Valentine waited through a vote—the new director was confirmed, and then the Senate ended session for the day with one of the most vaguely worded prayers Valentine had ever heard.

"Sorry it wasn't more interesting," Ducks whispered during the prayer. "Last week we had an impeachment trial. Those are always fun."

"Amen," the man behind said, though whether this was to cap the prayer or not Valentine never learned, for he left a moment later.

Ducks led Valentine through yet another Capitol Police checkpoint, this one with a bank of security camera monitors, but she seemed on friendly terms with all the men there and they made only a cursory check of his ID, and logged him in via computer.

These tunnels were wood paneled, with real door handles separating the garage-sized offices from the carpeted corridor. Soft music played through speakers hidden within the electrical and water conduits. She stopped at a door with a laminated plate that read SENATOR JOHN BEY, SENIOR SENATOR FROM OKLAHOMA, and knocked.

The door opened a crack, and Valentine saw a ferretlike man with a widow's peak. "Ducks."

"Visitor for the senator, Larry."

"Okay, but it has to be fast. He's got a party dinner to attend."

Valentine entered the office, lit by soft bulbs in tasteful lamps. The senator sat in a little chair by a porcelain sink, being shaved by an attendant while another staffer changed his shoes and socks. Valentine thought his face looked careworn.

A bodyguard with a holster bulging under his paper jacket stood in a corner with a good view of the whole room.

Ducks led him to the end of the room and Valentine checked himself in the mirror. "Senator, this is Major David Valentine, Pacific Command by way of Southern Command. Major, this of course is Senator Bey." She turned to the man with the widow's peak. "And this is Larry Decasse, the senator's chief of staff."

"Fourteen and counting," Decasse said. "I could use three more if we could just get the funding."

Valentine remembered hearing that Southern Command's commander in chief, General Phillips, ran his office with the help of two staffers and a communications officer, and had refused the protection of a bodyguard.

"I think I know your name, son. How can I help the Cause and the people I represent?"

"Sir," Valentine said, suddenly unsure about how one addressed a senator, "I've got two reports. One needs to be transmitted to Southern Command." Valentine laid the first document, his one-page report on finding Sir and relaying the message that Southern Command desperately needed Lifeweaver help, down on the desk.

"The second is more for your eyes, though I ask it to go to Southern Command as well. It concerns what can only be called war crimes carried out by Pacific Command."

"War crimes?" the senator asked, and Decasse hurried to the senator's side. "Who? What? We just voted a commendation for Adler for opening a new line to British Columbia."

Mr. A. "It's in the report. They slaughter Kurian populations. That's why Adler is so successful. He murders whole towns."

"It's not slaughter," Decasse said. "They're relocating populations. He's the most effective commander in the Resistance. Very popular on the Hill."

Valentine ignored the chief of staff and stared at the senator. "Call it what you like, it's deliberate murder of civilians. Lot easier to win battles when the other side can't shoot back."

"I don't like this," the senator said. "Staff, give me and the major here a moment of privacy. Yes, you too, Ducks. You're not in trouble—you did your job."

Everyone passed out into the hall, save the senator and the bodyguard. He wiped the rest of the lather from his face and tossed the towel in the sink.

"Major, you think we're insulated here from the world, and about as useful as your grandfather's third nipple. We've got channels of communication all over the country, even a couple of fake ones we let the Kurians listen to going overseas. But for all the folderol, Mount Omega is still wired into the world better than most any other place I can think of. I probably know more about operations in the Cascades than you do."

Valentine felt gut-kicked. "So you approve?"

"If you're asking me if I like it, no, I don't. Do I condone it? Yes. It's a hard truth of this war. We just lost a Freehold in the Balkans and as far as we can tell, the Koreans no longer exist. If it weren't for the Australians, bits of Alaska, and the del Fuegans, the Pacific Rim would be a giant Kurian circle. Southern Command got lucky, but it's about exhausted, and Denver doesn't have electricity anymore. The only victories being won are up in Pacific Command, and he's taking on the toughest, best-organized Kurians west of the Mississippi. Now's not the time for some kind of purge. We do those kind of blood sports here, but nothing that gets said or done in Mount Omega makes a damn bit of difference. I'm under no illusions about matters here. But if we're ever going to win this thing, it'll take leadership from men like Adler. There's even talk of making him commander in chief, if his plan to drive down into California succeeds. We haven't had a president since 'twenty-two."

The gut-kick turned his meal to bile. Bile that had to come up and out.

"Some leadership. Your speech code in the guidebook says that 'no person is to be addressed in a derogatory or demeaning fashion.' But murder is just fine for someone a couple hundred miles away."

Senator Bey's face reddened. "Sure, it's a silly bit of pantomime. But we can afford the niceties of civilization here. The trick is to get the rest of the country back to the point where we can sue each other over passing gas while someone else is speaking. I'm going to paraphrase Lincoln here. The objective is to win the war. If we can win it by killing every last person in a Kurian Zone, I want to win that way. If we can win it without killing anyone, even better. If we can win it by killing some and letting others alone, I'd be for that too."

A strong knock sounded at the door. "Senator!" Decasse's voice sounded. "The Capitol Police are here."

"Now what?"

Valentine suspected he knew what. The bodyguard went to the door.

"Yes?" the bodyguard asked as he opened it.

Valentine heard Decasse's voice: "Turns out Major—"

"We need to take the senator's visitor into custody. He's a deserter from Pacific Command," an authoritative voice said.

The bodyguard turned and looked at the senator. Valentine guessed that some protocol kept police out of the office.

What could he do, unarmed? Take the bodyguard's gun and shoot his way back up through Grand Central?

"I don't suppose Mount Omega has a sanctuary policy somewhere in this?" Valentine asked, lifting the guidebook.

"Too many people here already. There are families of representatives that go hungry at night."

"I'll go quietly," he told the senator.

The senator stood up and patted him on the shoulder. "Sorry, son. I'll make sure the report about your mission gets through. We want Southern Command to know you went out a hero."

Eleven

PB Camp "Sally," July: Valentine had seen dozens of compounds like these in his travels in the Kurian Zone; only the little buildings on the inside varied. Outside it was always the same: two rows of fencing topped with outward-pointing razor wire and a high observation point for the guards. Sometimes the houses were nice little prefabricated mobile homes, in other places drafty shacks where the women and children ran around on bare earth.

This one, oddly enough, was in an old church-school combination, made of stones as gray as a typical Cascade sky. The watchtower sat in the church steeple, and the fence ran in a great rhombus from the bricked-up side of the school to the old church parking lot, encompassing both the school athletic field and a small park opposite the church doors.

He came to the Sally as a Punishment Brigade convict, having worked his way through the abbreviated Pacific Command military justice system like a grain of sand passing through a worm's tract. Like the metaphoric worm, Pacific Command didn't have much in the way of brains or heart, just nerve ganglia that received Valentine as a deserter (he rode back from Mount Omega in an empty supply truck—heavily caged for transporting valuables east and malefactors west—chained hand and foot and under the watchful eye of a sentry in the cab cage) and processed him by a hearing where he admitted leaving his post without orders with the intent never to return. He gave a fine speech damning Pacific Command from the Bears following orders all the way up to Adler's Resource Denial methodology, but none in the hearing seemed particularly impressed. They convicted him and sentenced him to ten years in the Punishment Brigade. When he asked his lawyer how many men survived that long a term, he got a quiet shake of the head.

They put him to work with some other convicts in a chain gang blacktopping roads and felling trees. When they had 120 convicts together—the additions took roughly six weeks—they gave everyone a hose bath and piled them into a pair of seatless school buses for the trip to Pacific Command Military-Criminal Salvage Training—Sally.

"Okay, you cocksuckers, listen and listen hard!" the top sergeant yelled, standing at the head of the stairs with his back to the church doors. Like Valentine, he had a generous helping of Native blood and wore a mattress-ticking shirt and green camping shorts. Only the jaunty police hat had a military crest, the eagle head of Pacific Command.

Valentine and the others waited in groups of twenty, each under a police corporal. Ever since being handcuffed at Mount Omega, he'd given up on hope. He felt like a wrung-out rag, but still had enough intellectual curiosity to wonder what kind of bin he'd be tossed into.

"I'm Sergeant Kugel. You're going to hate me, this place, and every waking minute you spend here. The only way to shorten your stay is to follow orders. You stay here until I decide you're fit to leave, on the bus to the front or in a body bag. Your choice.

"We've got no officers, no la-di-da judge advocates. Just you cocksuckers and your PB training staff and some sentries with scoped thirty-aughts, who'll shoot you down from the wire just for the challenge of a tight grouping."

He took off his pistol belt and hung it on the church door behind him. "I'm going to save everyone a lot of time and mental stress. Any of you cocksuckers feel like taking a shot at me, I'll give you the chance right now. No hard feelings. Anyone swings at me after this big fat kiss of a welcome, I shoot the cocksucker dead and feed his balls to my Doberman. So now's your chance."

He stepped down to the bottom of the church steps and disappeared from Valentine's view, thanks to the rank in front of him. Valentine could see a bit of hat and that was all.

"Well? Well? I haven't had PT today—I could use a good sweat. All right."

Sergeant Kugel trotted back up the stairs and put his gun belt back on.

"You're all standing here because you're useless. You were useless the day the bitch that whelped you squeezed you out, and you're useless now, according to God and Court, which decided you're not even worth the brass a firing squad would expend. We'd float you downriver like shit, except we don't want to give the Reapers the satisfaction. So I'm going to make sure that though you may have been born useless and lived useless, you'll be able to die in a useful manner and following orders for once.

"One last thing. I don't want to hear any talk about how anyone is innocent. That's between you and God above. I don't give a damn, and I hate you all, whether your souls are white as a virgin's sheets or black as the witch king's pits. I'm here to send you out ready to keep the Reapers busy until a Bear team can take them down. There's no sick call, no off duty, and a bullet's the only punishment. We start in five minutes. I'm not going to ask if you all understand. Like the man said, frankly, my dear cocksuckers, I don't give a damn."

Valentine spent forty-nine endless days in the confines of the training school. After two weeks of almost solid physical activity—his only break was the two days he spent in the kitchens under the equally bloody-minded sergeant who ran the laundry and larder—the men began to break down and miss orders, stupefied with exhaustion.

He kept waiting for the pistols to come out, for an execution to set an example to the rest, but they lost only one man, a rapist whom the others called "Short Eyes." Valentine woke one morning and found his bunk empty. His name wasn't called in the morning roll, and nobody asked questions over breakfast. He'd slept at the opposite end of the bunk-littered school gymnasium, and Valentine fought hard to keep from being too much awakened by the inevitable noises of 120 men all sleeping in one room.

He made a few friends. Diaz, who had been caught raiding a Pacific Command depot—according to him, in order to feed his mother and sisters; according to Kugel, he'd been caught with copper wiring and electrical tools. Diaz never seemed to tire, and was always the first to offer a hand to help someone to his feet one more time. Then there was Smooth John Hollows, "Joho," who'd been caught peddling drugs but who had such an easygoing, friendly manner and a sharp sense of humor Valentine couldn't help but like him, or at least look forward to the next quiet quip out of his mouth, and then there was Tuber, a meaty, disproportionate Bear washout who'd lost his temper once too often and killed a man in a brawl.

After the eighteenth day, much of it spent on the broken-up old bleachers on the athletic field, which had been disassembled and turned into an obstacle course, the only way they could make it through their exercises was by teamwork. Pairs and trios of men helped one another up the shimmy poles and over the walls. Valentine divided the twenty-man team into groups of four and shoved them into places as they negotiated the course, then stayed with the slowest team. They'd get a rest break after ten circuits; the faster they got through the circuits, the longer the rest break. "His" platoon finished first.

When the mass could hardly walk without staggering, the sergeants made them crawl through everyone's least favorite stretch of the exercise yard: the mud pit and track circuit. The mud clung until it seemed that every man was carrying an extra thirty pounds for the trot around the edges of the wallow and back to the starting point for another crawl. After Valentine lost count of the circuits, he could rise only with the aid of Diaz and Joho.

"Wish they'd get some quimmies in this mud with us," Joho grunted. "I'd do some fast jackrabbit uh-uh-uh when lil' Keggo isn't looking."

Valentine remembered the shape and bob of Malia's mud-covered breasts, felt his heart break anew. That night drying mud flaked off his hair and into his dinner.

Then, remarkably, the tyrants gave them a day off. They distributed early apples and pamphlets with the history of the Punishment Brigade, its simplified rank structure, and the various sorts of specialty fields.

The Punishment Brigade mostly did high-risk duties: disarming unexploded ordnance, clearing minefields and booby traps, and doing forward signal duty or decoy work (the Kurians had some sort of special missile called a "screamer" they lobbed into the mountains now and then that homed in on radio transmissions), sapping missions, and "river watch."

The last was one of the most dangerous jobs in Pacific Command: guarding the rivers leading up into the mountains. The Kurians employed the fish-frog creatures Valentine had first encountered in Chicago, to guard water-girthed Seattle, and sometimes small teams of the creatures foraged inland. The river-watch teams inspected nets and kept an eye on white water, looking for a glimpse of the pale green bellies and shining goggle eyes of the Big Mouths. At night there was little you could do but keep away from the banks and listen for the *slee-kee, slee-kee* sound of their on-land breathing.

The next weeks were a mix of classroom, lab, and exercise. Everyone paid attention during class, asked questions; anything at all was better than pounding across the athletic field for the ten thousandth time. They were tested daily on their progress.

"Right answers, and I can even read it," Kugel said, handing Valentine back his test on *Eleven Ways to Kill an AV and Crew.* "Where'd you get the thing about hand grenades and electrical tape in the fuel?"

"Southern Command, Sergeant."

"Didn't know you were a habitual deserter, Valentine. Thought Pacific Command was your first. You desert PB and the only direction to go is to the Kurians, where they'll turn you right in to the Reapers."

Valentine looked at the ground.

"Why don't you give us all a big fuckin' shock, follow orders, and see something through for once?"

He passed on.

"What's the thing about electrical tape?" Tuber whispered, as Kugel yelled at some other PB—the involuntary recruits insisted it stood for "poor bastard"—about his handwriting and spelling.

"You pull the pin and wrap some electrical tape around the handle of a grenade. Gasoline dissolves the sticky. The more loops, the longer it takes. Then it blows."

Valentine glanced back at Kugel, who passed out another test and winked. Ten days ago, Kugel would have had him and Tuber jogging around the fence perimeter holding hands for talking among themselves.

The ordnance-disposal training was the worst. They used real shells and demolition charges, with just enough dynamite hidden inside to knock you on your ass with your ears ringing. Worse, you had to work through thick gloves and plastic safety goggles that were more scratch than lens.

Tuber was clumsy, and set off a shell as he and Valentine worked. Valentine expelled a deep breath as he picked himself up, but Tuber went berserk.

"Goddamn goddamn goddamn!" he screamed, spinning, throwing off his gloves, goggles, and helmet like a whirligig expelling sparks.

"You're dead, dummies," Corporal Pope, the bomb expert at the training center, shouted, not that every man in the platoon didn't know.

Tuber charged the corporal. Half the men in the platoon, including Valentine, threw themselves at him. He tossed two men off one arm, sent another reeling with a blow, tossed a fourth through the window.

"Chill, man," Joho squeaked, Tuber's hand gripping at his throat.

Corporal Pope reached for his pistol.

"What the hell's going on in here?" Kugel yelled, poking his head in the door. "Pope, stand down."

Tuber charged at Kugel, hauling Valentine along like a backpack. Valentine couldn't say what happened next, only that he and Tuber went over like a tripped horse, knocking aside tables and classroom stools. He turned and saw Kugel with a club across the back of Tuber's neck.

"PeaBees, hold this cocksucker down!" Kugel grunted. "Pope, get your foot on his neck. Don't let him get leverage!"

Valentine threw himself across the small of Tuber's back. With two men on each limb and Pope bearing down on Tuber's neck, they just managed to keep him facedown on the floor.

Kugel hurried to the classroom slop sink and ran a pitcher of water. He returned and upended it on Tuber's head.

"Tubelow! Tubelow!" Kugel shouted. "Stand down!" Tuber continued to struggle and Kugel took out his pistol.

"No! He's giving," Valentine said, which wasn't quite true, but Valentine straddled the small of Tuber's back, putting himself between Kugel's pistol and the back of Tuber's head for a few seconds. Valentine reached up and caressed Tuber's cheek. "Take it easy, Tube. Take it easy. *Itsy-bitsy spider climbed up the waterspout. . . .*"

Tuber relaxed.

"Fuckin' Bears," Pope said.

They chained Tuber in his bunk for the rest of the afternoon, just in case.

Graduation came, and they were pared down to 105. The 14 rejects, the perpetual screwups who were the kind that got other men killed, were taken away in a barred bus. Some said they were the smart ones; they'd spend the rest of their sentence in a mine or lumber camp. Others said they were being taken off to be quietly hung somewhere. The rest got tiny tattoos on their right biceps, done quick and dirty by the corporals, a little Roman numeral V and 775 beneath.

"You're PeaBees now," Kugel said, addressing them from the front of the church as they sat in the pews. They'd spent the morning cleaning the barrack, hanging up and cleaning the bedding, making everything spotless for the next "class."

"You're moving up to the front. The rest of your training will be in a school that'll make this look like kindergarten, the kind of school where mistakes make you dead. Ready to go make yourselves useful for a change?"

"Yes, Sergeant."

"Seven Seventy-five Company, you're finished here. Go and do right for a change, and maybe someday I'll see you back here."

He rolled up his sleeve and showed a fading blue tattoo: V with some blurry numbers beneath.

* * *

More buses came, the same seatless wonders in which the 775 Company rode, hanging on to bars fixed to the roof for dear life, swaying like a single mass in the turns. They were dumped in yet another depot, with the mountains ending to the west and Seattle's tower-dominated horizon blue in the distance. They ate militia sandwiches in an old IHOP. The men looked at the militia women with more hunger than they did their food.

The outnumbered women understood their power and used it kindly, distributing smiles and ignoring some of the bluer catcalls. Valentine smeared some honey on a biscuit and listened to Joho's chatter. The man was as happy as a warbler on a sunny summer day, giving running color commentary every time a militia woman walked by.

An officer in a beat-up old uniform and Windbreaker appeared at the door. He had two shining circles on his collar—Valentine guessed they were buttons or thumbtacks. "Seven Seventy-five Company! My name's Mofrey and we're going to the front. Form platoons on the road, column of two. Don't make me shoot anyone. Punishment for trying to desert PB is summary execution."

Four miles later—Valentine thought he smelled the rotting-plant smell of the bay now and then, faintly on the stronger gusts of wind, but it could have been his imagination—they arrived at an old hotel in the center of a partially demolished office park that served as the headquarters for the Punishment Brigade. A couple of curious NCOs looked them over; then they were brought into a warehouse. Holes in the roof at one end offered the only lighting, and a permanent mold farm on the walls and floor near the gaps the only decor. They were instructed to sit on the cleaner concrete at the other.

"Keep it down, you slugs," a sergeant yelled. "The colonel's gonna admit you to our ranks, God help us."

The warehouse had a little office near the truck bays, and Valentine saw a man circumnavigate some old HVAC equipment to the rail so that he could look down at them. There was something about his easy stance that made him look like a pirate captain watching his crew from a quarterdeck. Valentine blinked, almost unable to believe his eyes.

"Welcome to First Brigade, Seven Seventy-five. You're a different breed of soldiers, and you'll find a different breed of war up here," he said in a loud, clear voice. It was Captain LeHavre, Valentine's old superior in Southern Command's Wolves.

"Anyone doesn't want to fight the Kurians," he continued, "file on over toward the door and go outside. We'll find something else for you to do. It'll involve shovels."

He lost two more men that way. A few more looked longingly at the door, but seemed to feel safer staying with the rest.

"Good. Very good, Seven Seventy-five. Fourteen dumps and two shirkers. Strong bunch." He came down the stairs and joined them on the factory floor. Valentine saw three shining thumbtacks on his collar, arranged in a triangle. He still had his steady green eyes, and his belly was a little more pronounced on the otherwise muscular frame. "Who was born the farthest from Seattle?"

That was easy. A man named Bink held up his hand. He'd been brought up in Nairobi.

"Name's Bink, sir. I was born in Africa."

"You're the new Beefeater. If anyone has a gripe, think they're being treated unfairly, they tell you and you tell me. Understand?"

"Think so, sir," Bink said.

"Only thing I don't want to hear is how you don't belong in the PeaBee because you're innocent. Fate can be cruel sometimes—deal with it or step out that door and cry over a shovelful of shit. Now, platoon leaders: Give me Diaz, Valentine, and Wasilla."

Valentine, having been through the routine before, stepped forward.

LeHavre nodded once at him. "You'll find out sooner or later that Valentine and I knew each other back in the Ozarks. We were Wolves together. I trust him and so can you. But he and the others impressed your drill team back at Sally. Stay in front, you three—the captain's got some pins for you.

"We'll start you off easy here for a couple of weeks. We'll rotate out platoons to train with experienced companies. There's no weekend passes for PeaBees, but we make our own entertainment, usually on Monday and Friday nights. Calisthenics in the morning and then sports. More good news: You've got the rest of the afternoon off. We're going to get cards on all of you and then you'll see the Brigade doc. Be polite to her—she's the only woman in the PeaBees and she'll be cupping your nuts at the end of the exam."

That night Valentine dined alone with Colonel LeHavre in one of the hotel's "extended stay" suites. He hadn't changed much. The brisk, intelligent officer had slowed down a little physically in the intervening decade.

LeHavre, as colonel of the battalion, rated a personal orderly. He still ate the same food as the rest of the men; it was just brought to him and Valentine on a tray.

"Vodka?" LeHavre offered. "The best of the local hooch is called

Grand Inquisitor. Made by a bunch of Russians who escaped to Canada from Vladivostok. It's pretty good."

"No, thank you, sir."

"Eat first. Then we'll talk."

They polished off the hot food—smoked ham, applesauce, some dispirited green beans, and honey-glazed biscuits—in silence.

"I miss the fresh veggies from Southern Command," LeHavre said as they finished. "Going to say no to the Grand Inquisitor again? I'm going to put a little in that powder crap that passes for orange juice. Rad, an Orange Wallop please. Privileges of rank."

The servant went to the refrigerator and clinked glasses. He returned with the iced drink.

"We each want to know how the other got here, I guess," LeHavre said.

"They told me you led a party up this way, but you never arrived."

"My report must have been—oh, what's a polite word? Intercepted. You're the junior—let's hear your story first. That way I can enjoy my drink."

Valentine tried to keep the tale short, and concentrated on events from the point when he arrived in Pacific Command.

"It's still a group of warlords here. You know one of them, Thunderbird. There are others. Adler's united them, probably because he gives the appearance of victories."

"What do you mean, appearance?"

"What's he replacing the Kurians with? Nothing. He's just scorching earth in front of him, rather than behind.

"How did you end up in the PeaBees, sir?" Valentine asked.

LeHavre had Rad bring him another flavored vodka. "I'm not a drunk—two's my limit. My story's not all that different from yours. I came up along the coast, out of Grog country in Oregon. I was brought to the Outlook first. Lots of speeches and maps about areas cleared of Kurians. There was another Southern Command liaison there—he'd . . . oh, how would you put it? . . . He'd gone native. Singing Adler's praises. He introduced me to the man himself. I'll confess, even I liked him at first. Quiet, unassuming, but confident. Able to make a decision, suck up a wrong move and move on—you remember, I look for that. Eager to remain a civilian. Yeah, he impressed me enough so I joined. There was no one waiting for me in the Ozarks."

"Not even that little girl, Jill?"

LeHavre massaged his kneecaps. "Wolf duty really catches up to you when you get older. My knees are shot. But Jill would be tickled that you remember. I was told she sorta fell for a young, good-looking

Quisling. Yeah, I know. I wish I could have been there to look after her and her mom. But maybe it was the only way she could stay alive. She retreated with them."

"So how did you end up a PeaBee?"

"I saw the results of one of the Action Group sweeps. I suppose I had it better than you—I didn't see the Bears in action, just the results, an old foundation full of bodies. I had to use a pole to figure out how deep they went. Some of them were pretty torn up. Bear bloodlust."

"You blame the Bears?" Valentine asked.

"No, of course not. The Bears are just a better tool for this sort of thing. I know how easily it spins out of control. Again, not just Bears. I heard something about your massacre in Little Rock. You'd been arrested and then escaped, right?"

"Yes," Valentine said.

"Where've you been since? Keeping clear of the Ozarks?"

Valentine decided to tell him. Sooner or later the pain had to work itself to the surface and come out like a splinter. LeHavre was the closest thing he had to a guide in life anymore, and the colonel had lost someone he was more of a father to than Valentine had ever been to Amalee.

"I went back to the Caribbean, really to beach myself there. I'd met a woman there, with the Jamaica pirates. She ended up with a daughter out of it. But in the years I was gone, she took up with another man, both for her own sake and our daughter's. Good man, I shipped with him, and as far as Amalee is concerned, Elian Torres is her father. Malia, her mother, still . . . still feels something for me, but I can't say whether it's love or hate. I've got no business busting up a family. Malia wanted me gone, so I left."

He felt for Malia Carrasca. He'd shown up with Narcisse and Blake—heavily disguised, of course. What woman in her right mind wouldn't balk at such an arrival? It was easier to go than to stay. And after that, the long angry hunt for the killers of Mary Carlson.

"How'd your kid look?"

"Happy," Valentine said. "Little. But God, she can run."

"You did the right thing. I know you've got problems, Valentine, and hurts, but there's a long list of people who'd gladly switch with you."

Valentine had told himself that before, but it helped to have LeHavre say it. Valentine still respected him.

LeHavre took a breath. "Why'd you go down there in the first place? You didn't strike me as the type to give up on the Cause."

"The Cause abandoned me first," Valentine said.

"Whoa, there, Valentine. How can the Cause abandon a man?"

"You said yourself you'd heard about my trial. I ended up a fugitive from the place I'd given up . . . everything, everything to defend."

"C'mon, Valentine. You're mixing up people and places with an idea. I asked you this once before: What's making you take up the rifle instead of a tractor wheel or a book or a fishing rod? What's the Cause?"

"Being free of the Kurians," Valentine said.

"There you go. It's an idea, not a person or a place. People, well, people can be awfully little. I've covered a lot of land in my life. There's beauty and ugly, fertile and sterile everywhere. It's ideas that matter. Good ideas, right ideas. Ideas are bigger than any of us. They don't get old, and they sure don't issue orders to get anyone court-martialed. You think I've given up on the Cause?"

"I don't see how you're helping it as much here as you did back home," Valentine said.

"Valentine, I didn't get put here. I volunteered to be an officer in the PeaBees. Remember your first time out on your own? The Red River operation?"

"Distinctly," Valentine said.

"You told me that when you got those folks out, you really felt like you'd accomplished something. Even more than the Reaper you and your Wolves snipped."

Valentine didn't mention his spell in the Coastal Marines, when he was working as a mole in the uniform of a Coastal Marine Quisling, the refugees he'd rounded up . . . canceling whatever karma he'd built getting the Red River families out, or the Carlsons.

"I like PeaBee work. Being the picket line between the Seattle KZ and Pacific Command has its dangers, but there are opportunities too, if you ever heard that Chinese philosophy."

Valentine thought he saw the light beginning to break through the clouds.

"I'm still getting people out and up to Canada, or down into Oregon and east. It's a little trickier—in a way it's like threading the needle between two Kurian Zones—but it can be done. There's a Resistance Network in Seattle, a damn good one. They've got members at some key checkpoints. They get the people to me, and I take it from there. Every once in a while one of my PeaBees really distinguishes himself and then he goes too. There are advantages to being the one who signs the casualty reports. Want to help?"

"Can do, sir."

"My ears must be going too. That voice sounds like my old lieutenant."

Valentine spent the next few months leading his platoon through the different operational assignments as they trained under real conditions. Five veteran PeaBees joined his platoon to help the men learn, but even under their guidance there were losses. A man was electrocuted on a raid against an electrical substation. Even worse, on river watch, three men just disappeared, probably lost to Big Mouths, judging from the crushed plant life leading back to the Snoqualmie River.

But there were rewards to PeaBee work too. Valentine guided dozens of individual families—perhaps a couple of brothers, a wife, and child one time, grandparents with a cluster of grandchildren another, and two sisters with their collective broods—from rendezvous points in the Kurian Zone, then across to the PeaBee positions. From there they were brought to hiding spots, where the PeaBees fed them—who knew what kind of three-card monte shuffle LeHavre's Brigade Supply staff was playing with Pacific Command?

The whole 775 Company was reunited at the end of October, and in their first real operation punched a hole down "Highway 1," clearing mines that allowed a column of Bears, most likely an Action Group, to drive into the Kurian Zone. Valentine wished he'd left a mine or two.

Valentine grew to like their captain, a Canadian named Mofrey, whose grandfather had served with a regiment he called "the Princess Pats." Captain Mofrey still clipped his grandfather's little badge on his steel PeaBee helmet. Every time a Pacific Command regular told him to remove it, he did, only to put it back on as soon as the regulars had passed out of eyesight. All Valentine could learn of his reasons for being in the PeaBees was a conviction for "gross insubordination." Could an affection for an old badge land someone in the PeaBees?

He even saw Gide once or twice, usually on picket duty. She'd made it into the Pacific Command regulars, and they'd trained her as a scout/sniper. She still carried his carbine. The PeaBees were watching the Quisling positions from a railroad culvert in the predawn when they heard the password whispered.

They came just as alert as if they'd heard a rifle bolt being worked, but waited, and then next thing Valentine knew there was Gide, crawling through a plant-choked culvert with a scout in front and a scout behind.

She seemed as astonished as Valentine at the meeting, but for the moment pretended not to know him, and Valentine went along with it.

"Made it right to the edge of downtown," Gide said as they warmed themselves in a basement a hundred meters back from the railroad tracks, Valentine's platoon headquarters. All he could offer them was a hot mush trying to be oatmeal, with a couple of pieces of dried fruit broken into it. "Tough to get there. Water's out, because of the Big Mouths. Bridges are too well guarded."

Valentine was tempted to tell her that some of the bridges were watched by the Resistance, but they didn't cooperate with Pacific Command because of the depredations of the Action Groups.

"Were you just there to look?" Valentine asked.

"We can't discuss operations," one of the other scouts said. "Need to know, you know."

"Except to say girlfriend here is deadly with that gun of hers," the other scout said. "One time a Reaper picked up on our smell or whatever. She killed it with one shot. It just fell over and froze up. Never seen the like."

"Robie!" the senior one warned.

The scout shrugged. "Shit, PeaBees are still Pacific Command. Don't tell me you weren't happy to see the uniform comin' out of that ditch."

"Kinda friendly with the Pee-Pants, aren't you?" the senior said to Gide as she sat next to Valentine, back against the cold concrete brick wall.

Gide took off her helmet. She'd cut her hair almost down to the skin. "I knew him in another life. It's been too long, David. You can get in touch through Ranger Group, if they let you write."

Joho churned rather than stirred the mush on the little camp stove. "I'll do a damn sight more than write if you like. I've got six months' lead in my pencil, wantin' to get out," he muttered.

"Hey, Snakes," Robie piped up. "Whaddya call your gun again? 'Big David'? Any relation? This PeaBee packin' 'Little David' maybe?" The other scout chuckled.

Gide warmed her hands on the hot bowl of mush. "Need to know, guys, need to know. And speaking of secrets—" She turned toward Valentine, unzipped her camouflage Windbreaker, and unbuttoned the top of her uniform shirt. Valentine saw a leather thong around her neck, holding a little modified wallet. She opened it and showed the four remaining Quickwood bullets resting between her breasts.

"I think of them as four little guardian angels," she whispered.

November came in dark and blustery. Up in the mountains they had snow, but on the rim of Seattle's suburbs the brief days and lengthening nights of the season just saw more drizzle, only now it was a little colder and a lot more uncomfortable.

Like a branch snap that starts an avalanche, the next disaster in Valentine's ill-fated trip began with a sound. In this case it was the muffled roar of tires on wet pavement outside another church.

Valentine, Mofrey, and eleven "trustees" of First Platoon were waiting out the wee hours of the morning in the basement of a church that had been converted to a New Universal Church Community Center, but abandoned thanks to its nearness to the war zone. Valentine rested his head against the orange silhouette of a child. A border of colorful kids holding hands ran around the basement wall.

Mofrey always took Valentine on the trips when they were assigned to 775 Company. To the men, Valentine was just an officer who had a good "nose" for the enemy, pulled them back if he felt there was a Reaper in the neighborhood, and usually could be relied on to find a gap in the Quisling positions.

Eight Seattle residents were readying themselves for a run into Free Territory, two parents and their five kids, and a older aunt, the sister to the patriarch. They were divesting themselves of their bright-colored KZ clothing and flimsy galoshes for heavier outdoor work clothes, boots, hats, and jackets for the run to their safe house. Ordinary civilians in the Kurian Zone got only the thinnest kind of outerwear, perhaps to discourage exactly this kind of attempt.

The parents were obedient, the kids wary and asking questions as soon as they forgot that they'd been told to keep quiet. The Resistance Network member, a pinch-faced woman with nervous eyes, kept flitting back and forth between Mofrey and the family. Once they were properly dressed and fed, they'd cross no-man's-land under the guidance of the short platoon.

"They couldn't tell the kids until they left. Too much chance of letting something slip at what passes for school nowadays," the Network woman explained. "They're confused, naturally."

Valentine watched Joho clown for the kids, but expected he really had eyes for the oldest teen, a well-blossomed young woman with lovely hair who even made the shapeless KZ overalls look good.

Valentine heard the tires outside before the others, found his hand falling to the butt of his wire-stocked assault rifle. The rest of the platoon had to make do with hunting weapons or shotguns, little better than the weapons issued to the militia.

A sound echoed downstairs, an impressive rendition of an alley-cat screech. That was the signal for trouble from Spencer, a PeaBee with a talent for imitative noises, who was keeping watch from the choir balcony.

"I'll go, sir," Valentine said. He signaled two men to their feet and they hurried upstairs. Valentine wondered if his spell in Pacific Command's Punishment Brigade would start and end in a church.

Valentine saw Spencer framed against the balcony window, next to a pane of glass that had been replaced by cardboard and plastic. Valentine went to a different window, saw Pacific Command soldiers—worse, Bears—piling out of a pickup and setting up a clean alley of fire from what had been a bakery.

Valentine hurried down to the basement, waved Mofrey over.

"It's an Action Group," he reported.

"Here? Someone got their wires crossed. LeHavre wouldn't send us into an operation. Better run for it." He lifted off his helmet, ran his fingers through his hair. "Contact One," he said to the Resistance Network woman.

Now the civilians looked alarmed. Picking up on the anxiety, one of the kids began to cry.

She approached. "We've got to get out of here now, and quiet—"

Now wasn't soon enough. The door upstairs crashed, shouts followed.

Mofrey looked around.

"Get them ready," Valentine told the Network woman. He shoved his assault rifle into Joho's hands and hurried back for the stairs.

"Follow me," Mofrey told the First Platoon PeaBees behind him.

"Easy there, Delta Group," Valentine called to two Bears covering the stairs. "There are friendlies down here with Two PeaBee One. Understand?"

He came up and found the Bears lugging in communication equipment. Spencer was under guard, kneeling facing the wall, with his palms on top of his head. Another Bear urinated on an NUC Birth Drive banner. Valentine went to what he guessed to be a platoon headquarters, a radio being set up on the altar with a knot of Bears around it.

A Bear elbowed a lieutenant—Valentine vaguely knew him, Hanley—no, Handley, Valentine read from his Velcro name tag.

"Lieutenant Handley," Valentine said, coming up and saluting. "Reporting the presence of a squad of PeaBees from Second Punishment Battalion here, carrying out salvage operations, plus prisoners."

"We didn't know any of you were in this area," Handley said.

"You're just as much a surprise to us," Valentine said. "With your permission, we'll get out of your hair and get back east." Hopefully

Handley was the type who'd gladly accept the offer to have one less worry on a field operation.

Mofrey brought the rest of First Platoon up.

Valentine silently willed him to stand there. He tried to make a little "stop" gesture with his hand. Mofrey saw Spencer, still under guard in the corner, and hurried up.

Mofrey came up the center aisle. "I'm Captain Mofrey. Why's that man under arrest?"

Delta Group wasn't into saluting, and PeaBee troops didn't rate the honor from regulars anyway. "We thought he might be a deserter. Charlie, let him up."

The Bear lifted Spencer to his feet as easily as he would lift a toppled two-year-old.

Valentine heard gunfire a couple of blocks away. Handley checked his watch.

"Spencer, back with the others," Mofrey said. "Lieutenant, I have some civilians in charge. They're my responsibility, and I've no intention of letting you shoot them."

Valentine sagged, glad of the sentiment but gut-punched at how Mofrey went about it. Now the Delta Group lieutenant's decision was framed as a matter of disobeying orders or not, rather than simply seeing a minor headache disappear into the predawn.

"What makes you think you could stop us, PeaBee?" the Bear who'd lifted Spencer to his feet asked.

"They're a technical crew, hydraulics," Valentine lied, desperate to defuse the situation. "We've got a backhoe and a shovel loader we're trying to rebuild—"

"Voorhees, get me Thunderbird," Lieutenant Handley said.

Valentine moved. He chambered a round in the assault rifle, pointed it, not at anyone, but at the field radio. "Don't transmit. I'll disable the radio."

Bears and PeaBees all went for their weapons. Gun muzzles pointed in every direction but up.

"Chill, brothers," Joho called, sighting on the lieutenant. "Nobody's shot yet."

"Valentine, what the hell are you doing? Put that weapon down!" Mofrey said.

"Lieutenant, this could get crazy really fast," Valentine said, loudly enough so the church acoustics bounced his voice off the back pews. "I've no intention of hurting your valuable piece of equipment, as long as you let the PeaBees and the civilians walk out of here. Bitch to Thunderbird, bitch to Colonel LeHavre, bitch to Adler himself after we're gone.

The alternative is killing all of us and maybe one or two of you. Would you rather spend your debriefing bitching or explaining?"

Reports began to squeak in over the communications system.

"I need to answer these," the radioman said.

"Go ahead," Valentine replied.

"Valentine, you're under arrest," Handley said. "The rest of you, get the hell out of here. Take your prisoners, if they mean that much to you. Torgo, make sure they get out of the kill bottle."

"If you're going to place anyone under arrest, Lieutenant, it should be me," Mofrey said. "I'm in charge of this mission."

"Leave well enough alone, sir," Valentine said. Then to Handley: "I'll surrender my weapon as soon as they're out of here, Lieutenant."

Joho grabbed Mofrey, pulled him back. "Listen to the man. We got daylight coming fast."

When they were gone, Valentine put the gun on the desk and submitted to being patted down and restrained with plastic cording. The stress brought with it a hunger that gnawed at him. Being a Bear meant living with one's appetite as a constant companion.

Bears came and went, but the only one Valentine waited for was goat-bearded Torgo, who returned to report that the PeaBees had left the operations area.

He tried not to listen to the comm chatter. Then he saw a familiar pair of boots step up in front of him.

"Valentine, you're like a bad twenty that keeps showing up in my till," Thunderbird said. "Handley said you were here, but I had to see it for myself. You've done yourself in this time."

"Tell me something, Colonel. How did my father get all this started?"

"You've got more important worries."

Valentine found the courage to beg. "Please."

He clucked his tongue. "Oh, it wasn't here, not in Pacific Command. Kubishev told me about it, actually, never gave me any details. Don't know that you'll get the opportunity to look him up."

"Going to shoot me with the rest of the folks you're murdering?"

"God bless 'em, every one," Thunderbird said. "We'll pick this up in a few hours, Valentine. You'll be traveling, a lot farther than a trip to the nearest brick wall."

They threw him in a truck with a hood over his head, chained hand and foot and nudged by what felt like a shotgun barrel every time he rolled too far away from the side of the bay. But he could still hear. There were babies crying all around.

They traveled at a good speed for what he guessed was a little over two hours. To occupy his mind, he counted minutes and scored them off into hours. Routine soaked up fear like a sponge.

Then they parked and quiet women's voices talked as the babies were passed out of the truck, soothing and cooing over the "poor little things." He was the last to leave.

They kept him blindfolded as someone, a woman by the smell of her, fed him, stripped him out of his uniform, and gave him a quick sponge bath. They let him use the toilet. Then they sat him in a room with a ticking fan, hands and legs cuffed to brackets in an electric-chair-like frame. Valentine kept waiting for them to wire his genitals or fillings, but the silent workers left him alone.

Finally he heard someone enter. "Major Valentine?" a precisely clipped voice asked.

"Yes."

"Do you know my voice?"

"Can't say that I do."

"I'm Adler."

"Now I see why I'm tied down," Valentine said.

"Why's that?"

"So I don't go for your throat."

Adler chuckled. "Three experienced Bears with me."

"Okay, I can't kill you. Are you going to kill me?" Valentine wanted it out in the open, to know.

"Me? No. Another? Quite likely. Unless."

"Unless?"

"You see reason."

"I can't see much in this mask," Valentine said, trying to work it off with his jaw muscles and his cheeks.

"I don't want you to identify this place to the Kurians. We're turning you over to them."

Valentine felt his pulse quicken. "What does 'seeing reason' involve?"

"Forgetting all this ever happened. Rejoining Delta Group. I'll put you in a position where you can fight the good fight. As you see it. You'll hardly even know the Action Groups exist. You can fight the old-fashioned way, the useless way, wading into the enemy with banner unfurled. I have need of skilled officers who can keep the Kurian forces busy. You might be of use with the Big Mouths. They've been destructive as they've grown in familiarity with the waterways around Seattle."

"Let me see your face."

Valentine sensed a mass shift behind him, heard curtains being drawn. The mask came off, and there was the real heart and soul and mind behind Pacific Command.

Adler wore the patient face of a teacher, calm as a death mask, just old enough to be fatherly, just young enough for a spark. He had sad mortician's eyes, but there was a power behind them. Valentine felt the loom of the Bears behind, though what he could accomplish shackled hand and foot . . .

Maybe worst of all, Valentine liked him on sight.

"What did Seattle do to you? You're laying waste to everything he owns."

"I served him. On a whim . . . on a moment of appetite he destroyed my children."

"So now you're killing other people's children?"

"It's better than the alternative. A bullet ends the matter. Having your soul pulled apart, shred by shred, memory by memory, every awful act laughed at, every joy mocked—no one deserves that."

"I've always thought one's soul belonged to God."

"Maybe. Nevertheless, they partake of the distilled experiences of a life. Sip by sip. Stand with me. Or I fear you'll find out."

"How do you know so much about it?"

"He made me watch. He relished every detail. All because of a careless thought against him."

"I am sorry," Valentine said.

"Then you'll rejoin our war?"

"Your war."

For the first time he looked exasperated. "Word games. Fine. My war."

"I pound on the door while your murderers slip through the window."

"Not how I would put it. May I promise you one more thing? When Seattle is destroyed, my war ends. I will retire, disappear, live quietly somewhere. Pacific Command may fight on or hang itself."

Valentine bowed his head. "You've been polite with me, so I won't tell you where you can stick your offer."

"Now it is my turn to feel sorry for you. As to my 'offer,' I doubt it would fit. My staff calls me all sorts of colorful names having to do with anal retentiveness."

They stared at each other.

Valentine broke first: "So we're both too phlegmatic to get angry. Just out of curiosity, what's with the heroism stuff? I missed the chance at a lecture."

"The Action Groups can't get everywhere. We regularly send propaganda deep into Seattle, along with certain painless, lethal pills, encouraging the populace to do the right thing. I understand you even flew some to a very difficult-to-reach area. With luck, many of them will be used. Their names will be added to the hero lists and read out in our broadcasts. I still have a friend or two west of here. But my time is nearly up. I should have liked to bring you to another new-moon party at the Outlook. I believe you attended one before."

"I kept to my room."

"I'm sorry we didn't meet there. Better circumstances might have made our association a happier one.

"Farewell, David Valentine. Your theory about the inviolability of one's soul is about to be tested."

Twelve

Collection vans: Valentine had seen all varieties of them over the months and years of his trips through the Kurian Zones. He'd seen buses with shuttered windows in Chicago and long yokes for captives to be linked together in Hispaniola. He'd averted his eyes from vans in Wisconsin and armored cars in Louisiana. The principle was always the same, whether they rode on battered old suspensions across snow-dusted old interstates in the Dakotas or were pulled by a team of cart horses along an Alabama backwoods path: Separate those to be taken to the Reapers from the rest of society. Like so much of the Kurian Order, it was a simple mix of deception from the New Order and willful blindness in their subjects. Hide the contents of the stock trucks bound for the slaughterhouse and allow those who might be unlucky enough to see one in operation the comfort of telling themselves a lie.

Valentine had seen more of them than he cared to remember. But that chill November night was the first time he'd been put in the back of one.

They made the switch at midnight on a small, battered bridge over a river. Three Bears, in spiffy uniforms the color of a typical overcast, pulled Valentine out of a concrete bunker and chained him to two other unfortunates, a man in the lead and a woman just in front of him. The man wore thick flannel and was barefoot; the woman stood shivering in militia pants and a T-shirt. Valentine passed a note to the Bear in charge, a brief farewell to Gide he'd been allowed to pencil, thanking her for their weekend at the Outlook, and asking him to pass his regrets to Colonel LeHavre and Captain Mofrey.

Passing the note was made a little more difficult by the thick leather belt around his waist, and the attachment for the handcuffs around his wrist.

The Bears brought him to the east end of the bridge. Valentine's night-sharp eyes saw a similar party on the other side.

A flashlight waved up and down. One of the Bears waved his horizontally right and left.

"They're ready," an NCO said. "Let's go, dead men."

"And women," the one in front of Valentine added, tiredly.

The man in front sort of lurched forward. "Ahhh! Ahhha!" Valentine heard his handcuff chain rattling against the front fitting at his belt.

"Move it," the Bear at his side ordered.

"My legs!"

"Now they're stopping," a young militia with a volunteer armband said, his eyes pressed to some binoculars.

"You just gotta walk to the other side of the bridge. Nothing's going to happen to you there, not with our guys around," the lead Bear said.

The man wouldn't move. "I will, I will. . . . I can't, I can't. Can't!" the man stammered.

"Oh, balls," the Bear said. He and another each took an arm and they lifted him.

As they carried him he sputtered something about being really, honestly sorry. Why wouldn't anyone believe him that he was sorry?

At the midpoint of the bridge two prisoners were waiting, one in a bloodstained militia uniform; the other looked like a truck driver thanks to his ball cap with ROLLING COOPERATIVE emblazoned on it.

Quislings and Bears exchanged sets of keys. Valentine noticed that the harnesses were identical. While this was going on, a bottle moved west, a thick roll of newsprint east.

"You shouldn't be doing that, Bongo," a Bear chided his mate.

"I like to read their funnies," the one evidently called Bongo replied. "Don't read nuttin' else."

"Don't or can't?" the chained militia woman asked.

"Shut down, you," the leader of the column warned.

The exchange done, the Bears accepted the two and immediately unlocked them. One of the Bears threw the harnesses across his shoulder, presumably for the next midnight exchange. Valentine listened to the two Bears who'd carried the lead man talk quietly as they walked away.

"The one in the back, ain't he a Bear?"

"Think so. Seen him in the uniform at Fort Drizzle, anyway."

"Do they know that?"

"Like I care."

"Is it just me, or does this side of the river stink?" Valentine asked.

"It shakes in front, shitting himself," a female officer in charge of the Quislings said.

"Better you than me, pard," the man at the back of their file added.

The man at the front, who had perhaps feared a glowering Reaper at the other end of the bridge rather than a group of Quislings, was able to walk the rest of the way. Valentine suspected he had shit himself, as he was shaking something out of his trouser.

"Don't feel too bad," Valentine called to the front. "Those fellas back there do it all the time when they fight."

"Yeah, takes a lot of guts to gun down women and kids," the Quisling at the back said.

They were loaded into an old brown delivery van. Much of the front paneling was missing or cut away, along with the skirting. Whether this was for easier maintenance or a security precaution Valentine couldn't tell, though he knew collection vans were frequently wired with explosives. Duvalier had said something or other along those lines when they saw one in Kansas.

The Quislings rolled the door shut and locked it, leaving them in darkness. Valentine heard the engine start, half hoped for an explosion.

This was it. The last ride. Valentine was a little surprised at how calm he was. It was over, no more worries, cares, regrets about Malia and Amalee. What would Blake turn into, a fallible human capable of empathy, or a cruel, instinct-driven automaton?

He'd had a good run. Duvalier always said Cats never lasted. He'd done more damage than most. If every human piled into a van could just take one enemy to the grave . . .

The blank nothingness that yawned before him, a forever of oblivion, the world spinning along and he'd exist as a memory or a story or one of his many signed reports buried in some archive. He hoped his legs wouldn't fail him at the last—maybe he could stamp on the Reaper's instep—or would his bowels give way?

The militia woman pressed up against Valentine.

"Hey, buddy, can you work your fly?" her voice breathed in the dark.

"Pardon?" he said.

"Let's do it, right now. I can slip out of these pants."

"You're kidding, right?"

"C'mon, hurry."

"No. Thanks, but . . . no," Valentine said.

The truck picked up speed, lurched into a higher gear.

She slid over next to the other man. Valentine tried not to listen as he took her up on the same offer. The bench they sat on squeaked, or maybe it was the wheezy breathing of the man. Valentine smelled her sweaty sex in the confines.

Two distinct thumps as they toppled over into the bed of the van. Now Valentine could hear their chains dragging on the floor. The man groaned and gasped.

Valentine felt her foot touch his. "Offer's still open if you want a turn," she said. He moved his foot away.

"Hey, let me enjoy a moment, huh," the man said.

They exchanged names in the darkness. He was Colin, she Mona.

Fifteen minutes later they arrived.

The van idled, and Valentine heard voices outside. "I'll confirm with Pound," a man's voice said. "Three going in, right?"

"Three, assuming we don't have another fuckin' suicide," the driver said. "They're trade goods, but you never know."

"I wish I had one of those hero pills," Colin said in the darkness.

A bright light blasted into the back of the collection van, giving Valentine one of those instant, diamond-shard headaches a sudden stimulus up his optic nerves seemed to cause. Valentine looked down, saw a name scratched on the wooden seat between his legs.

Bob Barquist Feb 15 68.

Valentine tried to remember where he'd been when Barquist was taking his ride. Probably back in the Ozarks with Ahn-Kha, showing a group of leaders from the Production Resource how to grow heart-root in cold weather, to be eaten or ground up into pig and chicken feed.

He wished there were some way he could have sent one more message to Narcisse—some bit of rhyme to teach Blake—or Malia. Ali even. Would she sigh and say that he hadn't been careful enough?

He felt hands hauling him out of the collection van and they turned the spotlight off.

"I might be pregnant!" Mona said, showing evidence Valentine could only guess at as she pulled up her pants. "You need to take me to a medical center. I might be pregnant!"

They stood at a brick wall. The collection van was parked at a gate. Old metal letters on a clear stretch of wall read,

ELL VUE B TANI AL GAR ENS

Someone had added an *H* before the ELL.

The gap in the wall, big enough for two buses to pass, was closed by a yellow line of police tape. Inside Valentine saw some old, overgrown buildings. The park looked to be in ruins, but he could still make out old lots and paths.

"You guys got lucky," one of the Quisling guards said. He had flaps on his hat to keep his ears warm, and a short beard. "Only three of yas. Pound-o'-flesh always lets one make it out the other end alive. The way I see it is you've all got a one-in-three chance. Don't clobber each other right off the bat, or we'll give you a dose of bird shot, and then you'll never make it up the other end of Long Trail."

"I want to see a doctor," Mona said.

The Quisling in the hunting hat ignored her. "We use you all because you got that good old mountain-crossing spirit. All you've got to do is get to where them lights are. See it, way over there?" He pointed between two stands of trees.

Valentine saw a pair of red lights on twin poles, like the goalposts on a football field, glowering eyes staring at them across the lush plant life. If they were in fact goalposts, they were a good half mile away, maybe three-quarters of a mile.

"Strip," the Quisling ordered.

Soldiers stepped forward, released their hands so they could pull their shirts off. Valentine felt his skin retreat at the cold night air.

"Please, I could be pregnant. You never do this when someone is pregnant," Mona said.

Colin rocked on his heels. "Shut up, you idiot." He was breathing deeply.

"There's a Reaper in there," Valentine said.

"Good guess," the Quisling said.

Valentine didn't guess. He knew.

"Look at the weird burns on the back of this one. What did they do to you?"

Three Quislings were fiddling with their harnesses while others covered them from an economy hatchback with a machine gun mounted on the hood.

Mona began to cry. "Why can't I see a doctor?"

"Again, don't beat on each other," Hunting Cap said. "When the tape falls you're off to the races."

"No fair, they've got shoes," Colin said.

"No fair, they've got shoes," one of the Quisling soldiers mimicked in a school-yard voice.

"Get the rest of your stuff off. Shoes too."

They complied; what else could they do? Valentine put his arm around Mona, shared body warmth. "I hear it's not so bad. They hypnotize you, like a snake does a bird."

The tape fell and Valentine felt a sharp blow to the side of his knee. Colin had lashed out, and even now was running, the tape whipping free of his thighs as he headed across the overgrown parking lot.

Valentine felt a shove in the back, and he and Mona sprawled on the other side of the wall. Valentine came up to a crouch. The Quislings began to close the gate.

"I might be pregnant. You don't want to lose the baby!" Mona said, clinging to the bars.

A rifle butt came through and struck her in the stomach. She jackknifed, gasping.

Valentine helped her to her feet. "Let's go."

He looked back at the wall. A pair of heads watched them from the other side.

Valentine picked up a rock and sent it whizzing at the heads, but missed.

"Your buddy's already a quarter of the way to them lights!" someone shouted helpfully.

Valentine pulled Mona down the path. It opened up on what he guessed was another parking lot. The grasses and brush had been cleared here, and Valentine saw buildings on the other side.

"Oh my God," Mona said flatly.

Four figures in a line greeted them, like odd, plasticized mannequins with their skin removed, feet fixed in concrete. Elaborate layers of muscle made their faces a hideous salmon-colored patchwork. Valentine stepped up to one, realized it was a real corpse, covered in some kind of thick, clear plastic. The first one pointed, Uncle Sam–style.

DON'T BE CHOOSY, read a sign cradled in his arm.

The next one was scratching her head. Her sign was on a sandwich board.

PICK A WAY.

GUESS WRONGLY, said the third, its hands on its hips like an exasperated parent.

The fourth pointed to a little empty cement platform next to the others. RIGHT HERE YOU'LL STAY.

The parking lot trailed away to a path to the left. In the middle were the buildings, and to the right was another path heading at a ninety-degree angle away from the twin lights, paralleling the wall.

The left path or the buildings both led more directly to the goalposts.

The buildings would be the most dangerous, but there might be something he could use as a weapon there. Valentine tried to sense the Reaper or Reapers, but he was cold and his knee hurt and Mona was pulling him back toward the gate. "I don't like this game. I'm going to throw rocks at them till they shoot me."

"C'mon," Valentine said, pulling her toward the buildings.

"Let go, you bastard!" she cried, falling to her knees. "You're just bringing me so you can throw me into its arms when you see it, so you can get away."

"Suit yourself," Valentine said, letting go. She ran back to the gate.

He smelled the air, searched the buildings with his ears, heard only a clattering wind-chime noise.

Valentine passed wide around a boarded-up building facing the parking lot and into a courtyard. Doors were welded shut or barred with heavy padlocks. Other closed-off buildings, one marked CAFÉ, surrounded what had once been a nice little garden.

While passing through Wisconsin on his way to Lake Michigan, Valentine and his two fellow Wolves had skirted a big old still-occupied farmhouse where the owner liked to make decorations for his yard. Animals, gnomes, old ladies bending over and showing bright-painted polka-dot underwear, geese with wings that spun in the wind, even old Packer football helmets bobbing on counterweights as the breeze pushed them . . .

The courtyard between the buildings reminded him of that farmer's land.

Somewhere or other Valentine had heard the phrase "bone garden." If there was such a thing in reality rather than a metaphor for a cemetery, this was it.

The wind chimes Valentine heard rattling were human skulls, hollowed out with tibiae suspended within to add to the rattle. Wheels within wheels of plasticized human hands, some holding fans, others carefully cupped to catch the air, spun in the November breeze. Skeletons sat on benches admiring winter-dead flowers; at least here the gardens showed some signs of being maintained. Around a table outside the café, four skeletons held forks and spoons over fresh, reeking piles of entrails.

Part of Valentine was horrified, another taken by the intricacy of the wiring, another grimly followed a mental train of thought about what effect the Kurians were trying to achieve. He'd heard auras could be "flavored" by the emotional state of the victim. Prolonged terror might add some kind of seasoning to the psychic palate.

The tableau even showed a grim sense of humor. A skeleton stood in the classic Hamlet pose, wearing puffy breeches and a nailed-on feathered cap, holding a fresh-looking human head—it certainly stank like a three-day-old remnant.

Hamlet didn't have his sword, but he had a femur.

The tattooed Cat who'd taught Valentine some basics of hand-to-hand combat always made Valentine recite the first rule of unarmed combat: *Arm yourself.*

Or in this case, leg yourself. He wrenched the leg loose, spun and spun and spun it on its wire until the link weakened, then pulled it free. He went to one of the cement benches and broke it off at the knee end, giving himself a sharpened spike.

Several paths led off the courtyard and the buildings. Valentine could see the lights peering at him from across a vast, brushy field, bisected by cover. It was tempting to plunge into the bushes, but he suspected they thickened with what looked like Devil's Foot farther in. Even with a machete and thick clothing, he'd hesitate to hack through spiky Devil's Foot.

He chose one of the paths through the trees, and found it joined the path he'd discarded in order to get at the buildings.

To get to the trees he passed through a vaguely Oriental garden, at least judging from the architecture. The plants had mostly run wild, but there was still a bubbling, attractive-looking fountain.

The water smelled clean.

He reached forward.

A fortunate, foreshortened step saved him. He felt something brush his leg hairs, froze, looked down, saw a length of fishing line passing in front of the fountain. Valentine followed the wire to the trigger, then up to the overhanging trees, saw a big latticework like a spiky flyswatter ready to fall and cripple a hand dipped in the water. It looked flimsy; obviously it wasn't designed to kill, just to injure and cause pain.

Valentine decided to forgo the water, and stepped carefully onto the wooded path, every nerve alert. He willed his eyes into picking up every twig, every branch, every trap that might or might not be along the path.

There'd once been a sign, probably an explanatory map, at the beginning of the tree-flanked path. Now a human skin, face and hair still attached, was stretched between the posts.

DON'T RUN!
YOU'LL JUST DIE TIRED

read the helpful tattooed warning.

The crotches of the trees held human skulls with glowing eyes. Valentine glanced at one as he passed; the "eyes" were golf balls painted with luminous paint. Valentine decided to parallel the path after he found a shallow pit filled with sharpened wooden spikes smelling of fresh blood. Poor Co—

Reaper!

Valentine crouched, tried to lower his lifesign, tried to box up the cold and his sore knee. He gripped the splintered femur in both hands, left steadying it, his right on the ball joint, ready to drive it. . . .

He heard panting and saw Colin running wildly down the path, feet muddy, favoring one leg, but fear driving him through the pain. A cloaked Reaper, its face white-painted with eyes and lips blackened to imitate a skull, thin chest similarly decorated to enhance the ribs, skipped along behind him, raising first one long arm and then the other in a sort of dance.

"and i run and you run and i run and you run . . . ," it sang as it hopped.

Could he catch it unaware?

The Reaper halted, pointed a long black-nailed finger at Valentine. *"you! you wait your turn! gimpy's first!"*

Colin sprawled, tripping on the same hole that had injured him earlier. *"oh, you've tripped. get up, you're not finished yet. run run run little silly man."*

They disappeared toward the buildings, the Reaper harrying its prey like a dog driving a lone sheep.

Valentine angled toward the western wall. Twelve feet of brick, with trees well cut back, was topped with electrified fence.

"Don't even think about it," a megaphoned voice from the trees called. Valentine searched the timber, saw a hunting blind. "He's busy with the others. If you hurry, you'll make the finish line easy."

Valentine trotted back into the woods.

He ran faster as he saw the two red lights, broke out of the trees and up a long meadowed path, thick with night dew. Valentine saw more lines of fencing, angling toward the finish line. A couple of New Universal Church robed types stood before a candlelit table with food and bottles and a trophy cup.

But there was a cold piece of evil lurking just on the other side of the victory tape.

Valentine sensed a Reaper under the table, alive and pulsing. A final shock for the winner?

He couldn't say why that one little detail bothered him more than the nests of sharpened pungi sticks on the path, or the humiliation of being stripped in front of joking guards. He turned and trotted back along the path toward the buildings.

He found them on the other side of a little wall-less Japanese building, between two gardens filled with stones. The Reaper loomed behind Colin, poking him in the kidneys with a long, black fingernail, urging him toward Mona, crying, holding out one hand as a plea to stop and covering her sex with the other. Valentine could hear the breathy, high-pitched voice.

"*one two three four, i declare a food war. five six seven eight, the winner gets to make the gate.*"

The Reaper jumped and landed next to Mona, who tripped and fell.

"*you can take him. he's out of breath, wounded in the foot! go for his other leg!*"

Colin jumped on her, got his fingers around her throat.

"*now rape her! spread her legs, inside, inside, and i'll let you live.*" It hung over the couple, its cloak drawing a curtain around them. . . .

Valentine flitted between trees, put the cement of the little pagoda between himself and the scene.

"No! No, please! Oh God!" Mona screamed.

Something at the base of his spine woke up and twitched. It ran hot up his back, perched between brain and skull atop his head like a spider.

Valentine hopped up on top of the pagoda, and made the jump with the thoughtless ease of a house cat leaping to a kitchen table. Dirt and clinging plants fell, displaced by his weight, but before they hit the ground he was a gargoyle shape half-hanging from the pagoda roof.

Below, the Reaper opened its jaw and shot its tongue toward Colin's back, teeth following. Colin screamed.

The greenery hit the ground next to the Reaper. It turned its head; eyes followed the trajectory up—

And met Valentine on the way down.

He landed atop the Reaper, driving the femur down toward the great beehivelike organ that sucked down the blood. It reached up, backward-hinging arms moving for him, but Valentine was off it, moving on white-hot instinct, hardly knowing what his body was going to do next.

He swung a stiff-fingered uppercut, felt fingers break through skin, grabbed the Reaper under its hyperextended jaw, fingers closing on bone, dragged it off Colin, who had a gaping, tongue-sized wound in his back. Valentine whipsawed and the Reaper sprawled.

He held its white-painted jaw in his hands.

The Reaper rose, confusion in its eyes as its tongue lolled. Valentine cast the jawbone aside and readied his femur for another strike.

The Reaper turned and ran, but Valentine was after it, a wild predator drawn by flight, got on its back and drove the sharpened femur up through the gap left by the jaw.

Crying, Mona pressed her hands against the wound in Colin's back. Blood came up under her fingers anyway.

As the Reaper collapsed there was another, running from the woodland path in the direction of the goalposts, its feet a blur, a strange oversized leering jack-o'-lantern mask atop its head. Valentine picked himself up, left the twitching, dying, genetically engineered corpse, and ran toward the new one, ink-smeared bone in his hands. The Reaper slowed, perhaps not used to a man running toward it.

A mindless feral howl sounded from Valentine's throat. His heart seemed to fill his entire chest cavity, its throb rattling his ribs and collarbones. . . .

Some sane corner of his mind hammered out thoughts as fast as letters flew from a quick typist:

You don't know how to fight you great thirsty slug you've forgotten how, send all the puppets you want, you can no more fight than fuck time to face me, product of a warrior race bred and tested in ten thousand years' battle, scarier than any costume, don't run you'll just die tired . . .

The Reaper turned and ran. Its mask slipped, and it blindly plowed into a tree, lurched onward, tearing the mask free to run.

Valentine angled through the trees, yipping like a hound on a hot scent, caught up to it just outside the glowing eyes of the goalposts. It turned at the last second, threw up its arms to ward him off, and Valentine caught it at the knees with a diving tackle, knocking it down, felt claws open wounds in his shoulders as he drove his femur up between its legs. The Reaper didn't have sexual organs, but its skeleton had a gap.

Kill it so they send me another. And another . . . no.

Valentine fought to form words.

"You," he said, straddling the Reaper, feeling stronger than he had ever felt in his life.

He twisted the femur. "You, at the other end. Talk, or I make your puppet into a corn dog."

"sssstop! pleasssse."

Valentine withdrew the femur, and the Reaper lashed out with its free arm. He caught it at the wrist and twisted it until he heard a snap.

"Stop it," Valentine said. It was like talking in a foreign tongue; he had to force himself to make words. "I'll take your toy apart a limb at a time. Then I'll hang your churchmen from the goalposts."

"what do you want? i give you your life, i give the female her life, i give the man his life, just let my servant go."

"Are you Seattle? The head honcho?"

"no, i am but a keeper of—"

"I want to talk to your chief. King. Grand and Exalted Overlord, whatever he calls himself. The one in the big tower."

"he does not deal with your kind directly."

"Then through you. I don't care. Tell him I have an offer."

"what could a human give such as he?"

"Adler. The leader of the resistance."

The Reaper's slit eyes widened. *"impossible!"*

Valentine reached up, got his hand around its windpipe, felt the thick muscles that drove the tongue.

"grraack . . ." Valentine released his grip. *"yes, yes, cease and desist. i contacted, he assents. you shall have your meeting with his representative among the mortal."*

Thirteen

Mouthpieces: Every Kurian organization depends on layers of intermediaries between the Kurian Lords and their human herds. Seattle is no different.

All the layers of police, troops, secret police, church investigators, even diplomats to other Kurian Zones, report to one man's office in Seattle, and that man is Maxamom Silas. Impressive looking, with a good eye for clothes, and an even more impressive speaker and judge of character, he's something of a born second-in-command. Some in the know of the ins and outs of Seattle's realm believe him to be more important than the lesser Kurian Lords in the feudal conglomeration, especially with recent desertions of the Kurians supposedly guarding the borders of Seattle's empire.

He has his faults, of course. If an original thought ever entered his head, it got lonely and left. He's also a man who lives very much in the present day. "The past can't be changed and the future has too many variables," he's been known to say.

Maxamom Silas watches over his city from the old Space Needle, overshadowed by the greater Kurian Spire doubling the highest heights of the Seattle skyline, as if contesting Mount Rainier itself. Why he chooses the Space Needle as a location for the meetings of his highest military, industrial, and church leaders might be answered better by psychology than logistics or practicality or even sybaritic comfort—after all, he often weekends at the much more congenial Gates estate. He's earned the view. As a Seattle-born NUC altar boy, he impressed the church hierarchy enough for them to send him East for an education. He returned a bright young graduate of Harvard's Population Manage-

ment School, not inspired with any particular vision, but crammed with the latest skills and theories.

Silas receives credit for his division of the city into neighborhood-sized "quads"—each ruled by a Kurian. School and work and sports teams encourage quad loyalty. These in turn are gathered into "conferences" where a presiding Kurian clan works out squabbles. In theory, a human need never leave his conference; the whole of his existence is encompassed in the square miles that make up a conference, though he will sometimes travel to another conference to root for a home team in a championship, or listen to a political speech.

Seattle himself oversees the conferences as sort of a supreme judge. His conferences reside in his own massive tower, where they may be more easily watched and controlled. Treachery has been unknown since the great purge of Year Forty, when three leading conference clans were killed in a single deadly night.

It is this simple system that allowed Seattle to expand his realm in the 2050s, owning all the land between the Grogs in Oregon and the thinly inhabited coastline north of Vancouver. From the Kurian point of view, the apparently powerless "quad" role was attractive, for the number of human auras he had to pass up the food chain was strictly limited, and in return he received the military protection of Quisling formations organized at the conference level. While there is some dispute on the matter, Seattle can at least be credited with being the only Kurian overlord who regularly saw his fellow Kurians petition him to be included in his empire.

Until, of course, the advent of Adler and his brutal strategy. Adler would strike in secret, hard and fast, at the quad level of the Kurian Order, harassing and chipping at the vulnerable fringe of Seattle's realm. He avoided every trap laid for him, seeming to know which quads were strongly garrisoned and which were weak.

Even Maxamom Silas had few ideas of how to cope with the crisis. His expertise in security was limited to quelling dissent from within and breaking up organizations like the Resistance Network. After three conferences contributed to a "Guardian Army" that plunged into the mountains, only to dissolve thanks to desertion and harassing attacks from mountain-wise guerrilla bands, no further attempts were made to take the offensive.

But Seattle himself is not without the canniness of a hunted fox. He sent to his subrealm of Vancouver for the "Big Mouth" amphibian Grogs, and used the numerous waterways around Seattle to gird his realm, though a good deal of his productive capacity is now spent feeding

Grogs rather than trading with other Kurian Zones for the goods that once made Seattle such a pleasant place to live and breed.

Valentine watched Seattle through the outward-slanting windows of the Space Needle. He tried to imagine what the roads looked like long ago, filled with cars and trucks—the crushed remains of which now formed barriers between Seattle's zones. Now there were just bicyclists and a few motor scooters, making way for smoke-belching army trucks, biofuel buses, and the occasional gleaming SUV.

He'd first relayed the bare bones of a plan to a pair of skeptical military adjutants, but as he spoke they grew more and more interested. Then he spent a day in an apartment on what he guessed was a military base; BELLEVUE CONFERENCE IS THE FIRST WITH THE MOST read a banner hanging over an exercise field that he could just see through his grimy window. Later they told him that he'd need to speak to Chief Executive Silas' Regional Security Work Group. So they gave him soap and a razor, sent a girl in to trim his hair and nails, and gave him an afternoon to present his plan.

They shuttled him to the Space Needle in a motorcycle with a little encapsulated sidecar that reeked of sweat and tobacco. A cold front had parked itself over Seattle, and the normal drizzle had turned to sleet the previous evening and promised to do so even earlier tonight. From the road Valentine got a closer look at the Lord's Tower, as it was called, and didn't care for what he saw.

Five great shafts, laid out like the dots on the "five" on an ordinary craps die, rose straight up in shafts of blue green like a fountain frozen in time. Above the tallest of the city's buildings, the Kurian compartments, as Valentine thought of them, began. They looked like mollusks or barnacles clinging to a pier, rather than the spider-egg-sac orbs he'd seen in the middle of the country. Atop all, like a great mushroom cap, was the dome of Seattle himself. Valentine thought he saw trees up there but could not be sure if the green caps were vegetation or just some odd element of Kurian architecture.

"That must have taken some time to build," Valentine said as they parked beneath the Space Needle and the driver opened his canopy.

The driver shrugged. "My dad knew a guy from the conference who worked on it. Once the foundation went in, they grew the columns. Only steel in there as far as I know is remnants from the scaffolding."

The driver passed Valentine on to one of the military attachés he'd first talked to. They took an elevator up the Space Needle. Some minor earthquake damage had been patched over and painted, but otherwise it still looked fresh from the World's Fair.

Valentine idled in a waiting room, downing a mug of the best coffee he'd had since his last trip to Jamaica. Photographs of post-'22 reconstruction projects and the Victory-5, a super-fuel-efficient observation plane and light bomber produced at the Boeing works, filled the waiting area. A card listed an impressive set of specifications. The plane's lines reminded him a little of the gliders he'd trained on in Yuma, wide flat wings with little stabilizers at the tip, though with a heavier body and push-pull propellers.

He listened to a pair of engineers breaking for coffee, grousing about the state of the sewers. Seattle was only a third as populous as it had been pre-2022, and as the remaining humans no longer produced enough waste to keep the sanitary system working, they were closing off vast sections so as to divert into the still-working parts and narrowing pipes.

"You'd think PVC was gold, they way they stint," one said, sipping his coffee.

"The shit's gold, that's for sure. Energy wants it for the biofuel stills. Fisheries want it for the hatchery. Agriculture needs fertilizer. If they only would let us get a per-gallon rate, we could buy all the tubing we needed from the Oakland Bay Company. But no, 'waste' it remains."

Next trays of food—Valentine smelled fish and roast beef, along with onion and potato—came up the elevator and disappeared into the meeting room.

Valentine wandered to the observation rail while the Quisling leadership ate. A sharp lemony smell filled his nostrils, and Valentine heard a heavy, shuffling step.

He turned. A squared-off man, all right angles and pinstripes, stood on the observation platform, looking at him. He had golden rings on each hand.

Behind him was a big gray Grog, who evidently was the source of the lemony smell. Valentine couldn't remember ever seeing one of the long-armed grays so neatly trimmed and coiffed. It wore a kilt with sewn-in scabbards for weapons, and the butts of two rifles projected from its shoulders. Silver-capped teeth shone against lips greasy with roast beef juice, its tongue discreetly probing for trapped morsels.

"I take it you're Valentine," the man said, stepping up with hand out. He was about Valentine's height, but built a little heavier. "I'm Silas, chief executive around here. Kur commend you." He had what sounded to Valentine like an odd manner of speech, as though all the words were formed in the top of his throat and passed up through his nose as well as his mouth.

"David Valentine. You could get a fair price out of the Louisiana

Kurians for me, by the way." The Grog hovered as Valentine shook hands.

"You're not frightened of Grogs, are you? Silvers is well trained," Silas said.

"U-koos," Valentine said to the Grog, lowering his left hand toward the floor and bringing the right to the center of his chest. The greeting was a fairly universal one in St. Louis, but he didn't know if it applied out here.

The Grog slapped his own centerline a few times and hooted. Valentine saw an old white scar on his right breast, sloping down toward the Grog's navel.

"Introductions being over, we've got another hour or so of work after lunch. Sorry to keep you waiting, but we're running late. Then it's going to be all military, and you're first on the agenda. Seattle himself is curious as to what you're going to propose, you know. It would be in your own interest not to disappoint him. If I understand, you're some kind of assassin? You took the measure of two Reapers, unless I'm being misinformed."

"It was me or them. I'm glad Seattle is the forgiving type." Valentine felt shaggy and uneducated in the light of Silas' controlled diction.

"Nobody much likes the Bellevue clan. They trade with the insurgents and word gets around about that little exercise field. Unsettles the herd."

"You're one of the herd yourself, aren't you?"

"One body can always be swapped with another. But talent—that's not so easily discarded. Do you know what these are?" He held out his manicured hands, an NUC-crested brass ring on the left, a plainer one on his right.

"Brass rings."

"Yes. Word of advice, Valentine. Don't believe your own propaganda posters about freedom and all that. There's always been the rulers and the ruled." He tapped the glass in the direction of the city. "The Kurians aren't that different from other rulers throughout history, save for one twist. They want productive births and productive lives, just like all the others. The only thing all this slanging is about is their desire for, when the time comes, productive deaths. Reuse and recycling of strange and mysterious energies otherwise lost to the cosmos."

"If that's what you believe, then I hope I'm around when you go drowsy and forgetful. You going to strip off those rings and volunteer for recycling?"

"I've earned a ripe old age, and I intend for it to be a productive one. Sadly, I've not had time for children yet. Our aphrodisiacs have been certified for ninety-year-olds. But really, I didn't come here to talk about myself or the honorable family name. I wanted to get an idea about you, before plunging into all the hows and whens. I'm a little curious about what you want out of all this."

"Put in your words, I want to stop the unproductive deaths. Adler is slaughtering whole families."

"Both sides are exhausted from all the fighting. The Kurians never thought it would take so long to reorganize us. Every new eruption kills more in a few weeks than the Kurians do in a year. Waste, sheer waste."

An elegant woman in business dress, lovely eyes behind thick glasses, cleared her throat from the hallway.

"Mr. Silas, they're reassembled and await you."

Silvers took a long snootful of the air around the assistant and popped his lips together: *dop dop dop.*

"I look forward to hearing your plans, Valentine. Just don't think you can organize another mutiny here. We're not stupid."

"Never said you were, Silas. Rotten, maybe, but not stupid."

"You're not my idea of an ally either."

"We don't need to respect each other, as long as we cooperate. I'd make a deal with the devil himself to stop Adler's slaughter."

Two and a half hours later Valentine finally got a chance to talk, in the meeting room at the top level of the Space Needle. It rotated with the speed of a minute hand, slowly shifting from city skyline to mountains to the bay.

He stood at one end of a long, slightly curved wooden table, richly lacquered and the color of blood. Papers placed on it seemed to hover above their own shadows. The table could hold twenty-two at a pinch, Valentine guessed, but at the moment only four figures sat at it, Silas at the other end. Lesser operatives sat discreetly at the edges of the room, near phones and computer terminals, but Silas dismissed them for the day, keeping only those seated at the table and his secretary.

And of course Silvers, filling a battered sofa just behind Silas' chair.

"What the hell is a deep amphibious operation?" a general with heavy, burnished steel shoulder boards said. He had the fleshy look of a man who liked to do his generaling after a late breakfast and before cocktail hour.

"Hear him out," a uniformed woman with a raccoon mask of camouflage airbrushed across her eyes said. Her bristle-short haircut made one of Alessa Duvalier's self-administered razor jobs look vulpine. "About time someone talked about going on the offensive. We need more men willing to put their balls on the table, pardon the expression."

"Keep yours behind your zipper, Park," the fleshy general said.

"Let the man answer the question," Silas put in, and the table went silent again. Behind him, the city's skyline glowed in splashes of color, searchlights illuminating the old, empty office buildings as though they were national monuments. Lights dusted the edges of the city, washed down the road.

"I just made up the term," Valentine said. "But it describes what I think your 'Big Mouths' can accomplish, if the field training I received about their habits was correct. I read some news bulletins about their use in Florida deep into the Everglades."

"How many will you need?" a man in thick black wool asked. He had the fishy odor of a man off a long day at a gutting wharf. Valentine couldn't tell if he was in casual military clothes or civilian wear so rugged and severe it could pass for a uniform. His name tag was similar to the general's and that of the woman called Park, a black rectangle with white lettering; his read TROYD.

"I have to see them training to decide that. Do you train them?"

"We do," Troyd said. He kept his hands out of sight under the table, unlike the others, who were making notes or drinking coffee or tea.

"How are you going to get past the river barriers?"

"I know a little about the watch system," Valentine said. "Before my comrades delivered me into your little garden of horrors, I was an officer in the troops that supplied the river sentries. Dangerous work."

"That's why they had PeaBees doing it, no?" Park asked.

"Yes," Valentine said. "I even lost a few men to them in the fall. We never found the bodies."

"They've adjusted their fertility cycle to the salmon runs. Whoever eats the most gets to be female and host the fry. Sometimes they even eat the males, if the males don't swim away quick enough after the mate."

"That's a fucked-up way to do it," the fleshy general said.

Troyd shrugged.

Park snorted. "Make for a quieter world."

Silas cleared his throat. "Let's set comparative biology aside for now. We've learned what you'll need for the job. What do you want in return?"

"Some peace and quiet. A nice little house, maybe on one of those islands outside the bay there. A nice boat, not quite a yacht, but something I can use for travel or fishing. A few servants and a couple women to keep me warm on these clammy nights. But most important, one of those brass rings like you all wear so I get left alone."

"You? Settle with us?" the general asked.

"Not with you. Among you. I'm not going to be welcome back with Pacific Command. I'm under a hanging judgment with Southern Command."

"Brass rings aren't mine to give out. Speaking of which, there's going to be one awarded to our friend Troyd here at the next audience, for his work with the Big Mouths."

"And well deserved," Park said, rapping the table.

"Damn, is that this week?" the general asked, looking at his organizer book. "I may have to beg off—I've got inspections in Tacoma."

Silas kept his gaze on Valentine. "It's a boring ceremony. Speeches mostly, gives the TV station something to broadcast for a few weeks. I might arrange for a short interview. Seattle is most interested in the proposition, and he would be the one to promise a ring."

"I'm not doing it on faith," Valentine said.

"We're not so sure you can do it," the general said.

Valentine shrugged. "I wouldn't expect a ring to be handed out unless I accomplish the mission."

"I'm expected at a wedding banquet for one of my colonels. Can we wrap this up?"

"Hungry for your cake, or your droits?" Park asked.

"Not what you're thinking, Valentine," Silas said. "The maid of honor gets a more active role in military weddings around here, is all."

"Who gives a damn what he thinks?" the general asked. "Are we reporting up here or no?"

Silas nodded to his breathtaking secretary. "I'll call for a vote on the Valentine Proposition, and we'll adjourn." He touched a button on the arm of his chair. "Captain Chu, take Valentine back to the lounge."

"Suppose you vote the proposal down?" Valentine asked.

"You might end up in Seattle's tower anyway, but in considerably less distinction. But don't worry, a part of you will live on as a conversation piece."

Valentine went back to the lounge, smelled the nervousness on Captain Chu. Valentine wondered if the man expected to be stabbed with a stir stick. He felt too tired, too disgusted with himself, to put up much of a fight, even if the vote went against him.

Ten minutes later the door opened and he saw the French cuffs of Silas, a broad smile on his face. But he had Silvers with him rather than the statuesque secretary.

Valentine struggled to look nonchalant.

"The vote ended up unanimous in your favor."

"All four? I figured that general was hedging."

"Three. Friend Troyd sat at the table as a courtesy, but he doesn't have his ring just yet. I decided to seat the minimum for an official meeting of the Security Staff. I imagine the less who know about your project, the better."

"Wise of you," Valentine said.

"I want you to have dinner with me tonight. We'll get you cleaned up and into some decent clothes. When you're out mixing with the other ranks, your cover story is that you're an emissary from Catalina, learning how to handle Big Mouths. You know anything about Catalina?"

"Not really. Island off the California coast is about all."

"Don't worry, no one here's ever been there. Our only contact with them is for oil transactions, and the Energy Staff isn't scheduled to renegotiate for eighteen more months. Just pretend you're wealthy. Oh, and say 'awhoha' now and again."

Valentine rode back to the city in Silas' limousine with his secretary. The trunk of the vehicle had been heavily modified to accommodate Silvers in his own semicupola complete with the first Grog gun Valentine had seen since leaving St. Louis. This one was a piece of craftsmanship, twin barrels each with its own two-thick magazine sloping down at an angle, with a built-in firing shield. Silvers strapped himself into the gun and the seat like the deep-sea fishermen Valentine had seen in the Caribbean.

"That's quite a hogleg your bodyguard totes," Valentine said, looking through the tiny back window at Silver's hair whipping in the wind.

"That little apparatus came off an armored personnel carrier, initially. I think they're . . . ummm."

"Twenty-five millimeter, Thunder City Rangeworks," the secretary supplied.

"Anyway, they cost a lot. Oh, I'm sorry, David Valentine, Luty Loosh. She usually goes by Miss L. Top-quality English import, and almost as hard to get as a Rolls."

"I'll save you some time: Lubey Bush, Lusty Tush, Loosey Flush, Thirsty Lush, and combinations thereof," she said. Valentine detected a little bit of an accent now, and she tended to hit the first syllable of her words hard and sharp, like a determined pianist. Valentine felt like a drawling backcountry scrub compared with these elegant-sounding creatures.

"She was ill-bred enough to make herself so useful I had to keep her around—even after we got tired of each other," Silas said.

They took an off-ramp into the city, passed through a gate in a concrete wall, and pulled up beneath a well-lit turnaround, sheltered by a gold-fringed awning protecting a carpeted path to shining brass-and-glass doors.

"This is my pied-à-terre in the city. Let's get you changed for the better and then talk more over dinner."

"Whatever Silas says," Valentine said.

"I've heard that one before too," Miss L. said.

They rode up in an elevator that made the one in Fran Paoli's building in Xanadu seem like a freight. A little screen in the elevator showed the time, date, and outside temperature as it ticked off names and what Valentine guessed were locations every few seconds:

Vinson, B. COLTRANE MIL
Apporimatox, N. TACOMA 18
Rutig, A. (in transit 5)

Neither of the others paid any attention to the screen, so Valentine ignored it as well.

The elevator opened into what Valentine guessed to be Silas' apartment. It was airy and open, a Prairie-school foyer/living room combination filling two floors. Stairs passed up on either side to doors that Valentine guessed to be bedrooms, and glass filled the wall facing the bay. A patio filled with plants had a second floor to the left side.

"I like a drink after that many circuits in the Needle," Silas said. "You like Scotch, Valentine?"

"You're a brave man, Silas," Valentine said.

"Why's that?"

"You left your bodyguard downstairs. I'm a desperate insurgent. Suppose I went for your throat?"

Miss L. removed her jacket. Valentine saw a soft leather holster strapped under her arm, the shining butt of an automatic inside. "It's loaded with hollow-points," she said.

"Have to admire a woman who brings her own protection."

"I believe in redundancy," Silas said. "Speaking of which, Luty, see if you can find friend Valentine one of my suits from when I'm better about exercising and down ten pounds."

She led Valentine up the carpeted stairs and to a bedroom that had been converted into an oversized closet, complete with three-way mirror. Her heels clacked on the hardwood floors as she walked down the line of jackets.

"I'd like to see you in gray flannel," Miss L. said. "You're too serious for double-breasted. Hmmm, a vest will make you look like a pimp with that hair. We'll stick to a simple cotton shirt. Where are you from, again?"

"Minnesota."

"That's the one east of Wisconsin?"

"West of Wisconsin."

"Ah." She paused until he looked at her. "How old is your mother?"

"I'm sorry?"

"Just wondering if she was Old Regime or not."

"No, she died fairly young."

"I'm truly sorry to hear that. Here, try these. I'll give you some privacy. There's clean socks and underwear in the drawers. I'm sure Mr. Silas won't mind you taking a pair."

They ate off china in a restaurant with a French name filled with blue velvet and gold trim. Miss L. went home for the evening and Silvers took his spot at his master's shoulder. The Grog got his own bench behind a thin curtain and sucked down an entire tureen of soup, softly hooting to himself as the men ate. Valentine had salmon with dill and assorted greens, Silas king crab legs. Silas probed him, not about opinions of the Kurians and those who worked for them, but about music and art and books he'd read.

Over dessert they talked about what kind of sports Valentine enjoyed. Silas apologized for the size of the desserts, enormous slabs of cheesecake slathered in syrupy strawberries. "If I have a weakness, it's for sweets."

"Mind answering a question?" Valentine asked.

"That's foolish to answer before hearing the question."

"Why the VIP treatment?"

"You're not getting the VIP treatment. I am. You're just in the overkill."

"And the questions about jazz versus jug band?"

"Just trying to take the measure of you."

"I appreciate the clothes, but this isn't the life I want. I could never live in the shadow of one of those towers."

Silas laid down his delicate dessert fork. "Do you speak from experience?"

"I've spent years at a stretch in the Kurian Zone."

"Just because you make it sound temporary doesn't change facts on the ground."

"There's no such thing as never. I'm pretty sure some mathematician or other proved that."

* * *

Silas put Valentine up in an almost empty apartment in his building, with some apologies that it would be temporary. But it did have a bed and hot water, and it was warm and dry. Valentine looked out at the city through two layers of glass door, both locked and welded shut.

The next day, after a quick rundown on the public transit system from Miss L., they fitted him with a plastic-sheathed metal loop around his ankle. A twitchy technician issued him with an ID card and swiped it through a slot in a black plastic circle the size of a wristwatch face embedded in the loop.

"Okay, Valentine comma D. of the Catalina Island and Baja Principalities. Your TRFID transmitter verifies who you are every time you use the card. Just in case you lose it, it's useless to anyone else." He consulted a screen. "You'll be okay for travel downtown for a couple days. Wow, nice expense account."

"It's not going to electrocute me in the shower, or blow my foot off if I leave Seattle, will it?"

The technician raised his eyes. "Catalina must really suck, if they run it like a work camp."

"No comment," Valentine said.

"Naw, it won't do any of that. Go swimming with it."

He didn't swim, but he spent two days exploring Seattle, staying as far away from the Kurian Tower as he could. It seemed a technology-driven city, and Valentine couldn't understand half of the conversations going on in the cafés. Every other block had a technical college or a medical school, mostly filled with foreign students from Asia. Everyone had an ankle tag, except for a few arty types who wore theirs around their necks, and it was from one of these that Valentine learned the coding system. Black indicated foreign dignitaries.

"Of course upper management has theirs implanted," a youngish longhair cradling a leather-topped wooden drum in a relaxed lounge with the intriguing name "Earworm Café" explained. "Everyone's got to bear the mark of almighty Babylon." He worked on an old computerized music player with a portable light and a set of precision tools.

"Sez the dude who spends every other morning getting CI certification," a girl chided as she cleaned a table and collected discarded mugs. "Double Deck, you'll be wiring IDs to your own family before you know it."

"Go pop out another kid for the churchies, your royal no compromises," the drummer said.

She bared sharpened teeth and Valentine decided to pay his bill. And the boy's.

Back at his apartment he found a note.

"Don't forget audience tomorrow. I had the suit pressed and the shirt cleaned—Luty."

The next day Valentine stood in borrowed clothes under a cheap plastic poncho. Seattle's mighty tower soared above him, making him feel like an ant in the shadow of a redwood.

A vast plaza surrounded the tower, rimmed with decorative columns topped with pensive statues of Reapers that served a more discreet purpose as vehicle barriers. Inside the circle it was paved with red and gray bricks that probably formed some kind of design when seen from on high, perhaps a spiral of some kind. Valentine guessed that at least four square blocks of downtown Seattle had been knocked down to make the expanse.

A strange sort of scaffolding had been set up in front of the tower. Perhaps three stories high on its own, it consisted of two staircases leading up to a long, bridgelike platform, an isosceles triangle aimed at the center column. A television camera was perched halfway up the stairs.

The spectators gathered for the audience consisted of well-dressed functionaries in the front, and a mass of shaggy student types farther back, each of whom received a little paper ticket like a theater admittance. The Seattle Police, in waxy black leather jackets, herded the entire crowd into one narrow mass in front of the scaffolding. Silas went up to the television platform and spoke to the cameraman, who turned his camera out on the crowd. Silas looked through it as well, and the police had the crowd spread out a little at the back, and passed out banners that could be unfurled to hide the lack of numbers.

SEATTLE CITY OF DREAMS AND PROGRESS, read one. PACIFIC COAST BEST AND BRIGHTEST HONORS KUR. Then there was the eternal OUR FUTURE IS BRIGHT AGAIN in phony childish lettering, held up by uniformed Youth Vanguard troops, which Valentine had seen in every political rally he'd attended in the Kurian Zone. Duvalier always said that Youth Vanguard troop rallies were so filled with high-ranking Quisling pederasts and pedophiles that the banners should read *Our cherry is plucked again.*

"Why not just round up more people for the audience?" Valentine asked one of the cops. "That's what we do back home."

"That's what I tell 'em," the cop said. "Just give folks a day off so they can come into the plaza. Give 'em luxury coupons like they give those sweatin' kids. They wanna have their cake and eat it too is all. Can't lose ten lousy hours of work. What they do is give everyone a half day on Fridays so they can go home and watch the speeches rebroadcast."

"That many televisions around? We sure don't have that at home."

"Shit yeah. Back in the good times, before all the fighting with the insurgents, this was a sweet spot."

"Sorry to hear that."

He lowered his voice. "Getting so even a police badge ain't proof against a cull. Like I was—"

A blast of music from the speakers mounted on the scaffolding interrupted him. Valentine wondered if Silas had selected Aaron Copland.

Then a New Universal Church Archon began to speak. He led the audience in a hymn, "Onward Human Progress," and Valentine managed to drone through it; he'd heard it many times before in the Gulf.

Silas' limo pulled up to the scaffolding and he and Troyd got out. Silas, wearing an elegant camel-hair coat that stood out against the dull aluminum of the metal, led Troyd up the stairs, where after a brief introduction as "the skilled xenologist who is doing so much to reverse our recent misfortunes" Troyd walked up a set of railless stairs that seemed impossibly narrow to Valentine. It was tipped with a sort of pulpit, and from there, by leaning on the rail and reaching his hand up, he could just reach a sort of blister on the side of the tower.

Silas spoke, talking about battles recently won that Valentine had never heard of, except for a small skirmish that resulted in a raiding PeaBee company retreating from an old state trooper station. To hear Silas describe it, another Stalingrad had been won.

Troyd passed his hand through a shimmering wall of light and pulled it out, still dripping with what looked like liquid fire. He shook it off and held up his undamaged hand, and the new brass ring on his finger glimmered like Venus on a dark night.

Valentine half listened to the speeches, marking the placement of Reapers. Two stood at the bottom of each stairway.

Troyd descended the stairs more surely, and stepped to the microphones. With the TV camera on him, he gave a brief, halting speech, thanking Seattle for his generosity and leadership, as a banner unfurled from the bottom of the scaffold.

29 RINGS AWARDED IN OUR SIXTH DECADE
WHAT'S STOPPING YOU FROM GETTING YOURS?

With Troyd's speech concluded, the Archon stepped to the microphones again. He clutched the railing and sagged for a moment, but Silas helped support him. With that, he raised his head, and with his eyes rolling and cheeks twitching he spoke.

"My children," he said, giving Valentine an odd tingle over the difference in his voice. The Archon sounded a little like a stroke victim who hadn't quite regained the full use of his tongue. "Your Kurian friends and allies have this day placed one of your number among the eagles that soar over this lovely land of ours. He is an example to be followed, for he teaches us the virtue of cooperation and utility. The beings he directs to guard your homes may look fearsome to you, but consider how fearsome they must look to those who threaten our peace. Perhaps then you shall look on their strange faces and beauty. We, your Kurian friends and allies, know you have sacrificed to feed these beings, but who regrets a toe when a leg is saved?

"There are dark forces at the gates of our city, so long a symbol of the heights mankind can reach, with just the tiniest touch of a friendly hand. With these fresh allies beside us, we can look to better days ahead. Belief in victory will lead to work for victory. Work for victory will lead to an affirmation of that belief.

"Too many homes have been darkened by death in the last year. New medicines are even now on their way to church dispensaries to help you dispel whatever fears and doubts you may have. But these have not come cheaply. We must bring the new B-6 into production to meet orders already placed, and certain luxuries will, for a time, become unavailable. Your conferences will provide you with details of our plans to increase output. If we all push together, a very short period of sacrifice will put us back on the road to prosperity and peace. Meet these hardships, not as a burden among burdens, but as a challenge above self! Will you, my family, accept this challenge?"

"Yes," Silas shouted into the microphone. "Yes, yes, yes," he chanted, and the crowd took it up, perhaps eager for exercise to keep warm in the chill November air. The Youth Vanguard jumped up and down with each "yes."

After a few close-ups of people cheering, and a rowdy student or two lifting her sweater and T-shirt, the TV cameraman left.

Silas came down the stairs, chatting with Troyd.

"Wait for Valentine a moment, won't you, Troyd?" Silas asked. "I believe he's going to accompany you back to your wet little camp. Unless you want to come up and pay your respects in person."

Troyd looked at the ring on his hand, rubbed the skin. "No. I was touched once. That's enough for me."

"Then it's you and me, Valentine," Silas said.

"What, up there?"

"Of course."

"I thought I could just speak to one of the, the . . ."

"We call them avatars."

"One of the avatars," Valentine finished.

"He wants to look at you with his own eyes. All eight of them. Are you coming?"

Valentine nodded, and stepped up onto the scaffold stairs.

The four Reapers came up the stairs with them, boots loud on the metal steps. Valentine saw the TV man blanch as he placed his camera in a padded bag and frantically wound cables as the Reapers passed.

Silas hit a button by the microphones—another worker with a little silver television pin on her collar dismantled the microphones—and the stairs Troyd had used to climb up to the blister lowered and flattened into a narrow walkway, bridging a gap between the tower and the scaffold bridge. Valentine saw a slit open up in the tower wall, saw lips peel back as it widened.

He looked up at the blister in the tower. Some trick of light put six Reaper faces in various oddly shaped shards and panels of glass.

Two Reapers led them inside, ducking to go through the slit. Silas followed, hands held out a little for balance. Valentine walked the beam uneasily, more thanks to the Reaper following behind than from fear of a misstep.

They lost two of the Reapers at the portal. Valentine couldn't resist turning around and looking. Sure enough, there were lines of triangles like shark teeth, yet off bias like the blades of a ripsaw, deadly yet decorative bumps on the inner side of those lips.

Valentine was relieved to see the inside conforming to human ideas of architecture and design.

"The center tower is separate from the others?"

"At the level humans go to, yeah. People work full-time in here, you know. They use our technology to light the place, keep the air moving. Seattle used to be a popular piece of real estate for them. I learned they evolved in tidal zones when I was out East in Cambridge."

They passed through an inner, curving shaft. Valentine looked up, saw small spiky projections on both sides of the wheel within wheels. There more threadlike projections connected the two layers of structure. It reminded him of a cross section of a bone with the marrow cleaned out. Climbing it would be possible, he imagined, but a long and demanding ascent.

All the corridors curved and wound, so it was difficult to see more than ten meters or so ahead. The Reapers led them to another elevator, in what Valentine guessed to be the center core of the pillar. Silas put his key into the slot and Valentine heard a beep.

"You have to do it too."

Valentine got the same beep and a green light came on over the elevator. The doors opened and they got in, accompanied by the Reapers.

"two for audience, seattle level," a Reaper said to a speaker grid.

Valentine found it interesting that even Reapers had to report in to some central authority. Bureaucracy or security? Weren't these Reapers animated by Seattle himself?

The elevator rose fast enough for Valentine to feel the change in perceived gravity for a moment. Then he concentrated on swallowing to relieve the changes in air pressure.

The elevator opened out on a wide bay. A Reaper in a purple robe, his face hidden by hood and fabric mask, nodded, and Silas led Valentine out of the elevator into the plain, well-lit lobby. Valentine noted that the walls had a metallic sheen, and there were what he supposed were two-way mirrors on each wall.

"Silvers used to wait for me in this room. But he kept getting nervous around the avatars and soiling the corner."

"You feel like you need a bodyguard up here?" Valentine asked.

"You never know. A Grog's like a big, comforting dog sometimes. A dog that can shoot."

The Reaper pointed to a door on the right wall.

"Crap. I hate the tunnel. I was hoping he'd talk to us in the gardens. You're on your own, Valentine."

Silas hurried over to the door, waved at a camera lens—Valentine noted the door had no ID card slot—and it opened. Dim light, such as one might find under fifty or sixty feet of murky water, showed a room beyond.

"Go on. It's safe, until he decides it shouldn't be safe."

"See you," Valentine said.

Valentine passed in, ducking slightly to clear the door, wondering if another elaborate death awaited inside. Funny how even involuntarily one developed a fatalism about that sort of thing. Did they put some psychotropic in the food?

While touring a classroom once in Biloxi as a Coastal Marine, Valentine had to do "community service" in a classroom. The class had a small family of hamsters, and the hamsters had a little plastic warren of connecting tunnels and shafts and rooms. The room he stepped into reminded him of those shafts, save that it was in the shape of a slightly pregnant triangle and surrounded by some kind of liquid.

He thought he could see other shafts and rooms through the liquid, but they might have been decor, or models; the rather cloudy water—if it was indeed water—made it difficult to tell.

Valentine saw dozens of bodies floating in the liquid. Most were in the shape of the octopus-bat creature that Valentine knew to be a Kurian/Lifeweaver form. Wires or lines projected from their extremities and "necks" to a football-sized orb that glowed mysteriously now and then as the forms floated. Something about the slowness of the movements inside made Valentine decide the liquid wasn't, in fact, water.

Others shared the space with the aliens, gentle and predatory. Valentine saw a Grog or two, and humans. An encephalitic fetus, tethered both to mother by umbilical and to its own football, yawned and stretched.

"Do you admire my menagerie?" a voice in his head asked. It was slightly mechanical, and Valentine realized it was from an old battery-operated Ready Reader toy he'd heard Amalee playing with the last time he'd seen her. He'd given it to her when he arrived on Jamaica, and she proudly showed "Uncle David" how good she was with it already, dog and cat and hat and ball prancing, stalking, bouncing, or spinning across the faded screen.

Valentine decided to respond aloud. If he started having conversations with himself, or the Kurian, or maybe that floating fetus, he didn't like his chances of making it out of the tunnel a complete personality again. "Which one are you?"

"All of them. In a way. You have a well-rounded mind for your kind, Vaal-eyen-tine-Dee. Strong extremes of love and hate. I hope you know the narrowness of the balance point on which the scale rests. Oh, here she is. How are you, sweet boy?"

The last was said with his mother's voice. Valentine felt a piece of him fall off. "Don't do that!"

"Do what, you little pail of piss water?" an old drill instructor from the Labor Regiment asked. "Oh, I like him."

What am I here to do again?

"Bargain, I think," LeHavre's voice said. Suddenly he was eleven again, standing in the kitchen above his pantsless mother, blood all over the floor, tomatoes stewing on the stove.

"Oh, that was delicious, thank you," Father Max's voice said. "But my time is limited."

Valentine found himself on his knees in the tunnel, gasping like a fish, his heart pounding. "Stop it! Please!"

"Very well. Why are you wondering if some of these are *Dau'weem*?"

"I have old friends in Southern Command who have vanished."

"I assure you, they are not here," Ready Reader said.

"What is this thing?"

"Are you familiar with your concept of a phased array?"

"No."

"A team of horses, perhaps?"

"Yes, of course."

"It's the same principle. Joined minds able to do what one cannot. It helps me keep tabs on my enemies—and my allies. Which reminds me, which are you?"

"An enemy."

"I admire your candor. Are you here to kill me, Vaal-eyen-tine-Dee?"

"No. I can't imagine how I'd do that."

"You've proven yourself inventive in the past. But you must know your limitations. Watch out for Blake. He'll forget himself someday and kill you, I expect. These constructs have very poor impulse control. Speaking of impulses, you've got strong ones toward my old friend Adler. What kind of a man do you think he is?"

"A madman," Valentine said.

"You're wrong. In any case, he's set me back years. Not that years mean much to me, of course. I shall rebuild, better and more carefully, once he's gone. Sooner or later."

"I want to make it sooner."

"You do, of that I'm certain. Your wobbly little scale is quite tipped where he's concerned. I'd like to do it in Silas-Em's life span; he is a talented sort and I shall hate to lose him to age. This new generation thinks the most piddling acts of conformity merit a brass ring. Where is the desire for greatness?"

"Maybe you're breeding it out of them. Herd talk and all that. We've still got it in the Free Territories."

"Dream on, Vaal-eyen-tine-Dee," Duvalier's voice said. "Are you sure you're not mistaking free range for free land?" The voice shifted back to Ready Reader's. "Oh, and now we're tipping back for love again. You're more fun than a good treetop swoop on a breezy day, Vaal-eyen-tine-Dee."

"And my ring?"

"You do want it, after all. And food and a warm wet mouth and poke after poke into delicious juicy pussy and then a steaming hot bath. Are you toying with me, man, channeling the baser urges?"

Valentine kept fantasizing.

"Maybe you're not as interesting as I thought. In any case, I've no doubt you intend to go through with your plan. Your wish is granted. Adler's destruction would be worth eight-count of rings to me. Cross me and you will end up in the tank until your body rots. You can barely comprehend how long that will take."

"Don't forget my island."

"You'll find them cold and rocky after your Caribbean, but something can be arranged." Light poured into the tunnel. "You may leave now. Good-bye."

One of the human forms jerked as its tether balloon changed color. His eyes opened behind his mass of drifting hair and he waved. Valentine saw the eyes widen, and he tore his gaze away and fled back into the receiving room. The man floating in there was the Bear Rafferty.

"You don't look so good, Valentine," Silas said. "Did you see that little girl? Some comedian stuck a—"

"No," Valentine said. "I saw someone I knew, briefly."

"You need some air." He turned to the Reaper. "Can we go into the greenhouse?"

For a moment it seemed as useless as talking to a statue; then their escort Reapers moved to flank the other door. Silas waved Valentine over and it opened.

Valentine smelled fresh, humid air and open space. Above, a crystalline dome diffused and admitted light, whitening the sun a little. A red path covered with a no-slide coating led them up to a little prominence, with a couple of comfortable human lounge chairs before a pool, which flowed over into a waterfall somewhere below.

Staggered was the only word for what Valentine felt. The space was bigger than any stadium he'd ever seen, and filled with a winding archipelago that was half-bayou and half-beachfront.

Red and purple trees topped with bristles of tresslike leaves dropped green vines into the water. Spongy-looking yellow growths clung to the bare trunks of the trees, sending out vast, delicate webs to catch deadfalls from above. Wind swirled around the interior of the dome.

"This is a piece of Ehro, home planet of the *Dau'ar*."

Valentine felt invigorated. "I thought they came from Kur. Someone told me it was a dry, almost lifeless place."

"A castle under siege runs out of even rats eventually. But Ehro is where they evolved, I'm told. That oxygen's nice, isn't it?"

"I wish they'd go back to it."

"They can't, but then you know that, I expect. We're just a part of a bigger, older war. I worry sometimes that the *Dau'weem* will apply the same strategy to our planet that Adler does to the suburbs."

Something translucent buzzed by on pink wings. "They'd never do that."

"Remember what I told you the other night about nevers? I never wanted the role of interlocutor. I decided to take what they'd hand me and go out East, build an academic ivory town and seal myself into it. But you'd be surprised, once you learn the true history of the world, just what parasites those things that laughably call themselves 'Lifeweavers' are. I've got a book or two I could loan you."

"I've seen the propaganda. Your master's the real parasite. Black bloody leeches. Worse than leeches, leeches at least leave the host alive. The Lifeweavers are interested in conserving life, not devouring it."

"Tell that to Silvers. He says a disease killed most of his people back home. They didn't want the Grogs used to conquer any more worlds."

"Not every plague has a purpose," Valentine said. "Seems just as likely your own masters would use a tactic to get them to quit their lands, force them to hitch up with Kur to find healthy land on another planet."

"Kur hates purposeless death."

"I can agree with you on that."

Silas sighed. "They've accumulated wisdom we can't even guess at in their long years. They're going to guide us up to heights we'd never reach on our own."

"I've had enough of this view. And the heights. I want to go to work."

Silas looked at his heavy gold watch. "Good. You'll start tomorrow."

Fourteen

Grog troops: An easy path to promotion and power for any human with a military background is to volunteer to serve as an Officer of Xeno Forces. High rank and its powers and privileges come quickly to volunteers for the OXFs, but at the cost of a social stigma. Mixing with nonhumans leaves OXFs in a strange netherworld, secretly despised by those they fight for and openly by those they fight against.

Though the rumors of bestial mating rituals and cannibalism are unfounded, and can usually be traced back to Freehold propaganda or melodramatic fictionalizations, there's no denying that OXF attract their share of bad apples. Men who can't win promotion or fit in elsewhere sign up for OXF training, where standards are looser and faults overlooked.

Of all the odd troops OXF have led—or tried to lead—the actions involving Big Mouths evoke the most consistently chilling accounts. Sometimes the only evidence of one of their attacks is a strong fishy odor, bloodstains, and a few bitten-off heads, hands, and feet missed after the seaside scrum and feed. Almost ungovernable, and known to turn on their OXF leaders in victory, defeat, or starvation, they are perhaps the most bloodthirsty Grogs to fight or lead.

Yet it was these dangerous oddities that David Valentine led into one of the most daring actions of his career.

Valentine stood on the steady deck of the old Japanese factory-fishing ship, renamed the *Redeye Run,* in its permanent Puget Sound moorings in the east passage around Vashon Island and tried not to barf.

He'd smelled rotten fish before. He'd smelled sewage before. If it was possible to mix the two and come up with a third odor worse than the two component parts, the Big Mouths had discovered it in their hovels within the hulk.

He lifted his gaze from the open cargo hatches of the ship and looked at Vashon Island with its herds of sheep. The Big Mouths, when they wanted a change from seafood and crustaceans, had the run of the flat, muddy island and its flocks, stranded there for that purpose.

"Why this heap of junk?" Valentine asked.

"Mostly because the freezers still work," Finn Troyd said. Calling him "Finnegan" was a gilt-edged invitation to a punch in the mouth, and judging from the behavior of the OXFs on the ship, that was the civilized option. "You have to hand it to the Japs—they build industrial equipment to last. We've got a big supply of frozen emergency food. The last thing you want to do is run out of rations when you're handling Big Mouths."

Valentine nodded.

"Ready to go down and meet the gang?"

"I guess I'm dressed for it." Valentine, with the titular rank of captain, didn't bother with "sir's"—no one in the OXFs did.

They both wore old woolen pants and sweaters, covered by a layer of waterproof overalls and thick green plastic boots.

"Grab your S and S and let's go, then."

By "S and S" Troyd meant shotgun and shockstick. The shockstick was almost identical to the ones Valentine had seen and used in the Southwest, save that it had a longer and heavier rubberized handle.

They went down into one of the holds. The side of the ship was punctured below the waterline. Scale and rust gave some color to the old sides, and the barnacles and whelks were making inroads into the water pooled in the bottom of the hold.

The smell was even worse down here thanks to the confined space. Valentine looked around at the staring bright red goggle eyes of the squatting and lounging Big Mouths.

They were hard to describe. Scaled like fish everywhere but the mouth and belly, they had huge triangular heads that tapered off to thin hips, where they were equipped with the long rear legs of a frog, ending in flippers and residual digits—almost useless for gripping, according to Troyd. Short arms, mostly used for climbing out of the water and pivoting on land, had webbed, gripping toes. They had blue green backs and pale, tartar-colored bellies.

The hold echoed with the sound of their breathing, as they sucked air through gill-like openings: *slee-kee, slee-kee.*

They liked to position themselves against an object, an underwater rock or log, with their rear legs folded. They could execute fair-sized leaps even without something to push off, but when properly "sprung" they could cover thirty yards or more in a lightning-flash hop.

Valentine watched a larger Big Mouth come up through a hole in the bottom of the ship and crowd another one out of the way with a few threatening snaps of vertically hinged jaws.

"What keeps her afloat?"

"One of each of the holds, forward and rear, is full of buoyant stuff, and the slop barges to either side are fixed permanently as camels. Marker barrels, Ping-Pong balls, flotation foam from old life jackets and airplane cushions, coconut coir, just about anything guaranteed not to sink. You could rip out the whole bottom of this ship and she wouldn't go down. At least I don't think she would."

Pools of filth rested in the shallow water lapping in the hold.

"They like it dirty down here, don't they?"

Troyd shrugged. "The shit feeds the slime. Little fish and crabs feed off the slime. Bigger fish eat the little fish. The Big Mouths eat the crabs and bigger fish, leading to more shit. It's a regular circle of life."

A Big Mouth splashed around in the filth, wiggling its rear hips and hunching its back. "Lying around, eating, and shitting, that's about all they do when they're not in training."

Valentine noted that the full-grown Big Mouths had stainless steel rings at their forehump between the eyes and in a fleshy taillike growth between the legs.

"What are the rings?" he asked.

"Front one's a towline or tether line. You'll see how those work. Rear is attached to some gonad tissue—that's a control line. About the only way you can direct them is to yank 'em by the balls. But haul too hard on the reins—they'll swing around and try to bite yours off."

Troyd let Valentine absorb that factoid and then continued: "Okay, we've seen lying around and shitting. Let's go look at the eating and training."

They took a flagged motorboat over to a sheltered bay between Maury and Vashon islands. OXF, mostly male but with a few women, stood on little floating platforms heaped with white buckets, or paddled around in sea kayaks, or were pulled about lying on floats Troyd called "boogie boards."

"Hey, Finn, can I borrow your ring?" a man called from a platform. "I'm going into the city this weekend and I could use a little flash."

Troyd laughed. "You'll have to bite it off like that whatsit in the old movie. How are they working?"

"Good. Eager. Donaldson lost one this morning, though—it attacked him. The others already ate it. They didn't get a frenzy going, probably the big breakfasts you're issuing."

"Glad to hear it." Troyd tossed a thermos of coffee to him. "Be nice and share for a change."

"We're going to have to get you a sea suit," Troyd said as they pulled away from the platform. "The water's pretty cold in the bay this time of year."

He pointed to a platform next to the shore. "That's training. You'll learn the hand signals easy enough—there's only sixteen of them. We fire flares when we want them to attack. For the BMs, that is. There's another dozen or so the handlers use to keep in touch with each other."

"What about at night?"

"Same signals, with chemical glow sticks. The BMs actually respond better at night. I think they can see the glow sticks better than they do hands. Same thing with the flares. Just don't pull your flare pistol early—they'll see it and get all idgitated and go nuts because they think it means food."

"I need to know everything about capabilities. Especially speed in water over long distances, and on land."

"On a long haul they average, um, fifteen or twenty miles per hour. That varies depending on currents. They slow down a bit in really cold water too."

"And on land?"

"Land they move along pretty good, a fast walk. But they leave a trail like a mudslide. There's the smell and they lose scales pretty easily, so pretty much any idiot knows when some BMs have been through. When am I going to hear more?"

"What's in the buckets?"

"Positive reinforcement. The BMs go nuts for pork. Dog too, but not so much as a good fatty pig. We give them pigs' feet, snouts, heads, ears, all that stuff, when they do something right. After a successful action we'll usually roast a hog or two to treat everyone."

"I think I read somewhere that physiologically, human flesh is a lot like pig."

"They eat that too. They're always eager to go into action to get a bellyful. You've never seen creatures so eager for a fight. They don't give a damn about casualties either, just means more eating on the way home."

"Any land training going on now?" Valentine asked.

"Yeah, up by those old houses."

"Can we land this thing and take a look?"

"Sure. We'll even show you how to give a couple orders. Just watch your fingers when rewarding. Toss, don't give. These ain't a bunch of backflippin' dolphins."

Valentine spent the next six weeks training with the OXFs. They equipped him with a Chinese SG carbine, reliable enough but not much good beyond fifty yards on autofire or a hundred shooting over open sights. They accepted him as one of their own. OXFs saw a lot of wanderers pass in, decide the work wasn't for them, and pass on again to something easier—like lumberjacking.

He answered a few questions about Catalina Island, and retreated behind the old reliable "That's classified" when probed too deeply, though most of the questions revolved around the weather and the amount of sunshine. He hemmed and hawed during a couple of equivocal probes about needing people with experience handling Big Mouths back on the island.

One of the trainers opined that the Big Mouths wouldn't do well there, as they were cool-water creatures, but another man claimed the eastern shores of Florida were thick with thriving BMs.

He spent his days cold and wet and his nights in his fish-reeking quarters on the *Redeye*, with his hands and arms slathered in lanolin to restore moisture and keep his skin from sliding off the bone. The creatures' odor was all-invasive, all-pervasive, and seemed to be the one thing that quieted his appetite.

As he slept he got the uncomfortable feeling someone was watching his dreams along with him.

Eventually he laid out a detailed plan for Troyd, a route into the mountains that avoided the river-watch stations. It involved a series of upriver journeys and then short overland hikes, always to the north, where a new river would be picked up for a push of a few miles more inland, then another short overland journey. By this long, counterclockwise turn, they could hit the Snoqualmie upriver from the Outlook, unguarded by dams, falls, or nets.

"The BMs can do it. It'll be hell on the men, though. That's a lot of time in some very cold water. We'll need to bring chemical heat."

"How secure is Vashon Island?" Valentine asked.

"No one hangs out there if they know what's good for them."

"Good. I'd like to use that old airfield there. It's about the right size for the target. I was poking around in it the other day to check the interior. With a little fixing here and there, block one door and put in another, we could get the corridors right. We need to rig some lighting and get some interiors. Can you ask Silas about some drywall and some workmen?"

"Jeez, Valentine, these are BMs, not commandos."

"The less left to doubt, the better. Now, the last thing I need is a moon chart—"

While construction went on, Valentine spent his mornings on endurance swims with the Big Mouths. He practiced "driving" paired BMs behind a sea kayak, mile after mile, first up and down the coast of the sound, then up the White River.

Troyd worked out the logistics of the overland part of the raid. The BMs were used to short hauls in tractor-trailers, but the OXFs had to get them worked up to an hour or two.

Valentine agonized over the timetable with the man Troyd decided on as second-in-command, Lieutenant Burlington, another Canadian down from Vancouver. They started making test swims at night, taking forty Big Mouths up the lower end of the White, then camping on the old mudslide damage from Mount Rainier, then spending the day in a lake, then traveling overland a couple of miles more.

"What about getting them back?"

"If they get back, they get back," Burlington said. "They're basically expendable."

That simplified matters. Valentine had a hard time feeling much sympathy for the fish-frogs. At the first sign of injury to a fellow, the others ate it. A military operation deep behind the opposing lines became a good deal more practicable if one didn't have to worry about returning the troops.

"We've got to think about our getting back. I say we go downstream on the Green River. . . ."

On Troyd's recommendation they added a third officer to the team in case illness or injury removed Valentine or Burlington. Holly Nageezi, a tight little bundle of muscle who never seemed to feel the chill of the sound, had been an athlete for, of all things, a women's Roller Derby team. She'd been away from her quad on a night when one of the Action Groups hit, slaughtering every neighbor and friend she had.

Bad luck struck just before the jump-off. They lost three Big Mouths from the ones trained to go into the mock Outlook, when on a trial run in, Valentine forgot and pulled his flare pistol too early as they approached. The BMs became, in Troyd's words, "idgitated," and started attacking one another when he didn't release them right away.

Valentine talked with Burlington about replacing them with Big Mouths from the pool. "Fresh ones would probably just do what all the others do. I think it would be safe to bring them."

"But these have gotten used to going a couple days without feeding. Maybe inexperienced isn't the way to go. They might lead the others astray."

In the end, after talking it over with Troyd, Valentine made the decision to go with just the twenty-seven.

Then Burlington deserted on a dark, late January night, three days before the new-moon weekend. Nobody could say how he had slipped away.

He left a note. Troyd showed it to Valentine but kept it a secret from Nageezi. Burlington had suggested that the whole operation was a one-way trip for the human handlers as well as the Grogs.

Troyd and Valentine informed Nageezi of her rise to second-in-command and she seemed oddly pleased. "Doing's easy. Having someone notice, that's difficult," she said.

They inspected the gear together at a vacant Tacoma dockside warehouse that served as their jumping-off point, and saw that their team of twenty-seven BMs had a heavy breakfast of sheep-with-hooves-removed. Valentine had his carbine, a silenced .22 automatic he'd picked up at the downtown armory, and a heavy diving knife with a built-in wire snip, sharp enough to cut the leather leads between his kayak and the Big Mouths in case of trouble. He oiled everything and placed the guns in waterproof bags.

"Nap?" Nageezi said as the hours counted down to when the trucks would be loaded. She pulled her silenced .45 out of its holster and patted a spot next to her. "We're going to be doing it in the field."

"So get used to it now."

They nodded against each other, but it seemed to Valentine that neither really slept.

Loading the Big Mouths into their covered livestock trucks was comforting in its routine, indistinguishable from the dozens of times they'd done it on long training runs. Valentine rode in the first truck with a pair of experienced drivers, Nageezi in the second. A third truck followed, there in case of mechanical failure, carrying one more meal for the Big Mouths in the form of a heap of dead, mangy dogs. Valentine watched the soldiers in the guard truck sway along—for all the drivers and the guards knew, this was just another training run.

The weather turned nasty at the riverbank, a cold, lashing rain that turned everything dark three hours ahead of schedule. It came down hard enough that Valentine thought it would blow itself out quickly. The Big Mouths hopped into the river eagerly enough.

The drivers of the third truck, anxious at the sight of the snapping jaws, refused to toss the dogs to the waiting Big Mouths until Nageezi drew her automatic and promised the fish-frogs dog or driver.

And with that they were off.

The rain alternating with snow lightened up but never really ceased. It didn't make much difference on the longest river run, that first night. They waited out the day in a backwater of the river, with the Big Mouths either resting or probing the riverbanks for small game and waterfowl.

The first overland trek, almost six miles, went well enough. Valentine and Nageezi hiked what felt mostly uphill on a heavy portage through the woods, following in a trail flattened by the prowling Big Mouths with fiberglass kayak, paddle, and equipment. Anything that didn't involve buckets of ice-cold water being flung in his face seemed like a treat.

He and Nageezi huddled together in the snow as they rested the second day, eating preserved food—appallingly small portions according to Valentine's cold-sharpened appetite—the green and white mountains of the Cascades around them. They warmed their food over chemical heat and pressed close together under a thin survival blanket, recuperating.

The second night's run was a long, churning nightmare of white water as they were pulled by the strong swimming—or hopping, over some of the rapids—upstream. Nageezi had the knack of resting herself and her team in the occasional eddy better than Valentine, and by the time they went back into the water, with fresh chemical heat packs pressed to their feet and the small of their backs, he let Nageezi lead.

The rotten weather carried one advantage: It made observation from the banks almost impossible.

They waited out the third day at a lake on the Green River, with the Big Mouths philosophical about their empty bellies. They'd been trained to have a real gorge after penetrating the fake hotel built up in the airport on the third night. . . .

For the final night's run Nageezi took amphetamines. She offered a pair of white capsules to Valentine.

"Benzedrine?"

"I'm okay," he said.

"Suit yourself," she said, popping the capsules and following them with a swig of water from a big bottle.

Valentine would have just about given a finger for a thermos of Space Needle–quality coffee. He set his kayak in the current and took up the reins from the new team with winter-chilled muscles.

"At least the weather's broke," Nageezi said, smiling. "Seattle stopped the rain."

"That's a bunch of crap," Valentine said, irritated at her chemically enhanced cheer. "They don't control the weather."

"Screw yourself," she said quietly, but Valentine's ears picked it up.

"What's that?"

"Suit yourself."

She's a Quisling. What do you care what she thinks?

Because, for one night, you're a Quisling too.

Valentine could live with it. He just hoped the Outlook was filled with Bears fresh from a Resource Denial operation.

The Big Mouths swam excitedly up the Green River. They could already taste the hot pork they expected to be waiting for them. Valentine marked the end of a lake on his map, and broke a chemical light. He signaled for the last portage.

Nageezi took two more bennies at the end of the portage as they slipped into the Snoqualmie, heading downstream at last. Valentine unhooked the reins from his Big Mouth team. He could paddle from here. It would warm him up.

He visualized the bodies strewn in the streets of the housing block, the fearful families in the church, and tried to summon a little of the Bear energy for the final push, but it stubbornly refused to come out of hibernation.

They rounded a bend, shot past a few boarded-up buildings heavy with snow, and there it was. The Outlook.

Valentine paddled his kayak next to hers. "Let's get a little closer." He shook a chemical light and stuck it under the water and repeated a circular signal three times; the red-eyed amphibian behemoths gathered round the kayaks.

They pulled their craft to the edge of the river, beneath a substantial lip of land, Valentine hiding the chemical light in his vest. He checked his knife, and took his guns out of their waterproof plastic sheaths.

"Feel that ring on your finger yet?" Nageezi asked. They anchored their kayaks in the shadow under the earth and rock lip. A paved river path was just on the other side of a set of white-painted warning stones.

"Not just yet. I want to hit the Outlook first."

She checked the safety on her .45, worked the slide. "If I get hit, try not to let them eat me."

"Same here," Valentine said, trying to remember not to reach for the flare gun until all the Big Mouths were out of the water and hopping toward the entrances the way they'd been trained. He adjusted his rifle sling around his neck—the Chinese carbine had a hell of a kick and he wanted it tight against his shoulder. . . .

She peeked over the lip of the riverbank. "You know there's a tradition in the OXFs. If a commander falls, and the second still wins a victory, all the spoils go to him. Or her."

The gun flashed toward him and fired.

Valentine lurched away as the muzzle turned toward him—over a decade of being around guns taught one to keep out of the way of barrels—but even Cat reflexes weren't faster than a bullet. At first he felt a hard thump at the bottom of his right rib cage. Then he discovered he was in the water, bobbing toward the falls, blood warming the interior of his suit.

He saw a Big Mouth turn toward him. Its jaws opened and Valentine instinctively pulled his feet away, oddly calm.

The last thing he remembered before the jaws engulfed him was Nageezi's face in the dark, as she gestured, lifting a chemical light of her own.

She was smiling.

Fifteen

Bearfire: Ask twenty different Bears to describe the feeling of Bearfire running through their bodies and you will get twenty different answers. Some speak in terms of space and time, everything slowed down and yet compressed. Others describe it mentally, as a determined form of psychosis, where every obstacle, from a minor vexation to a hail of machine-gun fire, is overcome by boundless violence. Most describe physiological changes: heat, euphoria, a terrible driving energy.

Ask the same number of doctors to describe the injuries they've seen Bears survive, fighting on to victory and recovery or toppling only once what's left of their bodies falls apart, and be prepared to have a short book's worth of incredible stories.

This is one of them.

You fucking cunt!

Valentine realized he couldn't breathe or see, and all he felt was a horrible, slimy mess surrounding him, seeping into hairline and nostril, lip and ear hole.

Can't breathe, wet cold panic

And flipped around again, violently jostled.

Wet hot fear

—turning into

White-hot anger.

Valentine wriggled a hand up, closed fingers around the corded knife hilt.

Red!

He lashed out, hand and foot, head and arm. Stabbed hard with the knife handle, punctured, punched through resistance, then with a long backhanded sweep opened up the voluminous gullet of the Big Mouth.

It vomited him out before he could fight his way free, rolled away, stricken and thrashing.

Valentine broke the surface of the hard-flowing river, hurt as he sucked air, found himself bouncing, got his toes pointed downstream, fetched up against a rock, lost it, slid against another, caught it, losing his knife in his desperation to get a grip.

He pulled himself half out of the rushing river, saw a long leg flail as the wounded Big Mouth went over the falls.

He climbed up onto the rock, thought about his wound, reached, and felt the hot wet blood against his palm. The bullet had plowed one long furrow along his rib cage.

You'll live.

She won't.

He jumped to another rock, sucked a deep breath of air, felt pain again, realized his rifle was still bouncing against his chest.

He removed the weapon's final proof against liquid infiltration, a heavy-duty condom over the barrel, and found a stone to crouch where he could watch events at the Outlook.

A stream of sparks cut across the night sky, exploded into red light as a flare wobbled down, blown northeast by the wind.

The parking lot where Valentine had once watched a few drunk figures play basketball was alive with slithering, hopping, humpbacked shapes.

Glowing red goggle eyes fixed on the snow-dusted gables of the Outlook. Warm yellow light shone within, fell in checkerboard patters on the virgin snow in front of the hotel.

Slee-kee, slee-kee, slee-kee . . .

Mr. Norman Rockwell, meet Mr. Hieronymus Bosch. Mr. Bosch, Mr. Rockwell.

Valentine lifted his gun, chambered the first round in the magazine, sighted on Lieutenant Nageezi. An urge to run at her, grind her face into mush, was suppressed as he straightened up and felt the pain in his side. He lowered the front sight to her thigh as she paused behind a parked truck in the lot, Big Mouths flapping and surging around her.

No, she knows her business. Wait. Get back to the kayak. First-aid kit.

The Big Mouths knew their business too. They divided into three streams of hopping shapes. Leap-gather-hunch-leap-gather-hunch-leap-gather-hunch on their way to the front and side entrances.

Crashes, screams, somehow softened by all the snow. There it was, the mad music of gunfire.

He gained the kayaks and tore open a dressing, pressed it to his wound, found the surgical tape, and went to work.

A Big Mouth made it all the way to the roof of the Outlook in a single leap. Another chased a shadow on a curtain right through the window, crashing through window, frame, screen, and curtain. Valentine heard a squelching noise and blood sprayed on a wall, three quick arterial jets.

A man fled out the front door, uniform coat torn, one shoe off, running into the night toward the parking lot with arms pumping. A Big Mouth flung itself out the door after him, flew over the footprints he'd left in the snow, and fixed its mouth over his head as it landed, folding its prey like a clasp knife.

A soldier ran across the deck, heading for the wire gondola crossing the falls, spraying bullets from a pistol back through the door. Valentine sighted on him, but another shot rang out and Valentine caught sight of Nageezi's features in the shadows of a station wagon parked in the lot.

Gunfire shattered a second-floor window, peppering the station wagon, deflating a tire, and forcing Nageezi to flatten. Two men hurled themselves from the shattered window, hit the snow rolling, and came up with assault rifles ready. One poured a magazine into the Big Mouth on the lawn, tearing its still-gobbling head to pieces.

They ran for a red full-cab truck. One paused, turned to look up, and waved at something in the broken window as the other made it to the driver's-side door on the truck.

Valentine recognized Thunderbird's features as he turned, bathed in the light of the Outlook.

Adler was at the window now. He hesitated, jumped, fell for what seemed to Valentine an eternity, but landed lightly and with more skill than the Bears.

Nageezi popped up from behind her bullet-stitched car, aiming, but Thunderbird spun and tore her to pieces with a short blast of his assault rifle.

Adler seemed to flow over the snow-covered yard, legs a blur. Thunderbird covered him as he approached the pickup.

Glass exploded and a Big Mouth followed the glittering pieces out onto the lawn, drawn by the motion. Thunderbird put in a new magazine as the creature turned, watching Adler run as the truck came to life, gathered—

And was brought down by a long tongue of muzzle flash from Thunderbird's weapon. He took two steps forward, pumping more bullets into it, flesh flying everywhere in the night.

More screams, more gunfire, a grenade explosion within the Outlook, and the red truck backed out of its spot, Adler slamming the rear passenger door.

Another Big Mouth, having passed all the way through the Outlook only to emerge at the far end of the wraparound porch, liked the look of the truck and covered half the distance to it in a jump. Thunderbird turned, but something went wrong with his gun. He threw it down, pulling a pistol as the jammed weapon hit, and sidestepped for the turning truck.

Now it was Valentine's turn to sight, not at Thunderbird, or Adler, but at the driver of the truck as he reached out to clear ice from the windshield. He flipped the selector to single shot and put three 5.56mm shells through the front windshield into him.

Valentine ducked and changed positions. He came up again to see the truck rolling across the parking lot at the purposeless speed of an unpushed accelerator in drive, turning slightly to follow the path of least resistance downhill.

Thunderbird sprinted for the truck and Valentine fired at him, knocking him down. The Big Mouth liked the look of his fall and pounced.

The truck waggled, then turned, and Valentine saw Adler climbing into the front seat—too late. It bounced over the curb and nosed into the river, doors flying open as it hit.

Valentine splashed, slipped, recovered, and hurried toward the truck before Adler could escape. He saw a shape dive out the door on the opposite side, marveled at Adler's fluid athleticism. Ex-Cat? Valentine jumped up onto the river-walk path and pounded after him, saw Adler slipping and floundering on rocks, arms waving so fast in the light it looked as though there were three of them.

Valentine whipped his rifle behind him on its sling and launched himself into a flying tackle, brought down his quarry in a body blow that felt more like he hit a badly stuffed tackling dummy than a man.

He hauled Adler up by his slippery, oily hair and dug for the eyes, the nostrils, his left hand reaching for the windpipe and finding only cool squishiness.

But the blood was wrong—

"Turn around, Valentine," Colonel Thunderbird said. "I'm putting this right between your eyes. I want to see them empty as the bullet pops the back of your head off."

"Before you pull that trigger," Valentine said, turning and raising his hands, "have a look at this."

Thunderbird's blood-circled eyes widened; the pistol in his hand shook and lowered. Valentine held aloft the leaking, slippery body of a Kurian. Or perhaps a Lifeweaver. Or both. Only the dying mind, twitching as it passed into inferno, glory, or nothingness, could say for sure.

"Is that—"

"A Kurian Lord," Valentine said.

Valentine threw the corpse up at Thunderbird, then hopped into his kayak and started across the river, half expecting a bullet in the back. He chanced a look over his shoulder.

Thunderbird was on his knees, crying.

Two days later Valentine staggered into a motorcycle-cavalry depot in Maple Valley, scribbled a message to be transmitted to Troyd at the *Redeye Run*, and promptly collapsed.

He woke in an ambulance, and paid a brief visit to a hospital, where they found him suffering more from exhaustion and blood loss than any specific injury—though he did carry a recently healed bullet wound—and after feeding him, they sent him back to his old temporary apartment in Silas' building.

Troyd visited him, called him "ring brother" or something just as insipid—Valentine could never remember later—and dropped off a few personal possessions from his berth at the *Redeye Run*.

"Three of your Big Mouths made it back the day before you did. We found two more in Lake Sammamish, but they were making a nuisance of themselves and had to be destroyed."

"Nageezi got it in the parking lot of the hotel," Valentine said.

"I dunno about her," Troyd said. "You know we found one of Burlington's shoes in a bunch of BM shit? I'm thinking she chummed him after getting him to write that desertion note. You're lucky she didn't try to rung-jump over your corpse."

"I guess I am," Valentine replied.

He found he'd suddenly acquired a personal chef and regular visits from Miss L. to ascertain any needs beyond food and sleep. "Does the hero of the hour require anything else?"

"My ring, as soon as I'm feeling up to it."

"Does it mean that much to you?" she asked, looking a little disappointed.

"I went through hell to get it. Cold, angry hell. It's worth it to me."

Even Silas stopped by, with a gift-boxed bottle of brandy to put an edge on his constitution. Valentine suddenly couldn't stand his presence, and pretended to be overcome with yawns. Silas took the hint.

But he found himself leaving his bed, again and again, to look at the downtown skyline and the crystal-capped Kurian Tower. But how?

Once up and around and evidently with plenty of time and money for his recovery, Valentine walked into the student café he'd visited when touring Seattle, but unfortunately didn't see the kid with the drum.

He recognized the girl who'd fought with Double Deck, working behind the counter.

"Young lady," Valentine said. "Double Deck's not around, is he?"

"He's got class. I think he said he had to report to community center later. You might catch up to him there."

"How much are those T-shirts on the wall?"

She raised her eyebrows in surprise. "You don't look like the Earworm Café type. They're twelve dollars, two for twenty."

"I'll take six. But I don't have to walk out the door with them, if you'll just get Double Deck here."

"What do you want with him?"

"Babylon's going to make him an offer of extremely brief, extremely lucrative employment."

"If you're wanting to ditch your tracer for a night or two, you'll need an excuse." She stuck out a fleshless hip. "If the price is right, I could say you were tied up to me."

Thanks to a dead tracer and a borrowed mountain bike, Valentine made it to the north tip of Lake Sammamish. From there it was a fairly easy run to the borders of the Seattle Kurian Zone.

"We don't know how he kept himself fed," Captain LeHavre said. "There are a couple of theories, mostly flavors of shit whirling off the fan blades."

They spoke inside a sentry checkpoint just outside the headquarters, a little prefabricated set of roof and three walls built like an outhouse and just as cozy. Valentine didn't want his presence known to the men, so he waited until he saw a familiar face and hailed him from cover. He in turn got LeHavre.

"He liked to tour the nurseries a lot, where the babies grabbed in the Action Group raids would be taken. Seems like a crib death or two struck now and then. Some staff got suspicious at an Ellensburg orphanage and they all were 'disappeared.' "

"He had to have some help somewhere."

"There's a Kurian Tower out by the Grand Coulee Dam that might have been visited too. He kept going out that way to survey it with an eye toward taking the power station, but conditions never seemed right for him to give the go-ahead."

"On the inside too."

"I hope most of them took it in the neck at the Outlook."

"There's a witch hunt—maybe it should be called a wizard hunt, at that—going on right now. I hope Pacific Command doesn't fall apart again. Thunderbird and his Bears are all tainted by this."

Interesting as the political fallout was, Valentine's time was limited. "Speaking of Thunderbird's Bears, if you think a successful action would help restore things here, I have an idea or two along those lines. There's a dreary party being planned in my honor and I'd like to see it crashed. But you'll have to get the Resistance Network in Seattle and the Bears to work together. That's going to take a little diplomacy. One more thing. What are the chances of you helping me write a proposal that'll get a scout/sniper named Gide temporarily seconded to the PeaBees?"

"Can do," LeHavre said, and gave one of his dashing pirate-quarterdeck salutes.

Two weeks later, with plenty of notice about the date and time, Valentine stood tall on the field of honor.

Seattle's remade downtown around him, thanks to tricks of optics played on someone standing on the plaza, seemed to be bowing to the Seattle demigod's tower. The strange, clamshell-like growth extending from the central pillars hung in the sky as though suspended by invisible wires, linked to the pillars by joins so narrow they seemed to defy principles of engineering. No cantilevering, no braces, no suspension, assisted the mollusklike housings of Seattle's Kurians.

And above all the rest, a vast jellyfish-like shape, faintly luminescent like dying phosphors, squatted the home of the demigod, challenging even Mount Rainier for dominance of the horizon.

Madness, madness, madness. But Valentine wanted the ring. By blood and thundering rapids, it was his.

Despite the rain, the watching crowds seemed larger than usual.

Silas stood at his side, his elegant camel-hair coat taking the drizzle as if confident that it would be properly dried and pressed after doing its duty.

"Good crowd today, despite the cold. The so-called Radio Free Northwest reported the death of 'one of the leading minds of the Resistance,'" Silas said. "Our broadcasts have been reading locations and numbers of people killed."

"I wonder which epitaph he'd prefer," Valentine asked.

"Every lumberjack and longshoreman's ready to celebrate, it seems. Watch the stairs—they can get icy when it rains in this kind of cold," Silas advised.

"Don't let the echo from the loudspeakers throw you off either," Miss L. said, behind the pair of them. "Just do your speech."

Valentine had rehearsed it twice with Silas the night before. Not much longer than the Gettysburg Address, it would "get the job done," according to the mouthpiece. Valentine checked the words on the little laminated index card one more time.

> **I stand here, an ordinary man with extraordinary purpose. Today I've been honored with the highest award our saviors can give. But in the end, the sacrifice and struggle that went with winning this ring are meaningless compared to the service Kur has done for us. Kur bestows, with a parental hand that heals more than it hurts, a gift for those with the eyes to see, the new, universal creed that we aspire to: a united human family in harmony with itself and the planet it lives upon, stronger, healthier, happier in our new purpose. Giving up selfishness, I found plenty. Giving up knowledge, I found wisdom. Giving up independence, I found freedom. I thank Kur, not only for myself, but for all mankind.**

It had helped him take his mind off the coming ceremony. If he gave the speech he wanted, he would most likely end up looking like a fool for the few brief seconds of his remaining, violently concluded life.

Gears worked and the scaffolding rose and unfolded itself into place, a steel skeleton animated by hidden cables and counterweights. A banner hung from the central walkway.

SEATTLE IS THE FUTURE

At a nudge from Silas, Valentine crossed the plaza. The two Reapers at the bottom of the stairs, dressed in long dark robes like judges and wide-brimmed Pilgrim hats to keep off the rain, parted and pointed with their hands facing the tower up the golden stairs. Valentine wondered if anyone was to be marched up the black stairs. . . . He or she might just earn a reprieve.

If they showed.

Otherwise, he'd have to give Silas' speech. That would be quite a memento for the newsreels. David Valentine, former Resistance hero, praising the Kurians.

Valentine climbed the steps toward the multifaceted blister, saw a Reaper inside, something else, looming behind, like an octopus perched on a leather umbrella.

"Take my ring, David Valentine," the Ready Reader said in his head. Valentine found his hand moving up, passing through the glowing pane at the bottom of the blister.

His hand came back, suffused with light. Drops of rainbow fell from his hands.

Or was it just illusion?

The ring felt real enough, heavy, a little piece of a far-off planet weighing on his hand. He turned, was vaguely aware of cheering, and stepped toward the microphones.

Is a man just a big, talking bag of chemicals? A reputation? An aura?

No skirmish lines of men broke from the surrounding buildings. No trucks roared up the wide avenue from Mercer Island. The Resistance Network had failed, or Pacific Command had, no telling.

Valentine took a deep breath.

"I stand here, an ordinary man with extraordinary purpose. Today I've been honored with the highest award our saviors can give. But in the end—"

Did he catch a glimpse of light on one of the columns at the other end of the plaza?

"But in the end, all Kur offers us is death," Valentine said.

A Reaper at the base of the stairs twitched.

Ka-rack—Valentine heard the shot a split second later.

Another shot, and a Reaper at the base of the right stairs began to run up. It didn't make it a third of the way before it stiffened.

The crowd spread into chaos. Valentine saw men lifting weapons from beneath their heavy coats and ponchos.

It appeared LeHavre had gone one step beyond the plan for guiding the insertion of Pacific Command's forces into Seattle, and had decided to occupy the plaza before seizing it. But, then, his old captain had always been an improviser.

The Bears bellowed and shot into the air, driving the crowd toward the tower with noise and confusion. What it must have looked like to the Kurians above, he could guess—a mass attempt to storm their collective Bastille.

One Reaper stood at the base of the stairs stupidly; perhaps its Kurian had panicked and forgot what it was supposed to be doing. It jerked as a bullet struck, and immediately stiffened.

Score three for the Miskatonic armorer.

Gide missed with the fourth bullet as the Reaper ran for the stairs. Valentine backpedaled, expecting a final, brief struggle, but the Reaper threw itself inside the organic door, which opened and closed like a toad grabbing at a fly.

Below, the riot continued. Police whistles blew, but to little effect, as the Bears fell into teams, pushing panicked spectators out of the way as they streamed for the tower.

Valentine ran down the stairs, heading for Silas, who had hiked his coat up like an old lady lifting her dress to hop a puddle, and was running across the plaza.

Valentine gave chase, heard explosions from outside the column, a scattering of gunfire.

Miss L. separated herself from the crowd, flung herself on Silas as a police detail opened up with shotguns. As Valentine ran up she drew her pistol from its holster, but instead of aiming for Valentine, she pressed its muzzle to the back of Silas' head.

"Stay down, Sly."

"I need him at the base of the tower," Valentine said.

"Get up, Sly," she ordered.

"You doing this for his own good?" Valentine asked.

They hurried into the center of the four pillars, where the Bears, dressed in variegated civilian attire, now with camouflage vests and hats thrown over them, were prying up cobblestones to make barricades to lie behind.

Valentine saw Thunderbird giving orders, as Bears and PeaBee troops emptied backpack after satchel after bag of dynamite sticks and plastic explosive through holes being made in the concrete with power drills and portable masonry saws.

"We got most of the C-4 in Pacific Command ready to blow, boss," Thunderbird said to Valentine.

"Dunno if it'll bring the whole shebang down," a Bear feeding wire into one of the holes said. "Depends on how strong those supporting towers are."

"How did you get all that past the bomb dogs?" Silas asked.

"The dogs were in the Resistance Network too," Miss L. said.

"Not—not you too?"

"'Fraid so, Sly."

"This bang better work, or we're going to have a hell of a fight getting out of here," Thunderbird said.

"I'd like to avoid that if I can," Valentine said.

"What's the alternative?" Miss L. asked.

"We'll negotiate," Valentine said. "They've got something we want—those people and Lifeweavers I saw in that tank up there. We've got something they want, an intact tower."

"They won't listen to us," the Bear at the wires said.

"They'll listen to him," Valentine said. "Care to deliver terms? Not of surrender, just an exchange of hostages."

"What hostages do you have?" Silas asked.

"You, for a start. Maybe they grabbed a few others on the way here. Bridge sentries and such."

"I'm not sure I want to stand in front of Seattle and start naming terms," Silas said.

"Then we'll shoot you and blow the fucker," Thunderbird responded. His hand dropped to his pistol holster.

"I suppose I could try," Silas said.

"Good luck," Valentine said, and meant it. "If it doesn't work out, try and get out of the center tower. You've got fifteen minutes from when you disappear in that tower. Any troops show up on the plaza, we blow it."

Silas gulped, looked up at the towering mushroom cap. "I'll see what I can do."

Valentine watched him ascend the scaffolding, stopping to gape at one of the frozen Reapers. He made it to the door. The organic mouth admitted him.

"Can I stop loading clay into this tower?" one of the Bears on the demo team whispered.

"Sure," Thunderbird said. "Hope this works, Valentine."

Gide returned from her sniper perch, hugged Valentine. "Long time no see."

"Thanks for keeping the Reapers off me."

"They're your fancy bullets. You want the gun back now?"

"I think it's in better hands with you."

Miss L. checked her watch every two minutes, reading the time to Valentine. They heard trucks pulling up on the roads around the plaza.

Then the mouth opened. Rafferty came out, crossed the bridge from the scaffold, carrying a little girl wrapped in a blanket. "They're coming! They're coming! Turn off the bombs!" Rafferty called.

Seven other humans who emerged, rather shakily, still glistening with the solution they'd been suspended within, must have been favorites to the Pacific Command soldiers. Some of them cheered.

"I don't see any of the Lifeweavers," Valentine said. "Maybe this is a down payment against our leaving."

"Somehow or other, we'll make it back with the real thing," Thunderbird said.

"What is that, a kite?" Gide said, pointing up.

Valentine followed her gaze. Four shapes, reminiscent of jellyfish, drifted, circling down on air currents.

"Creepy-looking things," a Bear commented.

"Depends which side they're on," another said.

"What's that coming down now?" Thunderbird asked.

It was Silas, camel-hair coat flapping in the wind. Gide screamed. Valentine turned away when he hit.

"What was that, a bonus?" a PeaBee asked.

The four Lifeweavers drifted to earth, too exhausted to mask their native form. They couldn't even speak. It didn't stop the Bears from cheering them, nonetheless.

But one figure did not rejoice.

Valentine couldn't say how he crossed the plaza without being noticed. Perhaps he crawled from body to body, hiding among those police killed in the organized riot. But nevertheless Silvers stood over the body of his master. Valentine saw tears wet his eyes, felt his own throat tighten. Even Ahn-Kha wasn't one for tears.

Except once.

The Grog went down on one knee, put a hand against Silas' crushed face, bent down, and listened to the chest. He came away with the side of his face wet with blood.

A deep growl started in his throat. He took a blade out of his kilt and checked the edge with his thumb. For one horrible moment Valentine thought he was going to plunge the blade into his hairy breast, but Silvers made a quick, shallow cut, crossing the angled scar straight up and down, an even longer cut than the old wound. He went down on all fours and hurried to the limo, extracted his twin-barreled cannon from the cupola, and snapped on the harness.

Then he gripped the blade between his teeth and turned for the tower.

As he passed Valentine, he pulled back his lips and one ear flicked up. Valentine, unable to imitate the gesture, thumped his chest three times with his left hand.

Silvers snorted and chambered a round in each barrel. He climbed up the scaffolding, and a loud report echoed as he blew a hole in the door-creature. He worked the bolt on his cannon; then he jumped inside.

"Let's get out of here," Valentine said.

"I'll go talk to the troops outside the plaza," Miss L. said.

"Tell them that anyone who wants to march out with us is welcome," Thunderbird said. "No reprisals. No trials. No more Action Groups. We'll choke Seattle the old-fashioned way, with our bare hands."

Sixteen

Union Rock, Wyoming, July, the fifty-fourth year of the Kurian Order: David Valentine headed east again on a road even older than Route 66, escorting two of the four Lifeweavers rescued—some might say negotiated, others swindled—out of Seattle. The Oregon Trail had its posts and stops rearranged, but the old path is still much the same as it was in the nineteenth century, right down to form of conveyance, for oxen and horses have no octane requirements.

Instead of bringing pioneers west, it sees refugees plodding east and smugglers traveling in both directions. Like their forefathers of two centuries ago, the parties travel in groups for safety, guided by experienced mountain men. They travel armed and wary with good cause, for bandits and grifters hover along its length, and Reapers cover a shocking amount of distance in seven hours of hard running. All are on the prowl for the vulnerable and the careless who might be threatened or cajoled out of valuables, from transport animals to hand-cranked radios, even if they manage to hang on to their auras.

There's a small Freehold or two along the trail, sometimes filling a mountain valley, or some good ground in a river basin. Valentine, listening to stories of other wayfarers along the route, heard talk of a big celebration that always took place in the Wyoming United Grange at Union Rock. People from as far away as Denver, the Nebraska Sandhills, and the Wind River Freehold attended. Picnic tables erupted during the day on land, and fireworks burst overhead at night. News was swapped for news, knitting and quilting for items from the trader stalls, and any number of young people met and married in a whirlwind of celebration. It sounded like the old summer festival in the Boundary Waters, and Valentine delayed his journey a week or two to linger and attend. He could go south easily enough from there, and, he hoped, reach Denver, and Southern Command's liaison, by late July.

They joined up with a bigger train, made up of old automobile chassis pulled by trail oxen. There was already talk of what each party would add to the festivities, making it sound like a potluck dinner with attendance running into the thousands.

Valentine didn't have to get to the Ozarks. The Ozarks came to him. A party of Wolves was in attendance for the Independence Day festivities, recruiting out of a tent thick with tobacco smoke, pecan pies, and Texas chilies and barbecue.

Valentine had seen such displays before, like the welcoming feast on his arrival in Missouri fifteen years ago. *Good God, was it that long ago?* He watched a boy clear a pie tin with two fingers like a bear dipping honey. *Enjoy it, kid. It'll be brown rice and chicken twice a week with the Labor Regiments.*

"Another Sioux, you think?" a sunbaked female sergeant with her stripes inked on her suspenders said to a bronze-skinned youth with a ponytail that dwarfed Valentine's. "Be a good summer for us if he joins. I'm sick of teaching kids how to stretch their canteens."

"Ya hey there, friend," the AmerInd said, approaching. He raised his hand and met Valentine's palm hard enough to loosen a feeding tick, let alone trail dust. "You look like you know how to keep a scope zeroed. Thinking about using it on something bigger than antelope or wild horse?"

The Wolf at the food table hurried around it and into the crowd. "Bud above, that's Major Valentine! Tell me you ain't David Valentine, off Big Rock Hill and all." Valentine thought it an odd request. The goateed Wolf pushed forward and took off a battered slouch hat. "It's Hornsby, sir. We were in the rear guard on the march to Dallas, when the Razors were guarding the supply train. I helped you fix a bridge."

Valentine was grateful for the name. He extended his hand. "Hornsby. Red River. Good to see you again."

Hornsby made introductions to the recruiting team and guides. "I've got a couple more bodies for Southern Command. You'll want to keep an eye on these two. Meet Oberon and Titania. They're travelers like Father Wolf."

"I'll put us under your orders for the trip back, sir," the sergeant said.

"Actually, I think you're supposed to put me under arrest. But maybe I'll go with you as far as Missouri. I'll have to flake off there."

He'd let Styachowski know where to find him.

"Seen much of the celebration?" the sergeant asked.

"Just got in."

"Take a walk out to Union Rock. It's a sight to see."

Valentine saw the Lifeweavers comfortably installed in the Wolves' covered supply wagon, under constant guard thanks to the alcohol, tobacco, and firearms stored inside.

He wandered through the festival. A hundred or more separate parties seemed to be going on around a central broadway of trader stalls. Bikers congregated on their machines; black belts gave exhibitions of ice breaking for the kids. Ice cream was sold alongside bourbon and tequila. Teetotalers kept a distance from the stalls, and Valentine saw black-coated folk he guessed to be Mennonites, or maybe Amish. Games of baseball and basketball were in full swing on cleared patches of ground with equipment ranging from crude to commercial quality. Lively fiddles and bagpipes competed with accordion and tuba, but the biggest crowd was gathered around a pair of young, shaved-headed black boys creating an astonishingly complex rhythm with plastic produce buckets and drumsticks, with a few cowbells thrown in for gongs. When they finished, a preacher stepped forward and started an energetic sermon. Valentine listened to the mixture of oratory, showmanship, and gospel for a few minutes, then wandered off.

There was the profane keeping a discreet distance from the sacred. A little ways away from the rest of the camp some enterprising prostitutes had set up their tents under a sign advertising GENTLEMEN'S ENTERTAINMENTS, though their camp looked quiet for the moment.

Union Rock would be difficult to miss. It dominated the campsite like an unevenly risen bread loaf. A drum circle in tie-dyed shirts played, and passed around a joint, in its shade while a trio of barefoot girls festooned with beads danced.

There were any number of tourists walking around the rocks or climbing the more accessible parts. Valentine read an old pre-2022 landmark that mentioned this prominence as a popular stop on the westward-traveling Oregon Trail, which visitors often climbed to carve their names.

Someone had been hard at work since. A little path wound around the rock, traveled by families helping their children sound out the letters carved into the rock.

It was rather like a picture gallery, but the frames were shadow boxes, carved a forefinger's depth into the rock. Expertly crafted metal plaques were set into the boxes. Valentine moved down the line, reading with a little tingle running up his spine. The Ten Commandments, the Sermon on the Mount, and the Lord's Prayer, the Magna Carta, the Mayflower Compact, the Declaration of Independence, the Constitution and Bill of Rights, portraits of presidents and the postman Franklin, the Gettysburg Address, and an inaugural speech by Kennedy.

It wasn't limited to politicians. Valentine saw a young man busy making a rubbing of Shakespeare's *Hamlet* quartos, and Irving Berlin had sheets of music. Robert Frost had a poem about some woods on a snowy evening, and Valentine recognized O. Henry's "Gift of the Magi" in its terse perfection. Someone went to a lot of trouble to reproduce *Whistler's Mother* and a study of a troubled-looking Lincoln in bronze plate.

Above the gallery, in letters big and deep enough to be read from hundreds of feet away, some crammed between others, some in a single line and others in a block of text, there in a glorious hodgepodge stood phrases freshly whitewashed so they might even be read under a bright moon. In fact, the work continued—Valentine saw limber and energetic young boys and girls among the rocks with paint and brushes, cleaning and recoating so the words might gleam under the fireworks. Too many for Valentine to take in all at once, he had to move from quote to quote with care.

"WE MUST HANG TOGETHER OR WE SHALL SURELY HANG SEPARATELY." "GIVE ME LIBERTY OR GIVE ME DEATH." "I HAVE NOT YET BEGUN TO FIGHT." "A HOUSE DIVIDED CANNOT STAND. . . ." "THE ONLY THING WE HAVE TO FEAR IS FEAR ITSELF." "WE SHALL FIGHT THEM ON THE BEACHES AND IN THE FIELDS. . . ." "NO MAN IS AN ISLAND. . . ." "EVIL CAN NEVER SURVIVE, THOUGH IT MAY SEEM TO TRIUMPH. IT IS ONLY A QUESTION OF PATIENCE AND ENDURANCE." "I HAVE A DREAM THAT MY FOUR LITTLE CHILDREN WILL ONE DAY LIVE IN A NATION WHERE THEY WILL NOT BE JUDGED BY THE COLOR OF THEIR SKIN BUT BY THE CONTENT OF THEIR CHARACTER." "DOUBT NOT YOURSELVES, ONLY THE LIES OF TYRANTS WHO HOLD BUT A PROMISE IN ONE HAND AND A WHIP IN THE OTHER." "NO POWER FROM OUR POOR EARTH OR ANY OTHER WORLD CAN STRIKE DOWN THE GOLDEN LADDER BETWEEN YOUR SOUL AND GOD, WHO IS RIGHTLY CALLED THE ALMIGHTY." "OUR GREAT TEST HAS COME. WE MELTED IN THE HEAT OF DARKNESS AND DISASTER, BUT SHALL REFORM, AN AMALGAM GATHERED IN THE SWORD MOLD, HARDENED LIKE STEEL HAMMERED FROM THE FURNACE."

Valentine circled the rock twice, but kept returning to the Gettysburg Address. Its handful of words renewed him like the free ice water being passed out by the young "scouts" collecting valuables for the extension of the monument.

He had a single gold coin left. He palmed it and tossed it in the old plastic bleach jug as he accepted a hard plastic cup filled from the ice jug. "Please return for reuse," a childish hand had scrawled on the cup's side.

LeHavre was right. He'd made the struggle personal. It wasn't about this or that Kurian, or even some general's ego or his career. Even his family. They were all just caught in the whirlwind, a contest of life and liberty versus tyranny akin to those the men and women who had spoken the words described, even if the stakes were higher.

The Cause wasn't found in Southern Command; it wasn't the Cascades, or even this little band of July Fourth partyers. It was behind barbed wire, in the shadow of the Kurian Towers, in ugly little killing bottles like the Bellevue gardens. In a revolt in the Appalachians, led by a familiar-sounding Golden One.

That's where he'd be too.

He let the clean, cool water pass through his lips and wash him like the baptisms the firebrand preacher was even now attending to at the creek, and read again:

> **. . . that we here highly resolve that these dead shall not have died in vain—that this nation, under God, shall have a new birth of freedom—and that government of the people, by the people, for the people, shall not perish from the earth.**

About the Author

E. E. Knight was born in Wisconsin, grew up in Minnesota, and now calls Chicago home, where he abides in domestic felicity with his family, and assorted pets. He is the author of the Vampire Earth series.